Jack Juggler and the Emperor's Whore

John Arden

JACK JUGGLER
and the
EMPEROR'S WHORE

Seven Tall Tales
linked together
for an indecorous Toy Theatre

Methuen

First published in Great Britain in 1995 by Methuen London
an imprint of Reed International Books Ltd
Michelin House, 81 Fulham Road, London SW3 6RB
and Auckland, Melbourne, Singapore and Toronto

A CIP catalogue record for this book
is available at the British Library
ISBN 0 413 69570 0

Typeset by Deltatype Ltd, Ellesmere Port, Wirral
Printed and bound in Great Britain
by Clays Ltd, St Ives PLC

Contents

Author's Note

All the twentieth-century people of these tales are entirely fictional; but some of the events and dates and places are real. There were, for instance, festivals in Belfast and Dublin in the years given. Their participants and what they did there are my own invention. I have described fictional productions of imaginary plays on real stages in real years; and I have also invented some theatres, such as the Marylebone Showbox, the Stockwell Soldier's Glory pub theatre, the Pomfretshire University Drama Department. There *is* a Beverley Arms hotel (my great-great-grandfather was its landlord once); there is not, I hope, a Vermeer Hotel in Kensington; while the Gresham and Buswells are very well known among visitors to Dublin.

I never heard that any city-wide dramatic celebration of naval heroes was planned for Plymouth in 1972.

There is no restored Georgian theatre in Knaresborough, and none of the Knaresborough residents in these pages have ever existed. Nor do they exist in Richmond, where there is in fact just such a theatre: I have transposed it from one Yorkshire town to the other and made very free with its activities.

And so on.

As for the three 'period' tales (Eugene Aram, Albine de Montholon, and Fernão Lopes): I hold no brief whatever for the accuracy of their history. They are presented as the dream-creations of Leonore Serlio and Jack Pogmoor, who may not have fully researched all the details, and whose own lives necessarily impinge upon the phantom lives of previous epochs, rearranging them, distorting them. Very broadly, though, the tales are true.

My source for the account of arsenic on St Helena is *The Murder of Napoleon*, by Ben Weider and David Hapgood (Robson Books, 1982). It summarises the earlier discoveries of Sten Forshufvud.

A Grateful Acknowledgement

I could never have finished this book in the way I wanted to finish it, had not the AUTHORS' FOUNDATION (in 1992) awarded me a most welcome cheque for £2,000 to enable me to travel and carry out my research. I live in the west of Ireland; to write a long novel about England (or largely about England) needed constant trips by air and sea and, in England itself, by very expensive railway trains, to check historical sources unavailable at home and to collect a good deal of topographical data.

I had wanted to visit St Helena, which would have been fun (if it did not involve crippling seasickness; one can only get there by ship, and quite a small ship at that), but it proved too lengthy and complicated a business to be undertaken in time; I was thus forced to complete that part of the book without first-hand observation. I hope it doesn't show. Perhaps just as well: the cost would have swallowed up all of the award and more, and my English excursions might have had to be cut down . . . But I am grateful to the Governor's Office on St Helena for furnishing me with some extremely useful information about the island.

The AUTHORS' FOUNDATION and the K. BLUNDELL TRUST, administered by the Society of Authors, are great institutions for needy writers. The money comes from less-needy fellow writers who have taken thought for their colleagues; may I commend and recommend them!

J.A., Galway, 1995

For my grandchildren

Craig, Danha, Jade, Zak, Laura Bronte
and **Emily Carol**

for when you're all old enough to read it.

Now this bargain must I make with you, that you
will say hum and ha to my tale; so shall I know
you are awake.

(George Peele, *The Old Wives Tale*)

Night!
. . . thou hang'st fitly
To grace those sins that have no grace at all.
Now 'tis full sea abed over the world,
There's juggling of all sides.

(Cyril Tourneur, *The Revenger's Tragedy*)

Shall sickness prove me now to be a man,
That have been termed the terror of the world?

(Christopher Marlowe, *Tamburlaine the Great*)

A rape, a rape!
How?
Yes you have ravaged justice,
Forced her to do your pleasure.
Fie, she's mad.

(John Webster, *The White Devil*)

Introductory Anecdote

How Jack Juggler Made a Dream From a Picture
(1975)

Bid him come in, and paint some comfort,
For surely there's none lives but painted comfort . . .
Is there no tricks that comes before thine eyes?
O Lord, yes, sir.
Art a painter? Canst paint me a tear, or a wound, a
   groan, or a sigh?

(Anon, addition to *The Spanish Tragedy*)

1

There was a man called Pogmoor; Jack Pogmoor, theatre director; an Englishman. He lived in London.

He first became known in the late 1960s for his spectacular productions – modern plays as well as classics. He was sometimes called the Crêpe-paper Man, as so many of his best effects were created out of the most ephemeral materials. Another nickname for him was Jack Juggler; some people said because his shows looked like conjuring tricks. Others alleged different reasons; and in fact there was more than one story.

He abhorred any kind of heavy, literal, 'straight-line' performance, despising what he termed *prose-acting* – 'Always *poetry*,' he used to cry, in a rattling Yorkshire accent that an unimpressed newspaper-woman once likened to a helicopter with a loose rotor-blade: 'Keep it fluid, keep it fluent, keep it fast! Don't you bloody worry about your motivation: the movement itself gives the motivation.'

Actors on the whole were keen to work with him, but they were also afraid. There were complaints that he treated them as mindless marionettes. But once he had made clear the exact nature of their required 'movement' and drilled them in it with rattling voice and a notorious metronome until they were ready to burst into tears on the stage, then suddenly his whole process of thought fell into place, and they would wonder how they'd ever had any doubts. If, in their humiliation, they resigned from his casts, he wrote their names down with spiteful emphasis in a little black notebook and never employed them again, however excellent their reputations, however successful their performances with other directors.

2

As soon as he became rich enough, he began an enviable collection of theatrical pictures and illustrated books. One painting, a copy of a French work of the later sixteenth century, was a special favourite. Its original was attributed to Antoine Caron, designer of masques and pageants at the poisonous Valois court. It represented the Old Testament legend of Joseph, in several episodes, all shown simultaneously within a single architectural and landscape environment. There was a sort of great open-air stage, paved in red and white chequer-pattern, with painted and gilded arches and porches and turrets and obelisks and nude classical statues and flights of steps rearing up from its expanse. Yellow desert stretched across the background, to the foothills of a distant mountain range. The events of Joseph's life declared themselves, as it were, on miniature stages elegantly disposed about the great stage. The people of the events, small in scale but lithe, long-limbed and hurling themselves into a frenzy of passionate action, were exaggeratedly dressed in that odd mixture of everyday and Greco-Roman costume so popular with Renaissance artists. The whole effect had much in common with Pogmoor's own productions in full flow.

During his thirty-fifth year, 1975, Jack Pogmoor had a dream about this picture. It surprised him, and continued to surprise him after he woke up. Because in it he seemed to move *like a marionette* through every sequence of the story, so close to the figure of Joseph that he might have been Joseph himself: and yet the story was not quite the story he knew. He had no religion to speak of, yet he heard himself protesting in the tones of a rigorous clergyman against liberties taken with Holy Writ. And his words went unanswered – unheard, indeed, in all the excited bustle of rapidly accumulating sacred history.

There was also another voice, still, small, but completely dominating his own. It was inside his ear – no, inside his very brain – he thought it was an angel speaking, until the dream told him it was God. It ran a constant narration to every sequence of the Adventures of Joseph, as insistent and tiny as the gnat's voice in Lewis Carroll's *Looking-glass* book. (Pogmoor had once adored the Alice tales; but ever since his last postgraduate year at university, 1965, he had come to loathe the name of Alice – he had, as will be seen, a discreditable but sufficient reason.)

God said to Jack Pogmoor: 'Here to start the story. Little Joseph, swankpot child, kitted out in his many colours, boasting his superior dreams, the mark for jealousy and hatred, little King Shit who puts himself too high above his brothers – not real brothers, but half-brothers, nasty men – too high above his rude father. Only his mother loves him, so she gives him the sissy's coat. He despises her for her ignorance. He weeps.

'In his resentment he tears the coat off and flings it away, then hides in a hole in the ground lest they find him and flog the arse off him.

'Alone in the desert he meets a gang of marauding soldiers, Pharaoh of Egypt's security forces. They press him into their ranks. He is forced to march and drill to dreadful shouting of sergeant-majors and the tick-tack-tock of a metronome. He weeps again, in the open air on parade, in the thronged solitude of the deadly barracks.

'See, he has been observed. By Potiphar, an official gentleman, kind, scholarly, anxious to be loved (though he never says so). He winks an eye toward Joseph: "This young man will do very well as my confidential secretary. Come, little chap, I'll bring you home with me. I'll fix it with your colonel, don't panic." And in Potiphar's ornate house Joseph discovers happiness, he straightens his back at last, his young body fills out, he is *confident* and all-of-a-piece. Look.'

Joseph indeed confident, in a warm sunlit open-fronted room, carrying an armful of papers to his employer's desk. His employer's eye upon him with melancholy care; no words to express that care. Over against them, on a high balcony, a dark-eyed round-hipped lady leaned across the balustrade, her brave embroidered gown cut so low as to expose her breasts. She too watched intently.

'See, he is again observed. And woe, he observes the woman. How long before Potiphar's wife and himself are damning their souls in one bed? Not long, for Potiphar must depart on a journey. Watch him go, watch: ah, now the coast is clear!'

The fat rump of Potiphar's horse was just disappearing behind an obelisk. Potiphar's wife came down a staircase on to the marble pavement. She entered a porch with green and purple curtains hanging across it. Perhaps she called somebody in after her, perhaps she did not know her husband was gone, perhaps Joseph followed her without any call. There was a red wind gusting from the desert, too much noise to be sure whether either had spoken or not. The wind blew the curtains open and shut, open and shut: and there was Joseph inside with her, and behind her a wide, valanced bed. A sword was propped up in the corner – Potiphar's: not needed on his journey.

'For Egypt is a land of affluence and peace.

'It is midnight, new moon,' the voice went on with a change of tone, less a gnat now than a murderous hornet, 'new moon, but very dark.'

Yes, that corner of the picture *was* dark, deep blue-black like the darkest ink, although the rest of the sky, over three-quarters of the canvas, remained brilliant, full of hot sun.

'She asks, "Who is there?" He laughs and replies, "A loving husband, who the hell else?" So she reaches out and pulls him to her. Dead silence, save for the burning wind. Is the deed done, or isn't it? Dark, dark, we cannot tell. But suddenly she cries aloud, "NO!" She gives no reason. Cries once; and gives no reason. He leaps to the sword, heaves it and jerks it between their two bodies, he is stark naked and beside himself (were his clothes shed by his own hands or hers?), the blade rips at her gown, throwing it down about her thighs, there is blood on the blade, he has wounded her in the haunch. In comes her maid to help her, in a shriek and a rush, oh! oh!'

A haggard black Nubian woman, full tilt from the stairs towards them, anger, terror, and the armed guards, wildly bearded under Roman helmets, catching Joseph by the elbows, binding him, beating his face.

'—and flogging the arse off him. So.

'So Potiphar is home again; she shows the bloody wound, the bloody gown, the bloody sword. Explanations, excuses, apologies – useless. You could have been Potiphar's friend. He tried to be yours. You could have been his wife's friend. Could you not see, could you not *feel*? Gaol: and eventual death.'

The voice did not continue with the rest of the story, even though Pogmoor's memory insisted that Maître Caron had put it all into the picture – the voice had nothing to say about Joseph reading the dreams of fellow prisoners, Joseph reading Pharaoh's dream, Joseph released and given charge of the famine-prevention programme, Joseph in a royal mantle (same shape, same pose as Child Joseph in his many-coloured coat, grown wonderfully giant-sized), Joseph at last lording it over his filthy and suppliant family.

'Gaol,' buzzed the still small hornet again. 'Gaol, disgrace, death.'

After which, the Voice of God seemed to have finished with Pogmoor. He awoke puzzled, uncomfortable, not a little frightened. He had no intention at all of presenting any Old Testament play; that *Technicolor Dreamcoat* show had already been seen and enjoyed everywhere; so why this ridiculous phantasm? Was it to tell him that a Pogmoor dream might be as important as an Egyptian one? But neither *being* Joseph nor *knowing* a Joseph of any great significance, he was unable to see how. He thought that most dreams, perhaps all dreams, bear reference to one's past experience. This dream, in some respects, did; but it ought to have had a more positive ending. He ought to have been told about Joseph's ultimate glory. What demon of divine malice caused God, in that creepy fashion, to fall so abruptly silent?

3

Pogmoor's work-in-progress just then was by way of a partnership-job with the playwright Fidelio Carver, a drama of 'historical situation' that promised an invigorating range of political reference: Napoleon, ex-revolutionary, ex-Emperor, marooned upon St Helena, did he die naturally, or was he poisoned? And if the latter, who did it and how? A Swedish expert in toxicology had published details of his recent research: arsenic! – small doses, fed into the Emperor's body over a long period; and finally, the wrong remedy. *Coup de grâce.*

Carver had read about this and had immediately rung Pogmoor to suggest that it might make a play.

'You see, Jack,' he muttered excitedly down the wire, 'you see the point, this is a murder, assassination, execution, call it what you want, for the cause of reaction, the cause of revolution, personal revenge, work out what fits best, but completely successful, not only did they kill him but to this day, this very day, by God *they got away with it!* Murder will out! that's what the books say, that's what they all say, it's a commonplace of history, political killings might be good, might be bad, but everybody knows they've happened and frame their policies accordingly; but in this case, this man, the most crucial individual phenomenon of the age – the world just goes on just as though he'd died of jaundice. Which is what they did think he'd died of. Or most of them, most of them. *Only the murderers knew that he hadn't.* So where does that leave them? What to do next? Well, Jack? I say – Jack? Jack, are you there . . . ?'

Jack, after whistling to himself for a moment, said, 'Why not? Have a go then.' There was a real enthusiasm concealed in his clipped phrases.

'Oh, I've already begun. Tell you what, Jack, there's a most complex pro-and-con for the woman I'll call the heroine. Heroine, villainess, I can't quite tell yet, but listen: she's the wife of the probable poisoner, she's the Emperor's whore, how did she get there?'

'Where? You've lost me.'

'Into his bed, man, Napoleon's. Of her own choice, of her husband's scheming choice, or did Boney just catch her and force her?'

'Force? You mean *rape*?'

'Coercion, at any rate. You see, Jack, that's an element left barely decipherable in between the proper lines of written history. An open question, quite unanswered. Whichever way I *do* answer it, all the possible motivations take on a whole new pattern. I'm even thinking of calling the play *The Emperor's Whore*. I love it.'

'I'm not so sure that *I* do.' The tone of Pogmoor's voice had shifted a little bit *sideways* . . .

But within the week the pair of them began to sketch various scenarios. Carver was not much use at constructing plots, he was better suited to sharing his ideas with someone else. But he had a harsh feel for dramatic language, both high-style and gritty vernacular, he could slip from prose into verse and from either into the lyrics of song without any sense of strain, he could imagine sweet, sad, comical or ferocious confrontations between vivid individual characters or characters in the vivid mass: in short, he was ideal material for the manipulations of Pogmoor. They had already combined on a number of plays, large and small.

Whether Carver in 1975 was absolutely as pleased as Pogmoor to be trotting through his career in repetitive tandem is not easy to say. He kept his personal reflections very much to himself. After some months the Napoleon idea began to give the two men a good deal of difficulty, and tempers now and then were frayed. The playwright was a mousey grey fellow in his forties, some eight years older than Pogmoor. He had known Pogmoor for more than a decade, and they described themselves as friends, whatever that might mean in the volatile circumstances of their craft. They were in fact brothers-in-law; or rather, ex-brothers-in-law; in 1971, Carver's twin sister Leonore had become Mrs Pogmoor – an odd choice for both of them, many people thought; the marriage did not last more than a year and a half and there were no children. Pogmoor would ask after her whenever he and Carver met; on occasions he ran into her in her brother's company; all three were so polite and tactful that none of them could quite believe that their diplomatic protocol was capable of such success.

Carver's own sex-life might be called 'convoluted'. There was a time when everyone thought he was homosexual; but then he was noticed to be in some sort of connection with first one woman and then another; and then he seemed to share a flat with a Bengali youth, a freelance publicity-handler in the avant-garde arts scene. They had met when a play by Carver was presented at a pub theatre in Stockwell for which this Sulaiman prepared posters and press releases. But no one really knew what Carver was up to. Some people asserted he was either unusually chaste or a eunuch, and that all his 'connections' were exclusively for the pleasures of spiritual enrichment and good conversation. He liked to *chat*, it was said, but not with just anyone. If Leonore understood her brother's convolutions, and if (during the marriage) she had ever explained them to Pogmoor, Pogmoor held his tongue on the subject: that much can be stated with certainty.

Pogmoor himself was always a subject for gossip, not necessarily genial, and sometimes prurient. Only to be expected, after all; his professional persona being so egregious, his itch for publicity so acute. Few of the stories about him seemed to be backed by solid evidence. He rejoiced to make himself out an amoral hedonist, daring and defiant; which encouraged the paradoxical belief that he'd never really copulated anywhere to boast about. Yet he could not be dismissed as phoney: for who would dispute that his stage work was as good as the best, even though it was in places like Warsaw or Zagreb that it received its highest acclaim?

Whenever he worked with Carver, the result was perceived by the critics as *political*; which is to say, political of the Left. Many of the organised party-orientated Left did not agree: in their view the plays inclined to Anarchism, aesthetically determined and therefore irresponsible, reactionary even. Playwright and director strove rather too often, perhaps, to overturn monuments, mispronounce shibboleths, drive into brake and briar the sacred cows of *every* faction.

Pogmoor, towards the end of the '60s, had been at least a fellow traveller with a number of revolutionary groups. They welcomed him as an attractive *name*, a Useful Idiot (as Lenin put it); in general they got sick of him at about the same time that he lost his temper with them; and he was not at all reliable when it came to such essential routines as selling party newspapers, attending demonstrations, sitting for hours in grubby halls at strategy conferences being adjured by irate apparatchiks to 'face up to the task imposed on us, comrades, by the imminent Crisis of Capitalism'.

Carver was probably more sincere, more profound, in his revolutionary views; but quieter. He rejected facile anti-establishment attitudes; at the same time he firmly believed that no writer could join a political party without unacceptable risk of corruption. In 1970 or thereabouts there was a short-lived involvement with a radical agitprop theatre group, which perhaps had something to do with the Sulaiman episode of a few years earlier; it was generally regarded as out-of-character, artistically an aberration; he refused to talk about it afterwards. He did go on demonstrations – Vietnam, Ireland, Trade Union Rights, Civil Liberties, Censorship, Gay Rights, Nuclear Disarmament, Ecology, Anti-Apartheid, Anti-Racism, solidarity with various Industrial Disputes – and made no braggadocio. In 1981 (and unexpectedly) he was to be severely beaten by the police when they attacked a march against the Thatcher government over the IRA hunger-strike; it put him into hospital for a week.

But demonstrations and public meetings, even when peaceful, took a great deal out of him; it was only with reluctance that he engaged himself with them at all. From a sense of obligation, it might be thought? or perhaps of deep inadequacy which he could only overcome by *offering himself up*, an all-but-anonymous tiny footnote to the communal history of the age. As a playwright with his name now and then upon posters, he stood out (just a little) from the mass; as a political activist he attempted to embed himself into it – to make his mark, to avoid notice, all in the one gesture.

4

Pogmoor's dream about the Joseph picture had an immediate and disturbing effect on his work. He talked about the dream to Carver, inconclusively (indeed incomprehensibly) all through a pub lunch where they were supposed to be making preliminary decisions upon Napoleon. And soon afterwards he allowed his weekly meetings with the playwright to lapse. (They'd only been going on for a month.) He said to him, over the telephone, 'Look here, Fid, there's no bloody point. You've read the books, I've skimmed through the books, get sat down and do some writing, sitha! When tha's done it, put it i't'postbox. If tha's not got it reet well fettled, *I'll* side it up for thee. When I've time. Just now, I'd best see how I'm fixed.'

Carver gave a cross grunt and rang off. The brother-in-law as Yorkshire tyke was an irritating manifestation which he always refused to countenance. He knew well it was the cover for some minor deceit. In this case, he suspected Pogmoor was growing more and more interested in a classical production that had been suggested to him by the Royal Shakespeare Company and so was seeking to put the *Emperor's Whore* project either on hold or into the dustbin: only time would tell, and Fid Carver was always philosophical.

As it happened, Fid Carver was wrong. For Pogmoor had suddenly become conscious of something to which he had never before given serious attention. It was hard to put a name to it: Mortality? (In his mid-thirties?) Doom? Weird? Nemesis? Whatever it was, it was uncannily located behind the outside corner of his eye, like the parrot on an old sailorman's shoulder; he could not go anywhere, talk to anyone, do anything, without twitching his head to one side all the time, just to see who or what was there. He did not dare ask any of his acquaintances if they thought he needed therapy.

Nor did he dare give up Napoleon altogether. In fact, without telling Carver, he was reading every day more and more material on the subject. He spoke to his agent, Wally Overton, a man who worried about his clients' health and did his best to keep them clear of unnecessary stress. 'You can tell the Royal Shakespeare I want no more aggro about this damned *White Devil*; I'm in no mood to direct a Webster play this season; and besides—' (he put this as a kind of joke) '—sometimes a fellow has a devil of his own to take care of, twice as white, whiter than leprosy, Wally, twice as bloody, twice as dangerous.'

Wally looked at him anxiously. 'Oh dear. If that's the state of mind this Carver script's leading you into, don't you think you should give it a rest? Take a job well away – away from London, I mean, away from your chum. There's a festival in the autumn in Knaresborough, Yorks – home territory for you, Jack, yes? They'll have finished restoring this gem of a Georgian theatre; they want to open it with a musical about their local hero. Amateur cast, local author, local composer, just like the hero, but a really most beautiful little playhouse; and they've first-class financial backing. Jack, I can assure you they will pay you what you're worth. It might even be a kind of holiday.'

'It might even be a pain i't'bloody neck. Nay, I don't know . . . Who's the hero?'

'Eugene Aram, the murderer. Hanged, I'm informed, the same year that the playhouse was built.'

'Who's the author?'

'A guy of the name of Lobscott. Percy Lobscott. Ring a bell?'

'Never heard of him.'

Pogmoor avoided telling Carver about this offer. But he accepted it; and Carver found out.

Another phone call.

'Eugene Aram? Secret killing? My God, you can't! If you do, you'll exhaust the theme. At least, your own interest in the theme. Jack, I know you too damned well. And what happens to our Bonaparte then?'

'Nowt. He'll still be there. Marooned and all ready for us, with or without his harlot, in solitary rancour scanning the horizon. A strong profound theme has innumerable variations. I dare say a dose of Eugene'll do us both a bit of good. I'll tell you all about it, how it goes, *as* it goes, week by week while I'm away. Fid, it's germane, tangential but deeply germane, to all of what we've got in mind. Murder will out! remember? Eugene Aram killed a man in Knaresborough in 1745, got rid of the body, and took himself off to Norfolk. Where he worked as a schoolmaster with the highest reputation for pioneer linguistic scholarship, a most civilised easy-going gent; and then *fourteen years later* somebody dug up the bones. York Castle Gaol; the County Assizes; the gallows-tree on Knavesmire; the second gibbet, in Knaresborough Forest, to which the poor scholar's cadaver was lugged fifteen miles upon a jolting cart, neck twisted like a wrung-out dishrag, tongue lolling, teeth snarling, to hang there in chains till it *dissolved*.'

'He got caught.'

'That's right, Fid, he got caught.'

'I don't like it. It contradicts our chief idea. The whole essence of St Helena is that *nobody* got caught.'

'That's right. Odysseus in the cave of the Cyclops, the ravening ogre brought to his knees by the hand of Captain *Nobody*. Which is of course negative; unproved and unprovable, a mystical hypothesis. Maybe that's why I'm not quite so keen on St Helena, I mean not at present, not just yet, I mean not these last few weeks. Listen—' There was a long silence.

'Jack, I am listening. But to *what?*, I am forced to enquire.'

'Oh, shut your clever cakehole. You want a story of a totally successful killer. He is guilty in fact; is he guilty in his psyche? That's your theme, right? The inherent contradictions of political crime. *His* ambiguity, not *hers*.'

'Hers?'

'You know who I mean – the Emperor's whore – the wife of the poisoner – the White Devil of the Island of Exile. She's a marginal figure. If she's not, she'll over-egg the pudding. She ought to be, she must be *straightforward*: she knows of his crime or she don't. A willing accomplice or an unwilling accessory or plain-and-simple innocent-ignorant. Each of those ways is okay; but *you're* trying to have it all three. Bullshit.'

'That's how the story comes out.'

'Fid, I said bullshit. The *man* is your man. And your audience knows that he knows what he's done. Don't evade. Christ, you're so slippery, it's giving me nightmares!'

'I don't understand you—'

'Leave it, Fid, sodding leave it. Christ, I don't understand my own self.'

First Tale

How Jack Juggler Got His Name

(as told by J. Pogmoor, 1985)

Virgins, in vain ye labour to prevent
That which mine honour swears shall be perform'd,
Behold my sword! what see you at the point?

(Christopher Marlowe, *Tamburlaine the Great*)

Some suggestion of what might have been troubling Pogmoor in 1975 may be found in this document. But he did not start to write it until a whole decade later; we should not assume that when he dreamed his dream the conduct of his younger self would have appeared to him in quite the same light. He refers to 'allegations': in '75 they may have been no more than a persistent unease in his own mind. But by November '85 (when he was forty-five) specific charges had surfaced, some of them by word of mouth, with one instance at least of printed defamation. A paragraph in Private Eye *alluded to the National Theatre refusing him a production on the grounds of his 'reputed history of addiction to coercive legover among nubile thespianettes'. No option but the law – libel, slander, exemplary damages! His solicitor demanded an account of the relevant events. The version we have here is not quite that account: even as he sweated to lay out the forensic facts, Pogmoor was rewriting and expanding (and to an extent disguising) them, with an eye to an apologetic autobiography. He was indeed to* juggle-about *with autobiography for years; somehow he never got further than a heap of 'foul papers' clipped into file-covers and buried in different corners of his shelves as though he preferred not to remember where they were.*

1

For a start, and it annoys me almost more than anything else: I am not called Jack Juggler because of how I dealt with that girl.

It was a very long time ago, of course – *once upon a time*, indeed, for dammit you could call it a fairy tale! – and certainly the name did arise just then; and there may have been some overlap of meaning, among those few who knew a version of the story. But may I assure my suspicious readers (as I'm striving to assure my legal man, who gets the first draft of this effusion in *slightly* more legal language), it was the name of the play. The play made me famous, within a limited circle; legitimately so. I directed, Polly Blackadder was leading lady.

Allegations of *rape* are unbelievably wide of the mark. The word bears no relation to the circumstances that obtained. In the mid-sixties we were Permissive; had to be, if we claimed to promote the ideologies of the age; how should we know anything of the coming onset of Militant Feminism? Sometimes, I'll admit, one might have 'gone too far'. Two would have gone too far, in point of fact; and if things now and then turned out a little curdled, the chick as a rule was inhibitingly conscious of at least part of the responsibility, and made bloody sure she kept the bellyaching strictly to herself.

And besides, the allegations about this particular Blackadder chick were not at all true, as I shall show; it is perfectly noxious they keep floating to the surface to plague me; I am today a man of some status, some distinction, beginning to go grey, sexually more or less over the hill (or so I heard last week: some skulking little bastard passed it on to me, never mind from what airheaded young Ms Prunemouth). It makes me very angry to have to write it all down now, when I can't even remember most of it; but my reputation in the current atmosphere of feminist neo-Grundyism must be protected, or else, by God! I'll lose my career. So here you are.

I'll return to Polly Blackadder shortly: I have first to set the scene for her, or none of it's going to make any sense.

I repeat, the name they gave me was the name of the play. To be accurate, *A new Enterlude for Chyldren to playe named Jacke Jugeler, both wyttë, very playsent and merye* . . . , and so forth. It had been fumbled together in the sixteenth century (we're told the reign of Bloody Mary), based upon Plautus by 'Anon', a schoolmaster-playwright no doubt, hoping he'd encourage his pupils to enjoy Latin drama in the original language for its own sake. He took a certain risk by throwing out some sideways knocks at the Doctrine of Transubstantiation, but they would surely have been above the heads of his young actors. If any parents or fellow teachers had detected his hidden meaning and raised objections, it was so very vaguely intimated that he could plausibly deny it, retract absolutely if pressed, go to Mass with unclouded brow, and avoid any smell of ecclesiastical courts, heresy charges, smoke and fire and carbonised flesh in the marketplace. He was anyway historically lucky. Within a year or two of his play's appearance, Good Queen Bess came to the throne and changed the religion yet again. *He* would not have needed, in his Protestant grey age, to waste his time protecting himself upon reams and reams of paper against unjustified, uncorroborated, most malicious allegations.

They called me Jack Juggler because my version of the play in 1965 astonished my university associates with its vigour and relevance. We were all very concerned to be 'relevant'; revolutionary, no less. We were remaking our cultural values; yes, upon the framework of Mid-Tudor comedy if that was where our creative parameters happened to impinge. I cannot see that the name is anything to be ashamed of; I have answered quite happily to it ever since; indeed I've used it on my own account as a regular artistic pseudonym, and why not?

I would have been Jack in any case. I was christened Jonathan, and never liked it. Even as a child – an only child – I found it uncomfortably precious. 'Mummydear's little chappykins' with long fair curls, a daft Christopher Robin sailor-suit and such a sweet little sou'wester when it rained. The other kids did their best to make me cry at nursery school, would you believe; in all the dowdiness of their wartime-utility shorts and jumpers and their clipped back-and-sides haircuts as though the military conscription was already reaching out to them. What was worse, they laughed at 'Mummydear'. They ought not to have done; her (probably black-market) fur coats, her swooping elocutionary vowels, her lipstick, her peroxide permanent waves were no more than foretastes of a then unguessed-at Tory leader for whom in their prime they'd all be voting, with ravenous contempt toward the whole of England – except for the home counties and their own native *colony* of the home counties, north-country managerial suburbia. Rhododendron hinterland of the Huddersfield Road, Barnsley; 1880s villas, semi-detached, soot-black sandstone; plane trees along the pavement. My mother, being a bookie's wife, was discernibly a piece richer than their mothers, that was all; and *our* house was detached, neo-Elizabethan, lozenge-window-paned, half-timbered, 1920-ish; their mothers must have audibly despised her. But they aspired to her nonetheless.

When I grew a little older I found myself known as Johnny. My aunts on my mother's side all called me Johnny. Better than Jonathan, but not much. No one ever took a 'Johnny' seriously.

Instead, I demanded 'Jack', and in the end I got it. Brisk, brusque, masculine, and practical at all social levels. Let's not talk about Jack the Ripper – but Jack the Lad, Jack Tar (which even accommodated sailor-suits, though I was long beyond *them*, thank God), Jack the Giant-killer, Idle Jack, Jack-of-all-Trades, Lance-Jack (my actual rank in the national-service army), Every Man Jack in sweat and leather and a fine pair of bollocks? – why, the list was endless – no one fooled around with Jack, unless he was in the accusative case as Fuck-you-Jack-I'm-all-right, and *that* was a Jack well capable of fighting his own corner.

They did, of course, fool around with my surname, until I took pains to deconstruct it. Smythe-Pogmoor was impossible, except to gain a point or two in the hierarchical intrigues of the Chamber of Commerce tennis club; I can never hear it, still less write it (as now), without a shudder at the memory of my mother's pekinese all a-whimper and a-dribble in her plump arms against the pearls on her well-brassièred bosom. It belongs to her pre-war white telephone, and her dinky chintz telephone-seat with the area directory bound in mauve velvet. ('Hello, is that Perkinson's? This is Mrs Smythe-Pogmoor, number 3 Hydrangea Avenue. I am most dissatisfied, most, with the unpunctuality of your errand-boy. I distinctly requested the floral decorations before luncheon. My guests for my afternoon bridge-party are due to arrive in half an hour and there is not a bloom to be seen in my drawing-room. No, an apology is quite indefensible; I need a very good reason for your default, or my future custom goes elsewhere . . .') Double-barrels supposedly suggest a degree of aristocracy. All ours did was show that a deeply aboriginal and socially intimidated Pogmoor had married a pretentious Smith who had done her level best to make far more of it than it deserved.

I became plain Jack Smith as soon as I was out of the army and could have my own way in such things. Lance Corporal Smythe-Pogmoor had carried no weight whatever, officers sniffed and lower ranks deliberately put on chinless accents when addressing me. I do believe discipline actually suffered. On the analogy of the missing horseshoe nail, my very name could have lost a battle.

So: in 1960 Jack Smith got himself in, against the staunchest parental disapproval, to the brand-new Department of Drama in a brand-new go-ahead Regional University (superficially termed a Redbrick – more adequately, a Glassclad Precast Concrete – most adequately of all, an Extended Carpark Concept with Architectural Addenda). Upon reaching postgraduate level, he shed a second skin and lo! Jack Pogmoor. A change of name in the midst of 'theatre studies' was part and parcel of the trade-bullshit; we all had a good laugh at my rapid proletarianisation, and everyone seemed to agree it was damned good *Zeitgeist*. (Smith, after all, had been nearly as anonymous as 'Anon'.)

I'd better be careful here. While vindicating myself I don't want to be accused of libelling others. A fictional locality, if you don't mind, for my academic rambles, but not too far from home – the 'University of Pomfretshire'; which I hope will sufficiently indicate a half-finished campus laid down among windswept rhubarb and liquorice fields, the would-be intellectual centre of a bleak limbo of coalmines, scrapyards, asbestos-walled light-industry plants, several miles' bus-drive from our Barnsley or from any other of a half-dozen smoke-grimed similar boroughs. (I exerted every mental effort to make 'several' seem a thousand.)

Those who know me will doubtless know exactly which university, and if the cap fits I suppose they'll wear it; but as the public at large *won't* know, offended individuals will hardly publicise themselves gratuitously, considering how long ago the whole silly business was.

2

Before giving account of the play and its incidental hanky-panky, I'd better say a word about Polly herself, my ambiguous wee friend. She was a short dark square tough-jawed Scot from Edinburgh. Her father was a doctor, an untrendy GP of modest means. She had taken her degree in Classics at the university there, which did not (I think) boast a department of drama; so she came to us at Pomfretshire for an extra two years' postgraduate struggle, aiming obliquely at the professional stage, of which her parents disapproved. 'Play-acting', they called it, to imply that it was just possibly a reasonable hobby for a student but ought severely to be confined to her spare time, and if she were truly pursuing her studies she'd no business to *have* spare time. Even that was a great concession: they were serious Presbyterians, they had hoped she would have gone for medicine, or at least law; but as I say, she was tough, she knew what she wanted and meant to get it. Which is why I say 'struggle'. Her family tradition had striven to imbue her with an old-fashioned sense that all forms of entertainment were self-indulgent, and thus perilously close to sin, *per se*; while dramatic entertainment and its excitably intimate preparations verged at once upon one particular sin, what else but fornication? of course, it was notorious: observe in every Southron Sunday paper the theatrical divorce-suits. I don't suppose old Doc Blackadder ever said to her in so many words: 'A woman upon the stage is nae better than a harlot; lassie, tak tent!', or whatever. But the feeling was certainly there and she fought against it might and main.

She needed to be an actress, from God knows what queer strain among her genes. She would eventually seek a place in RADA or somewhere like it; but, as a careful Scot who built up her life in well-trimmed ashlar courses from a firmly-set foundation, she wanted first to ground herself in all the theory of the theatre, its philosophy, its place in society, everything, in short, that a college could supply. A generation or two earlier she would have had to run away from home to join a rep or a touring stock-company as assistant stage-manager and general dogs-body. Which might have been more practical; but grant-subsidised university, indeed postgraduate, education was now the cry of the time, and it rhymed very happily with her cultural prejudices. As of course with those of her father; he could not in the end withstand her.

Who would dispute she was a virgin, both by character and environment? Moreover she believed in it. Twenty-one years old.

She went to church every Sunday. Which was beginning to seem eccentric among students, even in Edinburgh; but she had been led there all her life and saw no reason to desist. Let me say, she was not ostensibly *devout*. She never talked religion, and she would never have belonged to one of those crawthumping campus Jesus-groups who ticker-taped all the freshers with smarmy 'good news' leaflets before they'd even found their way to library or cafeteria. She just went to Sabbath worship and told nobody; until somebody saw her – me. Her digs were in a sober terrace-house in the outskirts of Hardcaster (nearest town to the university), not very far from my own.

One Sunday – it would have been about the middle of her first year (my second, final year as a postgrad) – I was strolling out to buy my *Observer* and *News of the World* from Higden's corner-shop, and there she went, tip-tip-tap down the street in front of me on determined low-high heels, with a demure black dress of a sort of velvety fabric cut so taut and so close to her wide bum and strong shoulderblades that you could imagine she wore nothing but a varnishing of black shellac. On her head was a little green beret, from beneath which her short black hair clipped her nape like an undercap. She carried, discreetly, a small black volume, by the very angle she held it you could see it was neither a novel nor a textbook, but – amazing! The Book of Common Prayer? Ah, no: for in Lord Sidmouth Street she walked straight past St Etheldreda's to turn briskly into the porch of the Presbyterians almost next door, and I realised that Metrical Psalms would probably be nearer the mark.

I'd already made some small approaches: noncommittal, by the beastly standards of university courtship. Now I knew I had to have her.

'Have her' – exact words of my internal decision, but what did they mean? Screw her once, and say goodbye? Screw her once, and then again and again? Ask her to marry me; and perhaps defer screwing (if that's how she'd wish it) until after the ceremony? Or combine with her, body and spirit, in life and in work, for as long as it might last; maybe even go to church with her, to share with her what she thought important? All these answers, all mixed up. I felt so fervently toward her that I felt no parallel need to set my feelings side-by-side and sort them out, rejecting some, embracing others.

For that church was so lovely a challenge, invitation, provocation; I had been thinking about her a great deal already; but from that Sunday on, her decorous tip-tip-tap vibrated my inner ear by day and by night.

As for her acting? Frankly, I can tell you, it was great – which is to say, it *promised* to be great, she had of course a lot to learn. In Edinburgh, I heard, she had played Yeats's Deirdre with an urgent noisy power in a Dramsoc production that brought a rave notice from the *Scotsman*. It was then re-produced during the vacation as a Festival Fringe piece, when Harold Hobson of the *Sunday Times* all but fell out of his wheelchair in his ecstasy at her passion.

> Miss Blackadder [he gurgled] struck our hearts with horror and terror; I could think only of the young Bernhardt as described by Victor Hugo, '*c'est une guerrière atroce couverte du sang pourpre des batailles de Vénus!*'

I'm not sure of the French, but that was his general gist (I stole a crafty dekko at Polly's file in the Registrar's office, she'd enclosed a few press cuttings with her application form, of course).

But she told me, very seriously, that she really felt more drawn towards comedy; 'hard comedy', she said, whatever she meant by that. I don't think she thought of 'difficult'; 'hard' as opposed to 'soft', rather; a most Scottish concept and no mistake. Well, it would no doubt be the sort of comedy best suited to an atrocious amazon, purple with gore from Venus' wars; and so I told her. She nodded, peered into the dregs of her cup of coffee, smiled frostily, replied: 'You've been peeping where you shouldn't. I daresay you're quite right. But we first have to discover what roles are available.' This conversation took place long before I had a sight of those Metrical Psalms; without fully realising it, I had dipped my first foot into the whirlpool.

Six weeks or so after our chat I sat next to her at a student bottle-party, on the floor, listening to the Beatles: it was late enough at night, the horrid wine-cup of our hosts had been replenished several times with any number of ill-chosen liquids; most of us were well foxed; there was groping and inexperienced joint-passing. I put an arm round Polly's shoulders, she did not repulse me. Nor did she look at me. I worked my hand down to her left boob, still she made no move.

My language is as vulgar as my actions were, I know; but we *were* very vulgar at Pomfretshire in those days, vulgar and surprisingly young for our ages. I was only too well aware of it (would you believe, I was nearly twenty-five? *Barnsley* twenty-five), I strove hard for sophisticated maturity. Blunder upon blunder; shame, guilt, remorse . . . ?

I slid fingers into her dress. She shrugged; but with such strength I slipped backwards among the cushions and boozily let go my hold. 'Oh no,' she whispered hoarsely, and she didn't seem to be drunk or stoned at all. 'Oh no, Jack, that won't do.' She rose to her feet – I thought she was going to stalk out of the room – but no, she just went to another corner and sat down again, legs crossed, feet under her skirt, between two gauche first-year undergrad girls, one fat, one skinny, one snaggle-toothed, one with glasses, whom nobody wanted to grope. They conversed, if I heard aright, in superior tones about Terence Rattigan; and then, after half an hour, left the party, all three together.

Oh no, Jack, it didn't do. And I didn't think to try again until, as I said, I had seen her go into the church; maybe a whole term later, I'm not sure.

At all events, a good few months elapsed.

3

And then came the question of my final production; the stage presentation of the substance of my thesis, a series of not very original thoughts upon playwrights between the end of the Middle Ages and the beginnings of the Elizabethans. I had to find a script from that period and bring it to life, with whatever cast I could rummage up among undergrads and postgrads. Several of my colleagues were at the same game; there was Sheridan and Brecht and one of the new playwrights (Edward Bond?) busily about to be mangled for the benefit of Faculty and Student-body, all squatting like owls along the tiers of our small auditorium.

My problem was that every play I had been examining was composed in such stilted English, neither full-blooded Chaucerian archaic nor the broad sweep of Marlowe or Shakespeare, but somewhere awkwardly in between. The verses seemed scarcely to scan and the obscure topical references, perfectly okay in footnotes, made very little sense in performance to speakers or to hearers. How on earth would semi-trained students (semi-*literate*, my God) be able to cope with them? 'Bring to life'? It was a joke.

I was supposed to be a Director; to display myself as such, rather than as library scholar. As a library scholar indeed I knew I was no Dover Wilson. I had to prove myself in flesh and blood. I was therefore supposed to be able to find and instruct actors to embody my ideas. I had been scribbling away about early booth-stages, schools-drama, political patrons of acting companies for and against the Reformation, until I had almost lost touch with the boys and girls in the department. And clearly the boys and girls were headlong bent for Bond, Brecht and even Sheridan in preference to *Gammer Gurton's Needle*, or whatever else I could offer them from my cornucopia of unfunny old farce. It had to be farce. The serious business of that age of theatre – characters called 'Avarice-Policy', 'Adulation-Honesty' or 'Hardy-Dardy the Vice', all stiffly projecting their crude incitements to bad or good government – would bore the audience solid. An audience, if you please, that thought the Beatles were the crown of life, marijuana the food of the gods, and CND sitdowns the acme of democratic expression. And if the audience were to be bored, however skilful my stagecraft in the abstract, I would have failed at my first hurdle: what else is Directing all about?

I had, however, been cultivating Polly. My blunder at the party may or may not have been forgotten; but she was happy nonetheless to *talk* theatre with me for hours on end. She talked it very well, which was pleasure enough to be going along with until I could find some trick to bring our bodies to the bared sweetness of intermeshed proximity. Her own thesis was the Roman Theatre, Plautus and Terence basically, plus some heavy work on their Greek originals – and an appendix to deal with tragedy (not much, except for Seneca; she'd thought up a *theory* about Seneca-in-performance; I don't need to go into it). She did not have to finish the writing for another year; in the meantime she was greedy for parts in any play that happened to be going on. *Saint Joan of the Stockyards*, the Brecht I've already mentioned, was glittering before her eyes. She was altogether too enraptured by the 'integrity' of the humourless Marxist who was about to direct it, one Fred Owston, an authentic prole-by-birth from Mexborough.

I was resolute she was *my* actress. I had to wean her from the dire Fred, but how to do so when I had no script for her – let alone a meaty part? The Tudors, on the whole, were none too generous toward young actresses; why should they be? they never used them. Boy-players were but prentices, and scripted-for accordingly. I prowled and prowled around her with bright ideas and daft ones; and then, at last, I hit it.

4

Commissar Owston was already starring her in a disagreeably rigid one-acter by some 1930s amateur stalwart of the left-wing Unity Theatre. She played an impassioned partisan in the Spanish Civil War whose lover had to be shot as a fascist spy, and she had to give the orders: 'the necessary murder', and the play made no bones about it. Her role was indubitably *hard*; but not a vestige of comedy – maybe she'd welcome a relief.

There was to be but the one performance. I was backstage when the dress-rehearsal came to an end. She strode into the wings with real tears on her grim little face, and her spine still as stiff as a rifle barrel with the trauma of the firing squad over which she had just presided. Owston clasped both her hands in fervent but wordless congratulation; and then turned sharply away to give urgent political correction to the boy playing her lieutenant, a happy-go-lucky scruff, more like a national-service squaddy than the peasant ideologue intended by the author. So of course I did the proper theatrical thing and kissed her and breathed she was 'fabulous'. She let me do it, too; all high with her art as she was. She let me come with her into the women's dressing-room (there were no other females in the cast) and even let me help her unstrap her pistol-holster and bandoliers. I foresaw she would not allow me to unbutton her battledress, at least not fully; so I at once began to say what I had to say.

'I've hit it! *Jack Juggler!*'

'What? I thought you told me it was a silly play with nothing in it.'

'So it is, as it stands. But why leave it as it stands? It's one-third of a piece by Plautus, inconsequential, ending nohow. So why don't I put back the other two-thirds – or bits of them – and make a tight modern comedy out of it? From my point of view I'd be presenting a critical reassessment of a Renaissance playwright and his source material, worth – oh, twenty pages of analysis in my thesis. From your point of view—'

'Why should *I* have a point of view?' Her words were dry and detached, but I could see she was pleased.

'Because I want you to be in it. The two women's parts, as they stand, are perfunctory. But why leave them as they stand? Plautus made a plot of sexual intrigue, our 1550s schoolmaster censored it, didn't he? for the sake of his pre-puberty kids. Get it back in again, and give yourself a chance. You've thorough knowledge of the original—'

'*Amphitryo?*'

'Right; but *I've* not studied it with any degree of insight; I've only just thought of this angle; thought of it in point of fact as I watched you, twenty minutes since, while they showed you the twisted evidence that El Loco the Bullfighter was Franco's secret agent. Bewilderment, incredulity, love betrayed yet lust continuing, tenderness, rage, revenge – we need all of that, we can find it for you, you can do it – but comic, this time round, just like you've always wanted. Why, the situation's an archetype: the bloody bastard's been shagging the arse off you and when you thought that you knew who he was all you know now is that you knew who he wasn't!'

'H'mph,' says she, pert as a wagtail, 'Jack, there's no need to be coarse. Plautus wasn't coarse – not *unduly* coarse, if you know the Latin, *I* know the Latin. And neither is P.J. Regan.' (P.J. Regan being the ex-IRA Red who had confected the Iberian epic.) 'And I hope, if you do monkey about with this *Juggler* play, you won't be coarse either. I don't care for it, you know that; dear goodness, it's not necessary.'

Dear goodness.

And yet—

She said, 'Off you go, Jack,' highly businesslike, 'tits coming out.' She was indeed opening her jacket, beyond contradiction she meant me to leave the dressing-room, she believed she wasn't *coarse*? Oh, she'd changed over the last few weeks, Doc Blackadder would feel dourly satisfied he'd been right all along about the drama and its vicious influence.

Firm modesty nonetheless: she turned her back, and I turned to the door. She wanted of course to be alone to concentrate on her performance that evening, but she threw a parting word: 'Tomorrow, if you're serious. But I have half-promised Fred.'

'Joan of the stockyards,' I couldn't stop myself retorting, 'isn't a funny lady at all. She'd get on your nerves something dreadful.'

I made a noise with the door as if I'd absolutely gone through it, glanced behind me before I did go through it, saw in the mirror that tits were indeed 'out', such a very brief glimpse, eh, dear! (but one I'd never had before), and in the corridor who was there but Fred Owston? We glared. I told him his production was masterly melodrama. He told me the admitted crudity of the play was historically inevitable, and so was my bourgeois reaction to it.

As I went to the lift-shaft I heard him offer a respectful clearance of the throat outside the dressing-room, letting Polly know he'd wait there until she was ready.

5

I was more than ready. Onto my bicycle, back to my digs, and deep into the old compendium, Farmer's *Anonymous Plays*; together with Plautus (Loeb edition, the time-honoured school crib) which I'd whipped out of the library en route. Now that I knew I'd caught her interest – I'd never have had a chance even to *hear* about her bosom otherwise – I must get some preliminary notes down on paper and no delay.

You'll not object if for a few paragraphs I turn pedant and start summarising plots? Believe me, it's extremely germane.

❧ Plautus told a story about Jupiter (chief god), who wanted to lie with Alcmena, lovely mortal. She is a virtuous wife, so he cannot approach her direct. 'Oh no, Jove,' she'd snap, 'oh no, that won't do.' So to ease himself into her sheets he must disguise himself, by miracle, as her husband General Amphitryo, conveniently away at the wars. Mercury (assistant god) has disguised himself likewise, as Amphitryo's slave Sosius. His duty: to ensure that Amphitryo by some mischance doesn't come home unexpected and march into the bedroom left-right left-right to discover Lord God on the job, which would shock the whole household and give divinity a very bad name. Mercury-as-Sosius, therefore, and Sosius-as-Sosius begin the crucial action of the play when they meet outside the house and have a row. For, as you'll have guessed, the real Amphitryo *is* on the way home, while Jupiter and Alcmena are still at it. Mercury-as-Sosius persuades Sosius-as-Sosius by brute force that Sosius-as-Sosius is not Sosius, so who is he, the poor sod? – he's nearly driven into catatonics. It's an episode that lasts for five hundred lines, give or take; say twenty-five minutes of acting time. It's just the first misunderstanding of an accumulative comic series throughout the play – Amphitryos and Sosiuses running lunatic rings round each other, until distracted Alcmena (her arse well shagged-off, but who did it?) is finally consoled by miracle: Jupiter reveals himself in the standard-issue clap of thunder and her reward is to be pregnant with none other than the Infant Hercules, divine child and all your wives should be so lucky! ❧

The point is: hardly any of this was in 'Anon's' *Jack Juggler*, except for what I've called 'the first misunderstanding', False Sosius *vis-à-vis* True Sosius, which 'Anon' followed pretty closely, joke by joke and kicked-bottom by kicked-bottom, although he did prolong five hundred lines into something over a thousand. The two Sosius-types were the only identical couple in his script, and he made no attempt whatever to give anyone else a *doppelgänger* for sexual or any other purpose, or to introduce pagan gods or miracles.

❧ No Jupiter, therefore; and Amphitryo, prosaically, is a city gent (Mr Boungrace) who hangs around the Threadneedle Street wine bars; rather than go home to supper, he sends messages to his wife to come and meet him. Not surprisingly, the wife (Dame Coy) is an irritated body in danger of turning into a regular shrew. Their Sosius: a layabout pageboy called Jenkin. They also have a girl, Alice, Dame Coy's personal maid. Alice's sole contribution to the play is to launch into a high-powered denunciation of the absent Jenkin for his juvenile-delinquent behaviour, after which she goes off and doesn't come back; although Jenkin himself has earlier built her up, thoroughly to whet the public's appetite for her entry on stage—

> She simpereth, she pranketh, she jetteth without fail
> As a peacock that hath spread and showeth her gay tail;
> She minceth, she bridleth, she swimmeth to and fro;
> She treadeth not one hair awry, she trippeth like a doe.
> She quavereth and warbleth like one in a galliard,
> Every joint in her body and every part –
> Oh, it is a jolly wench to mince and divide a fart . . .
>
> *But it is a spiteful girl and never well*
> *But when she may some ill tale by me tell.*
> (etcetera)

—he is drawn to her and repelled by her; he erupts with these little bursts of under-age sexual malice which ought to mean her eventual emergence as a significant person in the plot; but they don't . . . And now: 'Anon's' Mercury, Jack Juggler himself, another City of London page, roughly resembling Jenkin, but employed in another household. He has it in for Jenkin (and indeed for Boungrace) over some street-corner vendetta, and plots to get his own back by assuming the exact disguise of his rival and causing all the trouble he can. The trouble, in effect, is a scrappy catalogue of domestic cross-purposes, with Boungrace and his wife missing their appointments, Jenkin (like Sosius) doubting his own identity, while everyone (except, alas, the peacock-tailed Alice) beats him up; and, finally, when the story has unravelled and one would surely expect Jack Juggler to be confronted by his double and/or the outraged adults (*Recognition Scene*, Aristotle would have called it, yes?) nothing happens. Jack has made his escape; and his tricks remain a mystery. As, I suppose, Transubstantiation was a mystery. If you can make Jenkin believe that Juggler is Jenkin, you are well on the way to make *anyone* believe almost anything else – for example, Bread is Flesh and Wine is Blood; or so the Epilogue obscurely hints:

> —simple innocents are deluded . . .
> And by strength, force and violence oft-times compelled
> To believe and say the moon is made of a green cheese,
> *Or else have great harm, and perchance their life lose.* ❧

Thoroughly scary totalitarian implications: whatever we did with the script, we'd have to keep those. Nineteenth eighty-four was less than twenty years ahead.

6

But how to introduce into 'Anon's' half-witted anecdote at least a proportion of *Amphitryo*'s complexities? Next day I asked Polly to come round to my digs in the evening to discuss it with me over a bottle of wine; she gravely declined with damnably downcast eyelashes, pretending it would be 'more convenient' if we met in one of the postgraduate study rooms, at any rate for a start. So we did, that afternoon, with lots of books and efficient pads of notepaper, and a wary ear cocked (on my part) for jealous interruptions by the likes of Owston. I was already beginning to think of *him* much as Juggler thought of Jenkin:

> —I called unto my mind
> Certain old reckonings that were behind
> Between Jenkin and me, whom partly to recompense
> I trust by God's grace, ere I go hence!

Dear goodness, yes.

(A state of mind not diminished by a certain physical likeness between us, less perhaps than that which linked the two pageboys, but I *had* once heard an undergraduate funny-bugger refer to us as 'Yin and Yang'. As a 'mature student', the looming Fred might have been five years older than me. But otherwise: we were both nearly six foot tall; we were both rather too fat, myself because I took no exercise, he because he took more than enough – all muscle, let him *rot* for it! college wrestling club and a cup-winner –; we both had blondish hair, although his was Stalinesque *en brosse* while mine followed Yeats's into one eye – or Hitler's, if you prefer it. He wore leather jackets, I slopped around in dufflecoat and Aran sweater; and he had the wire-rimmed spectacles.

Also, our West Riding accents. An effort had been made at home to rid me of mine; whereas his remained as shaped by the pit villages and railway yards of the Dearne valley, the tang of a smouldering slag-heap. I could talk broad enough when I chose to. Now that I was definitively Jack Pogmoor, I chose to more and more.)

7

Polly jabbed her biro dismissively into Loeb's creaking dialogue. 'There's a recent Penguin Classic just out, much better for stage purposes than this. Also, it reconstructs the missing Recognition Scene. You did know the Recognition Scene is missing from the ancient text? Between Jove and Amphitryo: it's crucial.'

So: she had the weather-gauge of me already. She was already fishing the Penguin translation out of her businesslike briefcase, and I hadn't known about it at all. I *was* aware the scene was lost; but it was a little late to tell her and be believed. I may have hissed between my teeth as a sign of short annoyance, but she ignored it and continued:

'If you think you can extend Dame Coy Boungrace so far as to make her a worthwhile part, you're going to have to create her hidden ravisher – logically, Jack Juggler's master – to fill up the plot. Are you interested in Mrs Boungrace? I cannot say that I am. She's a hoity-toity snot-nosed parvenue; developed on the lines laid down for her, she'll be a caricature of a 'certain-age' woman sneered at for her frustrated libido, mocked because she deserves all she gets, Gilbert and Sullivan couldn't do worse – cruel, to be sure, but the wrong kind of cruelty – I don't find it good material for genuine fun. Unless you were to dig at the text to alter her personality; but then you're outwith your original author's conception? Forby—' (I loved it when she talked pawky like a minister or an advocate out of Robert Louis Stevenson) '—Forby, such a metamorphosis must necessarily overcomplicate, overweight the structure, and introduce – h'mph! an entire new male character, gripping the initiative of the play's action at the expense of Jack Juggler?'

'Ah! and I've thought of that.' Like a wily privateer I had crossed her course now, and edged myself briskly to windward. Neither did *I* care to extend Dame Coy; she was too much of a piece with my own dear mother; I was not at all ready to dredge up my infantile inhibitions in public – maybe one day I would be, maybe after a year or two – you have to *work* for emancipation. Polly, I was hoping, would at length be of some help here; but not quite yet. She was right about the play's structure, though.

'Alice?' I said, tentatively. And then added strength to the suggestion. 'Alice Trip-and-Go, the playwright calls her. So let her do just that: amuse herself with young Jenkin, ambiguous, contemptuous, *cruel* – such a pretty little lad, she can't stand him, faugh! he's so mucky and idle; let her let him believe she's invited him into her privates. She gives him the eye, and switches it off again, he doesn't know whether to take her at her word or not. While he's floundering around, Jack Juggler in disguise gets in first. And then work it from there, with a well-made Recognition, and a proper leading-on to the guts of the Epilogue.'

Ha ha, with what a grin she received it. My own privates glowed within themselves, the palms of my hands began to tingle. She liked it! 'I like it. Oh Jack, I do like that! I could give you a firework of an Alice, so I could. But how old are these pageboys? As I read the text, they can't be more than about thirteen. Isn't it a wee bit, eh, a bit too—?'

A wee bit too raw for the body of the kirk? 'Oh, bump them up to sixteen or so,' I said carelessly, 'a pair of teenage louts who behave like silly kids most of the time and yet know what to do with the tarts, except Jack has and Jenkin most likely hasn't. Not so much pageboys as juniors in commercial offices? A suggestion of modern dress, easier to organise, cheaper, I haven't a big budget; modified by lots of jewels, plumes, gaudy painted boots, to *bring it up*, right?'

She approved of that too. I rambled on about my written thesis – connections with later derivations from the Roman Comedy – running forward through Shakespeare and so on, all the way to *Box and Cox*, and *The Prisoner of Zenda*, even – but she wasn't really listening. She now had a part she could fix all her teeth in and to hell with the academic fal-lals. One thing worried her. 'Who's to write it, Jack? You?'

Her tone of voice was not encouraging; but it was true. I claimed no talent as a writer. Far better to be the man who told the writer what to write, the creator of the Overall Concept. And already I had the answer. 'Carver.' I put forward his name without hesitation. 'He'd be well able to find a style halfway between Tudor rhymed couplets and Plautine vernacular – from the Penguin text, of course.' Fid Carver was the department's resident playwright that year; he'd had one piece already at the Royal Court, *succès d'estime*, and another on Granada TV; period plays, both of them, set respectively in early nineteenth-century Yorkshire and sixteenth-century Spain and spot-on for their surge of appropriate language. He was currently at work on a satire with a contemporary setting, a swashing blow on behalf of the TUC against the Red-baiting press, to be performed by a cross-department cast. Owston had sought to direct it as his thesis project; but then refused, because it was 'contaminated with romantic individualism' – which made me think it must be good. One of the lecturers was to take charge of it instead.

I had met Carver only in passing; I had not been overwhelmed by his muted personality and Brillo-pad beard; he worked busily in his digs and came rarely onto the campus. But I knew him to be swift and fertile and conscientious about deadlines. Polly thought him a fine idea. My tingling hand met hers across the table, clutched tight; our happy smiles spread mutually.

And then she went off, to tea in the cafeteria with Owston. Bloody Blackadder Trip-and-Go, and *the de'il run awa' wi' her!* Ha.

8

Rather than trek you through every last detail of our subsequent work on the play, conferences with Carver, casting, rehearsals, the spectacular performance of Polly herself, how much of it worked and how much in the upshot didn't quite work (but I've said already it made my name), I feel forced to re-examine my sexual circumstances, as they were, as *I* was, in those years of Lucky-Jimmery, lukewarm Nescafé at any pause in the action, Yorkshire landladies on the watch for lecherous misdemeanour like anti-terrorist police at today's airports.

To be frank I was (very nearly) as much a virgin as Polly purported to be. Barnsley Grammar School had been no school for amorists. And myself at Barnsley Grammar School had scarcely whirled a glittering torch in the adolescent social vortex, such as it was. In my last year we did a school play: *The Admirable Crichton*, wherein I thoroughly misunderstood my character of an elderly liberal peer in a Belgravian Edwardian context that meant nothing to me or to any other of the cast. (It was directed by a misfit teacher who spent his life yearning for Belgravia and its polite amenities; he thought we must all share his dream.)

Nevertheless the school's fit-up theatre, theatre (you might say) *in essence*, captured my spirit entirely: the perceived ideal of its settings as opposed to the inevitable disappointment of their reality, distemper paint on tatty canvas flats . . . J.M. Barrie's fairly ordinary notions of this place or that threw my mind wide open to hitherto unimagined visions of what ought to be possible – make an undiscovered world, here and now – a society salon, tall windows, great sweeps of curtain-draperies, chandeliers, where long-gowned ladies who swayed like tulips while their servants moved in counterpoint, stiff and edgy as clockwork dolls –

and then the outrageous contrast, all hierarchy dissolved into naked castaways on a Caribbean island; rediscovering themselves as gods and goddesses among wafting screens of bright green foliage full of hummingbirds, butterflies, shafts of unmerciful sunlight; white-gold beaches through gaps in the palm trees; and beyond them, purple ocean, the immensely distant horizon which might have been drawn with a glass-cutter. Here at last: my own dream! Not at all the teacher's, but just as yearning, just as apparently hopeless behind the *No Hawkers or Circulars* of complacent Hydrangea Avenue.

I was about to be theatrical! My vacant existence was now furnished with destiny, I would shape *my whole life* within the small incandescent space of stage and wings and dressing-rooms and unpredictable front-of-house. And to the ravens with the swotting-up homework which my ignorant dad used to shout about each evening: 'No, you're not going out, I won't have it, you've exams to settle into, qualifications, School Higher Cert or Standard A or whatever they call it; there's to be no laiking wi'lasses till then! My God, if *I'd* only had your chances as a young lad . . .' To chime in with his refrain, 'Mummydear', an obsessed parakeet: 'Jonathan, there is no substitute for Technical Qualifications which will Fit You for a Business Career; your headmaster's report was insistent; Jonathan, do you hear me? – algebra! What Reputable Firm is going to look at a young man who mopes over picture-books and cuts out little people like a baby?' She meant my second-hand volume of Gordon Craig's stage designs; and my Pollock's toy theatre, which she had hoped six years previously I would soon have 'grown out of'.

There were girls in *The Admirable Crichton*, fetched across town from the High School. After the show one of them kissed me, and I hugged and kissed her back. Because of my aunts and their prissy little daughters, I hadn't liked girls very much. Now, however, things were going to be different. Just wait.

And then I was called up to the army. I spent my service, *wasted* it, more precisely, at low-level clerking in an Aldershot administrative block. The weekend before my demob I got unexpectedly pissed with a couple of mates; some typist girls, civilians from our office at District HQ, attached themselves to us; a fierce unworthy episode of setting-to-partners and 'knee-trembling' took place down a back alley; dark muddle of suspender belts, khaki trousers, trapped underwear; I remembered very little of it in the morning. Much better did I remember the cautionary VD film we had all been shown during our first week in basic training; I worried myself sick about that, also about the gruesome possibility of young Cheryl becoming pregnant. Well, neither did I catch a dose, nor she (I suppose) a bun in her oven. Not that I ever checked up on the latter; but she made no attempt to check on *me* after I'd handed in the uniform and signed for my last rail-warrant, so at length I felt free to assume that the 'All clear', as it were, had sounded. Whereat I preened myself secretly upon my devilish man-of-the-world experience. And yet, at the same time, I felt the episode was repulsive. Animal noises, animal smell, animal taste in my gulping mouth. And I knew why: young Cheryl was a little scrubber, she had incited the whole business, her hands were at my buttons before I realised what she was doing; it angered me and soured everything. Next time, no such nonsense; sexual intercourse had to be better than *that*.

9

For my first three years at Pomfretshire I strove for a next time and yearned for it to be better. With surprisingly small result. Some youths might have avoided the issue, turned away from women, turned to their own sex perhaps. But I was choked with contrarieties, lust and disgust together – I was well read enough to discover the most flattering precedents – Shakespeare expending his 'spirit in a waste of shame', Catullus hating and loving on a self-inflicted felon's cross – I clasped them to my heart. I had been a timorous child; as a young adult I was morose and diffident. So much so (except in rehearsal-room, where I felt a buried power stir its bristles and begin to growl), that it's a wonder I didn't slip like a slug in a rainstorm between the bars of a drain-gutter and disappear altogether from academic society.

The chicks were as diffident as I was, nervously provincial, so serious about their degrees – unless they were *confident*: in which case they weren't interested in me, they simply saw me as a neurotic nuisance and never understood that in my own view I was a committed libertine, pursuing foray after foray. I began to make notes of individual encounters, analytical of my continued failure. Contradictory conclusions: I was too avid; I was too tentative; I had bad breath; I was too intellectual; I was too upper-class(!); I was a crude vulgarian reeking of Doncaster Races and 'Reliable Ron the Old Firm' (ineradicable Dad); and above all, I was too bossy, too possessive, too much of a bloody swankpot, like all the men who talked at large about becoming celebrated directors. And all of this was entangled with the futile name of Jack Smith. On the other hand, Jack Pogmoor – why, *he* would be something else! Just wait then, let 'em wait, till his Permissive plans matured. Devilish.

So you see, you must discount, when I write about myself and Polly, my misleadingly cool prose-style: it's a product of hindsight, that's all . . . and shame, guilt, remorse . . . blunder upon blunder.

10

Jack Juggler brought an immediate and most gratifying clamour of congratulation. There was a boisterous party after the show in the greenroom, for everyone concerned with all the postgrad thesis-plays (ours had been the last to be presented). Professor Altdorfer, head of department, who had always been rather brusque with me, thrust a bear-like arm about my shoulders and proclaimed (from his full experience of pre-Nazi German theatre) that 'such *pastiche* with political inthrust was very much like, very, certain singular and strong experiments of early Piscator' – he had not thought, reading my preliminary study-notes, that I would be able to bring it off, but I had and he was most pleased.

Even Owston grimaced grudgingly and muttered, as he swayed, bottle in hand, 'Aye, you made it work; I've to give you that; clever. I'm not the only one, it seems, with an eye to Bert Brecht. Though *I* prefer not to come upon him sideways. That Blackadder's marvellous though, ent she? Well worth all dirty tricks to get her.'

If he sought a drunken brawl I wasn't going to accommodate him; but I knew what he was driving at. Polly had worked with me because I had made a whole new play for her, especially for *her*. (*I'd* made it, not Carver, Carver was merely subordinate.) By the same token, P.J. Regan's opus had very nearly been a whole new play – unpublished, never professionally staged, wrenched out of its well-merited tomb by Owston's nostalgic zeal – and if Owston had been sharp on the ball to rearrange Fid Carver's newspaper-satire around Polly as vital heroine, he could have had her in that one as well. But the oaf chose to boast *political standards*, he'd thrown up his opportunity, he'd lost her, and by God he knew why. She could be in a Brecht classic at any point of her career, so I am sure she had calculated, but an original invention by Pogmoor must absolutely not be bypassed.

Baulked by my cheery smile, Owston laid aside the verbal meat-cleaver and tried a stiletto instead. 'Mind you, without Polly, your critique of the master–servant relationship would have spun out a bit thin, don't you agree?' He was as well aware as I was that the chief 'critique' in the play had been aimed against brainwashing, the Dictatorship-of-the-Proletariat model sitting equally with that of the

Counter-Reformation. Which annoyed him, I had no doubt; but not even Comrade Fred would want openly to justify such procedures as the Moscow Trials. Had I been paying more attention to the growth of British Trotskyism, I'd have diagnosed his political stance with greater accuracy. I guess his views were just then in transition. But if he wasn't a Communist Party member he was still a boilerplate Marxist. And no way would he give me credit for my discovery of the real 'relevance' of *Jack Juggler*. Once again, I ignored his insult. He seemed to think his left-hand praises for my production had been an adequate quid pro quo for the few kind words I'd passed the previous evening upon his *St Joan of the Stockyards*, and they'd not been all that sarcastic, either. He did know his business. So he finished with me abruptly, shuffling off to join in an outburst of Socialist Song from a knot of his *Stockyards* boozers.

There followed, almost immediately, a curious encounter with Carver's twin sister. I only mention it because I married the woman five years afterwards. A flourishing stage designer; she might have made the sets for our production (Carver would have preferred it); but students, of course, had to do it as part of their course. She was up from London to see the play; I had not had time to be introduced to her; Carver said she would be leaving early to catch a night-train to King's Cross. I had the impression there was some sort of trouble between them; I had the impression he had expected her to stay and was all on edge because she wouldn't . . .

Twins, I am told, do not need to be identical. But Leonore and her brother seemed to belong to different nations, let alone different families. She was like a gypsy with dyed blonde hair; except (as I later discovered) the colour was absolutely natural, paler than her Levantine skin, brighter than her shining teeth. Her lips were as rich as blackberries. She dressed like a gypsy, too, multi-coloured prints, a kerchief round her head, tinkling ear-rings, I think there was some sort of fringed shawl. She was taller than Carver, lithe and serpentine. A 'Veronica Lake' lock of hair escaped from her kerchief, hiding one pale blue eye and nearly half of her face.

She slipped suddenly toward me from between three or four chattering students, to accost me in a low hoarse voice: 'Dirty tricks?' (Embarrassing! she'd overheard the damned nonsense with Owston.) 'Well, boy, this is the business, you can't start too early.'

What on earth could I say to that?

She smiled in a very odd way, one corner of her mouth up, one corner down. 'Fid says you're clever, as well. *He* means it as a compliment. Why not? We shall see.' She made me feel so awkwardly young; it was rude and it was patronising *de haut en bas*, from thirty-three to twenty-five; she stood there and appraised me, like a housewife at a jumble sale with a second-hand bedspread. Her cold pale eye shook me open, as it were, stretched me against the light, and then folded me up again to replace me on the stall. (Not quite what was wanted: try elsewhere.) We were close to a window. She glanced quickly out of it. Whispered. 'Ah, my taxi! Dead on time.' And off she went.

I had just begun to say to her, resentfully indeed, 'It's very nice meeting you; you do have a verdict on the play?' I don't think she heard.

The excited casts and crews were getting drunk very quickly. Members of Faculty were indulgent toward them, for all the plays had gone well. Music was uproarious. Polly and Carver in a corner talked and talked and talked. I brought a bottle over; she put her arms round me and kissed me; then Carver had a lot to say again and she seemed to forget me. I sat back into my own corner and tried to make do with the girl who'd played Mrs Boungrace. But she was something of a whooping idiot, onstage and off; I yielded her without a pang to her regular boyfriend; I watched them dance the Twist (or whatever style of hands-off rearing-and-crouching had succeeded the Twist that year) for maybe half an hour. Polly came to me and kissed me again, this time with her tongue in my mouth. She said I wasn't to mind about Fid, everyone knew Fid was dreadfully sulky unless you let him talk, and 'Oh, I am so happy I can't bear to have anyone sulky, not tonight, Jonathan, no, oh dear goodness no!'

(Jonathan. How extraordinary. I knew I'd never told her my full name.)

While she was kissing me, and a wonderful long kiss it was, Carver left the room with a boy from the Edward Bond. I was mildly surprised he hadn't chosen one of his own cast to fondle, if that's what he had in mind. Only now it occurs to me: Playwright's Post-natal Blues! – when it is suddenly apparent that actors and director alone have between them created success, the poor bloody author left out of the reckoning for evermore. Polly's response to his garrulity must have convinced him of this. What had she said to him? Or rather, what had she failed to say? Had she talked about me all the time? Or worse, had she talked about Owston?

Because suddenly, she wasn't there. And neither was Owston. And neither were a lot of other young people. Some, I daresay, were on their way home, conscientiously conscious of the times of the last buses and the 9 a.m. lecture tomorrow. Others, in pairs, were wandering about the building. It was dark and empty everywhere by now, except for the greenroom revels. Some official arrangement had been made with the janitor; otherwise he'd have locked up long ago. Labyrinthine corridors and miscellaneous small rooms and large; shadowy alcoves; sensual possibilities. Old Altdorfer, breathing schnapps into my ear-hole: 'I have the agreement of our good Mr Brown that in one hour he clears all out.' (Who the hell was Mr Brown?) 'Hullabaloo is very good, for a short while; I am too old for it, already. Tell all these lively people, from me, well done and good night.' He loped blearily away, fumbling in his trousers pocket for his car keys.

11

I was unaccountably in the theatre foyer, the door to the car park on my right, the passage to the greenroom behind me, the entrance to the auditorium on my left up a short flight of stairs. I did my best to fix these positions, like a map-reader orientating himself. It was more difficult than it should have been. Something mobile in the middle distance was disturbing the symmetry. Owston, almost blind to the world, feeling his way down the short flight of stairs. His U-boat Oberleutnant's leather jacket was draped around his shoulders, his shirt-tails were out of his belt, his glasses had slipped to the very end of his pug nose. He held an empty bottle.

'Empty,' he grunted. 'Go to t'greenroom, get 'er another.' On the bottom step his foot seemed to falter under the weight of his ankle; he made a grab at the handrail, missed it, sat down on the stairs: 'Scots wha hae!' he bawled, as though the words were a Gaelic war cry. He rolled sideways on the stairs, bumped from one tread to the next, until he fetched up against the box office in the foyer. He ended snoring on the fitted carpet below the ledge of the little ticket-window.

I picked his jacket up; and put it on. I picked his glasses up and put them on. What on earth had come into my head to impel me to such inconsequent action?

12

Drunken folly? No: for I was not drunk. I'd taken on a quantity of wine and I still held a half-full bottle in my hand; I was certainly being unusually careful about how I disposed of my limbs, each movement well planned and slow; the seconds and minutes (hours, indeed) of my personal time were not going at the same speed as the hands of my watch – which already pointed to half-past midnight, yet when Carver and his lad went out of the greenroom I had noted it to be eleven forty-five, surely no more than ten minutes since? But my brain was *analytical*, its responses remained ordered and clear, no blurring whatever, I was perfectly capable of comprehending both Cause and Effect.

Cause: Owston, blotto and half-dressed – did he know his fly was unzipped? – vaingloriously declaring some Scottish train of thought in hazy continuity from whatever he'd been up to before he emerged.

Effect: suspicion, rage, grief, revival of baffled desire, deadly need to seize hold of the main chance.

And the main chance lay in the auditorium, that's where the bloody man had come from. So up the steps, Pogmoor, *now!* creep (like Jack Juggler) in another man's skin, spy (like Joseph's brethren) the nakedness of the land.

She was not exactly naked, but—

Let me first explain about the stage set. It was just as the actors had left it after the show, a 'constructivist' composite design built on a thrust stage and made up of rostra, scaffold-poles, draperies and odd bits of requisite furniture; a floorcloth painted all over with packs of cards, dice, snakes-and-ladders and in the midst of them two sly-looking boys in the costume of the Knave of Hearts, glancing askance at one another, Gemini-twins from a zodiac chart; slung overhead, a large banner, to display in strong calligraphy our author's '1984' maxim:

SYMPLE INNOSAINTES! – BELIVE AND SAYE
THE MOUNE IS MADE OF A GRENE CHESE:
**OR ELLS HAVE GRET HARME
AND PERCACE YOUR LIFE LESE.**

The lights were all out, stage and front-of-house, except for one small working-light, a hundred-watt bulb, hanging above the prompt corner. There was a bed, belonging to Alice Trip-and-Go in Carver's new 'seduction scene'. It had no function at the end of the play and was therefore trundled away on its castors into a curtained recess at the back. The curtains had been pulled aside; I could see the coverlet, a faint gleam. I stood on the top tier of seating and blinked at it.

Immediate indication that the bed was not empty: a ruffled teacosy of short black hair, Polly's hair beyond all error. Ah God and she lay there, draped in white as white as the coverlet. As near as dammit, a producer's dream of the Sleeping Beauty in a panto. But not asleep, for even as I stared she shifted her head and peered back, eyes narrowed to make me out against the shadows. Her left arm, bare to the shoulder, sketched a lazy-like gesture of welcome.

She had been in red blouse and black bell-bottomed trousers at the party. She must have returned to the dressing-room for one of her stage costumes, the nightgown – as worn in the seduction scene. (I remembered how at dress-rehearsal its material proved too transparent, revealing incongruous underwear. We talked about a flesh-coloured body-stocking. 'Or nothing at all?' I suggested tendentiously. She laughed, then pretended to be shocked, then appeared in performance with a minute pair of pale panties just vaguely discernible, and no sign of any bra. Courageous, delicious, also slightly nerve-wracking: Permissive and all as we were, the department had its proprieties . . . In the end, no complaints. Two strawberry ghosts of nipples were A-okay by everyone. And happily her parents preferred not to come all those expensive miles from Scotland to see their daughter *undervalue herself*.)

I ran my hand over my head, pushing my forelock back across my scalp. I came down through the auditorium as far as the edge of the stage – upon which, only a few hours ago, in response to my guiding spirit she had flickered and danced in the thrill of her art like a gleeful dragonfly. And where now she sprawled satiate, her excitement exhausted?

Not quite.

'"Scots wha hae", indeed,' she snorted. 'What an ignorant Sassenach remark – "he only says it to annoy because he knows it teases". And moreover: he says it to *Alice*. But Alice knows that you know, deplorlorable Mr Owston, you're not ignorant at all. You know all about Lewis Ca-carroll, we are *not* what we seem, through the glass-looking, dark – dark as a white rabbit's hole – you did find another – other – find—?' The word 'bottle' began to shape between her lips and died drowsily away. Eyelids closed, tipsy head dropped onto the pillow. How bitterly I surveyed her ingratitude. Wouldn't you?

'Come on again,' she said, 'come.'

Ah, here was my main chance with a vengeance.

'Ech, dearie dear.' (Her soft murmur had the precise mawkish tone of a kind auld wifie in a but-and-ben.) 'O Frederick, we really shouldn't.' (*Frederick?* The gorge still rises . . .) 'Should we?'

Well: we did. She permitted everything. She forgot about the second bottle. She was wanton and deliciously drowsy; but of course I was peremptory, and alas it didn't last very long; when we had finished, she fell suddenly asleep. So, like a fool, did I.

If I'd nipped away at once I could have *got* away, free and clear; she'd never have known. As it was, I woke up to find her furiously, ineffectually, beating at me with clenched fists, so distressed she seemed unable to speak. Nor did *I* try to converse. The best I could do was to drag myself sideways out of her reach and off that coverlet, and scramble from the theatre the same way I came in. Owston was still hugging the foyer carpet, a stinking brock in his foetid den. I dropped him his coat and specs. The last few gaggles of party-goers were still on their way through the car park. I cannot have slept for more than twenty minutes, but by God it was twenty minutes too long.

13

And what to say to her, the next afternoon, when I met her head-on, along the cinder path at the back of the Science Faculty? She didn't try to avoid me, either; she saw me in front of her and stepped quickly to cut off my retreat. Her face was as white as a scrubbed dishtowel, her dark eyes were two cauldrons from some Calvinist hell-pit.

She had rediscovered articulate speech, and lost none of her terrible anger: 'It's not something I mean to be silent about. You'll have your own justifications, I don't need to hear them, Jack Juggler played his part for real, and now he's at his shauchling cantrips, aye you used me on the stage to ornament your scabby glory, and then you just used me. For whatever it gave you, spite, jealousy, power. How would *you* ever suppose you could understand a man like Owston?'

Do you tell me Owston had *not* had her? That he and she had done nothing but giggle – romantic innocence and a bottle of claret? That until I made it different, she was all the virgin she ever was? That 'Come on again' had meant only 'come on and give me a wee wee kiss but there's no more you're going to get, you wicked Mr Owston, you'? For allusively, by implication, that's the fable she proceeded to maintain. Could I believe? If she was Owston's, she was mine, I was positive about that. Not only mine but anyone's; she was clearly an open sluice. But if she *hadn't* been Owston's, then – then she would never be mine. By what I'd done to her – *with* her – I'd lost her utterly. Blunder upon blunder . . .

My impromptu rebuttal seemed, as I spoke it, to be the complete clincher, I must have been temporarily unhinged to deploy such an argument, but—

By what quirk of feckless innocence, I vehemently demanded, had she abandoned her panties last night? She wore them during the play, no doubt she wore them under her bell-bottoms at the party. Upon the bed, beneath her nightgown, they were not: how could it have been other than deliberate? Had Owston said, 'Leave 'em behind'? Or had she thought of it all on her own? With lidded eyes turned to one side, not evasively but as though I were unfit for her gaze, she refused me a straight answer. Her choice of clothes was *her* choice, who was I to call her to account for it? The obliquity of her contempt stung my face and locked my tongue. She jerked forward to break away, I stood stuttering, I begged her to stay put for just one moment.

'Well?' she spat, swinging round at me on one heel. 'If you've more to say, say it and that's an end.'

I tried to apologise – for everything, actions and words, all of it – no use. I told her I loved her; without knowing whether I meant it or not. No use. My 'just one moment' was over. She began to walk, fast, hastening through a throng of students in front of the doors of a lecture hall. I chased her and overtook her between stunted saplings in a half-grown shrubbery. 'But what,' I pleaded, 'what – are you going to do, now? – I mean, could you – will you—?'

'Will I tell?' There were tears running down her cheeks, her bonny countenance all puffed and distorted. 'Tell who? Tell my parents? Tell the Faculty? Tell Owston? Are you mad? Who would *you* tell, if it happened to you? God knows, who *will* you tell? You'd better not, you're as disgraced as I am! One word, Mr Pogmoor, and you're dead.' I had to let her go then. She was in such a state, I don't suppose she even realised she'd begun mouthing like a hard man in a Leith Walk chip-shop. But she was right: it *would* be death, I could never find enough excuses. Not among the class of people who worked so serenely day in day out to make Pomfretshire a paradise of enlightened liberal values.

14

Two days later: a Sunday. From the window of my digs I saw her, there she was! tip-tip-tap once again down the pavement and round the corner into Lord Sidmouth Street, Metrical Psalms in her gloved hand, green beret slightly a-tilt upon her smoothly brushed round little head.

(I may have been drunk on Alice Trip-and-Go's mattress, although I know I've asserted I wasn't, but I was very well aware – on Alice's mattress – that someone else had just been where I came. All my five senses shouted it aloud; it required no missing underwear to stamp it with the seal of proof.)

For the remaining fortnight of that academic term and then through-out the next term, which was also to be my last (provided my thesis found favour, which it did), P. Blackadder attended all her seminars, acted in as many plays as she could, and moved about with ostensible cheerfulness in a group of female friends. Now and then I saw her with Owston – sometimes in Hardcaster, sometimes at the theatre in Leeds or Sheffield, once at a small demo to protest against the Vietnam War – but (overtly, at least) she did not keep him company on campus. He was directing no more plays, being incarcerated with the written part of his thesis, *Brecht and his Royalties and the Contradiction of the Cash Nexus, an Extra-theatrical Parable*, sweating to finish it by the required date. My own thesis likewise kept me close in the punishment-cell. Owston and I hardly ever spoke to each other; she and I, never. I gather she moved digs to a village called Backthorpe, four miles out of town; at any rate, she ceased to be a Sabbath feature of Lord Sidmouth Street.

Despite what she'd said to me, she did go and blab to her girlfriends. I got some very frozen looks from some of them; they must have heard at least a portion of the story. *Her* story, of course: hypocritical prevarication, from one end to the other. It is not so much that she told lies; she just presented herself everywhere, always, as an Untruth all living and breathing and shaking her tight little tail.

Look at it! She deceived me; before ever I deceived her; and without having to utter one single identifiable falsehood.

While we were working on the play she showed evidence of affection far above the needs of the job. She made it appear she'd left Owston severely alone since her last cup of tea with him – which would have been the day she and I decided on the shape of our rewrites with our four hands all a-tingle together. Afterwards, those kisses at the party; that unexpected 'Jonathan'. And yet, at that very same party, she and he were already arranging their dirty little rendezvous. On *my* stage set, with all the accoutrements of *my* production to enhance their fun-and-games. It cannot have been spontaneous. They'd been leading up to it for bloody weeks.

I'm a jealous bastard, I've often been told so, I confess it. Jealousy, in general, makes for hair-trigger sensitivity towards other people's attempted cheats. So how was she able so smoothly to smile upon me while all the time smiling with Owston, and yet never let me gather one hint? Probably because she gave no hint to her own self. She concealed herself *from* herself. As I firmly believe she did about what happened on Alice's bed. If she'd never been fucked before (which I sorely doubt) she let Owston take her cherry without any admission that such a cardinal event was about to occur, was occurring, had occurred. The following afternoon, by her manner if not her words, she *denied* it to my face. I believe it was an honest denial, according to her own lights. They were, after all, by a long process of descent, the lights of the manic John Knox: once she conceived herself as being among the Elect, her sins were predestined to wither even as she committed them. She'd done nothing with Owston that she didn't have a right to do: therefore she'd done nothing.

I don't say the same for myself. I'd employed a rash but cunning stratagem, found out what I hungered to know, and assuaged an overmastering desire. Because the end of it was not happy, it would have been better if I hadn't begun it: I found *that* out within twenty-four hours. But it could have developed otherwise, had she been what I thought she was, what she had given me such reason to believe that she *must* be. Might I not have drawn from her an unstinting acceptance of me, of my need, of my passion, define it how you will? In which case, I would have become odious neither to her nor to any of her friends.

15

At least one of those friends was only too glad to shovel odium all over me. Some sort of American (Italo, like Al Capone? – I didn't know her very well); her name was Carmilla, the same name as that vampire-woman in one of those Victorian shockers, and her behaviour was not far removed. Carmilla Costello, an intense long hank of female gristle, tall and thin as a radio aerial whipping in the wind with tatters of a grimy flag at its tip. Her field of study was costume design; brilliant at it, they said; she was at Pomfretshire on an overseas postgrad exchange scheme. Her frozen looks were the most glacial of all; but she never approached me, until the last day of my final term when we found ourselves in the revolving-doors of the library, me coming out, she going in. She scowled and bared her teeth at me through the glass as we circled round. I was so startled by the fixity of her gaze that I began to go round a second time; and so, to my horror, did she. Arriving once more at the exit, I jumped out and down the steps, anxious to get away from her as quickly as possible. For God's sake, she came out after me, ran after me, caught hold of the empty haversack which had contained my final load of books-to-be-returned, and hauled me to a halt. The haversack-strap twisted taut, a garotte at my adam's-apple.

'Bloody hell,' as I plucked to loosen it, 'hey, what the hell—?'

'You,' she gasped. 'You!' And she positively kicked me, driving her sharp boot from under the swing of her maxi-skirt so strongly against my shin I fell down with a yelp of real pain. 'If I had a blade like you had, I'd take stripes out of the thick of your ass,' she went on, not gasping now but screaming. 'Like, I'd drag down your britches and lacerate you! Jesus, you'd get no fucking hard-on, I'd slice through the strings of your nuts.'

I'd no idea what she was talking about. She was pure-and-simple raving crazy. And all this, if you please, under the eyes of a score of people, intelligent academics on their way out of a faculty meeting, who just stood there and wobbled, like penguins, open-beaked.

She too was aware of the crowd, she lowered her voice and hissed at me, bending down to be sure I could hear, my mouth and nostrils full of frizzes of her hair and damn near smothered: 'You rode to bloody Backthorpe, with two feet of *sword* in your hand, to lash her with the flat of the blade and fucking cut her, man, to cut her if you couldn't fuck her, to cut her and fuck her afterwards, to punish her for being Polly – punish her for what she was, is all, what she was and what she is – well, you didn't do so good at it, man – did you, you fucking Juggler? Like, oh, she was one too many for you. Goddammit, go punish *yourself!*' This time the toe of her boot caught me straight in the face; I was half-blinded and blubbering; and on the instant she was off, rusty mane flying unkempt all about her, gaunt elbows working like wings.

Would you believe nobody, but nobody, tried to stop her?

Fair enough, they stooped and bumbled, idiotically asking me had I been hurt and so on, carrying me in for first-aid (which I didn't really need, once the agony had worn off), but none of them enquired why she'd done it. There was an unpleasant assumption that she must have had very good reason – maybe some had heard most of her words – and in any case the least said the better. Only too clearly, there *had* been talk about me, yes! indeterminate inimical gossip, all spreading from the one Untruth.

16

But surely, not even the Blackadder at her most equivocal could deliberately have invented that gruesome and improbable fairy tale – what, me cycling out to Backthorpe, my sword of vengeance (from the department's prop-room?) clasped awkwardly against the handlebars, my vicious mind filled to brimming with weals and gashes and blood and sperm – and screams, no doubt, and pleas for mercy? And then somehow failing in my filthy attempt? If I was indeed, so to speak, the Devil, by what dark Geneva exorcism was she enabled to outsmart me? For truly I began to believe I had attempted some such ill deed but refused to remember it – why, four miles there and four back, it must have taken me well over an hour; could I have suffered so lengthy a blackout? Good Christ, was I a psychopath? Would anyone tell the *police*?

17

To this day I have never understood it. Not fully. Not all of it. But I have come to consider that P. Blackadder herself had little enough to do with it. Mind you, I did find out that the way she told her story, there was considerable transmutation of that brief confused beating she gave me when she woke me up. She left it to be inferred that *I* had hit *her*; perhaps I did, just a little, while struggling to get clear of her. Unwitnessed flurries and scuffles are hard to report accurately in hindsight. Anyway, she succeeded in labelling me as 'Inclined to Sexual Violence'. And Carmilla extended the notion.

I was to come across Carmilla again in my life, and again she was to do me damage. By God, twenty years afterwards, she is *still* doing me damage, or why am I writing all this?

She was in fact quite as mad as she looked. And so extraordinarily emotional that she (how shall I put it?) *subsumed* herself most of the time into the minds of certain people towards whom she had acquired either a deeply erotic empathy or a frenzied antipathy. Antipathy, Jack Pogmoor; empathy, P. Blackadder. Now – and here I'm afraid I'm bound to lose my more rational readers, but there's nothing I can do about it. I can only state it as I saw it—

It is unluckily true that at the end of the previous term I had entertained some highly prejudicial fantasies. That Sunday night, after my final glimpse of P. Blackadder as churchgoer – well, I lay in bed, neither asleep nor awake, and thought about her, dreamed about her, in terms of the utmost cruelty. Naked steel was certainly part of it, naked steel and naked flesh. My subconscious was a whirlpool, of blood, sperm and corrosive acid. And of course it gave me a hard-on. What the hell else?

But I swear to you: only once, only once with such vile turbulence. And never, after she'd moved to Backthorpe. Away in Backthorpe she made my heart ache; but distantly, a weeping melancholy, I couldn't see her there, couldn't imagine the house where she lived – and besides, in the interval I'd been home for three weeks' vacation. Didn't I tell myself, I was *soothed*? I did not go to Backthorpe, not on my bike, not in the bus. Nor did I ever walk there. Indeed, that final term, I was out and about very little; I had my thesis to complete; no, that wasn't the real reason.

Nor was it only Blackadder, or Owston, whom I feared to face. As a social being, for a couple of months, I had observably begun to collapse. But I do suspect it *wasn't* observed, by anyone beyond myself.

Meanwhile Carmilla Costello, unwittingly or with intent, extracted from my personality – from my soul, if I could understand just what 'the soul' might be – my entire and secret whirlpool, every detail of the misery of one abominable lonely night, and then made of it a concrete fact; got the date wrong, got the place wrong, brooded and brooded in silence and never even bothered to check it to find out was any of it true.

There were plenty she could have talked to – P. Blackadder's landlady, for one. She could for that matter have asked me. Which would have been far too easy for her, wouldn't it?

By contrast, to mention it to P. Blackadder herself was so difficult (if I guess right) that by God she'd rather die. I said she brooded in silence. Her longing for the Blackadder was surely almost totally silent, much more silent than mine had been. Devoid of kisses, devoid of touching hands, devoid always of direct speech. I daresay, if Costello *had* spoken, her questions as to Pogmoor would have been received with an enigmatic narrow-eyed glint, a sideways shift of the chin, a scandalised 'dear goodness'; by no means the best testimony to save my reputation. At all events, she preferred her empathy, her antipathy, her vivid vision of lovely Polly in peril of my appalling dream. Such terrible Yankee trust she had in the sincerity of her own intuition.

18

Nonetheless, I am doubtful about what I've just written. I don't want to suggest that the woman had magic powers. Whatever it was with her, it must be susceptible to scientific experiment. If the scientists haven't got so far, that's their hard luck – and mine. Also there is just possibly a run-of-the-mill explanation, one that would satisfy, for example, a police detective. My diary, inconsistently kept, some days two dozen close-wrought pages, and then weeks of no entry at all; I've lost most of it over the years; but at Pomfretshire in that epoch I do remember occasional insertions of bits and pieces of *poems*, broken threads unravelled from the tangles of thought I couldn't endure to expose in plain prose. I'm sure I wrote 'Blackadder'. Did I also write 'punishment'? *Details?*

Did somebody find it? Did Carmilla's bulging eyeballs have the run of my fool's-cantos?

Do you know? – *I really don't know*. Lethal whirlpools will suddenly vanish, leaving the surface bright and calm for the basking sharks to enjoy the sunshine. Once away from the university for what I hoped would be the rest of my career, I managed to forget the whirlpool. And therefore to forget whether I wrote about it or not. I have now, against my will, to attempt an agonising recall. But the writing, if there had been writing, is even today blotted out. So what could I say, to the run-of-the-mill copper? 'If you think the theory plausible, set it down as a statement, I'll sign it.' Which does not mean I accept it, or will not repudiate it when they produce it in court.

I hate to get bogged down in the problem of C. Costello.

19

The problem of Polly is work for a lifetime. As indeed it has so proved. For a long while I was not fully alive to the circumstance. Yet who else but Polly was imperceptibly enlarging herself inside my creative energy until at last I had to recognise her as the Emperor's Whore of my constant obsessions? Leave that for some other occasion, it didn't arise until much later; this is Pomfretshire, no more than that.

Carmilla's assault below the steps of the library was my humiliated farewell to the place, in public, inexplicable, a fluent source of sniggery anecdote. Even without it, there'd have been a cough against my name: 'left under a cloud', the regulation phrase. It didn't help that nobody could quite judge how dark a cloud, or what it signified. I guess it was dark enough to have prevented my getting any immediate university post, supposing I had been anxious to apply for one. My *Jack Juggler* achievement could not be denied. But there are ways of composing non-libellous references which leave very wide spaces between the lines for entire essays of denunciation to be read, as it were, in invisible ink. Professor Altdorfer paid great importance to 'personal relations with students'. He was not always fully aware of what went on under his dreamy old nose; but if anyone dropped him a hint he would certainly feel bound to act upon it. And then, of course, the coffee-time gossip at inter-university conferences, summer schools and so forth. Within a matter of weeks a whole network would have heard *something* of J. Pogmoor's suspicious behaviour.

But in 1965 the academic departments and the Real Theatre had far less contact than they do today; their respective scandal-networks were not yet fully intermeshed. I could look for work in Real Theatre on the basis of my directorial talent, and feel fairly secure that rumours of moral turpitude hadn't got to the bosses first. And if they *had*, would it matter a damn? An uncorroborated carry-on with an actress was an improbable bar to employment, provided it hadn't ended in the dock. Professional women (and young men, for that matter) were expected to take care of their own chastity if that's what they wanted; they weren't students any more, they must live without paternalistic shelter.

Nor would I need a character reference from Altdorfer. The only essential recommendation was *Jack Juggler*; and I knew it had been noticed. Certain emissaries from the professional theatre, agents, artistic directors, did visit university productions (sometimes with enthusiasm) if given due notice and the right amount of harassment. You had to be good at lobbying, self-assertion, political knack. I'd been sedulously studying those skills; my 'management' of Carver and Blackadder was evidence of my growing competence; and the next step was no great obstacle. I took pains: wrote letters, made phone calls, even button-holed several strangers at stage doors in distant towns, to ensure a discreet sprinkling of influential persons in the audience for my production. (And so, I may say, did P. Blackadder. Her career had still a year to go before it was really ready to jump off, of course; but she was no less sharp than myself toward a main chance, particularly when someone – as it might be myself – had stuck it in front of her thankless face.) And presto! I was offered a job – assistant director at a new civic theatre in one of the more apathetic boroughs of the East Midlands. It did not promise much; but I was told I could have a production of my own before the end of the season, quite sufficient to keep me in business.

They were as good as their word. I asked to do Carver's gutter-press play. He called it *Banner Headline*. It had not been at all liked when the university staged it – may I say, without Blackadder in the cast, for she was otherwise employed, having a ball-breaking go at *Lysistrata*, costumed by Costello, produced by a fervent lectur-*ess*. I backed up Carver's claim that the fault was not his text but a bad choice of director, the civic-theatre people had reservations but in the end approved of the script, and we pulled it into energetic shape. Such reviews as appeared in the posh papers were excellent. The *Guardian*'s provincial critic reached a positive high-falsetto of enthusiasm:

> Perhaps few of those who buy certain national newspapers can truly understand the strange genesis of what they read. If so, and if it worries them as much as it should, let me adjure, exhort, compel them to go at once to Mr Carver's intrepid exploration into the Sweeney Todd dens of our latter-day Fleet Street.

The result was a second production at the Royal Court, and I directed that one too. Carver of course had had work at the Court before; they'd turned down this play on the basis of its Pomfretshire flop. I was the man who saved it, for him and for them, and for me, and all within the year.

The wry-mouthed Leonore did the décor. She and I flyted continuously one at the other, biting our thumbs like the bravoes in *Romeo and Juliet*, but antagonism never burst into serious quarrel. Her sets were visually wild yet totally under control; they chimed absolutely with my own imagination; she was an even better designer than her brother was a playwright. (An opinion I took care not to convey to either of them.)

So indeed I was kept in business.

And from then on – why, I've *stayed* there, haven't I? And still will; if I'm granted a fair shake.

To hell with universities. And if my saying so should prevent one of them at this late date giving me any sort of appointment, such is Free Speech in the Island of M. Thatcher.

20

There remains a final question, a delicate one, which I have so far avoided posing, and which I certainly am not able to answer.

Did P. Blackadder really think I was Owston?

It's all very easy in a Plautine comedy to accept the convention that a character becomes the dead spit of another one, simply by donning a similar jacket or slicking back a streak of hair. True, she was tired out, physically and emotionally. True, she had much too much wine inching down into her hot little bladder. True, the auditorium was very poorly lit. But even so . . . Is it possible to credit that Owston's most personal, most intimate demeanour while in grips breath-to-breath with a young woman, his bodily movements, his involuntary noises, the very smell of the bloody man, would be exactly reproduced (from mere guesswork) by the likes of Pogmoor? I had done quite a lot of acting in my three undergraduate years; it had never been greatly praised, I knew myself it was not my speciality, I dropped it as soon as I could. I *did* try (that night) some mild imitation of Owston's slouching walk, his abrupt grunts, the fling of his heavy arms, but without any illusions as to its value. I confess I was knocked backwards with extremity of surprise to find such an impersonation unchallenged – which all but quelled my orgasm, until I felt how the Blackadder was preparing to luxuriate in hers.

Now: just suppose she indeed knew who I was? And decided to let it go. And then slept for a little, woke up, and decided – what? To fly into a fury, not because she had been most villainously deceived, but because she needed to know how I would react when she went through the motions of a villainously deceived woman. And my reaction was all wrong, wasn't it? I fled her bed without a word. Just as her fury had been without a word; and there surely was my cue, it was up to me to fill the gap. She needed me to speak and I couldn't think what to say. So many possibilities, so many altogether-different directions my life could have taken – her life too – both our lives – she and I together, oh most beautiful untrustworthy Polly! Such chances: and all vanished for the lack of a word. Remorse, guilt, shame . . . above everything, inconsolable *regret*. Dear goodness, let me not, ever again, at *my* age ever again, have to contemplate Pomfretshire.

Second Tale

How Carver (Being Dead)
Sent Word of His Life
(1992)

Sit nearer, sister, to me; nearer yet.
We had one father, in one womb took life
Were brought up twins together . . . I could wish
That the first pillow whereon I was cradled
Had prov'd to me a grave.

(John Ford, *The Broken Heart*)

It seems you would create me
One of your familiars
Familiar! What's that?
Why, a very quaint invisible devil in flesh,
An intelligencer.

(John Webster, *The Duchess of Malfi*)

Already in the First Tale we brought the story of Pogmoor forward by eleven years, to account for his state of mind in the mid-'70s. So also with Fid Carver. He had his own trouble. If dreams of ancient Egypt, seethed in a pot with the St Helena poisons, gave nightmares to Pogmoor, Carver was incapacitated even to think of Eugene Aram. Unlike Pogmoor, he hid it; he fell to shuddering inside his clothes, and no one knew. Until after a certain autumn night of an arts festival in Belfast: the night the sixty-year-old playwright met his unexpected death.

1

It was more like a suicide than murder, yet more like a deliberate murder than the swift and awkward misunderstanding that it quite possibly, disconcertingly, was.

Carver had been invited to the 1992 Festival by an academic he had never met, and only vaguely heard of (he had had very little to do with college personalities for many years) – a Dr Henrietta Taggart, of the Eng Lit department at Queen's University. She asked him to make one of a panel of writers and critics at a public forum to discuss 'Nationalism and the collapse of the Left'. He was suspicious of the invitation. He did not think the Left had in fact collapsed, except in the propaganda of the Right; and the plonking assertion of the forum's title made him wonder what hidden agenda was to be served. Before accepting, he put out a few queries around his Irish acquaintances, quite a large body of acquaintances but one that a *responsible* citizen (such as a Dublin TV news editor) could scarce call representative save in terms of contrariness and unpredictable subversion.

He found that Dr Taggart did not hide her agenda – everyone who knew her knew exactly what she was about. She belonged unequivocally to the Protestant-Unionist tradition of northern Irish public life and had been engaged throughout the 1980s in a literary campaign to re-establish that tradition in the face of what she perceived as a resurgence of cultural Catholic-Nationalism emanating from Derry and Dublin. She avoided any overt connection with political factions (although some of her personal relationships did give rise to malicious innuendo): her arguments were strictly and honestly confined to the interpretation of novels, poems and plays and of other people's interpretations of novels, poems and plays. She left it to be inferred by simplistic journalists that her arguments, extended, meant that the Derry–Dublin school gave objective aid and succour to 'IRA terrorism' and 'neo-Gaelic ethnic cleansing'. Whether the IRA ever read any of the texts upon which these arguments were based, was to her a question of no account. The aid and succour, if it did exist, was subliminally inhaled, as it might be noxious gases from some industrial plant apparently smoke-free and therefore disregarded by the public at large.

Carver concluded that her forum was designed to assail Irish Nationalism – no doubt by analogy with German, Serb, Slovak, Croat, Israeli, Bosnian, Basque or Baltic varieties – and to maintain a type of Leftism attractive to enlightened segments of Ulster opinion; segments who approved continued union with Great Britain but feared contamination from Orange Order drum-thwacking, Paisleyite bigotry, Ulster Defence Association crypto-Fascism. Segments, in short, who would have wished to be able to join, and vote for, the British Labour Party, if only the British Labour Party would stop messing with papalist-green messers, the likes of John Hume for example.

Carver did not agree with any of this; he believed, as an Englishman, that all of Ireland should be Irish and that it was his business, as an

Englishman, to say so. He thought that Ulster Unionism had been propped up for far too long by British cash, British troops, British blood. And that none of this propping-up was consistent with British Socialism, because it was utterly contrary to the Socialism of James Connolly (whom he revered) and because – to put it plainly – it created the very terrorism that it purported to restrain. He had written more than one play to say so; and had had a deal of trouble getting them produced. Some critics said he had damaged his ageing talent by crude espousal of the propaganda of violence. He had certainly damaged his bank balance; and his agent did not like it at all.

So he accepted the invitation, in combative mood. He would, as an Englishman, re-examine 'Nationalism' in terms of *British* Nationalism – as much as to say British Imperialism – and stick it as a pejorative label upon Dr Taggart's own school of thought; he would do his level best to turn the presuppositions of her seminar inside-out.

(She had also asked him to give readings from his work to a group of her students. He had an unproduced TV play – years old, but who gave a damn? – on the subject of the Fenian dynamite outrages in London in the 1880s and the consequent setting-up of the British Police Special Branch. He would read from that script to them and from that script alone: let them like it or lump it, it was good solid Carver, *tout court*.)

Thus by plane from Heathrow on a soaking wet Thursday afternoon to Belfast's Aldergrove airport; Dr Taggart met him in her car with jolly hospitality; took him out to dinner to introduce him to a number of his next day's forum-colleagues; argued with him quite spitefully until the wine rendered all of them more or less buzzed and the restaurant felt forced to eject them; and then drove him to his hotel where, all unaware, and with a jolly 'Goodnight!', she left him to his unaccountable end.

2

The Lord Chancellor Clare Hotel should more accurately have called itself a guesthouse, or even a bed-and-breakfast: it was small and cheap and inconveniently arranged, a rookery of tiny rooms partitioned amongst what had once been the middle-sized rooms of a middle-class early-Victorian terrace house in the Botanic Avenue area close to the university. Its fancy title was justified, perhaps, by a residents'-only liquor licence; although most of the late-night people crowded into the narrow lounge bar did not seem to be actually staying in the place. Carver had told Dr Taggart, in her car, that he needed to revise his notes for the forum before he went to bed – the dinner conversation had given him new angles of polemic – but his room was dark and cramped, with no solid surface to work at, only a wobbly dressing-table, and the chair had one leg shorter than the others, or so he seemed to think (unless it was the drink) – he would find himself a proper table in a corner of the lounge bar, deploying notebook and brandy-glass and ginger-ale bottle and ashtray in the faint hope that no one else would sit down too close to him. 'Henrietta: goodnight, night, night! and we'll slaughter each other tomorrow . . .'

It is probable he should have gone at once to bed and saved the revisions until breakfast-time. He scratched at the pages with the air of a man not fully in control of his words, or of the thoughts behind the words; a lonely hoar-headed rheumaticky man not at all ready for sleep and suspicious that the television on a shelf at the foot of his bed upstairs would either have finished its programmes for the night or would prove to be out of order. Never mind the damned revisions: brandy and ginger-ale, one glass, then two, and then three, was just the ticket, just the job, for a wet night on one's own in Botanic Avenue.

He grinned at a blundering fellow who came squeezing round behind him and into the seat beside him, clattering a glass against a freshly opened bottle of Bushmills whiskey. Late twenties or early thirties, round-shouldered, spotty white face, tawny teeth, tight white lips (so white as to be all but invisible) under a scrap of red moustache. Slop of his careless whiskey onto the back of Carver's chair as he moved, and all over the formica table-top once he sat down. 'Just the job,' said Carver fatuously, 'ticket.'

The intruder swung his head round; a startled glare: a snarling challenge. 'What's that? What? Job? You need be careful what you say to men around here. What in hell d'you mean, "ticket"? There's some around here have a bloody poor notion of a joke, so they do.' His hands were twitching violently and the bottle went on spilling. He wore a threadbare grey suit with a black mourning-band on one arm; a grubby striped shirt open at the top button, its frayed collar a size too small; a ratty black tie that had slipped sideways: he had the look of a useless clerk in a dodgy little business who expected imminent redundancy. He poured himself out a large dose of the Bushmills, gripped it as firmly as he could in his left fist and swallowed nearly all of it down; at the same time he shoved his right fist deep into his jacket pocket as though to stifle any independent tremors.

The glass door of the lounge opened into the hotel foyer, which in turn opened to the street. From Carver's table it was possible to see through the glass door to the street door, a solid panel with a security spy-hole. There was a thin *burr-burr* somewhere behind the bar. The barman put down a glass he was about to fill, left the bar, went out to the foyer, paused to peer thoughtfully into the spy-hole, and then set about unfastening the latches of the street door. It was the fifth or sixth time he had had to perform this evolution since Carver had begun on his brandy.

A dripping black umbrella came swiftly into the hotel with some very short person hidden behind it; the barman clapped the street door shut. By the time the umbrella was through the glass door into the lounge it was halfway-furled and being shaken from side to side, while rainwater sprayed all about. A small tumult of irritated evasion took place among the customers up against the bar. The short person, still out of sight, could be heard gasping apologies, but his umbrella-slide seemed to have jammed: he continued to shake and spray.

Carver, with his fatuous grin, sat motionless, watching, brandy-glass poised in mid-air. A sudden jolt, against his ribs, from the right elbow of the Bushmills man; brandy flew out of the glass across the top page of his notebook. He turned his head, moved his mouth – to make truculent comment, it is supposed – no words came. He must have seen the man's right hand on its way out of the jacket pocket – must have seen that it held an automatic pistol – must have seen the pistol under the table-top aimed approximately at the half-furled umbrella – must have seen the Bushmills man's left hand gripping the right wrist in a fierce effort to steady the aim. Must have seen that he, Carver, fixed between the assassin and the assassin's only way out, was altogether in the wrong place.

No one else in the room, at that stage, saw the pistol. What they did see was Fid Carver spring to his feet, scramble round the corner of the table, stand in front of the Bushmills man, bending over the table toward him with both hands slapped hard on the formica, and an ashtray knocked sideways to the floor. What they heard was Carver's voice, high-pitched excited contralto, screaming into the Bushmills man's face: 'Just the ticket, just the job, Jesus Christ, after all these years!'

As he screamed, the Bushmills man began screaming as well: 'Get out o'the fucking way, man, what the fuck d'you think you *want*?' – or something to that effect – later evidence was uncertain as to the contents of both screams – but everyone agreed how the Bushmills man cried '*want*' a split-second before his gun went off. Just as everyone also agreed that Carver, with four slugs in his gut, kicked and sprawled and jerked like a beetle impaled on a pin, unable to say anything in any way intelligible. Nor did he speak in the ambulance, on the way to the hospital. Nor yet in the hospital itself. He just died.

One of the witnesses, the barman, was to depose that *he* had heard, 'I'm only giving you what the fuck you fucking *want!*' He seemed very sure of this; but who could possibly be sure? – for behind the jammed umbrella another pistol had at once come out to send a single fatal bullet point-blank into the right eye of the Bushmills man.

Nobody admitted to even a glimpse of the umbrella-carrier's face. For he was out into the foyer, out through the street door, into the night, into the rain, before the crowd in the lounge had recovered from the shock. The barman should have known him. He had seen him through the spy-hole, why else did he let him in? He told the police he believed he was letting in a Mr McBride from Greenock, Scotland, registered hotel-resident for more than a week. But Mr McBride at the time was at the house of his cousin, one of those rarities, a Catholic policeman, who lived in Downpatrick, eighteen miles from the city; a strongly supported alibi, even though Mr McBride was little more than five foot tall and possessed a most notable umbrella.

The Bushmills man turned out to be a suspected member of the UWF (Ulster Will Fight), a minuscule but murderous sub-division of the Ulster Defence Association. His name was Elias Taggart: *vulg.*, Ly-boy 'the Plunger' Taggart. Henrietta was horrified: he was a sort of a cousin of hers, God help her! never mentioned in the family, an alcoholic disgrace, an ex-student of theology, an ex-inmate of Crumlin Road Gaol with a conviction for gross indecency toward small boys at a Presbyterian orphanage.

3

The Royal Ulster Constabulary found it hard to understand the part played by Fid Carver. He had, they thought, behaved as though he knew far more of what was to happen than was consistent with their first theory that he just observed a drawn firearm and hopped out at it like a bloody fool. The eye-witness discrepancies confirmed them in a growing belief that there must have been some prior connection with the Plunger Taggart: a connection already indicated by the (entirely coincidental) double link to Henrietta.

At the same time the low stature of the man with the umbrella reminded at least one detective of Jeremiah Gilhooley, nicknamed 'the Priest', or 'the Wee Priest', known and wanted for his connections with

AWRUI. (That is, the Army of the Workers' Republic of United Ireland, an IRA 'reject-splinter' so distantly removed from the paramilitary beaten track that it was said to collaborate with the hardest-line Loyalists for certain *semi*-political purposes, the drugs traffic, protection rackets on building sites, selective information-gathering for the security forces among both Provos and UDA, intermittent contract-killings.) But the Priest had not been heard of for some years. Perhaps he was out of the country.

All in all so much of a mystery, and the motivations so obscure, that fears were aroused of an undercover involvement, MI5 or something similar; a not uncommon factor in such affairs, one into which an ordinary policeman stuck his long nose at his peril.

It would therefore (thought the RUC) be a helpful exercise to run an unattributable briefing through the media. Which they did, within the week: discreetly hinting at (a) Carver's unfortunate *Sinn Féin*/IRA sympathies, deduced and grimly noted by the London Special Branch as well as by those eminent intellectuals who had endured him in the restaurant that evening; (b) his undoubted history of recurrent depression (he had, it appeared, been in and out of psychiatric treatment for a number of years); (c) the Plunger Taggart's reputation as a drinker always short of ready cash, as a regular incumbent of mental hospitals, as a notoriously unreliable activist on behalf of whatever he joined, whether a Presbyterian congregation, the Larne and District Sportsmen's Gun Club, or the UWF; (d) the vast amount of wine and spirits which Carver could be shown to have taken on board since his departure from Heathrow; and (e) the perfectly dreadful condition of Carver's kidneys, as revealed at the post-mortem.

Carver was still fairly well known; his death caused a minor flurry in the press. Most of the obituaries implied that he had long outlived the probably unjustified fame of his plays in the '60s and '70s; but there was an irony to be exploited, and journalists did their best to exploit it. 'Terror comes to terrorist plotsmith' – 'This gun was for real!' – 'Belfast last night gave chilling answer to the unrepentant English playwright who battened on Ulster's agonies from the revolutionary chic of his Kentish Town flat' – were the immediate kneejerk comments. Carver had reaped his just deserts: a melodramatic warning to any other British writer who dared breach the editorial consensus on the Matter of Ireland.

Once the RUC had had time to distribute their self-protective rumours, the notion of collusive suicide appeared in a few newspapers. Very soon there was an end to it; the public was assumed to have lost interest; the coroner's inquest was indefinitely deferred pending further police enquiries.

For 'enquiries' we should read a painstaking effort to *stifle* enquiries about the enigmas of McBride and Gilhooley. The Wee Priest's melodramatic reputation was at one stage floated in the media, and then hurriedly withdrawn – it seemed that a person or persons at a top security-level wanted him kept under wraps. A police spokesman got a rocket for rashly presuming to name him, while the media were induced with practised ease to ignore the indiscretion.

(Certain Irish journalists, those who really did know something about such affairs, were inclined to believe that AWRUI had never existed; it was no more than a useful figment evoked by the security forces to conceal the working of their own dirty-tricks department; the acronym was in fact a codeword for *unsolved, insoluble, better not even TRY to solve*. But to say so was disreputable guesswork; it made editors apprehensive; none of them ventured to print it.)

The Lord Chancellor Clare killings were thus put on the long finger – except by Fid Carver's sister, his only living relative. But before ever she could turn-to in the thunderclap of her grief, to answer the calls of the press, to organise the funeral, to dispose of her brother's possessions, to come to terms by-and-large with her terrible loss, she found she had a letter to read.

4

Carver had written it about ten years before, at a time when he had been undergoing a drastic course of mental rearrangement. A well-intentioned but fundamentally foolish Alternative Psychotherapist was trying to persuade him to abandon his career as a writer. Creative art, this clown insisted, was itself an expression of personality disorder. To be sure, for long enough, it had performed a necessary function: it kept Carver's brainbox from absolute internal collapse. But its superficial benefits were on the point of reversing themselves; every play the patient wrote, or attempted to write, or even began to think about, brought him nearer to the brink; he was approaching, in short, a terminal state of narcotic-addiction – not to drugs of substance but to the Pathological Fictionalisation of the Reality he Sought to Evade. He'd be better off digging an organic garden, subjecting himself to acupuncture, drinking a morning dose of his own urine, and spending several hours a day swopping infantile cries-from-the-buried-child with a circle of similar nutcases in closely monitored group-therapy sessions. Whether it cured him or not, it would at all events reduce his intolerable élitism, that most damaging 'Prometheus Complex' which compelled him to construct his own little people to play about with in his fantasy-world; as long as the latter continued, his perverse alienation was bound to augment itself in a rapidly ascending spiral of self-devouring cause-and-effect.

The 'Prometheus Complex' was the Alternative Psychotherapist's professional speciality; it had at one stage appealed to Carver as an exciting and apparently original idea, with vainglorious opportunities for boast-and-brag on the man's couch when nobody else seemed at all concerned by anything he said or wrote; but at last he came to see that it was driving him mad. In a fury of disillusion, he paid off the complacent charlatan. He scrawled filthy words all over the bastard's bill. He threw himself at his typewriter to hammer out into a long long letter his rage, and his fears, and his *genuine* self-devourings.

When he had finished it, he folded it without re-reading, thrust it into an envelope, licked and stuck the flap, and endorsed it:

> LENNY!
> Only to be opened if it looks in any way as if I've topped myself.
> If I've died in my bed or it's clearly a pukka accident, don't you dare to bloody open it, chuck it straight into the fire. It's nothing but a load of balls: truly. Dammit, girl, I *trust* you.
>   Dearest love to my dearest love – and you do know what *that* means!
>
> FID

Then he put it into another envelope, simply inscribed FOR MY SISTER LEONORE IN THE EVENT OF MY DEATH; he sent this to his agent, Jenny deVries, asking her to lay it away in her office safe and forget about it. Carver himself almost certainly forgot about it – blocked it out of his mind, indeed – as soon as his temporary paroxysms abated. For if he remembered, how could he have failed to recall and destroy it? such a deadly dangerous narrative; embarrassing too. And by no means impossible for someone to open it, for some unexpected reason, *before* he was dead. Embarrassment alone should have sent him straight to Jenny's safe; he was not, when in good health, a glowing heart-on-sleeve man; the thought of anyone, even Leonore, reading such neurasthenic prose would surely have corroded him with shame. And yet he forgot it? Or did something inside him really want it to be found? Was he madder than he thought he was, unconsciously manufacturing his own dreaded crisis?

In the event, the dutiful Jenny (with no idea at all of what the packet contained) delivered it as instructed. Carver had simply told her it was a memorandum of family matters; of no great importance, but Leonore would need to know.

5

Something about Leonore at the age of sixty.

Having heard (from an inconceivably insensitive phone call by the Belfast correspondent of a London tabloid) how talk has been running round as to the manner of her brother's death.

Having, for the last ten minutes, held his letter in her hand.

Having unplugged the telephone and double-locked the door of her flat.

Having not yet made up her mind whether to tear open the inner envelope. *Has* he 'topped himself'? *Could* he have? Yes, he could. But she does not believe it: her *twin*? – she would have *known*. She is terrified, even so, that he might have done.

She sits in her studio: a stage designer's studio on the first floor of a tall white Regency house, anomalous among dim Victorian terraces. A room busily accoutred with books piled on books, model theatres, perspective drawings, photoprinted working drawings, collage-patterns of different surfaces, cutout pictures of actors in costume and of stage arrangements from all periods of history pinned to softboard on every wall, posters of innumerable productions, photographs of innumerable productions (with and without actors) – and one huge dominant feature, an inexplicable twice-life-sized upside-down monochrome photo-blow-up (it fills all the space between two windows) of the vertical nude bodies of a pair of strenuous women, side by side fronting the camera, every inch of their skin tattooed or stencilled in a pattern of flowers and leaves, each woman with two fingers of one hand in the pubic hair of the other, their two heads in black shadow downward from their open mouths at the bottom of the picture, and their feet at the top dissolved in a white-hot glare of light.

She sits in her studio: immovably vertical, perched high on a draughtsman's stool, knees together, ankles tight together on one of the rungs of the stool, a long grey-blue gauzy skirt tight round her at ankles and knees, grey-blue plaits of hair pinned tight round her skull giving emphasis to her swarthy cheekbones, nose like a knife, mouth like a dried leather purse, eyes like white-blue pools in a wild expanse of grey-green. She stares past the giantesses' nudity, through the left-hand window, into the tossing, rustling, whipping and whining autumn treetops of Antioch Gardens, Kentish Town; seems to hear (rather than see) the lowering dark of the storm-clouds that pile in upon north London from the west. It will be sunset in half an hour; her brother's empty flat, just over her head, will never have a life in it again, however many future tenants pay their rent, move in their furniture, cook their food and guzzle it, run the bath, flush the water-closet, roll and rummage their sexual itches on the beds. Never.

She sits in her studio: as dark as an Egyptian, as bright as a Sheffield knife, blue jewels in the dark lobes of her ears. It would be hard to guess her age if we did not know it. She is certainly not young; but young men have turned about to gaze at her in the street. Young men have felt a lust for her sinewy loping limbs. Young men and young women. The graceful straightness of her stride. The very startle of her colour-contrast, storm-clouds and rainbow over against what is left of a sunshine sky. 'Never again?' she asks herself. Never.

Who could believe her to be twin to Fidelio Carver, that muted, scrub-bearded, diffident, middle-sized and middle-shaped, scarcely noticeable muttering man?

These twins were not even identical in name. Her legal name, supposedly, would be Leonore Pogmoor; there was no writ of divorce between her and Jack Juggler, they just ceased to live together and left it at that. Carver (with his accountant) worked out a more-or-less equitable financial settlement and persuaded them both to agree to it despite the peril of their angry temperaments. Ever since – eighteen years – she has been Leonore Serlio. 'Madame', when she feels grand about it (usually to overawe moneymen); 'Mrs' or 'Miss', for day-to-day convenience (she doesn't care which); she disdains the new 'Ms', 'bloody stupid for anyone born earlier than Auschwitz', she has commented often enough. Her mother's family, nearly all of them, met their deaths in Auschwitz – imperious Venetian Jews – *they* were the Serlios.

They were Carver's mother's family as well, of course: but who would believe it, meeting him? To all external intents and purposes, he has been only the son of his father – that is to say, the son of a stumbling Anglo-Saxon of a highly traditional kind, a Staffordshire rural vicar who was nonetheless an active member of the Communist Party and scandalised his parish with a bust of Lenin in a side-chapel of the twelfth-century church. A tedious preacher, but a fiery pamphleteer, he died of pneumonia after tempestuous weather on a hunger march of the unemployed. It was the very same day that the twins first went to nursery school.

Giovanna, the parson's widow, had been brought to England by *her* father in the 1920s. Mussolini was not at that stage hunting Jews; but Socialists were in very great danger. Signor Serlio had espoused (when already middle-aged) an extreme selection of the doctrines of Gramsci, thereby betraying his family. They scornfully cast him off; but still felt sufficiently kin to him to secure his escape from Italy and some sort of income for him in exile. They were very nearly too late. He was brutally beaten by Fascist corner-boys; his bowels all but fell out of his rectum when dollop upon dollop of castor oil flooded into them through a kerosene-funnel forced between his shattered teeth. This happened in a garage on the Livorno waterfront just before the ship for Tilbury was due to sail. His tormentors dragged him up the gangplank and dumped him – degraded, befouled, a reeking bundle of pain – into the arms of Giovanna. She had been told, 'Signorina, on board, on board! just a few small customs formalities to delay your father half an hour, he will be with you safe and sound in plenty of time . . .'

He gassed himself in London nine months later. The Rev. Cuthbert Carver went to his funeral; to say goodbye to a courageous comrade. So he met the comrade's daughter and what could he do but marry her?

Was the marriage a happy one? It was, at least, *unusual*. We might perhaps talk of an owl and a she-eagle cramped into the one small nest.

And nothing very different when we consider their two children. Giovanna survived her husband by no more than three years. (Run down on a country road by an MG sports car, the drunken son of a stockbroker roaring with laughter at the wheel.) After that, Leonore and Fidelio were brought up by an unmarried Carver aunt who did not like them; they hated her. She used to whip them on their bare bottoms with a cane, and lock them in their bedroom with a prominent chamberpot and no books and no food. She used to make them learn by heart great chapters of the Bible, the most punitive she could find. She denounced Jews, she denounced Communists, she denounced (worst of all, most particular of all) her own brother and his foreign wife. It was, she said, a question of principle; she took her stand by Church and King.

At the end of the Second World War she suddenly had mercy. Or rather, she lost patience, just as she lost her patience with the whole realm of England now that Attlee and his Levellers were in power. She came into a legacy and thus was enabled to send the twins to separate boarding schools, from which they wrote to each other every day until authority discouraged it. ('Unhealthy emotionalism . . . retrograde self-indulgence . . . stultifies the spirit of *school*.') When they were sixteen, the aunt for the first time permitted them home for the holidays, not caring too much whether they accepted or stayed away. On more than one occasion they told lies both to schools and to aunt. The aunt thought the holidays had not yet begun; the schools thought the children were secure in the aunt's house. Where they really were, how they stole the cash to get there, and what they were doing for those few knots of days alone together, was for ever their most precious secret.

They were not aware, until years later, of Auschwitz and the fate of the Serlios. Nobody told them. Had they been told, how would they have felt? Aunts would have been shamefully murdered. Aunts they had never seen. Could they, at that age, have had compassion for murdered *aunts*? At that age, they were very queer young people indeed, and not exactly likeable.

The boarding schools did not make them happy. Strange to say, in adult life they were both to agree that the most intense happiness they had known was between the ages of seven and thirteen when they lived in daily fear in the fearful dark house of the aunt. They could not tell why; but they *knew*. Doubtless the fear itself was thrillingly impregnate with its own sharp compensation.

In the teeth of the aunt's disgust, it was finally Clem Attlee (and his Levellers) who provided the grants to get Fid into London University and Leonore to Goldsmiths' College as an art student.

Then Leonore went to work in the theatre; and Fid found a job in the university library. He left it as soon as he could, to set up on his own, a professional playwright. (He had luckily been exempted from the national-service conscription, coming up at his medical with a quite unusually morbid urine-sample. No doubt he should have sought treatment for the condition disclosed, but he had no courage regarding doctors. He neglected himself, and continued to do so.)

About this time there was another fortunate legacy. Giovanna's uncle, old Daniele Serlio, died in New York. He had escaped the Final Solution by American residence at the outbreak of war, the family having prudently placed him there in order to separate the Wall Street branch of the Casa Serlio finance company from its Italian connection, in the event of Italy and the United States being on opposite sides of the hostilities. He thought of his niece with the utmost bitterness: the daughter of a Red, and the wife of a Red – indeed, as it appeared, a Red herself – she had not deserved his benevolent interest. Nor did her children deserve it. All the dollars of his personal wealth would go to Jewish charities or direct to the State of Israel. But on his deathbed he changed his mind. Every other living Serlio had been herded out of the world into abominable Night and Fog: yet these English twins were surely Serlios, *his* flesh, *his* blood? They could not be blamed for their mother. He *must* give them something.

'Something' amounted to a small annuity and two decayed town houses in north London. Lenny and Fid decided to refurbish the Antioch Gardens property and live in it. The other one, in Highbury, was already let to an old lady whose constant (and justified) complaints cost them a great part of their annuity in payments to jobbing builders; far more of a burden than an asset.

But at least they were independent. They no longer felt totally bound by each other's emotional need. There were people in the world outside: they began to *experience* them.

6

Having now for two hours held his letter in her hand.

Having not yet made up her mind whether to tear open the inner envelope.

Nor where: whether it should be torn here in her own flat, or on the second floor, in Fidelio's.

If she can decide to tear.

Perhaps first if she knows *where* to tear, then she can think about *whether*.

Not in Fidelio's. She cannot bear to go up there. Cannot bear to see the rooms. Dishevelled, spilling with books, food-gear amongst writing-gear, writing-gear amongst sleeping-gear, pictures amongst hanging clothes, rolled-up clothes amongst books, dishevelment always (for Dishevelment, read Security: for Security, read Love), because always, 'I'll be back in a couple of days, a weekend, a week, bloody housework'll keep till I'm home again,' and suddenly Always is Never.

Yet, *yes*, in Fidelio's. *His* letter, *his* voice, *his* walls ought to hear it. All of a piece, always, with *his* dishevelment, his.

Yet, *no*, because she cannot bear.

Therefore: in this flat. Where, in this flat? Where?

She climbs from the high stool, stiff. How long has she sat upon it? It is already quite dark. She switches the light on. Intending just this one shaded anglepoise on the wall above her head. But the flex is connected (how could she have forgotten?) through the multiple plug to all her working lights, at her drawing-table, her handcraft bench, her slide projector; the connection is ON: everything is lit, *flash!* yellow-and-white all over the studio, dazzling her, dumbfounding her, an explosion in her tight-plaited skull. OFF, at once OFF!

Not in this studio, no. This terrible tight letter from the tightening heart of a self-condemned man, a *dead* man already. She cannot read it in a wide bright space. No, she cannot bear.

The studio is the whole floor, except for kitchen, bathroom, bedroom. All three of them in alcoves, behind folding screens instead of walls. Kitchen, or bathroom? Bathos, absurd, almost degrading: to read it in the midst of pots, pans and cornflake packets; or towels, toilet-paper, soap. So the bedroom. But somehow the bedroom all of a sudden is making her afraid.

Nonsense. She *shall* go in there, must go. Pull the screen open, switch on one small bed-head light, slide the screen: and that's it.

Leonore's bedroom: she being sixty years old.

Very small, hardly space for her one wide high bed, one chair, one small table. Built-in wardrobe, built-in cupboards and shelves at all heights in the tight tall walls. No pictures, except a couple pinned to the bed-head: a small polyphoto strip of Fidelio when twenty years old, a small Indian-ink caricature (made in 1930 by a Communist artist at a public meeting) of the Rev. Cuthbert and Giovanna holding hands. Walls, wardrobe, cupboards, shelves, all painted matt black all over with huge yellow sunflowers. Yellow sunflowers all over the duvet. A tall mirror in the embrasure, where there used to be a window, at the foot of the bed. The room is not windowless: a small pane hidden among shelves, at the side of the bed, almost too small to look out of, enough for ventilation. Also among the shelves, backing them, backing their neatly arranged contents, narrow panels of mirror-glass; creating illusion – is what you see on the shelf really there? or is it outside through a window? or reflection? What's reflected? (Look! there's your head on the shelf.) A wide mirror all over the ceiling: makes the tight small tall room quite damnably queer; for such was Leonore's choice – thirty years ago? Thirty-five? Or was it Fidelio's? Didn't they giggle, clasp hot hands, the night they first thought of it?

Having still not yet made up her mind *whether*.

When that journalist rang her up, how he forced it into her brain – 'His cry to the killer, Miss Serlio, "After all these years!", so what d'you think it meant? "Just the job, just the ticket." Miss Serlio, Mrs Pogmoor, can you really insist he'd have hopped in front of a gun if he didn't mean to welcome the bullet . . . ?

'Mrs Pogmoor, *come off it!* – (can't I call you Leonore?) – if your brother really meant to be a have-a-go hero and intercept a shot aimed at somebody else, he could never have said what he said, check? Leonore, isn't it true he'd always been *implicated*? That if, for some bizarre reason, he wanted a job done on himself, he knew where to get it? Can you confirm he came to Ulster knowing he was going to meet, get drunk with, perhaps have sex-romps with, this lady professor with family links to the gunman . . . ?

'Okay, not IRA; but face it! IRA, UDA, UWF, AWRUI, they're all terrorists, check? Leonore, I have to put it to you: your brother was playing the field? Any links, can you confirm, with the Red Brigade, the PLO, the Libyan angle? Could blackmail be a factor? Was your brother, like, *gay*? This guy that put the bullet in, did you know he was a child-molester . . . ?

'Plus: we got a tip your brother had let himself wreck himself with nephritis – quite a jolt finding it out, for a bloke his age . . . ?'

—on and on until she realised she had only to put down the phone: so she put it down. And pulled the plug out.

But then, directly afterwards, by motorcycle courier, the packet from Fidelio's agent. Didn't it all fall into place?

Not possible to believe the journalist, the slime of his putrescent tongue seemed to ooze through the very earpiece of her phone, she had to take out a handkerchief and wipe it.

Not possible to believe; only possible to doubt. Doubt won't do.

She is down, flat exhausted, on her back, on her bed. Lets shoes fall to the floor. Opens blouse; she has to *breathe*. Loosens skirt at waistband. Props shoulders against pillows. Doubt won't do: finish it! One hand to hold the envelope, one hand to tear it open. Ah! and it's done.

A folded and refolded bunch of many pages. Flimsy paper, hasty typing, words crossed out with xxx's, words misspelt and not corrected, and he didn't even number the sheets. It *is* divided, very roughly, into chapters of a sort. She fuddles and muddles them, trying to find the right order. At last she has them ready; ah! she hates his facetious title. But let her read.

'LAST POST'

(i)   Schizo-Phantasist

Oh no, my dear, I'd never have done it, you know that, if only there was
some way I could see myself round it. There isn't; not now; it's quite
evident; no help for it.

All because of this bloody fool, the quack, the clown, the mounte-bank, the Alternative Schizo-Phantasist; and by Christ he has the nerve to blame *me* for fantasy-making! Lenny, you did tell me, 'have nothing to do with him'. And I've left you no chance to tell me *you told me so!* I've snatched that option from you, like a nursery chair from under your bum. (D'you remember, I once did? It was before we had to go to the Aunt, because Mamma came and screamed at me, I think I'd nearly broken your back, five, six years old, my first ever practicable *coup de théâtre*, I'd spent weeks working it out and it hurt you, nobody clapped, nobody laughed.)

Lenny, look here: I know I'm all-over-the-place, but this *is* a serious document. This charlatan, this quack, this bloody fool mountebank Alternative: he thinks, because I write about This and That, that I cannot endure a life where That and This take place, that fiction cannot be true, that truth cannot be created as fiction. I'd hoped he'd be a challenge to me; supine in his pretentious pad I could talk and talk and altogether prove him wrong. But Lenny, how can I? Tell him the true reason why all my writing has been true, but nonetheless has been *in disguise*? For so many years I never really told myself. Still less did I tell *you*. Wasn't that the worst betrayal?

And now: disguise again. Because although I now *will* tell you, after all it will not be *telling*. To tell is to be heard and to know that one is heard. Dearest heart, but I'm dead. How can a dead man tell? This letter is a sort of time-bomb, to deter me from ever taking the only sort of action that would make it go off. But now, you are reading it; now, it has detonated; therefore it has failed in its purpose. I'd do better not to write it at all. But I must.

I put 'time-bomb'? Subconscious, Freudian giveaway, and I put it in a serious document? I'm allowing myself a writer's tricks and I shouldn't. Because, you see, Lenny, there *was* a bomb. It killed people. I knew about it.

No I didn't. It had nothing to do with me, so therefore I didn't ask. If I'd asked, I would have known it had a great deal to do with me.

You could say (and I *do* say) that my voluntary ignorance was one of the killers. There are bones to be dug up. Not just the bones blown asunder by the bomb – or pulverised in a smashed-up Mini car, because that's part of the story too. *My* story; here's to tell it! because I don't think, any more, I can live with it much longer. I *was* able, through all my disguises, both to live with, and make words around it – around it, not *about* it – oh yes and I made money. All those plays, those 'explorations' of political deceit. And now, the Alternative! the damnable Schizo-Phantasist! why, he's stripped the disguise, snatched it, a chair from under my bum . . . CRASH. Far from proving him wrong, I seem to be proving him right. All my work, for ten years: Pathological Fictionalisation of the Reality I've Sought to Evade. (Bloody *gaol* that I sought to evade, though that isn't really the point.) Such a fool, but he was right.

He was right, yet he missed every connection he could have made had I been such a fool myself as to talk sense to him instead of red herrings. He suckered himself from the start like a snail onto my *Emperor's Whore*; a play I can't get rid of, I can't finish, it refuses to allow me to leave it alone, I've been tinkering with the text for years – will anyone ever be able to present it? So of course I had to tell him about it. He asked every conceivable daft question, where the idea came from, how long since I'd started working on it, who besides myself was engaged with the subject (meaning, I suppose, had it been given me out of the blue as a commission by some management, or whatever). 'Hey, wow,' he would exclaim, in that insidious false-Californian jargon he favours (his own voice, under-neath, is solidly Geordie). 'Wow! Napoleon! Why?'

(ii)   Shaky

Well, I lied to him.

I said that as Napoleon was the most crucial individual phenomenon of his age, it was important for a writer to come to terms with the Emperor's dimension. Not quite a lie in itself (which is why it has been easy to tell); only when presented as my sole and sufficient motive. The one thing I could not, would not, let the S/Ph chew in his bilious cud, was the crucial phenomenon that *nobody got caught*. By judicious omission, a most thundering complete lie. But it kept him so happy for hours.

'Hey, wow, Fid! unless – like – you're some kinda crypto-mad-Fascist, what gives that a groovy dude like you should wanna jerk yourself off on a dead terminator in a crazy hat, a half-pint serial-killer two hundred years old? Wow, this is heavy, what's coming down, man . . . ?'

What he thought was coming down was the sublimated power-craving of his precious Prometheus Complex which he was deter-mined to fix me with; he swung himself along with it from unstable premise to shaky conclusion and so from one conclusion to the next, each shakier than its precursor. He paused now and then to drag at his joint and pass it across to me; he called it 'getting cool so we can rap'. As you can imagine, I'd have preferred a Benson and Hedges.

'So where are you, Fid, in this drama of yours? Like, defeated, like old Nap in the snows of Russia, or riding Cloud Nine like the battle of – like – Leipzig? – shit, man, do I mean Austerlitz?' He meant Austerlitz, but didn't pause long enough for me to confirm it. He rambled on in wide digressions, taking in all manner of

obnoxious tyrannies, from Jehovah to J. Edgar Hoover, to Margaret
Thatcher indeed; and related them one by one to the inadequate
longings of the would-be creative writer.

But of course he didn't touch upon the play that really mattered
in this context, the one I didn't write, Jack Pogmoor's 'Eugene
Aram Experience' (its name was actually *Hermit's Hole*). For how
could he imagine that it had also been *my* experience? And if I told
him why, I was trapped. By God, he'd have a hold over me tighter
than his wildest dreams. Bones to be dug up? Bones *would* be dug
up. Serious-minded, intellectual Eugene, sitting cool and quiet at
his heart's ease, brought suddenly to horror and death! Fidelio, too?
No Statute of Limitations on conspiracy to murder.

And you never knew any of it, did you? Darling Lenny, I'm
telling you.

No, she has never known. She peers at these pages over and over again,
trying to bring the messed-up typing into focus. It is almost illegible. Oh,
miserable Fidelio, how hard it was for you to write it . . . how much
harder for her to read it. She doesn't give a damn whether wittingly or
unwittingly he killed or did not kill. The world is full of killers and most
of them never intend it. But that *she* should not have known, that he
should have *hidden* it, is truly atrocious. Perhaps it is time for her to
reflect. Had she known or hadn't she? Perhaps half of her had . . .
perhaps the other half was afraid to ask . . . herself and her brother are,
between them, one flawed character, arbitrarily divided, two heads,
eight limbs, complementary genitalia . . . that, too, is atrocious.

(iii)   Bare Bodies in the Bivouac

I betrayed you because I did not tell you. Now I betray you because I'm
telling you too late. Oh Christ, Lenny – how can I say it? – you *betrayed*
me. *Take it easy, I have loved you so much. Wait! Think! Withhold*
judgement.

This is a very fitful letter. But I promise you, from now on, not any
more. I shall carefully lay it all out, from the beginning.

Shall I call 'the beginning' that dark winter afternoon in the
cottage near Rugeley? The old widow-woman from across the lane
was getting us our tea because Mamma had had to go into town for
the weekly shopping. How clearly do you remember it? In *my*
memory, it's an engraving by an early Dickens-illustrator. *David*
Copperfield or some such. The pair of us at table, face-to-face over
boiled eggs and bread and butter, while Mrs Booth goes to answer
the knock at the front door. Outside the window, the policeman's

bicycle propped against the garden gate; on the threshold the policeman's voice in a distressed and ominous growl. And then Mrs Booth's cry: '*Dead?* You can't mean dead! Oh, the poor dear children. However are we going to tell them?' Well; we were already told. She didn't need to come back into the kitchen.

No. Maybe 'the beginning' began a week later. In Peterborough, the house of the Aunt. Such a neat, clean, dismal house, in its neat, clean, dismal edge-of-the-town edge-of-the-railway-yards street, yellow brick Victorian terraces, three-foot strips of front garden sparse with laurel bushes, dismal wallpaper indoors, dismal lino on the treads of the stairs, the piano in the front parlour which we were strictly forbidden to touch. So we touched it, and made music, and she drove us to our barren bedroom. Under a black-framed fly-spotted lithograph (Gentle Jesus suffering the little children), we undressed one after the other and bent over a bed for *our* suffering; one after the other, one watching the other, as the other squirmed and struggled and howled, the Aunt's hand as strong as a screw-press to force a small skinny body hard into the hard mattress, the Aunt's cane like a ribbon of fire. And yet, what we watched was not the *other*. The other was ourself. Your pain was my pain, mine was yours. My tears (in the bedroom with you afterwards; locked in and never, so it seemed, to be let out) were your tears, your tears were mine.

No. Let's try a third 'beginning'. Scrounging, sneaking, nicking, *liberating*, like a born Artful Dodger (which indeed I never was; I must have been inspired! by adolescent passion; what grown-up can fully recapture its shameless contrivance?), I had managed to convey that narrow bivouac-tent from the school cadet-corps store into my luggage at the end of term. Our foolproof plan of escape; it didn't fail us. I met you at Bristol station. We took the train to Barnstaple and then a bus along the coast toward Porlock, then the scramble up through gorse and bracken overlooking the blue blue sea. It was so hot we could not endure a morsel of clothing, even at sunset, even with all the flies, midges and creepy-crawlies. How could we have dared bathe naked in that waterfall, unthinking, unguarded? How could we have dared pitch the tent all alone without trembling for a sudden footfall, an intruder, an invader, a layer-in-wait? But we did: and we did more than that. The tent was so very narrow, the sleeping-bag narrower still. My hot sweat was your sweat, your bare body was mine, mine was yours, there was no *other*.

Brother and sister. True love.

Leonore tosses and turns, burning on the sunflower duvet. The gas-power heating is turned up to its utmost for this bleak autumn night; and its utmost in the bedroom-alcove is already like a baker's oven. She has ageing flesh these days, it needs to be well warmed. But the letter has been warming it too.

Without getting up, she takes off her clothes, crumpling them carelessly under and around her as she lies there. She looks into the many mirrors; and all of them say to her, 'So straight, brown, graceful a woman, how would anyone know her years, except for her hair, except for her dried dark lips?' Leonore says, 'Oh God.' At last, she is weeping.

In a flurry she swings her feet sideways, slides herself off the bed, crouches beside it, grovels with a key at a locked drawer, eighteen inches wide, in its high built-up base. Opens the drawer, fumbles about in it with one hand (the other hand tight around the letter), finds what she seeks, fetches it out. A long hardwood dildo, hand-carved and beautifully polished, two tiny painted eyes at its scarlet-painted tip: she made it herself from a red-figure drawing on an Athenian drinking-cup, a cup from a brothel-bar for insensitive drunken young rips and the slave-women they rummaged and rolled. Now and then the young men would lie back and watch the women (obedient to orders) roll and rummage amongst themselves, perched on the tops of tables, ungenerous spectacle but worth thinking about even so, worth paying to have pictured on a cup – slave-women who did what was called for, Persian women, Egyptians, Celts, *Hebrews* indeed why not? Twenty years ago, she made it? Thirty?

She lies down on her back on the bed. Strokes her belly. Lean brown thighs. Pale red-gold private mat of hair turning dark russet. (Should it not be going grey? *Will* it at last go grey?) Plays with the dildo. Lets the loose pages of the letter lie scattered on the smooth of her belly. Fid's memories, being *her* memories, are not to be hurried over. Let her make of them what she can, let her recapture the shameless contrivance of their youth – it's not impossible, not for *her* – let her pause (just for a while, only for a short sweet while) before she must read about betrayal.

Here, on her bed, warm tears on her cheeks, warm hand sliding near to her cunt. Ah, she is warm; ah, she is now so *hot!* till she bloody well sweats and writhes. Till her duvet is sodden beneath her. Till everything, here, in her bedroom, on her bed, is as hot and as wet as her tears, as her cunt for fuck's sake, as her godawful lonely cunt, alas alas alas, while she plays in it with the dildo which she made. Did she make it for tonight? Did she *know*?

Leave it; and let her read.

(iv)　　　　　　　　　　Packing It In

*Leonore, if you betrayed me, it was not in the way you most likely think I
mean. I am not talking of that afternoon in 1970 (Sunday 21st June) when
you tightened your arms around me and whispered between deep kisses:
'Oh my love, don't you suppose it's time that we dropped it, packed it in,
scrubbed it, forgot it and fucked off – each through our own door for ever?'*

To be sure, we were both unutterably depressed. It was towards
evening of the third day after the day of the General Election; Tories
were suddenly in unexpected power; an extinguisher of vicious
cant had been jammed down to quench what limited glow still
remained to the life of the country. Nonetheless, that did not quite
logically account for what you said; oh, I was so shocked I could
make no comment; just a feeble bleeting 'Why?'

You said something unpersuasive about us not being the ancient
Egyptian royal family. Incest, you said (you were bold enough to
use the word; I could never quite take hold of it), was no bloody bit
of good in this place, this century, and in the long run would get us
into trouble, 'drop us in shit-creek', you said in point of fact. It was
only by God's good luck, you said (did you ever believe in God? I
think not), that I hadn't 'knocked you up'. We were already thirty-
eight years old; a bit late to haul out pregnancy as an objection? I
said: not luck, sound management, I said: when we were kids in
that cadet-corps tent (where anything could have happened),
whatever of me entered you, my semen did not; ecstatic restraint
and you blessed it; who was the careful one, you or I? I said: since
those days, our techniques were all the more sophisticated, so what
in God's name (I never believed in Him either) was the problem?
You didn't answer me. I thought, on second thoughts, I didn't need
you to. I thought, you see, that I *knew*. And I thought that I
probably agreed with you, even though such agreement was a
gimlet in the pit of my pelvis.

The drive of your desperate mind, so I deduced, had nothing to
do with making babies and the well-publicised perils of inbreeding.

But everything to do with everything we did to pretend to
ourselves we were free.

That arrogant Schizo-Phantasist has compelled me to consider
disguises. (He has accused me of being 'in denial'. I laughed in his
face.) And certainly you-and-me (about which I have let him know
nothing) does have to be diguised, quite as much as murder. I
disguised it by encouraging people to observe that I was gay. I *was*
gay too, still am (I suppose), insofar as it's never been possible for
me to flirt with any woman but you, let alone have her fuck me,
without always the inevitable silent reminder running up my spine
to point out that she wasn't you; thereby there-and-then the

collapse of all my pleasure, to say nothing of hers. Whereas, because a man is so obviously not you, with a man the whole business was on quite a different footing. No such chill in the backbone, none. Mind you, not much sex either. Friendship and tenderness, when I could get them, that's more or less all. Sulaiman was an exception. I had real lust toward *him*, and precious little friendship. In point of fact, I didn't like him; far too smooth, far too inclined toward the main (financial) chance. God, I abhor commercialism. I really suspect he only let himself lie with me in the first place in order to improve his career.

So the homoerotic became a disguise. Which is mad of course; because for far too many it still needs a disguise of its own. But it didn't affect my writing. Sex in my plays, undisguised, has never been a difficulty. Sex came freely in, I've written of it as easily as a swimming fish, of its pleasure rather than its punishment, comedy rather than tragedy, absurdity not solemnity. I wrote a sentimental porno-farce about incest once; I could have written it more easily if I'd never *had* a sister, only dreamed about it. It was a play that no one chose to produce, not even in the free-for-all avant-garde club theatres. 'Too queer, in a queer sort of way,' they said, 'not quite accessible.' They meant they were scared of it. Rot 'em. It's true the Lord Chamberlain in those days was still censor for the regular theatres; but by the time we got rid of him, the style of the script seemed dated, other issues were coming up, I didn't bother any more with it.

It never occurred to me to tell you what I did or didn't do with young men when you weren't there. Nor did I ever ask what you did with young women. I guess I *knew*; just as you *knew* about me. I guess we ran on parallel lines, and no harm. No harm, at least, until June 1970 (oh yes, the 21st, the third day after Blue Thursday: goodbye, good old illusion of egalitarian social justice!). If friendship and tenderness, scattered vaguely all about (and now and then a bit of lust), were beginning to bore me, it was reasonable for me to assume they were boring you too. So when you said what you said, I was shocked, but not surprised. As so often throughout the years, you were taking the initiative. (Though God alone can say who took it in the cadet-corps tent.) We both yearned for a shadowy someone else: someone else who could really be our life. I wept, you will remember, shared the bath with you for one last time, got dressed, and went out to live in Highbury. The old lady had just died, and the house required an occupant.

I was not to know it already had several: but I'll come to that later. Just now, I'm leading up to *betrayal*.

(v)   Your Choice, your Whim

—to betrayal; and I've got to it. Jack Pogmoor.

Within less than a year you were married to him.

Did you shunt me out to Highbury (like an old dog to his kennel in the yard) because you knew you were going to get married? Or did you suddenly find, in Kentish Town without me, that marriage was a whim – my God, a *perversion!* – you could easily and excitingly indulge? You explained yourself by asserting you wanted to have a child, and you'd very nearly left it too late. Perhaps. But no child came. How hard did the pair of you try? You only gave it eighteen months.

Understand me, Leonore. The betrayal was not that you went for a husband. We'd made each other no promises. I myself, with a clear conscience, might have fetched a wife into Highbury, if conditions had suited.

You betrayed me by choosing *him*. Almost any other man in the world! and I wouldn't have done more than damn your eyes in private and break a few pieces of crockery. But because it was Jack Juggler I all but went out of my mind, I bloody near topped myself, went to the gardening shop in Holloway Road and actually bought weed-killer, got hold of wide-gauge sticky-tape to cover the cracks in the window frames for when I turned on the gas-cooker taps, tried to locate a cut-throat razor (and me with a beard moreover; I hadn't shaved it for fifteen years). You didn't know, did you? Our twin-telepathy wasn't working so good any more. One unilateral act of betrayal, and it buggered itself up. Ha! I was best man at the wedding, as jolly as a Seven-Dwarf when Snow White took her tumble with the Prince. Ha! and I kissed the bride; and the bride bloody simpered and sizzled, and *believed* me when I wished her all happiness.

But for five and a half years – not long, perhaps, but packed to overflowing – your husband and I had been a Partnership.

A Partnership without Eros, a Partnership without closeness in any personal sort of way, a Partnership only of ideas about theatre and of competence in making them happen. From the *Juggler* play itself at that anomalous think-tank we used to call 'Pomfretshire' (from the black dribble of a pomfret-cake, no doubt; though liquorice allsorts might have been nearer the mark, a bagful of highly coloured rubbish), through a whole rake of further projects, some successful, some not, a few of them aborted without acrimony, we had developed our own style and wore it like a Comanche's warpaint, formidable, inimitable. No call for you to be jealous. You had your fair accredited share in enough of what we made. Was I jealous, was Jack jealous, when you designed sets for other playwrights, other directors? It was all in the business, your right to deploy your talent wherever you believed it could be used. (But I don't say I wasn't jealous when Jack had a go at someone else's script. He didn't do it very often; and never with great *éclat*; he always came back to Carver; his instincts couldn't keep him away. And I'd always demanded his name on the contract, always, when managements asked, 'Who's to direct?') In the long run it was a question of trust.

Why should I say your marriage broke that trust?

Because, as I understand it, when a playwright and a director make the running together, they run jointly in the service of the play; they are telling the one story and together they look out for the actors, music, sets and costumes that will help them to tell it most cogently. But for director and designer to gang up in prior conclave is (to put it at the extreme) a double-barrelled pistol aimed straight at the playwright's gut. To put it at the *most* extreme; should they choose to convene the 'prior conclave' in naked bed, they are whores and thieves and slave-owners all at once. They do not seek to serve the story, they seek the story itself, as they lie there, to loot it and to master it; if the playwright's version should not obey them, they'll monkey it about till it does. The playwright shall bring them glory, or (conversely) 'let them down'; any bloody hack will do, for if one can't match up, there's always another, and another after him or her, those pathetic strings of scriptwriters as on the credits of Hollywood films, each name getting smaller and smaller as you come to the bottom of the screen.

(vi)   Artistic Differences

Do you tell me Jack-sodding-Juggler never intended to use you like that? If you do, I don't believe you: he didn't get daubed with such a nickname for nothing.

At Pomfretshire, you know, he juggled his way into *me*, when he saw I was having difficulty getting a director for my gutter-press play. I was depressed, I was vulnerable; he whipped in like a pickpocket's hand; scooped me up for his Tudor comedy and out of reach of Owston, and enlarged on his advantage. Oh, that's how the Partnership began, right enough; I didn't twig at the time; when I came to look back on it clearly, I found I'd gained as much as he had – so carry on, Fid, don't recriminate! *Trust*, though, was ill-advised. I had excellent reason to put trust in his eye for a script. In his other departments, I'd no reason at all, and should have known better.

The last work we attempted together before you announced your

engagement was my adaptation of Büchner's *Woyzeck*, commissioned by the National Theatre, not yet allotted a production date.
The NT had agreed that Pogmoor should direct it; he and I had
failed to agree the precise nature of the adaptation. We had both
made up our minds it should be something more than a straight
translation. Beyond that, we were into uncharted artistic differences: he said the play was too diagrammatic, he tried to have me
'Carverise' it, extending scenes and characters as I'd done with *Jack
Juggler*. I felt strongly that each scene as it stood (apart from those
unfinished at the author's death) said everything Büchner wanted
and needed to say. The only problem was the order of the scenes,
which scholars have always found doubtful. A different order
means a different emphasis, a different emphasis means a different
play. Does Private Woyzeck kill his mistress because he is a neurotic
misfit quite unsuited to army life? Or does the life of the army, in
itself and inevitably, drive the poor fellow mad? This was what we
had to decide.

Never mind 'diagrammatic': if it seemed diagrammatic, then the
Pogmoor eye was looking at it from the wrong slant; let him shift
his point of view and think of what the story might actually tell us.
He argued that the sets you were already sketching out for him,
your suggested system of moving them, called for a very particular
rhythm; my text should adapt itself accordingly, and this in due
course would reveal to us the necessary order of events. I retorted:
'Then her designs are premature and may be quite wrong.' He
fetched you in to back him up. You remember? We had supper, and
drinks after supper, and got on each other's nerves like a quarterdeck of rum-sodden pirates – there's prey to port and starboard but
the wind switching all points of the compass – which of the snarling
matelots is fit to set the course?

Which of them pulls the first knife? Which of them first stabs his
shipmate?

The production in the end fell through. Pogmoor blamed me. You
blamed me. Remember? For a set of cross-purposes that *could* have
been passed over (friendship and respect between colleagues,
water-under-the-bridge); it had been before, this time it wasn't. He
was juggling himself into *you*, and once again I didn't see it.

He wanted a new partner, and didn't want a playwright. Long
before the rest of them he followed a crafty hunch, foresaw a
dynamic new power-centre: designer/director teams to initiate new
work, create their own performance-scripts, advance the status of
both their professions. The flood of money into the arts was not
exactly running short but quick ears had detected a burbling in the
pipes. Newly subsidised theatre managements had to account ever
more closely (to a Labour government beset by Zürich Gnomes) for

their share of the taxpayers' devalued £.s.d.; less and less did they dare take risks. Writers *per se* were a risk. No knowing what we were going to say next. A strongly written play *argued* with the public; votes might be lost, complacency outraged, by irresponsibly sharp language. How long before authority realised that its cultural patronage served only to pay for the undermining of its own assertions?

Whereas spectacle (not just old-style 'décor' but the new Physical Theatre, mobile human bodies in unexplained and inexplicable juxtapositions) need not be tied to verbal precision; it could sidestep divisive ideology and thus approach the Standards of Excellence, the Cultural Values of ballet or opera; could astonish foreign visitors and then be exported for foreign tours, a plus-factor in the Balance of Payments; most useful of all, could disarm the Tory Opposition (keep the arts for heaven's sake out of meaningful politics! did we *want* Harold Wilson to lose the election?). Of course outlay must be matched by assured returns at the box office. Adjust play-texts to assure the returns, have them quietly approved (or vetoed) by designers as well as directors. Extinguishers here and now, and one of them onto *my* head: the bloody man's a bloody lefty, jam it down.

Crêpe-paper Jack had clear sight of the main chance (or thought he had) and moved himself in to take it.

And for you: what was in it for *you*? Bull to the cow in season, fair enough. And a frisky young calf the hoped-for consequence. My love, you had a right to hope. But why *Pogmoor*? Professionally, you had no need for him; you had offers and to spare from any management you cared to wink at. So it comes down to the personal, the improbably intimate, doesn't it? I grant he was grown quite attractive since his hobbledehoy Pomfretshire days. He'd lost weight, he looked more youthful, he bathed more often, he'd learned how to refrain from always boosting his own cleverness, I do believe he got to bed with actresses. Success had made him sexy, at least to the young and foolish. But how could *you* be taken in? Was there anything at all about the man that made you think him a suitable father for whatever little Serlio you might conceive? Like constancy? Sincerity? Warmth?

Dear heart, I am left no alternative. I am forced to conclude you *desired* him, at the most basic, the most lecherous level.

7

All of this he hid from her too.

For twelve years Fid let her believe that during the time he lived in Highbury their separation was more or less amicable; Pogmoor found another route towards *Woyzeck*, which Fid did not want to obstruct (so he said, and said quite frankly); as it involved Leonore and Pogmoor staying in Manchester for maybe twelve months while they formed their own new production company, brother and sister must necessarily be out of touch . . . And in the end was it not to be entirely resolved? Fid back again in Antioch Gardens, Pogmoor once more directing Fid's plays, Leonore (no longer married) serenely at work on their décor.

Whore, thief, slave-owner? *Pistol at his gut?* How can she not shudder and quake that that should have been his thought? But he did think it – twelve years! – he thought it and he wrote it all down – he wrote it down and addressed it to *her*. And now: from his bullet-torn corpse, he extrudes this thick vapour of hatred! (If the Aunt were still alive to mount the staircase, cane in hand, and watch her quake, to be sure the sour old biddy'd laugh her knickers off.) In God's name, how to cope with it?

Of course her marriage was no damned good, the worst mistake she ever made, of course it was prompted by an insane and sudden *whim*, a kind of gamester's desperate lunge to stake her total destiny upon – upon – oh! – Something Else, Some*one* Else, upon anything but what had shaped her hitherto.

Lechery, as well? It could have been. And if it was, why not? She had never known the full truth of a man's body – except her brother's, that enticing lobster-pot, so easy to creep into, so safe and so comforting until she tried to get out. From Pogmoor, each time he leaned near to her – and he did lean, a great deal – she inhaled a predatory reek, as from a half-fledged vulture, unique, irresistible to every spark of hair in her queer dark nostrils; she was suffused with curiosity. A treacherous young man, a grasping young man, a young man whose one-night stand could kill a woman's spirit for a whole season afterwards.

If she were to reshape herself so late in her life (she perceived thirty-eight as a *crux*: choose now or renounce all choice), it could not be by loose attachments, whether women or men. With women she had had plenty; they led nowhere but back to Fid. With men she was in a difficulty. Because she did not know them, it would take her a long time to learn. A broken succession of brisk tutorials? Useless; jumping in puddles, here, there, everywhere. But to launch into the sea of sworn permanence . . . ? Why not? Take a chance on it? GO!

Only so would she find the full truth.

Full truth did mean a 'little Serlio'. But also the discovery of the flesh of the child's father against her own flesh night after night till not a particle was withheld from her. If Pogmoor caused her to tremble (antagonism? abhorrence? or the reverse of them, why not?) then Pogmoor was the one she must choose. Anything less would be sheer cowardice.

Oh yes, she admits to lechery. After her wry-mouthed fashion, she certainly felt it; and then she endeavoured to inspire it.

She invited the man Pogmoor to Antioch Gardens on a blistering afternoon (June 23rd, the Tuesday after the Sunday, a taxi had just brought away the last of Fid's luggage to Highbury); he came sweating and unkempt from the glasshouse heat of the bus; she offered him tea and asked him would he not like a bath, he looked as though he could do with one? All very pleasant, hospitable, matter-of-fact. She had unscrewed the bolt on the folding screen that closed off her bathroom. Once she heard him well-settled in the water, she slid the screen and came in too. (Her bathroom was bigger than her bedroom, her bath the same size as her big bed.) Legs stretched between his spread thighs, cool water up to her breasts, she touched him with her toes and said: 'Boy, this is all that'll happen, this is as far as it goes: unless you say you'll marry me. Will you?' And then: 'Take your hands off! If you try to play it rough I can win. I've got hold of both your ankles. One tug, you fall backwards, you drown.'

She laughed as she spoke, but for a moment he seemed terrified. Then her busy toes tickled him and *he* had to laugh. 'Eh dear,' with a giggle, clicking his quick mind to and fro: 'Tha's got me trapped. Wait up, sitha, I've to think on. Marry? Why, I'll tell t'brutal truth, Lenny, sat here like I am, bollocks-bare and soaped all over, I can't see good reason agen it. Thee and me, lass, betwixt us, I'd say we'd mek a right good buckling. Tek a chance?' (Her own thought, exact: an omen, it was *meant*!) Thereupon he dropped his Yorkshire and added, most nervous and sharp, 'You might have left out that crack, that I'd try to play rough. I don't do it. Not even any more in my dreams.'

Did he assume it was all a species of lascivious joke? Nonetheless, he'd *agreed*. He'd accepted her; the word was spoken. Of course, at that point, *she* had to backtrack, helpless with trepidation. It took six months of deep baths (and drunken suppers and entangling bed-sheets) to impel them to the registry office, but they made it. There, in the first week of January, they pledged their public companionship.

He was never to explain what he meant by 'not even any more'. Although she asked him time and again, he evaded, he refused.

Two hurtful refusals, in the upshot, to destroy the marriage. First: he gave no explanations ever (any sort of explanation, for anything he'd done or did); he was not only treacherous and grasping but secretive into the bargain; unforgivable. Second: he denied her vaginal intercourse without premature withdrawal or the craftwork of a contraceptive. He did promise that one day she would surely have her baby; but every day the 'one day' seemed further and further off. She finally concluded he did not want to be bothered. For her, that was enough. No quarrel; but she finished with him, ended and done.

Old lechery, ended and done, leaves nothing behind. Desire? gratification? bathwater out through the plughole. Pogmoor is now just Pogmoor, man of talent and not to be trusted. 'Cheap!' She says it, aloud, 'Cheap, demeaning, it didn't happen.' What didn't? Don't ask. But she thrusts her Athenian scarlet-tipped foolishness down between mattress and wall and out of immediate reach; pulls her clothes back onto her, any-old-how, incomplete and furtive covering, hooks and eyes, the odd button, hiding herself swiftly from the scorn of her mirrors.

For meanwhile *(she must confront it)*, from June 1970 until Christmas '71, what horror was the life of Fidelio? She hardly ever saw him; when she did, he seemed matter-of-fact, day-to-day, run-of-the-mill; she asked him no great questions; for the first time in her own life it was possible not to think of him, not to wonder what he was doing. Today she *must* wonder. No bloody option. Oh, he's taken pains to ensure it.

(vii)   Old Friends in Struggle

The first party of squatters – one might call them the flying scouts – had been in the Highbury house (8 Malthus Terrace) for no more than twenty-four hours when I arrived.

The main brigade was on the march, expected any day; foragers spreading out from their various halting-camps, vedettes deployed. If I use these Napoleonic figures for them, it's because their operation was not at all spontaneous. They had planned it in the utmost detail, theoretically, ideologically; the practicality was not quite so hot. Their chief failure; preliminary intelligence. They knew the house-owners were absentees, but they did not know how far absent – how *near*, in point of fact. Nor did they know who the house-owners were. Standing well back in the ground-floor room, shadowed and invisible – it was a black thunderous evening of midsummer rainstorms – the advance-party saw me panting along with my two suitcases round the corner from St Paul's Road, through the gap in the dwarf wall where there should have been a gate, through the litter and jungly weed of the small front garden, up the steps. Perhaps I was a wandering evangelist, something like that. They expected (I suppose) I would ring the doorbell. If they did not show themselves, I'd wait a little, ring again, and sod off. It was a weekend, they'd had no time to buy a new Yale lock and fix it. The rattle of my latchkey was a total surprise to them.

Of course, they should have put the chain up. For such careless-ness, Napoleon would have drummed them out of his *Voltigeurs*.

In the hall I stood face-to-face with their *pro tem* leader – no, spokesperson, they were a Collective. Good God but I knew her! She knew me. It took both of us full thirty seconds to be certain. *I* was wearing a peaked cap, pulled low against the rain; my mackin-tosh collar turned up around my jaw. And over the past five years *she* had changed quite remarkably. Polly Blackadder. Good God.

What used to be her strictly trimmed casque of gleaming raven hair was now a thick drape like a mourning-veil, long fringe over her brow, long strands falling down across each shoulder to her breast, greasy and uncombed. She was plimsoll-shod, in very dirty dungaree trousers with a workman's ragged shirt worn outside them. Her face was hard and hostile, without makeup, indeed without soap-and-water. The last half-inch of a roll-up cigarette was stuck between her lips.

A slouch of confederates glided behind her as we stood there, a young man and a young woman, as scruffy as she was. They could have come out of a picture-book of nineteenth-century London low life, a street-corner ruffian and one of his drabs. I could smell marijuana. I could also smell a blocked-up lavatory; and there was rubbish all over the stairs. Through the open door of the front room I saw more rubbish, torn wallpaper, bare floorboards, some beer-crates and packing-cases, a transistor radio, a camping-gas stove, cracked cups and a filthy teapot. Irate left-wing posters had been tacked to the walls. A very new one, home-made and made in a hurry, yelled down at us from the first-floor landing:

ELECTION A FASCIST CON-TRICK!
FUCK THE TORY JUNTA!!
EXTRA-PARLIAMENTARY STREET ACTION NOW
TO SMASH HEATH'S FATCAT COUP!!!
Vive les Semaines de Soixante-huit!
Viva la Lotta Continua!

Issued by the *Viva-Vive Vindicators (VVV)*

Beside it was a home-made, made-in-a-hurry mural; a combin-ation of photo-montage and vigorous felt-tip drawing. It showed a sexy young Amazon in her birthday suit, charging with a garden fork at the new Prime Minister whose trousers had fallen down below his knees. A huge defiant VVV was inscribed across her buttocks.

'Right,' growled Polly at last. 'Great! Mr Carver, the bourgeois dramatist. He has the key, he has the confidence, I doubt he must opine he's the landlord.' The two confederates growled in unison.

Then all of a sudden she grinned, jumped forward and kissed me. 'Dear man, you're sodden wet, in with you, Fid, sit down; shall we give you a cup of tea? And we'll tell you what it's all about.'

I ought to have been pompous, denunciatory, outraged. I very nearly was. Dammit, it *was* my house; I was expecting to live in it, eventually in some comfort. But remember, I was deeply depressed that day, I was dreading my loneliness. They made me welcome, you see. I began to weep, for the second time since lunch. Not a great outburst of sobs; I was able to pass it off as a summer cold. I think Polly knew different, but she had the tact not to comment. She introduced me to what there was of the gang.

Cliff (Cambridge dropout and *nouveau*-prole) and Sonja (Dutch, an avant-garde actress from Amsterdam): hard-line Anarcho/Trots or not, they were affectionate young people rather scared of what they'd got into. Which is not to say they were not serious. Polly, by some years the eldest of the three, was exceedingly serious. The Presbyterian conscience had impelled her into strange waters, by way of Paris two years before. She had been there! she told me excitedly over the tea – on holiday, or so she'd intended. Of course she had to go to the Théâtre de l'Odéon, where the revolutionists held their headquarters. She was assaulted by the riot police and spent a day and two nights with twenty-five others in a blood-and-vomit-spattered cell. The gendarmes may have assumed such treatment would have frightened her off. They cannot have known much about her, her consistency, her capacity for deep productive anger. From then on she had seen 'theatre' in an utterly different light.

She had not given up her profession; an enterprising agent had found her lots of excellent parts on stage, in films and television; she could have become something of a star. But after Paris a good half of her belonged in the politics-of-struggle and no turning back; specifically the politics of her trade union, Actors' Equity. Here she aligned herself with the Socialist Labour League faction and fought all sorts of battles to radicalise the union membership. She would not *join* the League, however; she resented its critical attitude towards the Paris students. She'd have done better for her career if she *had* joined.

As it was, she was somewhat isolated; she made enemies among conventionally-minded actors; people were unwilling to work with her, lest she lecture them unbearably in the greenroom on their exploitation, or held up rehearsals by demanding neo-Marxist analyses of every decision the director announced. For instance,

cast as Miranda in *The Tempest*, she enquired why should Caliban be
made up ugly? We had only the word of his oppressors for his
repulsive appearance. There was no objective evidence for it in the
script, so why assume that Shakespeare intended it? Surely Caliban
was a Caribbean Indian of regular good looks, and a victim of
colonialist propaganda? Make anyone up ugly, it ought to be Ariel,
the running-dog, the *provocateur*. Thus she mingled Struggle for
Conditions of Work with Struggle for the *Content* of the Work;
which confused and annoyed everyone, not least the Socialist
Labour League. Employment opportunities began to fall off. Now
she had determined to thumb her nose at her agent's protestations,
to go her own way, do her own thing.

   She told me, still excitedly, that the squat was the home-base of
VEXACTION, an acting company founded only last month by none
other than that Fred Owston who had refused to direct my play at
Pomfretshire. She thought it amusing; my own laughter was not so
hearty, when I heard he was due to take up irregular residence with
three or four additional members, here in my house on Tuesday, or
maybe Wednesday. He had changed even more than *she* had; so it
seemed. For Polly had shifted from nothing-in-particular to committed revolutionism, while Fred (revolutionist already) had had
violently to turn himself inside-out inside himself, an agonising
process; so it seemed. 1968 for him too: the 'Year of the Pig', she
said he called it. Paris, Berlin, Prague and the Chicago Police-riots
had together so disgusted him with post-Bolshevik corruption and
party bureaucracy as to sling him absolutely Over the Top; so it
seemed.

   (Oh yes: Fred and Polly had been lovers ever since Pomfretshire.
She explained this to me in private later that night. And oh yes:
poor Polly at Pomfretshire had undergone some foul experience.
She would not tell just what it was; only that the memory of it
affected every choice she'd made since, political, personal, sexual,
artistic. Fred had brought her through it, a strong considerate mate
– although she never told *him* just what it was, either. After Paris
she had had to bring Fred through his own trauma. They were very
warmly bonded and I mustn't be sarcastic.)

   The aim and purpose of VEXACTION would be 'cultural disrup-
tion of mega-capitalist social norms'. Improvisatory, dialectical,
rudely topical, a medium of support for workers' struggle telling the
truth in a society of lies. They were all three very vague as to where
their funds would come from. They did talk about support by those
whom they supported; but I had more than a suspicion of small-
scale criminality. Exposing the injustice of bourgeois property-law,
no doubt. Dole frauds, shoplifting, credit-card swindles. Certainly
squatting. Somehow the whole thing was tied up with the Viva-

Vive Vindicators (whoever they were); the connection was left largely unexplained.

But my first preoccupation was the squatting. I could not make up my mind what to do about it. Except I knew within five minutes I was not going to turn them out. It wasn't just the cup of tea and Polly's guarded friendliness; I had begun to get a sudden *buzz*, almost the same as the first springing of the notion of a new play – without warning, inside my head, aha it's *there!* and where the devil did it come from . . . ?

The house was in shameful condition. They let me know their opinion of this: you and I, Lenny, were typical *rentier* shits, depriving oppressed tenants of rightful repairs and maintenance, and then letting a perfectly good building stand idle while thousands languished homeless all over the land. I did my best to expound the facts. How the aged Mrs Pole-Hatchet, after years of eccentric demand upon her landlords' purse ('*Jew-landlords*', as she made a point of pointing out), had suddenly refused us all access, claiming that our only reason for wishing to enter the house was to insert microphones to transmit her doings to Moscow. How she anxiously awaited murderers from Moscow, Politburo hitmen to avenge the late Colonel Pole-Hatchet's part in the 1919 war of counter-revolutionary intervention. How in the meantime she hacked and scraped at the walls, uprooted floorboards, pulled out electric wiring, in demented search for bugs already planted. How one day she attacked the milkman with a blunt paint-scraper, screaming that he was Zinoviev still mysteriously alive and come in person to cut her throat. How they took her to hospital, and how she died. No doubt we should have at once set to work to refurbish the premises, but we didn't have the money, did we? we had to postpone. We postponed it one day too many.

(viii)   Proposal

Did they believe me? They didn't say. They just nodded and growled and gave each other sceptical smiles, sidelong, waiting for my proposal.

I began with an analysis of the situation, trying not to sound too stiff in my verbal arteries.

(a) I needed to live in Malthus Terrace because I had nowhere else to live, never mind why,

(b) VEXACTION had nowhere else to live. I would like – no, I *needed* – to be actively helpful to anyone who challenged the current crap of the regular theatre.

(c) I was at a standstill in my work. The collapsed *Woyzeck* project was only a potboiler to 'mark time' while I sought an imaginative

break. This could well be that break. At all events, a weird coincidence; I'd be a schmuck not to see how it flew.

(d) If I let the premises be used as VEXACTION's working base,
would the collective in return:

  – pay a nominal rent, to help cover a portion of my costs?
  – leave me one small room, to work in, undisturbed?
  – allow me to keep in touch with – if possible, have some part
    in – whatever VEXACTION was at. Not as a 'bourgeois
    dramatist', bloody patronising both ways! but – to strike a
    random chord with Polly – as the man who made Alice Trip-
    and-Go for her, remember? Believe it: I was excited by their
    plans. Turned on. It went without saying, I wouldn't dream
    of trying to influence their policy. Unless they did feel I was
    needed? Shit, I meant no more than a spirit of solidarity.

They listened without meeting my eyes. A long silence. Polly
said, 'Alice Trip-and-Go is not altogether a sonsie recollection. That
apart, it sounds pretty good. Well-intentioned, which paves the
road to – ach, *ye ken weel whaur*. Too well-intentioned to be agreed off
the cuff. We'll discuss it when the others arrive. Meantime, Fid,
choose a room. Undisturbed? Aye, to be sure. We'll cock an ear for
the clack of your typewriter. I presume you've brought it with you.
The mighty playwright at his mighty task. No no, the *subtle* playwright at his *subtle* explorations; nae doot, a noiseless typewriter.
Till Tuesday, then – or Wednesday. Dear goodness, I can't wait to
see Owston's face.'

(ix)   Live and Let Live

*His face, neither on Tuesday nor Wednesday but in the small hours of
      Thursday morning, was a caricature of comic perplexity.*

Since breakfast-time on Monday I had been in and out between
Number 8 and the shops in the Holloway Road, stocking up with all
the things I needed, all the things I had forgotten to bring, to make
myself just tolerably comfortable. I had very little time to talk to
Polly and her pals; they too were out and about, hunting-and-
gathering, scavenging, prowling and lurking. They had mysterious
business in Notting Hill Gate and Brixton: I preferred to ask no
questions.

   Under the roof, at the back of the house, was a little room where
a servant must have slept way back in the 1820s. It held a fireplace
the size of a coffee-pot and a broken-down old bedstead on which I
laid out my sleeping-bag. I found a tea-chest in the adjacent attic
and a three-legged stool: I could read, type, and eat. I bought my

own camping-gas stove, a few bundles of faggots and bags of coalite, a boy-scout outfit of mess-tins and eating-irons: I could cook, keep warm if it got cold, and eat with delicacy. I bought food, as far as possible in tins and packets.

So much for my freelance self. For myself plus collective, I was able (as avouched householder) to secure promises from electricity and gas boards that supplies be eventually reconnected. I bespoke an electrician to deal with the damaged wiring. I ordered installation of a phone; a *pay*-phone, I wasn't having nonsense. I called a plumber in to look at the WC. I called a glazier, I called a shop that sold second-hand fridges. Mrs Pole-Hatchet's cooker was still in the kitchen, probably still fit for use, once we'd given it a good scrub, once the gas board had been kept to their promise.

I might even have managed to type some sheets of creative writing, if I could have created any writing to type. But I was too distracted by the thought of Owston.

The *reality* of Owston came barging up the stairs into my 'undisturbed' room before it was daylight and just after I had at last got to sleep. For hours I'd been kept awake by cramps in my leg-muscles, unusual itches, heavy sweat, macabre half-dreams. Now he comes flashing a torch into my face and pushing his great fist against my neck. 'Eh up,' he barks, 'Carver, what the bloody hell's all this then?'

He was as bulky as he ever was, but bearded like an Ostrogoth, long hair all over his shoulders, sweatband round his skull. His wire spectacles were as I remembered them, so was his leather jacket. He wore military macho boots laced up to the top of his calves. His thick trousers were military too, with green blotches of jungle camouflage. He could have been a Hell's Angel drafted for service in Vietnam.

'Jesus Christ, mate, you've fixed us into a right fucking deadlock. We can't get rid of you because you've taken the house in charge, neither the landlord nor *not* the landlord, more a kind of gracious host expecting obligations in return for hospitality, bourgeois shit and you've dropped us right into it. What the fuck was Blackadder up to, letting you pull her a trick like that? I can't think why she let you in. But neither, old son, can *you* get rid of *us*. We're seven, you're one; and *you've* got your liberal reputation to smirch, ent you? Live and let live: okay? Got a fag, have you? Right.'

Perplexity was already abating. He had shifted his lamp to the stool and my typewriter to the foot of the bed; he'd dumped his broad arse upon the tea-chest, knees spread, arms akimbo, jacket expansively draped, an ogreish version of Old King Cole. He lit my cigarette for himself with a rasp of satisfaction, blew smoke all around him, and settled down for a good long chat. I asked him did he know what time it was; he said of course he bloody knew, we'd got to sort out this question of mutual territory. He would put it to the collective with appropriate recommendations; it couldn't be dealt with too soon.

The chat was one-sided. 'Nominal rent? Not a chance. We're expropriating the expropriators, ideological imperative, no way will we accede to the cash-nexus. Commodity-transference, though, we *could* handle that. We buy the nosh, pay the electric, the gas, as much of the running repairs as we can, which ent much; *not* the rates, Christ no, not the insurance, those are all yours wi'knobs on. We're on the lookout for a motor, second-hand van, summat like that. We'll divvy up expenses there, you'll pay your share. We might need your name on the logbook. But we'll not see you short, okay? Next thing: VEXACTION's work. Would it *suit* you? Hard to believe. Nay but five year ago it wouldn't have suited *me*. Right then, we'll give it a try. If we don't like your input, we'll tell you to fuck off. Okay?'

And so, before breakfast, the collective amongst themselves agreed it with Owston; and then they had me in and we all ate bowls of cornflakes and all of them agreed it with me, give or take a few minor niggles. One being the question of drugs: as householder (I tried to make them understand) I'd have to bear the full brunt if they were busted by the fuzz. They swore that they'd swear I'd forbidden them to stash, carry, or use while on the premises. I had to take this at face-value, although it made me most uneasy. Similarly with their fell-off-a-lorry financial expedients and their sweeping guarantees that I would 'not be seen short'. At Pomfretshire I'd have taken oath that both Owston and Polly were dead straight on such matters. But that was then. Cross fingers and hope for the best.

The new arrivals of the collective were much like the ones I had seen already. The whole affair was fundamentally an ex-Pomfretshire undertaking; VEXACTION's founder maintained his erstwhile links. A student revolution had hogged the headlines at Pomfretshire the previous autumn. And now two of its People's-Power Cultural Committee were in London to join with Owston: 'Che' (a pop-poet from Wakefield), and 'HP' (a black girl of sixteen, who had not been on the roll of the university at all but had nevertheless slid herself somehow into the committee; an 'outside agitator', I suppose she must have been. In fact she was a runaway from a Bradford comprehensive school). The third member of Owston's party, Toe, or Theodosia, was Irish from Ballymurphy in Belfast, although she seemed to have lived most of her life in Luton. I'm not sure where Owston picked her up; he said she had professional experience as an entertainer. She was no older than the others, so the experience could not have been extensive. However: no pre-judgements. Cross fingers of two hands.

(x)   The Overt and the Occult

Let me make this clear: until Sulaiman Rahmat Ali came back into my life,
I had no reason to believe that Malthus Terrace was anything more than a
legitimate sideways jump in my career as a playwright. Eccentric, perhaps,
but in its own way logical: I hoped it would also prove fruitful.

Everyone at Number 8 was a member of VEXACTION, and VEXAC-TION was a public and soon-to-be-publicised theatre group. It was *not* the same outfit as the Viva-Vive Vindicators but an offshoot of the VVV; the VVV itself had personnel elsewhere (how many, I can't say) who had little enough to do with the craft of presenting plays.

VVV was a 'political tendency'; its constitution, if it had one, being communicated by individual contact. Anyone who shared its underground-extremist doctrine was entitled to take part in deliberations and to help shape activities. But it was impossible to know whether you shared the doctrine or not, until someone told you what it was; you weren't told until someone had reason to believe you would share. Nobody told *me*. When I enquired about it from Polly, she blinked at me from under her swart fringe and plucked a fistful of scurrilous leaflets out of a cardboard box: 'You'll get a fair idea from these.' I didn't. They were expanded versions of the posters on the stair-landing, loud-mouthed protest stuff, nothing at all specific.

In other words: a secret society, membership by invitation only and subject to vetting by a murky sort of central committee in Notting Hill Gate, or Brixton, or both. If in hindsight it appears sinister, I did not think so at the time. It took me quite a while to get the hang of it. When I did, I just assumed it was a kids' game of mystery-making; frustrated piss-and-wind had to acquire revolutionary substance somehow, so why not pretend to be Bol-sheviks of 1905? I myself was so frustrated by the political subtext of the *Woyzeck* disappointment, that any kind of 'barbaric yawp' against the System was roughly in tune with my mood. So you'll see I didn't worry about what I found out about VVV's activities – formally termed 'the Praxis' – ultra-leftist fly-posting; leaflets strewn anonymously in bars, music clubs, fringe theatres, students' unions and so on; enigmatic placards at anti-Vietnam War or trade-union or housing-shortage demonstrations, mixed in with the regular placards and slyly passed out for unwitting marchers to carry; braying letters sent at random to the press and to prominent individuals as warnings of the people's-wrath-to-come.

VEXACTION was the only really *open* activity; its manifesto would imply solidarity with the occult VVV rather than direct adherence.

In Number 8 we were so busy trying to get VEXACTION off the ground that deeper affiliation scarcely occupied our minds. Owston never mentioned such an encumbrance. But he certainly knew his trade. His first aim was to create a unified dramatic style; he set about it by having us read stories from the day's newspapers and immediately act them out, improvising whatever characters and interpretations of events came spontaneously to mind. Then we would analyse what we'd done. Then we'd do it again, more carefully, more aware of what it all meant. Then Owston himself, and Polly, representing respectively the traditional capitalist type-figure ('Grabitall') and the spirit of humanist-socialist-liberation ('Polly'), would take control of the action from their opposed points of view, interfering in the plot, squabbling and scuffling with each other, exhorting and supporting or abusing and blackmailing the rest of the *dramatis personae*, and very often between them diverting the original fable into quite a different course and a harshly unexpected ending.

After a few weeks' intense work we found ourselves with a string of playlets on all sorts of energetic and immediate themes, foreign affairs, industrial affairs, socio-sexual controversies, crime and punishment, war and peace. We could link them together or present them one at a time. The quality of the acting was variable. For example, Polly could do almost anything she was given; her archetype could turn into a typist in one piece, a mother in another, a festering old beggar-woman in a third, and still remain 'Polly', the strong small brave woman to enkindle the hearts of all of us. Owston was more limited; he was really only capable of swaggering in a top hat, roaring with rage and greed, dissembling behind the corner of his cloak and smoking a cigar like Groucho Marx. Toe was well able for an extravagant striptease or blues songs in an Ulster accent (so *that* was her vaunted experience! Luton pubs and clubs for a clientele of fitters and welders); HP was a born comedian who yearned to be a schmaltzy tragedian and too often lost good laughs by muffling them in the heartache of the stereotyped mournful clown; Sonja belonged to the 'reeling and writhing and fainting-in-coils' school of Performance Art and had difficulty with intelligible words (let alone her Dutch accent); the two boys were basically 'walking gentlemen', although Che ran a nice line in ad-hoc satirical ditties. I myself fitted slickly enough into the standard role of disillusioned *raisonneur*, mumbling and bumbling my way through webs of liberal pessimism; Grabitall's toady and Polly's butt.

Costume was rudimentary. Cardboard masks and outlandish headgear, otherwise our ordinary clothes.

You'll ask, what application was there for my playwriting talent? Well: after all the impromptus, final scenarios would have to be *fixed*. Carver's job to fix them. But at the same time to allow room in each fixed script for topical variation, spur-of-the-moment gags, new slogans, sudden response (verbal or physical) to contradictory audience-reactions. Polly laid great stress on sudden response. Uncomfortable for Owston, whose mind moved at a deliberate pace; he had to drive himself fiercely against the grain. So did I. It was very heavy going; it was hilarious good fun; and none of us could be sure of ourselves until we actually faced our public.

We first faced it in the first week of August (probably too soon, but we felt we had to nerve ourselves and make a *leap*) with a gig at the students' union of the London School of Economics, to enliven a Civil Liberties teach-in. The college was on vacation; but there were enough students around town, from the LSE itself, from the university and the polytechnics, to hire the premises for this urgent issue. The day's events, lectures, harangues, interminable debates, overshot their timetable; we performed in the canteen bar much later than we should have done; many young people had drifted there already to take refuge from the more boring items of the teach-in, and by that hour were very well oiled; they laughed like hyenas from the moment we made our entry, possibly at our jokes, more probably at *us*; halfway through the show (forty minutes of Grabitall coercing Ted Heath to 'restore the nation's moral stan-dards'), Toe's Dance of the Seven Freedoms – a most arbitrary version of what had been rehearsed – incited such disorder that the organisers begged us to finish, thanked us for our contribution, paid us our fee and hustled us off, all within the one hectic gesture. Toe, in bare feet (bare everything, not to put a tooth in it), cut herself badly on the broken glass as she ran out. Back to Highbury in a smoulder of anticlimax (our ancient van's self-starter failing at every traffic light), only to discover a day or two later that we had on our hands the makings of a mini-sensation. Hard agitprop, combined with raucous sex and a very low class of buffoonery, had hit them where they lived, or so it seemed.

We'd cautiously invited no critics; but the LSE students, behind our backs, did notify a handful of approximately radical journals. *Time Out* called us 'bawdyhouse Marx-n-Sparks on greased wheels with no brakes'. A prat in the *New Statesman*, annoyed, so it seemed, by me in particular (even though we'd presented ourselves anonymously), opined:

—rarely can a hitherto intelligent playwright have lent his reputation as well as his subfusc person to such crudely unthinking charades. The very bottom of the barrel of stone-age Red Rhetoric.

Which meant that my input must have been suitable. I was not told to fuck off; neither was I admitted yet to full membership of the collective. Nonetheless, I felt proud. My life in the theatre was suddenly *reborn*.

And just as suddenly, our invitations began to arrive.

To begin with, we accepted them all. Sometimes, from a sense of solidarity (and to confirm our political credentials), we agreed to waive the fee. A dangerous precedent; once it became known, sponsors who could afford to pay tried any excuse to avoid it.

One such was an Irish club in Kilburn in the middle of October. We brought them our Irish piece, no more than twenty-five minutes, in between the *ceilidh* music and the national-liberation ballads. It largely depended upon Toe's information, or should I say her highly partisan readings of other people's information? Its subject was the recent Falls Road curfew: the British Army in Belfast (supposedly to protect Catholics from Protestants) turns a cat-in-the-pan on receipt of the election results, comes rampaging into Catholic houses, beats Catholics up, inspires Catholic riots, inspires recruitment into both branches, Official and Provisional, of the recently split IRA. In short, the Tory government as the terrorists behind all 'terrorism'. (The Kilburn club, we were discreetly notified, leaned towards the left-leaning Officials.) Great success, storms of hot Fenian applause, drinks on the house: and no money.

Owston and Polly fell to wrangling with the club secretary, in outrage that a 'whip-round among the lads' would do just as well as the agreed cheque. It was damnably embarrassing, it made me feel like my own fatuous-liberal character in the play, it drove me to a table well away from them to sip Guinness until they'd sorted it out . . .

Before I looked up at his face, I knew it was Sulaiman beside me, his willowy stoop toward me in exquisitely pressed safari-jacket, the soft tap of his dark-amber fingers tip against tip, his burgundy-red cravat. He was smiling like a djinni from an Arabian Nights bottle, long eyelashes sweetly flickering over his soft and soulful eyes. 'Poor Fidelio,' says he. 'So very unseemly. I do suspect, don't you? that your group needs a finely tuned and most diplomatic public-relations chap. Shall I help?'

I don't remember which was the stronger, the surge of sexual shock, or my more rational astonishment at his presence (so apparently incongruous yet so take-it-easy, so why-ever-not?) in this unexpected place. I could not imagine how he thought he could help. VEXACTION and the Fergal O'Hanlon London-Irish Association were managing a neat little ruction all on their own; why on earth would either side accept his interference?

He saw at once what I was thinking. 'My dear old fellow, they haven't told you? A very particular consonant, very tidily extracted and triplicated from *almost* the last gasp of the alphabet – VVV, my surly darling – ring a bell?'

(xi)   The Bounds of Likelihood

Uncanny, was it not? that Polly and Owston should pick on my *house to squat in, out of all the empty houses in London. It could never have been predicted. Not by any sort of theory of average probability.*

But Sulaiman, once I was able to consider his reappearance in a less hysterical, more controlled fashion, was quite within the bounds of likelihood. He had always hung around little do-it-yourself out-breaks of the arts, theatre especially. The area of his interests was small, the number of people and places limited, we were sure to run up against him soon. He was always up-to-date, always on-the-make, not a trendsetter himself but a trendsetter's sniffer dog. And undeniably VEXACTION was becoming a trend.

As for his familiar relationship with the Irish club, that too upon reflection was not hard to understand. National independence, and armed struggle to obtain it, were part and parcel of his childhood environment, he knew all the jargon, he understood the per-sonalities. His father, a wealthy merchant and landowner in Krish-nanagar, had been active against the Raj around the time of Sulaiman's birth; although he was a Muslim he had determined to stay on in what he hoped would be an ecumenical India. But the aftermath of partition brought the burning of his country house and the fanatically cruel murder of two of his servants: communal violence interwoven with peasant revolt. It drove him to emigrate to East Pakistan. He left his son behind in Calcutta to be reared by relatives as an enlightened secular nationalist. Pakistan, a sectarian state, disgusted him – despite its necessity as a refuge, despite those two-thirds of his property that lay within its frontier.

The milieu in which his son chose to spend his student years was not altogether what had been planned. Way-out leftists (Maoists indeed), intellectuals, artists, sexual nonconformists, subversives in hiding from the law. The young man proved an old-fashioned wastrel in a decidedly new-fashioned way.

His father must have paid for his transference to England (prompted no doubt by the Calcutta police); and then paid for him at LSE until he saw he was never going to graduate. After that, Sulaiman was on his own. If bedtime with me in Stockwell in 1968 was any criterion, he managed very well. *Adept* is the word that comes to mind.

He was certainly adept at handling VEXACTION's gripe about our fee. After ten minutes' soothing talk – on the one hand, my dear fellows – on the other hand, old boy – now, Polly, my love, hold horses! much to be said on both sides – he produced a most efficient compromise, a reduced cheque *and* a whip-round, amounting to a five-quid surplus over and above the agreed sum.

Then he conveyed me, no less adeptly, to the far end of the bar. He allowed me to buy him an Irish whiskey, with soda and a reheated sausage-roll. (Defiance of religious taboo was integral to his self-presentation, and Kilburn was a safe enough place for it.) I was hoping he would not ask me to spend the night with him. I feared I could not say no; I was sure that I *ought* to say no. He was so beautiful, so persuasive, so destructive to my peace of mind. During the weeks of our past-and-gone affair my writing had fallen demeaningly to pieces – except for shapeless little gut-poems of doomed voluptuous indolence, dialogue-fragments of lovers deceived, miserable laments for corrupted hearts and priapic loins – I'd torn all of them up the day I said goodbye to him, and flushed them down the bog. I truly thought I *had* said goodbye.

'Goodbye', 'no': short words, untrue words, cancelled as soon as uttered. Or as soon as the next opportunity came smiling to sit beside me on an Irish Republican bar-stool.

'Polly and Fred,' he murmured, 'do feel that my presence in Highbury would be pretty productive all round. They had wanted to confine house-room to the actual actors, but now they appreciate how my very particular talents in instant proximity would be much to general advantage. (Forget my silly joke about VVV nonsense: you didn't get it, my dear, it wasn't funny anyway.) They say, first the collective must make its decision, most mandatory, a matter of principle, goes without saying. But I don't want to drop out of Brixton until I have the say-so from *you*. Individual say-so, dear Fid, no hang-ups, no ill-feeling. Can you resist?'

Dammit, no I couldn't. That very night the slippery bugger came to instal himself in Malthus Terrace. In the back seat of his jade-green Mini he'd had his bedroll all ready and waiting. Dammit, it was wide enough for two.

(xii)   A Reminder

Something about him always reminded me of you, Lenny.

Of course not his dark eyes and black hair. But his hands were so
like yours, so capable, so swift and quiet. And his long taut legs.
And his mouth, whether smiling or grim. His smile above all, a little
crooked, yet brilliant, yet secretive, so like yours. But you, I always
trusted. Even when most deeply besotted, I never trusted *him*.
Deep-sleeping ominous migraine, my awareness of his essential
contradiction. Revolutionary principles – if indeed they were principles, not just a trend – set against his inherited wealth? it didn't
add up. His father died in '67 and left him *lakhs* and *lakhs* safe and
useless in banks at Dacca and Calcutta; he couldn't get at them
without going there; he couldn't go there (so it seemed), either to
East Pakistan or to India, without risking arrest; for as long as he
stayed in England the main chance stayed alight in his eyes like a
beacon on a far-off mountain.

                                8

'Bloody fool!' shouts Leonore, out loud.
   Why, Fid knew him, saw through him! yet sodomy yet again with
him at the drop of a sausage-roll? October, he gives the date. Did she tell
him *before* October that she and Pogmoor were setting their own date?
Yes she did, she sent a postcard, a rollicking great Santa Claus of a
beefeater in Kodachrome, grinning beside the gate of the Tower with a
scrawny American matron. Insensitive? Sure. But how could she have
known? when the bloody weeping fool refused to inform her of the
truth of his feelings? Want to bet he'd been holding that postcard tight in
his inside-pocket, all soggy with his tears, as he pissed himself in Kilburn
and succumbed?

(xiii)   So It Seemed

Sulaiman's pretence that he had come only to assist *VEXACTION was not
to be borne out by his behaviour at Number 8.*

To begin with he kept out of our way, easily and tactfully enough;
now and then at mealtimes offering us suggestions about publicity,
improbable schemes for suborning various media-persons, and
news of gigs he was hoping to fix for us. Through his contacts at the
Kilburn club he was trying to arrange another, much more important, Irish evening in Liverpool. We would need extra material for
it; our Falls Road play must be revised to incorporate all the

developments of the past four months. He designed a striking poster and some politically aggressive fliers, and ran about town in search of printers' competitive estimates. This went on for ten days.

On the eleventh day, a sudden change: with manifold and diffident apologies, he interrupted one of our workshop sessions. Apologies or not, the interruption was a fact, and it signified. Sulaiman was effectively in charge. Maybe not in charge of the practical theatre-work; but very much in charge of *something*. If he'd been acting deferential, from now on (he made it clear) he expected to be deferred to. And he was.

He called a meeting for after lunch, of three selected persons; Owston, Toe and Sonja. Our afternoon work was postponed to make room for it. The next day, he called another meeting – Toe and Polly only – and once again no afternoon work. This went on for several days, until (so it seemed) all the collective had been closeted with him, in varying individual permutations, upon business which they kept to themselves. When I say 'all the collective', I mean *I* was never invited into these confidential little huddles.

It was not as though I hadn't had a hint of an inkling. The night before the first of his meetings he spoke to me in bed. Gentle fingers feather-light on my cheek as though he feared I would go to sleep before he finished what he had to whisper: 'Fidelio, I need to tell you,' he was breathing into my ear, 'you need to be told, I think. This is of course just *us*. For tomorrow, amongst all-and-sundry, your Sulaiman won't be quite what he has seemed. Does not Anglo-Danish Hamlet say "an antic disposition", to keep very good friends off the track? Absolutely the same thing with *this* nonsense. Bengali-Paki-Anglo Sam, d'you see—' (They'd called him 'Sam' at the LSE; he liked it and kept it going; 'Sam Rammit' became his working-name; he believed it eased his contacts with chaps-in-the-London-street.) '—d'you see, Sam takes his lessons where they're learned, classic Shakespeare as useful as anywhere. Just don't you be surprised, my dear.'

I suppose I thought (half-asleep, satiated, hard put to withstand an unbearable sense of waste) that he meant we were not to go bragging through the rooms downstairs about our sex and sexuality. Fair enough, but pointless; *I* never talked of such things, if *he* did I hadn't heard him. Everyone must have known he'd brought his bedroll up to my garret, and a fat lot any of them cared. But that wasn't his meaning at all.

For after that night he moved his gear out of the house. I don't know where he was sleeping. Perhaps back again in Brixton. In one way a great relief to me; in another, a scalding torment. He would turn up daily at Number 8 in the course of the morning, proffer apologies, issue instructions, call his meetings. I noticed that for every meeting he contrived to include either Sonja or Toe.

The 'antic disposition' was to keep *me* off the track, not the others; it followed I'd been quite mistaken as to the sort of track he'd been talking about. VVV, I concluded, was playing its secret games. I felt very uncomfortable; the more so as all sorts of changes were taking place in the work itself.

For instance, after a meeting with Polly and Sam Rammit (Sulaiman from now on was irremediably metamorphosed), Owston announced that our production values were not up to snuff. We had to become more *professional*. There'd been complaints of inaudibility: we'd need amplifying equipment. We looked dingy, T-shirts and jeans were a drag, man: we'd need properly designed costumes. Che and his concertina as our instrumental music was a drag, man, a fucking drag, face it: we'd need at least a drum-set and an electronic keyboard. Some of our venues had been badly lit: we'd need our own lighting. Sam Rammit was exploring ways and means to lay hands on all this stuff. I pointed out that we had not hitherto had the money to pay for such fundamental (and to my mind, undesirable) amendments to our style; did we have it now? If we did, where had it come from? If we didn't, how would we get it? I was told that that was irrelevant, bourgeois, divisive; ways and means were being explored. The collective, so it seemed, was happy to acquiesce.

There was the business of the transport. I had no car of my own – or rather, I had, but my sister had it (in Manchester, oh yes). VEXACTION's van being registered in my name was advantageous to me, no question; as a rule I had been in charge of it, making sure it was maintained, driving it on most of our trips, driving it for my own personal use whenever I needed to. It was a horrible little beat-up box of rusty old iron fitted with insecure seats; I don't know how it would have scraped through if we'd been faced with an MoT test; all eight of us (nine, if you include Sam Rammit) could just cram into it with bumps, bruises, petrol fumes and nausea. Sam Rammit's Mini was rarely used; he was protective of it to the point of uncomradely individualism. Owston had a motor cycle but normally preferred to travel with the crowd so we could all have the benefit of his hectorings en route. Now, so it seemed, Sonja and Toe were to assume responsibility for the van; I would only be the driver when specifically requested. Toe at the wheel was dead dangerous; Sonja smoothly competent. I did not really mind, the vehicle after all belonged (*de facto* if not *de jure*) to the collective as a whole, but . . . Are you surprised I felt uncomfortable?

Carmilla. You'll know Carmilla Costello better than I do, I think. Didn't you have dealings with her at a later date, just before you and Pogmoor broke up? To me she was a very scatty Irish-American who was at Pomfretshire the same time as myself. She'd spent the intervening years back home, Boston or wherever, but now she was in England once again. Owston told us she was undertaking our new costumes. She and Polly had been in constant correspondence (so it seemed), they knew almost everything about each other's business. She rented a pad south of the river, Clapham or thereabouts, where she'd set herself up as an alternative dress-designer, devising gear for the Carnaby Street rag merchants, psychedelic tat, Kama Sutra medallions, sweatshirts, mini-skirts, headbands and so forth, items of printed cheesecloth with erotic emblems (Taoist) or ruthless slogans (Maoist). She was more off-the-axle than ever, darting briefly into Malthus Terrace at irregular intervals to spout psychobabble and revolutionary spleen at us, leaving kitbags full of fabric-remnants cluttering up the hall, sticking Californian rockband posters or R. MILHOUS NIXON: WANTED FOR MURDER notices on our walls, suddenly and inex-plicably pulling people's trousers down to take measurements of the inside-leg. She gave us no chance to discuss her intended designs, and her language was even fouler than Owston's.

Polly became very morose: uncooperative about quite small details, such as the arrangement of our daily roster for cooking and washing-up. There was a coolness between her and Owston.

The Liverpool gig took ages to organise. First it was to be on this date, then on that; and nothing else could be scheduled until it was confirmed. The venue itself was in doubt. There was talk of a club down near the docks, of a community centre on the edge of Toxteth, of a pub out at Huyton with a well-equipped concert-room. Toe would spend hours on the telephone, snarling her Ulster sarcasm at 'Paddy O', 'Mickey Mac', and someone called 'the Priest' who was surely not in holy orders. It was never made clear what precise organisation she was dealing with, and her phone calls usually ended with the person at the other end talking at great length while Toe nodded her head and interjected, 'Yeh-yeh,' 'Jasus Christ,' 'Understood,' 'I'll get back t'youse,' at intervals, finally ringing off and running into the scullery to report herself to Owston with not a word of explanation to anyone else. Then we would be told of yet another change of plan.

Then Sonja suddenly announced she had to go to Holland. Only for a week, she said. Whether family business, boyfriend difficulties, or something to do with our work was not exactly stated, although all three possibilities were floated for the rest of us to pick up if we wished to. Sam Rammit, so it seemed, organised her tickets, by KLM flight outward, by the Harwich ferry back; much *sotto voce* argument between them as to exact dates and times. On the day of her return I was asked to take the van and pick her up at Liverpool Street. She arrived off the boat-train with several very heavy bags, astonishingly accompanied by Carmilla.

Their hair was uncharacteristically under restraint, they wore smart tailored suits, sheer stockings, high heels – hats, moreover! as though they'd just come out of church. I hardly recognised them. Had Carmilla been to Holland too? Or had she just met Sonja at Harwich? Neither of them bothered to say. They told me brusquely to drop Carmilla off in Clapham; but first she diverted me to a boarded-up Brixton shopfront where she knocked at a side door. A dirty young man in a string vest with a Zapata moustache came quickly out and took delivery of most of the baggage without so much as a mumbled greeting. At length across town to Highbury; with Sonja in the back of the van peering nervously out of the rear windows. Did she think we were being followed? I asked but she wouldn't say. All she *did* tell me of the trip was that she had been so seasick she had blown her mind, only she had 'good shit to smoke on open deck where no one smelt. Most of it gone before Customs-search, thank God. Hey whaddaya know, I have a stash of it still in my fanny! Don't worry, I don't smoke in your virgin house.' But she did and she knew that I knew that she did. She was a wiry little creature with thin pale-yellow hair; when she was anxious she would huddle her arms to her chest and shiver all over like an ash tree. She was shivering a lot these days.

Oh God, why didn't I say anything?

9

Because, thinks Leonore, you were too scared of what the answer would be. You were demoralised by the likelihood that you'd have to break away. Your life in the theatre, suddenly reborn? You had found, with VEXACTION, that no longer were you *writing* plays: you were actually *making* them, acting in them, strutting your stuff, hilarious good fun, 'subfusc' was a jealous libel – or if it wasn't, you had to disprove it – above all (she supposes) the galvanic flash between drama and audience was for once under your own control. And now it began to look as though some of that audience was acutely controlling *you*. Well, you had a right to be frightened. You could not bear to go back to what you'd been doing before: but the alternative was to be urged like a bullock to the abattoir into narrower and narrower passageways, sliding on slimy floors, hearing unaccountable screams from out of the darkness ahead. Once you spoke, you were rejected. Fail to speak, you go on and on, until speech becomes impossible.

You had thought that at last you were joined with your own people. Now you discovered that *they* did not think you were one of them. You did not dare to demonstrate they might have been quite right.

And in any case, they were in your house. Neither their host nor their landlord, you were hooked, hung, and dried.

She thinks he was a bloody fool but she does not really know what else he could have done – given all the circumstances, given what *she* had done and said – no, she's as numbed and as baffled as he was.

(xiv)   Night Train to Liverpool

With only twenty-four hours' warning, the Liverpool gig was finally on.
Last-minute preparations were a panic of frantic cross-purposes.

And bang in the middle of them, a quarrel blown up out of nothing between Carmilla and Owston and Polly.

It began with the costumes. They were still in Carmilla's studio, nearly complete but not quite; and she needed to work on them right up to the hour of departure. So we could not try them on, or even see what they were, until our arrival when we unpacked. Also, the additional gear, lights, sound-boxes, musical instruments: they'd been obtained but we had only half of them at Malthus Terrace. The remainder were in Brixton, awaiting collection. Carmilla's own car was in a garage down the Wandsworth Road with some chronic defect that needed its usual repair; she declared she must have the van for all sorts of odd pick-ups; she must have it before it went to Brixton, or else (she said) no costumes at all.

It could have been adjusted, given a little patience and collected thought; but Polly chose to argue that the costumes were not top priority, Carmilla would have to wait. Carmilla's response was to turn upon Owston, accusing him of brainwashing Polly in accordance with his own vile agenda, a shit-pit out of which he had never been thoroughly dragged: 'Moscow-line jello-junk! it don't matter that *over there* there are guys who risk their lives every day against the pigs? against your fucking Nazi khaki? bottles and rocks against guns? – like, Christ what the hell goes on?'

Polly said, abruptly, 'If we have to be down the rabbit-hole, we could do without the Queen of Hearts ordering everybody's head off. Piss off, would you please, and shut up.'

I did not know what either of them meant. Polly was extraordinarily tense, and when Carmilla burst into tears and clutched her by the arm in an uprush of almost amorous penitence, she shook herself free, escaped into another room and slammed the door behind her. At which point we were aware of Sam Rammit, rigid and grim in the hall. Toe was with him. We hadn't seen him for nearly a week, and she'd been out of sight all morning. Now he'd arrived just in time to hear the row; he asserted himself directly.

A few short orders, no chance to dispute them. The van at all costs must be ready to run north overnight, with all the gear, repeat *all* of it, including the costumes. Owston and Toe taking turns at the wheel. Because of the gear in the van there wouldn't be room for everyone. Fid Carver to go by train, a bloody slow train, 'Apologies! leaving Euston at midnight; but you might be needed here between seven and half-past ten. Okay, Fid? Good.' Carmilla wouldn't be going at all; we'd have to deal with the costumes ourselves when we got there, 'to make your own bloody good sense of them and no belly-aching': he supposed we had the nous to cope with it? He himself would travel in his own car, with Sonja as co-driver, no passengers, his back seats must be kept vacant in case of a surplus of gear. We'd rendezvous at six in the morning in the concourse of Lime Street Station, perhaps have breakfast if the buffet was open. And then we'd find our way to wherever it was we were going, probably the Huyton joint, but there were still a few phone calls to make. 'Okay: let's get on with it!' Or did Owston want a last rehearsal?

Owston did; it filled up the afternoon. The revised play was very ragged, and the work was exhausting. When we finished I went to bed for an hour or two before going for my train. I didn't know what the others were doing, or where the van was, or whether Carmilla was still sobbing and cursing. I decided I would eat my evening meal at Euston and let everyone else make their own departures as best suited them. In fact I was *not* wanted; I got up at about ten and walked to the tube with my holdall.

The Liverpool train was at the platform some time before it was due to leave. There were not many passengers; no second-class compartment-coaches, only the long ones with tables; I did find a table to myself. I stood and waited for the guard's whistle and watched all the railway business, my head out of the open top of the window. It was a mail-and-newspaper train that stopped all along the line, but I could see a few sleeping-cars further up. If there'd been more spare cash in my pocket I'd have asked if there was a vacant berth. My nap in Malthus Terrace had not been sufficient – disturbed by shoutings all over the house and runnings up-and-down stairs – I didn't relish six hours on a damn silly seat too short to lie down on. Besides, a large party of scouse-mouthing drinkers had come in at the other end of the carriage; they looked as though they were going to be rowdy.

There was the guard, flag poised, whistle up to his lips. And there – rushing past him with a porter, a pile of tottering bags on his trolley – was Blackadder, wild-haired, flustered, furious, quite contrary to plan, very nearly too late into the bargain!

I called out to her; she saw me; and made straight for the door of my carriage. I ran to haul her bags in, we just got the last of them when the whistle went, the porter slammed the door, the train moved off.

'Don't ask me what I'm doing,' she gasped, 'I haven't the breath to tell you. Look . . . look, Fid . . . look: I have a sleeping ticket. Couldn't get to the right car or the train would have gone. Just help me along the corridor; we can sit down; I can tell you.'

It was a single-berth cabin; she must have spent a fistful. I had not realised she was such an epicure. We got all the dunnage inside, she actually *tipped* the attendant, she bolted the door and we sat.

'There was no room in the van,' she said. 'They sent me with these at the last shitty minute. Why was there no room in the van? Ah, Mr Carver, you'd be prudent not to enquire. But I doubt I'll have to tell you. Something's been happening, you see that? Aye, he sees it. Aye, but does he go on to see that someone's bloody *bauchled* it? Fauch!' When she was truly disgusted, her vocabulary became most obscure. Non-Scots had to guess her meaning. Incompetence, I deduced. Owston's, I thought, from her tone of personal outrage. She'd been much the same throughout the afternoon's rehearsal, and poor Owston had borne the brunt. His love for her was dog-like, whether she kicked him or petted. There'd been precious little petting these last few weeks. I did not like the man much, but at times I was sad for him, his grouchy aggression carried its own heavy price. Yet who would have thought he could have forced himself so successfully into VEXACTION's impromptu techniques? And led them, indeed? Surely Polly had been his instigator – no, more than that, his inspiration. She had brought something out of him, bright and alive, which his snailshell of working-class self-consciousness had closed off from the world for years: she might have given him more credit when things got difficult.

My judgement was specious: I had not known just how difficult. Now, I was to be told.

She indicated the pile of luggage with a vehement flick of the back of her hand. 'Dear goodness, what's to be done? Fid, this is *not* what VEXACTION's supposed to be about! If all this clamjamphrie is not in the van, what is? Sam Rammit inveigled him, I warned him how it would be, he didn't even want to tell me – Fid, he kept it secret from *me*.' She clapped-to her mouth like a letterbox, near choking with screwed-up dismay.

I promoted her by asking, 'Who kept? What? Fred? What did he keep?'

'Aye, Fred, who else? Frederick, self-sufficient Mr Owston, sixteen-stone phallic symbol from the colliers'-rows of Mexborough! But of course I found out. Not from him, even though he loves me, not from him, not even in bed. You'll have observed, Costello loves me? She never says. But she does, always has; and she shows it by spilling the beans. She didn't *need* to be in bed. Mind you, we never were. I've just sufficient of the lesbian in me to return the friendliness without the flesh, they call it prick-teasing when it's with men. I daresay I'm that too. Used to be, at all events; you'd have thought I'd have learned my lesson.'

This was all very disjointed. Better not to interrupt. She was coming to the heart of it.

'Mind you, Costello's quite daft enough to tell everyone, pickle or mickle, hither or yon, love 'em or not. Dear goodness, she'd even tell the fuzz. How could anyone believe her secure? Yet it was she they let fix it up from Boston, her friends shipped it over, she had Sonja take delivery in Rotterdam, and herself and Sam Rammit have shoved every lump of it into the van – *our* van, *VEXACTION's* van! – and in Liverpool it's all up to Toe! Would you trust that girl Toe with fippence-ha'penny to buy sweeties? Never on this earth. Never. But they have!'

I was listening in stone-cold dread. Knew where she was going before she got there. Knew suddenly far more about Toe than was ever exposed by her hee-haw jackass guffaws, by her fat buttocks' bump-n-grind among broken glass and hooting students. That unwholesome squashy face under a dingy orange afro-mop (like a goose-egg in a fistful of coir) had been livid with controlled purpose, and she didn't give a damn for any of us. Only for Ballymurphy and its rage against the Brits. Because she'd lived as a Brit, hadn't she? in Luton? she'd read all our newspapers, she'd undergone at first-hand our cold bloodymindedness, our halfwit insistence that no one was right but ourselves.

Carmilla? Carmilla was the American Dream, a hard-nosed entrepreneur with a patriotic conscience – or a with-it set of vibes, which these days was much the same thing. T-shirts, mini-skirts, guns, all grist to the mill; except guns as an item of export would be closer to family tradition. There'd be a hard-nosed Boston daddy, émigré relic of the Black-and-Tan war very likely, and a goon-squad of Boston brothers. Little sister would have angered them two years back, by her hippy contempt for Mayor Daley of Chicago: now she had a chance to make amends.

Sonja? International paranoia. (Probably justified.) Too many drugs to think straight. (At least beyond the immediate moment.) Craving for excitement. (And now she's in her own Hitchcock script.) Skinny little Sonja was a mess she couldn't get out of.

So was I.

'I suppose it *is* guns?' I croaked. 'Fetch 'em to Liverpool to get 'em into some sort of cargo, for some sort of boat for Belfast?'

Polly nodded. 'Oh, they need them in Belfast,' she said. '*You'd* need them if you lived there. *I* would. Don't we say so, in our own play? VVV's doing useful work. But VVV is *not* VEXACTION. VEXACTION's doing useful work. To mix them and muddle them, like this, to compromise everything, it's – oh God, it's just – just so fucking thoughtless *stupid*, I can't believe it ever began! – VEXACTION will be ruined, VVV will be ruined, because neither bloody party understands their own part. *Bauchled!*'

'Sam Rammit, cutting corners?'

'Sam? Fauch. The Ganges genius. So sharp you could shave with him. Sees an insecure new theatre group struggling like tadpoles to turn into vigorous wee frogs, and all he can think of is – 'they've got guts and commitment, they've got touring gigs, they've got a van! let's hijack them for secret couriers, who'd ever suspect?' *I* suspected, me. And Mr Owston told me lies.' For a second time she clapped-to her mouth.

Then she opened it, unwillingly, but determined to be accurate: 'No. Not quite lies. It's just he didn't tell me the truth. *Suppressio veri, suggestio falsi*; I was gey gleg at the Latin, Fid, when I was a caller young lassie, you'd never credit, never.'

It was heartbreaking to hear her talk like a withered old woman, it was no more than half a joke, she meant it and she looked it, sick, haggard, grey-faced.

Again she remembered to be accurate. 'Dear Fid, I'm not the only one, am I? I should have thought of it before I spoke. Like me and Owston: yourself and Sam? Oh Fid, I'm so sorry. But I doubt he said never a word to you, under your wee quilty, away upstairs, with your stang betwixt his hurdies? Did he? Did you *ask*? Well, it's all done, we're the fall-guys tonight, so we are, and we just have to hope for the best. Fingers crossed.'

She sat crouched over on the edge of her bunk, smearing her eyes with a whole handful of black hair, getting the ends of her hair into her mouth, snorting catarrh at the back of her nostrils. I put out a tentative arm to embrace her, a degree of unhappy comfort, but she didn't need it, not now. She sat up straight and practical, shook the hair away from her face, gripped me briefly by the wrist. 'See her, Fid, this won't do. We're not safe here, the two of us. I've only the ticket for one berth, questions might get asked. You go back to your carriage – no, not the one you were in, nearer than that, the next one to the sleepers, there's plenty of spare seats, Should anything happen before we're in Liverpool, you'll be in touch, at hand. Keep your eyes open, lugs too. Go.'

It was as well that I went. The attendant in the corridor was just about to tap on the door.

(xv)   Suspended Animation

What could I do, but wait till we got to Liverpool? Once arrived at
Liverpool, I could take myself in hand, and consider, in Liverpool, what to
do. Until then . . .

Until then, I huddled into my corner, immediately next the entry to
the sleepers, suspended animation, trying to read, trying to keep my
mind quiet. The latest *Plays and Players*; I'd bought it at the Euston
bookstall. I was not really capable of taking in the words. But I tried.

I even tried to read an interview with Pogmoor. He outlined the
manifesto of his new company (and yours, Lenny; yes, there was a
picture of you, narrow-eyed and dishonest like a fortune-teller at a
fair). A socialist co-operative, he alleged, fully professional, fully
committed, Arts Council grant guaranteed, and a new collaborative
script (a version of *Woyzeck*, how gratifying!) already optioned from
three of our new breed of young playwright – Messrs Abel-Nottidge
(Christopher), McCoy (Alex), and Saltmarsh (Bill). Not one of them
older than twenty-five; all of them so excited to be working with
exciting Jack Juggler; all dropping hints, without precise definition,
in the direction of Physical Theatre, 'we seek to empower *all*-usion'
(quote from Pogmoor) 'rather than *ill*-usion or *de*-lusion'; all of
them proclaiming loud distaste for Tory rule and for the Theatre of
the Establishment – and yet (quote from Pogmoor) 'only by our use
of the Language of the Enemy can we infiltrate and at length take
over' the Theatre of the Establishment, corrupted as it was, but not
quite irredeemable . . .

All of them – beyond argument! with their eyes on the main
chance. Saltmarsh, McCoy, Abel-Nottidge: Shadrach, Meshach and
Abednego. No fiery furnace was going to burn *them*. Between the
lot of you, you'd already decided the name for the company, right?
'There are **M**ore **O**f **U**s than **TH**em!' (quote from Pogmoor) – so
you thought you'd call it MOUTH. No: MOUTH-71, to give it a
sense of futurity. Or maybe a sense that it wasn't meant to last
beyond the end of next year (this year, remember, was still 1970).
But nice. I was in no position, not any longer, to assert that
VEXACTION was nicer; nevertheless I—

10

Leonore is not impressed by her brother's retroactive scorn. Between
then and now he was happy enough to adjust himself to MOUTH-71.
Let him cease recrimination and get on to *what happened*! She skips
pages, finds his next chapter-heading, urgent to know what she never
knew. Ah! here we are: Rugby.

(xvi)   Broken Journey

*This was a train that stopped at Rugby for something like thirty minutes,
while trailers of parcels clanged up and down the platform, porters yelled
incomprehensibly, and the station lights flickered in storm-wind and snow.*

In London it had been drab dirty rain, cold enough indeed, but we
were into December, we were heading north, what else could be
expected?

I did not expect Fred Owston. And it seemed he'd forgotten about
me. He came humping himself through the coach from the bottom
end, a few minutes after we pulled out of Rugby. Huge and
unwieldy, sprinkled with snowflakes, in his leather coat and (of all
things) his motorcycle crash-helmet, peering left and right as he
swayed up the gangway, checking on everyone there.

When he realised it was me, he jerked to a halt and showed his
teeth, all the melodrama of Grabitall confronted by a militant
worker: 'God's Christ,' he spat, 'Carver! What the hell are *you* doing
– oh! – right – of course. Blackadder: where is she? She's got to be
here, *Blackadder!* Don't tell me you've not seen her!'

I explained where she was.

'In a sleeper, a fucking *sleeper*! I've got to talk to her, God's
Christ—!' He surged forward to the door; and of course found it
locked. 'Oh, of course it's fucking locked, keep the proles out at all
costs, never let the sweet dreams of the ruling class be disturbed.
But what the hell will we do? The silly bitch is stuck there till
Liverpool! God's Christ.'

He was swearing even more than usual, in a dreadful state of
consternation, jerking all over; he slammed his gloved hand against
the door, gave up in despair, flung himself into the seat beside me.
Whatever I might say to him would be a mistake; I kept silent. So
did he, for three edgy minutes; then he ground his teeth and
growled, 'Totally fucked-up, finished, capped! – God, it's all blown
wide open, she mustn't go to Liverpool, we can't let her go!' He
ended on a strangulated shout, simultaneously springing to his feet.
I do believe he was about to bang and bang again on the sleeping-
car door for the attendant and so demand entry to Polly's cabin, and
damn whatever risk there was in making himself so conspicuous.

But the door opened of itself, and Polly came out of it. Her face
had been grey, now it was chalk-white. A blue holdall was slung
over her shoulder. She saw Owston first and then me, did not greet
either of us, but slid in behind the table, furtive as a ferret. 'Oh, well
might *you* be here,' she hissed at Owston. 'You do know what was
in those bags I brought onto the train?'

'Nay, there was nowt in 'em, masks, costumes, microphones, a
spotlight, a pair o'snare-drums – that's not the fucking issue! Polly,

it's all gone rotten. The van never left London. Toe had a call from t'Pool just as we were due to set off, that highly prudent little bugger they call the Priest. Christ, did I say rotten? Why, Liverpool's fallen apart! Mickey Mac was arrested at teatime, with a bloody great pistol in his pocket, right bang in the middle of Dale Street. Paddy O's house has been raided, they've lifted his wife and his brother, no one knows where *Paddy* is, let's hope they never will. Aye, they did, they sprang a trap, and you know what Toe told me? – they thought we'd all be in it, us, the van, everything. It's just plain bloody lucky we'd such a foul-up about dates. The last date the fuzz was given was yesterday morning, they were twenty-four hours too soon! But that's not the worst—'

'Of course it's not the worst.' She bit her teeth onto each word as though her mouth were full of grit: '*I'll* tell you the worst, Owston, I've just this minute found it out, it's—'

I don't think he heard her. His own news was too catastrophic. 'Number one: all this stuff, explosives as well as the shooters, it was never meant for Belfast at all. Toe let the truth out this evening, in a panic, when she'd heard from the Priest. Booby-trap bombs and fucking mayhem, all over the north of England. Never mind the fucking military! it's working-class shopping centres, cinemas, public transport. Totally in contradiction with all the ideology, the analysis, perspective, they swore to us we all shared! Totally against all assurances. God's Christ, we've been took for a ride. Took.'

He kept repeating 'took', stuck in the groove, 'took, took'.

I couldn't bear it. I clutched him by the end of his muffler: 'Owston, for God's sake, will you tell us number two!'

He started to laugh. It was horrible. 'When you think about it, why shouldn't they? Face it: *we* call ourselves comrades, *they* call us Brits. "Useful idiots." It's a recognised tactic, I knew it, I've used it, and I didn't fucking see it right under me own nose.'

'Owston! Number *two*!'

I was pulling him by the neck, his helmeted head rolled backwards and forwards. He went on laughing. 'Oh aye, number two. I wor saving number two for t'last. Number two's both short and sweet. Sam Rammit is card-carrying filth – Special Branch? RUC? MI5? CIA? – who cares which? – I'll spell it you in five words, *Ahdge-ent-pro-vocker-tewer* and that's him – that's your Rammit, that's your ardent spirit of the Third World Revolution. He's been roasting us on a fucking spit ever since he got to bed with Carver. So what about it, Carver? What? Do we tear your throat out of you now, or wait while we've chucked you off o't'train?'

He may not have meant it; not meant it for more than a moment. Polly told him to hold his noise. He remembered himself and shut up. I remembered myself; I let go of the muffler. Polly's turn to talk: 'You can keep it till presently, how you know all that, and why's it so, forby how you came here. But if Rammit's what you say he is, do we suppose he's worth his pay? If he was, they'd have us all in the net, and they haven't. Consider it, we've still got a chance, but—'

'A chance to do what?' I asked. Was she going to suggest we could still shift the guns to Belfast?

'A chance, you gawping gomeril, to be rid of what I've found in my sleeping-berth. "Nowt," he says, "not the issue, not the fucking issue?" Well—'

Well. After I'd left her, she'd had *qualms*, that was her word. Having learned she could trust nobody, not even her lover, she was not going to trust the baggage. She opened it up and searched. All clear: until she unzipped the blue holdall. Now she had it on the seat beside her, between herself and the window, covered by her left elbow. 'I would value an opinion,' her voice was shaking but calm, 'if we can do it without being seen – I think we can, there's no one near us – upon the nature of certain parcels herein. Fid, get out of the way. Owston, change places with him. Keep it *quiet*, damn you.

'You've been in the army, Owston, staff-serjeant of Intelligence, were you not? So what the devil d'you think *this* is?'

She opened the bag where it lay, still shielding it with her upper arm. He leaned across the table, looked inside, put a hand inside, sat paralysed. 'Plastic explosive,' he muttered, aghast. 'I didn't even know we had it in the van till half-past ten tonight. No way, no fucking way, should it be here.'

'No way, but here it is. And I've been set up with it; and you, my big bonny beard, you've set *yourself* up with it, fauch!'

'Will you close that fucking zip!'

'It's closed. Owston, from now on I don't want a word out of you except when I ask for one. Your Intelligence Corps experience has had every chance to make plans, we've seen the result, so no more of it. And no more of your fucking swearing, it gets on my nerves. I'm the fall-guy, the patsy all these weeks, the one that you and Rammit chose to defecate upon at your leisure; something's to be done about it; I decide what; you'll do it. And this goes for you, Fid Carver, you're part of it now whether you want it or not. Just listen, the pair of you.'

Her father was a doctor, I'd heard. She'd inherited his authoritative style; and I daresay his sangfroid and capability. First to elicit the symptoms, then diagnosis, then prescription.

Symptoms and diagnosis. (I'll run them together because they were all mixed up between what Polly knew already and what she could assemble from the incoherence of Owston.) Just after I'd left for Euston, the collective, *en bloc*, took two minicabs and Owston's motorbike to Brixton, to the shopfront where Carmilla had left the bags that day. (Those bags had been innocent enough – a blind, in fact – theatrical paraphernalia from Sonja's old Amsterdam company which had closed down and was getting rid of its effects.) The real guts of the 'gear' came from Holland by cargo-boat, wooden boxes full of pistols, Armalite rifles, ammunition. They were in a lockup garage in a mews near the shop; so were those VEXACTION items which had to go to Liverpool; the van was there, half-loaded; there too was Sam Rammit's car. The boxes were so obviously not part of VEXACTION's drama-requirements that Cliff began to kick up a row. Che and HP joined in, and Polly supported them. They had to be told, she insisted, they could *not* be allowed to involve themselves without full knowledge and free choice.

Whereat they were confronted with a *fait accompli*. Owston put them on their mettle as revolutionary activists: there were times when the propaganda arm must merge with the executive in the interests of the working class, or were they going to chicken out and throw all militant principles to the wind? The defence of the Belfast ghettoes was paramount. Not only a duty but a *privilege* to assist it. He opened some of the boxes to prove his point. He had not expected plastic explosive as well as firearms (indeed he was quite shocked to see it), but if plastic had been called for, plastic would be delivered. For who were VVV, that they should be so arrogant as to restrict the legitimate arsenal of the beleaguered Irish People?

HP at this point decided she'd had enough. She was only a kid, after all, and black. She was terrified of explosives, terrified of rape and murder if she fell into the hands of the pigs; she'd no trust that white 'comrades' could keep her safe. She had a boyfriend in Camberwell, a songwriter from Jamaica, who had been pressing her for some time to take her talent and her beauty out of VEXACTION and into Black Culture where she belonged. She seized her moment, slipped away from the garage, went off to find him.

Toe and Sam Rammit were wrangling and roaring over the date. Rammit had not realised until the previous day that Liverpool had demanded a postponement. He told Toe she'd betrayed him: he'd been notifying all sorts of useful people in Lancashire and Yorkshire that if they wanted to see VEXACTION, Tuesday was the night, and suddenly it turned out to be Wednesday! She had put him 'up the very devil of a tree!' His word 'betrayed' was a dead giveaway – *isn't it always?* – if any of them had noticed it in the confusion. They remembered it afterwards, too late.

The loading of the van continued. Gear and people together (even without HP) were too heavy for its ramshackle chassis.

Rammit, in a rage, refused to take any more of this 'bad bad bad *bandobast*!' He expected them at Lime Street at six in the morning: if they weren't there, he was done with them for ever. He pulled Sonja into his car and scorched off up the Stockwell Road.

It was nearly half-past eleven: if one of the group were to hurtle to Euston, there was just time to catch the train. Polly volunteered, taking with her in a minicab every bag she could manage – every innocent bag, or so she thought. Owston was anxious to keep her out of trouble: *he* made the selection. (She decided on a sleeper out of sheer bloodymindedness, and paid with VEXACTION's floating fund.)

After she'd gone, it was discovered that the van would not start. Cliff had some ability as a mechanic. He fooled around with the engine for the best part of an hour before getting any result. No sooner was it working than Zapata-moustache came in from the shop to call Toe to the telephone. It was the Priest, demanding she ring him back directly, from a phone-box in the street, reversed-charge to a 'secure number' she'd committed to memory some time ago. So she did: the Priest told her about the police action in Liverpool, he told her on no account to make the journey, he told her to use her own wits as to what she should do with the gear, he told her there'd been an informer and he was sure that it wasn't at *his* end. Let her look to it.

Upon hearing all this from her, they at once began to accuse each other. But Toe, from her close working with Rammit, put two and two together, it *must* be him, of course it must! No one else could have made the mistake of alerting the cops a day too soon; no one else knew as much as he did about all aspects of the operation; indeed the operation was largely his idea. As also were the logistical details of the campaign in England for which the weaponry had always been destined. She admitted she'd known the said details from the very beginning; she realised at once she should not have admitted it; but she *had* admitted, and that was it. She defied her gobsmacked colleagues. She swore at them, she told them they could do what they had to do, she didn't give a fart from Paisley's arse for their scruples.

Owston was quite sure what *he* had to do. To warn Polly! Had he time? The midnight train stopped at Watford, Berkhamsted, Bletchley, Northampton; so it would not leave Rugby until half-past two, he could be there on his bike if he rode like hot shit. The snowstorm all but baulked him, but he made it. Here he was.

No, he'd no notion what the others had finally decided, or what was going to happen to the van. Che had suggested they might all meet at 'the Gate number two'; Owston was sure Rammit didn't know about it; if Rammit didn't know, he couldn't have told the filth. 'The Gate number one' was VVV's Notting Hill Gate hangout, no good, finished, wide open. But 'number two' was nearly a mile

away, private information, personal, a hippy joint up the far end of
the Portobello where Che used to go for his cheap hash and easy
pussy, the heads there were cool, maybe there'd be no hassle.
Maybe.

In the meantime, what of the blue holdall?

Polly asked, 'Will it blow up?'

Owston said, 'No way. No detonators. Unless it's unstable with
age. *I'm* not going to unwrap it to find out, no way.'

It was now time for Polly to *prescribe*.

First, we must separate. Owston (she decided) must get off at
Crewe, the next stop of any importance, catch a train back to
Rugby, climb onto his motorbike, and – carefully, carefully – fetch
himself to London to 'the Gate number two'. She would continue
her journey as far as—

'Hey, no! No way, Polly, *no!* God's Christ, Polly, I love you! Not to
the fucking 'Pool – Rammit and the filth'll be waiting there – I can't
let you go to—'

'You certainly can. I'll be noticed at once if I abandon that sleeper
before the end of my ticket. The wee man there has a beady eye;
the more I tip him the worse he wonders. Or *almost* before the end
of my ticket. Suppose I tell him I never realised this train stops at
Runcorn, and Runcorn's where I really need to be?'

At half-past five on a winter's morning? Where would she go
from there? It wasn't an impersonal great junction like Crewe. If
the station staff saw her leave a train from London and at once
make arrangements to take the next train *to* London, they'd think
she was mad, they'd be bound to remember.

'Those bags are the problem, I'd as soon carry a ball-and-chain
. . . I'll bring 'em by cab to Runcorn bus station and take the first
coach to London. If there's no immediate coach, it won't be safe to
hang about. So I'll quietly leave the bags in the shelter (there'll
surely be a shelter, perhaps even a waiting-room), walk across
town, catch a local bus to – tickety-tick, where? Chester, Warring-
ton, Stockport? Dear goodness, I'll do a tour and come to London
via somewhere else, let the bags be lost property, they can't hang
me for forgetting my bags. I did do a tour once in that part of the
country, playing vicious Mrs Dudgeon in a disaster of a *Devil's
Disciple*. Isn't that what we are,' says she, suddenly as spry as a
magpie, 'three little devil's disciples wanted for conspiracy to murder? – we should tell it to Milhous Nixon.'

You see, once she'd made her rigmarole of a plan, all her *qualms*
were to be compressed under a bloody silly joke. Mine weren't, not
by any means. There was a terrible logic about the future of that
blue holdall.

Looking hard at me – and yet *not* looking at me, if you see what I mean? – she now made a dangerously dry statement: 'It's been carried and jolted and flung about as far as this and it hasn't blown up yet, so probably it won't. It's not at all kenspeckle, not at all heavy, it could be hidden almost any place. The question is where. What are the stops between Crewe and Runcorn?'

I refused to be thrust into it by unchallenged consensus. 'The question,' I said to her, 'is not where but *who*. Miss Blackadder,' I said to her, as firmly as I could, '"full knowledge and free choice"? – I have the one already, be so good as to afford me the other. I have never had part in the secrets of VVV, I was never within your doors at Brixton, if Sam Rammit wants to frame me he'll have a job to make it stick. Which is very good reason for me to tell you and your fun-and-games to *shove it*, here and now. Don't speak, please, I've not finished! It's also good reason for me to lift up your poxy holdall and lift myself with it right out of your sight—'

As I was talking I stretched my arm across the leather lump of Owston, across the narrow table, and gently eased the holdall from under her elbow. I took my own, rather smaller, holdall down from the rack. (It had nothing in it beyond spare underwear and a book or two, all unmarked; a few toilet necessaries; a VEXACTION script which I transferred to my pocket.) I squeezed it and zipped it into the top of the other one, crazily wondering how plastic-without-a-detonator responded to being squeezed. But two holdalls on one man would look slightly odd; slightly odd was too odd for safety.

I kept talking all the time (I had to or I'd have fouled my trousers). '—I mean *right* out. Don't ask. Don't ever come back to Highbury. Any of you. Whatever you've left in the house, identifiable as yours, goes out with the garbage, I'm sorry. I'll report that van as stolen, by persons unknown. So if Toe's still in charge of it, you can give her fair warning. That's it! have a nice trip – as they said to Marco Polo—'

With a jolly grin (a damned apoplectic rictus) for the benefit of other passengers if they chanced to be awake, I slung the holdall to my shoulder, my duffelcoat over my arm, and reeled off down the train. I didn't stop till I got to the very last carriage, where I shut myself in the WC and gave way to acute diarrhoea.

I suppose I could have at least thanked them for all the good things about VEXACTION. I suppose I could have kissed Polly goodbye – after all, she'd kissed me hello, my first evening in Number 8. But no; I felt far too savage. But perhaps they'd understand. My relieving them of the holdall was in its own frightful way an expression of gratitude, even a kiss.

As the train rumbled slowly northward, and the snow thickened on the carriage-windows, I turned over in my mind all I could remember about Rammit. He wanted, very earnestly, to go home to his own subcontinent and the money that was there for him. This could, in the long run, be managed; most easily if the British Foreign Office were to arrange things on his behalf with the Indian and Pakistani governments. For a clear guarantee from the latter that all their charges against him would be dropped, he was ready (I guessed) to do anything he was asked to do by anyone in Whitehall. The spontaneous creation of a way-out revolutionary group, and the use of it to uncover an entire IRA unit, would be no more to him than a rather stiff quid pro quo. (And most convenient, once he was home, for his private CV and his relations there with the political police.) No more? Not quite 'no more'. He had no need to seduce me to get himself into Malthus Terrace. He had no need, having got there, to keep me out of all his dirty deeds. Was it possible he was truly fond of me? I wanted to think so; and yet, at the same time, it was a very ghastly thought. Sam Rammit, Sulaiman Rahmat Ali: a very ghastly young man. And beautiful. I would be re-picturing his beauty, between waking and sleep, every night for every year afterwards.

If Crewe, as Polly said, was the 'first stop of any importance', Rugeley was a halting-place of no importance at all, except for its own inhabitants. And ex-inhabitants. I knew that the train would pull in there, to drop newspapers and mailbags; it might just as well drop me.

(xvii)   Bandits' Cave

How well do you remember Rugeley, Lenny?

We were both so very small when we left it. And no doubt between then and now it would have been enlarged and rebuilt and generally mucked about with, like everywhere else that grown-up people hold fixed and beloved in their minds since childhood. I'll tell you what *I* remembered. On the roadside to the north, about two miles from the edge of the town, a sudden twist of thick hedgerow at the corner of a lane, with a plantation of fir trees behind it. You'll remember it too, you must do: we used to hide in and around the plantation for Bandits and Ambushes, we used to picnic there on hot afternoons with Mamma.

Lenny, you *must* remember! that piece of trash in his red MG swung round that very bend the night that Mamma walked home with the shopping. He swore in court it was a blind corner. I knew, even then, it wasn't. We could always see the traffic coming, so long as it didn't come at us on the wrong side of the road . . .

I was the only person to get out of the train at Rugeley. There seemed but one man on duty in the station; he was occupied with

the packages from the luggage-van; the exit barrier was open; I
walked quickly and softly out into the snow. I am almost sure no
one saw me. Certainly no one saw my Liverpool ticket. At that hour
the streets were perfectly empty. If a policeman was on the beat, he
must have been taking shelter somewhere, who could blame him?
The snow came from the east, I was headed sideways to it, north. I
could walk with comparative comfort, cap down over my eyes,
duffelcoat hood pulled up on top of the cap. Nonetheless, a mile and
a half beyond the last streetlamp, in pitch-dark relieved only by the
glint of the snow, seemed one hell of a distance. I was worried in
case they'd built houses all out along the road. They had, up to a
point, but open country did begin just about where I needed it. And
the hedge and the plantation were exactly as they used to be. So
was the little gate at the end of the hedge. And so were the three
hundred yards of bracken, bramble and gorse on the slope between
the plantation and the stream. Even in December it was the densest
imaginable tangle; and of course I had no torch to find my way.

Lenny, I *remembered*. I didn't need to see, or not with my ordinary
eyes. I met myself, there on that road in the dark, met myself at the
age of six, and myself at the age of six gave me back the eyes of my
childhood – just as they had been – just as bright as I remembered
them when I myself was only six . . . The Alternative Schizo-
Phantasist has urged me ad nauseam to 'rediscover the hidden
child', thereby (he pretentiously claims) to 'let go of my pain, fear
and anger'. But the programme had already been reversed; the
hidden child rediscovered *me*; it was lurking there near Rugeley
where it always lived, waiting to hurt me, enrage me, terrify me
and finally persuade me to triumph over what it had done. Was this
quite what the Schizo-Phantasist had in mind? To 'let go'? For
Christ's sake, the bloody child held on and held on and would *not*
be shaken off! Nor was it alone. You were there too – although you
didn't know you were there, you thought (that night) you were in
Manchester in bed with Pogmoor – or with Shadrach or with
Meshach or with Abednego – or with their wives or their mistresses
– but you weren't! You were staggering forward, leading your
brother by the hand (he was six years old and thirty-eight, all at the
one same time), through deep snow and rabbit-holes and scalding
tearing thorns, two miles outside of Rugeley, half a mile from our
old home; I let my feet put themselves where they told me they had
been long before, following *your* feet until you led me – how could
you fail? – to our own old 'secret cave'; more of a burrow than a
cave, but it was still there, still heavily covered by untouched
masses of undergrowth, and nearly full of drifting snow. And that's
where I buried the holdall.

I left my own holdall inside it, having some very vague (and surely useless) idea about forensic analysis and traces of explosive. I grovelled below the snow in freezing hard soil until at last, with bleeding hands, I'd made a scratch of a hole, just deep enough. A dog might dig it up? Or worse, a pair of children, at the same games as ourselves. *Unstable with age . . .*

Do you remember the 'bandits' dinner-table'? That slab of stone too heavy for you and me to lift together, lying amidst the bracken just below the cave? I felt my way to it and dragged it loose. Brambles were grown so closely around it that I realised no child could have played on it for a very long time. I pulled it into the cave and pressed it down over the buried holdall. It covered it completely; and then the snow would cover the stone, just as it was covering my footprints; and then the brambles would grow in the spring; and maybe – very possibly – just a chance – I'd done my best – maybe the secret would be kept.

Between the fir trees, with dead bracken stuffed against the cold into my clothes and shoes, I fell asleep like a derelict tramp. I doubtless nearly died like a derelict tramp. In my icy wet misery I had a very queer dream. I dreamed I had set the stone in place as a memorial to Mamma. I cut her name on it with what seemed to be the iron beak of a mediaeval actor's devil-mask, and then coloured in the hollow letters with blood that came out of my penis.

By daylight there was a thaw; by the time I was able to lurch out onto the deserted road and limp towards Rugeley, it was raining so hard that the damage to my appearance would scarcely be noticed. At the railway booking-office I pretended to be a hideous itinerant Scotsman with a hangover – I can do the accent pretty well – a piece of mischief, in point of fact, a private homage to Polly Blackadder; but it would serve to confuse police enquiries. I had the feeling that police enquiries would be waiting for me at Malthus Terrace. I also had the feeling I was going to be very ill.

(xviii)   Hogmanay

Wrong on both counts. I was ill, but not very ill. And the police made no move toward me at all.

I rang them up, in point of fact, to tell them the van had been stolen; they received the news serenely, a matter of tedious routine. I was uneasily puzzled by their inaction; the more so when it occurred to me that as the whole affair was an undercover carry-on, undercover cops would hardly be behaving like CID from the local nick. They might not approach me for ages, but that did not mean I was not under surveillance. And of course they might pounce at any time. I would have to decide, should I be very cautious, or very bold? When I felt better, I would make up my mind.

After two days spent largely in bed, with constant whiskies and Lemsips, I did feel a little better; and I tried to adjust myself to Number 8 with nobody in it except myself, and to adjust myself *to* myself going through the old motions of a professional playwright at his daily work. Then you sent me your definitive wedding-invitation – that beastly beefeater postcard had been no more than a loosely phrased hurrah. So a day or two of razors, weed-killer, speculations about gas-taps, the very sump of the sink of misery, and then – well, it was Christmas, wasn't it? I looked up some of our friends; I actually went to a few parties. I thought I ought to be seen, in a low-profile sort of way. I telephoned you in Manchester, talking pleasantly about the wedding plans, your MOUTH-71 plans and so forth, as though nothing out-of-the-way had been hap-pening. Do you remember any oddity about those conversations? I think not. I did my best to be casual.

On New Year's Eve I was at home, watching the TV. The phone rang at about eleven o'clock, a woman's voice with an Edinburgh accent. 'Mr Carver? I imagine you require a wee dram to signify the feast of Hogmanay? I know you take such matters seriously. Seriously, you need to come. The pub immediately fornent the Highbury–Islington tube. Ten minutes, I'll expect you.' She rang off.

Damn her! how *could* she? Had she no sense at all? Yet I did not dare not to go. 'Seriously'? What had happened?

As soon as I entered the crowded lounge I saw Polly at the far end, keeping a seat for me, with two whiskies on the table in front of her. She began talking even before I sat down, as though we were in the middle of a chat that had already gone on for some time. 'This is no way to break bad news, Fid. I'm not sure it *is* bad news. It certainly isn't for me, but you'll have a different perspec-tive. Don't look surprised, an agreeable seasonal drink, nothing tense about it whatever: but Sam Rammit, d'you see? is dead.

'Sonja too. I'd say he *ought* to be dead. But not her. Stupid meddling girl, but not to be dead.

'It seems they were in his Mini car, somewhere outside of Birmingham, they skidded at speed off the road, down an embank-ment, into an electricity-pylon, no chance for them, none. Faulty brakes, the police said. Did you ever know him tolerate the slightest gremlin in that car of his? Dammit, once a week he had it in for bloody overhaul. Accident my granny. It was fixed!

'Don't say anything if you don't want to. Sit quiet for a minute. Oh Fid, I'm so sorry.'

She put her hand over mine, forcing it to stop trembling. She was very kind and gentle. Fixed? Could I believe her? Like all extremists, whether left-wing or right, she supped up conspiracy-theory as though it were her mother's milk. And maybe with good reason. If Rammit were a double-agent, he had two sets of people to betray: therefore two sets of people who would seek to betray *him*. To the Irish Republicans he was that worst of all miscreants, the hired Informer. To his occult masters in government service, he was a bungler, a 'bauchler', an Unhelpful Element, and a man who knew too much. If either party decided that he ought to be dead, he would be. And he was.

But what about us? Secret murder is a desperate thought. I had never so much as contemplated it as a plausible reality, despite all the films I had seen, all the scripts I had written. Polly suggested – if it *was* the IRA – surely we were clear of it – the van and its load had been got to them in the end – she would not say how, but certainly not via Liverpool – I gathered Toe had 'dealt with the matter'. If, on the other hand, it was government – much more likely, for why had the lying story been put out about the brakes? – then she thought it would go no further – their purpose had been served – VEXACTION was disbanded, VVV vanished into thin air – for our own sakes, if nothing else, we *had* to keep our mouths shut. The end of Rammit, indeed, might well mark the closing of the file. Which did not seem very probable to me. But it was all so uncouthly mysterious, perhaps she was right.

I had thought she and I would not be talking ever again. Now that we were, there were questions I would like to ask her. First, though, I should tell her something. 'The holdall's okay,' I said.

A mistake. 'What holdall was that? Yes, I will have another drink, Scotch again. Thank you.'

If she didn't want to know about the holdall, she wasn't going to enlarge upon the rest of it: Owston, VEXACTION, Toe and the van, or the gear in the van. I was to be left in mid-air, as it were, just as I had left her when I walked away from her down the train. Such uncertainty gnawed at my heart; I would have to come to terms with it.

But her crafty evasion was a backwards kind of compliment; it was clear that she trusted me. She was a woman of fine character, I had always believed so – noble character, I would even say. Nonetheless, there were areas of darkness: I mean, her *truth* was not quite everybody's *truth*. She was remarkably clever at skating over a sequence of apparently indisputable fact, constructing (as she went) her own quirky version of cause-and-effect. For example: when exactly did Carmilla tell her about the gun-running? How often had she let Owston make love to her once she knew he was deceiving her? And how and when did she let him know that she knew? I couldn't ask her, she wouldn't tell me if I did, she may or may not have known the answers herself. Perhaps she *needed* her own ambivalence. Actors often do. It's no less useful in politics, 'legitimate' or 'underground'.

So instead, we talked theatre, professional prospects, cosy scandal; absurd under the circumstances. When I mentioned MOUTH-71, she seemed to shy away. It was as though the name of Pogmoor were taboo; I don't know the reason. Myself, I would have liked to discuss him. To get him out of my system, I suppose.

I was no longer angry that she'd called me. I recognised she herself had taken a risk in doing so. I believed now she had done it from her goodness of heart – simply in order to keep me decently informed, to allow me the chance to accommodate my personal loss. There was more to it than that, of course; she and her friends would be anxious to find out how 'secure' I was, how strong were my nerves in the aftermath of all we'd experienced. I did not begrudge her such assurance; she must have understood I had the same worries in reverse. We were *all* going to be worried for God only knew how long.

Upon midnight, we kissed each other for the 'Happy New Year'. And then away, in our separate directions.

For the *what* New Year?

(xix)   Civic Duty

To be careful? To be bold? I decided: bold.

The security-spooks were no doubt confident I was successfully intimidated from any further concern about Ireland. They had made a bloody fool of me, I must by now have learned my lesson. So I had; but perhaps not quite the right lesson? Associated I may have been with the criminal coup they had sponsored; but I still possessed my Civil Rights; one of them was the right to demand Civil Rights for the Irish. I would show them I was not to be deterred from deploying it. Despite our brief VEXACTION play, I knew shamefully little in detail about that country; now I would concentrate upon finding out all I could, and making public what I found. Meetings, demonstrations, letters to the *Guardian* – full-length plays, I would go so far. I could not risk incriminating myself, I could not incriminate the ex-VEXACTION crowd; but otherwise I refused to be silent. Oh indeed, I'd let them know 'lessons'.

In August they brought in internment in the north of Ireland; rumours about torture began to seep through the screen of official mendacity.

I went, full of civic duty, to a public meeting at a community hall in Camden Town; where I listened in growing frustration to a totally inconclusive platform of protest – Irish Nationalist tub-thumpers, Labour Party careerists, indefatigable Trot manufacturers of workerist boiler-plate. There was a great potential for British support; this was not the way to mobilise it; *our* nasty army, *our* disgraceful government, would never be disrupted by the roaring and bleating that was going on that evening.

I decided I had nothing effective to contribute to such a precooked and self-serving package of futility. I moved to the rear of the hall, almost ready to leave, but hanging about for an extra minute in the faint hope things might improve. I was not the only one to do so. A hand across the cleft of my bum, a hoarse voice into the turn of my neck: 'D'youse ever have to hear such a rake o'hoors' melts? Sure they all think they're safe enough this side o'the water, safe enough and bold enough, yah. I've a mind, so I have, to flash my cunt in their faces.' It was Toe, and be damned to her for an incorrigible blowfly! musky and husky and gross as she always was, with mascara like a duck's footprints and a poultice of scarlet lipstick very nearly from ear to ear. 'It's enough to throw your dinner up, just! Let's split, I mean seriously, c'mon.'

'Seriously'? Oh God, not again. Polly was one thing; Toe altogether another. Toe was bad trouble. But I did not dare deny her. We went out by different doors, to meet again (as though by chance) a few hundred yards along the road, beside the canal at Camden Lock, where we looked at the sunset and sat down as though to admire it on a romantically placed lock-lever. Uncluttered open space: we could see all around us. She leered from left to right, forward and back, spying out (as she put it) for Special Branch in any alcove of neighbouring architecture. She decided they were all in the community hall, still taking their copious notes.

'Okay,' out of the corner of her mouth. 'We need to know, have you heard from the cops about the van?'

As it happened, I had. Months before, just after Easter, the Southampton police, of all people, had rung me up to tell me that the vehicle was found; down at the docks there, burnt out and written off after an unwitnessed accident. They were very abrupt, and gave me no details. They told me I would shortly be getting a visit in London from an officer of the Met, who would sort out the 'paperwork' with me on their behalf, whatever that meant. It frightened me very much; I even considered fleeing the country; but I reflected that if they were really onto me they would never have telephoned first. At all events, no such officer turned up – and indeed, to this day, I have seen neither hide nor hair of him . . .

'They mention the bomb?' she asked.

'Good God! *Bomb?*'

'Aye. Two fellers blown to pieces, and a woman on the dockside, stewardess from a cruise-liner, seemingly.'

'Why wasn't it in the papers?'

'It was, but 'twas all lies, *and* it was way back in February. Sure, they took their time about making that call. The tale in the press was a pair of drunken bowsies drove slapbang into a pile of drums of inflammable chemical in a cargo-yard at dead of night. The wee girl had nothing to do with it, she was waiting for her boyfriend, for a short scratch of a knee-tremble in the dark. No one had told her it carried the death penalty.'

I did remember having read something of the sort; but I'd never made the connection.

She went on to give me what she claimed to be the inside story – on unimpeachable authority (she claimed), so unimpeachable she was not free to identify it. The dead men were security-spooks. They had filled the van with explosives timed to go off on another wharf an hour later, to devastate port installations and any ships berthed alongside; thereby to incriminate the Official IRA, at that time the branch of the Republican Movement most respected by the British Left. There was (she claimed) far too much respect for the Movement in Britain to suit the books of certain people close to government; they were planning to float a whole great raft of repressive legislation, clamping down on civil liberties, shutting off free speech – in effect, as hindsight tells me, to anticipate the Prevention of Terrorism Act of 1974. Public opinion had to be prepared, bewildered, softened up: what better way than by the panic of an IRA 'mainland' campaign? There was no such campaign – nor indeed would there be, until the Official IRA bomb at Aldershot in February '72 and then not again until the Provo London bombs in '73 – so they had to invent their own.

But someone had second thoughts, at a Very Top Level. For a start, the premature explosion diminished the propaganda value (no grave material damage had been caused, and the stewardess was a Malaysian or something, with no relatives in the UK). Then the press might discover the secret-service links of the two men. Then again, any attempt to connect the van with 'known IRA activists' could dredge up the embarrassing name of Rammit. Finally, it crossed the mind of the Very Top Level that no one knew *why* either faction of the IRA had so far failed to bomb in Britain. Had they not been able to organise the logistics? Or could it be a principled political decision? Until this was fully clarified, it might be highly dangerous to set them an example, irresponsibly to escalate with no clear view of where it would lead. So forget it! abort it! muffle the media! tell the clowns in the local copshop to stop their enquiries forthwith.

Toe swore it was all true. But could I believe her? And why was she telling me? I had been given to understand that the matter of the van had been 'dealt with' by her, Toe; so what the hell was all this about spooks in the driving-seat?

My fluttering protests only set her to snarl and to run off one of her favourite streams of sarcasm. She had indeed delivered both van and contents to 'a reliable man in the Midlands', the night of the Liverpool fiasco. Well, he wasn't reliable, was he? She guessed he'd been 'infiltrated'; someone'd have to do something about that, someone (she thought) would have it in hand, she didn't know, she might never be told. But I was a Brit, wasn't I? and *I* had to be told – if only because the Movement would from now on have no more dealings with sympathetic Brits, and if the likes of my fucking self had any fucking notions of offering further facilities, I could fucking well stuff them and sod off. Unreliable Irish were one thing, felon-setting Brit messers quite another. She laughed; a friend's warning, she said, she'd always fancied me, she said, only she knew I was a queer, but keep my bullshit for the *Guardian*: 'Keep it for your own crowd, don't bugger us about,' she sneered. 'This is serious business. And now that you've heard it, you'll *know* it.'

My indignation at her total distortion of my conduct was ruthlessly cut short. She poked me in the ribs like a Ballymurphy crony at the conclusion of a grand old gossip, gave a cackle of low complicity, and strutted off (in her purple hotpants and fluorescent green tights) toward the Chalk Farm tube.

I still did not know whether to believe her or not.

(xx)   Bones

I had consoled myself for all the muckup of VEXACTION and the Liverpool train by assuring myself that I had in some sort been a bit of a hero.

My disposal of the holdall was an act of great self-sacrifice, putting myself in considerable jeopardy, something to be secretly proud of. Even after the conversations with Polly and Toe, I tried to maintain this assurance. To an extent, I succeeded. I had done what I had to do: now it was high time to re-emerge to a respectable career; to make my peace with you and Pogmoor; to embrace as worthy colleagues Shadrach, Meshach and Abednego; to acknowledge the pretensions of responsible dissidence put about by your MOUTH-71. I contained my own deep secret – I had proposed myself as a revolutionist, I had halfway been accepted – if in the end it fell to pieces, I had no need to shoulder the blame – let the climate of this terrible time do that, we were all infected equally by the gathering miasma. I had at least *striven*: I could be proud.

Proud? Of young women dead, who should not have been dead.
Sonja. The stewardess. Spirited, ardent creatures, deep in their
graves or in crematorium ash-jars – they had lovers, they had
families, who would never know why or how they died, and *I* could
never tell them – rotten bones, unaccounted for, buried in falsehood, buried to be forgotten as a deliberate act of policy. (As also
my own cruel lover, and the anonymous two rats of Southampton.
As also the holdall, deep in the Staffordshire earth.)

So convenient to imagine they would never be dug up.

11

Is Leonore to believe *any* of this? The whole of his story seems to have
been a pack of lies. But whose lies? He admits he was deceived. Is it not
possible he continued to be deceived, that he continued to deceive
himself, and that he eventually took to his typewriter in order to deceive
her? But what he writes next, she can check from her own memory – if
she can be sure she does remember it – it was a time in her life she has
preferred not to have to think about—

(xxi)   MOUTH-71

Toward the end of 1971 I finished my first 'Matter of Ireland' play,
Poison-Voices.

'Matter of Britain', really, insofar as it demonstrated the effect over
several centuries of official propaganda befouling the national view
of the adjacent island and its people. I called it a 'mini-epic',
meaning a wide sprawling landscape of conspiracy and falsehood
confined within some ninety minutes' acting time. Two basic plots:
(a) the researches of a London journalist who seeks to write a series
of articles on Irish politics and culture, and (b) the devious uses to
which her conclusions are put. A framework of outsize melodrama
contained the strands of plot, partly because I like melodrama, and
partly because what was going on in real life was damned
melodramatic of itself, as who should know better than I? The script
no doubt was influenced in style by my work with VEXACTION,
but (need I tell you?) it stayed pretty damn clear of VEXACTION's
work with VVV. An objective summary, I considered it, an *Englishman's* summary: and where was the English theatre which would
want to put it on?

Jenny deVries, in her bouncing Falstaffian way, gave her instant
impersonation of the worst kind of hard-nosed agent: 'Lord,
nowhere!' she harrumphed. She condescended to expand: 'My

dear, you have to face it: no one is going to accept this sort of stuff unless it's a paean against *violence*. But the whole of your script is *justifying* violence. Or isn't it? If you really think it *isn't*, then you've not made your viewpoint at all clear, darling. Darling, you must face it: you might have got away with it last year. But people are really *sick* of all the riotings and shootings and bombings and all that absolute *shit*. I saw in the paper, my dear, that there's been already a thousand explosions in Ulster since I don't know when – January? – and a hundred civilians murdered, poor lambs, and fifty security forces – though God knows, my dear, and haven't I always said it? any boy that joins the Army ought to know what to expect! and the government are perfect *pigs*. But seriously, Fid, the situation makes me sick, my dear: and I really can't guarantee to place your script at all.

'Quite apart from anything else, all your characters are so – so *ruthlessly determined* – on *both* sides of the question. You don't have a single person who has any sort of *angst* about what they're up to: it's *not* psychologically convincing, or at any rate not *attractive*, and the actors will simply *hate* it.'

For all her florid eruptions of old-fashioned West End gush, Jenny knows what she's talking about. I could not dismiss her opinion. But the play was a considered statement: right or wrong, I was not going to alter it. I told her so; she groaned. Then she bounced around her office, taking a phone call from a client, making another one to a management, sweeping her vast derrière about between her desk and the clutter of her side-table and the clutter of her bookshelves and her coatstand and her wastepaper basket, like a jovial mother-hippo in a child's playpen, until she had distracted herself sufficiently from the matter-in-hand to be able to return to it with a more positive response; she asked had I thought about MOUTH-71?

'I know you mistrust them, and I know it's very personal with your sister and that Pogmoor man and so on, and they don't pay at all well. But Chris Abel-Nottidge is one of my writers and he *was* rather pleased with that extraordinary *Woyzeck* he and the other two elaborated on and Pogmoor directed. You'd have done it far better if you'd kept it in your own hands – but there was a *vitality*, and the critics seemed to like it.

'So maybe we should send them this *Poison-Bottle* or whatever it is.' Jenny always misnames plays that she wishes you hadn't written. 'They might have the spunk to do something with it. But they *are* a 'co-operative', so don't say you've not been warned. All I ever try to do is to try to help my writers to *live*; and they *fight* it, they all fight it, I simply can *not* think why . . .'

Yes, she *did* know what she was talking about: there *is* something

wrong with the idea of a theatrical co-operative, when it includes
everyone down to the electrician, but does not include the temporarily contracted playwright; and particularly when it does
include another playwright on the permanent strength – you know
very well who I mean, that Cambridge cockalorum Bill Saltmarsh,
aka bloody Shadrach, whose tantrums over the *Woyzeck* project had
driven Abednego into DTs (however much he glossed it over to
Jenny) and sent inoffensive Meshach into a dugout in the
Dolomites (is he out of it yet, Lenny? or have we *all* lost sight of the
poor bugger?). Most co-operatives, in fact, are hidden dictatorships;
and (I suppose) when MOUTH-71 accepted *Poison-Voices*, I rather
hoped this one would be, with Jack Juggler well installed to stop
the buck.

Not quite how it turned out.

Rehearsals were very difficult, and the crucial pre-rehearsal
period, when the script had to be thoroughly pummelled and
wrenched into workable shape, was quite as bad. The main difficulty was that the company's previous, and only, production had
not so much been *Woyzeck* as – to quote its actual title – *The Woyzeck
Variations*. Each of the three authors (or should I say 'adaptors'? the
borderline was very vague) had written his own one-act play
loosely attached to the original story; and then they were slotted
together by Pogmoor – as far as the acting-style went – and by you –
with an overall Visual Conception that quite honestly annoyed me
intensely. It made me think of Inigo Jones drowning Ben Jonson's
masque-scripts in a deluge of baroque upholstery. Everybody, you
see, had a finger in the pie: but *Poison-Voices* was quite different and
it had to be done differently, whether you wanted to or not. I was
still far from sure of my own material; I simply did not dare to let
bright ideas from all points of the compass drag it off-balance before
I myself could understand and mark the essential proportions of the
argument.

Shadrach had far too much to say, and damn his eyes seemed to
think he had a right to compile his own variation of my story, as
though *I* were Georg Büchner, 134 years dead. From his infant-
prodigy standpoint, perhaps that's more or less what I was.

The actors kicked up shit (just as Jenny had foreseen) and I truly
cannot say that you, my lovely sister, were any help at all. Every
time I succeeded in getting Jack away from all of you, and did my
best to come to some sort of understanding with him about this or
that particular point – as: if a self-proclaimed good-guy is really a
villain, please have him signal it from his very first entry, *don't* try
to be bloody subtle about it, it is not, repeat *not*, that sort of a play! –
he would seem to agree with me, and then sneak away somewhere
and mull it over with you, or with Shadrach, or with the stage-

manager, and then in the end they'd leave it all up to the cast, who only wanted to be *liked* by the audience but didn't understand what was likeable and what wasn't.

I called it 'abdication of responsibility', *they* (with great parade of virtue) called it 'Socialist principle'. VEXACTION had given me a bellyful of that, thank you very much; and I didn't believe a word of it. I don't think half that company of yours would even have voted for the Labour Party; but they jolly well could recognise the butter-side of a piece of bread.

(Not that I blame them: their butter was getting scarce, to say nothing of the bread itself. But so was mine, if this went on; I was *not* in their co-operative; if my play was a flop I was finished for the next twelve months; *they* had a new piece by Shadrach to settle into; dammit, it was already being cast!)

You've known all our life that I do not find it easy to assert myself. I make what I regard as strong demands, only to find that people have taken them as tentative suggestions. And when I start to insist upon them, I become shrill and unconvincing, like a wet maths master we had at school – he used to allow the class to get totally out of hand, until he could stand it no longer; a quavering announcement, that 'if we did not behave he would have to – to – put his foot down'; a further interlude of adolescent rough-house; and finally, screams and bellows as he threw a pile of books at the head of the wrong boy and sent two more of the wrong boys to report themselves to their housemaster.

Now in previous productions this defect of mine did not matter so much. Pogmoor in those days was pretty much on my wavelength; he did not have to concern himself with the establishment of an ideological image for a new kind of acting company; he was able to concentrate upon, he was able to understand, what intuitively I wanted (and what the play needed) without my having to stir myself up in order to stir up trouble about it. At the same time, I was close to *you*; you and I had been talking about the scripts from before I even sat to write them; we *knew*, each-to-each, the colour-scheme of our two minds.

But not in Manchester, not with MOUTH-71, not with the *Poison-Voices*.

I had (as I've mentioned) been sorely afraid that you and Jack J. would be ganging up against me. To some extent you were; but I also observed you were ganging up against each other, choosing your allies from the rest of the company, with bloody Shadrach as a trimming makeweight, now for you, now for JJ. You two formed your own power-blocs, he was the Third World, while I – I was the *underclass*, the destabilised peasantry that Third World political fixers lead, delude, repress and (ultimately) massacre.

Oh yes I was! and you, if you're honest, will admit you never
noticed it. You just thought that wretched Fid was being grouchy
and jealous and tedious and self-indulgent and that rehearsals
would proceed much better without him. Didn't you? Your exact
words, if I remember, after a quarrel we had when I first saw your
model for the set. Pogmoor came between us to agree with me on
nit-picking details but to support you over the general concept:
neither of you had the wit to see that the general concept was just
what was wrong. The details were no more than symptoms.

Well, I saw what was at the heart of it. That marriage of yours
was not working. I deliberately kept my distance from any
intimacy, I had to: both of you kept *your* distances so markedly from
me. So I did not know the problem between you, and I did not really
care. Was I glad or was I sorry? Sorry: because the disharmony was
damaging the production. Glad: because I'd never wanted you to
marry him in the first place. I wished all the time you'd find an ad-
hoc reconciliation until at least the first night of the play; and after
that would you please split with my blessing?

I saw Shadrach come out of your bedroom in the Midland Hotel,
when *I* knew very well that Jack had had to go for the night to
London. (Why were you in the Midland Hotel? you were surely in
Manchester long enough to have found a flat? but you and Jack
chopped and changed domestic arrangements like a disaffected pair
of cats trying to settle in a new house.) I thought, 'Ah! that's a
Symptom. Who's *Pogmoor* been with overnight?' I saw Pogmoor in
a Chinese restaurant with – what was her name? – Bríd: that icebox
of an Irish girl who played the Dublin tourist-guide. I thought,
'Symptom again; but just *what* is the General Concept?'

So eventually the play was shown. Our first performance was on
February 3rd, 1972, half a week after Bloody Sunday in Derry,
when the paras ran amok and gave murder a bad name. The British
media ran amok too; lie after lie; the troops displayed 'commend-
able restraint'; the IRA opened fire first; nobody was shot who was
not first seen to be holding either a gun or a bomb. Whereupon the
plain people of Dublin massed in front of the British Embassy and
gloriously set fire to it. We assumed, for a short while, that the
timing of the play was spot-on. What better occasion to demonstrate the corruption of our national understanding? But of course
if the national understanding was indeed so corrupted, then
audiences and critics would congenitally be unable to understand
the play. Which they were: it got lousy notices.

There was a tour, following the advertised policy of MOUTH-71,
playing small theatres, community centres, trade-union halls, up
and down the industrial north and the Midlands. I should have
said, there was an *arrangement* for a tour; for in fact it did not take

place. Or it only took place at one or two of the announced twelve venues. All the rest sent urgent messages, some of them imperious and indignant, others worried and apologetic, saying that the play was dangerous (it would encourage IRA bombs), or that it was subversive (the local police were putting on pressure), or that it was sectarian (prods and teagues in the local labour-movement would be set at odds by it), or merely that they'd heard it was of no 'artistic excellence' and – as cultural standard-bearers of the politically conscious working class in the area – they'd rather not be seen to condone our bourgeois rubbish.

There we were; the tour collapsed; the co-operative met in conclave. The question at issue: should *Poison-Voices'* projected London season (three weeks at the minuscule club theatre attached to a pub called Soldier's Glory, south of the river) be proceeded with or not? It was supposed to be the culmination of the tour; without the tour, would we be fit to confront the capital? *The Woyzeck Variations* had confronted the capital with great acclaim; but word-of-mouth had prepared its way. *Our* word-of-mouth dug potholes in the road and scattered broken glass on the tarmac. Opinions were divided; no decision was immediately reached. (Or so I was told afterwards, being only the co-operative's hireling and not invited in to deliberate. I was also told that three-quarters of the meeting was taken up with circumlocutory arguments pro-and-con a new name for the company. Should it be MOUTH-72, now the New Year had passed? or should '71' be retained as a statement of the date of foundation? or was it better to drop the date altogether and call yourselves plain MOUTH? I preferred the third solution; it chimed very happily with my acrimonious reflections; but of course it was none of my damned business.)

The Soldier's Glory dilemma was still unresolved, when all at a blow we were slammed in our midriff by the libel action.

No! *my* midriff; and no bones about it. You've said 'our' in so many conversations on that subject ever since (and I haven't contradicted you until now) that perhaps you need a reminder of what actually happened.

A columnist for a right-wing newspaper, one Barney Brewster, an insidious creepy-crawly, took it into his head that a character in the play was a portrait of his putrid self. Well, even though 'portrait' might be something of an exaggeration – I prefer 'caricature' – I would not be candid if I denied that I had him in my mind. But Barney Brewster is tall and corpulent, the man in the play was short and slight; Barney Brewster is a bugger from Bournemouth, the man in the play hailed from Gateshead and sounded like it; Barney Brewster is a great big toad, the man in the play was a greasy little earwig – I thought on the whole I had avoided direct defamation, and I warned Pogmoor to avoid it likewise, for Barney Brewster is vindictive and everyone who knows of him knows it.

I did of course incorporate certain pastiches of the Brewster style into the journalistic effusions of the man in the play. I also told the story (very well attested the other side of the Irish Sea) of how Brewster went to Dublin to make a senior government official rat-arsed with drink and deeply compromised with collusive tarts in an MI6-sponsored massage-parlour in the Clyde Road; he then tape-recorded every word of the silly man's maunderings; to regurgitate them later as an 'unattributable' statement of Prime Minister Jack Lynch's position on the Northern Troubles. I thought on the whole that not even Barney Brewster would want to stand up in court and say, 'Yes, m'lud, that's how I write; and oh yes, quite certainly, that's how I get my political scoops.'

I was right: on the basis of the play and only the play, the obnoxious creature would have had no case. But unfortunately someone in MOUTH-71 had an eye to *significant décor*. Six-foot-wide photo blow-ups of newspics and articles about Ireland were pasted up around the stage, extending to the auditorium and foyer. Pride of place, bang up against the bar, was given to a two-page spread by Brewster – his views on the Irish views on internment – the very piece for which he went brothel-trawling in Dublin. There was also an extremely large picture of Brewster himself, together with a hostile profile of him from the (very left-wing) *Black Dwarf*. He was, in legal terms, identified; and everything else about him in the play, *true or untrue*, therefore contributed to the defamation. For exam-ple: the Dublin tale (by his account untrue) became a lying reflection on his journalistic standards. His actual words, where loosely quoted, became a (truthful) reinforcement of the lie. If I'd given the man in the play a wooden leg, it would not have abolished the identification; it would only have strengthened it by indicating malice and implying allegorically that the real Barney Brewster was incapable of walking straight. Such is the law. *I* didn't make it. It very adequately protects rogues against fools. And even more adequately it provides a substitute for official censorship where political dissent is to be quashed and no protest aroused.

I ask myself to this day who exactly in this case was the original 'fool'. I was vaguely aware that Brewster's name occurred with prominence in the décor. I should have been *sharply* aware: but at that stage of rehearsals my attention was taken up with a tiresome piece of miscasting that threatened to destroy the impact of Act Two Scene Three, and I failed to take note of the full implications of what was being posted on the walls. No doubt I assumed that you and Pogmoor were aware of my warning and had it all in hand, no doubt I had absorbed just that much too much of the Spirit of the

Co-operative. Not to put a tooth in it, I abdicated my responsibility.

Pogmoor was no doubt anxious to prove his revolutionary credentials by tackling the Tory press head-on with his production, tackling the Tory pressmen in a deadly personal manner. He knew (because you'd told him) that I'd earlier extruded a few offhand sneers against MOUTH-71 and its principles; he refused to be outflanked from the left by odious comparisons with VEXACTION. He knew precious little about VEXACTION, but what he did know made him defensive.

And no doubt *you* never thought about the problem at all. You just said, 'blow-ups, press cuttings, okay! So many square feet, such a height from the floor, should they be black-on-white or white-on-black? and what's the best colour for the background?' You left the exact content of the excerpts to the co-operative. At that juncture, the co-operative meant Shadrach, diversifying from his work of publicity and programme-notes. The actors, bless their hearts, were committed to their bread and to their butter, whoever might be kind enough to spread it – which is to say, to their performances and to keeping well in with the director – that's *all* they were committed to.

I was served with the writ, myself alone, author. I at once contacted Lewis Hinge, as much a friend as a lawyer; he asked me frankly, 'D'you want to fight it?'

I told him, by golly I did. 'Bloody well fair comment,' I said, 'Barney Brewster is a piece of dung under a spotted bow-tie and I'll expose him in open court.'

He told me I hadn't much of a chance. He said, 'This play of yours is too friendly to one at least of the IRAs, the Marxist one, alas; this is *not* the right season of history for that sort of sympathy. A British jury will eat you alive. What's happening with MOUTH-71? Shouldn't *they* have received a writ? You do know, if I'm acting for you, I can't act for Leonore? Possible conflict of interest. Sad.'

But MOUTH-71 had not received a writ. Brewster must have calculated he could make *my* malice apparent in court – of course he knew about VEXACTION's repertoire and my earlier attack on the gutter-press in *Banner Headline* – while suing a whole theatre company might bring him too much odium from the liberal public at large. (Remember, Thatcher in those days was but a dimly perceived 'Milk-snatcher'; full-scale cultural counter-revolution was on nobody's agenda.)

The company therefore appeared to be free and clear. It seemed to me (I do admit Lewis was not so sure) that if they had the sense to take down the blow-ups from the foyer and so remove 'identification', they could go on with the play in legal security until they were officially injuncted. I did hope they would dare to go on.

I trusted that they would go on. An attempt was being made to silence free speech, they claimed (as a company) to stand up for free speech, they claimed to confront the powers of reaction, they could – if they had but the guts – become a focus of solidarity and enkindle the British theatre as a genuine Voice for Truth. The play posed the Rights of the British and Irish working class in stark opposition to the Irish and British ruling-class Conspiracies: it was impossible for me to imagine that MOUTH-71 would run away from such a challenge.

(Oh yes, I'd been well soaked, only too well soaked, in the confrontational sweat-bath of VEXACTION. Despite all, I hadn't given myself anything like sufficient time to dry off.)

Pogmoor came to me as blithe as a budgerigar: he (on behalf of the co-operative) had consulted *his* solicitor. The latter's advice: get rid of *Poison-Voices*, get rid of the trouble-making author, or MOUTH-71 will be ruined. The Arts Council, no doubt, had also been offering advice. The Arts Council (not yet fully Toryfied) was still in principle enthusiastic for the Challenging Role of the Playwright, but was beginning to worry: it had received a complaint from a Tory MP *and* from the British Army (GOC Northern Ireland) about its funding of the work of this particular playwright who *inter alia* accused British soldiers of torture. The Arts Council had weathered the storm, but was not about to sail gaily into another one. So Pogmoor (on behalf of the co-operative) abandoned the production: he talked to me most plausibly about the actors and their jobs, if they appeared to defy the legal system they would all of them be finished, he had no choice but to act like that notorious American general in Vietnam who destroyed a town 'in order to save it'. Pogmoor would suppress the work in order to preserve the workers – that is to say, all of the workers except me. An intelligent realistic Socialist standpoint, he most seriously believed it, the only one possible under the circumstances. I told him he was Ramsay MacDonald; he said, nonsense, he was *Lenin!* – Lenin always understood when to *reculer pour mieux sauter*. So I left him to his French and came to you.

You said, if MOUTH-71 (as publisher of the play) was sued, and lost the case, all the individuals of it would be liable – as well as myself (as playwright) who would be liable *by* myself. There'd be two distinct sets of damages to be paid to the man Brewster. And you and I (jointly but separately) could say goodbye to all our property. Whereas if you could be kept out of it (with the rest of the co-operative), Antioch Gardens would be safe. At the expense of Malthus Terrace, if the court ruled that house to be mine. But the court might not rule it. You'd been advised, you informed me, that with some dexterous legal shuffling, Malthus Terrace might be passed into *your* name – no indeed, not Pogmoor's, I need not be afraid of *that!* – and then, if I lost the action, why, presto! I'd have nothing to lose. I asked, who advised you? You replied, 'Lewis would have done, if he'd deigned to talk to me. I've had to take all my worries elsewhere. And there's Jack's lawyer, of course.' (You'd been asking around.) 'Let's go for some *strategy*,' you said. 'It's high time we all played it clever.'

So *I* said, I *had* to say: 'Okay.'

I remained sole defendant, bore all of the bloody brunt, and MOUTH-71 (even so) lost its grant for the next twelve months. The Arts Council, reluctantly, had had to cut and run. Fuckup.

No need to tell you more about the course of the libel suit. You know well enough how it dragged on for the next five years until finally it was settled out of court. You know very well how it caused my reputation as a reliable playwright to fester like a cat's corpse in a cesspit. Let me only, for present purposes, give a quote from C. Dickens:

> —the protracted and wearing anxiety and expense of the law in its most oppressive form, its torture from hour to hour, its weary days and sleepless nights – with these I'll prove you [*so rants Ralph Nickleby, so also ranted Brewster*] – and break your haughty spirit, strong as you deem it now.

As it was in 1838, so also in 1972. I could have used some comrades.

(xxii)   A Dried Pea

I was relieved, though, about one thing.

I had *not* wanted to go, with the play, to the Soldier's Glory. That little theatre was where I first met Sam Rammit: it was surely superstitious of me, but the thought of its stage and dressing-rooms shrivelled my balls to the size of a dried pea.

(xxiii)   Machiavellian

I got away from Manchester as soon as I could and dug myself in at Highbury, in outrageous winter, in a bone-biting fog and chill of Jacobean vengefulness; I was a veritable upas tree of a Machiavellian malcontent, I should have worn dead-black raiment, pulled my hat over my brow, let my stockings down-gyve *to my ankle, whitened my knuckles on the haft of my dagger.*

I blamed it all on your marriage with Pogmoor. I made up my mind to bring that marriage to an end. Only thus would you and I be as we were before; only thus would he and I ditto.

How to do it?

To begin, you were already halfway there. Okay, he complied with your sleeping with Shadrach; okay, you allowed him to eat sweet-and-sour pork with career-climbing actresses and tickle their twats with his chopsticks or wherever his fancy lay. But there must be a line you'd draw somewhere.

How about—? you and me! the bivouac on the slope of Exmoor, the royal house of ancient Egypt? I could not believe you'd told Pogmoor about that. Nor could I believe his north-country inhibitions would ride him easily over the circumstance. I had to let him know. I didn't know how to let him know.

In the end, I decided that the simplest way was best. I could not tell him to his face; it would be so obvious what I was up to, and then there would be no chance of him and me ever working together again. Moreover, he'd tell you that the news had come from me, and how would *you* react at my betrayal of our joint secret? Yes, *I* was now the one determined to betray. Unlike you, I was fully aware of what I did; unlike you, I made no excuses to myself. I was bloody well *of evil purpose*, and I gnashed my teeth gleefully, I thought it all out and I did it.

The simplest way was best; before February was over, I wrote him an anonymous note.

So cunning I was, I took the train all the way to Pomfretshire to post it from the campus mailbox. It was a regular poison-pen piece, made up of fragments of print, all different sizes, cut out of the *Yorkshire Post*. He would suppose (so I calculated) that it came from someone at the college who remembered us from the old days and had hated us ever since. There were probably several candidates; I recollected great jealousies; I also recollected one or two very right-wing lecturers (Eng Lit, not Drama, decent Franz Altdorfer would never have sanctioned their appointment) who fiercely resented all the theatre of the 'committed Left', in particular how Pogmoor and I had so insidiously 'politicised' the historical integrity of *Jack Juggler*. Maybe whoever it was had been following the fortunes of MOUTH-71. One of our two *Poison-Voices* tour gigs had been at Chesterfield, not so far away, it must have been talked about, even seen, although I hadn't noticed any college faces in the audience. Anyway, I was quite sure that Pogmoor would think Pomfretshire, he would never think Fid Carver, and neither (in the upshot) would you.

And it worked, Lenny: didn't it? Within four months he walked out on you. Did he ever tell you why? No, of course he didn't, he was *traumatised*. If he had told you why, you would inevitably have told *me*. But you didn't, and after a while – why, we all became good friends again. My evil plot had worked and I never knew a moment's remorse.

12

Ah God, this isn't right. This was not how it was. The facts were quite otherwise. (Yet her brother's unlovely memoir is of itself a *fact*. It must be taken on its own terms. Leonore has not expected the terms to be so mean-spirited.) Did he spend all his life, from 1972 until now, in the positive belief that Pogmoor left her because she had been incestuous? 'Four months', was it? between the anonymous letter and the final break-up? Fid seems better on chronology than herself; but her impression is decidedly different, she is sure it was two months.

She is also sure that Pogmoor never read that letter.

It was sent to Antioch Gardens, where she had returned after the *Poison-Voices* débâcle. MOUTH-71 was winding itself up, in its original form: Pogmoor was getting out of it, she was getting out of it with him. Bill Saltmarsh was about to take over, to reconstruct the constitution of the co-operative, to cleanse it of all traces of irresponsible ultra-leftism (while retaining its northern provincial and approximately proletarian identity) and to put in train a solid programme of 'high standards of excellence' – all in order to seek re-entry into the good graces of the Arts Council. Its name was to be changed to MOTH – '**M**irror **O**f **T**orn **H**umanity' – Saltmarsh was a sentimental romantic, despite the sex-n-violence of his acrid dramaturgy. Whether or no it should be MOTH plain or MOTH-72 (to keep some connection with its beginnings) was still under discussion. Pogmoor was sick of the whole issue; Leonore was unwilling to retain any closeness with Saltmarsh. There was a *Mrs* Saltmarsh, an actress, neurotic, possessive and young, who wanted to join the company; she showed signs of making trouble.

When the letter arrived, Pogmoor was still in Manchester, undergoing a series of meetings with Saltmarsh, an accountant and a couple of lawyers. He had asked Leonore to glance through his mail and phone him about anything important. So she opened this particular item, with its Pomfretshire postmark, read it, and sat looking at it. Disgust was her first emotion; then alarm; and at last curiosity, which did not conquer the other two but effectively served to subdue them. There was no heading on the letter; it went straight to its nasty intent:

· !**BEEST** + 2 **BACKS**! ·
· broun & **WiTe** · skrauney & greesey · smoo**T**hface & **H**ariyface ·

Twin & Twin · sisTer & BroTher ·
Wich ones' on Top? · & were Does our Jack fiT in? ·
· inbeTween or UnderneeTh or SaT asTrid like a KasTraTid GiNNyPIG? ·
· You Ougrht to know, Jack, · if you din'dT know, **NOW YOU DO!** ·

The ignorant spelling must be a blind; for the phraseology was quite
literate, rhythmically literate, in an oddly old-fashioned way. 'Beast
with two backs', indeed. Scarcely what you'd call a tabloid-reader's
metaphor. Just as Pogmoor was supposed to do, Leonore deduced
'English Department'. But she'd no idea *who*; nor could she work out
what next.

It was horrible to think that Pogmoor might thus be possessed of her
own most precious secret. But maybe he need never be. No reason to
believe such a letter would be sent more than once? But then again it
might. God help her, if he ever read it, he would *know* her through and
through, she could never face him again, and yet he'd have the power,
psychological power, to make her do whatever he wanted.

No way could she speak of it when she called him on the telephone.
And what next? Silence and more silence. And never knowing when
it might not be broken. Or maybe her secret ought not to be a secret?
Ought never to have been a secret. Maybe she *should* tell him? Maybe.
Not yet, though, not just yet, take it slowly, think about it.

Enormous possibilities, in every sort of relationship . . . even as
between a Mr and Mrs Pogmoor . . .

So not yet.

13

And bloody hell, it was Fid all the time. Such *viciousness!* yet good God,
what can she do but laugh? Poor love, poor silly dead love. And he
thinks he was 'greasy', and he thinks she was 'scrawny'? Oh lord, how
babyish! but perhaps he was right.

14

He *was* right about one thing: the marriage had not been working, not
for a long while. In fact it began to go wrong almost as soon as it
commenced. But an ill-suited couple can continue together for years, if
there is something material between them to hold their interest (in this
case the theatre company), and if no particular pretext for a terminal
quarrel should suddenly spring up and take them unawares. Neither
Pogmoor nor herself felt inclined to regard passing infidelities as

pretexts of this sort, though they were not unscathed by them. The intense collaborative work of dealing with, first, the *Woyzeck* play, and then Fid's temperamental flourishes during the process of *Poison-Voices*, blunted their jealousies over nights spent in other people's beds; maybe both of them were but seeking brief relief in those beds and finding it; maybe, had the company stayed on an even keel, both of them would eventually have settled down to its routine in the north for at least another twelve or twenty months of slowly evaporating toleration.

But then the routine fell apart. The future was wide open and perilous. Pogmoor, Leonore knew, was soliciting work once again with the big subsidised theatres, with the film industry, with television. He was rarely in Kentish Town, indeed to all intents and purposes had ceased to live there; she too was out and about looking for freelance contracts. About ten days after Fid's play was brought to an end, and about a week before he sent his anonymous letter, she succeeded in landing one. She was appointed chief designer for a large-scale civic and community festival in Plymouth: there was a pageant of the town's history envisaged, and a series of plays about famous naval heroes – Drake, Hawkins, Nelson and so forth – to be presented in a disused covered dock in Devonport. What was left of the ancient seaport after the World War Two bombings was to be decorated like Granada in fiesta-time. The whole affair was the brainchild of a livewire among the generally philistine Plymouth businessmen, a Tory councillor who had his eyes on the parliamentary nomination next time round. He had found a patriotic dramatist, a competent writer (aged fifty-five or so) who blamed his comparative obscurity on the undercover Marxism of the theatre/TV establishment and the political venality of the critics. This man's claim to fame was a 1950s J. Arthur Rank filmscript, *Arctic Attack!*, about the sea-battle of Narvik Fjord; he adored the Royal Navy and was determined to bring to the festival all those traditional values long spat upon by his younger rivals in the profession, values long eroded under the dust-storms of Socialism, 'totalitarian permissiveness', 'underdog whinge and scrounge'. He was more than the festival's playwright; he was its artistic director as well; and was personally responsible for choosing Leonore.

It was a very odd decision. He knew perfectly well what work she had been doing lately and with whom she had been doing it. If she had been at all sincere toward the ideology of MOUTH-71, she was the last sort of person he should employ. But he had already fallen in love with her, from her photograph in *Plays and Players* – an utter absurdity of emotional self-abandon, a spinning *pas seul* of middle-aged venery, his shuttlecocking rebound from a recent accusatory divorce. Having fixed up a meeting with her, he was able to persuade himself that all in an afternoon the force of his personality would impel her irresistibly from the false spirit of MOUTH-71 to the true one of Drake, Hawkins, Nelson and (not the least of 'em) himself. His conceit was as strident as his persecution-mania.

He expected, in his old-fashioned foxy-gentleman way, to seduce her during the course of the work – or maybe after it, he was an impetuous fellow but cautious, even when turgid with desire. Perhaps, if he were to find that he had really *recycled* her into accepting his egregious principles, he might steer her towards divorce and then marry her. For he too had in mind the parliamentary nomination, not realising in his political naïvety that it was already bespoke. Impetuous, cautious, self-deluded, insensate; his name was Maxwell Prosser; a commissioned naval paymaster at the Devonport dockyard during the war, he would have preferred to have captained a submarine, but the Admiralty thought not.

Leonore saw through him, all in an afternoon, greedily ate the lavish and pretentious lunch he bought her, reckoned up the financial potential of the job, accepted it, and decided that under no consideration would she ever make love with him. But she might let him think that she might, if it would hasten the contract and fetch in some money up-front. She had lost quite a bit on the Manchester enterprise; and looked likely to lose even more, the way Pogmoor's negotiations were going. Her 'gambler's desperate lunge' had all but bankrupted her; no more impetuous tricks! the *crux* of her advancing years had turned out to be no such thing, she would never become a mother, she would never change her wanton habits, she had lost Fid, she had nothing else to search for, except the deep pleasure of work well done and the superficial pleasures to be grubbed up from its earnings.

This man Prosser had work for her, high earnings, high prestige, if all fell out aright; indeed it was the largest and best-publicised single project she had ever been asked to undertake. She was going to need some help.

The ground floor of the house in Antioch Gardens must become a regular workshop-studio, a full-time assistant should be installed there at once, preferably a live-in assistant who would always be on call, either to pop down intermittently to Plymouth or to take charge while Leonore popped down to Plymouth. She foresaw an entire springtime of heavy toil in London before Plymouth itself became her centre of operations. The date of the festival was scheduled for late August; let her hire a capable person on a six-month contract; it looked as though something like two thousand costumes were going to have to be designed and made, to say nothing of the built sets and the street-decorations.

Who came up among the applicants – most convincingly by far the best of them – but Carmilla Costello?

Leonore retained a vague memory of her from Fid's time at Pomfretshire, the same impression he had had: a talented but 'very scatty' expatriate, never quite at one with British manners and social habits even in the most informal bohemian surroundings. Leonore knew nothing of any involvement with VEXACTION, and Carmilla did not tell her. Carmilla's CV was impressive enough without it; and it seems (if Fid's memories are accurate) that VEXACTION never used any of her work. Leonore now realises how Carmilla deleted VEXACTION from the CV as an unpleasant mistake; like Fid, she must have had a bad fright. And a very bad shock from Polly, for did not her longed-for Polly deny her at the height of the crisis? 'Piss off, would you please, and shut up' – the poor woman must have felt herself blown into fifty pieces all over her own street-map of Clapham.

Leonore recollects the quick intensity of Carmilla's erotic approaches; they began almost as soon as she gave her the job; they began *with* the job, in fact, as though Carmilla assumed them to be part of it. There was something not quite canny about this, some hint of irrational mental speed-up which the new assistant herself neither expected nor fully understood. Leonore at first was unwilling to respond; she always disliked *responding*, the loss of initiative disturbed her; but in this case she could think of no good reason to refuse. Carmilla was desirable, in a skinny, stringy, muscular, unwashed sort of way; an affair with her would provide Leonore with a temporarily secure emotional base from which to keep the slimy Prosser at a distance; and after Pogmoor's continual evasions, after the vapidities of Saltmarsh, after Prosser's unappealing restaurant-expertise, Leonore was thoroughly hungry for the tingle of feminine nerves.

Nonetheless Carmilla's nerves were very nearly too much for her. She wonders now, as she wondered then: had Carmilla ever successfully propositioned a woman before? She talked like an experienced sexual buccaneer; but there was a kind of last-ditch frenzy – yes, a 'gambler's desperate lunge'! – about her total contempt for psychological foreplay. Her astonishment at Leonore's acceptance of her advances was so palpable it was almost pathetic. Her love-making, too, was desperate, as though she knew it could not last, as though at any moment Leonore would suddenly turn upon her and tell her to – well, to 'piss off'. This was irritating; it tempted Leonore to be cruel. (Just as Pogmoor had been cruel to Leonore?) As Leonore was already irritated by the reactionary rubbish of Prosser's festival and by her own bad conscience at having agreed to be part of it, harsh little scenes took place, hurtful snubs, sarcasms, shoutings and weepings. They were no more than momentary, but nasty enough for all that.

Leonore was thrown off-balance by Carmilla's 'inside knowledge' of her. Telepathy with a twin brother had a natural flow to it, sometimes it was there, sometimes it wasn't, it was a matter of strong but imprecise feeling, impossible to quantify; moreover its existence and its nature were plausibly affirmed by scientific research. (Just then, it was *not* there: she had no idea what Fid was up to, nor did she wish to find out. Nor did *he* make any contact with *her*.) Carmilla's intuition did not seem natural at all; it was more like the surveillance of a spy. To take a trivial example: she always contrived to know where to phone Leonore if the latter was away from the house without having left any note on the memo-pad as to her movements. Of course, Carmilla may well have rung every number she could think of and only caught the right one at the end of half an hour. But when she *did* catch the right one, six times out of ten she was able to say just who Leonore was with, why she was with them, and what was the *emotional tone* of the meeting. Thus: 'Hey, I was sure you were with that Prosser guy, but the mayor of Plymouth's there as well, isn't he? Honey-child, for Chrissake don't let him con you about dressing-room facilities at the sports-ground, we gotta have enough space for five hundred, and that asshole's trying to bullshit you, Leo, just because you're a woman, I know he is, I fucking *know* it, and Christ! Leo-honey, you haven't called the bastard's bluff . . .' Intelligent deduction? elimination of impossibilities? it did not always hit the target; but it was spot-on sufficiently often to create a certain disquiet in a gullible mind. Leonore did not believe herself to be gullible. Carmilla was playing tricks.

But Carmilla also knew, without being told, too many of the reasons for the chill upon Leonore's marriage; her malevolence (indeed her unspoken panic) toward the absent Pogmoor was vicarious and gratuitous; it went far beyond the bounds of his wife's churned-up resentment.

Did Carmilla have an intuition about Fid? Carmilla, of all people, must never find out *that*! Let her believe she'd replaced a husband, but on no account must she know that neither she nor anyone else could ever usurp the *brother's* right. Even though the brother was no longer where he used to be, his heart was Leonore's heart, inviolate. Which if

Carmilla understood, Carmilla would run mad, would she not? Carmilla would never rest until all was brought down in catastrophe.

Carmilla's design work was everything she had claimed for it; but there was something – what was the word? – *askew*.

Altogether it was the most awful mess; and Leonore, having created it, became guarded to an extreme degree, secretly guarded, taking very good care to hold a slight but deliberate distance, even when seeming most thoroughly reckless; she indulged herself in her love-affair, but *observed herself* as well, like an actress in a passionate role who always must keep open a prudent thought for the audience and ensure her fellow player stays properly downstage.

15

One thing that Leonore is *not* able to recollect: when and how she destroyed the anonymous letter, once she'd read it and decided to defer taking action. She thinks now that it may have arrived more or less coincidentally with the arrival of Carmilla. She knows she had it razor-edged in her hand while she talked on the phone that day to Pogmoor; his other letters (which she was briefly describing and summarising for him) would have gone into their various folders or else been set aside for posting on. She was fearfully upset, and her memory has muddled it all up. Did she drop the letter there and then into the wastepaper basket? If she did, she'd have torn it up, how could she *not* have torn it up? Was she distracted – distraction upon distraction – by Carmilla, perhaps, or another phone call? – and idiotically left it, to lie for a time on her table? Did Carmilla see it? For if Carmilla *did* see it, then Carmilla knew about Fid *before* she made love to Leonore; and did she also assume that Pogmoor knew too?

If Leonore can work all this out, it should explain a great deal. Particularly what happened later, two months later, strange words, criss-cross of baffled rage, counterpoint of misconceived violence: a dire four-cornered encounter between Pogmoor, Leonore, Carmilla and an improbable little woman called Chudd. Antioch Gardens, the first of May; she remembers the date exactly, because the date was the origin of the incident.

On April 29th she had a phone call from Pogmoor. He was coming home the day after tomorrow, and expected to stay for some time. This was tiresome, but scarcely avoidable: essential business must be discussed. Leonore no longer felt *married* to him; but on the other hand he was no stranger, certainly no enemy, her home was still his. She was anxious not to have to resolve the contradiction; not yet; sleeping dogs, let them lie. ('Only pray he's not been sent a copy of that damnable letter! If he has, the filthy curs are awake.') He was driving up from Manchester, he would arrive at lunchtime, maybe earlier if the motorway were clear: he was aggressive at the wheel of his Fiat. So at lunchtime he'd be bound to meet Carmilla.

Was this a problem? Carmilla had been in Plymouth; she was on her way back to London when the call came; she couldn't have known about it, could she? Now Carmilla and Pogmoor had not met since the former settled in to Kentish Town, indeed not since Pomfretshire. (Leonore had heard nothing about what might or might not have happened between them at Pomfretshire in the '60s. In fact, it was years before she *ever* heard.) The situation was therefore embarrassing; but sheer cowardice to be paralysed by it. Let him come. And don't mention him in advance to Carmilla; don't mention Carmilla to Pogmoor; no advantage in prematurely stirring trouble . . .

The next afternoon Carmilla had an inspiration. 'Who's gonna be Queen of the May?' she suddenly bawled, apropos of nothing, while both women were bent over drawing-boards very busy with a set of sketches; even though it was Sunday, they were at work; the sketches had to be finished by mid-week. 'You'n'me, Noreen-honey, why don't we crown each other?' Leonore, used to working alone, rarely spoke in the studio; Carmilla preferred to have music on the radio, interspersing it with loud and arbitrary ejaculations which might have been intended to start a conversation, if Leonore chose to reply. As a rule she did not reply, until they broke for a coffee or something to eat. Neither of them made a difficulty of this asymmetrical discourse; Carmilla could retain her opening phrases in her mind for an hour or two and return to them as if she'd only just uttered them, while Leonore all that time would have been chewing them over and was able to come up with some approximately relevant continuation. ('Noreen-honey' and 'Leo-honey' were Carmilla's alternative modes of address to her; sometimes it would be 'Norry-honey', sometimes 'Honey-Lo', in a crooning Deep South accent, as of a devoted black nurse in an Ole-Plantation romance. Carmilla was not yet thirty, about eleven years younger than Leonore.)

In this case, over sandwiches at five o'clock, Leonore burst into Tennysonian song: 'You must wake and call me early, call me early, mother dear, for I'm to be Queen of the May, mother, I'm to be Que—' and then broke off to hunt for the mayonnaise.

'Yo!' cried Carmilla, 'before dawn, yeah? I guess Chudd's an early riser, why don't I see if I can throw it?'

'Chudd who? Throw what?' But Carmilla changed the subject. Leonore concluded a surprise was being prepared; the younger woman loved surprises; Leonore was not fond of them but was kind enough to endure them for the sake of amorous harmony. She kissed Carmilla fondly and opened a tin of tuna.

Monday morning, May Morning, forty minutes before sunrise, there was a ringing and banging at the front door.

'Who the hell is that at this hour?' (It couldn't be Pogmoor, surely? For the moment she had quite forgotten Carmilla's 'surprise'.)

'Christ, but it can't be – no!' For an instant, Carmilla, still slubbered with sleep, looked deadly white and frightened; and then jerked herself into full consciousness. She forced a laugh: 'I thought it was – the drug-squad, yeah? but I'm clean, more or less, yeah . . . Okay, no hassle. No hassle, Honey-Lo, it has to be Chudd, is all.' She rolled out of the bed and wriggled into one of her poncho-like wraps. 'How's about you grab some clothes, fix some coffee, I'll let her in.'

Leonore padded obediently and blearily about the big room, and fumbled with coffee-things; she could see through the window a van parked opposite the house. A sort of scurrying beetle was lifting boxes and tripods and coils of wire and light-fittings of various sorts out of it, while Carmilla ran to and fro carrying them into the porch.

Great performance of bringing all this impedimenta upstairs, Carmilla panting and giggling and dumping it piece by piece on the floor. At last the beetle came in with the last of it, threw it noisily down inside the door and threw herself into a chair saying, 'Sod it, what a staircase, cow; you should get yourself a fucking hoist.' This was Chudd, Camera-Guru, highly alternative, highly professional, highly expensive. A double portrait by her of Carmilla and Leonore was to be Carmilla's Mayday surprise love-gift, the Crowning of the Queens. And it looked as though they might well be all day having it taken. (Okay! if Pogmoor didn't like it, Pogmoor could bloody lump it.) Chudd was laying out a white line of cocaine; Carmilla would have some too; Leonore preferred to stay with her Gauloises.

Abishag Chudd (she never used the 'Abishag'; always the surname alone) was famous in Carmilla's circles as photographer, pornographer, occasional drug-dealer, Swinging-Sixties icon, grotty psychedelic genius, Age-of-Aquarius image-maker, sexually ambivalent voyeuse and general oddball. Leonore's circles knew the name but did not actually know *her*. She had some deformity, neither dwarfism exactly nor a hunched back nor a crooked pelvis, but it kept her low to the ground on what appeared to be unusually short legs; her shoulders were very broad and her arms like a wrestler's; she hid all this under a swirl of long garments which totally disguised her shape; all you could see was a dark-brown withered face and a cropped or balding bullet-head covered by a beaded skullcap. She might have been any age between thirty and sixty; she might have been a man or a woman; she might have been of any nationality from the West Indies through North Africa and the Levant to the East Indies. She herself, if asked, described herself as 'a non-specific multiple-ethnic. Wanna make anything out of it, cow?' Sometimes she said she was born in Gibraltar, sometimes Malta, sometimes Singapore. Her eyes were black and bloodshot behind huge hornrims; her accent had a tinge of Australia; now and then she dropped into what might have been Arabic; as a rule she had little to say, she communicated by laughs, grunts and swearwords; the laughs were like the sudden braking of a juggernaut truck. Her impressive personality suggested a grafting of Henri de Toulouse-Lautrec upon a cathouse madam from Cairo.

Half an hour of brooding silence, and then, as though at a message from the gods, audible to her ears alone, Chudd erupted into rapid movement. She sprang and scrambled all over the room, clearing the furniture against the walls, dragging lamps into place, erecting a kind of gantry from two aluminium stepladders, light girders and expanded metal, laying out (underneath the gantry) half a dozen three-foot squares of foam-rubber with a wide black cloth spread on top of them, and unpacking a box of paints and brushes.

Carmilla explained that Leonore and herself were to strip, have their bodies painted by Chudd, and lie side-by-side on the cloth in whatever posture Chudd preferred. The camera would be aloft; the ensuing pictures might be interpreted as women lying down, or women standing up or even women standing on their heads; the lighting would make them mysteriously ambiguous. The concept was Carmilla's, its detailed execution would be entirely left to Chudd. Once Chudd accepted an idea she brooked no further intervention; Leonore must do what she was told.

Leonore was alarmed. This was not the sort of camera-session she particularly wanted Pogmoor to come in upon. But it was still only breakfast-time, a damned early breakfast at that, of course they'd be finished before noon. On the whole she thought she liked the concept. It was sexy, it was disgracefully self-indulgent, and she wanted to please Carmilla. She said, 'I like it, on the whole, maybe yes, or maybe – why the hell not? D'you know, I think I will sniff some coke. Let's try it, then, Horsecollar: GO!'

Her pet-name for Carmilla had been 'Horsecollar' since the morning after their first bedding together; she did not choose to explain it. Leonore never flattered any of her lovers except Fidelio; her endearments were always abrasive.

Chudd's pleasure in the body-painting was extreme; throughout the lengthy process she hissed between her teeth like a stableboy with a currycomb, she patted and fondled and stroked but did not speak. When she considered herself finished, she abruptly dropped brush and stencil, gave gleeful great slaps to two pairs of slender buttocks and barked out: 'Down! On your sides, facing! Great, fucking fab, yeah gorgeous, boy-o-boy. Tell you this much shit, the two of you, you'd never fucking guess one was older than the other, you could be twin sisters, fucking teenage, legs like birch trees, yeah, shit-hot torsos, *svelte*!'

She leaped up onto her gantry and bustled and rattled about, this position, that, crouching above them leering and peering, viewfinder, light-meter, dirty bare brown feet hopping in their flurry of draperies from one girder to another until she found her first shot. Now she was talking all the time, photographer's fervent patter, shot after shot, ordering their hands this way, their mouths that, to the right to the left, up down, inside, between, 'Keep it cool, keep it sexy, warm it, warm it, fucking *hot!* keep it up to her, cow, that's the way, yeah *that's* the fucking way, now ease it off, off off away, fab, great, yeah, boy-o-boy, cool—' and so on and so forth.

For brief moments she would pause, fling herself with foul-mouthed mutterings down the ladders and around the room, adjusting her lights, bringing out more lights, pitching reflector-screens into new places, hurly-burly of spontaneous decisions achieved at lightning speed. And then she was aloft again for another series of objurgations, adjurations, rapid shots and lascivious moanings.

Leonore and Carmilla blushed, giggled, squawked, played shamelessly with themselves and each other, and slid about on the foam-rubber like dolly-birds at a rock band's orgy. This was what Chudd wanted; if it made a good picture, then *go with it*. 'Fucking teenage' was an exhilarating thought.

As the coke-induced high wore off, the morning imperceptibly wore on. They grew tired, they grew lazy, they threatened mutiny; but Chudd, their serjeant-major, would grant them small respite. Once Chudd was on the job, she did not falter; a commission was a commission; all three of them must work at it until she was sure she had got it *right*.

16

Pogmoor of course held his keys to the house and to Leonore's first-floor flat where the session was taking place. The locks were well oiled. Chudd overhead was clattering out her patter and moreover had a Thelonious Monk LP turned up little short of full-volume on Leonore's record-player: so none of them heard him come in.

Leonore saw him first, just inside the room, corpulent and ugly, open-mouthed, staring at her, staring at Carmilla, lifting his breadloaf face to stare upward through his spectacles at the bogle-like bespectacled Chudd. 'Castrated guinea-pig'? no better phrase.

Leonore in her confusion started to scramble to her feet. (It could not possibly have been later than half-past bloody ten? He must indeed have had an open road.) Carmilla's forearm shot up, strong as an iron bar to pin Leonore to the mattress: 'Still, honey, still! Lie still and let him look.' Carmilla's teeth were bared at him, a wildcat's teeth, a jackal's, the fangs of an angry cobra.

Chudd from her gantry vomited the filthiest language, slamming the cap onto her camera-lens, swinging her stumpy legs to bring herself down to floor-level; the session was dead, interruption marked an end, man, end, a sodding cunt of a fucking *end!* – bad trip, heavy scene, shit coming down, man, *kill it* . . . ! She started to dismantle her equipment, racing backward and forward, mouthing, deliberately creating every possible degree of hubbub. She was affronted. She meant it to show.

Breaking free from Carmilla's arm, Leonore on all fours made towards Pogmoor to cut him off into the bedroom-alcove; she had to talk to him alone. He side-stepped her, took three swift paces across the floor until he stood over the sprawling Carmilla; he bent down to her; he matched her snarl for snarl; he spat in her face.

Carmilla screamed and taunted him, crying out incoherence about twins – he had come to look for twins? and Christ he'd fucking found 'em, but sister and sister not a brother on the fucking scene, not an asshole of a shitty brother, not a shit of a man's prick in the whole asshole pad—! It made little objective sense. Except to Leonore. Leonore, from where she crouched, could not see Pogmoor's face, could not judge how he reacted; but she jumped to the conclusion, in the haste of half a virulent minute, that whereas heretofore he had *not* known her secret, now he *did* know it, he *had* to know it! Carmilla had just given it out. Carmilla had betrayed.

That was not what he was on about. 'Dyke!' he was saying. 'Cuntsucker!' he was saying. 'Splatterer! Fucking psycho with your lying tales, did you tell her about Backthorpe, did you tell her about the bicycle, did you tell her about the sword, about cutting with the fucking sword, of course you did, you! you long streak of cholera-flux! it'll take me six weeks to scrub you out of my floorboards, up and out of it – NOW! – or I'll break your scaly legs off!' He had her by the ankle and was levering her violently about – in a way that made it impossible for her to get up and go, even if she wished to, but the drench of his fury quite doused his practicality.

Did she think Leonore would help her? But Leonore now saw Carmilla as nothing better than a reeking streak – with scaly legs fit to be broken, hair to be pulled up from the roots, eyes gouged, neck wrung – Leonore hurled herself onto her with never a word in her mouth but murder in her claws – Pogmoor, astonished, fell back – and Chudd like a black-widow spider jumped horribly onto his shoulders.

In the end, of course, there was no murder. The two naked women, quite unpractised in unarmed combat, hurt each other for a short space, only to roll apart, dribbling and sobbing. The man in his fleece-collared motoring-jacket staggered backwards about the room until the bundle of draperies with the squat little creature inside it was scraped off against one of her own stepladders. The stepladder fell down; what remained of the gantry fell with it; a lampstand toppled over; the shocking clang of collapsed aluminium brought everyone to a panting halt. And silence. It was a very heavy scene, and nothing to be proud of at all.

Carmilla picked herself up, grabbed an armful of clothes, and fled from the flat without even putting them on. If she ran bare and painted into the Mayday streets of Kentish Town, Leonore knew nothing of it. She was gone and that was all. Let her take her frenzied treachery elsewhere. In due course she'd have to be sacked. And another assistant hired. Leonore had never liked her. How foolish it was, and how evil, evil, evil, to grab your bouts of love from a person you don't like. Leonore was weeping; and Chudd with morose contempt continued slowly to pack up the gear.

'Get out,' said Leonore to her husband. 'I need to get dressed.'

'And you can't do it in front of me?'

'I *won't*,' she said. 'Out.'

'Out, you fat bullshitter,' put in Chudd from behind all her boxes. 'don't you know when you're not fucking wanted? Bad vibes.'

Pogmoor looked bleakly at both of them, shrugged, growled, and went upstairs. To his own space, which used to be Fidelio's space and would be again. Chudd, with an unexpected gentleness, put out a large hand, lifted Leonore to her feet, drew her into the bathroom. Inside, she ran hot water, helped Leonore into the bath, helped her shower and wash (without speaking) until all the body-paint was off, the scratches and bruises dabbed with Savlon. She wrapped her in a bathrobe, and led her back into the big room. She put on the electric kettle; she found a jar of instant coffee; she asked, 'Milk? Sugar? Big cup, small?'

'Don't bother with the coffee. I'll give you a hand to bring your gear down.'

'Don't you bloody touch it, cow, you'll be dropping it all over the stairs. Christ, woman, look how you shake. If you want to gimme something, you'd be better off writing a cheque. A whole morning's work and it costs. You gonna buy the fucking pics? Not you. Not her. Terminated, wasted, fucking lash-up, yeah? kaput. That's where it's at.'

'No, no,' Leonore's voice was breathless and ragged; she strained to keep it level, to express herself with firmness, 'no, but I *shall* want a picture, a big one, a blow-up. Big enough to fit between those windows. Bring me some prints and I'll choose. You can ring me. I'll pay you now for your time. *She* should be doing this, *she* was the one that fetched you here, it was supposed to be her money, but I don't know where she's gone, I don't know where she'll be, and I never *want* to know on this earth.' No tribute to Carmilla that she ordered the blow-up but a signal to Pogmoor: an angry manifesto, she would cover nearly one hundred square feet of wall with it, defiantly she would show him her body and Carmilla's every time he came into the room. He alone would understand *whose* bodies and why she put them there, for she knew that the faces were so lit and painted as not to be recognisable. (Carmilla would understand too; but Carmilla was not coming back; Carmilla would never see it.) 'Okay,' she said, 'what's the total?'

Chudd told her. An exorbitant sum, including damage to the light-unit, a buckled step on the aluminium ladder, a great L-shaped rip in Chudd's underskirt, and the cocaine which all three had consumed. Without comment, Leonore wrote the cheque (mad! it would empty her bank-balance); and then sat silent while Chudd went and came, clearing the gear in several journeys to her van. As she left the room on the last of these, she turned her head sharply, to bark out a laugh: 'That's it then?' she asked.

'That's it. Thanks for the bath.'

'That's where it's at, cow, that's where it's fucking at.'

The session was over. End, dead, kaput.

17

Shortly after midday, in Pogmoor's room upstairs, Leonore told Pogmoor, 'I want you to leave. I don't want argument. I want you to leave this afternoon. I don't want explanations. I don't want to know what you and Costello had between you at Pomfretshire or anywhere else. I don't want expostulations. And I don't want hostility. I want you to leave this afternoon, and not to come back, ever. Except as a friend of Fid's, if you *are* a friend of Fid's, and then you'll be a friend of mine. Just now, you see, you're not. But I don't want an enemy. Please.'

Pogmoor opened his mouth to argue, to expostulate, to explain. But he looked at her face first, and so saw how she was looking at him; he closed his mouth, growled, shrugged, and turned away to find suitcases.

She would have said nothing more, but there was one thing she *had* to ask. 'How come you told me that you never played rough?'

He already seemed ashamed; at her question he shrank, he almost folded up, a broad heavy man giving a close imitation of a dried-up onion with its inside all gone bad. He stammered and cleared his throat, he took off his glasses, he twitched his head this way and that. If Chudd had noticed *her* shaking, now *she* could see Jack Juggler on the verge of breaking asunder. What was wrong with the great booby? At last he found an answer, but to be sure it gave her nothing: 'There are times,' he said, 'there *were* times . . . Bloody hell, I don't have to tell *you!*'

The last spoken words of their marriage. But that evening when he had gone from the house and taken his movables with him, she found a letter on the occasional-table in the front hall. He'd addressed it to 'Madame Serlio'; it began very pompously – Pogmoor was capable of the utmost pomposity when he found himself backed into a corner –

> After considerable interior ratiocination, I have decided to write to you *honestly*.
>
> I hate and I fear the deception of women. I admit you have never *tried* to deceive.
>
> I suspected from the beginning that our marriage was a mistake. But the factors of error were always apparent, indeed you laid them open (from the beginning). You were honest, *Caveat emptor*: I was clearly to be put at an absurd disadvantage, by –
>
> 1) The disparity of our ages.
>
> 2) Your zeal to pile upon me the premature fardels of fatherhood.
>
> 3) Your curious delusion that the décor of a play should

determine all ingredients of its production (instead of being but one of them and as flexible as all the others).

4) Your singular sexual experience, never entirely comprehensible to me, but unilaterally rigged up in the prompt-corner of our relationship as a sort of measuring-post against which I seemed always too *short*.

5) *(– or should it be 4a?)* Your brother. You quarrelled with him and immediately proposed to me. For which of his qualities, his achievements, his activities, his unspoken and unspeakable numinosities, was I expected to stand in as his *understudy*?

Eh what? did he mean he had always known about Fid and herself? At any rate, always *guessed* at it? She read and re-read item 5 (or 4a), several times over; that was certainly the meaning he intended her to take, why else should he say 'numinosities'? She went to a dictionary. *Numinous: suffused with feeling of a divinity.* Was that or was it not a Jack Juggler euphemism for 'orgasm'? And coupled to 'unspeakable'—? Oh yes! he *did* mean.

In which case, he hadn't minded. Oh, he minded *now* all right, but *now* was not *then*. She need never have feared the poison-pen letter. She could have *laughed* at Carmilla's betrayal – no, she couldn't! for Carmilla had believed herself to be holding a lethal weapon, she was happy to use it, her essential virulence remained unmitigated, the wounds on her sly body from Leonore's furious hands were justified, oh yes they *were*.

But then came the thought – if he'd known it all the time, why hadn't he said? Because quietly, carefully, he had concealed and *saved up* his knowledge of her secret to use it against her if ever occasion served. His malice lay in wait for her, yes? Okay, to send him packing was justified, justified! She'd always thought him treacherous: now she had proof. (As treacherous as Carmilla; the mask pulled off both of them and all in the one short day. Jesus! but it was as well she found out.)

And now came a rapid change of the letter's tone – pomposity mutating into something like hysteria – lecherous hysteria at that:

> D'you think I was *jealous* of HER? Because she slid about starkers with you in front of a camera? You've always played such games, why *should* I be bloody jealous? No! And you'd better believe it. The other day on the phone – if you'd said to me, 'Don't arrive too early, there's a lesbian photocall and we want to be private,' I'd not have left Manchester till well after lunch. Or else I'd have asked you, 'Why don't I come and watch?' You well know you'd have been worth watching, all floral from tit to toe, golden skin, green leaves, gilded nipples?
>
> That's to say, if it had been anyone but HER.

Not jealous, not an ounce of it! just rage, hate, and frenzy that SHE should have made you one of her marks; and I know why she marked you; because years ago, years! she marked *me*; she wanted to get at me, I don't know why – I tell you, I don't know why, so don't ask. She *dreams* things, she dreams other people's dreams, she's quite mad. She's mad enough to make *me* mad. *You* went for her tooth-and-nail, she made you as mad as I was, so let's have no damn nonsense about 'Oh, I never knew you played rough!' I don't know what she meant about 'swords'. I do *not* know what she meant about swords, she dreams about cutting people up, paps and arses, blood and sperm, whirlpools. She's foul and she's mad. Look, you don't have to see me ever again; but I beg you, don't see HER.

Carmilla meant nothing about swords! 'Swords' had been Pogmoor's word. But 'whirlpools'? 'Blood and sperm'? Leonore began to wonder, was another poison-pen on its way, from Pomfretshire like the first one, to tell about Jack Juggler? Because Jack had his secrets too, and if these were accurate hints at them, he had even better reason to hide them than *she* had.

And yet, she still wished, for no possible good reason, to be friends with the fulminating clod. To love Fid and be friends with Pogmoor. Despite everything, the work that she and Pogmoor did together had been good work – not only because the critics said so – she *knew* it, deep down in her, somewhere (so she told herself) in between her crooked little heart and her bloody useless womb.

Was her work with Carmilla good? If it was, she was an idiot to have brought it to an end. But inside her, deep down, between yearning womb and battered heart, she was – oh, let her face it! – she was not at all sure.

And Pogmoor had a vile crafty needle to stick into *that* vein, hadn't he? See how he signed himself off!

—I think I shouldn't have attempted this letter – except I *do* need – it's important to me if not to you – vital – I *do* need to let you know that I DO NOT accuse *you* of deceiving me, not you, you were never one of THEM! I knew what I was marrying and I fell for it – because of the work, it was GOOD WORK! – it should continue.

But this Plymouth job – oh no. Shift yourself out of it, wry-mouth! Reactionary crap – we know all about Prosser and his sponsors – well, *I* do, surely *you* do? – the devil trying to nick our best tunes—

they do *not* understand your work—

> all they know is how to pocket your name.
> They don't deserve it, get it back.
>
> *See you! JJ.*

He was a very very troublesome man; but she would *not* let him ruin her life. If she thought about him and his juggling any more, that's exactly what he'd do. So forget him. Forget Carmilla. Let them both be mad together but a long way off, a long way off – *please!*

So evil to sleep with those you could not like. Why *did* she do it?

18

Unwillingly, resentfully, like a miserable seven-year-old dragged upstairs to be punished, she did most seriously consider Pogmoor's strictures about Plymouth. She did not shift herself out of it; instead, and before she had had time to make up her mind, Plymouth shifted *her*, and gave her no chance to argue. On April 28th, Friday, two days before Carmilla announced the idea of her 'surprise', she (Carmilla) had wandered into a restricted area of the naval dockyard. Perhaps by accident, perhaps not; it was no part of her brief from Leonore. The police picked her up and held her for questioning for a couple of hours. She established her identity and her connection with the festival; they let her go, with a warning. On her return to London she did not think fit to tell Leonore. She had had one of her bad frights, she thought Leonore might sack her, she must have worked hard all the way back to London to delete the mistake from her history.

But the Ministry of Defence Police did not delete it. On an afterthought, they ran her name through files, and then asked for it to be run through the secret files of the Special Branch. The Branch must have come up with a cross-reference to Sam Rammit. (Or so Leonore realises, in 1992.) The Branch got in touch with the Plymouth politician who was organising the festival. They probably did no more than breathe the word 'subversive'; he was not the sort of citizen to demand they should justify it; he immediately told Prosser to get rid of her forthwith. Prosser rang Leonore; and reported back to his politician to say that he understood the woman Costello to be no longer employed on the contract. But Leonore had wilfully hired her; and Leonore was therefore *marked*, if not as a subversive herself, then certainly as a person whose judgement of subversives could not be depended upon. The IRA bomb at Aldershot had only recently gone off, asinine murders of five women-cleaners, a clergyman, a gardener, by way of a botched reprisal against the paras for Bloody Sunday; nor was it many months since

British revolutionist bombers (the 'Angry Brigade') had been hustled off
to gaol; no one was to be allowed to take chances. Prosser blustered
about free expression but was curtly instructed to stuff it, he was an
intellectual wet, he was an airy-fairy do-gooder, he was soft on
saboteurs. His own contract would be under review.

Again he rang Leonore, to tell her he could not keep her on the job.
She informed him she was intending to resign anyway, thank you very
much; and now she could safely fuck off without fear of being sued for
breach of contract.

Two weeks later it was announced that the festival was postponed:
financial problems had arisen, Plymouth patriotism must accommodate
itself to the major national need, monetary retrenchment. Prosser
disappeared, to be next heard of on a Mediterranean yachting trip with a
typist; and Leonore asked Lewis Hinge (still her solicitor in personal
matters) to initiate legal action to get back all the money she had laid out
on materials for the décor. Hinge said she hadn't a hope.

Another two weeks, and Carmilla was among those lifted in a drugs-
bust at a flat in Hackney. It was rumoured that Chudd had set the fuzz
onto them; Carmilla seemed to owe Chudd a swathe of bread for a dud
dyke-porn photo-gig as well as for her smokes and snorts; and Chudd's
contacts with the drug-squad were notoriously sophisticated. Not that
Carmilla was convicted, or even brought to trial; the Home Office
received an indication from the Special Branch and deported her
without delay to the United States as an 'undesirable'.

19

It all happened twenty years ago; Leonore finds it hard to recall these
long-gone events in sequence, except when a gaudy 'set-piece' is
presented to her mind's eye – thus, for instance, Chudd's Mayday comes
clearly into her consciousness, an intricate tableau filled with vehement
blow-by-blow detail, twopence-coloured like a miniature scene on the
stage of her husband's old toy theatre.

(The toy theatre remained in Antioch Gardens when he left; he did
not bother to pick it up, even though it was his childhood treasure. He
and she were in the middle of making a new ten-minute play for it when
MOUTH-71 disintegrated; he cut it, as it were, adrift; he felt it had
become part and parcel of his married life; as such, he said *goodbye* to it.)

She has been able easily enough to reconstruct what led up to the
tableau, and the tableau's immediate consequences. The difficulty is the
subsequent consequences. She knows she had a hard time getting

enough work quickly enough to keep her solvent. She found the work
before long and immersed herself in it to the exclusion of almost
everything else; she was alone for about a year, she guesses, deliberately
alone, seeking no 'off-duty' companionship, male or female, and
certainly no sex. She thinks of it as the period of her temporary 'nun-
existence', not quite *non*-existence, but pretty damned close to it. She
imposed it on herself as a sort of atonement for Plymouth. She was
wrong to have had that affair with the anguished Carmilla, but she
would never have embarked on it had she not already compromised
herself with Prosser. She thought a lot in those days about her Serlio
grandfather – she began to feel as though she herself had carried the
castor-oil bottle to the Livorno dockside, a female Saul of Tarsus holding
the bigots' coats while they set about lynching St Stephen. She took to
reading the Bible, a book she had rarely opened since her schooldays, a
book she found hard to forgive. It had been an instrument of tyranny in
the hand of her aunt; now she began to explore other uses for it. Not so
much to 'find God', as to find *herself* by contemplation of other people's
search for God – or, for that matter, their sturdy defiance of God, their
incorrigible evasion of his irresponsible demands. Jezebel interested
her. Judas made fertile her imagination. She wished she could have had
a word with Delilah. Jael and Cain caused her to shudder – why should
one be congratulated and the other thrust out into the wilderness? Did
Bathsheba ever know how her husband came to be Killed in Action?
And what exactly happened to make Potiphar's wife cry 'rape'?

Then came a slow process, shorn of memorable tableaux, whereby
imperceptibly Fid, Pogmoor and herself achieved a cautious reconcilement. This was penny-plain, not twopence-coloured: taciturn forget-
tings, tentative approaches, undemonstrative small acts of forgiveness.

She does remember two specific *junctures*, after each of which a
definite shift of attitudes was apparent.

Pogmoor suddenly wrote to her, enclosing a new draft of the
abandoned toy-theatre play, he had finished it on his own – would she
like to draw the scenes and figures? She wrote back – 'yes'.

❧ It was a sardonic paraphrase of *The Wife of Bath's Tale* from Chaucer:
how a knight of the Round Table, condemned for rape, is granted his life
by Queen Guenever on condition he can solve the riddle, 'What thing is
it that wommen most desyren?' After long and fruitless search for the
answer, he meets a hideous hag who tells it to him – 'Wommen desyren
to have sovereyntee.' The death-sentence is withdrawn: but then he has
to keep his promise to the hag, to defer to *her* sovereignty. She exercises
it by demanding he marry her. Appalled, he submits; he shares her

repulsive bed; he forces himself to make love to her; lo! she is young and beautiful. ❧

Originally, in Manchester, this story had been Leonore's choice, a rather frantic plaything to distract her (and indeed Pogmoor) from her jejune affair with Bill Saltmarsh. Saltmarsh had *not* fulfilled her hopes, she had *not* conceived his child, nor did it look as though she were going to: and yet she still clutched at him. *And* he was young enough to be the son she would never have. ('Repulsive bed', oh yes: but where was the magical 'lo!'?) Pogmoor in those days had been rudely offhand both towards Chaucer's tale and Leonore's emotions. Now, it seemed, his mind was changed, at least as regards the story. His new script was very sceptical, even within the rudimentary limitations of the toy-theatre form. For example, it implied that the charge of rape was a frame-up and Guenever knew it but went along with it because otherwise her own adultery with Sir Lancelot would have been exposed; nonetheless it gave scope for witty little drawings in the style of fourteenth-century manuscript illuminations; Leonore was very happy to busy herself with them. And of course Pogmoor had to come along to have a look.

Once he was in the house on wary collaborative terms, if only for an hour or so at a time, it was hard to retain ill-feeling. And soon he began to drop in without reference to the toy theatre. The marital break-up was not discussed on these occasions. Lewis Hinge (in consultation with Fidelio and Fidelio's accountant) was sorting things out at a proper distance; Pogmoor's lawyer dealt with Lewis; Leonore's property and income had never been merged with Pogmoor's, so there were no very rancorous difficulties; nor was it necessary for Leonore to meet Fidelio.

Until one day Fidelio rang her up. He said he thought the house in Highbury could advantageously be sold, would she talk to him about it?

When was this exactly? Probably well on in 1973: but Fid's recollection of it is no more precise than hers. It was a strange period in the lives of both of them – neither of them, on the surface, committed to anything very much; both of them suffering hangovers after a surfeit of impetuosity—

(xxiv)   'Behold, it was Leah.'

I needed money very badly, what with the libel suit and its wretched
consequences. I had bad associations with 8 Malthus Terrace and you had
no associations at all. So why not sell it?

But our two houses were all that was left to us of the original House of Serlio; they were not to be disposed of upon accountants' advice or lawyers'; you and I must meet, face-to-face. You agreed.

Malthus Terrace was in your name by then, so it must be you to put it on the market. The legal device was thought up in order to save it; now it was a question of saving *me*. And yourself, indeed; I had heard that after you'd had the decent good sense to unhitch your boat from that cut-price Captain Hornblower down in Plymouth, your name became slightly blotched – 'she doesn't hold true to her contracts', etc. – and some sort of a hint of subversion which I didn't understand – the Dirty Tricks department was making free with you, I suspect – people you had snubbed had spooks to do their business for them? Whatever it might have been, you were in much the same plight as I was; we needed to put our heads together.

I was rather surprised you decided to make no bones about it. You said to come round and see you, so I came. I found Jack there. At least I think I found him there; his toy theatre was certainly there, maybe he called later in the evening? For an instant I thought you were living together again – my plot had come to nothing! – but then you told me the upstairs space was vacant, and brought me there for our chat. I wondered if this was a hint. Particularly when you proved so compliant about selling Malthus Terrace; I had not expected it. If there were legal problems relating to the Brewster case, Lewis would deal with them, you said. You were very cool and easy – frigid, almost, but not hostile.

Then we all three had supper together, you, me, Jack, talking coolly and easily about anything but our own inner feelings. Well; it was a fresh start, after a fashion. An odd sort of conversation, though. You kept on and on about a biblical anecdote that somehow had caught your fancy, Jacob and Rachel, how he so patiently served her father for seven long years before he could marry her, and then found that his veiled bride was in fact her sister Leah. In the end he got Rachel but at the expense of seven more years. Patience and hard labour. Were you directing this at me or at Jack? I could not be certain. But you did repeat, as I left the house to go back to Highbury, that the upstairs flat was vacant. Jack left the house at the same time, I was relieved to observe, on his way to Chelsea – Whitesmith Street off the King's Road, a new flat, he said. You managed to suggest he'd been living there for some time. You did not need to tell him what he already knew, you must have intended the information for me.

So I took you at your intention and turned up two days later with my baggage. You just said, 'Here you are then, I expected you yesterday. The electricity's been turned on and the telephone's connected. If you need anything, give me a knock.'

There I was, reinstalled. It was all very painless.

Two years, was it? that we lived there, working, me upstairs, you down, never getting in each other's way, not quite at arm's length, but not holding hands either. You did pluck a series of moderately prosperous jobs for yourself out of the general stewpot, none of them spectacular enhancements of your prestige, none of them to your discredit. (I *was* glad about your Plymouth failure: we all have to whore a little in our business, that's understood, but we don't have to do it in the absolute gutter.) We sometimes went out together, brother and sister, very correctly, demurely, to a show or a film or concert, to a restaurant, to walk on Hampstead Heath.

One night you asked me in to your flat for a drink after the theatre. One drink became several; and at last you said, 'Bedtime.' I was fool enough to think you meant it, I put my arm round you to bring you into your sunflower alcove, but you checked me with an unexpectedly strong hand against my chest. 'No,' you said, 'don't. This is Leah,' you said, 'not Rachel. Upstairs, Fid. Go.' I deserved it, did I not?

Patience; and hard labour. If Jacob could do it, I could. Could *you*? I asked no questions about your personal life; I know various friends, male and female, came now and then to your door; more of them and more often as time went on; I tried not to feel morbid about them. I looked up the story in Genesis: 'Leah was tender eyed; but Rachel was beautiful and well favoured.' I'm not too certain that your eyes *were* tender just at that moment; implacable, I'd have thought. But they'd been tender most of the evening, so I had to remember that and make do with my memory. The book also says, 'Leah was hated.' Yes, that had been true when I first went out to Highbury. Not any more.

'Let's pack it in.' Three or four years since you'd astonished me with those words; it seemed a whole generation ago. But my anonymous letter had undone your betrayal-by-marriage (I don't need to regret it, you were a far better woman once Jack Juggler skidded from under you); your professional betrayal (MOUTH-71) had undone itself, and Brewster's lawyers made sure of it. I now had no vindictive reason for resenting your withdrawal from me, so I loved you and accepted it and lived like a monk. Well, not entirely like a monk. There were *liaisons*, not important, I kept them quiet, I won't list them.

I got on with my writing and tried to market it. I offered the BBC a couple of radio plays dealing with Ireland – 'Do remember, Mr Carver, our drama will be accessible to listeners in Ulster, we cannot present anything that might *inflame* the situation there . . .' Statement of policy from a very high official: does he now suppose the 'situation there' to be noticeably quenched, seeing he rejected both my scripts and yet had the nerve to tell me they were excellent strong pieces? One TV play was accepted, a gloomy sixty minutes about the suicide of a gay clergyman. The Sheffield Crucible Theatre put on a bloodyminded crosspatch fragment of psycho-history in which I'd tried to probe the private life of Oliver Cromwell; and Jack directed it without much flair (but I doubt if anyone else could have done it better); you were not available as designer. I sketched and scratched at a sequence of grotesque one-acters, in the Gothic manner of Ghelderode, contrasting fables of mistaken identity: I fancy you and Jack had given me the idea with your toy-theatre playlet. But I never got them to come together, they are even today a work-in-progress somewhere at the back of my filing-cabinet. At least, I was still at it. Aged forty-two and as grey and decayed as a Hemingway fisherman, rowing through the doldrums with never a wind to catch my sail, industriously sweating myself to no apparent purpose. Until I thought of the Napoleon story: and all at once came all alive again.

(I seem regularly to be 'coming all alive again' – I came all alive when I joined VEXACTION, I came all alive when I got stuck in to *Poison-Voices*, I daresay I'm a manic-depressive? No! I'm just a writer, that's all that I am, it's the rhythm of the job, you could call it Fair Wear-and-Tear.)

(xxv)   Off at a Tangent

Whereupon Jack killed me dead by going off at one of his tangents,
croaking his bogus broad Yorkshire and swerving himself around till he
fetched up with Eugene Aram.

He said he'd had a dream. We all of us have dreams. *I* have bloody dreams.

No, it was more than dreams. It started in 1975 with that *White Devil* the RSC were tempting him with. A big boastful Jacobean job, with the full resources of the company, a flagship production; he could not resist it. However much he claimed to be gasping to work with me again, he was unable to regard me as *imperative* – my Cromwell play had convinced him I was something of a late-'50s has-been – he had been very annoyed that that production had not had better notices – he refused to blame himself. He would work with me (oh yes) if he had to – but if Stratford wanted him for Webster, then he didn't have to, did he? Fid Carver was a nice guy but quite at his ease dangling for ever on the long finger, slowly twisting in the wind, no trouble to anybody, dear Fid. While Jack Juggler in those years was ton-up along the crown of the highway.

He offered me a handful of prospective largesse: if he could do well with *The White Devil*, then he'd have thrust a good stout foot into the RSC for both of us. *The Emperor's Whore* (once it was written; I hadn't even started it at that stage!) would be sure of a place there, we needed an upmarket production if all my bright ideas for the story were to come to full harvest. I didn't argue; I crossed my fingers and muttered, 'That'll be the day.' I just crossed a pair of fingers and thought, 'Upmarket? After VEXACTION, after *Poison-Voices*, do I believe in upmarket any more? Or at any rate, do I believe in such phenomena for *me*?' I was thoroughly indecisive; Jack knew I was indecisive; isn't that why he was telling me his lies?

And then he dropped the Webster. Quite unexpected; it caused talk; was he having a nervous breakdown? Certainly there was something very odd going on with him. I found a clue to it in due time: I'll come round to that later. I want to talk about Eugene Aram.

Amateurs in North Yorkshire? It couldn't be a nervous break-down, or he wouldn't have embarked on any new work at all. Jack was neither a fool, nor a professional messer. Everything he undertook, he intended to go into with his utmost, I'll grant him that. So it was not credible he embraced this cultural project of the rural middle classes as a rest-cure. Amateur or not, it was nonetheless a *project*, and he'd give it all he'd got. Perhaps he felt he needed to revitalise; the same stirrings that I'd had when I pressed myself on VEXACTION. Or perhaps, as he attempted to tell me, the Aram story appealed to him as a dry run for my St Helena play. (The last thing he said to me, before he went up north, was that he thought I should find a new title. '*The Emperor's Whore* won't do, Fid. Nay, I can't tell you why; I just *feel* it. Don't you?')

But the Aram story and the Napoleon story were not the same story at all.

Did Eugene really believe he had covered all his tracks? He cannot have believed it. What, to murder a man in Yorkshire, bury the body, and sod off to Norfolk without even changing his name? Such a jackass didn't deserve to have a play written about him two hundred years later. No, his psychology was far far queerer than that. He must have known, *must!* that the buried bones, like *all* buried bones, like the Dry Bones in Ezekiel's valley, could be called up to life in the twinkling of an eye, at the clang of an invisible trumpet:

—behold a shaking, and the bones came together, bone to his bone. And the breath came into them, and they lived, and stood up upon their feet, an exceeding great army.

Fourteen years they had waited underground, assembling their accusation. As long as Eugene lived, they had something to say to him and oh! he was very well aware of it. And now, such an age after his death, they are saying it, daily, to *me*.

(xxvi)   Iron Mask

Today the Schizo-Phantasist hauls them out into the glare and the eyes of my mind are blinded.

I besought Pogmoor to leave Eugene Aram alone; but how could I beseech him with any plausibility, any rational argument that would carry conviction? How was *he* to know that once he'd spoken of this project, *and for all of the time that he continued to speak of it* (let alone work at it), it would clamp my skull, shut my mouth, break the teeth in my bleeding gums, compress my throbbing temples, the Iron Mask of a torture-crypt in a Gothick Romance?

Now, today, the shock once more. Repeated, redoubled. The Schizo-Phantasist has crept out of the shadows like an ogre from his den, to poke, prod and pierce and to utterly dismantle my—

(The end of the chapter disintegrates into a mass of deletions; the carriage of Carver's typewriter has apparently stuck, and the ribbon as well; words are typed and retyped one upon the other, some of them without sufficient ink. The sheet of paper is crumpled and ragged. It seems to have been jammed in the roller and torn free with a violent pull.)

20

Leonore cannot continue with all these pages yet to be read, scores of them, more of them, all over her black-and-yellow duvet. She strews them away from her, worn out by the burden of each cumulative paragraph.

Maybe later. After a sleep. She gets up to go to the bathroom, to hunt for sleeping-pills. Surely there are some left over, from that period of tension last year? Ah! here they are. As she puts on her spectacles to make out the very small print of the label, she is beginning to wonder, should she give herself an overdose? No: not tonight, at least. She must first come to the end of Fidelio's letter. After that, perhaps tomorrow, after breakfast or after lunch, she'll reconnect herself and have a think, she'll consider it again.

For tonight, nothing worse than a grapple with sleep. Could *anything* be worse than sleep, if she dreams as she fears she will dream?

Third Tale

How Leonore's Dream
Gave Shape to
Eugene Aram
(1992)

Lady, you see into what hands you are fall'n;
'Mongst what a nest of villains! and how near
Your honour was t'have catched a certain clap,
Through your credulity . . .

(Ben Jonson, *The Alchemist*)

Or, if you will, how Leonore's dream gave shape to Cordelia.

For the overriding image, the continuous voice through her twelve hours' drug-induced slumber, is of this small and eager woman at a candlelit writing-desk. Leonore knows nothing about her, has never even heard of her, but from the start of the dream she fully understands that this is 1766, that Miss Cordelia Pole-Hatchet has been a friend of Eugene Aram, that she is inditing her memories of him, and that somehow – apparently without speaking aloud, for her lips do not move – she sends every word of them into Leonore's ear. A quill-pen flashes over quires of bright white paper; Cordelia's face and moving hands are as bright as the paper in the golden pool of candlelight. Beyond and all around is thick black dark.

Cordelia (at a guess) is forty-odd years old, dressed in a plain grey gown, her abundant auburn hair pinned up neatly at the back of her head under a little white cap. She wears light spectacles with tinted lenses, which now and then slip down her nose and have to be jerked into place with a fillip of the fingers. Sometimes she is not writing: Leonore seems to see her at an easel, painting in watercolour; or at a polished bench, handling chemical apparatus, retorts, test-tubes and so forth; or out on the leads of a house-roof under the stars, peering upwards through her slim telescope on its elegant tripod. Again, the pair of candlesticks will be placed upon a harpsichord, and Cordelia is making music. But all the time the narrative runs on: a vivid quick flow of meticulous words, presented with all the certainty of long-considered fact. As her story proceeds, its images become the images of the dream.

It should be said: Leonore's knowledge of Eugene Aram does not go beyond those fragments she picked up from Fidelio's disturbed talk when Jack Pogmoor went to Knaresborough. Nearly all that she hears in the dream is quite new to her. She believes it, every word, even to names, dates and places, which may well be fallacious – she knows (in her dream) they may be fallacious, yet still she believes, in the way that dreamers will. She believes it: she watches it happen.

1

It is now seven years since the late unfortunate Mr Aram was apprehended by officers of justice and conveyed away from King's Lynn. Concerning his fifteen months' sojourn here, his fruitful membership of the King's Lynn Philosophical, Historical and Literary Society, his intercourse with the other members (not least, with myself), and the impression of his character as generally bestowed during that time upon the citizens of our fenland seaport, I am commissioned by the ladies and gentle-men of the Society to render a complete memorial – insofar as my own recollections may be considered even-handed and accurate. The said memorial to be submitted, under a dignified dedication, to the Hon. Horace Walpole, Esq., of Strawberry Hill, Twickenham, our distinguished Member of Parliament and renowned connoisseur of the historical, the marvellous and the grotesque. Mr Walpole's recent and sensational fiction, *The Castle of Otranto*, encourages us to hope that this true tale of a former constituent will agreeably stir his fantasy, even to persuading him that there lie hidden in the arcadias of rural England events no less horrid and strange than those which his muse has drawn from the mysteries of a popish continent.

The Society, moreover, in sponsoring my humble pen, has laboured to refute the demeaning accusation that Mr Aram's crime was in some inexplicable way connived at or concealed by any of its members or associates; or that we in Lynn did not, and still do not, accept the evidence produced against him before the Jury of his peers. He came amongst us, as we thought, a man of clear conscience. His parts of scholarship were manifest, his manners unusual but specious, his conduct to all appearances beyond reproach. I must confess that, upon first hearing that most terrible indictment against him, I was perfectly incredulous; as I know were many others. I read, in the news-sheets, the testimony of the prosecution and his own argument of defence; I maintained (for a brief period) that the latter must surely prevail; and yet I could not but remember certain instances, certain untoward signs, certain *portents* even, which thrillingly gave me pause. In short, by the time the learned judge delivered his charge, I was fully convinced of the prisoner's guilt. He had slain, he had concealed his deed, for fourteen years his immortal soul had lain buried in falsehood even as his victim rotted underground with never a prayer said over him. Moreover, I was strongly angered that he had so insidiously betrayed my maiden confidence; I rejoiced to be informed first of the verdict and thereafter the sentence.

'Whoso sheddeth a man's blood, by man shall his blood be shed.'

The red offence of Mr Aram had incarnadined all our names; we were in a manner *implicated*; it is my sombre duty now to cleanse us in the course of this veracious report.

Nota bene:

Before accepting the said duty, I laid down a certain condition. If truth is to be told, it is to be *my* truth, in accordance with the perceptions of *my* character, for it is *my* hand (not those of the Society in committee) that sets a-flow the ink upon the page. In order to cleanse from one attributed fault, we must first be fully scoured of all other: these papers shall not lie open to suspicion of genteel euphemism. The corollary, therefore, is possible hurt caused to excellent individuals by my portraying them in a less than dignified light. I have a reputation (slight but well-attested) for the *feminine trick* of pleasant satire. I think it harmless but salutary; I wish to tickle rather than wound; I apologise in advance without any admission that such apology needs to be proffered.

2

It is no more than fitting that I should be the one to give this story to the *literati* of our island kingdom. I was more closely acquainted with its subject than any other in Lynn, save perhaps for my much wronged brother, the Rev. Paulinus Pole-Hatchet, D.D., sometime Master of St Guthlac's Academy. Because poor Paulinus was the man who indeed brought Mr Aram to the town (induced thereto by most excellent recommendations from masters of schools in our metropolis and elsewhere), he necessarily bore the brunt of the subsequent revelation; his health broke; he must give up his pupils and take to his bed after an apoplectic stroke, and so he remains to this day, helplessly in need of my unremitting care.

I well remember the day of Mr Aram's arrival, soon after our Christmas holiday of 1757. Paulinus had written to him in care of the establishment where he was last employed, saying, 'So and so are the staged coaches you should take to Lynn from London, they discharge at the Duke's Head inn, inform me of the day of your journey and my sister or one of my people will greet you there and bring you to the Academy.' He could not go to the inn himself lest his classes be disrupted, he having no assistant since the unexpected illness of Mr Overton; the very reason indeed of his sudden search for a new man. Although I took my turn in instructing the boys, I could be spared on that particular morning, so off with me to the Duke's Head some ten minutes or twenty before the advertised coming of the coach. It was two hours late, by reason of the heavy snow.

Eight frozen passengers dismounted. Only one of them seemed likely to be the scholar I looked for, a severe personage in black with a most carefully curled and powdered wig and a pair of horn spectacles. To whom I advanced myself, all smiles, only to be taken – I blush to say it! – for a trull of the waterfront about to board and seize a prize. 'Jezebel, avaunt!' I declare he cried at me. 'Is this the filthy welcome King's Lynn affords its aspirant physicians?'

(He was none other, as it turned out, than young Doctor McCoy, whom soon we were all to know so well as a devoted member of our Society. But at that time he was aloof and diffident, apprehensive of his position among strangers, fearful of what he had ever been told were the loose morals of an English harbour-town, homesick indeed for the sturdy right-eousness of his native Londonderry.)

Hardly had I disembarrassed myself of the deleterious impu-tation when a most maladroit individual uncoiled himself into the snow from the very baggage-basket at rear of the coach, long thin shanks like spider's-legs groping in all directions for the step, one hand wavering in the air with an unwieldy portman-teau, while the other clutched a broad-brimmed soft flat hat in the execution of a sort of man-o'-war's flag-signal. His clothes were appropriately subfusc, and clean enough to be sure, but crumpled and ill-fitting as though flung in error upon the wrong body. I dare say for his disproportionate limbs no garments could be found to suit, unless measured and made by a master-tailor too costly for impoverished scholars to frequent; at all events Mr Aram, in all the time I knew him, never dressed himself other than as a scarecrow. He was tall beyond ordinary; he stooped. His features, pitted with the scars of smallpox, were gaunt and almost fanatical, as I might picture St Guthlac himself (patron-spirit of our Academy, he who dwelt solitary in the days of the old Saxons, a moping hermit of the hostile fen). I took him to be of early middle age, no more than six or seven years older than myself. In fact he was fifty-four. If he seemed less, it was because he wore his own ungrizzled hair, cut too short for a queue, and he rarely troubled to powder it – a barbarously plebeian affectation which did not at first sight encourage favour.

'My old dad,' he used to say, with his accustomed Yorkshire roughness, 'was a crop-headed gardener in shirt-sleeves and sackcloth apron, why should *I* make pretence of a better habit? He knew flowers, edible herbs, root-vegetables. I know books, that's all the difference. If we thrive, it's for our knowledge, not our mode. Take me or leave me.' And then he would laugh.

By his laughter, he was transformed. He laughed now, in the Duke's Head yard, at the awkwardness of his own descent from the cheapest compartment of the coach (where he must, by-the-by, have suffered excess of cold); and, worse, at *my* mistake with Dr McCoy which alas he had both seen and heard. His hilarity for the moment offended me; but I discerned such good nature in it, I was forced to laugh with him. By the time we had climbed into the Academy's four-wheeled chaise and John Lobscott had whipped up the horse to drive us home, we were already warm friends (I believed), although I must admit to a *guardedness* as to how my good brother would receive him. Paulinus was ever a stickler for correctness of deportment and decency of the outward man. 'We teach our boys to be gentlemen,' he would pronounce to their parents. 'Scholarship that lacks the graces is an ugly distortion, as misplaced as mere foppery without intellect to stiffen it. We attempt, above all, to inculcate Balance.'

3

To pronounce myself 'warm friends' with one of the opposite sex, so soon upon our first meeting, lays me open (I cannot deny) to a charge of forwardness: but pray consider my situation. My father, a country curate, exhausted his savings in the education of Paulinus at Cambridge; thus was I left with no fortune to bring to a husband. Neither did I possess those charms that of themselves attract suitors. Before I was six-and-twenty I had resigned myself to lifelong spinsterhood. But I did not repine; I had ever a love of learning and an aptitude thereto; Paulinus established his Academy; he showed no inclination toward matrimony; why should I not join him as housekeeper and scholastic amanuensis? The politer people of Lynn were, within their limits, both cordial and cultivated; we came together often in our modest Society for the improvement of our mental powers; I had all that I believed essential to fulfil my aspirations. Nay, a woman of independent accomplishment may be the better for a dearth of suitors, knowing how ill her amorous expectations must ride with an authentic zeal for enlightenment. I could count myself happy in my state, that of a Blue Stocking (to employ the cant expression) who already approached the meridian age of thirty-five.

And yet not happy: it is hard to find friendship where love has been renounced. There was a dryness. In the end – and it grieves me to admit the fact – it had almost become a burden. The good humour of any gentleman, any *man* indeed, who might rally me at sight uninfluenced by long acquaintance, was immediately grateful to my spirit. No doubt I received the same with a rashness most fit to be condemned.

Mr Aram made me laugh: he laughed again, and so did I.

My fears as to my brother's reception of him were not confirmed. After a short and most natural shock at his appearance and manners, Paulinus speedily recognised the true depth of his auxiliary's attainments. For Mr Aram proved more than an acquisition to any mere grammar school; he was a scholar in his own right, a philological theorist of the highest rank, and that without benefit of either university – indeed without recognition *from* either university, a circumstance which had long soured him. He would frequently denounce 'the bed-bugs of Oxford and Cambridge', by which he meant the slovenly dons. He knew he was greater than any of them.

Several days after his arrival, the stage-wagon delivered his books to our door, great cases of deal boards, an entire library outnumbering even Paulinus's pedagogical collection: many of its volumes (I believe) of some rarity. He said he needed them not for his teaching but his writing: he had already a large treatise more than halfway completed, *Aram's Comparative Lexicon*, modern and ancient, of English, Celtic, Latin, Greek and Hebrew. The Celtic was his particular delight, whether in its Gaelic, Welsh or Breton variants; he sought to demonstrate its relation to all tongues derived from the Latin, together with certain tributary admixtures from the Greek, an argument strongly opposed by conventional scholarship. No less in controversion of accepted points of view was his insistence that Greek did not give birth to Latin; rather had both languages their independent sources (as also the Celtic) in some aboriginal speech hitherto unidentified – perhaps, he suggested, Persian or even Sanskrit, were it possible to trace them back to their own primitive origins. He held a vast correspondence with servants of the East India Company, unhappily with small result: our merchants and soldiers in the Orient knew curt ejaculations for the turning of sharp bargains, the anathematising of lazy natives or the softening of brown-skinned damsels toward lecherous ecstasy, but had neither interest nor skill in the intricacies of verbal roots.

All this I had direct from Mr Aram's own lips in the hours set aside from schoolroom curriculum. His enthusiasm, reciprocated and re-enkindled by mine, knew no bounds: he achieved what I might call the very merriment of devoted learning. So hearty a contrast to my heedful and plodding brother! Paulinus, though most dear to me, was in no sense a man of intellectual spark. He knew his books thoroughly and conveyed them with diligence to the boys. Alongside Mr Aram, however, he could only be seen as a pedant.

He discerned it himself; and must have felt an occasional jealousy. At all events, his esteem for Mr Aram was impeded by knobs of suspicion. He took me aside (nigh upon our breaking-up for Easter) to enquire, in a halting voice, 'Cordelia, my love, you are as intimate with our new usher as anyone might lawfully be; has it occurred to you that his vehement mind ought to have fetched him at his present age to a far higher station than that which he occupies? I am cognisant of his having taught at a multiplicity of schools – and each one in a different town. Why did none of them retain him for longer than a few terms?'

I scarce knew how to reply; I too had asked myself the question. There were possible answers, but by no means conclusive, and they threatened to entangle me in tendentious prevarication. My conscience was troubled and I dared not shift the brunt of it upon my already burdened brother.

To come to the problem step-after-step: Mr Aram, though so brisk and jolly, did not seem to have the trick to make himself beloved by more than one or two of the boys – those whose own parts of learning sufficiently responded to his and who therefore became his favourites. With the rest he was hot and impatient, ironical at their expense, a grave mistake in any schoolmaster. They felt a resentment, and expressed it in covert mockery. His meagre flesh and great stature gave him the name amongst them of Long Lankin – from the savage protagonist of one of our old country ballads, which told of atrocious murders committed many years ago by a master-mason defrauded of his fee.

This nickname, innocuous of itself, was not without disquieting consequence. One darkling evening of late winter, it had so chanced I was in my linen-closet; through its window at the side of the school-house I heard some verses of the 'Long Lankin' ditty being sung across the playfield – by little Tommy Whitesmith, imp of mischief indeed, but never a child that intended severe harm. They ran something after this wise:

> Said milord to milady as he mounted his horse:
> 'Beware of Long Lankin what lives in the moss.'
>
> Said milord to milady as he rode away:
> 'Beware of Long Lankin what lives in the hay.
>
> 'Let the doors be all a-bolted and the windows all pinned
> And leave not a hole for a mouse to creep in,'
>
> So the doors was all a-bolted and the windows all pinned
> 'Cept one little window: and Lankin he crept in—

It was a most melancholy tune, and Tommy chanted it with a gruesome glee, his unbroken treble rising high and fierce to match the ferocity of the fable. He was strolling through the dusk arm-in-arm with some young friend – Bob Gotobed the carrier's son, I think. Bob, who had no voice to boast of, listened to the song with admiration and perhaps fear, giving vent to weak titters of laughter.

The playfield was otherwise empty, all the boarders at supper and the day-pupils gone home to their parents. By no extension of the school rules should those two have been then where they were. I was about to call wrathfully down to them and mark their names for Paulinus's report, when I apprehended Mr Aram was there already: suddenly standing, tall and black, against the thin yellow light that yet lingered over the bleak fen to southward and the reaches of the Great Ouse river. (Our school being beyond the edge of town with naught between us and the open levels but a low paling, a drain-dyke and pollard willows in a scanty screen.) I apprehended also that the boys were aware of their usher; and that Tommy sang that song of plain purpose to prick at his ears.

It was often Mr Aram's custom to take his solitary walk when school was over, asking for no companion, and telling no one where he went, whether over the ferry into the pathways of the fen towards Wisbech or Downham Market, or through the dunes in the direction of Hunstanton. Our servants told that now and then the country people would encounter him striding at great pace with clouded brow and bitten lips, arms tight behind his back or in windmill gesticulation as he muttered to himself and grunted beast-like – they said 'spells'. Not at all: for did he not rehearse in his mind the matter of his treatise? such furious brain-work as must always to labouring folk seem uncanny and of no good usage. Upon this particular evening he was just returned from such an exercise; he heard the song as he entered the gate, and paused to listen.

With no warning, he sprang forward, arms out from behind his back like the jaws of a mantrap. He seized the wicked Tommy in their grasp and held him fast. Bob Gotobed uttered a scream, swerved sideward, and fled from the field. Mr Aram paid him no heed; he had the one he sought; he dragged and worried the child willy-nilly across the trodden grass to the door of the Usher's Lodge, a cottage of one storey where he (Mr Aram) had his quarters adjacent to the school-house.

'Boy!' he was crying out in ungovernable passion. 'Boy, you are a viper, a poison-tongue beneath a bush, a fang into my heel, by G–d but I shall teach you conduct!' So straight into the Lodge and the door slammed shut upon them. I could hear the shrieks of Tommy Whitesmith, even within walls; my spirit in an instant sympathy trembled for his terror; at once I abandoned my linen, ran down the stairs, out of the house, toward the Lodge, determined to intervene. My brother was gone into town, there was none other to take action, discipline (I well knew) must of course be maintained, but surely not to harsh extremity. If Mr Aram were immoderate, control should be imposed; my duty, nothing less.

Let me delineate the discipline. My brother laid down strict rules. For heinous misdemeanour he kept a manifold birch-rod with which, at his discretion, *in loco parentis*, he might flog a boy until he bled. The assistant master had no such weapon; a light cane for peremptory correction, that was all. If the cane seemed insufficient, then the delinquent must be sent forthwith to Paulinus with a formal statement requesting the greater chastisement, a ceremony (may I say) but rarely initiated. My brother was ever merciful and encouraged mercy from his subordinate. I was sore afraid that in his rage Mr Aram had forgot his place.

Indeed he had. When I burst into the Lodge I found him with his coat off, all a-sweat with exertion, as he flailed with his cane upon the squirming howling child, striking him promiscuously from the backs of the thighs up the buttocks to shoulders and arms, nay, even unto neck, head and face. If I did not know him better I should have thought him monstrous cruel.

But I could tell well enough this was no calculated spite, rather an unmastered frenzy from I knew not what concealed cause; I could tell well enough he would repent it most bitterly. I caught him by the forearm, caught the cane with my other hand, prevailing with my utmost strength until he came to himself.

'G–d's mercy, Miss Cordelia,' he gasped in his consternation, 'what have I been about, what have I done?'

The tears ran down his cheeks as he bent over the unhappy boy, whom he took in his arms and soothed and cherished. 'Forgive me, my little man, it was too much. Yet surely you had need of some small pain to awaken you to the error of your deed?'

'Deed?' whined sullen Tommy (and reason enough he had to be sullen). 'All I did was sing a song, should you handle me like a madman for that? Just because I'm no d–mned darling of your irregular verbs, like some that I could name? Miss Cordelia, should he handle me? I declare he hath cut my a–se very nigh into three parts! G–d's blood but my father shall be told.'

'Then tell him, Master Whitesmith,' came straightway my sharp answer; I would not brook such oaths and threatenings, even granted the provocation, from a pup-dog of scarce thirteen. 'Tell him if you will; but first I shall not fail to inform Dr Pole-Hatchet; your manifest naughtiness has increased of late so greatly I do not doubt the Master's birch will very soon be brought to hand. How say you to that, young man?'

To which, as I guessed, he had *nothing* to say. He stumbled out of the room, snuffling, and made his way to where he ought in the first place to have been. The Master's birch was a deadly horror; only to name it served to reduce the most unruly. (We were not, after all, an academy like that dreadful Eton, to harden gentle boys into criminal young lordlings by unstinting flagellation and abuse – a true cause, I do believe, of disaffection among the common folk and the violence of the mob against their so-called betters.)

'So now, Mr Aram,' once we were alone, 'I think it were best you should explain yourself to me, and conceivably save yourself an ill scene with my brother. Lord preserve us, sir, were you out of your wits?'

He was slow to speak, breathing heavily. At length he groaned, shook his head several times, and commenced a low-voiced *apologia*.

'Out of my wits, Miss Cordelia? With sorrow I must say, perhaps yes. Are you aware of the nature of that vile and pernicious song-ballad? It makes trivial the foulest of crimes, narrates without compassion the conspiracy of a soulless wretch, vindictive murder for the sake of gold under pretence of extorting justice – of neither victim nor perpetrator does the song say anything good, the one is a mere cheat, the other a bloody brute, nor is the victim even the victim but the innocent wife of the intended victim, innocent wife, innocent child as well, an entire calendar of futile slaughterhouse.

'And this devil-broth of misguided rhyme to sound so sweetly, so angelic, yet so wanton upon the tongue of a stripling who on Sunday in parish church will sing God's Psalms with an equal sweetness? When I heard him I heard Lucifer in the Garden of Paradise, perverting in dulcet tones the very knowledge of good and evil, yea the very knowledge of knowledge itself, for the undoing of our first parents.

'For my immeasurable ire I profess myself truly penitent. I should have considered before I struck. Like Our Gracious Lord Himself I should have allowed myself time to tell myself, "he knows not what he does". Miss Cordelia, what would I not give to make amends to that affectionate confiding child?'

I thought he went too far. Tommy Whitesmith was no doubt affectionate, and perhaps at some time had even been so toward Mr Aram, but he sang the song as an act of mockery. To that degree, most certainly, he *did* know what he did. I said as much.

Mr Aram began to laugh, not quite at first his accustomed merry mirth, more a saturnine growling and rasping; but then his demeanour eased, his mouth loosened, his eyes glowed, and he clapped his bony hands one into the other like a man in good spirits once again. 'Aye, he meant to mock, of course he did, the cunning fellow! All preceptors worth their salt must learn to take jape and jesting from unfledged sparrowkins; why, it's part of our livelihood, no one knows it better than I. D'you think I held it against him? D'you think *that* was the cause of my outbreak? Nay, Miss Cordelia, never. Had Long Lankin – which I'm well aware is the fool's name they have for me – been owt other than a vicious homicide, I could have endured it year upon year without malice or surge of rage. I am for sure of a clumsy shape; I am built to be laughed at; but just now I could not bear that such an ancient murky cruelty should lie behind the laughter. Aye, aye, 'twas very wrong of me. In my heat I did not think. See; I surrender my cane. Will you speak, please, to Dr Pole-Hatchet; tell him upon my honour I do not use it from this day forth.'

He put the rod into my hand, and bowed as though taking his leave . . .

But it was for me to take *my* leave; which (after a while) I did. He had his handkerchief up to his cheek; in the tumult the skin had been cut, from lip's corner to just under the eyelid. You cannot seize a man's cane without *tumult* . . . For myself, I was alarmed, confused, in several sorts of moral quandary.

Back in my closet amid bedsheets and pillowcases I endeavoured most seriously to think. My great liking for Mr Aram had received an abrupt check. Could a man, who had done what I had seen him just now do, continue to be trusted for the guidance of youth? He claimed to have been outraged upon grounds of moral principle: well and good, had the song-ballad been sung by myself or my brother, though even then (I would have said) the morality was over-scrupulous. But when a silly boy gave voice to it, only to be treated as though he planned a murder himself, how could one be reconciled to an outrage so out of proportion? Was Mr Aram a fanatic sectary, pretending to conform to the service of the Established Church in order to obtain employment, yet adhering in private to some outlandish conventicle? Bear in mind, he was a person of peculiar characteristic: neither a gentleman-scholar like Paulinus, nor a common usher (as had been his predecessor) to teach by rote with no true erudition. Who could guess whence such an hybrid might draw notions of divinity? He was as discomfortable as an atheist shoemaker: you knew not what he might say next.

If this should be the case, it were bad enough indeed. But there was even a worse case; one to introduce dismay beneath the roof of any academy. I considered the caresses with which he had comforted the weeping boy, the perfervid words he had let fall – 'affectionate', 'confiding', 'so sweetly, so angelic', 'yet so wanton'. I considered the boy's own phrase, 'd–mned darling of your irregular verbs'. Was it possible Mr Aram might conceal in his bosom unnatural cravings, whereby he would view his pupils with an eye of jealous lust, and walk his schoolroom like a sultan making choice in the *harem*? Such danger of carnal crime must at once be extirpated, were there any solid reason to suspect. Fleeting indications, disturbing signposts (one might say); but more than that? I could not in all honesty aver it. Nor could I destroy a man for a mere fault in temperament which might prove to reach down no deeper. The whisper alone would blacken his name for life. A direct accusation could lead him irremediably to the gallows, and yet he might be innocent for all that. I had little enough faith in the equity of courts of law once paederastic vice came into the indictment: popular prejudice there rides roughshod, wisest judges are not immune.

It is now clear to me, looking back over these eight sad years, that I myself was very far from being a 'wisest judge'. I had an instinct, I ignored it, I let myself cloak it in a vague determination to put some questions (discreetly) among the boys, and otherwise do nothing precipitate. From their answers, even from Tommy Whitesmith, I found out little more than I already knew, and no more than I have stated above. Mr Aram had his favourites (*darlings*, if you will, but I could not discover that the word had any meaning beyond the natural scorn of the sportive child for the bookworm); those who did not like him made the worst of it, as boys do, flinging themselves with gusto into the utmost excesses of satire; he had in general been most sparing of corporal chastisement, and had never shown enjoyment of it; nor did he make a practice of invoking religious sanction in support of his own authority. In short, there was nothing against him, except—

'Except,' as I told Paulinus when he opened his doubts to me as aforesaid, 'except his sudden temper, which would seem quite unpredictable. It would explain his frequent change of school: he is ashamed of it, you see, dear brother, and once he has given way to it he may feel himself *branded*. The letters of recommendation made no reference to such a flaw?'

'They did not. Some of his former masters did say, or rather *imply*, that I should find him a "queer customer", but that was in the light of his obsession with his lexicon, which doubtless they mistrusted. There are many schools where an usher is kept chiefly to enforce order and therefore discouraged from intellectual searchings: St Guthlac's has never been one of them. I do not hear that Aram was *discharged* from any of his posts; he left of his own choice; and perhaps for the reason you have offered.

'Well: he will beat no more boys, we have that assurance. His shame in this instance is not his own secret: he knows that we know, and that hereafter we will be on the watch. A pity, in one way. If the usher does not cane, then the Master may have to birch, and truly I do not care to do it. Let us hope the boys will recognise that seeming leniency must not be abused. I have lately given our deplorable Whitesmith several thousand lines of Greek imposition; 'twill keep him safe within doors till Maundy Thursday. After that, we shall see.'

I forget what more I said to Paulinus; but I certainly refrained from any hint of my fears of nonconforming religion (which would have been most grievous to him); I felt already they were ridiculous. Still less did I broach the evil cask of paederasty, which remained, as it were, in the cellarage. There was nothing ridiculous *there*, but I had now my own reasons for discounting it.

Between the incident of the 'Long Lankin' song and my conversation with my brother, I had made other enquiries than those tentative ones I undertook among the pupils. I did not commence them as a deliberate inquisition; I found them arising – and being answered – in the natural run of my intercourse with Mr Aram. Suffice to say, I became persuaded that young creatures of the male gender did *not* arouse his flesh beyond the ordinary pleasure that anyone, man or woman, might derive from association with glowing youth. He admired all beauty, in his own strange way, and may at times have expressed his praise in awkwardly chosen words – his reclusive scholarship keeping him short of a shrewd knowledge of the world's opinion? – at all events, I absolved him, I need say no more.

Nonetheless, the 'Long Lankin' song was the first of those *portents* to which I have already alluded. It occurred in the month of March, 1758. For the narration of its successors, let me refer to the journal I began in the second half of that school term. (I do not know why I began it; save that suddenly I found the day-to-day of my life of far greater interest than formerly; perhaps I was half-conscious of some dread, some threatened doom, some thundercloud about to break? I write now from hindsight, always easy, rarely reliable. If my journal contained *fore*sight, I did not know it as I set it down.)

*

Cordelia now transcribes straight from the journal, selecting certain passages relevant to her theme and omitting others. A superficially unremarkable editorial process which Leonore does not remark, until slowly it is borne in on her that many of the omissions are in fact directly relevant and omitted for that very reason. Leonore is able to know *this (without knowing how she knows); she is able in her dream to know the exact content of such sentences. Cordelia is engaged in something well beyond the fair discretion of an editor: a tricky game of self-censorship, an attempt to pull wool over eyes, an attempt to rewrite history, to save face, to lay quiet an entire* cortège *of disquieting memories.*

The 'relevant' material that Cordelia leaves out is here left in: between square parentheses, each portion in its original place, just as it came to Leonore.

4

April 1st (All Fools' Day):
I informed Mr Aram that the Philosophical (*etc.*) Society is ready to vote upon his admission, should he come with me thither this night, myself and my brother to be his sponsors. High delight at my news, when I assured him of a favourable ballot.

I say to him, in deep confidence, I have every trust he will curb his temper during meetings of the Society, eschew his irony, subdue his mockery, and recollect we are a country town, we are not the *virtuosi* of London, some of us may even be stupid (yet despite that, true seekers of science). He laughs, says he knows it, says he is *aware of the date*, says stupidity even in London is not banished from learned company. But I am sure he understands me very well. He has been solitary for so long, he has quite lost the gift for social ease among assemblies of the polite, but he yearns for it, so he says: I believe him.

He was grateful, most grateful, for my help. And in the evening he was very well disposed, pleasantly taciturn, humorous with the ladies, decorous with all the gentlemen, particularly Mr Abel-Nottidge (our Rector, *aetat*. 76) who is always so swift to take offence. On returning home, he thanked Paulinus in well-framed measured periods. Most gracious altogether, a very good impression.

[And grateful, most grateful to *me*. Late at night I find my way by a dark-lantern across the grass, once I'm positive brother Paulinus sleeps safe; I heard him snore; bare feet so the stairs have not resounded. No moon. I am like Guy Fawkes. Mr A. in Usher's Lodge wide awake and a-waiting. As hirsute in his bed as a cadaverous Giant Blunderbore. Ah! his gratitude in the Usher's Lodge: and mine too, for his. Impossible such a stark wild-man loved boys' limbs more greedily than women's, impossible. I absolve him.

Nay, absolved already two weeks since, so why did I think of it still? Could my very suspicions have become my *prime mover* of concupiscence? that the one touch of his hand when he gave me his well-renounced cane, the one touch of that same cane when I switched it against his cheek (from who can tell what drastic impulse?) and he seized it as fierce as a wasp, and whipped it back at my haunches – could it be such zanies' games were enough to set afire all this quick-match?

Yet they did: and we have blazed, and we blaze yet again. He thought me at first a virgin, was astonished when I told him, 'No.' I have not yet told him how, when, with whom. That must wait, for a later time. All he knows: it was so long ago, so long beyond *almost* remembrance (so many arid years, such a desert of dry heart). If virginity were renewed through disuse of fleshly sport, I'd be unscathed Diana by now. Or would have been, two weeks since. Ha-ha.]

Mr A. has agreed to prepare a short paper, to be read to the Society. Upon the Celtic survivals in Britain, linguistic and other, subsequent to the coming of the Saxons. He says there has been much digging, of significant potsherds, brooches and so forth, in *tumuli* and the foundations of churches. We all of us look forward to it with the utmost of pleasure. None more than the Rector, in whose churchyard was found the sarcophagus, believed Roman, during the reign of Queen Anne. He keeps it before his threshold like a horse-trough. Uses it, too, *as* a horse-trough. Mr A. very scornful to hear this: I was hard put to it to have him stifle his snorts.

Palm Sunday:
Paulinus and I have our long-threatened short talk concerning Mr A.* Paulinus's gnawing questions. I set his mind at rest.

> [My own mind *not* at rest. Dark-lantern night again. Talk with Paulinus has aroused, once again, my doubts. Am rid of them, as ever, by *G–d knows what* in the Usher's Lodge. So lovely, so transcendent, both he (Mr A.) and *it*; his laughter, his loins, his crafty heart, the very roughness of his pock-shotten cheeks. Should I feel shame we are so hard at it upon a solemn feast of Christian observance? 'Ha!' quoth he, blasphemous. '*Hosanna* within the gates of Zion? *Hosanna* within *thy* gates, my pretty duckling!' And he an old man, very near. Strange that in this Academy, with such store of brisk young blood, I gave way to no temptation; why, how many times have I seen (inadvertently) our boys as they bathed in the river, and yet from that sight no stirrings – or none that I could not o'ermaster? 'Duckling'? His Yorkshire endearment, barbarous. Very well, and I can quack. He himself a raucous drake: feel him *surge* across the pond!]

* *as told above, in the body of my narrative* (C. Pole-H.)

Good Friday:
A day of profound heart-searching, and distress—

> [—as it ought to be, by common practice of religion: but so much of the *personal* has been added thereunto, that I hardly know how to write of it smoothly. Prayer and meditation, atonement for sin, do not today seem sufficient recipe to bring me peace and loving-kindness: I have been upon my knees at my bedside for hours. Ah Jesus! and all useless. What, oh what am I to do?]

Paulinus (by invitation) preached at Morning Prayer in St Margaret's, the boys now released for the week. Mr A. and myself therefore attending, especially to hear him; although our own parish is All Saints. His text from the First Lesson of the day, Genesis, XXII, 10, the sacrifice of Isaac.

> And Abraham stretched forth his hand, and took the knife to slay his son. And the angel of the LORD called unto him out of heaven, and said, Abraham, Abraham; and he said, Here I am.

Already during the Lesson, as the Parish Clerk attained this verse, I had become aware of Mr A. beside me all a-shudder and groaning to himself. I stared in surprise; he gave a 'hem' in his throat, set his handkerchief to his mouth, and seemed politely to expectorate therein. I took it he was troubled with a phlegm, and after that he made no disturbance until my brother ascended the pulpit. But upon his pronouncing his text, Mr A. once again began to move. This time without control: he heaved himself to his feet, gripped the rail of the pew with clenched hands, swayed like a man in a swoon, and half-fell, half-strode, across me as I sat. 'In good time did he call,' he was *hiccoughing* behind his teeth, 'but why only unto Abraham, why? Have no others been thought worthy of the heavenly intervention? Unjust, unjust, unjust . . .'

Whereupon, already free of the pew and into the aisle, he dragged his way through the amazed congregation to the porch and thence out into the Saturday Marketplace. Beadle and pew-opener ran after, also Dr McCoy, conceiving him stricken with illness. Paulinus halted his sermon, thrown aback, seeking my glance, unable to comprehend the event. I thought he signalled me, 'Go follow them,' for which no need, I was upon my feet even as our eyes met.

Outside the church, sprawled on the flags, Mr A. in a species of fit. Beadle fanning him with his cocked hat, pew-opener running to the pump for a cup of water, Dr McCoy preparing to bleed him. Mr A. stirs, pulls himself upright, shakes away the helping hands, stares livid at the physician's pocket-lancet. 'G–d's sake, sir,' says he at last, 'd'you add knife to bloody knife? Take it away and be hanged!' Dr McCoy, most displeased, was nevertheless courteous, in his dry consequential manner: 'Mr Aram,' he enunciated, 'if that was not the first warning of a constitutional seizure, I know not what it was. You'll be so good, sir, as to permit me feel the beat of your pulse.'

Having counted the pulse, he turned upon me, ''Tis all very well, ma'am, to have introduced this gentleman to the Philosophical Society, but I would recommend him to deploy some philosophy of his own, that he may be the more amenable in his dealings with other persons of science. His organism has sustained a brief internal shock, I would *not* diagnose intemperance as the cause, without better knowledge of his habits, but if he drink wine let him immediately leave off, if he smoke let him set aside his pipe, if he company with wh–res let him lie a-bed alone.'

[A fallacy of the mind, created by my guilt? or did he look at me most sharply as he spoke? Could he have known? How *should* he have known? it is not possible. Well, I stood brazen, no change of my countenance at all. I met neither *his* eye nor Mr A.'s.]

'For his diet,' he continued, 'I prescribe *etcetera etcetera,*' rattling on at some length about the blandest foods in smallest quantities. 'In the meantime good rest and quiet till your Academy shall reassemble, and make sure he do not delve into his books. Phantom blood, phantom knives, even though from Holy Writ, have disordered his imagination: after intense study, a frequent phenomenon.' So I called out John Lobscott from the church and we brought home Mr A. in the chaise.

As we put him to bed he said to me: 'That McCoy is a d–mned blockhead. In Holy Writ there are *no* phantoms. I should have thought, of all folk, a canting Irishman would have known better; does the agony of Christ's Cross-day mean naught to them over there? Have they not throughout history enough agony of their own? Ah no, but he's a Protestant who'll disbelieve (over there) all or anything that he's told any Papist might believe. For myself, each Good Friday puts the nails into my hands and feet, strong Protestant though I be. Pray leave me to my lonely prayers.'

[John Lobscott, obedient, goes. I linger, in the Usher's Lodge. I do believe he has a mind, even now, for *G–d knows what.* ''Twill be a half-hour ere your brother return,' he whispers. 'Broad daylight be d–mned,' he adds, quite mad for it. All his piety about nails, nothing less than sly hypocrisy? Surely not, for he weeps, trembles, is (most manifest) not yet clear of his seizure. I refuse him, what else? for I must ask, I do ask: 'You said "unjust", which I heard distinctly, though the others maybe did not. I beg you, dear sweetheart, explain. To your darling, to your duckling, I beseech you, do not close off your torments to *me*!'

Whereupon he makes known to me, what I had in my soul most darkly feared: *he has a wife.*

He has left her in Yorkshire (he will not tell me the town); nay rather, he says, she left *him*; walked stridently from his house there, declaring (outright and most grossly) she had a far better *bolt* for her *hasp* in a cobbler's shop just down the hill and at once she meant to go for it, bag and baggage and no forewarning! Which outrage to his honour cast him at a blow upon the world. In a sense, he confesses, the angel did call unto him; for he withheld himself from slaying upon the instant either her or her foul lover. But yet the angel did *not* call at the season it was most needed. Were heaven's justice truly just, his (Mr A.'s) first f–ck with that malicious bitch would for sure in happy time have been prevented; thereafter no bad marriage; thereafter no adultery. (Nay, there were many children, and yet adultery after all.) 'Unjust!' he says

again, and Christ's Passion was also unjust, he roars: 'for could not
the idle angels have called out unto Pilate? *of course they could,
d–mn them*, they were slugging in their beds, quite careless of all
their duty – oh indeed, 'twas well for Abraham! But Lord Jesus
and unlucky Aram, why, we must weep forlorn!' So he raved: I
left him to it. No dark-lanterns ever again. Finished.

And finished, too, my most secret hopes that MRS ARAM, in the
upshot, might joyfully become my name. His wife, wh–re or not, is
still his wife till death do part! and now he 'companies with
wh–res', and I am one of them. The only one? How can I tell? I
should have known, I did know. I am indeed no *virtuosa*: straight
stupid, such is me. Abominable, beastly, cruel-selfish old man!
Why did I not cut off his stiffened t—l, the first time he had the
arrogance to show it me? I might have done, yes; I was angry
enough against him that evening (or said I was).

And lo! my journal's pages are be-sodden with tears; they fall to
pieces under the stab of my pen. High time to return to the *dryness*.]

*

So much, then, for the second *portent*. Of itself, it seemed to
signify little, beyond a strange certainty on the part of Mr Aram
that Providence had in some manner *failed* him at an hour of
great need: perhaps, as in private he pretended to me, the
occasion of his ill-conceived marriage. Which contract most
evidently preyed on his mind; his life remained 'forlorn' for ever
after. At the time I had cogent reasons to believe him. Even now
I do not *dis*believe; but it was not the entire story, and I am
persuaded he only told it me for a purpose of deceit.

The third *portent* arose directly from his paper upon Celtic
survivals. To this day I do not fully comprehend what happened:
there was a remarkable discovery, which ought to have pleased
him; instead it seemed to hurl him into an indecipherable
chiaroscuro of dread.

As follows—

*

5

June 23rd:
The Society met in All Saints' Rectory, home of our President,
the Rev. Jas. Abel-Nottidge, M.A., who took the chair. Mr A.
read his paper. A thesis of curious learning, weaving a warp of
philology, history, religion, the principles of architecture (*etc.*)
into a woof of superstitious legend: I know not what portion of it

be true and verifiable (by further search in divers libraries, by sedulous excavation of ancient graves), or whether we should attribute its apparent extravagances to his own wild strain of speculation. Many of his arguments hang upon strange texts in the Celtic tongues; and forasmuch as no one of our circle knows those languages save himself (and perhaps Dr McCoy, though Dr McCoy most carefully sat mum), we are much at disadvantage. A *galling* disadvantage to some of us: Mr Saltmarsh, the architect, was as scarlet in the face as a drummer-boy's jacket by the time Mr A. concluded.

> [I too was sadly galled. Not (as Mr Saltmarsh) because I felt my historical preconceptions contradicted, but because – had Mr A. not so brutally exposed to me his *falsehood* – I should have had, would have had, some part in the preparation of the paper; a sharing of the adventure of his deductions and relevations; a far better understanding of the documents from which he worked. Since that desperate Good Friday he and I have scarce exchanged five words; and then only in regard to the internal economy of the school. Thus, by my unheeding salacity, have my very parts of scholarship been diminished. Woe alas.]

Mr Saltmarsh, an all-knowing pursy little gentleman, comes in with his dissent before ever our polite applause has ceased. 'Mr Chairman,' says he, 'may I earnestly ask our most interesting colleague, how the d—l he believes he can refute the late Sir Wm. Dugdale? Dugdale, an antiquary of unimpeachable authority, says positively (I forget where but I can find it) that all stone churches in England are of Anglo-Saxon building, or later. No warrant whatever for Mr A.'s brusque assumption that the Britons in the time of King Arthur left any such structure behind them. Stone edifices (or brick) are either Imperial Roman or Teuton or Norman. Between *anno domini* 400 approximate and the arrival of St Augustine we have no relics, none: the savage remnants of fallen empire dwelt and worshipped under perishable timber or else they rehabilitated ruins. Citations from Gildas or Taliesin or – who was it? Aneurin? – are not to the purpose: those "Celts", if they existed at all, were Welshmen and wrote solely of Wales.'

Mr A. swung his long body side-to-side, fists quivering, all on edge to rebut the rebuttal; but Mr Saltmarsh was by no means finished. 'Mr Aram!' he goes on. 'A small challenge to you, sir. Are you familiar with a Lincolnshire hamlet of the name of Goodluck Chapel? Some twenty mile from here, over against Spalding. I hazard rather too far for your celebrated long walks?'

'I have heard of Goodluck Chapel, sir. An island settlement in the depth of the fen, is it not? You surmise aright: I have not walked thither. Well, sir, what of it?'

In brief: Mr Saltmarsh was engaged in the rebuilding (to a Palladian taste, at behest of the local squire) of Goodluck Chapel's ancient church. His demolition of the chancel had revealed much older work than could have been predicted, within the outer casing of the walls. 'Their decoration, as I deduced from heraldic emblems cut into the stone, would be of the epoch of the Wars of the Roses; but behind that, without doubt, very early Anglo-Saxon. But by *your* thesis, Celtic. There is an inscription, I have endeavoured to read it, perhaps you can do better? Ride out with me tomorrow; examine what I have found; let us contend, upon the site itself! What do you say?'

'I say, sir, first, that whatever the date of your suppositious inscription, which may indeed have been placed by Saxons on a wall already extant, you should consider the name you have spoken. The word "Chapel" immediately shows that the sacred edifice came before the village and gave to the village its identity. It was not, to begin with, a parish, but a settlement grown up around a very primitive holy place: I would guess, a place of pilgrimage. Then, "Goodluck": an obvious corruption of *Guallauc*, a name familiar from the chronicles of the Celtic Nennius, who writes:

> Hussa reigned seven years. Four kings fought against him, Urien and Riderch Hen, and Guallauc and Morcant. During that time, sometimes the enemy, sometimes our countrymen were victorious— [*and so on and so forth.*]

'Hussa was an Angle who conquered in what is now Northumberland, *circa* 600 or thereabout. The four Celtic kings, I assume to be a Grand Alliance, drawn from all the east parts of the land. Guallauc may well have brought fenland contingents to the war, and upon his return from victory he dedicated his chapel as an act of thanksgiving. Such at least is my hypothesis: I will gladly come tomorrow, seek to confirm it, and we shall see. That is to say, if I have leave from Dr Pole-Hatchet?'

Paulinus at once gave him leave, and offered to make one of the party. 'What about you, dear sister? Shall not you too ride out with us? I think, for an occasion so deeply interesting, we could grant the boys a holiday? I could ask my friend the Master of the Free-school to lend one of his ushers to keep our boarding-pupils out of mischief between breakfast and supper-time. A game of football perhaps between the two establish-ments? Let me send John Lobscott directly to make the arrangement.' He seemed in gay fettle at the prospect. (There were times when even Paulinus was prepared for a species of *frolic*. I suspect he had a hidden wish to see Mr A. put down.)

> [I was torn, I will admit, between an anxiety to view the antiquarian discoveries, and a repulsion from Mr A.'s close company. If Paulinus and I and he were to cram together behind John Lobscott in the chaise, it must needs be very close: so I began to make my excuses. But then Mr Saltmarsh suggested a better disposition for the journey. He had his own especial 'great chariot' for site-visits, with a place in it for Mr A.; and he vehemently proposed to dispute all along the road with continued and rancorous controversy (Mr A. agreeing thereto, in a high mood of anticipated triumph). Dr McCoy expressed a wish to come, and so did Mr Abel-Nottidge. They too could be accommodated with Mr Saltmarsh and derive all the benefit of the vigorous pro-and-con. After that, there seemed no cause for my refusal.]

We were to be a veritable Expedition: picnic hampers were discussed, my easel and colours and sketch-book became a *sine qua non*; Mr Saltmarsh would of course bring with him his portfolio of measured drawings of the old church in its original state; Mr A. had his portmanteau of books; Dr McCoy almost quarrelled with the Rector over which of them would select the wine. Our tryst was for a half-past five *ante meridiem*, and the weather promised excellent fair.

As we broke up our meeting, a good hour later than usual, Mr Saltmarsh threw a Parthian shaft: 'Guallauc? An absurdity. Every soul in Goodluck Chapel knows full well it is called for St Guthlac. Why, Guthlac for many years made the island his lonely home. I'm amazed you're not aware of it, considering the name of your school! Or do you dare, sir, to contend that St Guthlac was *not* a Saxon?'

To which Mr A. gave no more than a creaking laugh and reserved his reply for next day in Mr Saltmarsh's great chariot.

No sooner had we entered the Academy gate than Paulinus was amazed and then furiously angered to find in the playfield a great bonfire a-blaze, our half-dozen boarders crowded round it, leaping, dancing, skylarking, scene of the loosest ill-discipline. He drove them sorely to their bedroom, calling to John Lobscott to fetch him at once the birch, for by H——n he would follow them up there and make some examples! 'That finishes all thought of a holiday!' he bellowed; never thinking of *my* disappointment. Nor did it look as though Mr A. would be given his leave; thereby disappointment for our Society into the bargain, and moreover at the very last minute. Untoward contretemps indeed; but at last, all was well. I was able to remind him that on every St John's Eve the boys had permission for their traditional midsummer fire; in the exhilaration of the evening's doings, he had let himself forget the date. 'Ha! but I'm a woolgatherer. My apologies, Cordelia. John Lobscott, return the birch to its pickle; and shall we see, can we not find some supper? Devilled chops, Aram, what d'you say? For tomorrow is your great ordeal. A glass of brandy?'

> [I plead sleep and go to my room. My brother and Mr A. at chops and brandy until all hours: why should I care? It would have been a night most auspicious for the device of the dark-lantern, the very summit of the year, the boys' cries of merriment out beyond the Lodge, their lively features all a-glow in the red and lurid magic of the flames, the smoke in every nostril, the crackle of the burning faggots. It would have been: it is not.
>
> I cannot be so dishonourable as to seek ways to ensure his dismissal, and yet I do not know how he and I can continue on the same premises, living here, working here, intolerable. At least, and I am thankful for it, we do not have to sleep beneath one roof. Once into my bed, I can forget the Usher's Lodge. It is as far from me as the dales of Yorkshire. Strange dales, unearthly garden, a Paradise in reverse, where *hasp* can find *bolt* so readily (by simply striding out for it? indomitable, malevolent, fit to be envied); and yet souls can be expelled therefrom, as bitterly as any old Adam.
>
> Cordelia, enough! To bed, woman; try to sleep.]

June 24th (Feast of St J. Baptist):
Our excursion proceeded under brilliant sunrise, the dawn mists fading into the brightest glare of heat as soon as we passed the ferry. Across the empty fens the roads run straight as a schoolmaster's ruler—

> [—or his cane, if you will – or the weals that his cane might leave. A voluptuous violation of the smooth skin of the virgin land. Of the *more-or-less* virgin land. Such thoughts are unwholesome: an end to them.]

Not an object in all that expanse tall enough to cast a shadow, save for the innumerable windmills whereby water in rainy seasons is continuously pumped out to keep dry the reclaimed acres. A prodigious illustration of the craft of the engineer, and (to my eye) an uncanny distribution of geometric man-made shapes against the shapeless *flat* of nature. Chess-pieces with whirling arms poised not quite at random (on certain squares, but not on others) of the chequer-board of drains and dykes. Without surveyor's chart to match objects in three dimensions with the single dimension of ink-drawn lines, the overmastering design is obscure; and uncanny because each windmill seems not so much an *object* as a queer *person*, spy, dogger of footsteps, dangerous guardian of endangered secrets. You pass by the one and he sends his message to the next, each circling of his sails to mark a word, or the *thought* of a word: 'Here they come. Who comes? Be ready for them *when* they come; and pass the news to your distant fellows.'

Such silence, moreover. Only the horse-hoofs, the carriage-wheels, the gathering wind, the trickle of water through the sluices, the birds, the groaning cattle afar off on the wide pasture – and the snarls, barks, coughs and grunts of Messrs Aram and Saltmarsh at their everlasting contention in the great chariot twenty yards behind.

We stopped to eat a morsel and rest the horses at what must be the most sordid public house between Norwich and Lincoln. More contention from A. and Saltmarsh as we sat outside the porch and drank our ale (not tempted to venture indoors because of the stench of the taproom, the grim demeanour of its host and his few customers, unwashed and inimical to strangers); Dr McCoy was now part of the argument.

He had at some stage of the journey decided that 'Goodluck' meant neither Guthlac nor Guallauc, but Goidel (*id est*, Gael). Thus far he was at one with Mr A.: the name did indeed denote Celts, but *his* Celts, from Ireland, who must have made some invasion unrecorded by historians and left their own linguistic mark to prove their presence.

No, not unrecorded, for – 'Irish, in Roman times, were called "Scots", were they not? Picts and Scots infested Britain. Why else the Wall of Hadrian? Well, they breached that wall, here they were!' He insisted, furthermore, that 'Chapel' meant no sacred edifice but was again Gaelic, corrupted: '*Capell*, noun substantive, a horse. Our hard-galloping Hibernian gentry overpowered here, they held dominion, sirs! Would G–d it had never ceased: the malefactions of Norman Popery would then have been unknown in these islands, the Battle of Hastings would never have been lost, the Battle of the Glorious Boyne need never have been fought at all!'

So eccentric a view dumbfounded his hearers. Old Mr Abel-Nottidge was nonplussed, as well as vexed at the introduction of all-too-recent and tendentious politics. 'Irish Popery due to the Normans? My dear sir, this is not good sense.'

'Goidel,' snapped Dr McCoy, 'Goidel, sir.' He smacked his lips over his tankard with an utter self-satisfaction (while Mr A. laughed and Mr Saltmarsh gnashed his teeth); he refused to dilate further. All he would add was, 'We shall see.' Mr A. having already said as much to Mr Saltmarsh the previous evening, our enlightenment did not progress.

The talk then turned to last night's bonfires and the observances of St John's Eve. Dr McCoy, drawing upon what he said were the beastly habits of papist peasants in his own country, held that a *human sacrifice*, by burning alive, was the origin of the fires (to secure a fertile harvest); and that such a horrid rite was even today accomplished in certain mountain regions of Donegal, although disguised as social protest. A cabin, he claimed, belonging to a landlord's servant (by necessity obnoxious in an impoverished rural neighbourhood), would be burned by night with all its inhabitants, unless some friend had afforded them warning.

The perpetrators are termed Ribbonmen or Whiteboys, from their peculiar costume, white hoods with holes for the eyes, or masks of entangled ribbon worn over cork-blackened countenances, which serve of course to hide their identity from the law; but he firmly believed there is also a derivation from the robes of the ancient Druids. 'Their bloodthirsty lust is now turned against Protestants, but that is no more than the accident of history. The principle remains the same. I would add, that these outrages are commonly accompanied by a nastiness of lubricious licence which must be seen to be believed, the women of the townland in a state of inebriation divest themselves of garments fornenst the heat of the blazing thatch until their nudity (*etc.*) – while the screams of the murdered wretches (*etc., etc.*) – I shall spare Miss Pole-Hatchet's blushes, you can imagine it for yourselves.'

'Seen to be believed?' I asked. 'And you, Doctor, *you* have seen?'

'Ah. No. Not to say *seen*, madam, no. But affidavits have been sworn before magistrates of repute; sure the details are well known to every dog in the street; and government takes no action, none; Dublin Castle is a byword for complacence.'

Mr Saltmarsh: 'They kill by the calendar? Well-away! and you are able to testify that the murders occur upon Midsummer, invariable? Does no one in Ireland slay his foe at another season?'

Mr A. (much moved): 'Be d–mned to the pair of you and your speculative tittle-tattle, I beseech you, sirs, no more of it! I gripe within my bowels at the very thought. What, to bandy argument as to whether a wicked massacre is of the Druids, or of the Pope, or of a squalid local vengeance? by G–d, but you make trivial, I close my ears to you, you are impertinent!'

I tried not to remember (but was unable to forget) Tommy Whitesmith and the song—

[—and all that came thereafter. There is a silver-grey cicatrice on Mr A.'s pallid face. He told Paulinus (when the scar was new) he'd been stung by a sapling-branch as he thrust his way through thickets in the course of a 'celebrated' walk. He told him in my hearing. I moved not a muscle, I was shameless, though inwardly stirred.]

Mr A., quivering with passion, slammed down his tankard and stamped off into the yard, calling to the hostler to have ready the great chariot, we had loitered long enough. Abashed, our gentlemen fell silent; one by one they rose from their places. We set ourselves again to the journey.

The day had clouded over, with a high wind from the west, and drops of rain beginning to fall. The cover of the great chariot must be unfolded. The chaise was furnished only with an insufficient half-hood: Paulinus and I doomed to a soaking.

[Dr McCoy, seeing this, makes offer to exchange places with me. I said, no, I enjoyed the rain (which I do not) – anything to avoid being seated with A. But A., at that juncture, gave out a crack of sudden laughter, forcing his old good-humour as it were against the grain: 'I'm for the chaise, I've disputed myself dry, let me ride in the wet for G–d's sake and take benefit,' and he was there beside Paulinus before the doctor had time to move. I declare he *winked* at me. Sensibility, or satire? His every gesture enigmatical.]

So we proceed, myself in great chariot, where I lead Mr Saltmarsh to tell us of his plans for rebuilding the church. More argument, but mild, as to Palladian against the Gothick styles, much to be said for both, and nothing to cause distress.

I have for some weeks been in the mood to write a play in regular verse. Attempting, that is to say, to summon up such a mood. I think of that, as we blunder along. (The road hereabouts has notably deteriorated.)

[Regular verse must surely be wholesome. Dryden, Addison, Dr

Johnson, not (on the whole) Shakespeare: my mind filled with
them, as well as with the styles of architecture, its turbulence is
lessened, very nearly set at rest.]

In this deep region of the fen, the reclamation is far from
complete, the windmills are fewer, the dykes more widely
dispersed. Our route now lay largely along an uneven causeway
with meres and swamps on either side, black and ominous in the
pouring rain. Dense clumps of dark bullrush extended beyond
sight; the heavy clouds seemed to sweep their tops, like a man's
huge hand that threatens to caress a woman's hair (but with no
good intent). Our excursion had lost its gaiety.

They had called Goodluck Chapel an island. So indeed it
almost was; hundreds of years ago would have been so entirely,
approachable only by boat. I have said the windmills are queer,
uncanny: to observe this low solid rise of dry land amid the fen is
to redouble the sense of unease.

Imagine, pray, a sombre pyramid, not more than two miles in
circumference. On the summit, the church, mantled in ivy,
surrounded by yew trees, its tower a broken tooth, never
finished by the original builders, with unglazed windows like
eye-holes in a skull, and battlements and pinnacles upon but
one of its four parapets. (The other three being left, irregular, at
varying heights; not parapets at all, in fact, but simply the *tops of
old walls*.) A crazy graveyard, close under the church, hemmed
in by the yews, with old crosses and slabs tumbled slantwise
down the slope of the ground.

There could have been no more than two dozen houses –
hovels of clay and thatch – stuck into the sides of the pyramid as I
have seen a child's flattened mud-pie embellished by chips of
flint. Between them, almost hiding them, a thick scrub of
untended bushes, hawthorn, hazel, brambles, overwhelming
the yards and outbuildings of these few decrepit farms. No
cultivated fields to speak of: rank pasture running down into the
fen. No gentleman's house either: squire and clergy live
elsewhere. Goodluck Chapel is a *dependent* parish, served by the
curate of a pluralist vicar and availing only of such patronage as
can be spared from more prosperous folk.

Yet the squire has decided to renovate his church. I wondered
why? Mr Saltmarsh shrugged, shook his head: 'I think Sir
Reginald was one of the few to grow rich from the South Sea
Bubble. In the sunset of his life he expends his wealth upon
Italianate follies, but not without communal advantage: if my

efforts at the church should please him, he proposes a model
village, to be erected on the south slope there, where you will
see a sort of ledge. The workmen already are clearing it to
provide a paved road, a more immediate way to attain the
church porch. We must dig out several score of ancient graves,
and demolish two or three cowsheds. The inhabitants resent the
work: they are not to be persuaded of the truth of their new
brick houses. When they see them, they'll believe, perhaps. If
Sir Reginald lives so long.

'Now, ma'am, gentlemen, we are forced to leave the carriages. There is no access save by the footpath.'

We trudged, in the rain, through the mud, up the narrow
winding path, where already Mr Saltmarsh's men had dragged
their scaffold-poles and sledge-loads of stone. Deep ruts,
draught-horses' hoofprints, heaps of horse-dung, the splintered
branches of uprooted thorn-bushes: an uncomfortable
approach indeed, which befouled us to our very hips. The heavy
footsteps of Mr A. were splashing close behind me.

[Too close. I sweated in the sultry deluge, and his breath was on
my neck.]

'G–d, G–d,' I heard him muttering, 'but this is an ugly place! Far
better had we stayed at home.'

At the church we found the foreman. He touched his dripping
hat-brim to Mr Saltmarsh. 'Very little work today, sir, bloody
wet, bloody useless, maybe it might clear, maybe not. I'd
ha' rather you'd brought your gentry on another time but it can't
be helped. Bloody trenches full o'water – watch that plank,
ma'am, it an't fixed! – right, sir, here's the wall what you was
talking about last week, I've hung tarpaulin across the carvings
to keep 'em fresh against the weather. Harry, where are you? A
pair o'steps, lad, quick sharp! and shift this bloody sheet.'

The tarpaulin was pulled aside, upon the inner face of the east
wall of the newly unroofed chancel, just above the altar. The
stone reredos (Mr Saltmarsh's 'Wars of the Roses' work) had
been chiselled away from its backing, to reveal a rough rubble
surface interspersed with courses of ancient brick; there was one
slab of freestone, asymmetrically placed. Thereon an indubit-
able inscription, badly damaged. We climbed, apprehensively,
to a wavering scaffold, to examine the relic more closely while
the rain ran into our collars.

The lettering was coarsely cut, large sprawling debased-

Roman capitals, clear enough to the eye where they had not been marred by first the affixing and then the removal of the reredos. I pencilled them down in my saturated notebook:

```
       ✠ / – RA– – / p. AN–MA. s. / ✠
    – – – – – – – US / MA–IST – – – US / –CLINGORUM
       AEDIF–CA– –R/DOM– – / DE–
       – – / – – – – / – – – – – – – / – – –
              HLACO / ERE– –T–
                     ✠
```

Mr Saltmarsh did not permit us to attempt our own interpretation, but most officiously read out aloud each phrase as he reconstructed it, with a translation and commentary subtended. Thus: 'Dedicatory cross. Then, ORATE Pro ANIMA Sua (pray for his soul); a second cross; Someone or Other's name, nominative case, illegible; MAGISTRATUS (magistrate, or chieftain, or thane); ICLINGORUM (of the Iclingas, or Icelings, or Hicklings, the Saxon family to which our Guthlac belonged); AEDIFICA-TOR DOMUS DEI (builder of a house of God, or *the* house, or *this* house); something or other or something else, illegible, a whole line. And finally: GUTHLACO split between two lines, and then EREMITO (to or for Guthlac the Hermit); cross dedicatory yet once again and that's it!'

'Meaning,' says Mr A., 'that this Someone or Other illegible was a kinsman of said Guthlac and built the church to commemorate him. Right.'

'Oh right, sir! quite right, quite.' Mr Saltmarsh was positively chirruping. '*And*, by my examination of the features of the wall itself, of the nature of its masonry, within remarkably few years of Guthlac's death. We are in agreement so far? Or I hope we're in agreement. You shake your head. Why?'

'The nature of the masonry. Those are very clearly Roman bricks.'

'Of course they are. The Saxons used them often. The remains of some temple or military camp, no doubt.'

'No.' Mr A., dogged, sullen indeed, twitching his scarred cheek, frowning around him as he spoke, none of the *merriment* of his scholarship here. It did not seem to me he had his mind fully concentrated: yet his argument was fluent enough. 'No, sir. I maintain Roman bricks first of all denote Roman building. To state otherwise, you must *prove* otherwise. And *Christian*

Roman building may be said to be British, therefore Celtic, of the very last days of Empire, when officers from Rome itself were no longer to be found here. This church had been constructed over two hundred years before Guthlac set foot within the fen. By whom constructed? Guallauc of course, he— Did I hear someone calling me? Ah no . . . no, I can't have done . . .'

For an instant he was all abroad, rolling his eyes from left to right, cocking his ear. With a shiver he resumed his theme.

'No, it is apparent: the Hicklings came to an ancient building and they set up their stone, perhaps at Guthlac's own desire, a pious affirmation of the founder of the shrine – whom they signify by those letters, H-L-A-C-O, not the dative but the ablative, *'by'*, not *'to'* the man; d–mn it, sir, he *built* it! and he's not Guthlac at all, he's Huallacus, from a perfectly conceivable Latinisation of Guallauc, abbreviated, misspelt, what else would you expect from a Saxon? The which would of course be abundantly proven, were the fourth line of the inscription not obliterated by your stone-masons' chisels. And the final word won't do: *Eremitos* is Greek, not Latin; the E and the T are most doubtful. I would read ERECTO – noble; or even REGALE – royal. Either of them appropriate to a Celtic king. I care not if you *do* sneer, my judgement is not—' He was all of a sudden most violently agitated. He started to shout at the top of his voice: *'Something's gone wrong!* What? Where? Who makes that noise?'

He leapt from the scaffold and he ran through the church to the porch like a man at an alarm of thieves. There *was* a noise, too: a strange howling from outside, mingled with angry cries and oaths of remonstration. A dog, several dogs, had set up a wild clamour.

We all followed him, with greater or less despatch: myself, very nervous, in the rear.

Outside, below the graveyard, we found a milling of workmen around an old woman, ragged and filthy, who tore at their faces, beat their bodies, with turkey-claw hands. The dogs, excited by the scuffle, raced in circles, snapped and sprang. (Birds too, a whole flock of them, low among the tops of the yew trees, anomalous in such wet weather, stirred by the disturbance into agitated flight. Ravens?) The foreman was endeavouring to bring an end to hostilities by swinging out at all and sundry with a four-foot length of lath. The descent upon him of the gentry succeeded where he failed: a moment's silence, the catching of breath, and Mr A. took the old woman by the throat.

'Virago!' he screamed at her. 'Bitch, witch and conniving harridan! Did they find what you have hidden, did they dig it, did they dig it *up*?' He held her high in his great paws, her feet off the ground, kicking, while he shook her like a colander of greens. It must have occurred to him then that the oddity of his words and behaviour required explanation. He dropped her in the mire. (But the birds and their tumult continued.) He turned sheepishly to meet our gaze.

'I could hear, from within the church, the commencement of the ruction. They did dig something up. Ask the foreman if it be not so.'

The foreman was hesitant, but at last became articulate. 'In the cowshed, sirs, yonder, I'd a chap with a pickaxe breaking open the stone base of the manger, according to specification, to find bedrock for the new road. On account o'the rain, we'd to leave off from the open-air trenches, they was filling as soon as we dug. But the cowshed having some of its roof still, I thought we could – like – make a start there, under shelter. It seems the old woman has her reasons against it.'

'Nonsense,' snapped Mr Saltmarsh. 'She is already paid good money, by the agent of Sir Reginald, to obviate all claim. The cowshed is for us, to do with what we will. Don't you know that, woman? Speak.'

She crouched cat-like, glowering and mouthing, her red eyes fixed upon Mr A. '*Finders*, so they say, is to be *keepers*, so they say. Him that dug didn't yet find. *He's* found—' (and she shot out her claw at Mr A.) 'so let him keep. What he's found, old Nancy's lost. Old Nancy don't want money. Old Nancy only wanted to sit where she sat, and talk to it. Now she can't, not for ever. They've pulled off the hat, and there, oh! the head and it's bare, bare, bare. Old Nancy never saw it, only heard of it, heard tell: and now she won't look, can't look, don't *want* to look to see it. What you can't see, you can talk to. What you *can* see, kills you dead.'

On all fours, she crawled whimpering past the corner of the cowshed. She caught hold of the wall and heaved herself to her feet. Then she was *merged*, with the thickets, with the veils of rain, invisible before you'd count five. The dogs, all a-whine, went after her.

'Who was it, the fool at the pickaxe?' Mr Saltmarsh put the

question with threatening emphasis: somebody had to be to blame. A young fellow stepped forward; he was bewildered, his hair in his eyes, his pleasant face lacerated by the assault of the old crone. 'What did you do, man, to tease the poor mad-woman? Have you no sense of decency?'

'Master, I did naught. Two strokes of me pick, three, I'd to tumble the stones and that; why, I'd not but just begun, when she's onto me from behind, master; come flinging herself out o'nowhere. *I* couldn't deal wi'her, nor could all the lads. Betwixt her and them dogs o'hers, I don't know which was worst. Eh, look at me, I'm all gore blood.'

'Ask him *what he found*!' Mr A.'s voice was now a deep-seated croak; barely to be heard. But everyone heard.

'Found?' said the labourer. 'Naught. I'd no *time* to find. Two strokes, maybe three; an't I told you, that was all?'

Without more words, Mr A. strode into the cowshed. A general crush to follow him. He went down on his knees in the dung at the far end of the building, furiously to grub among piles of straw and a litter of sticks and stones, the wreckage of the manger. He ripped more stones out of their rotted mortar, tossing them behind him as though they had no greater weight than walnuts.

'I have it! I have it!' he gasped. 'What's this? This is no bedrock!'

He had made himself a space the width of his spread palms, a flat surface under the jumble. A *stone* surface, roughly chiselled, with markings incised – a pattern of spirals like the whorls of a fingerprint, they covered the stone all over.

'Pickaxe! Crowbar! Get it up! *We must know what's beneath it!*'

It took thirty minutes, longer, to clear the slab completely and to prise it from where it lay, the strength of all the men being thrown into the work, levers and wedges hastily improvised. It was a vast irregular rectangle all in one piece, some seven feet long, a good yard broad, between three and twelve inches thick (depending where you measured). With a *crash!* it fell over on its side and split in two.

Some of the workmen had been growling in a heat of great good hope about 'caskets full of treasure': what lay at their feet had been, once, a human being. (Surprising? I expected it. Logical anticipation, at the edge of a graveyard. Poetic necessity, upon a day of such volatile passion.)

[*My* passions, or Mr A.'s? Against my will, am I his Mirror? Since we first saw Goodluck Chapel, miles ahead of us on our dreary road, I was oppressed nigh to swooning, and could find no reason beyond the weather. But the weather, I well knew, was *not* the reason.]

I write 'human being', but what we gazed on was a horrid bundle, bunched up in a long hole, or trench, as deep as a man's body to his shoulders. This cavity was lined with stone and so skilfully daubed with clay as to keep out the wet for – how long? Long enough to dry and shrivel (rather than rot) the cadaver's flesh; it hung upon the bones like a ragged wrap of purple-brown leather tight round a broken basket. Almost the shape of an old basket, too, lying sideways, knees bent to the neck – I was about to write 'head': there was no head.

Or at least, we saw no head; until suddenly Dr McCoy – down in the pit first of all of us, *ex officio*, his professional function – found a grinning ghastly sphere tucked in at the pelvic-joint, in the angle between upper thighs and what would have been belly (had the entrails survived like the bones).

'Good G–d,' exclaimed the doctor, 'he was deliberately decapitated.'

'He?' (Mr Abel-Nottidge.)

'Oh, he has to be "he", rector. Quite apart from anatomic proportion, there is even a shred left him of the nether skin of his scrotal sac, or was till it came away in my hand. His genital member I do not discover.'

He held up a piece of *something*, like a fragment of potato-peel with a bristly tuft adhering. He was rummaging the corpse with that butcher-shop callousness so notorious among those who *walk the wards* of our Free Hospitals, plucking out bones and putting them back, searching, so it seemed, for I could not imagine what.

I was appalled, but keenly curious; so also, everyone else. Whereat my brother decided (to my very great annoyance) he must utter on my behalf. 'The lady is feeling faint. I shall ask you to desist. Doctor, will you kindly – ah – arise from the grave. This is a matter for the civil authority. A coroner's inquest, an indictment for murder, a—'

Mr A. laughed aloud, a gross bellow that at length subsided into a spasm of gulps and snorts. The doctor, too, was smiling: 'I do not think an inquest would be overmuch concerned with a murder perhaps a full millennium old. There has been partial mummification, due no doubt to some property of the soil. Nay, I cannot say *how* old: but sure of a most primitive age. We have not a case here of one of your common low criminals who must huddle away his evidence into the nearest declivity. No, sir, this interment was pursued with ceremonial care. Pagan care, not Christian; unless one of you saw a cross on the grave-slab. I did not.' He scrambled to his feet and tried ineffectually to brush the dirt from his sodden garments. 'I'm after looking for some article of clothing, or jewelry, a belt-buckle, the tag of a lace, anything, to afford us a date. This dust in the bottom of the pit, this mould, I apprehend is the remains of whatever he was shrouded in. There seems a great quantity of it; were it sifted, we might yet discover—'

Understanding at last the potential of the situation, every gentleman of our party was into the hole in an instant. Treasure? Yes, of course: but treasure for *savants, connoisseurs*: priceless rarities as opposed to the dross of vulgarians' guineas and sovereigns. I thought of boys ducking for apples, and then (as my gorge rose) of woodlice in a gardener's seedbox: the spectacle was ludicrous and bred mockery among the labouring-men.

But in the end, success. Mr Saltmarsh, with a yelp of joy, holds up a detached finger-joint. Upon it, blackly tarnished and almost indistinguishable, is definitely a ring. At the same moment my brother discovers what he hopes is a part of a bronze knife-blade; and a minute later Mr Abel-Nottidge brings to light three small links of a chain, gold perhaps, perhaps from a neck-ornament; there is cheering and whooping and smacking of good friends on the back. The Philosophical Society has justified its existence; why, the *Royal* Society, no less, will be astonished to read our report!

Out of the pit, all but one of 'em, clutching their spoils of triumph, the old Rector ponderously hauled therefrom by a half-brigade of workmen and set to rest on a chance milking-stool till *angina pectoris* cease to threaten him. Mr A. still a-grovel at one end of the hole. Then he lifts himself, *ululating*, a solid object in both hands, the size and shape of the crown of a round hat. 'Why, you missed the very best!' he crows. 'A subsidiary excavation at the extremity of the great one, and in it – observe! It is an Urn. Receive it carefully, two hands please, *yours*, Miss Cordelia, yours are the safest, here!'

[The request was specious, I ought not to have accepted it; my hands were not the safest, they were shaking more than anyone's with all manner of emotion. I knew what he did; he offered me a love-token, mute reconcilement after deadly breach of faith. Such

height of overweening! and yet – I took the urn, and pressed it
gently like a babe to my bosom, while he climbed to stand beside
me. He received it again from me (our eyes for a brief interval
meeting; neither he nor I flinched from their intercourse); he
carried it out of the shadows to examine it with sedulous zeal.]
He said, 'The lid is sealed with clay. Too fragile to be opened until
we are safe at home. I will take it directly to the carriages, here is
straw and an old sack, it must be packed with the utmost
diligence.' He packed it and hastened away. The rest of us went
back into the church: Mr Saltmarsh was desirous we should
thoroughly understand the present progress of his renovation.

When we departed from Goodluck Chapel all our faces were
as the face of the valiant Duke of Cumberland upon the field of
victorious Culloden. The villagers assembled (though I did not
see old Nancy) to stand and gaze at us as we drove off, the men's
hats in their hands, the women each a-curtsey with a very
proper deference. Gratuities were distributed. But I thought that
all *their* faces held a certain apprehension, a vicarious compassion mingled with cruel delight, much as in the streets of Lynn
when a malefactor goes to the gallows. There was not a bird in
the wild dark sky.

Mr Saltmarsh suddenly said, the coach-wheels beginning to
turn: 'Gadso, with all his foolery about Guallauc the Celtic king,
he never sought to explain how the Saxon chose to call himself
AEDIFICATOR DOMUS DEI! The nominative, d'you mark? in
apposition to the illegible name. It is the *crux*, and he can't get
around it. Leave me alone with him a few short hours, I'll put
the fellow down even yet!'

But Mr A. was in the chaise, we were in the great chariot, the
'putting-down' would have to wait. It still rained, harder and
harder, every mile of our journey homeward.

June 25th (early morning):
Last night upon our return, weary, I wearied myself still further
by compiling the account for this journal, anxious to set all
down before it went from my recollection. Today, as soon as I
rise, I must add a number of paragraphs, for between my
finishing the previous entry and my long-postponed sleep, a
conversation took place; I had not the energy to write of it at that
late hour.

A conversation between myself and Mr A.

[Dark-lantern. Yes, I yielded.

His light in his window, past midnight, staring (as it were) across the grass at mine. If candles can be in collusion, why not human beings? One male, one female: bare feet out of the door, over the grass, tap upon *his* door.

He opens to me, fully dressed, his garments dried but still spattered with the detritus of the far fen, greeting me with no words but a giant fervour of all his blood, upon hearth-rug in front of parlour fire. He does not take trouble so much as to curtain the window – until I writhe from his grasp and myself make assurance of our privacy. No words – not words *as such* – for a whole hour by the beat of the clock of my heart.

Small-clothes on his shanks again, his buttons made fast, he speaks. With a curious formality: his tongue unlocked, but it might have been almost a stranger's—]

—he preparing (as it were) to read me an addendum to his philological paper: 'Miss Cordelia, you have been so good as to call upon me ere you sleep, therefore I must tell you about the urn, and show you.'

'The urn, Mr Aram? I understood all the rarities from Goodluck Chapel had been transported to the rectory, the *mortal remains* included, for safe storage on behalf of the Society. To divide the acquisitions is an unfortunate precedent. You do not mean to keep the urn as your personal property? Mr Abel-Nottidge is unlikely to accede.'

'Mr Abel-Nottidge does not know. He thinks it is with the rest, strapped up inside the picnic hampers. He was immensely fatigued; he will not be prowling there tonight. Tomorrow, he shall have it, with my apologies. You see, I took the liberty of opening it in private; for *I* found it, *I* alone was *directed to it*, its secret is *my* secret. Enough: I shall tell Mr Abel-Nottidge and all the others that it was empty. And that its presence in the grave can only have been emblematical; perhaps to signify the dead man's soul? I shall say, "We can never know."'

'Empty? Ah, what disappointment! We had all hoped for some clue to the meaning of that strange burial.'

[He looks upon me fixedly, until I redden from head to toe. To dress myself in his presence is an awkwardness to me, foolish, I am aware; the *ease* of such doings shall only be learned by calm practice; the light from the fire is glaring. At length he nods his head as though confirming to himself some sardonic speculation; he reprieves me from the ordeal of his eye.]

He abruptly turns his back and is busy at a cupboard. When he faces me again, I am ready for whatever he will show. His tea-tray. Upon it, on a white napkin: the urn, the lid of the urn, a flat tablet of yellow bone resembling the blade of a chisel, and a small dark cylinder like a Spanish *cigarillo* with a thick twisted knot at one end. All of them laid out in an exquisite precision.

Speaking rapidly and soft, he picks up each item to demonstrate its quality: 'First, the urn itself, and its cover. Geometric incisions in the clay round the top of the vessel, an asymmetric decoration which (by comparison with potsherds found elsewhere) may eventually establish the date. Triangles, you see; spirals, as on the stone. I am no expert in ancient ceramics. But Celtic, of a sort, I am sure. Now, for the contents, for indeed there *were* contents. Two of them. And perfectly unfitted to pass into the ken of that ill-conditioned Irishman. If he were to see *this*—' (he holds the '*cigarillo*' daintily betwixt finger and thumb '—why, to begin with, he and the Rector would suppress all publication of it, in the interests of propriety. D'you know what it is, Miss Cordelia?'

'I have not the least idea. Will you tell me? or do you baffle me, as it seems you intend with the poor doctor?'

'He will baffle himself if I give him the chance, but I won't. Moreover, he is unsafe with delicate pieces. Didn't you see how he ravaged the cadaver? the nether skin of the scrotal sac – bah! Did he think he was a man-tearing Bacchante?—

[—'or did he think he could match *you* in your honeypot ecstasy?' I have to look at him twice to ascertain he has truly said it. But he winks: his barbarity dissolved (as on previous occasions) into incorrigible good-humour just a handbreadth short of derangement. Mutual derangement, and of scandalously mature years. We both laugh.]

'You see, what we have here is the complement to his clumsiness, the very article he failed to find, the genital member itself with the scrotum attached, humiliatingly withered to less than half its proper size.

['You will not wonder why I show such an object to you, and only to you? Had you brought no dark-lantern to my door, you too (my duckling) would have been kept in the dark.]

'Whoever cut it off must have cut off the corpse's head. In life or after death, who can say?

'At all events, I am convinced that that burial was of a human sacrifice with concomitant sacramental mutilations, and the less Dr McCoy knows about it the better: I will not allow him to pervert these ancient mysteries for an Irish Ascendancy faction-fight, to stir Dublin Castle against the desperate wretches of

Donegal, G–d's blood, it is a blasphemy!' His voice shoots up the register; he is as angry as he was in the forecourt of the alehouse. It is as though he were speaking of pieces of his own flesh, demanding respect for them from a world of ignorant bigots—

> [—and in truth, I think he is. Only his 'duckling' can receive his revelations with the awe he believes to be their due. Once again his concupiscent wink as—]

—he strives against his passion and returns to a moderate manner: 'But all this is of small interest to a lady, and not entirely suitable. Leave it aside, and let us look at the next item, the last item, the item of greatest importance which I, and only I, have the essential erudition to comprehend. A tablet: do you mark it? Here is a lens. Examine it closely, and tell me what you see.'

I obey him, peering with some puzzlement at the narrow strip of bone. 'I see three engraved lines the length of the tablet, six inches each approximate, running along it on both faces.'

'Good—

> [—my pretty duckling, good!]

'And what else?'

'A series of notches against the lines, again on both faces of the tablet, some of them touching the lines, some of them crossing, in groups of varied numbers, and at more than one angle. Very similar to the notched tallies employed by illiterate tradesmen to add up their accounts. Is that what it is? The relic of an ancient marketplace?'

'You have it very nearly, but not quite. Say "library" instead of "marketplace" and you've hit it exact. These notches are called Ogham: they are the alphabet of the Druids. They have hitherto been found on monumental stones in various parts of Ireland; I know of none in Britain; I know of none anywhere on so small and portable a surface. Nor of such great age; every other discovery of 'em seems to be of Christian date, when the Druids were no longer priests but merely poets and genealogists. Our blockhead antiquaries still look upon this alphabet as occult and indecipherable: tell 'em it can be read, and they'll give you the lie. Nonetheless, it *can* be, it *has* been! and who should know it but myself? for *I am the man that accomplished it!*'

He is dancing like a mad Jack Tar round and round his parlour.

> [With a huge guffaw, he pounces, throws me forward over his ottoman, flings up my half-fastened petticoat, and bolt-into-hasp *a tergo violenter* 'til the vigour of our excitements can no more.

> Sprawled there even thus, plump and beast-like, a white doe in
> heat to anyone's eyes who should chance to walk in upon us, I
> conscientiously make shift to apply my rational faculties.]

'Mr Aram,' I beg him breathless, 'do you tell me indeed you
are already possessed of the message of the bone? For love of
H——n, sir, speak quickly, the suspense is unendurable.'

'No, not already, not yet, no. I have elucidated each character
of the inscription. But the language is archaic (although Celtic,
and Goidel Celtic at that, though do not whisper it to the
physician!), it is very hard to interpret, there are drastic
abbreviations, I need time,' he ejaculates, 'more time, much,
much, much more time . . .'

> [He breaks away from me then with a deep groan. Disconcerted, I
> roll over and turn my head to observe him.]

He leans against his writing-desk with brow supported on one
hand, all his vainglory gone in an instant. I fear I have displeased
him; I put out my own hand to touch him; he shies from me.

'No, it is not your fault; I am oppressed by my own doubts. It
may well be I have utterly mistaken the language, or that
Ogham in Ireland has a different significance from that of this,
its British variant. I was too quick, just now, to praise myself; the
fireworks of my delight should have been kept for a – for a less
dark occasion.'

I do not understand him, and I say so with asperity.

'But no,' he repeats, 'I have stated it is not your fault. I am too
tired tonight to continue my work. Tomorrow. I need time.
Please believe me: if I unravel with success, you shall share. I
thank you from the bottom of my heart; but I pray you, please
leave me to my broodings.'

I am vexed with him; I expel myself with urgency from his
door, slamming it—

> [—imprudently loud, ah woe! if my brother should have heard?]

—and so into the school-house, up to my room, onto my bed,
like a great girl in a morbid sulk. I apply, however, my rational
faculties; ill-feeling begins to abate. After all, he is a man of
science, therefore liable to these reversals of temperament. He
claims he needs time: out of compassion, I shall grant it him. Let
me wash, as is only decorous; put on my nightgear; and sleep.

June 25th (as continued, late at night):
By morning I was settled in my mind. Mr A. (with all his
vagaries) is my friend and I determined to treat him friendly.

Events did not accord with so sanguine a forecast. Today has been a day of sad relapse indeed after all the exultation.

Firstly, my brother sends word by the housemaid, even as I am dressing, that his ride home in the half-hooded chaise under unremitting rain has inflicted a severe chill – he does not think he can rise from his bed. I hasten to him to find it only too true, he has high fever and will need several days' nursing if it is not to become something more perilous. He tosses fretfully on the pillows: 'You and Aram must do your best. The top class is into Herodotus, the third book; the middle school may proceed with their Caesar and quadratic equations; set the little boys hard at parsing, they are culpably deficient, and 'twould do them no harm to learn by heart as many portions of *Paradise Lost* as will fill up the time till I return to them. Make sure that Aram does not neglect the Scripture class. Old Testament, the first Book of Kings, we had just reached the murder of Naboth, "Hast thou killed, and also taken possession? In the place where dogs licked the blood of Naboth shall dogs lick thy blood, even thine . . . Hast thou found me, O mine enemy? . . . Because thou hast sold thyself . . . sold thyself . . . to work evil in the sight of the Lord . . ." What evil does *he* work, in the dark of the night? Crying out like a wolf, slamming and banging his cottage door, past one o'clock, nearly two? Does he *walk*, to find more corpses? Shall he piss against the wall, like Ahab's issue, and so be cut off . . . ?'

Thus he rambled in delirium of his fever, while I soaked cloths and laid them cool across his poor head.

But I cannot soak cloths and teach in school at the same time: I sent John Lobscott into town to fetch Mrs Brewster, the by-the-hour nurse, a far from reliable woman, and costly; but someone must watch at Paulinus's bedside. Dr McCoy also sent for.

Mr A., to my consternation, is also unwell. The under-housemaid went as usual to the Usher's Lodge to clean his rooms, he being supposed to have joined the boarding-pupils in the school-house for breakfast. She comes running to me in alarm to tell me his door is locked and he will not open to her; he cried out he will be better presently, but what is 'presently' when all hands are required to do duty here and now?

It falls to me to conduct the entire school by myself. I have done this before, once or twice; it is difficult but I have my system. When I choose I can be as draconian as Oliver

Cromwell. The first thing I do is to open the punishment-book, with a slam and a bang. Second: to write names in it for heavy impositions, boys I see smiling and whispering, ring-leaders. One of them for the birch (when Paulinus shall be strong enough); I heard what he whispered: 'Maybe Cordy-cat'll take us bathing if it turn sunshine this afternoon.' I can accommodate myself to 'Cordy-cat' ('tis no worse than 'Long Lankin'); but a lout who has been shaving his face for twelve months is not to be tolerated when he couples my name with a bathing-party, the implications are unequivocal.

Mr A. does not appear. And I have not a moment of time to go seek him. He has been told of Paulinus's indisposition? I send John Lobscott to remind him. Once again the word is 'presently'.

The nurse arrived, before ten. No Dr McCoy. At last, as we ate our dinner (beef-stew and dumplings; *burnt*, an evitable mishap due solely to my enforced absence from the kitchen), his elder partner, Dr Hinge, comes huff-puffing along in his stead, with apologies and a most tiresome story.

Dr McCoy and Mr Saltmarsh have fought a duel!

It seems they had high words in a tavern last night, both of them fatigued by the Goodluck Chapel jaunt, and both of them still at odds over Goidels and Saxons, human sacrifice and associated nonsense. Dr McCoy, suffering (like my brother) the effects of yesterday's weather, found the wine went immediately to his head. He denounced Mr Saltmarsh as an impostor, and held him responsible for the ills of Ireland. Mr Saltmarsh gave his opinion of Ireland and the Irish. Dr McCoy struck Mr Saltmarsh. They went out accordingly at first light to a ruined windmill a mile from the town, with two foolish drinking-companions as seconds. Victory for Dr McCoy seemed assured – for are not all Irish gentlemen skilled duellists from the very cradle? – but his frenzy was such that he shot wild. He received Mr Saltmarsh's ball through the shoulder.

Dr Hinge has him safe a-bed, but avers that he (McCoy) will do no more doctoring for some considerable time. This is very bad news. Dr Hinge is *not competent*; and I fear for my brother's condition.

Dr Hinge also tells me that Mr Abel-Nottidge is quite paralysed with the rheumatism, and the Curate must perform his work for him at least until the end of the week. The 'bundle of bones' we fetched from Goodluck Chapel is filling the Rectory with a foul stench (says Dr Hinge) and should be burned before it spreads infection. Whether Mr Abel-Nottidge will follow this advice, indeed whether the Society will agree to his following it (he having no rights of personal property in the cadaver), is a question hardly to be answered while everyone is laid up sick.

I ask Dr Hinge to go to the Usher's Lodge and examine Mr A., once he has been upstairs to Paulinus. He does so; but returns dissatisfied. Mr A. let him in, but cursed and swore at him and refused to be let blood. It appears he was not a-bed, but striding up and down the Lodge in nightshirt and top-boots, very feverish. Dr Hinge does not know what ails him.

John Lobscott complained of the flux; and asked to be excused his afternoon duties. He believes he caught cold to his belly while driving the chaise, but avers there are other reasons as well. Last night he had terrifying dreams. Thinks old Nancy at Goodluck Chapel 'put the *eye* on him'. I do not know how he can say this. All the business with old Nancy took place while he was a full quarter-mile off, waiting with the carriages at the end of the causeway. But I had to excuse him: better not to have him about the place at all than to see him in constant fear of shitten breeches. A superstitious oaf.

In afternoon school, two more names for the Master's birch. I am not so much Oliver Cromwell as King Henry VIII: I dislike myself extremely.

Cook informs me that Mr A., having refused to attend both breakfast and dinner, has called through his window to the stable-boy to tell the kitchen to send over a poached egg for his supper. Cook feels 'put upon'; she maintains (with justice) that if he is well enough to eat an egg, he is well enough to have it in the dining-room with the boarding-pupils in the proper fashion of his employment. Mr A. has not ingratiated himself with the female servants; they believe him to be 'turned-up nosed' and 'a walking dictionary'; his satiric laughter (which so softened me from the start) is taken by them as an assertion of superiority. Quite different from Mr Overton who deferred to them 'as an usher ought to'. Mr Overton in fact had them like white mice in his pockets, soothing them, flattering them, setting their eyelashes all a-flutter—

[—and G–d *knows what* went on in back offices after sunset. At least there is no fear of that with A. But why should I care if there were? Even the righteous Paulinus had a tenderness for last year's parlour-maid. Cordelia, Cordelia, with everything at sixes and sevens, this is no time for hypothetical jealousy!]

Nevertheless, having seen to Paulinus (no better, but not appreciably worse), I leave the boarders to evening studies under hazardous supervision of their prefect, and strike out across the grass to the Usher's Lodge. He is either ill, and therefore a-bed; or in health and fit for his work. I intend to be *draconian*.

I knock at his door: no answer. I peep in at his window: he has the curtain drawn. I knock again and shout like a constable. Still no answer, so I act beyond good manners: I have a key to the Lodge door—

[—obtained with A.'s knowledge as an aid to the dark-lantern exercises. Paulinus of course has always possessed a spare key, but I know not where he has left it; he is unaware that *I* have one; I can only hope this episode will not cause him to find out.]

I open the door and go boldly in. The parlour is in disarray, with last night's candles burnt out and their wax-drippings all over the furniture. Books and papers scattered broadcast. If he is not in the parlour he must be in the bedroom. He is.

And impervious to my entry, to my voice. He kneels on the unmade bed, with his back to the door, in boots and nightgown (just as described by the doctor), stooping over something that lies among the crumple of sheets. I approach him most gingerly; there is that in his posture which frightens me, a rigidity, a feeling of *trance*. I remember his seizure in the church. I extend a timorous finger and tap him very lightly on the elbow.

I thought he would have murdered me!

So swift a whipping-round, not of his head alone but his whole frame, cat-like, dog-like, *footpad*-like indeed. 'Who?' he breathes, staccato. 'Who? Do you *dare*? You were in the hole, so stay in it! Or I'll cut your cut throat!' He shoots his hand out toward his razor, close beside him on the dressing-table.

I did not stand on dignity. No place here for *draconian* pose, the Master's sister demanding that the usher resume his duties, no. This was seizure, and dangerous, he saw me but with stone-blind eyes. I leapt a pace backward, my mouth faltering open and shut.

'Mr Aram, no! It is I, I am—

[I am your duckling! Sweet Eugene, I beseech you! my love, do you not *know* me?]

—I am only here to find what ails you. Please tell me you know who I am!' He pauses, one knee on the bed, one foot on the floor. His dreadful eyes recover their sentience, his outstretched hand trembles and slowly withdraws from the razor. In his throat a sound of vomiting choked back, a snort of catarrh behind his nostrils, while by degrees the snarl of his lips is metamorphosed to an awkward smile.

Absurdly, and half-laughing, I ask him, 'But why boots?'

He replies in a shaky voice, trying hard and overtly for a common-sensible tone: 'I've had to visit the outside privy many times since the small hours, there's a mucky floor there that's never cleansed, it's no place for slippers, I'd be glad if you'd get those wenches to do a proper job. Idle baggages, one and all. I sent word for a poached egg. Did it come?'

No, I told him shortly, it did *not*. I told him all I meant to tell him when I knocked at his door.

[But I tried to tell him humorously, as an anxious but indulgent lover. His state of mind is not to be trifled with; but it may be improved by a kiss. He accepts the kiss; but as I give it him—]

—I observe what he has in his bed. The bone tablet and the *other* item, and the urn. And with them, sheets of paper and a pencil. He has, in this constrained posture, been afflicting himself with his Druid-script. And driving himself mad thereby.

If a poached egg will help him finish, he'd better have it and be done. I tell him so; and go to fetch it. To reproach him is useless, I must *succour* him and that's all.

I prepare the egg myself, thereby affronting Cook, and make haste to ensure he eats it. It is served (very nicely) on a slice of toasted wheaten bread, accompanied by a cup of tea; he deals with it in little more than one mouthful. He turns again to his Ogham, and will entertain no questions about it; when I ask him does he think he will be in school tomorrow? he shrugs abruptly: he cannot, will not, say. Do I imagine he's gaoled himself here in the Lodge for a frolic? 'This is a matter of such great import that I – I am bereft of words to say *how* great.' No, I am *not* to be party to his analysis: 'I regret it, Miss Cordelia, far more than I can tell you; please believe me, it is impossible. Please go.'

Until detestable Good Friday, he took me with him step by step through all the arguments and proofs of his philological work. Despite last night, I did still hope that that brief Elysian partnership was now to be resumed.

[I am fool enough to mumble something plaintive about 'dark-lantern'. He looks at me absently as though the word has no meaning for him; then recollects himself, smiles, shrugs again, says, 'Tomorrow, why not tomorrow?' – so careless a toss of his answer toward me – does he even know *what* he says? or will he (tomorrow) allege he uttered no such thing?]

I have not the heart to repeat my remonstrances, his duty to Paulinus, the needs of our Academy. He would be acting just the same, had Paulinus himself burst in and dismissed him from his post. He is *in thrall*, and unattainable. Tomorrow I will have no choice but once more to encompass the whole of the school by myself. Unless I borrow an usher from the Free-school: inconvenient, for their curriculum is not ours, neither is their fashion of discipline, and the boys will be tempted to play yahoo. I return to the school-house with an ugly headache; I find the boarders defying the prefect, rolling and tumbling in a pell-mell; punishment-book again, and all of the wretches at last to bed. Myself at last to bed, after entering this misery in my journal and then looking in upon Paulinus. He is asleep and Mrs Brewster (in her armchair) is asleep. They are snoring like two fat pigs: I hate the pair of 'em.

June 26th:

Nothing this morning any better than yesterday. Paulinus still sick. Mrs Brewster complaining of her victuals. John Lobscott still sick. Mr A. still *self-gaoled*. The boys restless and froward. Cook evil-tempered. Myself with my last night's headache. Dr Hinge came to see Paulinus. Saying, two days at least before he'll look for an improvement; he let Paulinus's blood, examined his stool, smoked an obnoxious pipe in the drawing-room and departed. The usher from the Free-school arrived, late, and started shouting at the boys about *hic, haec, hoc*. I left him to enmesh himself and retired for an illegitimate nap.

Astonishing! At dinnertime, when we were all around the table, eating boiled mutton (shamefully gristly) and greens (not properly washed), Mr A. wandered amongst us, like a distracted traveller seeking direction as to how to find the Cambridge road. No apology, the merest catch of the head toward me, he took his place and received his mutton and sat silently forking it in. The meal over, and all dispersing to the schoolroom, A. caught me quickly by the arm and whispered: ''Tis done, I have unravelled it, oh G–d what is to be done now?'

Allowing me no chance to speak further with him, he donned his square-cap and gown (which Paulinus will have him wear, for reinforcement of the usher's status, even tho' he be no graduate. *Mendax quamquam venialis*: the parents prefer it), and so into the

schoolroom amongst the boys; he would (it seemed) conduct his
lessons but not with any briskness. By all appearance he was still *in
thrall*. Noting this, I asked the Free-school man to stay with us until
end of afternoon. I did not think Mr A. was to be trusted on his
own, not just yet. But they can surely between them manage well
enough without me. Another nap: I too am quite unwell.

During the afternoon I vomited several times and fell a-
shuddering with feverish chill. Possibly (as to my stomach) the
mutton: I would wish to think so at all events, a general
infection is not to be contemplated.

When school is finished, I compel myself to rise and seek out the
Free-school man to thank and reimburse him for his services. He
has somewhat to say to me, and a difficulty in saying it. At last:
'Miss Pole-Hatchet, is Mr Aram entirely *orthodox*? I could not but
overhear him with his Scripture class at the far end of the room. He
was telling them very strange things about King Ahab and
Naboth's vineyard. He suggested, obscurely, that Naboth *deserved*
to be slain, for vaunting his ill-gotten riches when the kingdom at
large was impoverished after the drought. He said kings have a
responsibility toward the Greater Good, and that murder might
not always be quite what it seemed to be. And then the boys teased
him and he waxed incoherent concerning the queen.'

'Jezebel?'

'Her. So he broke up the class, setting them instead to practise
copperplate until the bell. I think he felt a confusion and did not
wish to continue. Perhaps he came from his sickbed too soon?'

Perhaps he did.

(I told none of this to Paulinus, not even that Mr A. has been
ill. I did not wish to trouble his mind, when he is so troubled
already by his own enfeeblement; he must be let think that all is
well with the school. When he recovers will be time enough to
consult with him.)

[Dark-lantern, but reluctantly. Will he receive me? and in what
manner? I am determined there shall tonight be none of his
evasions and none of his *G–d knows what*: we either talk with an
utter seriousness, or I go straightway out of his quarters. Well, I *am*
expected.]

Mr A. is uneasy, like a man who hears rats behind the wainscot.
'We must talk, I have no quiet, it is all so – so very *arbitrary*.' I ask
him, what has he to tell?

['Tell?' says he. 'The Ogham? Not yet. I will tell you of the Ogham
once *you* have told *me* – once you have told me how you lost your

virginity and why it led your life to nothing until – until I came to Lynn and it led you to me. When I know *who you are*, I shall be the better able to confide in you; you have concealed things and laid things open all at the one same time; it has not been honest. So talk.'

For this, I had not bargained. But if he wishes it so—

'Mr Aram, I was sixteen years of age, studious, not beautiful, diffident and with a hidden soul. My father, a widower, ministered in the parish of Wells-next-the-Sea, the small harbour-town on the north Norfolk coast. With much ado he found husbands for my three elder sisters: as for me, he despaired. My brother persuaded him to let me follow my intellectual bent, and between them both they instructed me in all their own learning. For some further branches of knowledge they found a tutor or two, parishioners who would be paid for their small services with the produce of our orchard or what not, a landscape-painter once a week (for example), and the church organist. Also the young master of a Baltic trading-brig used to come, to discourse of the practicalities concomitant with geographical theory.

'Ezekiel Booth was his name; his ship (the *Dear Sweetheart*) was all winter in dock, being masted and rigged anew after heavy storms; he spent many an hour in our house. He was strong and bold, with long fair hair, his queue hanging down to his belt. He had a passion for the science of navigation, a great zeal to practise it in waters far beyond Europe. He talked to me of the Caribbean, of the oceans of India, of buccaneers and privateers, flying-fish and dolphins, pagan peoples with dark skin, their naked liberty, their seductive dances. He had no more seen these wonders than I had; but he knew many seamen who voyaged amongst them every year; he would recount their tales to me, we would speculate together upon their likelihood.

'My father took note of this closeness. It disturbed him; he put an end to the lessons. A common sailor was not for me: were I to marry at all, it must be a gentleman or nobody. Not that Ezekiel had said a word about marriage. But I had *hoped*; and my father saw it. I turned my mind toward drinking poison.

'Then the *Dear Sweetheart* was ready for sea. A wandering cruise ahead of her, to Stockholm, Danzig and other ports; she would be gone a long time. But first my Ezekiel was to make a short voyage round the coast to Lowestoft, for a particular cargo and to try the new rig. He devised a secret scheme with me: I was about to go a visit to an aunt who lived in Lowestoft, but on the way (at Great Yarmouth) I would leave the coach. His vessel would put in to Yarmouth, for no other reason than to take me aboard! I would thus arrive at Lowestoft *by sea*, telling my aunt whatever story I was able to invent. A mere jaunt of a day or two only, as improper as it was imprudent. Nay, wicked, I knew that much.

'I also knew it was not for my beauty he conspired with me, but in heedless delight at my youth and my eagerness. Whereas *I*, upon his quarterdeck, seeing him bare to the waist, swarming the shrouds to the very masthead, his tail of golden hair flung out behind him along the breeze, was enraptured altogether. Marriage, no longer a hope, had ceased to be even a consideration. I was on the sea, with *him*, a voyage everlasting, I gave no more thought to it than that.

'It was for *me*, he swore, his brig was named, which could not be true, and I knew it could not be true: then he said "*re*-named" and I would believe it even to death, even until after the clasp of his round arms in his cabin-cot had eased, and he set his lovely feet on the planking and murmured gaily, "Arise and dress!" for we were sailing into Lowestoft port.

'There you have it. The *Dear Sweetheart* went on without me, toward Denmark and the Skagerrak. But she met a norther in the Bight that piled her up on Heligoland: nearly all of her crew came home, and two mates, but not the master.

'There you have it, Mr Aram: what the d—l d'you make of it? *I* made a three months' child. Neither my father nor brother so much as guessed it. An old sludge of a woman who sold fish at our back door saw me, saw how I was, and pitied me because I'd been kind to her. Some herbs in some hot liquor, and some probing and some blood, on a pile of rotten sacks in her cottage: that which had been made was cancelled, annulled, repealed like an unjust law, cured like a filthy infection, sent into such oblivion that never never can I forget.

'Dear sweethearts indeed, the strong man and the unshaped babe.

'I have a most grievous headache, I have answered what you asked, I'll hear no more questions, no comfort, nothing. Ezekiel Booth was beautiful. You are an ugly old spider. Perhaps you are my punishment for *him*? Yet you and I are both eager (as he and I were eager); *youth* is not a point, ever again, upon the compass-card.'

This was the first time in my life I told this story to anyone. Because I told it for the first time I write it down for the first time, a deed of self-torture, of *probing*, of *blood*. Blood (that is to say) instead of ink, from the tip of my pen. After eighteen years I am open, I have opened myself; and to *him;* first my body, now my heart. It is as though now I am doing what I so yearned to do at Lowestoft such a long time ago, to remain aboard that ship and sail away and never come back. But then I would have sailed with my Ezekiel (and drowned with him, why not?); whereas now—

I did conceal; I have revealed. So what about *him?*

'You ask, what the d—l do I make of it? No more than I expected to hear. You had a great grief and you hid it. Hid yourself with it, in a hole, in a pit, like a hermit, in a *jar*. Since I came to Lynn, since you came with me to Goodluck Chapel, you can hide it no longer. Just as *she*, at Goodluck Chapel, could hide it no longer.'

'She?']

'The old hag. You saw. She knew the grave. How? Quite

rational, of course it is. A deep-desert place, even in the midst of our England, will be inhabited by aboriginals; they no more think and live like we do, than we can live and think like – like the cannibal Laestrygonians of whom we read in Homer's book. The headless gelded man within the clay of that fenland island has been remembered by the people there since the day they laid him under.'

'What? For a thousand years?'

'I'd say twice that number. Not impossible at all. They've had little else to talk about. The Romans came, the Saxons came, the Normans; the language changed; but the peasantry stayed as they were, breeding only amongst themselves, and telling their children the same stories that their mothers had told to them. Then comes Sir Reginald, Sir Reginald brings his architect, the architect brings a pickaxe, he brings me; behold! the *good luck* of Goodluck Chapel is laid open to the wind and rain. Our good luck? *Mine?*'

He brooded for a moment, muttering that it was conceivable he'd been wrong about Guallauc, maybe 'Goodluck' meant just what it said . . . 'Or maybe it means both, maybe it means everything, Guallauc, Guthlac, Goidel as well, a name that shifts and slides to accommodate all who should use it? When language is *aboriginal*, it makes a mock of lexicography, turns a scholar like myself into an ignorant child.

'All over England there are corpses in the ground, each one of 'em (if we only knew it) waiting ready to arise and signify his own frantic history. Sometimes they're quite forgotten, at other times most appallingly remembered. In Yorkshire, for example—'

He broke off and sat silent.

'Yes, Mr Aram? Yorkshire?'

He waved (as it were) Yorkshire away from him; waved *me* away from him almost; and sat silent.

[This is not satisfactory, I have been open; he is still closed.]

What he says is 'quite rational', no doubt of that. But there was much at Goodluck Chapel that seems to me beyond reason; at any rate beyond the ordinary reason of such as ourselves, school-keepers. He is as conscious of it as I am; he evades. To press him further would defeat itself. I must manage with what little he has given me.

Then he bethought himself. 'You wanted to know what the

Ogham has to say to us? I am sorry, it says nothing of any sense at all. The writer of the tablet was making a magic, she—'

[Again I must ask—]

'She?'

'I perceive her as the direct ancestress of hag Nancy, that's all. A magic – quite literally, a G–d–knows–what – it has the form of primitive poetry. I transcribe into irregular English verses, I'll read it you: it makes no sense.'

Despondently he fumbled among scrappy bits of notes until he found his latest draft. He had (it seemed) made no fair copy, not yet, not even for *me*.

'It says, but approximately, for there is the widest ambiguity to nearly every combination of the signs upon the tablet – first line of the six lines:

> *'Deep underground*
> *I have been found.*

'You see, already it makes no sense. A magic laid down alongside a buried corpse would be only for the corpse to read, to himself, to the gods of the Other World – who knows to whom? It was sealed, it was not expected to be studied by living beings. But the inscription implies directly the reverse – it implies a discovery – it implies (in short) me.'

There was panic in his voice.

'Please read it,' I said.

'Maybe I have mistaken it. I was all day and all night at it. I cannot have mistaken it.'

'Please read.'

'Second line of the six:

> *'The birds have told you where.'*

'Birds, Mr Aram?'

He ignored my question, and went on. 'Third line:

> *'How did you dare?*

' "How did you dare?" How *did* I? How? Fourth line, on the reverse of the tablet:

> *'For now the birds*
> *Shall tell you more.*

'More?' he cries, 'but *what* more? What? My G–d, they tell me *nothing*!'

No surely! was this all? For he had begun to fold his paper, first in two, then four, then eight, till it was becoming a tight little wad between finger and thumb. But I thought I had seen additional writing—

'Mr Aram, there *is* more. What is the rest?'

He looked at me fixedly, a dry blank countenance which might have been drained of all hope. 'Ah,' a heavy sigh, 'the rest of it. That's the difficulty.' He seemed to bow himself to an inexorable consequence. He unfolded the wad, slowly, deliberately. 'The fifth line of the Ogham, fifth? Why, 'tis a horrid instruction:

> *'Cut b–ll–cks from heart*
> *And heart from head—'*

He tried, with small success, to speak in an easy tone: 'Pray forgive the obscenity. The original, at that point, is exceptionally unambiguous, I must write it as I find it, my apologies. The Druids were not prudes; to them the source of life was both carnal and sacramental; the flesh was spirit; the spirit, flesh. We are Christians, we think otherwise—'

[—'or *do* we?' He added these three words with the queerest twist of the lips. If it were one of his licentious hints, it was entirely inappropriate: even had I a mind tonight for such, my aching head would disallow it. I shot him a suspicious glance. No, I concluded, he spoke from no twitch of lust, but from a deep unquiet mind, to himself rather than me.]

After a pause: 'Sixth line, final line, conditional to the instruction, meaningless:

> *'If you, like me,*
> *Would die before you're dead.*

'Very well: there you have it, and what the d—l d'you make of it?'

I make nothing of it, of course—

[—except drearily to wonder whether the cold German Ocean, where the bones of my Ezekiel lie, is also one element with the air; whether the fishes and the birds are close kindred, scavengers both (one might say). I seem to see seagulls, circling, calling, over grey-green wave-tops along a barren sandy strand where fragments of ship's timbers are scattered, half-buried.

I thought *I* had died before my death. I thought *I* had died when

Ezekiel died.

    Upon the day his wife left him, A. (doubtless) felt the same, why would he not? It is ridiculous this Ogham-script should so bring him back to it. I haven't patience. And I am not well. There is too much I have to write in my journal; I *must* write it, all of it, before bed. Pain, sickness, probing, blood . . .]

He sits trembling in his chair. I go from him, directly.

June 27th:

Dr Hinge says Paulinus improves, the fever has abated. If there is no relapse, he may resume work tomorrow. Mr A., sickly still, but dogged, comes to breakfast with the boarders, and thereafter takes his place in the schoolroom. I assist him with various classes. He is friendly to me, but distant. Regretting (I am sure) that he showed me that 'magic' last night. I cannot share his fear of it: it makes even less sense than the inscription itself. Is it possible he did not translate, but *invented*, so enthralled by the task of turning the brief symbols into verse that he has unwittingly created his own G–d-knows-what? In which case, his only fears are from his own imagination. The ancient grave has not spoken to him. So what *has*?

    My health is little better. I vomit, run with the flux, endure migraine.

    [No thoughts of the dark-lantern, so long as these ailments continue. Which is as well, because *he* is so d–mnably queer. When I am recovered, we shall see.]

I have been troubled about those boys' names I wrote down for the birch. Two of them were sheer excess of temper on my part: easy to grant a reprieve before Paulinus is returned amongst us. But the other one, the 'bathing-party' insult, was a different matter: young George Saltmarsh, the architect's orphan nephew, destined to take articles in his uncle's practice. A great ability at drawing and painting: I gave him some instruction last year, but abandoned it when his idleness disgusted me. He has since grown most insolent, I think dissolute. A strong flogging might check his ill courses before it is too late. But to reprieve two and leave a third condemned, because his mischief appeared aimed more directly at me, would show myself too swiftly vulnerable to taunts against my womanhood (as well as appearing both partial and unjust). Mercy, then, for all three or none of 'em. I decided, all three. After evening prayers I take the delinquents aside. The *two* are truly grateful: they've been livid-pale, terrified, for forty-eight hours. But Geo. S. simply smiles at me, contemptuous. Have I made a most dangerous mistake?

*

Now for the fourth *portent*, that of my play and its staging. It hung directly upon the third, although several months elapsed between them.

Mr Aram, during those months, conducted himself in the manner expected of him: he was punctual to his work, with a taciturn and ghastly good humour, to all appearance wrapped up (when not on duty) in the compilation of his lexicon. He had no further fits of rage against the pupils, who came to accept his oddities and ceased to provoke him. His spirits, by and large, were subdued; but Paulinus was well pleased. And then came the Long Vacation: three or four of the boarders, their parents dwelling overseas, stayed in the school and required supervision, so my work diminished less than I could wish. Mr Aram travelled to London and elsewhere, pursuing his researches in various gentlemen's libraries.

The outbreak of sickness went no further, we all of us recovered from it by degrees. Mr Abel-Nottidge took the advice of Dr Hinge: the ancient cadaver was had out of the Rectory and removed to a coach-house in the rear of Mr Saltmarsh's premises, he (Mr Saltmarsh) having leased the building to the Philosophical Society in order to house a small *museum*, a most liberal initiative, for which we were all most grateful. A glass case (purportedly proof against the outer air) was built to contain the cadaver. Mr Aram placed the urn therein 'to keep the old fellow company' – though not its contents: those remained his secret, and I shared it, a collusion tainted with moral qualms (not seriously to trouble me, but there *was* some malpractice there, and I hoped it would not become known). His work on the Ogham inscription subsumed itself into his lexicon-notes; he did not speak of it to me again.

Dr McCoy and Mr Saltmarsh made up their undignified quarrel, agreeing to differ like gentlemen. Both recognised their inebriety on the night in question; both regretted it and proffered correct apologies to the Society. The doctor's ridiculous flesh-wound soon mended, even despite the administrations of his colleague Dr Hinge.

During my short hours of leisure throughout vacation I set myself in earnest to the writing of my play. I was not *drawing a bow at a venture* like the soldier who slew King Ahab, but aiming at a positive mark. The Society needed funds for the conversion of the coach-house to museum; to further this important cause it was proposed to arrange a Christmas Entertainment, a Benefit at the ancient Guildhall, wherein at certain seasons a theatre-stage with proscenium would be sumptuously fitted up. I was the only member of an active poetic ambition, and when the question of a suitable play came up in our discussions, I *thrust* myself forward with no false modesty.

For some reason (unaccountable to me at the time) I found lodged in my head the idea of a fruitful plot:

∾ The Death of Ibycus, that ancient Greek poet murdered by brigands on the road to Corinth, on his way to display his art at the festival. The criminals are in the theatre when his non-appearance is discovered; they reveal themselves by their horror at the sight of a flock of birds; they remember those very birds having hovered about them as Ibycus lay dying beneath their swords. Something like the king in *Hamlet*, conscience caught by his nephew's play, 'Give me some light! *etc., etc.*' Except that the Grecian rogues are not stricken by the entertainment itself, rather by a circumstance external to its presentation. ∾

I had never written a play before. I discovered myself burdened with a surprising degree of toil, pleasant in fulfilment, wearisome in the execution.

*

6

September 7th:
The Academy reassembled today, boarding-pupils having come in last night, day-scholars this morning, all together for morning prayers and first school. Mr A. back from his wanderings, by a coach that arrived before dawn, to greet me at breakfast with enthusiasm – for his own busy researches and the prospect of my play.

[We have, unknown to Paulinus, exchanged letters during vacation. In mine to him, I've been telling him only that the play is to be performed and I am the author, I did not let slip its subject lest declaring it too early should enfeeble my imaginative *grasp* – a childish superstition. In his to me, great lists of all the ancient and outlandish texts he's pursued, and much of what he's learned from 'em. The Sanskrit, in particular. (He found a wealthy Nabob who'd bought illuminated MSS wholesale in Bengal, for their vivid miniature paintings of bare-breasted women! with not a thought of the literature they contained.) Our correspondence, on both sides, augmented by protestations of sensual affection: I fancy we've both been afraid that absence might turn to indifference. We neither of us quite trust the other. An irregular love is necessarily unstable; therefore huge my relief at the ardour of his embrace (in the boys' cloakroom, between breakfast and roll-call, a perilous place indeed).

Dark-lantern tonight, of course of course.]

September 14th (after supper):

[Dark-lantern last night, for the third night this week, and tonight again (surely) as soon as I have finished my journal-entry. If this continue, it will be *seven* nights in the week, and my fatigue will become manifest. Paulinus already sees me yawning; he believes me over-strained. I have told him it is the result of administrative confusion quite natural to the beginning of term. An excuse that cannot last.

Last night, when *G–d knows what* had run its sweaty course—]

I carelessly mentioned Ibycus. Mr A. very odd in his response, picking me up smartly, why? how? what books had I been at, that this story adhered to my pen? He said he did not like the tale, it was sensational, lacking decorum, it would not fit the Dramatic Unities, Mr Addison would never have handled it; he said it smelled of *The Beggar's Opera*, the sordidities of highway-men, quite unsuited to our Society's reputation. I told him the intent of a Benefit was to fetch the people into the theatre. Addison's *Cato* was highly regarded but John Gay became rich. I laughed at his scruples, but he did not laugh.

[Indeed he turned over in his bed, growling. A sulky beast; I pulled the sheets back and slapped his a–se with his slipper, hard; and so fled to my own bed. Tonight we shall see, did it enkindle him or turn him against me? But I am not to have my work denigrated while it is still so unformed. Was it not he in the first place who encouraged me to commence it? He should have waited to hear more from me about how I will proceed. He is, after all, less dismissive toward the school-boys; his patience with *their* clumsy attempts improves every day, so why not with those of his mistress?]

September 14th (as continued, late at night):

Mr A. contrite, he sees now he was wrong to try to dictate to my muse. Ibycus, if I must! (says he), he will graciously suspend judgement. I, in return, agree that his criticism has something of good value. A classic tragedy on this theme, in regular verse obedient to the Unities, may very well not be possible. If I cannot do it, I won't. So we come to a harmony once more.

> [It *enkindled* him. (I thought it would, bearing in mind the Tommy Whitesmith episode.) More of the same. And much laughter.]

October 1st:
The regular verse no trouble to me; but I ought not to employ it in every scene. Brigands, for example, must speak prose. Also, they sing songs: *The Beggar's Opera* no bad model, whatever Mr A. should say. I am finding much comedy in the byways of the tale. The whole piece, despite my best intentions, becomes rapidly as irregular as Shakespeare. Ibycus himself is tragical, of course; his murder must harrow the audience. But the conclusion – a band of ruffians in a crowded theatre (*alfresco*) milling about among the bewildered populace, staring at the sky while all others stare at the stage, cowering, scrambling, seeking to hide anywhere – is it not an absurd thought? Surely the manager would endeavour to have them hurled from the precincts, long before any could tell the true reason for their panic? We see such in our own theatres, and the cause is invariably *gin*. I am rewriting many scenes in the light of these thoughts. I now perceive large portions of what I've already written as pompous beyond all measure.

October 16th:
Mr A. insistent I show him my script. I refuse. He shall read it complete, before anyone else of the Society has a glimpse of it: that is a promise and he must content himself! He asks me, is there a part for him? I tell him what is so far decided: the paid actors of the stock company from Norwich (who will be here upon their touring-circuit) are to play the chief characters, and our members (if they wish) can be allotted the subordinate roles. I have a lengthy *dramatis personae* list, there will be mouthfuls of passion for all. I think (though I keep it to myself) that Mr A. might well be the Second Murderer. First Murderer is a little man, devilish and sly, a perfect part for Mr Bones of the company. He needs a foil, tall and grotesque, who impedes his evil schemes with occasional bursts of conscience. (I steal the idea from *Richard III*, the murderers of Clarence.)

The play is to be read next week to the Society. If it is finished. Will it be finished? Yes! even if I wake all night, writing and rewriting.

> [Therefore, alas, an end to the dark-lantern, but only for a short space of time. Last night I brought him his old cane. He did not know I had kept it. Why had I kept it? One of my secrets: I seem to have so many, I hide them even from myself. There is a kind of madness in it. Cordelia, regard yourself! all your pursuits, hitherto, have been more or less rational. The Blue Stocking denotes feminine reason; it ought not to be betrayed. Can playmaking (of its very nature) be an insidious *Judas-trick*?]

Paulinus is as hopeful as a child, on my behalf. Speaking strictly, his Holy Orders should prevent him from either taking a part in the play or attending its performance; but he says it is for a Charitable Cause and thus the rules do not apply. If this be so, the Rector himself might just possibly be persuaded to *walk on* as the High Priest of Apollo!

October 25th:

My play is finished! I have given my MS (in this last hour, at after supper) to Mr A. Tonight he shall read it: tomorrow evening, the Society as a whole shall hear it read. I have called it:

THE UNCOVERED CORPSE
or,
How the Birds cried 'Blood!'

(by a Gentlewoman of King's Lynn)
an Historical Ballad-Tragedy, never before performed!!

I suppose the playbill will be worded with a greater elaboration; but this will serve well for the title-page.

I have made a number of late alterations to my plot. For example, the Second Murderer (one Phaon, a sea-going pirate as well as a brigand upon land) now attempts an affair of the heart with the Confidante of my heroine Sappho – Sappho the sweet poetess, whom Ibycus loves unrequited. Sappho's place in the story is a contortion of history, I admit it without shame; but to dramatise *any* history is in itself a process of fiction.

> [This particular fiction brings about most happily a contrast of modes of love. Sappho rejects the *flame* of Ibycus, because she has previously loved another poet, Alcaeus, with unhappy result. Poets, she declares, should honour each other's verses, not strive for an amorous connection (which too often will destroy the very

springs of the verses themselves). Meanwhile she yearns distractedly for the crude embraces of Phaon, while giving her tender heart to her Confidante: Flesh as opposed to Spirit. Whereas Ibycus claims that *his* love would comprehend for her both Spirit *and* Flesh. A delicate question and I trust I have handled it with delicacy. (Sappho's *softness* for her fellow females being well known among persons of learning, it need not be emphatically stated.) She, of course, will be played by Miss Greengarden of the company, whose beauty has entranced me ever since she played in Lynn last year. If *I* play the Confidante, a neat correlation of temperaments may be achieved; I call her (for a certain reason) Naucrate, 'mistress of ships'; that love should entangle her with an eager Poetess and a Villain at the one same time lends her dialogue a pathetic ambiguity. She is not entirely guiltless of the murder; yet her guilt is unintended. She has something of a limp or a hunched back, poor woman.]

But none of this of any consequence, if the play is not liked.

[No dark-lantern for Mr A., until he tells me what he thinks of it. Oh, faintness, tremors and nausea, I cannot wait!]

October 26th (ten minutes past five o'clock post meridiem):
I am in my room, drinking tea, when the parlour-maid brings me a packet: inside it, my play, with a note from Mr A. Woe! he says no more than—

> *Madam:*
> I have read every word of it with increasing dismay, I sorely regret I ever told you my preliminary doubts of this story. For I deduce you have been at pains to *confirm* them through and through. You are a lady of such parts that your action can only be attributed to malice aforethought. You knew what I distasted; quite deliberately you have given it prominence.
>
> Thus you'll understand it will not be possible for me to be present at the Society's meeting tonight. Nonetheless, may I offer, both to you and to the membership, my honest hopes for whatever you might conceive to be a signal of your venture's success—
>
> > *yr. most obedt. E.A.*

He despises me.

No! he insults me, because I would not share my writing with him. No! he is deeply jealous: he would have wished to write a play for the Museum Fund himself and was too late to get his name in.

I despise *him.*

But tonight I shall not flinch. The Society may mock if it chooses. *What I have written, I have written.* And they shall hear it!

October 26th (as continued, near midnight):

Mr A. reckons without his host! The Society was so loud in its praise for *The Uncovered Corpse* that between its plaudits and my own exhaustion after my reading of it, I nigh swooned on the Rector's Turkish carpet. And such leniency toward the irregularity of style! for Mr Trampler (actor-manager of the company) was in our midst, and he pronounced it 'superbly adapted' to the public taste of King's Lynn. The austerities of Addison and other Augustan tragedians have never 'gone down' with our local audience, he said. He said my muse combines the jocundity of Gay with the harsh *home-truths* of Geo. Lillo. None happier than himself to oversee the presentation on our boards. (He, of course, will play Ibycus. A more mature reading than I looked for, but one must suffer one's characters to be embodied by such bodies as are available; and who can doubt the skills of Mr Trampler?) Rehearsals commence one month today. Paulinus is as proud of me as though I were Britannia and he King George!

Upon our return home, I send John Lobscott with a brief note to slip 'neath the door of the Usher's Lodge, informing Mr A. of the Society's opinion and stating (with a correct courtesy) that if he change his mind, his participation, assistance and advice with the play will be welcome, despite all. I am careful not to seem to *triumph*.

> [And be d–mned to the dark-lantern! I have shaken off all need for it, I am an Author in my own right! Were it consonant with good manners, I would *strut* the streets of Lynn like Penthesilea the Amazonian Queen.]

December 7th:

All the actors are now in town; they have set up the stage in the Guildhall; rehearsals are proceeding apace. The orchestra to be directed and the score arranged by our famous Dr Charles Burney, choirmaster and organist of St Margaret's, scholar and historian of music, a close friend of the illustrious Handel! School at St Guthlac's is almost abandoned, so many of the boys being required to take part in the play – we need a great crowd for the scene of the festival at Corinth, and their best voices as Chorus are requisite throughout. Paulinus (as Polycrates, Tyrant of Samos) is at the theatre, rehearsing, day after day. Mr A., crosspatched and sullen, must teach all the classes on his own.

The role of Phaon is now given to Mr Bones, who's kicked his

heels against First Murderer. He said Phaon (his supposed 'foil')
has all the 'fat o'th'ham' and ought not to be left to an amateur.
Lacking Mr A., I do not repine at this change of plan.

[But I have an uneasy feeling that Miss Greengarden nourishes a
similar jealousy as between Sappho's role and Naucrate's. She is a
young woman (alas not a *gentlewoman*) – I should say, rather, a
great girl – of unfeigned and luxurious charm; any offence lying
between us would be deeply distressing to me. She invites me to
sup with her tomorrow night, after her performance in the present
play (Desdemona to Mr Trampler's Othello; I saw it last night; she
drew my hottest tears). 'Twill be very late to venture from home;
but so exhilarating are these days that all petty conventions may
lightly be thrown to the winds!]

December 9th:
[Unable last night to make up my journal, I combine the entries
for two days.

When I walked (with John Lobscott as linkman and escort) to
Miss G'g.'s lodgings, a cold wind was a-stir with flurries of sleetish
rain. Miss G'g. told him not to return for me, as her landlady's boy
could easily fulfil the office; this pleased him of course, lazy man!

She gave me a dish of whitebait, with a quart of porter, and rum-
punch to follow. Simple fare but sustaining, the fishes admirably
crumbed and fried; more than a sufficiency of lemon and onion-
slices, and fresh bread. Notwithstanding the exertions of her stran-
gulation (on the Moor's fatal bed but one half-hour earlier), she
spoke exceeding lively; suggesting a host of amendments to our
scenes which do indeed materially improve her part. Nor do they
seem to diminish the pathos of mine. She shows kindness in her
jealousy, recognising that her comparative youth and beauty will *of
themselves* cause her to dominate the stage, therefore she does not
need to 'mutilate' Naucrate's lines – she used the word herself with a
very pretty deference. She admires me so much, she says.

By two o'clock of the morning, the wind had increased to a
powerful tempest and the street outside was a torrent, all the
lanterns blown out. She said I must not attempt to go home but
stay in her rooms until day. The punch had dizzied my head; my
cloak was not full proof against such weather; the house was neat
and *cosy*; I did not demur.

She has but the one bed. Narrow though it was, it invited me
deliciously. We slept in secure comfort, and embraced with a
mutual candour. Strange that I had taken her for Mr T.'s mistress!
She confided she is much of a mind with my Sappho; why should
cantankerous men have prior right to the warmth of women's
arms? I feel no shame for this affection; whereas, with Mr A.—

Cordelia, peace! write no more of it, you're done with him.
Today, however, I am not so sure.]

I am *torn*. Mr A. of a sudden accosted me in the lobby of the

schoolroom with another of his notes, pushing it into my hand
and surging away to his Greek class. Its wording as abrupt as the
manner of its delivery.

> I have been (for three dire weeks!) *deep underground*: now *the birds
> have told*. Indeed they have *told more*: you having writ your tragedy,
> they cry me upward toward it, I cannot deny them. The tablet of
> bone spake truth; I tried to ignore it; I tried to hide from my
> premature death; I cannot do it. Let me speak. If not tonight,
> tomorrow: I will not be peremptory.
>
> [Dark-lantern? Cruel woman, I'll await.]

What to do? I am torn.

December 10th:

I decided: I must see him. I have not the heart to rebuff an
authentic penitence. His letter moreover made me fear he may
be out of his wits.

> [If so, *my* fault. Maybe I can restore him. Dark-lantern therefore,
> in great trepidation: a fierce cold night which made me shiver all
> the more. Was there danger? But if I failed him there would be
> worse danger, for I see him every day willy-nilly, he could break
> out against me anywhere.
>
> If indeed 'twas for my love he's been running mad, he scarcely
> showed it, neither by gesture nor carnal touch. And as for his
> words—]

—he says only he has been re-examining the Ogham. He had
stubbornly endeavoured to 'hold himself together' contrary to
the admonition contained therein. Mortal error. Instead (he
says wildly) he has his orders from the birds, he must 'cut into
three and so die' – *id est*, leave his rational part and his
considered affections to the school-house and the Usher's
Lodge, and hurl himself regardless into the whirlpool of theatric
creation. His comments on *The Uncovered Corpse* (he says) were
of the study and its lamp-oil—

> [—and distorted by what he took to be 'perverse spites of Cupid'
> behind the shape of my play, behind my refusal to accede to his
> literary opinions. (His only word tonight of our love!)]

Plays (he says) belong to the stage; upon the stage and the stage
alone can he enter into mine. Hence this strenuous change of
mind!

I am nonplussed. Birds? What have birds to do with the
business? The absurdity that *birds* in an ancient inscription
(dubiously translated) should adjudicate yea or nay upon the
principles of modern drama! Of course our museum is the cause

of the play, and the museum turns his mind to the inscription. But also—

'Goodluck Chapel? Those birds there? You think *they* told? Collect yourself, sir! how *could* they?'

He looks me direct in the face. 'Madam, at Goodluck Chapel I saw not one single bird. Are you mad? It poured with rain; they were in shelter, as is their wont, keeping their plumage dry under the leaves.'

Which is a lie, I am sure of it.

However, if he wishes to be connected with the play, let him come to the Guildhall. There are many small parts yet to be allotted, many small duties he can undertake. Mr Trampler will be glad of his help.

I am very very angry with him, the more so as it is now too late for him to be cast as Phaon.

[The 'spites of Cupid' drive me out of the Lodge. I think he would not have me go; but he lacks the means of persuasion. His mouth seems to be about to frame words, his hand to reach for his cane. I allow him no time for either. Shall I be able to bear it when I see him with all his whims at the Guildhall? Am *I* mad? He dares to ask me! *Cantankerous*, Miss G'g.'s word. Yes. And as mad as a soaking raven.]

December 15th:

Mr A., during rehearsals, has behaved very well. He has cheerfully shouldered the task of marshalling the boys. As their usher he has an authority over them which they would not so easily accept from the stage-manager. He also plays a small part, that of the Master of the Revels, introducing the Corinthian Festival.

Mr Trampler asked him to lend his services to the stage-manager in general errands. He has done so with eager despatch. Until today, when an odd thing happened. Certain costumes from the company's stock had been lodged with Altdorfer the pawnbroker. (Mr Trampler, like all actor-managers, is never very far from insolvency; or so I am told by Miss G'g.) Mr A. was commissioned to go to the shop and redeem them – the Society paying, as they were needed for the play. To everyone's astonishment, he violently refused, saying that Altdorfer was 'a d–mned Jew and a rogue and own brother (were he to reveal his right name) to another d–mned usurer in Soho, London, who

cheated me once most abominably! I have only to look at him to
know the face! Never never will I enter his doors!'

This was nonsense. Altdorfer is certainly exorbitant, but an
exorbitant German of the Lutheran faith. He came to Lynn years
ago as supercargo on the *Dear Sweetheart*, and stayed here to
establish a business. I know him quite well. His son was taught
at St Guthlac's. If any brother of his dwelt in London, I am sure I
would have heard of it. He is a merry man and very garrulous,
when not behind his counter. Mr A. was excused his mission: a
dislike of pawnbrokers is no capital offence, however disproportionate. And he had Mr Trampler's sincere sympathy.

> [To Miss G'g. again this evening. She is not in tonight's play, so she
> can give me several hours. Her rum-punch (which I should avoid!)
> incites me to tell her something of my dealings with A. I do not
> name him to her, merely speak of 'old Blunderbore'. She consoles
> me for my unhappiness, kissing me *(and so forth)*; counsels me
> strongly against him. Needless advice: I know it all already. I also
> talk of Ezekiel. She tells me many of her own sad adventures. Now
> I am her *confidante* in life as upon stage. We weep together.]

December 16th:

Consternation at rehearsal. Mr Bones has fallen sick of a
grievous quinsy, is unable to utter, and (so says Dr McCoy) must
resign his part forthwith to save his throat. So why cannot Mr A.
be placed as Phaon, according to my original wish? Mr Trampler
doubtful – the part is too great for an amateur (*etc.*) – but he can
think at short notice of no better plan. Mr A. assumes a childish
reluctance, and then a no less childish submission to fate. He is
not happy, that much is clear. He has something to say about the
speed with which he must learn the lines (*etc., etc.*), but no one
believes him and no one heeds him.

> [He is unhappy because Phaon is to lust after *me*. I know this
> without his telling me. Much of my intent in this fictional *amour*
> has been spoiled for me by recent events. But let it be.]

December 17th:

Mr A., as Phaon, does not read as I had hoped. He *understates* his
lines d–mnably. Miss G'g. can do nothing with him. I've no
choice but to speak to him in private, which I do not wish to do.

> [I ambush him backstage, and reproach him with vigour. In return
> he informs me that G'g. comes 'bloody-well at him' just as his own
> wife did, while I (fleeing him in the play) mimic thereby my flight
> from him in life. In both cases, he is unmanned. He could tolerate
> 'the Greengarden' if only *I* were more responsive. By which token

he hands me a piece of poetry, his own translation (says he) of one of the few poems known for certain to be by the hand of the historical Ibycus. I am fool enough to read it:

> Whereas the flowers of the quince and the vine bloom only in the spring *(a fair description of 'em in two stanzas: I summarise)* . . . the poet's love blazes for full twelve months in the year . . .

> —wild Venus sends it raging forth,
> Thick-dark and shot with lightning fire
> A storm-wind from the rock-girt north
> To strike my limbs in ruthless ire,
> To twist and wring my heart 'til all its blood be dry,
> To whirl me from my feet! Demolished, here I lie.

Deeply troubled, I thank him and assure him that I will do my best to insert the poem somewhere into my text. I had not known that any of Ibycus's work in fact survived. Nor had I guessed that his muse was twin-sister to Mr A.'s wicked brooding at its worst. Even so, we play no dark-lantern tricks tonight, and let him not think we do.]

December 18th (as written on the morning of the 19th):
That vicious youth George Saltmarsh has disgraced the Academy.

I blame Mr A. He was supposed to keep good watch over all of our boys who were at work in the Guildhall. Yesterday Paulinus remained in school, and left them in A.'s charge with what should have been an adequate confidence. Young Saltmarsh was sent to the wardrobe in the undercroft to bring up his costume (he plays the Master of the Revels now that A. is Phaon) for inspection by Mr Trampler prior to dress-rehearsal on the 20th. He failed to return; and *at last* was discovered dead drunk in a gin-shop with a chit of a young seamstress attached to the company, whom in vain he was striving to ravish. The money for this debauch came out of the actors' dressing-rooms; he had abstracted it while they worked!

Mr A.'s excuse for his fault in supervision: he was aloft, helping to rig ingenious wires between the rafters over the fore-stage and the sky-borders behind, for the flight of the practicable birds. No one asked him to do this: his aid was officious. Even the stage-manager says so. Mr Saltmarsh (Snr.) promises to repay the stolen money, and sends immediate word to Paulinus, demanding that he discipline the nephew. 'With your utmost severity,' he adds. Rehearsals half broken up in consequence of this calamity. Mr A. marches Geo. S. back to the school-house, cuffing him along King Street, Queen Street and Lath Street into the Bridge Street, and all the way through the South Gate – most

ludicrous spectacle. Miss G'g. greatly agitated: 2s. $9^1/_2$d. of her
own small moneys is gone from her purse – she is not sure she
can trust Mr Saltmarsh's promise – 'My dear, in this business
they'll cheat us, if they can, every time'—

> [—and she prays me to console her. Rum-punch for the two of us
> in the parlour of the Duke's Head, at my cost, until the call-boy
> shall come to warn us of resumption of work. She tells me she is to
> leave the company as soon as my play is over. She goes to London,
> a professional engagement at Drury Lane! – nor is that all.
> *Marriage!* forsooth; and at once, in the New Year, to a prosperous
> metropolitan actor. 'My dear, I don't *want* to, he is a crab. But he
> has money, which I have not; and influence with Garrick, which I
> desperately need. The part at the Lane is nothing, a mere Con-
> fidante to Kitty Clive's heroine. Who the d—l wants to be a
> Confidante?'
>
> *I* do. But it's finished. Ah, she might have told me before!
>
> Ah, but she is sweet to me. Brings me later to her rooms, more
> rum-punch, more tears, more warmth, *and so forth*. I leave her
> early, I have my lines to con for the looming dress-rehearsal, so
> has she.
>
> So why do I not con them?
>
> Why, tonight of all nights, do I set out to carry that d–mned
> dark-lantern to where it ought not to go, ought *never* to have
> been?
>
> And why, halfway there, do I turn madly about and stumble
> back blubbering to my room, leaving footprints in the snow for
> anyone to see in daylight? For I don't con my part: but wake and
> toss and walk all night. My memory for my lines is gone,
> absolutely. Nor am I able to sit to my journal.
>
> Between breakfast and morning school I do at last sit to it. Thus.
> I wonder I write it at all, being brought to such a pass. More snow
> in the small hours: no footprints, be thankful!]

December 19th:

> [I ought to have restrained every thought, every hope, every beat
> of my heart today, save those in the service of my play. What! the
> dress-rehearsal, and I (author and actor) so infamously distracted?
>
> But immediately after morning prayers – at which I abased myself
> and wept (I trust unnoticed) – Paulinus, with dour solemnity, declared
> the punishment of Geo. S. Not only the Master's birch, but the birch
> *coram populo*, before all of St Guthlac's assembled, a most terrible
> innovation and a mark of the utmost shame. For did we not know, all
> of us, were it not for the benevolence of the school, the penalty by
> public law might very well be the gallows? At his uncle's angry
> insistence, the boy (though a day-pupil) had spent the night in the
> school-house, locked in a garret. Now John Lobscott, rod in hand, led
> him trembling amongst us. They would bend him across a carpenter's
> saw-horse, tie him there wrist and ankle, and unbreech him.

As my brother (a very Tyrant of Samos in all truth) announced these degrading preliminaries, he made a quick sign to me: I was not to be a witness.

I should have gone to my room.

Instead, I quietly entered our little wash-house across the yard. From its window it is possible to see into the schoolroom window. I could not see everything. (The face of Mr A., for example, was out of my vision.) I saw enough; and I heard. The heavy strokes, one by one; and I heard the young Mohock roar. I thought Paulinus would never finish, so cunctatious, so implacable, the rigour of his just wrath. And then, when he wearied, he handed the rod to John Lobscott and John Lobscott carried on. Blood.

I came out of the wash-house to feel and taste my *own* blood; it was running down my chin: my lower lip (somehow) was quite bitten through. As I leaned against the wash-house doorframe to recover from my urgent shudders (my *ecstasies*, though I shudder to say so), I saw that I was seen. Our kitchen-maid, a foolish slut, stood and stared at me from the corner of the yard. I sent her about her business: but I wish she had not been there.]

No work at the Guildhall during the day – at any rate for the actors – Mr Trampler and his stage-manager are setting up scenes. In the evening we all assemble for a full look at ourselves, in costume, in front of the refurbished flats. The *noble* characters are dressed as Romans from the company's stock. Romans, or Greeks? Mr Trampler says they were all the same. It would seem their men wore breastplates, periwigs and plumed helmets; their women, plumes and hoops. (The theatre has its proper tradition: we scholars must accommodate ourselves thereto.) The *lower* personages assume the clothes of present time: Phaon comes on as a gaudy sea-rover, Naucrate as a lady's maid.

The scenes, also from stock, are temples, palaces, wild country and so forth, much as one's always pictured 'em. I had my doubts about a Peasant's Cottage for the First Act: it looked to me ineradicably *English*, as it might be that alehouse on the road to Goodluck Chapel. Mr Trampler says it's all he has; so let it be.

There is a difficulty about the practicable birds: the mechanics of their flight. I am assured it will be solved before tomorrow.

Home to bed, faint with fatigue. (Mr A. will be all night at the theatre, *very busy*, I am sure.) But verily I do believe that my lines are secure in my head!

December 20th:
Dress-rehearsal, at last! throughout the afternoon. Naught went gravely amiss, but neither was anything *quite right*. Miss G'g.

laughed when I wept for mistakes: she said *all* dress-rehearsals proceed thus – if they do not, then disaster (inevitable) before the audience next day. Superstitious minx.

> [She *lied* to me, by omission, when she kept from me so long the ill news of her betrothal! I cannot hate her, but my love is curdled. She was cruelly *masterful* on stage today, in a way she never was before. I found it hard to assert my Naucrate against her. Will she behave so, tomorrow? Thank G–d we have but one performance.]

The worst bungling was with the birds. They did not fly at all! The stage-manager swears he yet has time to amend the machine; Mr Trampler in a towering rage with him; Mr A., interfering rascal, shouts at everyone, even *me*, demanding that the birds be 'dropped' as a piece of practicability, let Ibycus and the Brigands only *seem* to see them fly! But that would lead the public to think 'twas hallucination: absurdity, I'll have none of it, it falsifies the fable. No! there *must* be birds: what else is the theatre for, but to SHOW just as much as to TELL?

Mr Trampler requests us amateurs to take our costumes home and wear them for a little, tonight and tomorrow; we know not how to be at ease in 'em (he says); we are *lumps*, we need practice.

Mr A. all of a sudden declines to stay behind to give help again to the stage-manager. Says he needs to con his lines: not so, he has them perfect. He is sour about those birds, that his advice should not be taken. I suspect the stage-manager is glad for his absence.

December 21st:
HORROR!! AND SHAME!!!

> [His absence from the Guildhall meant his presence in the Usher's Lodge.
>
> I wrote my yesterday's journal-entry and so prepared (slowly) for bed. G–d's Chr–st! I was unable to keep my hand from the dark-lantern. And when I got there, through the falling snow, such frenzy and pain between him and me, *demolishing* our two selves before the piled-up logs he had a-blaze in his fireplace! Even tho' we were attired, in a foolish hope to make merry, as Naucrate and Phaon, not a crack of our old laughter, only punishing to hurt. Wild Venus raging forth indeed. Abominable, yet exquisite. I must have slept, afterwards; crouched up heedless among his boots and his portmanteau; for I crept back to the school-house only one quarter-hour before the morning bell awoke the boarders. Almost on all fours. This is base deterioration, far far beneath his true qualities, or mine. And then—]

—the performance. Oh, how am I to write of it? First, in the Quarrel Scene, I smacked my hand into G'g.'s poor face as fiercely as I could: we had never rehearsed it so. She took it without a word; her eyes alone betrayed her, wide open with shock, hot tears springing to fill them.

After that, a smooth course: till we arrived at the Murder Scene. Phaon's conscience, though well expressed (he delivered his lines with a biting strength), kept him so far 'up the stage' that the First Murderer had the action all but entirely to himself: again, it had not been so rehearsed. As Ibycus lies dying, first appearance of the troublesome birds: what would they do? To my amazement, the stage-manager had rid himself of the stuffed creatures that kept sticking on the wires. Instead he used black rags, no sort of solid shape at all, but they whipped and quivered high up above the fore-stage with sinister speed, a brief flash of 'em and they were gone. Mr Trampler, when the scene closed, came past me in the wings, grinning with professional pride: 'Why, they even frightened *me*. Just you wait, Miss Pole-Hatchet, till you see 'em in the Theatre Scene!'

A little later I observed Mr A., white-faced, mopping his brow. He had *hid* himself, almost, in a dark recess behind the prompter.

But he came out of it, acting vehemently, out of control, filthily! (his comedy beastly vulgar, his tragic speeches the nadir of rant) until the Theatre at Corinth. This scene was 'full depth', a high stage-within-the-stage, whereon the Chorus sing a song, while the Grecian audience fill up the middle space. Naucrate makes one of the Grecian audience. On the fore-stage, the two Murderers, arriving (as it were) late. I therefore had my back to them when they first appeared. Their cry, 'The birds of Ibycus!' alerts us all, we turn to see – and *what* did we see? The black rags (to an Awful Music) swirling and swooping round and round, from side to side, only a foot above the Murderers' heads; the wires had been re-rigged between the acts; the effect was as Terrific as the playbills had sworn it would be; and Mr A., at the very climax, had a seizure.

I CANNOT FORGIVE HIM.

The play had to be stopped. Phaon, in the final scenes, is crucial to the knotting of the plot. Phaon, in the final scenes, lay raving backstage, impossible to calm or rouse. He mouthed about 'the Man' who flew at him (so he said) from among the birds. 'The Man in his bloody bones.' 'The Man without his head.' 'The Man without his b–ll–cks.' It was dreadful to hear: and woe! *my play was stopped*.

Our imbecile King's Lynn public laughed and jeered as they pushed out of the building.

> [I shared Miss G'g.'s dressing-room. She changed her clothes in silence, nor could *I* speak to *her*. I was there before she came in, my hoops off, my stays undone, my shift dropped from my shoulders, unable to proceed further for the depth of emotion: I sat with my back to her, burying my head in my arms. Certain marks on my skin, bruises, *and so forth*. At last she must have turned and seen them; she came behind me, touched them lightly. 'I warned you, you foolish child,' she said. Her voice was compassionate. (But 'child'? She's full ten years the younger.) 'And don't think I don't know who he is—]

'I wish *I'd* had the handling of him. But to tell truth, I *don't* wish. *G–d knows what* such a Saracen might not have done.' Thus Sophia Greengarden. Her acquaintance with A. goes no further than his antics in the theatre. But she sorrowed for my sorrow. And went out: to make haste and catch the night-coach to London.

*

All this I have described may be thought more than a *portent*. A skilled thief-taker (his attention once drawn to Mr Aram's demeanour in regard to *The Uncovered Corpse*) would very probably have chosen to trace the usher's life back through the years for as far as it could be found. But which of us in Lynn had the qualities of a thief-taker?

We saw only a fellow townsman, unloved perhaps, but respected, who was suffering a sad affliction. Dr McCoy blamed himself, saying too much had been said and done at Goodluck Chapel for a taut precarious intellect to absorb with any safety. He diagnosed brain-fever; and kept Mr Aram close in bed for several weeks. Paulinus asked me to take charge of his nursing. I did not wish to do so; I was so bitter for the ill fortune of my play; but how could I refuse?

The patient, as it chanced, wanted none of my services. In his delirium he cried out to my brother that I had 'smothered him with wings and feathers', it was time I crept in under, under the trees, out of the rain, and at last into a hole in the ground, or else like himself I'd be strapped to a saw-horse by that pistoleer McCoy and (with a shriek) *'have her a–se cut into three!'* Let them

send, he beseeched, for old Brewster, her costs could be drawn
from his wages, for surely he would soon improve. He grew a
little calmer, kept repeating 'surely surely', and rolled and
sweated in his sheets with groan upon groan.

*

7

December 26th (Boxing Day):
Mrs Brewster says Mr A. is much better. He sleeps without
raving, eats his pap without a vomit, has not pissed his bed for
three nights. I do not much care. But for Paulinus the news is
good; the queer sickness cast gloom over his Christmas entirely.
Our vacation-boarders kept the feast with their usual joy; my
brother and I were sore put to be jolly with them. Today many of
the day-pupils came with their cheerful impudence to solicit
Christmas Boxes. I tried to laugh as I gave them the annual new
pennies, brightly polished by the housemaid; it was not easy.

[I had not thought George Saltmarsh would be one of 'em. After
his crime he was expelled the cast of the play; since the flogging I
had no sight of him till this morning. It was still, I observed, some
hardship for him to walk. He was sidelong deferential to me, *butter*
(the adage has it) *not melting*, as he made his mouth into a sly smile
and begged a favour: a few private words. He had come for no
Christmas Box: he had one for *me*, he said, he hoped I would
accept it as a token of his remorse.

I did not trust him. But the uncle is a tiresome man, the boy is
without father or mother, and Paulinus did deal with him most
fearfully. It was not for me to continue his punishment. So in we
went, to the drawing-room. He laid on the table a small scroll of
paper, neatly tied with a bow of ribbon. Wondering, I loosened the
knot. It was one of his own drawings, a most delicate pen-and-ink
with tinting of light watercolour. An apprentice attempt at the
quasi-caricatura of Hogarth, exhibiting great accomplishment.

I would have ripped it up before his eyes; but I lacked the presence
of mind. I could only stand and *goggle* at it, the blood fiery hot in my
face. Then I sat (for fear of swooning) and looked at it still.

I must write what I saw, though it puts me on the rack. There
was a bright fire in a dark room, illuminating two figures who
faced half-away from the spectator: a short plump woman and a
tall lean man. I am ashamed to describe their postures, save only
to say this—

Insofar as they were clothed at all, she wore gartered stockings
(*blue*) and a prim white cap of starched linen, with the hint of a

pair of spectacles beyond the turn of her right temple, while he
had a piratical bandana swathing his cropped hair, a cutlass stuck
into a sash, ear-rings, sea-boots. The rest of their garments lay
tossed upon floor and furniture. There was a cane in her hand and
stripes from its application across those parts of their bodies which
civil society (by decent convention) keeps hid.

'Miaow, miaow,' says Master George, 'Cordy-cat! you didn't
suppose mouse Abby'd hold her trap shut?' (Abby being the
kitchen-maid, ah mercy!) 'Those that peep through windows can
be peeped at in their turn.'

I looked again at his monstrous picture. Without doubt: he had
seen. Had the curtain not been drawn? It *must* have been drawn.
Maybe a careless gap, one fatal inch, or half an inch . . . who else
had seen? Abby?

'Not her. She consoled me for the birching, enabled me so
sweetly to get into the stables by night. Coming out again through
the garden, I saw a lantern on the prowl, went after it. Sneak-jack,
y'see, me. Very vengeful, y'see, me, Ecod, I'll not be treated like a
brat of thirteen!'

He might have been fifteen, approaching sixteen, but he spoke
as a man of thirty. He was big enough for a man of thirty; a
dangerous man too.

'Your own eyes,' says he, 'can tell you my improvement in
drawing from the life; aye you banished me your paintbox and
easel, but I kept it up, *didn't I?* self-instructed, aye and diligent
beyond all your expectations. Because that's what I want to be,
Hogarth is most admirable ingenious, but *I* have the power to rise
higher! Michelangelo! Italy! I know it! Oh, I *need* to go to *Italy*, so
why won't dear uncle permit me?'

He laid a hand on my rump. A fumbling hot hand, both
lecherous and boyish enthusiastic; I dared not do other than suffer
him. He gabbled close into my ear: 'All he'll say at this present, I
must bide in this d–mned Academy for your Pharisee brother to
flog me to death if he chooses, for your brute of a bloody old usher
to knock me about in the open street! Why, now he says I'm not
even fit for his piddling peddling drawing-office, though he'd
sworn I could go there at turn of the New Year. Ecod, I'd run
tomorrow, take ship, and never come back. But Cordy-cat, Cordy-
cat, I don't have the blunt!'

I told him (quavering) that his manifest talent did deserve a
sojourn in Italy, he did have a power, he did have a genius, it
ought to be perfected. I would most certainly speak to his uncle. I
gained courage (observing his foolish joy at my praise, observing
him somewhat shamefast, indeed he took his hand away); I added
that he should understand I was not to be coerced; his picture
would convince nobody, for who would believe it other than a
nasty little exercise of his own squalid phantasy?

He ruminated, and then said: 'McCoy. The spud-eating doctor:
he'd believe anything of *you*. I heard him tell m'uncle, being these

days d–mned good bottle-mates with him, that "Miss Cordelia's apparent prudery was physiologically contradicted by the creases in her round white neck." A medical fact, he said, an infallible token, "begorrah and bejabers, the comparative warmth of the *mons veneris* is ever reflected in the parallel throat-glands". Oh yes, McCoy and old Saltmarsh are vainglorious every night together, didn't they stand each other's fire and come out of it with plumes of honour? D–mned bawdily they talk with all their pedantry, I can tell you. Betwixt 'em they can ruin you, they can ruin this genteel Academy. So you go to m'uncle, persuade him, and that's it.

'Keep the pretty picture, I only meant it for your mirth, I can always sketch another one. Merry Christmas, ma'am, tra-la-la.'

His drawing *has* improved. Let him once be given the chance seriously to set his mind to it, would his character not mend as well? A regular apprenticeship in the *ateliers* of Rome could be much the best thing, surely? – and for all of us.]

January 7th:

Mrs Brewster and her sister take it turn and turn about to watch in the Usher's Lodge. Costly. It is said he is sinking into the blackest melancholia, eats, sleeps, groans, but never speaks a coherent word. The less he speaks the better, I cannot bear to think of him.

[A week now since school recommenced. Geo. S. absent. The day after Boxing Day he was carried away by his uncle, to Lincoln where the latter has a contract for a terrace of houses. It is this fetching of the boy all over the country that unsettles him, I do believe. This morning they returned: I go speedily to see Mr Saltmarsh. I make the nephew's case to him, Italy, prolonged studies, experience of the world, fellow artists, an adequate subsidy, (*etc.*, *etc.*). His reply exceeding tetchy: 'What, ma'am, should I pay for the hobbledehoy to *profligate* through foreign parts and nests of popery? What would he find there but a dose of clap? Most certainly not! I'm astonished at you. Tomorrow morning, first thing, he re-submits himself to St Guthlac's; I trust he'll be firmly dealt with.']

January 8th:

[Geo. S. creeps up upon me (against all school-rules) as I take sight of the stars through my telescope on the roof. Very meek, to all seeming, much cast down by the uncle's refusal. I show him the heavenly bodies; but their majesty does not awe him. Instead he tells me softly (while peering through the eyepiece of the glass) that he knows the Academy to be 'woundy rich and farting guineas. Find a way to the Pharisee's strongbox. Set me free.'

St Guthlac's funds are in the bank under sovereignty of my brother's sole signature. No doubt a foolish boy would not have understood this, but a boy who'd play chuck-farthing with a woman's secret shame must nonetheless be mollified. I endeavour, without scorn, to explain about banks, and drafts upon banks: I am right, he has not understood. And the obstacle turns him savage. He swings from the telescope and smites me, left and right across the face until I fall. Very nearly absolutely from the roof. He leaves me to my terror, saying he'll think what to do next.]

February 1st:

[Yet again I transfer some small money into Geo. S.'s hand. He comes to me quiet and private, sometimes daily, sometimes after two or three days, to leech upon my thin annuity. How long can this continue? Yet while it continues, he will be silent. Oh G–d!]

February 12th:

After nigh upon eight weeks' sickbed, Mr A. at last claims to be 'feeling fit for school'. Suddenly grey and aged, all his merriment vanished away, he slouches through the rooms like a down-at-heel broker's man, avoiding all eyes, teaching his classes with *sotto-voce* rancour, setting names into the punishment-book at the smallest breach of order. He has *died before he's dead!* Paulinus says, if this goes on, he will assuredly give him his notice. 'But let us first see if he mend through convalescence. For very charity, Cordelia, we cannot just cast him off.'

I have not spoken with A., nor can I. I abhor him too deeply – for the destruction of my play—

[—for the corruption of my generous love – for my consequent deliverance into the hands of young Saltmarsh.

And all this while, from young Saltmarsh, not a word. Nor offences against school discipline, nor aught else remarkable. Now and again a quick smirk at me, now and again a quick lick of his glistening chops, a quick rubbing of fingers and thumb together when there was no one to see it but me. And of course the speechless acceptance of coins.

But this afternoon (dark and wintry) I went to work in my private room at chemical apparatus. I had no sooner lit the spirit-lamp than his evil leering face sprang out from the shadows: ah! he was lying in wait for me, crouched like an ape behind my racks of retorts.

'Miaow, miaow! you're mixing poison? I wish I had the trick of it; won't you teach me? Old Aram was in school today. Breeding violence, worse than ever: *I* saw his rhinoceros eye. Ecod, in the open street, where I'm known to every tapster, he kicked me and twisted my arm, it's nigh on two month since but I'll never forget it . . .

'Something else I'll not forget, now that I've just remembered it: Cordy-cat! my fizzpot uncle went to town in the summer vacation. D'you know, he told McCoy he saw that fusty old usher of yours all a-prance and a-swagger down the middle of Covent Garden in a feather-tufted tricorn, a purple-brocaded coat and a wh–re on either arm? The b——r's got more money than you'd think! Of course, we should ha' known: he's books enough for fifty, piling his shelves like fish-creels. If he should be so rich, then where does it come from, and why does he work as an usher? Cordy-cat! it's not consistent.

'So I'm going to find out. When I do, I'm mortal sure I'll have a hold on him far tighter than I'd ever be able to fix with a naughty dirty stiff-pr–ck picture. Ecod, he'd just *laugh* at my picture! Why should he care a button o'sheep-shit if the Pharisee throws him out? D–mme, the bloody man could buy and sell you Poll-Pole-Hatchets, retail, wholesale, barter and swap. If m'uncle tells the truth, and I think he *does* . . .

'Cordy-cat! a word o'warning. You do *not* talk to Aram about this. Blow your mouth off just once, and the picture and the tale behind it go straight to the medical Irishman. Because *you* don't laugh at the picture. Oh no no no, no joke about the picture at all.'

His hand up and down my rump and a shockingly painful pinch.]

February 13th:

[A sleepless night (again; how many more?). I dare not talk to A., and yet it must be prevented. There is something very wrong, very dangerous here, my G–d! I am repelled by him but he *has* been my lover, am I to let him be tracked by a half-shaped doltish blood-hound pup, tracked how, where, to what?

(In Covent Garden? Two wh–res and purple brocade? Can it be true? *Of course it's true*. Tho' I daresay outlandishly exagger-ated . . .)

Lord, Lord, but what to do? Dear Jesus, I am penitent. So tell me, I implore you, what to do . . .]

February 14th (St Valentine's Day):

[A sleepless night, what else?]

Mr A. has resumed his old habit of long walks. And short ones as well, one must suppose. For during these past three days he has never been on the premises, never, except for precise hours of tuition, the regular meals, the prayers and so forth. A dreary *phantom* of an usher; and Paulinus is much perplexed.

[Dr Burney (who of his good nature comes weekly to give the boys music-lessons) sends to say he is a-bed of a fenland ague: is it possible I could supervise his pupils on his behalf, as I have often done in the past? I send to him, 'yes': but I wish I could avoid it.

Geo. S. is one of 'em, he purports to study the harpsichord.

But I cannot avoid it, indeed *must* not. I have made up my mind. If my Gracious Saviour did not answer me and *tell me what to do*, then Another One did. I have my Advice; it came to my heart in dead of night like the flutter of a bat; its implementation is not to be postponed.

I sit beside Geo. S. at the instrument while he strums and thumps and makes pottage out of the beauties of divine Purcell. I say little to correct him; I am too concerned with what further I am to say to him and how soon I will have to say it. At length he so muddles a series of chords that harmony and melody are both lost together; he slams his hands flat on the keys and giggles. His ordeal (for the week) is over. Mine is about to begin.

To be brief: I lay two guineas on the lid of the harpsichord. And then, as he pockets them, *I offer myself to him.*

I cannot meet his eyes lest he see the despair in mine. I add only, 'Choose your time, George, choose your place, and for as long as you like, on condition you do not proceed with the *hounding* of Mr Aram.'

He sticks his fat finger into the corner of his mouth and giggles again. Does he mean yes? Does he mean no? 'Ecod, she's not forgotten the date! a Valentine,' he splutters, 'and twice as old as Abby if she's a day.' He suddenly runs out of the room.

What have I done?]

February 18th:

[Sleepless night; and dreadful dreams. How can both statements be true? But they are.]

Mr A. was out all night. To be brought home in the morning huddled up in a farmer's gig, exhausted, wet, his clothes thick with mud. The farmer declared he had found him half-drowned in a dyke, some ten miles out of town. He himself told Paulinus (abruptly) that he'd had a stupid fall and sprained an ankle. But a quick wash, a change of clothes, a stout stick for his limp (he avers), and he's ready for the morning's work. Against all protest, he lurches to the schoolroom and leads his class on their trudge through Cicero. Or allegedly leads 'em: in fact, he sits blankly while boy after boy misconstrues.

[Abby is Geo. S.'s messenger. Is he prepared to spare me nothing? I know not what she knows of the matter: she simply comes to me in the pantry and blurts out that '"Master George" says the chapel of Red Mount, tomorrow night, eight o'th'clock, ma'am; and not to bother with an answer, he'll know it when he knows and so will you.' It is impossible to discharge this girl. I am in *her* hands as much as his.]

February 19th and 20th:

Quite incapable of writing my journal last night: so two days' entry together.

[The Red Mount chapel! That haunted ruin, an ominous pinnacled

eight-sided tower three hundred years old, on a knoll in the waste-
ground just inside the town's ramparts, scrub-bushes, black ivy,
thistles and nettles all around it and not a decent man's house within
cry . . . I walked there alone and hooded; hazardous. There were
thieves about, drunkards, did they call to me? I sped past. And yes,
he was there before me, squatting upon rubble with a candle in the
dark vault. I saw him smile like a sleepy Priapus. Jesus, believe me!
and forgive: I had even had amorous hopes of him; he is handsome
in a callow way; he has sudden fits of childish pathos; some of his
drawings have displayed *tenderness*; his long yellow hair is the same
colour as my Ezekiel's. I was determined to make the best of it.

  I might as well have tried to make the best of *Caligula*. (But
imagine a Caligula quite unpractised learning his trade by trial and
error.)

  Abby was there. Foul. She watched. She helped. I write no more
of it. FOUL.]

Today I have been very ill; I kept my room. Mr A. is unwell; he
stuck himself into the schoolroom and stayed there. He was only
pretending to teach (says Paulinus), and the Academy as it
presently stands is no better than a hedge-school. What parent
(if he knew) would not ask to have his fee returned?

March 8th:

  [Yet once more to the Red Mount. Worse tonight than ever it was.
And I gave him my last guinea. I have no more until quarter-day
(the 25th). I must borrow in advance for next week. From the
bank? From Paulinus? What excuse can I make to him? What will
he think? Somehow, somehow, somehow, this business must
have an end.

  If A. would go away? But he won't. 'Tis past all intellectual
acceptance I should protect such a slubberdegullion at such cost,
but I do: I am *strapped to the saw-horse*.]

Even were Paulinus to take courage and outright discharge his
d–mned usher, I cannot think A. would obey him. He's a
distempered old dog in a kennel, that's all, nose on his paws and
a chain around his neck. Loose the chain and he won't even feel
it. He'll just lie there fixed and shivering, and growl—

  [—and growl and growl. And growl growl growl – I write the same
word all over again – ink all over the bedsheets – my stupid pen
masters me – my stupid pen is about to spli—]

*Cordelia's journal at a temporary finish: a tailing-away of blots, smears, ragged
black squiggles and rents in the paper, as though very small birds with their claws
dipped in ink have had their squabbling run of the page. After a gap of some three*

weeks it resumes. Leonore, still dreaming, recaptures a glimpse of Fidelio's letter,
where it broke off in much the same way. Which writing is which? Typescript for an
instant seems to merge with quill-pen handwriting; and then they separate . . .
Cordelia's entries continue. There is a gap of some three weeks.

8

April 1st (All Fools' Day):
I had to ask to know the date. I've been collapsed into fever, into
coma or delirium or even death, all this time. Dr McCoy was
called in; Mrs Brewster (turn-about with her stone-blind
drunken sister) has been with me without stint; she says I was
'gone from us, body and brain, just like you'd been *took* by the
fairies. Just like that poor Mr A., but *he's* not been rightly given
back yet, you see.'

> [Oh G–d! what did McCoy make of the dire tokens scored into my
> private flesh? – I cannot think what he might not have found. But
> the man's a fool and prudish: a fair guess he never stripped me of
> my nightgown. Mrs Brewster's another matter. She must have
> seen to changes of linen? Mrs Brewster believes in the fairies. I
> spin her a raving tale; how I was lured into Mumchance Coppice,
> by a mysterious dancing light and dragged in the fog for hours
> through brake and briar. Quite without astonishment, she says she
> knows Mumchance Coppice, I'm not the first to be so mishandled
> there, she recognised the signs. So did the sister, when told of 'em.
> I ask what did Paulinus think when she told *him*? She says she did
> not tell him; nor did she tell McCoy: parsons and doctors are all
> one when it comes to 'long-toothed ignorance'. Let it be.]

Just after I wrote the above, Paulinus comes in to sit with me.
He has more on his mind than my symptoms: the Academy goes
from bad to worse. He has had to hire a pair of by-the-day ushers
(myself being deadly sick and Aram so ineffectual) and neither
of 'em a ha'porth of use.

> [And then, quite *by-the-by*, he suddenly tenders a most wonderful.
> piece of news. Mr Saltmarsh has gone to live in London, for the
> lengthy rebuilding of a Norfolk nobleman's town-mansion des-
> troyed by fire; 'tis a huge opportunity, his first in the metropolis; *he*
> *has taken his foul nephew with him!* 'Just to keep the young rip "under
> his eye". Stupid leniency, in my opinion; the lad's conduct has so
> improved since his Yuletide chastisement, he needs clearly the
> constraint of the school. Yet maybe we are the better without him.'
>   Glory to God in the highest, on earth peace, goodwill, goodwill!
> I AM SAVED.]

April 2nd:
Whether the doctor approve it or not, I am up on my feet and about! So weak I must cling to the furniture, but my heart is all vitality and Lord! there is so much to do.

> [First: to rid my life of Abby. Simplicity itself. She's a cruel little drab, I have no scruples. I lose a gold ring; it is found in the band of her wretched straw bonnet where it hangs on the scullery hook. John Lobscott (in presence of witnesses) is the man to discover it. If she leave Lynn directly without a word to anyone, I promise I'll not send for the constable. If I *do* send for the constable, they'll hang her; she knows this; she flees like the wind. I AM SAVED.
> And then next—]

—the entire reordering of this sadly debilitated school!

*

In that same week the Sheriff's men came up from Yorkshire and arrested Mr Aram for murder. His victim was one Clarke, a shoemaker. This creature, twenty-four years ago, had seduced Mrs Aram; thereafter, a long time after, accruing wealth in plate and jewelry through a fraudulent trick. The trick was not his but Aram's; Aram told him what to do by way of impostures and supple deceits; Clarke like a fool put trust in the man he'd cuckolded and did just as he was told; all unaware he was enmeshed in an engine of slow-calculated and complex vengeance.

For dishonour of adultery, Eugene Aram required Clarke's life. For his overmastering scholarly need to *buy books and yet more books*, Eugene Aram required Clarke's treasure. Two birds with one stone.

On June 24th, 1758, even as we drove home in the rain from Goodluck Chapel, Mrs Aram called upon the Knaresborough justices, bearing a small silver casket. She claimed it had been found in the garden of the house once inhabited by herself and her husband. She claimed it had once been the long-vanished Clarke's. She claimed it was sure evidence of a most atrocious crime, a crime much suspected and often discussed but never brought to proof. The justices deferred the matter, saying the casket was suggestive but no more. Where (they enquired, and not for the first time) was the corpse?

The corpse was uncovered upon December 21st, the very day of our misfortunate play. A skeleton, doubled-up knees to chin, its head severed, in a place called the Hermit's Hole.

(This, above, is what I now know and believe from the

revelations at the York Assizes. For what I believed and knew *then*: let my journal's blinded pages show it forth, to the dismay of my heart as I copy them.)

*

9

April 5th:
MURDER. PREMEDITATED.
    Impossible; but so it is.
    They came to the school at first light, two of them (with the King's Lynn constable), broadswords and pistols in their belts, darkness in their faces, iron in their rigid wrists. They found the under-housemaid scouring the doorstep, they sent her to fetch me out of bed, they sent me to fetch Paulinus out of bed, they showed him their warrant and told him their errand so harshly, so bluntly, that he sat himself speechless on a stool and permitted them to do what they would.
    They went straight to the Usher's Lodge, broke the door in without knocking, snatched Mr A. from his sleep onto his feet still in his nightshirt, clapped on the manacles, threw his clothes into his portmanteau, and ran him and portmanteau together through the garden, through the school-house, into their coach and away, like journeymen butchers with a skin-and-bones old bullock.
    None of us would have even known why, had not John Lobscott sped after them to the bridewell. Jesus, believe it! he was too late. Already all formalities were done, and the coach (with A. inside it) was well on its road for the north. Our constable explained the reasons: a secret murderer was a dangerous man, no leniency, no delay, no pretext for evasion or escape. (That Mr A. should be a *clever scholar* only made the severity more needful.) The two Yorkshiremen had arrived after midnight; they cannot have been in Lynn for more than four hours. They knocked up our magistrates at two or three o'clock. And there and then they'd have aroused St Guthlac's, save only for the good sense of the constable. 'At least wait,' he remonstrated, 'till Dr Pole-Hatchet has his servants abroad. Don't ye know, 'tis a *gentleman's* house?'
    I myself, so concerned for the state of my brother, had no more than a glimpse of Mr A. as they hustled him forth. He looked wild; I thought he *laughed*; he did not look surprised.

If he did kill, then he killed for no excusable reason, and by no acceptable method. Had he run through his wife's lover in a duel, or beaten him to death in the violated bedroom, all the world would have understood, he's a strong-tempered man. Instead he allowed him to take her away – not to the New World, not to France, not even to London, but five hundred yards down the street. And then – years later – how many years? *ten?* – he plotted a secret slaughter; and he plotted to enrich himself.

It cannot be the truth. He is practised against by occult enemies. Fabricated evidence, witnesses forsworn. So why does he seem to know – always to have known – that this morning's calamity was writ in the Book of Fate?

Dr McCoy, called in to Paulinus, says a mild apoplexy may be followed without warning by another, and then another, perhaps fatal. We must guard him most heedfully. He don't seem to know where he is.

April 6th:
On Paulinus's behalf, I have closed the school. I have sent the boarders home, or (where that is not practical) I have moved them into lodgings in the town. I do believe we are ruined. By Whitsuntide it may be possible to reconsider, reassess. All depends upon Paulinus's health; the auguries are bad. As for *my* health, why should I care?

> [For once again good John Lobscott has been opening his ear in the town. He discovers a most shocking circumstance. Shocking to *me*, that is to say. All others (thank G–d) will have failed to comprehend. For—]

—the constable enquired of the officers from York: granted that the Knaresborough inquest indicted A. for Clarke's death, how did they know to come to Lynn for him? Had he been writing to his wife, or what? I give their answer as John Lobscott gave it to me—

'None had heard of him in the North Parts, no not a whisper, not since he first *made his lucky* all them years ago, years. Seemingly he never bode in the one place, but ever shifted and roved hisself whenever he began to be noted. They tracked him to this town and that; then to London, they thought, but no further. Folk who knew him had died, or moved away, you know how it is. Then a young gent in Harrogate Spa got a letter, writ from Lynn (about the midst o'this year's February) by another young gent what he'd met in the Pump Room a couple o'seasons since. The young gent from Lynn had been with kinfolk as was taking the Harrogate waters, you know how it is; so they'd made friends. Very well, says this letter, there's a queer schoolmaster-chap from Yorkshire as is causing all manner of questions in Lynn; Harrogate Spa's in Yorkshire; maybe you'd ask around and see if aught's known of him? 'Twas a long shot, to be sure; but seeing as Harrogate Spa's no more nor five mile from Knaresborough – *well!* D'you suppose, ma'am, it might ha' been one of *our* young gents?'

> [I do not need to suppose. I know.
>   'About the midst of this year's February.' Upon our first cruel tryst at the Red Mount, he had either written his letter or had made up his mind to write it, whether I sacrificed myself to him or not. No doubt there will be a reward. Slavering bloodhound indeed, and a bloodhound of *treachery*.]

I cannot collapse again; my brother's life is under threat; I have my duty, I must do it; I can *not* collapse again.

Monday of Whitsuntide:
Tomorrow, with hardiest effort, we re-establish the Academy. Paulinus is able to teach, if we wheel him in his chair to the schoolroom, and leave him there no longer than an hour at a time. We have a new usher, he who was oft-times lent us from the Free-school, and has some knowledge of our system. Our number of pupils is reduced by two-thirds.

All our friends of the Society state that they always knew Mr A. to be some species of criminal, and *we* should have known. Nonsense.

A letter for my brother, from A. in the York gaol. He writes that his innocence will be manifest at the July Assizes; he has an argument that none can put down:

> Who is to say that the bones that have been found are of man or of woman, let alone of this one man Clarke? Who is to say they are not that very *hermit's* bones, who gave his name to the cave where they were found? Or if not the hermit himself, then some ancient devout person who sought burial in so holy a place? All this region of Yorkshire is chock-full of unaccountable bones: I have spoke of it to Miss Cordelia, she will surely remember? Our antiquaries here are compiling me conclusive lists.
>   Moreover this is not the first corpse to be uncovered and taken as Clarke's. The only direct testimony comes from one Houseman, a suborned ruffian who has sworn he was my accomplice. Through cross-examination his malice will appear; he too has been bedfellow with my loose wife! Ah Christ! why do not the laws of England allow counsel into Criminal Court to defend as well as prosecute? I shall

question the witnesses as zealously as I can, but God knoweth I have small forensic skill. Pray for me that I be not o'erpowered, that the Bench be not partial against me! For they say the Yorkshire folk are most certainly partial against me; they have ever a coarse jealousy of all learned men; why else did I depart from this county? they will shoot out their tongues from the jury-box.

I write now, under your favour, to beg you or your gentle sister to send a sworn affidavit as to the cadaver of Goodluck Chapel. 'Twas a very like case unto this, and can do me naught but good. I write also to those others who were there; but I sorely fear their jealousies. Reverend sir, toward you, toward Miss Cordelia, I have no fears, only confidence.

Yr. most obedt., most unfortunate svt.,

Eugene Aram

Post Scriptum:
Moreover, who is to say that Clarke is even dead? He vanished from his home place, as I did. *I* am not dead. Or *am* I?

I answer him, *per pro.* my brother (who is too much enfeebled to deal with it), promising the affidavit, and bidding him be of good cheer.

['Twould be a comforting letter enough that I send him, were there no more betwixt us than matters of scholarship. As it is, it must seem to him but a cold communication, for I bear in my mind that the gaolers are sure to read it. Which surely he's aware of: I hope so. In the margin I dare to write this:

Dark-lanterns give strongest light, but not everywhere.
May yours at this dreadful time be so well directed
that it shine out its beam to most excellent bright purpose!

Perhaps he'll take my meaning?]

This evening, the old Rector called to see us, to wish us Godspeed with tomorrow's *restoration* of St Guthlac's. Inadvertently (I hope) he clouded his benevolent intention by referring to Mr A. as 'that miscreant'.

He is troubled by a phenomenon in the Society's museum: Dr McCoy has reported that the Goodluck Chapel cadaver has begun, very swiftly, to disintegrate, even though supposedly protected by the glass case. Already it is little more than a heap of dust.

Which reminds me! – (I did not note it in my journal at the time, being altogether too distressed) – the *genital member* of the cadaver (preserved by Mr A. in spirits, in his bedroom-closet) was thrown into the midden by the housemaid when she cleaned out the Lodge after his arrest. She did not know what it was, of course; when she told me, I said she had acted correctly. The Ogham-tablet, on the other hand, has entirely disappeared.

All his papers were seized by the magistrates to be forwarded to York upon the doubtful possibility they might contain evidence. Whether they do or not, I suppose they are lost to him for ever. All his work, over all these years, pursued in the teeth of such academic prejudice: it is *tragic*!

June 21st:

> [A letter, most unexpected and affectionate, from my darling G'g.
> She has heard of 'your Blunderbore's weary trouble': 'tis the only
> topic of the day in London. She does *not* say, 'I told you so.' She
> commiserates, with great delicacy. Her marriage is *'assez ennuyeux'*,
> her husband (though useful for business) is a dullard when not on
> the stage, and she suspects him *'avec les jeunes garçons'*. But when,
> she asks, do I write another play? Let me send it to her, she will
> show it to Garrick, for *The Uncovered Corpse* (though not suited to
> London) had so much in it of good that she truly believes I might
> 'succeed where the unfortunate many have failed'! Well! I *shall*
> write. I have no time, absolutely; but ideas in abundance.
>   Perhaps a Tragi-comedy of Sensibility, about an innocent girl
> ensnared by two men, a malcontent of an antic pantaloon and a soft-
> skinned young rake, and how she strives to play them off, the one
> against the other, while still in search for her long-lost true love (far
> across the sea)? But who is the true love? Ah! there I shall need to
> think deeply. Classical, or modern? Is it not the Ulysses story, and my
> heroine a sort of Penelope amongst her suitors? But is 'Ulysses' a
> man or a woman? I wish, I wish I had more leisure to think.
>   But I am a woman most bitterly betrayed; only through my Art
> can I achieve consolation. I shall write. Nor shall I *send* the play: it
> must be fetched to her in person. How I long to embrace her again.
> My beloved.]

June 22nd:

Yet another letter from York gaol, again to my brother, again I must deal with it myself. A. is in wild concern about a new witness they have 'rummaged up', a pawnbroker from Soho, Mordecai Serlio. Serlio is to testify that plate and jewels were sold to him (little by little) by a Yorkshireman in 1745, during the course of several weeks' Hebrew lessons which he gave to the said Yorkshireman. At first he conceived nothing wrong, a parcel of silver spoons, a diamond brooch or so, passed in part-payment of the instruction. A poor scholar might well be compelled to render payment in kind. But the quantities of precious ware soon began to exceed the worth of the lessons—

> —he has deposed that he felt suspicion, but could not credit that a mere
> thief should be so zealous for arcane knowledge. Therefore he stifled

his qualms, and (by his own false account) continued to receive the goods, paying out good money over and above his agreed fee for tuition. Here I shall have him: what! he made no attempt to cheat the 'poor scholar', enlarging the price of lessons, diminishing that of the treasure? threatening exposure if the valuation were not taken as given? A Jew, and so honest! No juryman in York will believe it.

If this is not believed, why should aught else of his tale be believed?

When they fetch him to York, they say he will *recognise* me as he whom he knew so long ago. *Fourteen years?* It will never be credible. Moreover, the names are different, there can be no *prima-facie* case, I am Eugene Aram, the Jew's pupil was 'John Pogmoor', it is the freest speculation and utterly without proof. If he say he do recognise me, it can only be because the thief-takers of London have a hold over him, he must be known as a Receiver, he will forswear himself to save his life!

But I pray you, go forthwith to that Altdorfer in Lynn: get from him an affidavit to expound how the corrupt officers lie heavily on those of his trade, I am sure he hath experience, let him tell the court how often *he* was incited to swear falsely to stolen goods! Many times, I am sure of it; if only he will dare to speak. All I need is a few words to discredit the Soho Shylock, I know naught of him, *naught*, save his monstrous and gratuitous mendacity!

Yr. most obedt., *etc.*, E.A.

I will speak to Mr Altdorfer; but I have no hope of a serviceable statement from him. I do not believe him to be under any such 'blackmail'; and if he were, he would hardly acknowledge it! Ah woe! how they weave their nets to enfold Mr A. Since the case of Jonathan Wild, no metropolitan peace-officer can be deemed candid; surely those of York will know that to be so, but they are bound to hide their knowledge for the sake of a 'guilty' verdict – any trap to catch a rat, so they'll think. Alas, alas for truth!

June 23rd (written at five o'clock, post meridiem):

[Has coincidence of the date (St John's Eve, with all its reminders) brought this horror upon me today? No, the thought is superstitious. I banish it; only to supersede it with another one, no less irrational: the vileness of my secret mind has *conjured up* the very Fiend – GEORGE SALTMARSH IS RETURNED TO LYNN! I did not know it when I awoke this morning. But the vileness was there already, for—]

—I was suddenly certain, oh most *vilely*, calumniously, and unaccountably certain, that all the portents had a meaning, and Eugene Aram must be guilty. Eleven weeks I have lived under the persuasion of his innocence, I have asserted it to all comers, I have written him letters (*per pro.* Paulinus, always), I have signed affidavits, and prayed. Is it the Father of Lies, or is it

Another, who has infested me with these more-than-doubts? Whichever it be, I lay on my hot pillow and saw Aram transparent, as it were a chemist's retort-glass three-quarters full of a dried foam of hideous blood. I sprang from bed before dawn and ran out, to do what I never did in the whole of my life, I walked six or seven miles all a-purpose to see a man hanged.

Lazarus Chudd, a low footpad, was to be gibbeted in chains upon the scene of his latest crime, the murderous robbery of a poor old woman (of her purse and sixpence in it and her two buckled shoon and her shawl). It was on a lonely path to the north-east, out betwixt the sea-coast dunes and the woodland beyond Castle Rising and the hamlet of Wolferton; a salt wind blowing sand in the faces of the crowd – not so much a crowd as an evil clot of drooling mooncalves from the back-hovels of Lynn and from the villages. (And birds; black and flapping, soaring out of the treetops to see would there soon be dead man's meat for their beaks!)

Chudd made a sort of speech – or rather, he blubbered aloud – admitting his guilt and excusing it, telling of his own poverty, of the *looseness* of his harlot wife, the starvation of his children. He said he had robbed for their bread. (The children's bread, not hers: all *her* nasty earnings went on gin. I saw her at the gallows-foot, with the children at her skirts. Their appearance congrued with his words.)

I thought vindictively of A. He is accused of desiring *books*, to enable him to write a great *book*. Is a murder for books better or worse than a murder for bread? (Cordelia, you have never lacked for books! Were your father a rude gardener instead of a clergyman, dare you swear, hand on your *womb*, that your intellect's lust could never suck you into savage temptation?) Yet, yet, to take it bravely, sincerely in the Light of Christ, murder for books is but murder for worldly *fame*. The Roman emperors lived by such fame, tainted fame, villainous, the day-to-day 'glory' of Caligula.

> [Vindictively, I thought of A.: after all he had brought onto me, I did not *wish* him to be innocent – let him jerk at the rope's end (I thought) for as long and as painfully as the miserable Chudd, let him likewise blubber beforehand, let his continence likewise fail him so that he trickle like a tap as he too stands a-quiver in the hangman's cart, O Lord G–d!
>
> At which infamous moment, I recollected the wash-house window, I cast my eyes sideways, and horror! there he is – Geo. Saltmarsh. He comes before me grinning and kicking up the sand

with his boots. Dismounted from an elegant curricle, attired like
an arrant fop, he pulls off his d–mned hat and he bows.

'Cock-a-doodle! Pho! here's a charnel of a place to find *you*!' (He
has acquired a most singular lift to the lip, showing more upper
teeth than could possibly have grown there.) 'Ecod though, 'tis
woundy suitable. I'm still at the life-drawing, y'know: same two
figures, same theme. I was about to come to see you: just to tell
you how hard it'll be for you, should you be known as a
murderer's tail-hole. I know not what happened to Abby. But that
old monkery-popery chapel lies ruinous and wide-open still; there
tonight then, eleven o'clock, bring some bottles at the Pharisee's
cost. Why don't the pair of us get thoroughly foxed?']

Yet, yet, Aram is innocent. *He* at least is no Caligula. My friend,
and I denied him, and now like St Peter I do *see* myself. (Cock-a-
doodle.)

June 23rd (as continued, long after midnight):

[I denied; I must be punished. So I took him at his word: two
bottles, to contain *schnapps*. I know, from hard experience, he
drinks *schnapps*. I fill them from Paulinus's keg in the cellar (his
'Rotterdam Special'). According to McCoy, Paulinus will never
drink from it again. Ardent spirits are mortal to a man in his
condition. But tonight, they are the fire of my life. One bottle is
entirely for myself.

I fetch up the other one to my chemical apparatus. I have never
(knowingly) made such a compound before; I read in a book that it
is not *per se* a poison, but when mixed with strong liquor it turns
the slow poison of alcohol into a searing fierce quick one. I cannot
wait until Geo. S. at the age of (say) five-and-twenty should drink
himself down to the grave. I have no means of knowing whether
the book be right or wrong. But I do know that if those 'life-
drawings' be seen by my brother, my brother will assuredly fall
dead.

I am at the Red Mount prompt to the hour. Lacking his dirty
Abby, will he come to me alone? If not, my plan is baffled; to
conceal it, the tampered bottle must somehow be spilt.

As it chances, he *is* alone. (Glory be to the F., to the S., and to
the H.G.! if that be blasphemy, forgive, *forgive* . . .) He is also quite
drunk already. I take my bottle, he takes his, we swill our
inflaming draughts and tear at each other's clothes, all in accord
with his custom on these occasions. It is possible I am a little too
ardent; he looks at me strangely: 'Ecod, but she's *learned*
something!' he chortles, and drinks again. It takes perhaps fifteen
minutes to render him powerless. I empty the remainder of both
bottles over him, smash them on the flagstones, heave him on top
of the litter of broken glass, cut his neck at the artery with one of
the fragments, and let his blood run spurting out of him.

With sufficient *schnapps* inside me to make possible my deed, I

have rather too much to dress myself with decency, to walk easily
home. But there are the bonfires in the town, blazing like the
Glory of G–d; outside of their light the darkness is the more
intense, hell beyond heaven, I always maintained that hell was
dark, thick dark, despite the fact you burn in it. They say a she-
murderer is burned rather than hanged. Or is that statute now
repealed? Who cares? He was *not* murdered! he betook himself
with his vices to a lonely sordit place; after the departure of some
base companion he stumbled naked among his own bottles and –
who cares?

There may be gore on my undergarments. (My bared body was
splashed, I think.) I can be rid of it come daylight, and wash myself
likewise, ere ever the servants are risen.

I think the housemaid heard me come in bloody drunk. Who
cares? She knows, none better, that chronic sickness in the house
craves occasional breakings-forth. 'Tis Midsummer Games, she's
not sober herself. Or if she is, she need not be. I told 'em all, 'divert
yourselves', who cares? for I can write these words legibly, I can
(as though nothing had happened) give the lessons to our bloody
pupils – nay, will have to, in some three hours' time.

Meanwhile, I wake, I vomit, my room swims around me as I
endeavour to make shapeless notes toward the argument of my
new play, hazily seeking some plausible shape for my Penelope,
the hapless, the forlorn.]

*Leonore's dream straggles away: loose ends, inconsequential riddles. What, for example,
of Cordelia's first hearing the news of Eugene Aram's execution? What of how the law
dealt with the corpse of young Saltmarsh? What of the years between 1759 and 1766? –
how did Cordelia continue her life in King's Lynn, her friendships or otherwise with the
members of the Philosophical Society, her friendship with Sophia Greengarden, her
playwriting, her apparent maidenhood, the secret complexities of her Truth and her
Untruth? And what (if he ever read it) did Horace Walpole think of her modern-day
improvement upon* The Castle of Otranto?

*The dream straggles away; Leonore wakes up. Slowly she remembers: the last
portion of Fidelio's letter is strewn about waiting for her – her task for the day. And
when she's done it – more days, one after the other, for year after year, and each with
its meaningless task? Or no days, finish with them, cut off the whole damn nonsense,*
follow *him*, GO!

Fourth Tale

How Aram (Being Dead) Had Made Dreams for Fidelio Carver

(1992)

. . . (like a murthering piece, making lanes in armies,
The first man of a rank, the whole rank falling)
If you have wrong'd one man, you are so far
From making him amends that all his race,
Friends, and associates, fall into your chase:
. . . y'are for perjuries the very prince
Of all intelligencers; and your voice
Is like an eastern wind.

(George Chapman, *Bussy d'Ambois*)

1

It is a lowering dark morning in Antioch Gardens, winter's approach a full month before it is called for. Sheer malice, thinks Leonore, but she also thinks: 'What the hell?' This gloom is at least appropriate; and how much worse, had she had to prepare herself for Fidelio's funeral and unbearable condolences amid a merry spendour of late sunshine and all the children a-chirp on Parliament Hill? After days of stunned lethargy, she is now brisk; she is able to confront the dawn; she is able to confront (after a fashion) her bereavement. Thank God she seems old enough and (with a little deceitful contrivance) pathetic enough to off-load onto others the heaviest complications. Lewis Hinge has flown out to Belfast to confer with the RUC about the release of the body from forensic requirements, and its transport to London; while Jenny deVries will be sorting Fid's professional papers. Apart from this letter of his, this incongruous *Last Post*, this 'Iron Mask' (as Leonore now thinks of it), he really appears to have had few papers that were not professional.

Jenny is to arrive in the course of the morning to look through whatever he left in his flat upstairs; there may be some personal letters, probably embarrassing – Fidelio rarely answered letters without weeks of procrastination, most of his incoming correspondence would consist of aggrieved complaints about this wretched habit – otherwise there will be little beyond heaps of unopened junk-mail, a mass of socio-political propaganda in newsletters and pamphlets, and the regular communications of his work incompetently stowed away in a filing-cabinet.

His will, Leonore is assured, is safe with the conscientious Hinge who will be in touch with her about it soon; she knows her brother has left nearly everything to her. With the exception, perhaps, of some small unexpected legacies (she cannot think to whom – whatever they are, they will certainly be out-of-date). The will was made years ago and has never, as far as she knows, been revised. She would not be surprised to find a bequest of £100 for the funds of the VEXACTION company, or for something equally absurd and defunct.

She is today well capable of dealing with all these thoughts. She is brisk, grim, self-mocking, noisy. She bangs cup and coffee-pot down on the table, she sloshes hot black unsweetened coffee from spout into cup and from cup into mouth like a hurried traveller in a railway-buffet. She lights a cigarette as though it were a firework; she drinks and smokes alternately, jerkily, for no more than half a minute. She is forgetting her dream, completely; she *makes a point* of forgetting it. Even as she assures herself that that is what she is doing, she jumps up from the table and hunts, upon impulse, through drawers in the kitchen dresser, pulling out cookery books, electrical-gadget handbooks, three-point plugs and adaptors, shoe-cleaning equipment, until she finds what she so abruptly wants – a handful of motoring-maps.

She shuffles them deftly about on the dresser-top; she gets to the Fen Country; and that's the one she shakes open. She had a holiday there, once, years ago, didn't she? Ah, there we are – King's Lynn, and there is Spalding, and *there* quite near to it, is Something-or-other Chapel – she was sure she remembered, but she hasn't got her glasses on – yes, here it is! Fool! she reads '*Moulton* Chapel'. Goodluck Chapel? no such place. Of course not, how could there be?

Damned dream, of no importance, nothing at all, *nothing*, from a plastic phial of pills, that's all, forget it: go back to his 'Iron Mask'. He took long enough to write it, at least do him the courtesy of skimming it through to the end.

Snorting with irritation, she whips into the bedroom and at once onto hands and knees, scraping on the floor for sheets of typescript. Never mind about last night! this morning is *business*; and Jenny will be here in an hour. Fidelio's last chapter (xxvi) dissolved itself like a nervous Breakdown; the start of xxvii should be its Cure.

(xxvii)   'Go-to-Bed!'

Sorry about all that, Lenny. No more of it, I swear. From now on it's an even keel. I've had a crap, I've had a shower, I've had a cheese-and-pickle sandwich, there's half a pint of coffee in a mug at my elbow: we start again.

Eugene Aram was not able to cover his tracks. I have now, I hope, made tolerably clear the tracks that *I* had to cover. So I suppose you're able, as you read, to picture my trepidations? Bear in mind! this was 1975. We are dealing with the year after that slaughter-house bombing in Birmingham; the year they railroaded, as I am now convinced they did, six innocent men into gaol for it (their shoddy trial was just finished when Jack broke the news to me about Yorkshire, and I hadn't believed a word of the police evidence); we are dealing with the year after the Guildford and Woolwich bombs (again a set of wrongful convictions); we are dealing with the year in which the 'Balcombe Street Gang' were bombing and shooting all over London (and were finally to claim Woolwich and Guildford, only to be told they must be lying). Sam Rammit had known well what he was up to: from his employers' point of view, his only fault was to be premature. All this outrageous mayhem, as he and they had correctly guessed, brought about the scandalous knee-jerk of the Prevention of Terrorism Act, scrambled through parliament with no discernible opposition, eradicating our already eroded civil liberties, and most important of all, establishing – no, confirming! – a *climate*.

I knew all about that climate, *Poison-Voices* had fallen foul of it before it was fully in place, and it was not going to do me any good in the courts with Barney Brewster. The last thing I wanted was Jack Pogmoor obsessed for two or three months with *murder-will-out*. It would not have mattered, had he taken himself permanently north and ceased to bother me. But instead, he was hooked on the ludicrous notion that I would need to know every step, twirl and turn in his dance of Eugene Aram.

Maybe three weeks after we first talked about it, he invited me to his Chelsea flat to discuss 'possibilities'. He had been up in York-shire for much of that time, and I thought that he might have disliked what he found there, that he might be having second thoughts, that the possibilities were in fact Napoleonic possibilities – indeed he loosely hinted as much. I thought it stupid not to go.

I walked straight into an exploit of the Balcombe Street crowd.

(I should not say *their* exploit, for it did not form part of the indictment when they came to trial, but it could be called an indistinguishable photoprint.)

Lenny! imagine: a misty moisty early-autumn evening, about eight o'clock, that half-hour of dusk between sunset and lighting-up time when visibility is at its most deceptive. Some street lamps were shining, others were not, as though the man in charge of the switches might be sitting down with a lazy cigarette, reading his *Evening Standard* and not paying proper attention. Similarly some of the passing cars had their lights on, but not all of them. I walked from the tube at Sloane Square, along the King's Road, to turn to the left into Whitesmith Street. It runs down towards the river, two nondescript terraces built in the early Victorian period for lower middle-class landladies to let out in lodgings, two floors of respectable families, single gentlemen (shabby-genteel) above, the odd artisan with wife-and-kids in the attic; they were now expensively gentrified with the yellow front doors, window-boxes, and well-tended miniature gardens between each set of doorsteps. It was the first time I had been there, though I daresay *you* knew the place with some familiarity? Pogmoor must have been doing himself well to have bought a pad in such a milieu; his neighbours (I was thinking) would be young stockbrokers, upper-crust layabouts, starlets, models, politicians' doxies, gay film-producers, bachelor mandarins from Whitehall. He lived about twelve doors down the street, on the right, nearly opposite a 'discreet' restaurant with striped sunblinds over close-curtained windows: *Les Toits de Montmartre*, the sort of highly selective cookshop that does not deign to display a menu lest the *hoi polloi* give it a bad name by standing outside it anxiously calculating prices and counting the cash in their pockets. All tables would be reserved; patrons' orders no doubt suggested beforehand over the phone.

There were very few people on the pavements; a man in a leather jacket doing something to the engine of his silver Porsche, two languid leggy blondes trilling their laughter under a plane tree, an Electricity Board fitter up a ladder examining the top of a lamp-post where the light had apparently failed. The fitter's mate sat in a van beneath him, its nearside door open, a box of tools laid ready open on the curb by the front mudguard.

I took all this in without consciously noticing it; I crossed the road behind a black Rolls-Royce with a chauffeur at the wheel (he had arrogantly parked half on the pavement and half off); I walked casually along checking the numbers on the front doors; I found the one I wanted; I set my foot on the bottom step. I was turning my body but I hadn't turned my head. I saw two men come out of the

Toits; they caught my eye by their movement and the sudden glow of the restaurant lights behind them as the door was opened. They had just put their dark overcoats on and were shrugging and shaking themselves into them; bulky overcoats, superbly tailored garments of authority and power. The shorter of the pair had a large pale bald head with grey streaks of hair brushed across it, an unhealthy puffy face, thick grey lips, goggle-like spectacles with colourless frames; he seemed to be staring at me as though I had no right to be in the street when he chose to appear in it and he could not imagine why some underling had not ordered me off. My impression of his friend was less defined; a sense of swarthiness and a military cast to his thin features; I was aware that the chauffeur had got out to open the passenger-door of the Rolls.

A man on a motorcycle was advancing up the street from Cheyne Walk, a courier perhaps, in leathers and visored helmet, travelling slowly, turning the faceless sphere of his head from side to side. He passed the *Toits*, and slid to a halt. He was exactly between me on Pogmoor's doorstep and the two restaurant-clients halfway to their motor. His helmet-front was aimed towards them (more precisely towards Puffy-face who was a few steps behind the other); his right hand was off the handlebars and moving up across his chest.

A very loud voice suddenly screamed from the heavens – well, it must have been from the top of the lamp-post, it must have been the electrician – but it felt like a divine portent: *'Go-to-bed!'* all in one mouthful of intimidating warcry.

Puffy-face and his chum dropped instantly out of sight behind a parked Cortina; their chauffeur flung himself into a crouch with a pistol in his hand; the electrician's mate was out of his van with what I now know to have been a sub-machine gun no less; and the two trilling girls, with a squeak, ran to hide among floral tubs in the front patch of the nearest house.

The chauffeur fired his pistol; directly at *me*, as it seemed, I don't know how many shots but his aim was not good because one of them shattered a ground-floor window in the house next-but-one to Pogmoor's. The electrician's mate (on my side of the street) was simultaneously letting fly with a burst from behind the cover of the back of the van; the motorcyclist too had a pistol out; his bullets (as I saw later) went all of them into the Cortina; I rolled into a ball on Jack's doorstep, thinking what a small amount of noise all this shooting actually made, it sounded just 'crack crack crack', scarcely dangerous at all. In the movies they must put up the decibels for dramatic effect; I'd heard better on Guy Fawkes night.

Then the 'courier' revved up his machine; and *that* made a roar like a natural disaster, thunderbolts, earthquakes, as he tore off round the King's Road corner. Machine-gun bullets followed him, but nobody had hit anyone, as far as I could tell. Pogmoor in his first-floor living-room, running to his window at the sound, saw only what he thought to have been a near-miss of a street accident. He thought it must be me, absent-minded, almost killed by a motorbike; he hurried downstairs and opened his front door: 'What the hell are you up to on the deck, you bloody fool? Playing at hedgehogs? Fid! get up—!' His mockery trailed away as he saw the electrician's mate cradling his gun, glaring round for fresh targets; as he saw the chauffeur putting his pistol back into his coat; as he saw the dark-faced military man standing erect in the shelter of a portico with a pistol of his own. Puffy-face, whoever he was, had a very slick squad of minders, the accuracy of their shooting was less spectacular than their speed of reaction, but no doubt they had *frightened* their quarry – if that's what the motorcyclist was . . .

Police-cars zoomed into the street. A loudhailer told us all to stay exactly where we were – a necessary order, for people were running out of houses and generally floundering about. Coppers, in uniform and out of it, deployed in every direction, setting up a cordon, corralling individuals, taking statements. An angry little detective confronted me and Pogmoor. Who were we, where did we live, what had we seen? our employers' names, our places of work? quick-sharp, let's have some answers! I made the mistake of asking him what had happened. He looked at me suspiciously, he said, 'What d'you *think* happened?'

I made a worse mistake; I told him what, *at that moment*, I really did think. (All the above description is of course a piece of hindsight; I was totally flustered at the time.) 'I heard someone shout a word, "Gotobed", just like that, was it a codeword? and then for no reason they all started shooting; him, him – *him* too, across the road – all of 'em, they shot first, aren't you going to arrest 'em?'

He said, 'What was your name again . . . ? Okay, Mr clever Carver, if you want to be nicked I'll nick you. *He's* nicked. Take example.' It was the fellow from the Porsche, on my side of the street, just by the King's Road corner; they were manhandling him head-first into a patrol-car. I was not aware he had played any part in anything. Maybe he hadn't. What the hell was going on? There was no sign at all of Puffy-face, nor of Dark-face his saturnine shadow, the Rolls was on its way out towards the river and dangerously fast on the wrong side of the road, the electrician was down from his perch and he and his mate were telescoping their ladder, hoisting it onto the van's roof, like any pair of workmen putting an end to a routine job, not a gun to be seen in either direction, only fuzz in battalion-strength clearing everyone back into the houses.

I looked blankly at the blank face of the law. 'Now shut your fucking mouth and lissena *me*!' he commanded. 'Shots were discharged by a person unknown at a person or persons unknown, and you didn't see which persons nor how many shots nor anyone shooting back. How could you see? you were in a flat spin, you were shitting yourself, *weren't* you?' He raised his baleful gaze to Pogmoor: 'Where were *you*?'

'I was inside.'

'Oh, you were? Very sensible. You know each other, do you?'

'He's just called to see me.'

'How long's he going to stay? What's-your-name, Carver! how long d'you mean to stay?'

I told him, about an hour. He said, right, at least an hour, not to leave the house for sixty minutes and no smart-arse crap from either of us, was that clear? He said he'd be calling back. Then he went off to browbeat the two girls.

Jack pulled me hurriedly into his front passage. 'Good God,' says he, 'did we *see* it?'

'*You* didn't,' says I, 'and I really don't know, I really do *not* know whether I did or not. For God's sake get me a drink.'

I felt faint, I felt sick, I felt that that plainclothesman knew all about Sam Rammit, I felt too that he knew that *I* knew – I was a washpot of irrational terror. Jack Pogmoor, of course, wasn't. For him it was no more than regular Chelsea fun-and-games, sensational, no doubt, bizarre, but just the stuff to make his evening. And of course he wanted to talk about nothing else.

He informed me (as if I didn't know) that we had witnessed a classic stake-out, a predictable target had cunningly decided to eat at his regular nosh-house – perhaps they'd had him at it every night of the week – but tonight the assassin struck, they were absolutely ready for him, they missed him, did I think he'd got away scot-free? did I suppose the arrested Porsche man was indeed a confederate? why were we told we couldn't or mustn't trust the evidence of our own senses? and who did I guess was Puffy-face? Pogmoor guessed the head of MI5 or some such, who else could be the reason for all the frantic hugger-mugger? who said 'conspiracy-theory' was the first sign of madness? what did I bet there'd not be a word in the newspapers – should we put on the telly and see if the Nine O'Clock News had any—?

None of this was of interest to me; it was *part of me* already, it had been ever since my last chats with dear Polly and horrid Toe. It was impossible to tell Jack; I let him switch on the television, though my whole soul revolted from it. There was a very short item, quite on the lines of what the detective had instructed us to believe. An *incident*, they said. It was implied that the IRA might have been involved. No report of anyone's arrest. No suggestion that the motorcycle had been chased any further than Pimlico.

'That's enough,' I said, 'more than enough. If the cops come round again I want at least to have done some business before they carry me away.' Jack took it as a joke; I gave it that inflection; but it wasn't, you'll understand, Lenny, it was *no bloody joke*, no.

But he obliged me, assuming I was under some shock and needing normality: he explained what was going on in Knares-borough. He had *not* had second thoughts, Eugene Aram was tightly preoccupying him, and damn-his-eyes, he was asking for my help.

'This chap Percival Lobscott, he's a doctor and a local historian, he knows all about his subject, but he's not got the first notion of a workable script. I'd give over the whole damn thing, if it wasn't for that smashing new theatre – or old theatre, really, they've made a beautiful job of it, everything absolutely spot-on, groove-and-flat scenery, forestage with two doors in the proscenium, stage-boxes right on the forestage, chandeliers (with electric bulbs: fire-brigade regs!), winch and hanging platform for flying in heavenly appearances, I'm just wild about using it, Fid! I'm all of an archaeological witter. But oh what a sludge of a script. You've got to rewrite it for me, got to.'

'Didn't I tell you I don't want to? Didn't I tell you I was neck-deep in Bonaparte? And besides, what'll the author say? I suppose he's had a lot to do with the theatre restoration; if I know these small-town notables, his own neo-Georgian script on his redis-covered real-Georgian stage is the zenith of the poor bugger's life, I can't possibly take it from him. You've got a responsibility: you were hired by him and for him, who are you to sell him out?'

'I bloody well do not know why every time I meet you you accuse me of selling someone out! Let me tell you, it's damned offensive.' He was red in the face, genuinely furious. 'But I'm not going to quarrel. We never have in the past—' (Good God, did he mean it?) '—we don't need to now. I have absolutely no intention of asking you to replace Lobscott. What I want you to do is to replot his play for him, sketch a new synopsis of scenes, organise a proper confrontation of characters, and then let him write his own dialogue for what you've sketched. You can do it with your eyes shut.'

'Can I? You always told me that plotting was my weakest point—'

'That was before I met Lobscott.'

'—whereas *you* knew all about it and could always put me right. You're getting me to do for him what you've regularly done for me. Why bother? Cut out the middle-man, sketch your synopses your own bloody self.'

'Ah no, not so easy.' He was smiling and leering and winking,

Jack Juggler in the midst of a scheme, evading his manipulators, manipulating his impotent friends. God, how persuasive he can be! 'It won't do: I'm a director. Lobscott's been told I'm a *famous* director; which makes him dead nervous; he's been told that all famous directors devour decent strong plays and regurgitate meaningless pap. I'm not saying he's wrong; a lot of what he says is exactly what *you* say, so it has to be true, hasn't it? He can hardly bear to hear me tell him that even one single line of his writing might just possibly be redundant. But a playwright could tell him; a *famous* playwright, all the better. *You* could tell him. Oh Fid, he'd respect *you*. And don't you see, if you told him, you'd be saving him from *me*? I'm asking you to make his script director-proof.'

There was a ring at the doorbell downstairs, the police coming back as they'd promised; I rose to go and answer it, glad of the interruption, apprehensive of what it might bring; I was harassed from two flanks; I knocked over my gin-and-tonic.

Jack put a hand out to stop me, pressing me into my chair. 'I'll go, I'll let 'em in; while I'm doing it, take time, lad, think on. Don't show thissen a right miser wi't'talents tha's been gifted with.' He had the door of the room open but stood in it, grinning down at me to overpower me before he left, a ponderous wise old codger from a 'trouble at t'mill' TV series: 'It's a challenge for thee – sympathy, tact, solidarity, integrity! – why, this Doc Percy could be Fid Carver twenty year sin'.'

'Oh yeah? How old is he?'

'Now I'll not say he's young. He might be forty-five. Young in terms o't'trade, though. Like, think of him, Fid, your blushing apprentice; fettle thissen into him, do it!'

He was down at the door for a good minute; I obediently thought on; oh, I was disgusted, a script-doctor at *my* age! So that was his view of me. Intolerable.

The little detective had brought a colleague with him, a senior colleague by all appearance, in whose presence he kept quiet and glowered. This man was no older than thirty, tall and spare and disagreeable; a whining refined voice like the draught in an ill-fitting window; an ineradicable sneer pulled his lip up under his nostrils. He wore a thin beard; pale-brown oily hair straggled over his striped shirt-collar.

'Mr Fidel Carver,' he announced, with emphasis on the incorrect name as though already he lined me up with Castro, 'Mr John Pogmoor.'

'Jack,' said Jack.

'Jonathan, actually; we ran a check. And Pogmoor's not quite the full name? But have it as you like it. A playwright and a play-producer. Meeting in Whitesmith Street for a theatrical conference.

Why in Whitesmith Street, why at this time of night? A bit out of working hours, isn't it?'

This was weird.

'Whitesmith Street? I live here—' bumbled Jack, as flummoxed as I was.

'We ran a check. It says Antioch Gardens. Both of you. You're related.'

'Your archives are out of date. *I* live in Antioch Gardens, *he* lives—'

'He lives here, he's just said so. I'm not deaf, Mr Carver, and I don't give a fuck for the archives. Except for one point. The nature of your relationship, the link that might bring you together; a Mrs Pogmoor, Leonore?' (He carefully pronounced it 'Lee-anne Orr'.) 'Some intriguing cross-purposes with Royal Navy security in regard to that lady, or hadn't you heard of it . . . ? Well: if you say not, I have to believe you, no indication to the contrary, not yet. Forget all that, it's immaterial. How many plays have you written?'

He was looking at Pogmoor. Pogmoor turned, bewildered, to me.

I stammered. 'I – I can't tell you exactly. Is it important?'

'Not if you say not. Believe you me, Mr Carver, I have no fucking interest in the plays you might write. I only want to know why you lied to this officer, on the doorstep, an hour ago. Did you think it was a scene for the theatre? Did you think you could invent it, whichever way you'd decided you wanted to shape your plot? There was very nearly a life lost, very nearly two lives. Don't you suppose you're being frivolous, a little bit too fucking *frivolous*? Mr Carver, I am talking to you.'

I know it was weak of me, but I could not meet his hard blue eyes. They were mad eyes, deliberately psyching me; his entire mad rigmarole was intended to shatter me; it was close to succeeding, much too close; and the little man behind him was prowling Pogmoor's bookshelves in a deliberately distracting fashion. I was weak; I was distracted. I said fatuously, 'What d'you mean, lies?'

The little man swung away from the bookshelves, flipped the pages of his notebook, and grudgingly joined the party: 'What you said, to begin with. You identified certain behaviour from certain individuals. Whereas your *reconsidered* statement, taken down directly afterwards, went on the other hand as follows:

'My name is F. Carver, I am a playwriter, self-employed, of 33B Antioch Gardens, Kentish Town; I observed at approximately twenty-hundred-oh-seven hours shots fired in Whitesmith Street by a person unknown at a person or persons unknown.

I have no political affiliations and am as frightened as the next
man by terrorist outrage.'

'I never said that.'

'Did you not? Then how come,' sneered the tall beard, 'how
come, Mr Carver, my colleague has it down that you did?'

'Your colleague—' I began, but he did not want (or need) to hear.
His agenda for the conversation was already determined.

'Mr Carver, are you familiar with the Prevention of Terrorism
Act? You ought to be, you're an educated man, they say; but no
doubt in all the glamour of backstage triviality, you gave it a miss,
so I'll tell you. There are draconian penalties for the very heinous
crime of supplying aid and succour to men-of-violence, did you
know that? The penalties begin with a thorough going-over in a
dead secure police-station during a period of several days without
access to a lawyer, it's a part of my job that I really enjoy. Now if
you persist in saying that you saw what *I* know you couldn't
possibly have seen, you will be giving most definite aid and succour
to a gang of fucking animals. They will squat over their pints of
Guinness in Kilburn or wherever they fester, they'll jerk themselves
off into it, oh yes they'll be that chuffed that *you* should have
chosen 'em to make 'em leading actors in your rotten little panto.
I think you'd better stick to what my colleague's written down. If
you've anything to add – well, I'm sorry, I can't hear it, I do seem to
be a little deaf today after all, it must be the damp weather.'

Had he finished? I think he had; but his sidekick found a book – a
copy of *Poison-Voices*, a scanty paperback issued not by my regular
publisher (who mistrusted its commercial potential) but by a shoe-
string operation of the very far Left, working out of Tufnell Park.
'One of your plays, Fidel? What's it about then?'

The tall beard took it from him and studied the blurb on the back.
He did not read it out; I remembered what was printed there; I
would have preferred him to have got his hands on any other of my
writings but this—

A document of the savage confusion of 1971, the year of
internment, *Poison-Voices* analyses many strands in the tangled
web of Britain's imperialist propaganda-machine. Repression in
Ireland is stringently related to reactionary policies nearer
home— *etc.*

He looked at me askance. 'Would you sell me this?' says he,
blinking at the price-sticker. 'Two quid fifty.'

'No, he wouldn't,' says Jack. 'That's my book and I've only got
the one copy. You can buy it in any good shop. Try Collett's in the
Charing Cross Road.'

'Two quid fifty?' says he again. 'Hardly worth it at that price. In
the meantime, I'll leave you to your "conference", your theatricals,
while others of us get on with a responsible job of work.' He turned
to go. 'You see, I could not care less for dramatic effusion. Just so I
know the names of 'em, Mr Carver, that's all. Good night.'

'Wait a minute,' erupted Pogmoor like the damned silly idiot he
can be when he's not checked, 'how about us knowing *your* names?
You never bothered to tell us, you never bothered to tell us your
rank.'

'Sorry about that.' The little man cracked his face into an
unprecedented smile. 'Of course, sir, I should have said. I'm
Detective-Sergeant Grubbet, CID. And this is—'

The tall beard wasn't having any. 'You can call me a *public servant*.
If you require any ID, I'll bring it when I bring the search-warrant.
If I bring the search-warrant. Just my joke actually, why should I
want a warrant? Good night.'

Upon their exit they left the door of the flat open. We neither of
us spoke until we'd heard them pass the street-door.

Pogmoor said, 'You weren't much good. What are you going to
do about it? Blatantly illegal from beginning to end!'

'I don't know what I can do. Their word against ours. Two against
two. Besides, if I start anything, it'll only rebound on Lenny. You
heard him: the old Plymouth business. Some sort of delayed-action
frame-up, I've got to keep her out of it.'

'That sneering tall bastard was no ordinary copper. I'm not sure
he was a copper at all.'

'Special Branch.'

'That, or a spook. Well, he's got you proper frit, hasn't he? So
where will we start? Will we ring Civil Liberties? Write to – to
Freedom, Peace News, Republican News, Workers' Press, – the *Guardian*?
Look, Fid, it was a damned outrage. You mustn't let it lie.'

But I did. You understand. I hope you understand.

And moreover, within an hour I had agreed to read the Eugene
Aram play and see what I could do with it. Why? Because the
man's talk of frivolity and rotten little pantos had hit me where it
hurt. He said 'responsible', he said it intensely, that was his view of
his job. *I* had told Pogmoor he was responsible towards Lobscott. He
had told *me* I was miserly with my gifts. Very well, so I too was
responsible. If Jack needed help, if Lobscott needed help, who was I
to stand aside while they fudged a shoddy job in a beautiful
bandbox playhouse? No Special Branch man was going to tell *me*
about the 'glamour of backstage triviality', I'd show him. What a
stupid egocentric thought. But I had it; I acted upon it.

2

Leonore remembers: most of this experience was recounted to her by Fid that very night, as soon as he got home; later on she heard of it from Pogmoor as well. She was alarmed but not surprised: deep inside her, inside that strange 'twin-sector' of her mind, she knew that something had happened, *knew* before a quarter-past eight. (Indeed she rang Pogmoor's flat, but got only an 'out-of-order' buzz. She saw the Nine O'Clock News and kept on ringing, to no effect. She rang the police; they said they had no information.) This was the first time she had been thus *in contact* with her brother since – since the day she spoke of 'packing it in'. Neither man made any reference to *her* name in the mouth of the 'public servant'. And both of them gave her to understand that they had expostulated with vigour against the breach of their citizens' rights. *Suppressio veri, suggestio falsi*: about par for the course with those two, she reckons.

She also reckons that even today Carmilla's behaviour at Plymouth (supposedly in her name) is still threading its way through a number of significant files. She thinks about the curiously offhand attitude toward her of the RUC, only days ago, when they phoned her with the news of Fid's death. She thinks about that snide journalist from Belfast. She thinks about quite a number of similar small hints: why, she has been a marked woman for two full decades, ignorant of it, innocent, and her ears never burned, not once.

(xxviii)   *Hermit's Hole*: Three Fictions

> *I read the play; I made some notes for it; I went to Knaresborough.*

You already know a good deal about all this; I talked to you at the time about my difficulties with Lobscott's script, did I not? But you never knew what happened in Knaresborough, just why I came suddenly home in such a state?

Okay then, from the start. Of course I was nervous at meeting this Dr Lobscott; but Jack told me not to worry – he was easy enough to get on with when offered sufficient respect. He deserved respect; most certainly as Chairman of the Mother Shipton Playhouse Trust, responsible for the re-creation of the old theatre. The building had been known about for years; parts of it had long been used as stables, coach-house and grain-store (and then as a garage) at the bottom of the yard of a hotel adjoining the market-place; but from Lobscott alone came the obsessive curiosity that discovered the old proscenium and half a tier of galleries hidden behind lath-and-plaster; and Lobscott alone had the energy to initiate the heavy process of restoration. (Mother Shipton, by the way, was an oracular wise-woman of early-Tudor Knaresborough; I was surprised their first play would not have been about *her*. But then, with Eugene Aram, there was coincidence of date: the theatre's foundation and his execution were municipal talking-points all in the same year.)

The doctor turned out to be a bland, polite, inwardly ardent gent of about the same age as myself. To the devil with Jack Juggler and his blarney – an apprentice? perish the thought! For this chap despised all professional theatre-people, writers, directors, the lot; cultivated amateurs were (for him) the only guardians of the long-debased mysteries of the national dramatic tradition. He spoke of the Royal Court, the NT and the RSC as New York novelists in the '30s used to snipe against Hollywood. I ventured to drop the name of Brecht; I might just as comfortably have farted aloud at one of his regional medical boards. Whatever would he have said to VEXACTION?

Jack was quite right: the script was like its author, polite and bland as all-get-out, and yet with a bite inside it, a coiled serpent in its bowels somewhere – but how to lay hold of it?

To start with, I'd have preferred it not to have been a musical. But that was a *sine qua non*. The local talent was highly musical, they performed annual oratorios, they performed *Oklahoma*! or Gilbert and Sullivan or even Mozart with truculent zest. Their voices had to be used, or all their interest would disappear. And the composer was jolly good, in a boisterous brassy way, with a sound understanding of old English folk-song airs, a sort of noisier Vaughan Williams. He was a young music teacher from Harrogate; I felt he could be trusted, once the lyrics were set in order.

But they could not be set in order until we were sure of the plot.

❧ Lobscott had written his play on the assumption that Aram was probably innocent. A financial swindler, perhaps, but never a murderer. He accepted his hero's ingenious archaeological defence: that the remains in the cave were of the Middle Ages or prehistoric, and that Daniel Clarke had simply done a runner. Aram and his accomplice Houseman never successfully possessed Clarke's treasure at all. There was, in short, a frame-up; instigated by Mrs Aram, a woman of most secret and exceptional malice. ❧

Well, I daresay she might have been. Jack did not wish to think so: the secrecy of such a character was either so foreign to his experience that he did not feel fit to lead an actress to explore it, or else he knew so much about it that for his own peace of mind he dared not risk its exploration. He shied away from explaining, whether to Lobscott or to me; he merely declared that he preferred Aram guilty and the play to be a study of a thoroughly unscrupulous man, shameless, remorseless, a Marlovian high-aspirer who plunges like Lucifer from the top of Fortune's Wheel.

❧ According to Jack, the young Aram in Yorkshire sees nothing but a deadly life in front of him; he knows himself a genius, he'll do anything to prove it, to hoist himself out of the yokel mediocrity of a bleak coarse market-town. He marries a blatant harlot, fully aware that's what she is, the passing mistress of more than one influential rural magnate, a calculated step up for him, and he never cares whom she sleeps with. She adopts the role he gives her, but with a genuine affection. All he can think of, is how to advance his learning. She does her best for him. But her supposed openings for patronage do not fulfil their promise; he seeks a more certain way, first he swindles, then he kills. One of her lovers disappears; she suspects murder from the start; she is distraught; her affection turns to hate; but Aram is gone – no one knows where – there is no corpse and no proof. And then there is. Houseman spills the beans, and Aram turns up in King's Lynn. Jack refused to go along with the conventional interpretation of what happened in King's Lynn – the diligent schoolmaster of quiet virtue and earnest scholarship, inwardly harrowed with guilt, a version deriving from Thomas Hood's poem and Sir Henry Irving's angst-ridden stage-adaptation. Aram might be apprehensive, he might be regretful (the proceeds of his treasure-theft have eventually run out), but his pride in his crime remains undiminished. His pride in his intellect determines his 'ingenious defence'. And when that fails – 'You can't hang *me!* by God, I AM EUGENE ARAM!!' – he tries to commit suicide; he fails at that too. So to the gallows. Still defiant. Apart from the power of this overweening character, the main thrust of the play (said Jack) would have to be the process of detection. The macabre finding of a dead body, Mrs Aram's declaration that it must be her husband's, Houseman's incautious denial – if he knew nothing of any murder, how could he know that this corpse could not possibly be Clarke's? Pressure upon Houseman, full confession by Houseman, the discovery of the second body in the depth of the 'Hermit's Hole'. ❧

The problem with Jack's scheme was that Lobscott would never countenance it, for one or all of three reasons. First (which I believe indeed was the serpent in his gut), the doctor had liberal ideas: unlike so many of his Knaresborough neighbours, he was passionately opposed to the reintroduction of capital punishment. He believed the hanging of an innocent Aram to be strong propaganda for his cause. Second, he could not accept Jack's venomous deprecation of Yorkshire's philistine bourgeoisie. Was not the playhouse project itself a demonstration to the contrary? And third, it was all very well ranting on about inordinate Lucifers, but Lobscott knew he was no Chris

Marlowe. I could not see (and I said so, having skimmed through the script) how he'd ever summon up the needful strength of language.

The two of them were at a deadlock, which is why Jack brought me in. Of course he did not tell me this until I was fully committed. What he wanted me to do was to write a brand-new scenario, incorporating the best of Lobscott, the best of Pogmoor, and as little as possible of transparently recognisable Carver. I told him it wouldn't work. He offered me more and more money; he appealed once again to my sense of *responsibility*; he finally told me I was a has-been and he'd have to send for Abel-Nottidge. In a state of desperation, I succumbed.

With the utmost contortions of my reluctant imagination, I raked up a feeble little changeling-child of a tale.

❧ Aram is not innocent; there is a murder; Houseman commits it; Aram is at worst accessory after the fact. (Nor is this proved at the trial. Upon such slender evidence he should never have been hanged: which took care, did it not? of Lobscott's capital-punishment preoccupation.) I saw Aram relentlessly drawn into the crimes of the insidious Houseman, while pretending to himself that nothing of the sort is happening. He needs to buy books, he longs to buy books, he closes his eyes to all else. And the essence of the plot is his attempt to pretend afterwards that nothing really *did* happen. Not so much guilt, as guilt unendurably repressed. Just as earlier he has pretended that his wife was perfectly faithful until Clarke out of sheer boastfulness thrust her adultery into his face. Aram's attitude toward her should be crucial to the play's meaning – is it *his* fault or *hers* she has betrayed him? did she always mean to do it, out of bloody perversity, or did she suddenly make a wild throw of the dice in order to get clear of all her hindrances? – she is the one, not her husband, who is strangled and torn in the close-enfolding quickset of North Yorks. Why, married to my Aram, she might just as well be the wife of Percy Lobscott! ❧

For I observed young Mrs Lobscott was not a contented lady. I think she'd been going to bed with Pogmoor; but that was no business of mine.

(xxix)　　　　　*Hermit's Hole*: One Reality

I told Lobscott I would like to see the site of the murder, proven or alleged: an anchorite's cave, what could be more evocative?

He hummed and hawed, of course. If Aram was innocent, then how could the cave be important? He suspected me of sensationalism, the very vice he most feared from Pogmoor and myself. I

explained to him, as gently as I could, that drama of its own nature
was a sensational activity. And particularly so in the context of an
eighteenth-century playhouse, constructed to create the hottest
possible relationship between the actors and their public.
Emblematic scenery at the rear of the stage, I pointed out, and
roaring passions on the forestage right in the lap of the audience! If
all that he wanted was an earnest documentary, then he ought to
be writing for television.

He sank into a sulk over the remains of his chocolate-meringue
gâteau. We were sitting at the Lobscott dinner-table, he and me and
Pogmoor and one or two Mother Shipton Trust associates and the
composer – to say nothing of Jacqui Lobscott with her long silences,
her thick burnt-sienna pageboy-cut with its coy fringe in front of
her eyes, her foot under the table seeking, I suppose, for Pogmoor's
and finding (disconcertingly) mine. Watching Lobscott sidelong, she
gave a twitch to her narrow lips – indrawn lips, nervous, I didn't
like the look of them – and she eased back her chair. 'Coffee, a
liqueur, in the drawing-room? Poor Percy's got the hump. If we
move he'll shake it off.' Her rising scale of genteel laughter struck
me as particularly false.

Among the chintz in the drawing-room she said nothing, while
Pogmoor held forth about the exceptional power of the intimate
small stage – a redundant gloss upon my own words, but it served
to fill an awkward gap. A Mrs Kippax, star of the recent *Oklahoma!*
and ebullient young spouse of a facetious young solicitor, said she
could not believe Eugene Aram hadn't done it: she'd never trusted
over-earnest teachers since that dreadful man in Thirsk ran away
with the grammar school's Oxfam contributions. After which we
had local scandal (rewardingly juicy) for something like an hour
and a half. Lobscott forced himself to be hospitable, correcting
errors in other people's stories with fastidious persistence. Suddenly
his wife sprang to her feet: 'Why don't we go there now?' she cried.
'Why don't we see the cave by moonlight? Percy has a key, you
know, *ex officio* from one of his Important Committees. It'll only
take us forty minutes. Tristram and Jennifer are asleep, poor little
creatures. Young Debbie can babysit while she's doing the washing-
up.' (They'd had a girl in, to help with the dinner.) '*Avanti tutti!*
come on, people! come!'

She was not taking no for an answer.

It was a smooth balmy Sunday night at the beginning of October,
the clustered hillside town silent from top to bottom (save for the
wolfpack yelpings of a motorcycle gang holding its meet in the
marketplace); the harvest moon like a giant orange presided over us
slightly blurred through veils of gauzy haze. We came out of
Lobscott's precise and white-pillared Regency front porch straight

into a steep street that turned itself within a hundred yards first into a steep footpath and then into a flight of steps, leading down under the loom of the ruined castle along the ravine of the River Nidd. We walked gaily two by two above the water's edge for about half a mile, Lobscott's wine and liqueurs fuelling our bird-like chatter. Pogmoor walked beside me: 'Bloody pretentious, don't say I didn't warn you, the first time they invited me I found everyone in bloody dinner-jackets. I was wearing denim. Well, they learned their lesson. Informal tonight, tweeds; sweaters and no ties, even. Not the ladies, though. Eh dear, not the ladies. Knaresborough *haute couture.'*

The path narrowed, I slipped back a pace to allow Mrs Kippax in all the rustle of her bare-shouldered gown to whisper into Pogmoor's other ear. Just behind me were the Lobscotts. *Sotto voce*, they were having a savage little row. I heard him say something about 'playing the whore again, my love?' to which she replied, 'Never on Sundays, Sunday is *Percy's* day for playing with his little self. And how dared you try to pretend that you didn't know where the key was?' Then more loudly, 'If you won't talk to your guests, I will; I want a word with the real playwright.'

I felt her arm into my arm, her moist hand tightly enfolding my wrist. 'That Pogmoor man's a boor, don't you think so, Carver? Look at him there with Katie Kippax. He's your friend, Carver? so tell him, why don't you? that sweet Katie's not available; room in her life for two men only, one of them's Tom Kippax, the other runs a strawberry garden on the Boroughbridge Road. I've got lots of room in *my* life. Poor Percy has no room at all. Will you take his play away from him? If you do, you'll break his heart. So please don't. *My* job, Carver, nobody else's; but maybe I'm trying too hard?'

How could I answer her? I pressed her hand consolingly, which was surely a very bad idea. In the last stages of the dinner party she had swigged at the Calvados as though it were cider. If the path hadn't had a stout railing to it. I think she'd have pitched into the Nidd.

More fits and starts of her intimate hoarse voice – we might have been lovers for years – 'This cave, you know, you're quite right; it'd make a wonderful stage-set, Gothick horror, ghosts, everything. Exactly the place for a murder, I told him, he wouldn't listen. He keeps insisting there was no murder. "All right," I said, "a love-scene. Exotic erotic perversions, don't tell me," I said, "there's nothing of *that* sort in your silly old story?" I suppose Carver's written some of these full-frontal modern plays where all the cast strip bare-arse naked? Let me tell you, it wouldn't do for the Mother Shipton Playhouse. That's why I don't belong to the drama group. Otherwise, I'd be only too happy to – poor Carver, I'm embarrassing you, aren't I? Yes I am; I'll shut my mouth. Naughty little Jacqui, what *is* she to do?'

Her husband pushed in front of us, to make a surly production-number of unlocking the door of the cave – the 'Hermit's Hole', hollowed out of the steep side of the ravine – St Robert's Cave, he formally called it – St Robert's Chapel – carved from the living rock into the semblance of a building, with a groined vault, arched niches, pilasters along the walls, altogether about ten foot deep, nine wide, just over seven foot high. We all crowded in. Lobscott had a big motorist's hand-lamp, with which he lit up for us the recesses of the chamber. His dinner guests ooh'd and aah'd – none of the party had been there by night – we were like children at Hallowe'en.

He gave us a concise lecture (at least, he said it would be concise and then forgot his promise):

❧ The original natural cavern had been inhabited for several years around AD 1200 by the original hermit, St Robert of Knaresborough, during part of which time he shared the place with outlaws on the run. He was apparently devoted to the protection of delinquents from the terrors of King John's justice; he in turn was protected by his manifest personal sanctity; the king even granted him forty acres of arable ground, which he divided into rent-free allotments for the sustenance of the landless poor. After his death he was buried in the cave, or near it; and a couple of centuries later the chapel as we saw it was hewn by the Knaresborough monks to commemorate him. The chapel as we saw it was not quite what Aram would have seen. In *his* day it was a dismal neglected hole laid open to all the elements, an object of local superstition. ❧

Just the spot (as Mrs Lobscott had said) to bring a man whom you wanted to kill.

We were very much pressed together in the airless narrow space; Mrs Lobscott had her hand surreptitiously inside my flies; her husband was droning on; I was sweating with embarrassment (as Mrs Lobscott had deduced); embarrassment became claustrophobia, a sickening thick substance of panic scooping itself into my head until rational thought, as it were, was forced out of me at ear-holes and nostrils.

Pogmoor kept asking, 'Just where did Houseman say they buried the corpse?' Lobscott tried not to reply, but in the end admitted it was just inside the entrance. *I* was just inside the entrance, with Katie Kippax's husband behind me, a fat boutique-owner called Dolores-I-can't-remember-what against my left elbow, Pogmoor plumb in front of me with his heels on my toecaps, and my hostess up to her tricks to my right. I was standing on the very mark and I could not bear another instant of it. I think I gave Mrs Lobscott quite a bang with the back of my fist as I shoved her to get past her; I certainly nearly overset Tom Kippax; but I didn't care a damn, I was out in the open air.

Bear in mind! I remembered that the murder was committed on February 8th. I'd read nothing about the weather of that day; but I stood outside the cave and all the others stayed inside and *I saw* it as it had been in 1745. I *saw* a night of blizzard snow. Three men, meeting together, with dark-lanterns, for nefarious purpose. Clarke has obtained treasure by fraud; Aram and Houseman are to discuss with him how to dispose of it; Aram has a knife, Houseman has a club, they quarrel (who can say why, in the whirling dark?), the snow-flakes filling their eye-sockets, the black river in roaring spate at their feet – who can say which one strikes first, which one strikes the most blows, did they cut off his head? Did Aram castrate him? (There was no knife, and no wounds from a knife, in the historical record; but I saw them, yes I did.) I'm sure Mrs Aram was not there. But *did Aram think she was?* did he (as I did now, as it were, on *his* behalf) have a sudden hallucination that this was not the Hermit's Hole but his own bedroom and he was hacking insanely at Clarke whom he'd taken *in flagrante delicto*, knowing at last – if for only a moment – the full shame of a man who has depended on his wife's shame for all these years for nearly all of his own meagre benefits? Did Aram in fact turn Houseman's methodical crime-for-material-gain into his most per-sonal crime-of-passion, unbalanced, unexpected, a debauchery of blood? Did he? He must have done. This was reality. *I saw.*

How did I know there was a snowstorm? Why, I saw them bury the body deep under a gathering white drift. And *I* buried it; at Rugeley, tearing my fingers among frozen roots and briars; *I* did; reality; I saw myself do so.

I don't know what happened after that. I did not fully come to myself until Pogmoor and Lobscott were laying me down into my bed in the hotel. Jack fatuously asked about calling a doctor; Lobscott told him with asperity that *he* was a doctor and adequately able to recognise the effects of sherry, claret, Calvados, the bite of the open air, a crowded enclosed interior and the open air again, all combined in quick succession. I kept on talking (in a queer Scots accent) of the intense cold of the snowstorm; they both looked at me as at a madman; Lobscott ordered me to shut up! I'd be perfectly well in the morning; and Jack said, 'Why, you bloody fool, you're tight as a tick.' And then, in a whisper: 'Did you know you had your prick hanging right out of your trousers? Our Knaresborough's bloody got to you and no mistake! Eh dear.'

The next day I stayed in bed until lunchtime. I lay neither asleep nor awake, hag-ridden with hangover symptoms, experiencing dreams of a sort, or visions, or visitations of ghosts, I don't know what, but they were filthy. Now why do you suppose that the revenant Mrs Aram who had followed me from that cave to creep about the edge of my bed (whining and snuffling, venting her misery with small chirrups of laughter, sniping with cruel words, pulling up her skirt to show me her private parts) should not have had the features of plaintive Jacqueline Lobscott, but of you, Lenny, *you*? Even though she behaved like an exaggeration of Jacqueline Lobscott, and Jacqueline Lobscott's behaviour was surely what set going my – my fainting-fit, shall I call it?

And then in my semi-delirium I found myself watching the play – *Hermit's Hole*, no doubt about the title, and it was clearly being performed on the Mother Shipton stage – but it wasn't Lobscott's play, it wasn't Pogmoor's – if it was my own half-drafted version I must since yesterday (without being aware of it) have inserted the most drastic amendments.

❧ For it was all about St Robert, how he gave Eugene Aram sanctuary, and Eugene Aram brought into the cave a vicious gang of fellow outcasts, until the saint himself became infected by them, became leader of their deadly band, announced (to a burst of Handelian brass-and-percussion) that from now on his lonely hole was the 'Bandits' Cave' and he gloried in it. Something or someone 'bare-arsed naked' called Mother Shipton was there too, a flitting fleeting ominous bird-like shadow; she moved so fast I could hardly see her, with a rustle and a rattle and a harsh croak, as dry as a skein of shed snakeskin. ❧

I thought Aram had the look of Fred Owston; and St Robert (in his milk-white monkish cowl) seemed to me to be a dark Bengali.

A good lunch in Knaresborough's famous fish-and-chip shop (enjoy the tourism while you can, Carver! I had to eat and I *did* eat) gave me strength for the rest of the day. But it was no more than a short-term cure. By night-time I understood the Eugene Aram story was impossible. Impossible, I mean, for me. A talented young chap, Abel-Nottidge for example, could surely make good sense of it, and let him take his own chance with Lobscott. Indeed, with Mrs Lobscott. I sought out Jack Pogmoor and told him my decision. He was very disappointed; he said, 'Stay around anyway, at least till mid-week, there's a meeting of the committee on Thursday. I did hope, you know, Fid, you'd sketch a bit of strict class-analysis into the man's play. Do that for me, Fid, *please*, before you bugger off.'

No one can say I am not diligent. I agreed to what he asked, I even spent many hours during the next two days struggling with the script, endeavouring against the grain to prove to myself that I was not making a mountain out of a molehill. It was no use. I have suffered often from writer's block; but it normally hits me when I am at the very beginning of an idea, with nothing substantial already written that can give me a foothold onto the next stage of the work. This case was quite different: Lobscott's play existed, from beginning to end; I had made up my mind how it needed to be changed; I had a regular budget of notes to that effect; all the job required was a properly laid-out synopsis. And I just could not make it. I kept visualising St Robert, I kept hearing Mother Shipton, they were not in my synopsis, they were in no *class-analysis*, they would not go away. And furthermore they tortured me, more, more, more than I can tell you – seven years ago, Lenny, and I cannot, I cannot tell—

I called once upon Lobscott, on the Tuesday just after lunch, a time (he had told me) when he would be neither in his surgery nor out upon house-calls. There was an ambiguity in his dialogue; the social motivation of his villain Houseman – a mere begrudging lumpen-prole, or the consciously corrupt agent of the cynical magistrate? I had to put it to him personally, diplomatically, in terms of theatrical effectiveness, avoiding Marxist jargon. And I had better keep quiet about my throwing up the job – Pogmoor clearly had not mentioned it – Pogmoor was the one who had hired me – it would not be fair to him to blow the gaff prematurely. Lobscott's manner was abrupt, not bland any more at all. He half-answered my query in an awkward flurried manner as if all that he wanted was to get me out of his house. I thought at first he was ungracious because I'd spoiled his weekend dinner party; and then I heard a grievous sobbing from somewhere upstairs. I had obviously broken in on a domestic *situation*. I made haste to take myself off.

I remembered I had to drop a note to Jenny deVries, in response to a question of hers about my old *Banner Headline* play and its amateur performance rights. I went into the post office at something like four o'clock. I bought a letter-card and moved to one of those shelves along the wall to write it. A woman in a hooded mackintosh was already stooping there, addressing a letter of her own. She did not turn towards me; she was wearing dark glasses; but I saw enough of her profile to know it was Jacqueline Lobscott. I also saw a bloody great yellow-purple bruise across her cheekbone and all round her left eye. Subconsciously aware of my presence (I suppose), she put her hand up to conceal her face as she leaned on her left elbow and wrote. Then she finished writing, and did turn. We looked at one another for an appreciable part of a minute. 'Hello,' I ventured, 'it's – it's a nasty wet day—'

She swung her head sharply away, ignoring me completely,

swung her body as well, moved swiftly to the postbox, dropped her letter into it and went out into the street.

If Lobscott had been beating her, she did not wish for condolences from me.

Or perhaps she did wish; and I was too uncouth to take the hint? Should I have followed her, caught her up, escorted her to a teashop to listen to all her woe? The matter troubled me: until next day when I ran into her again, walking briskly toward me from the top of the town. This time she did acknowledge my existence, with the shortest sourest smile you can imagine. Her bruise was now almost invisible, well tended no doubt from her husband's medical stocks, and adroitly covered with makeup. I said, 'I'm sorry about Sunday night, I really was quite ill for a few minutes, claustrophobia, I should have foreseen—'

She interrupted me with frigid condescension: 'Oh, it surely does not matter, Carver, we all have these turns, don't we? *I'm* sorry too: I did not quite understand your category.' And that was the end of that conversation; she immediately bypassed me and swept down a side-street.

My *category*? Had someone told her I was gay? (Jack, in all likelihood, for whatever devious reason.) At all events, she'd concluded that my fainting-fit derived from my abhorrence of her feral sexuality. She was righteously insulted, and she was not entirely wrong. But that was not the whole of it, not by a long chalk. Oh dear! and I was just beginning to wish I knew her better.

On Thursday I told Jack definitely I was taking the midday train to London (change at Harrogate and Leeds). He could excuse it to the committee how he liked: best, on the whole, to explain that I was ill. I *was* ill, dammit to hell. I'd write my own apologies when I got home.

(xxx)   The Fruits of My Own Infamy

There was a terrorist-alert at King's Cross, barriers going up all over the concourse, police pouring in from everywhere.

I thought at first it was an identity-check, that a suspect was supposed to be arriving. But no: there was a bomb in the station. (Alleged bomb: it was never there at all, as far as I ever found out.) The train should have been stopped, perhaps at Finsbury Park, or in the last resort in the Gasworks Tunnel, but the warning came too late. British Rail, dead on time, had brought us brightly into the thick of it. Shouting inspectors, shouting policemen, hustling and herding – the very smack of the abattoir, all we lacked was cowdung splashing up around our feet – we were frantically channelled away from the normal exits, reversed in our course, sent stumbling along the main-line departure-platform in the general direction of York, and thence across the suburban tracks beyond the outer end of the train-shed through a narrow wicket to where the Midland Road meets Phoenix Road and there's not a taxi nor a bus-stop nor a tube. I'd no serious luggage, and a good thing too. People were losing theirs all over the shop, losing children as well, losing their heads: the cops were in such haste they transmitted panic the way an opera-singer sprays his spittle.

I was no more scared than the rest of 'em; which means I was bloody scared. They say, in these events, that the Brits keep the stiff upper lip. Afterwards, yes. But there and then? – well: a huge six-foot carnivore in an old-time bowler-hat, with the cut of a Grenadier Major at least, heaved himself so hard against me in his effort to get further up the line that he knocked me down prone and would you believe? – trampled over me. I daresay later that evening he told his friends in the club how we all had to stand firm against the terrorist. At any rate, he *trod* firm; I thought he might have broken my back.

At the wicket there was a huddle of fuzz, yelling 'Come on, come on, move it!' and handling us through from one to the other like Stakhanovites at a conveyor-belt. It was a regular running-of-the-gauntlet; and the last officer of the gauntleteers, in plain clothes after so many blue uniforms, was a man whom I'd already met. Only three weeks ago, in Whitesmith Street. The 'public servant', still with his beard, still with his eye upon me and his assumption of a secret knowledge of everything I'd ever done.

Did I expect him to stop me and ask me once again for my name? ('F. Carver, I am a playwriter, temporarily *un*employed, of 33B Antioch etc. . . .') I don't know. I just stood there, a rabbit in front of the python. And I am absolutely certain he remembered me. His hard blue eye told me so, it said (without words) that here I was experiencing the fruits of my own infamy, I had experienced them already in Chelsea, next time I would *not get away*. Then a constable shoved me and shouted, somebody's suitcase caught me hard at the back of my knee, the 'public servant' turned from me with exactly the same movement as Jacqui Lobscott in the Knaresborough post office.

Like Cain I blundered hopelessly toward a horror of solitude, out into the wilds of Somers Town, wondering had they shut down the Underground, or should I strike across to Hampstead Road and catch a bus?

There's a bus-stop just short of Mornington Crescent. From the side I was coming, you have to go over the road; there's no pedestrian crossing. Hampstead Road has a lot of traffic. It was just after dark and raining hard. I was dazzled by the lights of the cars reflected in the wet; very hard to judge speed and distance. I waited for a lull, I took my chance, I ran.

In the middle of the road was the 'public servant', standing facing me, his arm raised; he reared up like a dead stateman's civic statue, one hand (Napoleonic) in his breast, the other held palm toward me. Of course, he was not there. He would still have been at King's Cross of course, I understood that. Neither were *you* there, standing beside him, very nearly as tall as he was, but facing the other way, your back toward me, your back. Now I knew you were neither of you there. I just *saw* you there, that was all. I had plenty of time to dodge round you; the road was empty enough. There was a fast car coming from the left, and a big lorry from the right.

I had plenty of time; I stayed put where I was; and I waited for the lorry.

The lorry had time too. Because he swerved, and only hit me with the corner of his nearside wing. I suppose he would have hit the car, except that the car also swerved and ran up onto the pavement, *crash* into the pole of the bus-stop. (I didn't see that, of course; they told me about it later; the man in the car was stunned, nothing worse.)

I never quite lost consciousness, and nothing important was broken. Blood, tar, stones and shreds of clothing driven into my skin all up one side of me from ankle to ear. You came at once to the hospital, I was able to tell you I was a bloody damn fool of a jaywalker, and you said it was Jack's fault, exhausting me in Knaresborough with nonsense, sending me home with nothing done, a total waste of time, a 'non-viable project' as you'd always known it would be and *I* should have known so too.

So now I am telling you: it was nobody's fault but my own. I had, in one split-second, decided to stay put where I was, in the hope (though I did not *think* about hoping) that the lorry would kill me.

After my discharge from hospital I was utterly depressed. You thought it was reaction following the 'accident'. You thought it was because Christopher Abednego had supplanted me on Lobscott's play. You thought it was because you had been Leah for far too long, you were losing your love for me, I was losing *you*. Whereupon in my convalescence you came to the conclusion you were Rachel after all; you rented a cottage in North Devon between Exmoor and the sea; you took me off there in the gathering winter; and we lived like a husband and wife. We said it was just as though we had never 'packed it in'. But that was not true. We had secrets, one from the other. So our own secret was devalued. We could not put words to it, but our bodies were aware of our disquiet. *Exactly like a husband and wife.*

I guess I've always been under-sexed; you, perhaps, over. This disparity was somehow balanced out (call me, for the sake of argument, algebraical '$x - 1$', and you '$x + 1$', together we made unqualified 'x', which seemed about right for both of us) – but only for as long as we remained tied twins with no secrets but our own single secret. When that changed, everything changed. So it was not so paradoxical that '$x + 1$' should be the one to say 'pack it in', the one to define herself as Leah, while '$x - 1$' pled in vain against those bitter decisions . . .

You spent all that winter inventing exquisite little people to play with in the toy theatre. Every tale you made up for them was sadder than the last one. Each one was more or less biblical, but presented with a variety of historico-literary backgrounds: mediaeval, Arabian Nights exotic, E. Allan Poe melodramatic, *belle époque* pornographic. Not one of them now ended with the laughter of women triumphant – they all had the same theme, lost love and betrayal – (I recollected the poems I wrote at the time of my first affair with Sulaiman!) – not so much Tragic Theatre but the Theatre of Menopausal Pathos – all the more poignant for its jewel-like Lilliputian scale. Whereas *I* spent the winter trying to write about Napoleon on his island, and the woman with whom he slept there, and did she guess or didn't she that even as she fucked him (or endeavoured to *extract* a fuck from his deteriorating carcass) he was slowly being poisoned, and that that was the very reason she'd been pointed towards his bed? Two tricks played together against him who'd been lord of Europe, and both of them entwined like a game of Cat's Cradle.

If I did not try again to kill myself, it was only because I was unable to solve the St Helena riddle. I had to discover the truth about *that* before I could CUT IT ALL OFF.

(xxxi)   What Now?

Because throughout the next few years I fussed and messed with Bonaparte,
because thus I stayed alive, I was able to work at other things as well.

Jack directed some of them; you designed some of them; with one of them neither of you were involved. In the present context, that's the significant one, my television drama series on Ireland. You'll remember quite a bit about it, so I don't need to go into detail. Only my friendship with a very strong producer at BBC2 enabled it to be written in the first place. He then paid me the compliment of fighting for it every step of the way. We had to accept some compromises with the censorship; but in the end we got it made. Then we had to fight to have it shown. Again, certain compromises,

many postponements; but it *was* shown, at the beginning of last
year (1981) neatly in between the two H-block hunger-strikes. Tory
MPs and Ulster Unionists put furious questions in the Commons,
and Thatcher, Prime Minister, paid us the compliment of regretting
(from the despatch-box) the 'lack of judgement' of the BBC, a
compliment which did little good to the BBC and some immediate
physical harm to myself.

   Mind you! I was *pursued* anyway. 'Furies', you could call them.
They have failed to assume a definite shape, except when I have
dreamed (approximately once a month) about that spectre of a
'public servant' holding up traffic and sneering; that's all he ever
does, with his meaningless east-wind voice, his slinky pinstripe suit
and obnoxious amount of dandruff. But while I sleep, while I wake,
there are the Furies all the time, uncertain of their own selves,
trying to be the shattered corpse of Sonja, trying to be the shattered
corpse of a Malaysian stewardess – whom in life I never saw and
therefore cannot recognise – trying against all logic to be Carmilla.
When Carmilla seems to be about to be there, *you* are there too, so
is Polly Blackadder. Can you explain that?

   They drove me to write that drama series.

   They drove me to take part in that H-block demonstration in
London where some of us got cut off and bludgeoned by the police.
This was not long after the drama series had been released; my
name would have been noted as the author of it; I am in no doubt
at all that the bluebottles who hit me so hard knew who it was they
were walloping. I saw the 'public servant' somewhere in their
midst. He might plausibly have been there; I might have imagined
him; I was no longer able to distinguish the difference.

   Again then, the hospital, a whole week of it. Not a suicide
attempt this time, of course. But of course in a way it was. Most of
the march had obeyed police instructions and avoided Trafalgar
Square: I did not *have* to go with the dissidents, the barking militant
roughnecks, they did not expect me, they would never have missed
me, they are simply not my scene. But I went with them
nonetheless. To join with their banners and slogans – (*'Thatcher
Thatcher murderer! Shaft the Tory cunt!'*, etc.) – was perverted self-
indulgence, and I got what I wanted to get, but not enough of it.
Pain but no peace. And still my pursuers had failed to find their
shape.

   Afterwards, what was left? Napoleon, obsessively. And nothing
much else. I started to suspect that this interminable project was not
a proper play at all but a pretext to postpone my death. Which is
why, when I heard about the Alternative Schizo-Phantasist – how
he was into deep analysis of creative artists' creativity – I thought I
should give him a try. Not very sensible: such people are no sort of

use if you go to them determined to tell lies. As now I have found out.

Would he have been any more helpful, if I'd let him know about you and me? I did gabble on about my boyfriends – even Sulaiman, with all the VEXACTION bit left out. Also my attempts at girl-friends. I gave him some juice on the subject of Jacqui Lobscott, which excited him quite a lot. He wanted more and more physiological details of these sorry tales of sex; but he never probed their context. For instance, the Lobscott story – I don't think it struck him that the exact nature of *Hermit's Hole,* so intricately interwoven with it, was the determinant of my flight from her. Had her husband written any other play, she and I would have – God, I don't know what we'd have done, but for sure it would have been utterly different.

Okay, so I live with my Furies. One day, face to face, I shall see them full-frontal, and then (alas) you'll have these papers in your hand.

Mind you! I'm not the only one. Between Napoleon and Jack there are a number of spluttering short-circuits, just as between Aram and me. Not that *Jack* thinks of suicide. Oh, *he'll* juggle his way out of any trap, any labyrinth. But I do think there is one maze from which he has not discerned the exit.

He evaded Napoleon, then he came back to it, then he evaded it again, more than once, more than twice. At the time of his first evasion, he also evaded *The White Devil*, and I heard a queer tale about that. One of those middle-aged young sparks at the RSC, talking to Jack about the proposed production, about who should play the lead:

'—out at Pomfretshire, when you were there or just after, I'd come down from Cambridge to spend the weekend with a girl I'd been at school with, I saw this perfectly *eldritch* performance of Lysistrata – Polly Blackadder, whatever happened to her? She was around a number of theatres, quite spectacularly for a year or two, and then she disappeared. Politics, was it? or did she get married? Our casting-office card-index on her just tapers away . . . It's a long jump from Aristophanes to Webster, but she had a kind of 'hidden agenda' in her personality, which makes me think that if we *could* just possibly chase her up and find her for Vittoria Corombona, she could—'

Whereupon Jack exclaimed, '*We?*' – and went berserk. Nothing to do with Polly as such (or so I was informed); but an outburst of outraged protocol that the RSC had so far forgotten professional principles as to invite him to direct a play without allowing him to choose his own cast. Which was odd, for he had worked often with actors who were on company-contract, and had never objected if their roles were recommended to him by management. And when I say 'berserk', I do mean berserk. He threw a carafe in the office, and swept a typewriter onto the floor. They had to call house-security to frogmarch him out of the building. Through his agent, through his solicitor, he made his peace; it was all hushed up. 'Temperament,' they said. I suppose it was. But subsequent happenings have caused me to wonder. I don't know why I bring it up here, it's hardly *germane*, as Jack would say—

What now? Oh, my darling Lenny, I don't want to write any more. I'm so bloody tired, I'll just leave it. I'm sure I'll get to work again and forget I ever did *write it. And then you'll never read it. I do hope you won't read it, it doesn't mean much anyway. Bloody tired.*
            Good-bye, my dearest love, see you soon! – Fid.
         XXX XXX XXX XXX XXX XXX XXX XXX XXX XXX XXX XXX
(etc.)

3

The last few lines of his letter are in his own handwriting, very sprawly, and the great sprawl of X-kisses fills up all the space at the bottom of the sheet.

What now, indeed? Leonore sits for an hour, re-reading the document, shuffling the pages into order, numbering them properly, making notes in a methodical fashion of the salient events and dates – but noncommittal notes, non-incriminating – thus simply (for example), *Rugeley, 1970, 'into December', date uncertain but first snowfall of year probably* – which ought to be enough to guide her if she feels the need to check them out. There are seventy-odd pages, close-typed, quite as long as many a high-art novel: can he really have written it all in two unbroken sessions, as he appears to claim? He hasn't come back to it to revise it or make a fair copy, he was obviously working off the top of his head, off the top of his emotions, perhaps it *did* all come in a run, half a decade of his life, exhausting him by not only the labour of setting it down but the strain and pain of recollecting it.

Okay, so how much of it is true? She supposes that at any rate he meant what he wrote when he wrote it. Suicide: he did mean it, when he wrote. But were not his Furies, as he calls them, exorcised by the act of describing them? To be sure, he did seem to be in a very bad state in 1982. But after that, in '84, there was a grim professional crisis which he weathered with great resilience. It involved her as well, and Polly Blackadder indeed, and Jack Pogmoor at his worst: Fid was heavily embattled, reviled in many quarters, his Napoleon play ruined, and never word nor apparent thought of self-murder. Thereafter, in recent years, has he not been as normal as ever he was, writing for his living when he had the inspiration and the energy, hanging about moodily when he hadn't, an undemonstrative little house-boggart (which is to say, familiar spirit), growing stiff about the hips and stooped as to the shoulders, not in particularly good health? At irregular intervals, sometimes long, sometimes short, she shared her bed with him, a cherished treat for both of them with the minimum of sexual intercourse.

They just loved each other, nothing worse; and they were growing old. (Old? Until this year, less than sixty? Don't niggle: it's all relative.)

Not a flicker of a whiff of any Furies. Except – ah! yes, two names. Four years ago? She can't quite remember. No, she does remember: five. 'Toe', she remembers; 'the Wee Priest'. She remembers a message for Fid, a reminder of those two names, out of nowhere, inconsequential, it had worried her, he called it a joke, he had laughed and she thought it *was* a joke. Now she's sure it wasn't; but what had it meant? It did not mean suicide, or he'd have killed himself five years since.

Murder? Ah God, how can she know? Can it *ever* be known? Not without exposing the whole of this *Last Post* of his, this unworthy 'Iron Mask'. Ah God, she can't do that. Ah God, she ought never to have opened it. It has told her far more than she wanted or needed to hear.

And curiously, murder (which you'd assume to be so urgent) seems now of small importance. Some rancorous shadow-men may have killed him on purpose. Or not. However it was, whatever they intended, their gunstrokes left alive for her his scorpion-nest of thoughts, the worst thoughts he'd ever had; and they pierce her, they are pitiless. Ah God, she has no shield against them, not any longer, ah God she is too late. *She* should have written to *him*. Ah God, did he suppose that her thoughts were never scorpions? She begins to count the wounds she could have inflicted had she only had the time and an equivalent malice of memory . . .

Yet she never would have done it – never for his pain, never for his punishment, no. Too ashamed. Or else too proud. Either way it was matter to be kept to herself. She has, throughout her life, tried her best to *mind her own business*. Which she did not learn from her mother; her mother talked to everyone about everything, so unstintingly, so easily, so contemptuous of all restraint. Leonore was *made* by the Aunt; so, after his fashion, was Fid.

(Her dream last night troubles her beyond any of all this. She is aware of her own vices; flagellation has never been one of them. Has that cruel

cruel Aunt come back from the grave to inject her in sleep with posthumous renewal of a lonely woman's lusts out of pre-war Peterborough? Or maybe Leonore herself is in her own way as cruel as the Aunt? Fidelio, after all, wrote 'betrayal' in his letter, many times, many times, and she *did* betray, didn't she? And then why did she dream that Eugene Aram had called himself 'Pogmoor'? Surely it should have been '*Carver*'?)

What now?

She goes downstairs and out into the backyard, lets the seventy-odd pages loose into an old galvanised dustbin, pours white spirit over them, sets them on fire. She stirs them with a bit of stick until they are all black carbon, and then she bends over the bin to crumble what is left of them into powder with her hands. Her hands are as black as midnight. She smears them down her face and down her clothes; and laughs. It is beginning to spot with rain; another half-hour, and impossible to set anything alight.

What now? Funerals and so forth. Hideous. But she thinks she can face it. Pogmoor, she knows, will not be there. He is in Australia. And by God she is glad of it. There is no one to try to console her except comparatively distant creatures, such as Jenny deVries and Lewis Hinge, who will be compassionate but undemonstrative and can be dealt with without scenes. It may not in fact be necessary for Leonore to weep in front of others: that, she thinks, is the main thing.

There is Jenny at the doorbell now. Should she wash off the black ashes, or let them stay upon her person as an archaic emblem of grief? Italian? Jewish? Mediaeval, certainly. The bell rings again; there is no time to wash. Let Jenny make her own interpretation.

4

The day after the funeral she has a meeting with Lewis and Jenny: Fid's business affairs, his will, what to do about it all. She sits silent and lets them tell her; they are both very trustworthy and sensible. She signs everything she has to sign. And then she says: 'Lewis, can we afford a private investigator? Someone in Belfast, just to re-examine what happened? Belfast is – well, what it is – so I'm sure he won't find much. But the police there are not accountable: I really ought to know from a sharp mind on the spot just how many lies and what sort of lies they might have been telling. Please fix it. That's one thing: now, the second. I am not going to kill myself.'

Of course they express a horrified astonishment that she ever could

have thought that they would think so; but she pays their protestations
no heed. 'They say when a twin dies, the other one cannot live. It's very
likely true. I *know* it to be true. But I intend to let it happen *as* it happens.
Okay? In the meantime I have work to do, I have the whole of Schiller's
Wallenstein to make sketches of from start to finish, I'm bloody well
behindhand. I've got to go. You've both been so good, so very very good,
thank you so much. Thank you.'

She walks erect out of Hinge's office and goes straight home. At
Kentish Town tube-station a motherly black woman, collecting the
tickets, speaks to her: 'Oh luv, you look so sick, are you sure you're in a
fit state to go out in the street? At your age you gotta take care.'

Leonore replies, 'It's the change of weather. Rheumatism. Thank you.
Thank you so much.'

An investigator is hired; and discovers little to the purpose. *Wallenstein*
at the National Theatre is a big hit with the critics. Leonore, in early
spring, has some time to herself. She takes her car and drives north,
upon a whim, to visit Rugeley. The cottage where she and Fid lived with
their mother is no longer there. Mrs Booth's cottage has gone as well.
They have been replaced by a new estate of yuppy commuters' houses,
architect-designed, and already rather shabby – only half of them
occupied: the recession, she supposes. At the corner of the road where
her mother was killed there seems to have been no change. The
plantation is still there, and the bracken-filled wilderness behind it.
Leonore does not dare enter the wilderness. She just crosses herself, as
though she were an ineffectual Christian, and hopes that no fool with a
bulldozer will come attempting to shift the 'bandits' dinner-table'. But
in truth she has no care for the land-grabbing money-grabbing
speculators and their fuck-you-Jack employees who have wiped out her
childhood home. If unstable explosives are waiting for them, is that any
worse than the gun that was waiting for Fid? Or the sports car that ran
over her mother? If she had a gun herself, she might forget her promise
to Jenny and Lewis, on this spot, this very spot, here and now. She
wonders at herself for her callousness, her entire lack of responsibility;
she wonders, is she going off her head?

She drives on.

Her whim takes her south-east, to the Fens. First to Peterborough,
then (she so intends) to King's Lynn later in the day. In Peterborough
she finds the Aunt's house much as it was, dreary, mean, surprisingly
small; it is nowadays a good deal come down in the world, its dirty-
curtained windows giving her the evil eye in an evil little street. An
unkempt disgruntled girl squats under the fleeting sunshine in the open

front door; her very short blue-denim skirt is ragged at the hem, she has a fag in her face and a can of lager in her hand. There is a dirty baby-buggy between doorstep and pavement, a dirty baby half-asleep sucking a dummy. The girl stares at Leonore as Leonore stares from the car. 'You want summin, missis?'

'No. Sorry. Nothing at all.'

'Then piss off.'

Leonore drives on.

She never gets to King's Lynn. Her mind is so full of the Aunt's house and the Aunt – all the fifty-year-old misery – that she takes the wrong route out of town. Every signboard says Ely and Cambridge; of King's Lynn never a mention. She fumbles with her map, but somehow she cannot unfold it to the appropriate section; her fingers are trembling and irresponsive. She decides to go on, following the intermittent right-angled turns of this minor road across the empty flat huge beet-fields, with immensely tall brickworks chimneys here and there in groups, dark against the darkening sky like sombre politicians at the Cenotaph. Eventually she must find a properly designated road, or a village, or a person to ask.

To her left appears a continuous run of wire-mesh fencing, twelve feet in height, with rolls of razor-wire along the top. She becomes aware she is being hectored by periodic noticeboards—

Ministry of Defence Property
KEEP OUT

There are glimpses of hangars and ancillary buildings and a squat control-tower in the far distance; the uncouth horns, palettes, spatulas, spears and gargantuan forks of radar apparatus, as well as a traditional wind-sock. She thinks she can see jet-fighters lined up on the concrete apron. Then there is a red-and-white barrier stretched out across the road a hundred yards in front of her, and a large painted arrow.

MoD Security
Civilian Through-Traffic
COMPULSORY DIVERSION

She obediently, unthinkingly, swings to the right, round the corner of an unexpected grove of low trees; she is at once in something like a village green.

It is by no means a traditional village, for she observes that all the buildings are of approximately the same date (the 1950s, she guesses); they are not only uniform in style but are uniformly spick and span, as are the expanses of cropped lawn in front of each semi-detached house, as are the white bollards, whitewashed curb-stones, red-and-white rings round the bases of the lamp-posts. She realises she is surrounded by the married quarters of the air base; a wave of hatred floods her gorge, hatred out of nowhere for the Military/Industrial Complex; for its essential purposes of death and terror, multinational and businesslike; for the suburbanised 'decency' of its outward image; vicariously, for what it did to her brother, and (at Plymouth, very nearly) to herself. For what it did, seventy years ago, in Livorno, to her grandfather. For what it did, in Auschwitz, to almost every other Serlio.

Unstable explosives: whatever their provenance, whoever may claim to be their owner, their murderous potential is the bread of bloody life for the M/I Complex; Leonore can *not* allow them to lie hidden and disregarded. She should have done something at Rugeley; bloody well she knows she should; it is not too late now; she'll do it now. Next to a small supermarket at the edge of the green is a telephone kiosk. She pulls up beside it, jumps out of the car, takes the phone off the hook and dials 999 – 'Police!' She tells them where the holdall is buried, tells them how to get there and how to find the slab of stone, tells them how long the explosives are in the ground, begs them to inform their colleagues in Staffordshire, 'Quick,' she says, 'today, at once, no delay, oh *please!* anyone could find it and die!' She rings off after talking too long, far too long, *dangerously* far too long – but she must, must, make sure the topography of Rugeley is properly understood, for otherwise . . . She rings off, she has given no answer to sceptical cracklings at the other end – her name and address? where she is calling from? the source of her information, please? She rings off; she's done her duty – or a facsimile of her duty – by the citizens of Britain and the Furies of unfortunate Fid.

She leans on the bonnet of the car, taking great gulps of breath and retching into the gutter. (Were her directions fully understood? Why didn't she ring the *Rugeley* police? – ah, she's made a mess of it!) Anyone observing her might imagine she is drunk.

They might imagine other things as well. The sunshine today glittered bravely for as long as it lasted, but it did not last very long, there have been showers and blustery squalls, the spring brightness is deceptive, almost winter each time it clouds over. Therefore above her jeans and blouse Leonore has put on a loose-knitted sweater, a knee-length cardigan-coat, a thick muffler; her grey hair is done up roughly into a bun and squashed in under a flattened woolly cap. With the strands of it that keep escaping from the edges of the cap, her spectacles reddening her nose-bridge, the cap itself pulled down over her brow, she has something of the appearance of a mad mushroom on a long stalk. Her wellingtons are thick with mud from when she had to have a pee in a field several miles back near a place called Ramsay Mereside.

All told, she does not look like a serviceman's wife; if this servicemen's green here were not deserted, she might well expect curious glances.

As she slowly climbs back into the driving-seat, a little girl of about nine comes running out of the supermarket. Not a pretty little girl: unappealing and spotty, drab stringy hair tied too tight beside each ear into bunches like a pair of worn-out shaving-brushes. Her trousers and zipper-jacket, of ill-assorted pastel shades, are too small for her and decidedly grubby. She holds a large plastic checkout bag in both arms against her narrow chest: it is full of groceries to the point of spilling over and all but conceals her face. She seems to be in a panic hurry, she plunges across the pavement, the lace of one of her rotten old plastic trainers is dragging on the ground, it catches in her other foot, she falls full length. All the contents of the bag shoot out onto the curb; a sauce-bottle smashes; so do a couple of pots of jam; potatoes and apples roll everywhere. A sliced loaf drops in sections from its paper wrapping. The clingfilm protecting a dollop of minced beef bursts and the meat slides into a dog-turd. It is clearly a monumental disaster.

Leonore leaps to pick up the howling child, and to help her reassemble the shopping. She offers some words of comfort, but the little girl will not be consoled. 'Oh, me dad, me dad! me dad'll kill me when he knows!'

'Maybe he won't, dear; maybe he doesn't have to know. Why don't I come home with you now and explain to your mother? I'll tell her it was only an accident; I'm sure if I talk to her she'll understand and not be angry—'

'Me mam's gone, she's gone away, she's never coming back, there's only me dad and he'll kill me! I know he will, he always does—'

Leonore has never engaged herself unprompted in any class of public agitation. She has adhered in theory to the social ideas embraced by, for example, MOUTH-71; she has vaguely described herself as a Greenham Woman Everywhere without ever having picketed a missile-base; she has sent money to Anti-Apartheid or the NUM strike-fund; and she refused to pay her poll tax for nearly eighteen months. But the idea of standing upon principle between actual persons representing unjust authority and their victims and subordinates – this she has never felt able to do. The very idea is abhorrent to her. 'Only me dad' is a physical threat, a psychological threat – abhorrent! she can't face it. But suddenly she knows she *is* going to face it. She has a rapid scriptural recall, almost inconsequential but not quite, secular rather than pious, as acute as it is momentary: a little girl, Jairus's daughter, dead on her bed, everyone (church and state) *laughing to scorn*, and yet – *he took the damsel by the hand, and she walked*. She can not, she will not, let this child go home alone. Scarcely a minute since, she pusillanimously fudged the phone call about Rugeley. But Fidelio is gone, she has nothing in the world now to lose, let her not for God's sake fudge *this*.

'What's your name, dear? . . . Marigold? Well now, Marigold, where d'you live?'

Marigold points, blubbering, to a house almost immediately opposite. Leonore humps the supermarket bag under her left arm and with her right hand lays hold of the child's hand. She leads her firmly across the road and onto the path that runs over the lawns.

The front door of the house is open; the light is on in the hallway; a thick-set man of thirty stands silhouetted against it. He is in air-force blue trousers and undress blue jersey. Very short hair, a clipped fair moustache, an expression of strenuous severity bordering upon the manic. One hand is behind his back; he brings it out with deadly menace; Leonore's heart turns over as she sees it is gripping a cane – more exactly, a parade-ground swagger-stick with highly polished white-metal knob and ferrule.

We should say something about this man before Leonore finds out about him, because she is not going to have time to find out very much. He is Corporal Gus Macro, of the RAF Police. A few years ago, as a serjeant in the Parachute Regiment, he was injured in an IRA bomb-ambush in County Armagh. After his wound was healed, a psychiatrist's report upon him stated that another tour of duty in the north of Ireland would be totally detrimental to his shattered nerves, and recommended his transfer to a non-combatant branch of the Army. He could not face life in khaki with the prestige of active service denied to him; he obtained his discharge; and immediately joined the RAF. His medical record did not inhibit him from home-base disciplinary duties: duties which he embraced with intemperate zeal. Some time after he had extended them to domestic affairs, Mrs Macro ran away from him to a hostel for Battered Wives. She tried to bring their daughter with her, but the corporal prevented this by force.

At present he is waiting to hear from a solicitor whether or no she can successfully sue him.

He takes a step forward, seizes Marigold by the wrist, jerks her away from Leonore, snatches the bag of shopping from Leonore's elbow with the hand that holds the cane, and glances briefly at the mess inside it.

Chillingly, deliberately, he lets it fall upon the doorstep. 'Right,' he says between clenched teeth, 'you know what you done and you know what's to be done to *you*. I told you what you should of done when drawing rations out of store. You're idle, you're filthy dirty, you're stupid, you're a bitch and a whore's bitch, what *are* you?'

Marigold, the voice of a zombie, without so much as a split-second pause: 'I'm-idle-m-filthidirty-m-stupid-m-abitch-annanorsbitch.'

'Get yourself indoors, drop your pants, bend over the coalbox.'

Marigold, choking with terror, scrambles up the step and into the house. Her father follows balefully after her. He has not looked once at Leonore. He slams the door so hard behind him that the bang of it jolts the latch loose and it swings again half-open.

Leonore, left blankly outside, incompetent and conscience-stricken, hears the child scream once, and then twice.

Leonore abandons all good sense. She has *dreamed* this, has she not? it is little Tommy Whitesmith. But that's not what she's thinking of. She is thinking of Marigold and also of the Aunt. She comes into the corporal's house and into the corporal's kitchen and she hurls herself at his back. She has *seen* this, has she not? it is Chudd on the back of Jack Pogmoor. But that's not what she's thinking of. She is now thinking only of the Aunt. The corporal, on the other hand, thinks at once about ambushes; and he's an expert, a trained man, his reactions are unimpaired. (Or that's what he will subsequently tell the court.) He slips like an eel from her grasp, he springs sideways round the kitchen-table, he lashes at her face with the swagger-stick, he drops the stick as she totters backwards, he grabs hold of an electric iron and brings it down with all his strength upon her skull.

He is astonished to hear the siren of a police-car, just then, at that very moment, just outside – what *has* he committed? And how did they know of it so quickly?

Two constables come running in – they hear Marigold scream and scream – they are bewildered, this is not what they are there for – but they come. They had a message that some sort of bomb-warning, possibly a hoax, has been traced to the phone-box, they were on patrol in that identical area, they made haste – and the phone-box is empty. Instead, there is a dead woman, a small girl in a state of hysteria, a frantic man trying to fasten up her poor little trousers for her, and wet blood on the iron and on the floor-tiles.

Corporal Macro, blurry-voiced, drooling and spitting, tells them he was attacked in his own hallway by a Greenham Common-type lesbian bitch, let them not think he don't know about them; he was stationed at bloody Greenham his first posting in the Raf, they're all in it together with the fucking Paddy terrorists, let 'em not think he don't know about *them*. He says, 'She tried to interfere with my kid, fucking sexual pervert, that's all she fucking is, know what I mean? know what I mean?' His words are not consistent; but the constables write them all down. They have cautioned him, but he hardly notices it. He rambles on and on about the lesbians in the IRA.

Meanwhile Leonore has found her way to Fidelio – or perhaps she has found it is impossible for her to find it, found (in short) that there is nothing there to find.

Fifth Tale

How Jack Had to Juggle in the Labyrinth
(as told by J. Pogmoor, 1986)

Ay, you shall bleed . . .
. . . nor bear I in this breast
So much cold spirit to be call'd a woman:
I am a tiger; I am anything
That knows not pity. Stir not!

(Beaumont and Fletcher,
The Maid's Tragedy)

Leonore's violent death mirrored an earlier and strangely similar assault, in the spring of '86, when another human skull had suddenly been cracked (but not by a smoothing-iron) in an outburst quite as arbitrary as Corporal Macro's; and her ex-husband Pogmoor was involved. He was neither victim nor assailant, but stood as it were hapless in the wings of the blood-boltered stage, his hands and his clothes splashed red before he knew what was afoot. The statement he had made for his solicitor in November '85 (the matter, more or less, of our First Tale) was overtaken almost immediately by these hair-raising circumstances.

Here too there was a link with the events of the 1960s: profound cause-and-effect and far more deleterious than any paragraph in Private Eye. *The solicitor, Gabriel Garsdale, a contract-manipulator with small experience of criminal cases, felt queasily at sea: all he could do was urge his client at once to make a further deposition and to hurry up about it. Pogmoor must now furnish the continuous history, not just the preliminaries, and effectively bring it up to date; for he was enmeshed (Mr Garsdale insisted) in an escalating scandal of sinister implication. All current work or hope of work must go by the board until he had thoroughly cleared himself. (En passant, in regard to the previous deposition, a depressingly significant Counsel's Advice had just come in: actions for defamation against the* Eye *or the*

National Theatre were 'unlikely to succeed, given Mr Pogmoor's talent for implausible self-whitewash and gratuitous denunciation of third parties'.)

A private investigator could be hired to explore some of the opaque background; but any discoveries thereby made must *be supplemented by Pogmoor's own account – 'And Jack, it will not do, unless it's obviously truthful. An end, if you please, to your curlicues of prevarication. Jack, no evasions: I am warning!'*

He might more easily have warned an echo not to repeat itself. But Pogmoor did his terrified best; he sat and wrote.

(As before, what he wrote has been partially re-juggled *for an eventual wider readership; his tone and the essential facts remain much as he submitted them to Garsdale.)*

1

Truthful? Obvious? Oh lord, Gabriel, bloody hell. Where do I start?

Jacqui Lobscott's tried to terminate her husband.

Hit him seventeen times on and around his head, face, jaw and upper torso, with the sharp-angled edge of that heavy glass ashtray, badly aimed, clumsily wielded, as he lay on his bed in the Vermeer Hotel in South Kensington. The police pathology-people counted the marks, the dents, the gashed contusions – they came up with seventeen. They never get it wrong, do they? So let's agree that seventeen is the truth. Let's agree that it's true that she did it. She doesn't deny.

Let's agree that it's true that Percy Lobscott is now in a coma in the Charing Cross Hospital and may or may not come out of it. So *his* view of the 'obvious truth' plays no part in the present proceedings.

Let's also agree that it's true she's told the CID and thereafter her attorney (a Ms Wanhope, is that the name?) that she did it because of Lobscott's physical brutality. Her defence will be Self-Defence; but she's changed her first simple account; now she is blaming it on *me*!

Let's be truthful about this, if truth is the name of the game: she did not give the blaming-Jack-Pogmoor bit to the *police*; she told it to Wanhope, last week, in the Visitors' Room of Holloway Prison, after all the length of time they've been holding her there without bail and after all the many earlier interviews she'd doubtless had with Wanhope. Time enough, one might say? to brood upon and elaborate her story: not exactly to 'make it all up' – 'deconstruct and re-edit' would be a more accurate form of words. 'Something snapped,' is the end of the story, of *both* of the stories, all she could see was a species of 'red mist' – no, all she could see was the hexagonal ashtray sitting grinning on the bedside table. And suddenly it was in her hand and Percy Lobscott was a gory lump.

Obviously true that this has been *said*. Didn't Wanhope write it down and pass my name to the Crown Prosecutor, notification of an unexpected defence witness? So J. Lobscott said it, which we agree is the truth (the legal profession has never been known, has it? to put words into the mouths of its clients); and J. Pogmoor has to answer it. I've already had to answer it to the cops; for of course they wanted to know just what I had done to be cited in this incriminating way; and now, for my own safety, I have to answer it to *you*. Lots of lawyers' work involved, lots of fees, lots of pretty and ingenious pleading? So here is the point where we come to the end of what is 'obviously truthful'. Nothing at all, after this point, is obvious; for we have to consider just what exactly she did say and why; if *I* say it is not the truth, how far can I honestly say she's been telling a pack of lies?

No evasions, okay.

No *what*?

For God's sake, who do you take me for? GOD? D'you think I'm omniscient, d'you think I'm ubiquitous, d'you think I've got eyes in my arse? D'you think I can possibly *know* the truth? D'you think, in such a context, I am able to define what truth in fact *is*? If I'm anyone apart from my own chaotic self, you'd do better to say 'Pontius Pilate' – he put that very same question, *did not stay for an answer*, and was happy enough to be in a position to wash his hands. I'm not allowed to wash mine; I've got to tell it whether I know it or not. I'm no better off than that girl in the fairy tale who was ordered to spin gold out of straw.

D'you think I can sleep with a woman in 1975 and then not again until 1985 and that everything she intends or assumes during that interval of time, or that passes between herself and her husband, will be 'obvious' and apparent to *me*? D'you think it was 'obvious', any of it, even when I was with her? whether eleven years ago or *this* year? – for example, the true meaning of those meaningless syllables she might mutter and cry while we clenched ourselves in secret together? D'you think that the rosebush will gasp, to the bumblebee as he roves among her petals, reliable data about anything but the sweetness of the manufacture of honey? Or will enquire which should be sharper, the thorns on her stem or the dart in his busy little twist? In short, Gabriel, let's face it, when I heard what she said to me upon any of those occasions, how could I hear what she *thought*? I believed we had a relationship of a specific, if incongruous, kind; I believed she believed so too; now she tells the world we never did, it was altogether different, and (what's worse) I, J. Pogmoor, was aware of it all along.

I am genuinely baffled. If you want, you can call it 'evasion'; but it's not.

Brass tacks, and here we go.

Let me first summarise the prosecution's story and then J. Lobscott's and thereafter I'll extend into detail; and you'll see whether or no I can feel safe in the Old Bailey witness-box.

(As for what the tabloids will do to me when I get there . . . what a hope. And as for the black books of our Great Leader's Victorian Values! the new 'public opinion' which even in the theatre comes clustering like flies on a cowpat . . . God, but they've done a job on us since Thatcher's two great election-wins – Gradgrind plus Bowdler plus an arsenic dash of Ananias-and-Sapphira – or to put it more concretely: the glittering dentures of my late sainted mother combined with the harsh tonsils of the Feminist Left, aren't they made for each other? and yet they won't admit it. What a hope.)

> ❧ *Prosecution case against the Lobscott.*
> *They don't believe in any 'red mist': they make out she bashed her*
> *wretched husband thus:*

She had come up to London with him, not to keep him company, but deliberately on J. Pogmoor's own territory to renew an old adultery with the said Pogmoor – to establish it indeed as a permanent phenomenon. In Knaresborough, years before, during the production of *Hermit's Hole*, P. Lobscott had winked at his cuckolding; but then he'd decided he would wink at it no more; and she – 'for the sake of the children' – had agreed. In the Vermeer Hotel his eyes all of a sudden are opened: Jacqui and Jack are still at it! For he finds her naked in a stained and rumpled bed in the middle of the afternoon, sees (and smells) the clear signs of very recent sex, recollects he has just seen the man Pogmoor at the corner of the fifth-floor landing as he (P. Lobscott) came waddling along to his room . . . The whole horrid sequence falls shockingly into place; and he loses control. He goes for her with his fists, his walking-stick. (She showed the police the rasher-sized bruises, and she'd been bleeding from nose and mouth.) When he finishes, she crawls shivering into the bathroom, just as she is, and huddles herself down, pressed close against the tiles. (There are some bloodstains of hers between bidet and bath; the forensic people checked them out.) He decides to have a short nap until they're due to get ready for dinner; he believes she is ashamed; probably she weeps and pleads; at all events he supposes she'll stay put, cowed and miserable, waiting for whatever comes next.

That's not what she's about. To be sure she is quiet; but quietly calculating, dangerous.

She gives him time to fall into a doze, which he does, because (a) he's had a heavy lunch with the publisher of his forthcoming book, *Old Nidderdale Days and Ways* or some such; (b) he's emotionally wrung-out; and (c) he's a conceited bastard whose twisted mind is set at rest by the pleasant thought of his wife's humiliation. Then she hits him and that's it.

Carefully premeditated: no nonsense about any 'red mist' or fighting back against his violence for her own safety. She stayed half an hour in that bathrooom and then crept softly out to do him in at her leisure. No doubt (the prosecution will say) the *entire scenario* was premeditated. She told J. Pogmoor— ❧

(Indeed she did, I can't deny it.)

❧—that Percy would be away all afternoon; although in fact she well knew he'd return at about three. So she intended to be caught, not actually in the very act, but immediately afterwards with all the evidence still there to drive her husband into his ogreish rage. Proof of this? She'd a phone call from him a quarter-hour before he returned, enough warning for J. Pogmoor to escape; but also enough to allow *her* to get dressed and tidy the bed, and she didn't even *try* to do so. ❧

(I remember that call, it induced no great panic. I left at my leisure. Too much leisure, very nearly: for such an old fart, his arrival was surprisingly speedy. How he recognised me, I don't know; he emerged from the lift as I trotted into the service-stair and I suppose he got one good glance at the characteristic breadth of my back. The *receptionist* saw me as I went out through the lobby; quite apart from Jacqui's statement, the cops know that I was there!)

❧ Her motive for setting her husband this little trap was not perhaps, in the first place, to provide an opportunity for her to kill him. The CID have deduced that it's most probable she schemed for a divorce. By taunting Percy with the intimate squalor of infidelity, she hoped she might force him to let her go – she admits she asked him to do so, often, in recent years, and he always refused – he never made his reasons clear – he *said*, 'for the sake of the children,' but did not phrase it very convincingly – nor was he known to have strong religious principles – psychotic possessiveness? a mixed-up malice of revengeful lust? desire for domination? sheer hatred both of her and of himself? – who knows and who cares? to the police it isn't really germane.

But as he beats her he reiterates (in effect), 'No divorce, on any account!' She knows now he must die; she confirms her own courage to herself in the bathroom; Plan A is replaced by Plan B; and the ashtray is just where she left it after she and her paramour had smoked their post-coital Dunhills. ✤

So – that's what they're throwing against her; it's a pretty black indictment; it may (to tell truth) contain a morsel of truth, give or take two or three major misreadings. I do know her conduct was far from spontaneous.

At the time of arraignment she spoke of her automatic response to her husband's most shocking attack; that's all that she spoke of. But if the jury can be led to believe the attack was provoked on purpose, she has to think of something better. Ms Wanhope keeps telling her, 'We have to think of something better; no way were your actions "automatic", don't you see?' So: a long history of Percy's recurrent brutality? Well, yes, but . . . how to prove it? Who in Knaresborough can back her up? She thinks about that and decides it might be difficult. Her Knaresborough circle was always a spiteful crowd, Jacqui Lobscott the most spiteful of all; and now her gibes and witticisms have bloody well caught up with her. None of her 'friends' are going to testify that the punctilious Dr Lobscott was a repetitive wife-batterer.

And then, unexpectedly, in prison, she meets someone who gives her the clue! (Guess who? You'll never believe it. I'll come to that in a minute.) Someone to whom the name of Pogmoor is familiar. Pogmoor, the man from Pomfretshire, notorious, disgusting – and *Inclined to Sexual Violence*. Why, of course! and at once a whole new story becomes possible.

✤ *Defence case, as embellished under the advice of Ms Wanhope.*
According to this account:
When J. Pogmoor was in Knaresborough in '75 to direct *Hermit's Hole*, he and Jacqui came to bed together by mutual consent. They were genuinely in love, or thought they were. Percy was aware of it, he knew he was a bore and allowed her (in those days) to fulfil her desires discreetly. J. Pogmoor stayed in the town for several weeks. At the end of that time he and Jacqui admitted to each other that what they'd thought was true love was a passing swell of hot wet daydream and 'really, my darling, we had better let it pass, for everyone's sake, Percy's

sake, the children's, hadn't we?' They said goodbye, very melancholy, very tender, and wished each other all good fortune.

Until the end of last year when J. Pogmoor had occasion to go to Knaresborough once again. He offered to renew the 'misconduct'; indeed he called an Extended Run, a Revival by Popular Demand, with arrogance and complacency. She reminded him of their previous self-sacrifice and assured him she meant to abide by it. Furthermore she had promised Percy, no more lovers. Through the intervening years, 'for the sake of the children', her husband had ceased to condone, he had remonstrated painfully when she went on deceiving him with one or two other men, he had been violent, she had forgiven him, he had forgiven her, they had patched up a harmony 'for the sake of the children', she had pledged him her word. Hearing this, J. Pogmoor lost his own temper, he got a hold of her with great big hands, a gross and repulsive bloated hold, which she was incapable of squirming out of. They were alone, at a hotel (where she met him by appointment, solely in order to persuade him in decency and friendliness to go back to London and forget her for ever). She succumbed. She wept; she felt defiled; but she also felt guilty; perhaps (she thought) she had no right to refuse him, having originally claimed to be in love with him; so she permitted him, again and again, through all of one night, and she liked it less and less every time she lay down under him.

And then she and Percy travelled south for a week in the capital. Percy had not only his publisher to see, but J. Pogmoor as well – they were to discuss the production of another of Percy's plays. J. Pogmoor came one afternoon to the Vermeer when he well knew that Percy would not be there. She was foolish enough to admit him to the bedroom; grossly, repulsively, with bloated overwhelming strength, he repeated the 'misconduct'.

When the phone call was put through, J. Pogmoor ran. Percy enters; he's seen J. Pogmoor at the top of the stair; he finds Jacqui in bed and tear-blotched, all in shock at the sight of him, scarcely able to move; he jumps to the obvious conclusion. He pays no heed whatever to her account of J. Pogmoor's coercion, the *rape!* yes, she uses that word. For the first time since the precarious *harmony* was patched up (in about '81?), he reverts, and with interest, to his violent remonstrances. More violent than ever before, until at last he is out of breath and the rain of blows comes to an end. He orders her into the bathroom, yes *just as she is*, while he takes his nap. He does not want to hear the slightest movement, the slightest word, through the open bathroom door, not even the flushing of the loo. She is not to get dressed until he decides to shower and shave, and then they'll go out for their dinner. He expects her to be slavishly obedient. In the past, after his assaults, she has been. Not now, not any more, this time it is not *her* fault, it's Pogmoor's, absolutely! most grievous injustice gives her sudden and implacable strength. She grabs the ashtray, etc. . . . 'red mist', etc., etc. . . . and rings room-service to tell them what she's done. ✄

(Now, is not this far better for her than a tale of a relapsed adulteress quite coldly inviting her husband to the actions of an ogre, and thereby providing herself with every excuse to get rid of him? For if I overwhelmed her by sheer physical size – I'm not only a rapist but an *obese* rapist, goddammit! is that what she's been telling to Wanhope? she knows well I'm no fatter than eleven years ago – yet *if* I overwhelmed her, then of course her husband's rage becomes entirely unreasonable.)

✄She has done her level best to convince P. Lobscott of the truth, he blindly refused to listen. Instead of love, warmth, compassion, solidarity, support, all she got was a pair of fives and a thick stick and the vicious indifference of a marital Captain Bligh to the results of a deep-sea keel-hauling. What *could* she imagine he would do to her next? She absolutely needed half an hour, on her own, to think it out. Which he gave her, without realising what he gave. She crouched in that bathroom, turned the whole vile business over in the whirlpool of her mind; she was thinking; she was weeping; she was thinking again – she knew without question she was doomed. This man would go on hitting her for the rest of her life. Whatever he might have been once, Percy Lobscott from then on was a torturer for the pure hell of it, and she'd never be safe. Never. ✄

Were I her brief, I'd be much inclined to call it a clincher. Furthermore, it's a clincher for *me*. If the defence-witness Pogmoor does not admit he's a rapist, then it will certainly be suggested (and maybe even proved) that he's an accessory – or accomplice – to Attempted Murder. She's got a fifty–fifty chance, with such a double-cross of an argument, to scrape up a partial acquittal – and good luck to her, on certain occasions she was very delightful to me, I do truly understand her dilemma, it gives me nightmares to think of her in gaol.

But either way, poor Pogmoor *goes down*.

Any hope for *me* from Knaresborough? All I'll say till I've told you the full tale, is that the only form of testimony from any one of her genteel friends will be such as puts Jack Juggler into chokey for the rest of his life.

2

In the evening of the day it all happened I had my first visit from the CID, unpleasantly represented by a distempered yapping dog of a detective-inspector who seems to model himself on that Lestrade in *Sherlock Holmes*. His ideas of subtle questioning are primitive in the extreme: 'When, Mr Pogmoor, did you put Mrs Lobscott up to it? In Knaresborough at Christmas-time or did you wait till you'd got her in London?' (Jacqui had not yet thought of the rape-scenario, remember.)

I just said, 'What?' I said, 'No, I never did.'

He said, 'That's not quite her story.'

I said, 'What *is* her story?'

Her story can have been no use to him as regards myself, beyond an admission I'd been to the hotel, for all he could say was, 'I have reason to believe—' and so on and so forth. Bluff.

I kept on saying, 'No.'

He felt unable to retort with 'Oh yes' as often as he would have wanted to, unless he took a truncheon to me; it was early days for that, I suppose. He'd nothing on me and he knew it, barring the faint hope he could scare me into an immediate confession. So he told me with the utmost menace he would see me again shortly. 'And don't leave town without informing us. You'll be sure of that? – *sir.*'

His second visit, last week, was a damned sight more frightening. This time he made a deal of ceremony with cross-talk to his sergeant and the sergeant's notebook and all of that. He told me the rape-story, in a deadpan monotone, and then snapped out: 'Your comments?' Of course I began to deny it, an absolutely monstrous confection, how dared he put it to me that I ever would have—

Oh God. I suddenly realised, bang in the midst of my expostulations, that he *wanted* me to deny it, in order to be certain that his original notion was correct. But by then it was too late; in any case, I couldn't *admit* it, could I? As I think I've just written: the bloody clincher, no less. So I tried to shuffle away from it, by asking him hotly where on earth such a story came from.

To my surprise, he told me. He needed to tell me, in fact, because my youthful reputation was a strong point in J. Lobscott's argument, and he guessed he'd have to test it.

'Are you aware, Mr Pogmoor, of any reason why a woman called Carmilla Costello should seek in such a fashion to blacken your character? You'd better be frank with me. Because I warn you, if you're not . . . Whichever way the coin spins, *you're* in a fix. Best think before you speak. Quite happy to give you a moment.'

I could have done with much more than a moment.

I daresay I should have visited J. Lobscott in Holloway: chivalrous, no? But I thought it would be injudicious; and I thought so all the more when I heard all this.

Not even P. Lobscott, regional playwright, could invent such a plot. That that venomous Costello, deported from this country in 1972, could have come back under a false name, been arrested at Greenham Common, been thrown into clink pending a second deportation, and there met a hysterical creature who talked about *me* – why, it's totally implausible and yet I have to tell you it's the 'obvious truth'.

I'd already been almost sure it was Carmilla who put the rumours round of my perverted deviations, Carmilla whose sulphuric tongue compelled me to write you that earlier submission about Blackadder. And now it was Carmilla whose extra-sensory perception snuck her up to the Lobscott's lug-hole during exercise-hour or therapeutic-association (or whatever enlightened get-togethers they have for remand prisoners in a women's gaol these days) – Carmilla lets her know, and makes sure she lets Ms Wanhope know, the sort of man I'm supposed to be – and the man I'm supposed to be is exactly the man Jacqui Lobscott requires to make her story stick!

You do realise there'd be no such story without Carmilla to intuitively create it? A triumphant feminist parable is what she thinks she's discovered and a heroine commensurate with that Judith of Bethulia who smote off the head of the arrogant heathen general just when he believed he had her totally in his power . . .

You do realise Carmilla broke my marriage up, don't you?

You do realise that Carmilla, ever since she—

No! I've written it all before, or most of it, I appreciate it's scarcely germane, I fully understand I have to write now about the Lobscott, but I can't avoid the Blackadder, I can't avoid Fid Carver and his creepy Napoleon play and—

Carmilla and a needle-clicking Madame Defarge of a solicitor have knitted this whole story into the Lobscott's imagination; stitch by stitch I have to unpick it. All I can say of their fable is this. None of it is absolutely false. And yet it is not true. I shall have to take it slowly. There's all sorts of other stories mixed up with the full narrative and it won't make any sense unless I include them. When you've read it, you can extract what seems useful, get me formally to swear to it, and put it through to Ms Wanhope to see what she makes of it. I'm still waiting to hear from her; bloody Lestrade said she'd be wanting to see me; I gather she's been in touch with *you*: but I am a 'hostile witness' (if that's the legal term? or is

it only in the USA? they go on about it a lot in courtroom movies), and
I'm damned if I go near her without your protection. Will you be
allowed to come too?

I told bloody Lestrade that I'd answer no more of his questions until
I'd talked with my lawyer. He barked out a kind of laugh and said, 'Of
course, Mr Pogmoor. Quite as expected. *At* your convenience. Good-
day.'

Well, I've talked to you. And now I'm writing it. God knows when
those cops'll be back. I wonder do they *want* to let me wait, 'twisting
slowly slowly in the wind', what d'you think?

3

But it's not really Carmilla, it's *Polly* who came back into my life. I'm sure
I should have mentioned this in my first statement to you; but to be
honest, I couldn't face up to it. I have to face up to it now, 'no evasions',
right? or else I'm shafted. You see, I met Polly again, had quite a bit to do
with her in fact, I believe I know where she is now (geographically,
spiritually, a long way away; oh my God, yes indeed), but what would be
her attitude toward *me*? Important question: for if she could state on her
oath that Carmilla's deposition to Wanhope is no more than a load of
manure insolently dressed up as a psychological profile, then maybe
J. Lobscott's fantastic accusations will recognise their own falsehood
like Judas in the potter's field, and (just as he did) self-destruct?
Unfortunately, I don't think that that is what's going to happen, or even
what *could* happen, you'll discover why. But you'd better have the full
package, here and now, off my chest, out of my gut, clear conscience,
ruat caelum! oh God, what a mess. And it all looked so hopeful to start
with.

4

In 1983, September if I have it correct, I was in Dublin at their annual
Theatre Festival, at the helm once again of my own touring company,
the remote descendant of the old leftish MOUTH-71 which mutated
into middle-of-the-road MOTH. You remember, you dealt with all the
fallout when Fid C. with *Poison-Voices* ran us head-first into a libel action
from Brewster the fascistic hack, the bootboy of the *Sunday Slime*. As we
endeavoured to reverse from a very dirty cul-de-sac, the troupe was
scandalously taken over by that finagling little Saltmarsh, master-
minding his coup within the bedsheets of my own dear wife. Leonore

found him out within a very short space of time, but by then it was too late; he'd dissolved the very heart of the company with his pandering to the sort of audience that needed quicksilver-voiced Sloane Ranger actresses stripping off on Riviera balconies to embody 'the helpless *tristesse* of the capitalist ego' – that's not a quote from a review: Saltmarsh's own programme-notes . . . So he milked the company for a year or two and then took himself off to Hollywood, whither his melioristic style had been pointing him all the time. After him, they jogged along, one artistic director replacing another; and every season a little less cash, costively extruded from a belly-griped Arts Council. Then at last they had some sense and asked me back.

I'd had an acrimonious and quite unnecessary quarrel with Fid Carver which had put a halt yet again to his Napoleon play; I was therefore at a loose end and glad of the opportunity. The first thing I did was to change the name of the troupe. MOTH had become ridiculous – **M**irror **O**f **T**orn **H**umanity, indeed! perfectly impossible in the high-jingo aftermath of the War of Thatcher's Face, we didn't want to inspire *compassion* for burnt corpses on Falklands/Malvinas, we had to hit at the deceit that had murdered them – and yet not quite announce it with a trumpet-call that might (if unlucky) emerge as a mere rude raspberry. I was still childishly sold on acronyms and I tried to find one that would quietly indicate our full intention and yet still carry a hint of MOUTH-71 and MOTH. I thought of MERDE, I thought of MURK, but they sounded too sordid. Expressive of what I felt: but (imagewise) deeply dysfunctional. In the end I came up with MAFFICK!:

> Dictionary definition:
>   '*verb intr.* to rejoice with hysterical and patriotic boisterous-ness *(from the public reaction to the Relief of Mafeking, 1900).*'

> Official reading:
>   **M**asks **A**nd **F**aces
>   **F**or **I**nternational **C**rowds and **K**riticks!

> Private reading (internal company use only, *not* to appear in press-handouts):
>   **MA**ggie **F**atcher should be **F**ucked
>   with an **I**ce-**C**old **K**ukumber!

—yes, well . . . it was sufficiently *ambiguous*, the company at the time were highly delighted by it; so we all smirked at one another (with one exception), and adopted it . . . yes. Our committee – *note* 'committee', I was having nothing more to do with any shape or form of collective, not after I'd seen how a Saltmarsh could manipulate it – our committee had decided, as a prime item of policy, to tour the plays abroad as much as possible, hence the 'International' on our masthead. And indeed, our first production, Chris Abel-Nottidge's *Deepwater Dread*, had its actual première at the Dublin Festival. Eh dear, when I think of the consequent aggro, I don't wonder I'm already as grey as a ram's backside. For the play was all about the sinking of the *Belgrano* battle-cruiser, which demolished the peace talks with Argentina and thus inaugurated the whole grotesque Malvinas slaughterhouse.

ᐁ Chris told it from the Argentine point of view, which is to say his central character was a Buenos Aires conscript, sent to sea in a World War Two rust-bucket to wage the War of Galtieri's Face, his fiancée (a radical student) having previously *disappeared* after a raid on her home by the death-squads of the Junta. There was cross-cutting in and out of the war-rooms of both nations, and a wealth of well-researched documentary detail. ᐁ

It was not at all a bad play; Abel-Nottidge is a capable man. In terms of language and therefore vital spark, I did think it lacked something, and it encouraged too much 'prose-acting'; I could not help but be nostalgic for Carver. The Dublin critics were appreciative – their own prime minister had denounced the *Belgrano* atrocity, thus infuriating M. Thatcher – and his electorate on the whole was pleased to hear him do it. Remember, it was only three years since the hunger-strike in the Long Kesh H-blocks. Or *do* you remember, Gabriel? When the Irish remember, the English forget; when the English remember, it's only because someone is due to be punished with the firmest of Firm Saxon Hands. And at once a Firm Hand began to descend upon MAFFICK!

Nearly every Brit newspaper (among those few that know enough to cover the Dublin Festival) offered some sort of condemnation of our presumption – what! did we dare present such an 'anti-British' play in a country which had evaded its duty not only in the Falklands but also against A. Hitler? I tell you true: the Tory editors (as opposed to their far more sympathetic reviewers) were steaming, they sniped at us in leading articles and had us assailed in 'occasional columns', they asserted that 'IRA godfathers' were conspicuous in the first-night audience, they printed letters from ordinary-decent-playgoers asking why a Question was not put down in the House. So of course a question *was* put down, and the Minister in charge of the 'Arts' answered it by saying that while the Arts Council was totally independent and would never exercise censorship, it must consider most carefully the expenditure of public money on what *should* be, under the right conditions, a valuable cultural export accruing national prestige overseas – in short, 'Don't let me hear of this irresponsible MAFFICK! ever again being paid to prance and dance on a foreign stage!' The better our play, the worse our offence, naturally. It was bloody *Poison-Voices* all over again: but this time we had properly prepared ourselves.

To start with, we did not have Fid in his VEXACTION-mode telling us where our consciences lived. Our arrangements could therefore be made without narking and nit-picking and sweeping accusations of sell-out. We had deliberately taken a calculated risk; all we had to do to mitigate its results was to consolidate the position upon which we would fall back; we had no serious qualms. Which is not to assert we weren't worried – privately – I'd say one or two of us were in and out of the loo like a relay-race every twenty minutes. But our name was now notable, amongst those who count in such matters, as a token of intellectually consistent (indeed 'responsible') artistic dissidence. Our overseas contacts were well satisfied – most of them in fact were already in Dublin for the festival, and we began fixing travel-dates within twenty-four hours of the play's opening.

I was able to meet these bods at the International Conference-Seminar, a prestigious event (as everyone told everyone else), and an integral part of the festival programme. It was elegantly bedded down among the classical courts of Trinity College; it was accorded (without too much meaning) the title of *Theatre and Performance Art: a European Dimension*. Directors, playwrights, actors, designers, academics, critics, fund-administrators, financial entrepreneurs – droves of them had been invited, and quite a number had actually arrived, to be hailed by the local establishment as a big boost for 'the arts-in-Ireland as a significant factor of state-of-the-art Euro-culture'. All the nations of the EEC were represented; with guest-observers from America, Australia, the 'Socialist bloc', the Third World and all over the place. The public were admitted at a steep enough price; there were simultaneous-translation facilities; and a host of diligent chits, students, out-of-work actresses, daughters of dons no doubt, to scurry about on their little feet *tip-tip-tap*, attending to our every need and perhaps (if we were lucky) our every desire.

According to advance publicity, the conference-seminar would be a vital exchange of creative ideologies brimful of new ideas to challenge the accepted conventions: 'a crucible' – if we were lucky – 'of stimulating cut-and-thrust'.

Realistic appraisal: the whole gathering was a hard-nosed *trade fair*. Creative ideology had very little to do with anything that went on.

5

How was I to know that a woman, once known as P. Blackadder, was an undisclosed infiltrator within this marketplace or *soi-disant* 'crucible'? But not at first, not quite at first; something else (no less germane) had to happen before I fell across *her*.

6

MAFFICK!'s conference input was (a) a paper read by myself – subject: *Prose-acting and Poetry-acting, what they can do and can't do for the playwright's script* – and (b) our leading actress as chair of a panel to debate *Sexual Politics in Mainstream Theatre*. She was Antonia Button, a nuggety growling thug, upwards of thirty, energetic, short-statured, buck-toothed, in my opinion disagreeable; but she took direction with great flexibility and never gave way to nonsensical 'temperament'. Her contribution to the panel-discussion would no doubt be a well-thought-out steeplechase of acerbic allocutions: she reckoned herself an expert on the theme. (It was she – for who else? – who'd declined to be amused by the in-house interpretation of our acronym.) There was also, of course, our play, in a small avant-garde arts-centre in an alleyway backing onto the Liffey quays. Conference participants were supplied with free tickets to any of the festival shows if they put down their names in time; and MAFFICK!'s PR woman busied herself making sure that all the important ones had their names clearly down for *us*.

When I say 'the important ones', I mean not only agents of venues, but reps from commercial firms which were interested in providing sponsorship. The Arts Council was about to fail us, we had to look to 'enlightened capitalism'. The PR woman and myself were hard at work collecting and collating these characters and ruinously treating them to drinks in the Shelbourne Hotel or after-show Chinese suppers. At the same time we ran a parallel chase among some very recondite cultural foundations; and after a few days we began to put together a tenuous jigsaw of promised contributions, nearly enough in sum to keep MAFFICK! on the road for another six months – which ought, we thought, to cover the run of *Deepwater Dread*, but insufficient to hold the company together after that. This was good, but not as good as it should be. If we could not manage more than one MAFFICK! production, we were not really a company at all, but an ad-hoc bunch of individual artists primarily concentrating on what jobs would turn up for us afterwards: a state of mind inimical to any rooted development of style and team-identity. When I say 'team-identity' I mean of course 'Jack-Juggler-identity'; I had a desperate urge to get stuck into it, here and now for at least three years, with a tight little *permanent squad* (give or take the usual number of defectors and new recruits) until I was truly able for the first time in my career to *fix* my own dramatic vision, consistent, coherent, and to spread it about the world on a succession of stages. Hitherto all my work had lacked a sense of continuity. I was forty-three years old; if I did not define myself now, I probably never would. I kept thinking of Napoleon, and all the talks I had had about him with Carver. Napoleon had *fixed* his vision before he was out of his twenties. How the hell did he manage to do it?

All I needed to make it possible was one bloody big lump of a *renewable* subsidy. *Deepwater Dread* had already opened; the first reviews were generally promising; but the murmurs of right-wing disgust from over the Irish Sea had started to buzz in my ear, like that sonofabitch gnat in *Alice Through the Looking-glass*, an insect that's been invading my dreams since I don't know when – some sort of pre-pubertal trauma, I suppose, I've always thought Lewis Carroll ranked with Edgar Allan Poe or Mary Shelley rather than with the normal run of children's authors . . .

One bloody big lump! I well remember how it came. I was staying with the company in a dismal bacon-and-egg private hotel in Harcourt Street, thriftily keeping costs down and holding the boys and girls together; I dragged myself into breakfast on the fourth morning of our run. I had to deliver my paper to the conference that afternoon and I still was not sure I had it right. A great deal might depend on it, in terms of the Jack Juggler identity; it had to convince a jaded and self-centred audience that there really *was* such an identity, that it was worth a bit of cash to see it fully expressed and that MAFFICK! was the proper vehicle to express it. So I firmly refused to sit down with any of the actors: let them call me stand-offish if they wanted to, I would eat at a small table with only a single chair, and the *Irish Times* was spread out between me and the rest of the room. I was therefore very annoyed when another chair scraped the floor; Mandy Cakebread, our PR, placed herself decisively onto it, the red queen overpowering a chess-board. She whisked aside my newspaper without the briefest pretence of courtesy.

'Mandy, will you kindly fuck off.'

'The devil with that, Jack. I had my breakfast an hour ago: I'm here to disrupt yours, and I'll expect to be thanked when I've finished. You gave me a job; I've done it; if I don't tell you now, you'll be lost to me all day; so fucking listen to me, can't you?'

'God, woman, keep it short; I've more than enough to think about.'

'Don't eat that rasher, it's a most peculiar green colour, and they've given you burnt toast: you have to adopt a strong line in a dump like this. No, it is *not* far too early in the morning. If you hadn't wasted the night with God's most implausible German, you'd have strength enough now to show respect to your metabolism.'

This was as bad as a breakfast with Leonore; no, worse, for it was devoid of any subtext of sex, even of quarrelsome sex. Mandy had her own husband and let us all know he sufficed. I'm sure she sufficed him. He was an oldish accountant employed by an audio/video-distribution firm; he was just then seeking early retirement. I wondered was he wise: every day all day with Mandy, and no means of escape? I said: 'God, I can't stand it . . . Oh, very well, I must admit that Dr Schwarzkopf was useless. He claimed to have access to all manner of UNESCO loot but I couldn't pin him down to so much as a pfennig. At least you could have given me a hint.'

'I did; and you ignored it. Too damned arrogant, that's your trouble. So arrogant, I suppose, that you've never even noticed the name of Cordwain.'

'Which is where you are quite wrong. I know all about Cordwain. He's not interested in anything beyond bog-bumf and condoms and the multiple seduction of duchesses. Okay, he sponsors pop groups, he owns a grotty soccer team. I never heard he gave a toss for the theatre.'

'He comes from Yorkshire, same as you do. He plays his cards very close to his chest: I can deal with you, I can deal with him. Jack, I have already dealt.'

If this was true, it was very big news, but I wasn't going to let her know I thought so, not until she'd thoroughly explained. Levi Cordwain was what the press call a whizzkid tycoon, chairman at the age of twenty-six (Napoleon almost beaten to the post) of a sprawling multinational that had indeed begun with toilet-paper and non-pharmaceutical bedroom/bathroom products. He had since diversified so widely that almost any manufacture related to 'lifestyle' now came within his financial scope. He was the grandson of a Leeds upholsterer, an immigrant from Lithuania at the time of the Tsarist pogroms, who enlarged himself by sheer hard work into the 'Furniture King of the North' (*Yorkshire Post* obituary). Levi had turned out to be a very gaudy type of businessman;

an Oxford-educated sideburned playboy with the looks of Valentino and a zest for the upper classes that bordered on the brazen. He was never out of the gossip columns; nor would I ever have thought that his taste in entertainment ran within a mile of MAFFICK!

'Oh, but it does,' persisted Mandy. 'He's just not made it known, that's all. He put quite a pile into one or two West End musicals recently; and he listened very hard when the Arts Minister called upon private enterprise to invest in *serious* theatre and lift the burden from the public purse. Clarence—' (Clarence was *Mr* Cakebread, I think a pet name, I hope so) '—Clarence heard on the grapevine that Mega-Cordwain plc was about to take over Videovox and that Videovox weren't contesting it. Clarence told me and I told *him* to keep awake and do his bit for us, so when he was sent to Mega-Cordwain to give *their* accountants the rundown on Videovox's state-of-play, he took advantage of the coffee-break to put in a wideawake word. He actually met the great Levi himself, open-fronted satin shirt, hairy pectorals, golden medallion and all.'

'When was this?'

'About a month ago. We'd already commenced rehearsals.'

'Why the hell didn't you tell me?'

'Because I didn't know what would come of it. I may have been born in Penge, but I can play *my* cards quite as tightly as any tyke, Jack. You'd not have been pleased if I'd fired up all your hopes and then in the end had to piss on 'em. Would you?'

I had to admit I would not. She further explained that young Cordwain was coming to Ireland that very day, apparently to buy racehorses; also, so it was rumoured, to consummate his conquest of the daughter of one Shaughnessy, president of Shannon Crystalware, a company that handcrafted a line of highly upmarket perfume-bottles and shared a power of good business with Mega-Cordwain.

'Christ! he's not coming to the play?'

'He might, Jack; and what's more to the point, he might even come to your lecture. What time will it be? Five o'clock? You'll be finished by half-past six, curtain-up is at nine, two and a half hours for you to woo the bog-bumf tsar and win. Don't look so panic-struck. Clench your fists, grin your grin, and you'll do it – it's a doddle.'

Her confidence in me was more unnerving than flattering. I pushed my greasy breakfast aside and tried not to gag. 'Who told you about Maria-Goretti Shaughnessy? Surely Cordwain would never have mentioned her to – to your Clarence? Or would he, dammit? What sort of bloke is he, really? I really will have to know.'

'Well, he is the sort of bloke that would mention Maria-Goretti to Clarence, what else can I say? He's totally unstuffy, and yet thoroughly secret. You and he'll get on like a pair of magpies, one for sorrow, two for joy, so I say to you: grin your grin!'

If all turned out well, I owed Mandy and Clarence (particularly Clarence) a very special treat for their efforts. But Clarence wasn't at hand, and all I could offer Mandy was an extra pot of coffee from the kitchen of the Salve Regina Guesthouse, to be added to my bill as an earnest of future gratitude. Hypothetical gratitude; I didn't like millionaires; only too easily, come the evening, I could alienate the man and balls up the whole business.

As for how my paper went . . . I wouldn't call it a flop; to be honest, it proved a respectable bore – but then it had to, hadn't it? All the lectures of that conference were bores, because few (beyond a handful of sanguine students) were concerned about anyone's theories but their own. Each participant came equipped with a personal agenda and gave but one ear to the others'. On my way into the lecture-hall – an intimidating Palladian *aula*, almost a throne-room, with an apse, a vaulted ceiling, a dazzling black-and-white marble pavement and acoustics like the inside of an Orangeman's drum – I saw a noticeboard on an easel; a conference poster pinned to it; sellotaped to the poster, a last-minute programme-addendum. Announced for the morning of the final day of the conference: a women's troupe from France to perform, in this same *aula*, a *Nameless Comedy of Nameless Females* ('in several languages and none'). They called themselves '*Les Femmes Savantes*'. Their piece would be very short, I deduced, for it was immediately to precede Antonia Button's panel, as it were the text to a sermon. (Because of Ms Button, I would have to attend whether I wanted to or not. I didn't want.) A member of the troupe was to take part in the panel's pronouncements. As also – I blinked with irritated shock – was the 'well-known English playwright, author of *Poison-Voices*, Fidelio Carver'.

Of course I had no right to either shock or irritation. But my relations with Carver had lately been such that I would have preferred not to meet him for a considerable length of time. And I certainly would have preferred him almost anywhere other than laying down the law at me amongst a batch of didactic feminists. Besides, he'd want to know all about MAFFICK!, and I did not look forward to telling him how we planned to obtain our money. I was all too aware of Fid's views upon capitalist support of the arts. It was obviously impossible I should *ignore*

him: we had had much too much to do with one another for too many
years. But . . .

The thought of him dogged me all the way through my discourse; I
lost my place twice; a page of my paper slipped from lectern to marble
floor without my noticing, and I blithely jumped the gap without
noticing *that* either, to produce (if anyone listened at all carefully) what
must have been a monumental non-sequitur. It could have been worse,
for I was clapped at the end as though I had delivered a truly important
statement; questions from the house were intelligent and – more to the
point – answerable; and I no sooner left the dais than my right hand was
vigorously seized by two strong warm appreciative hands, the mitts of
Levi Cordwain, no less, who rushed me away from the hall, across the
great court, under an arch and into a limousine before I'd had a chance
to take stock of him.

He was surprisingly small and very pleasant to look at – a *sexy little love-bug* some of his women might well have called him – with such an
overwhelming rush of disconnected conversation, that one was
seduced, one was tempted to overlook his sharpness; sharp as a
surgeon's lancet and his brown liquid eyes took in every single thing
within their range even as his words hopped, bounced, sprang from this
point to that, genial, inconsequential, subtly condescending and above
all most masterful. Simultaneously I was put at ease and painlessly
terrorised. He addressed me as 'Jack', I had to reply with 'Lev', I had to
admit I'd dropped a page from the lecture – oh, be sure he'd not failed to
observe it! – I had to admit I had not been to bed with any of the
'conference dollies' – did that raise me or lower me in his opinion?
impossible to know – I had to give him an immediate summary of what
Deepwater Dread was all about – 'Not to say I won't be there, Jack, not to
say I won't be listening, but sometimes first impressions in the theatre
are – God, you know it as well as I do – you pick up some daft oddity
about the way an actor walks and then before you know it half the play's
gone over your head – the first time I saw *King Lear* I got myself totally
confused all the way into Act Three trying to work out how, if he'd
already divided his kingdom into two whacking great parts for – for
Goneran and Regal? – how he was going to manage if the third dolly –
Cornelia? – tops 'em both by telling him she loves him best of all? Lousy
way to run a boardroom, bad preparation, bad, because, don't you see?
all he was doing was delegating his subsidiaries, I do it every week, but
you do have to allow for every possible contingency, wouldn't you say?
surely *you* find the same thing with your acting company?'

I did not dare be pedantic; I let his mistakes in the princesses' names go

uncorrected. Had he got them wrong on purpose to test me, or were
such petty details the sort of thing he *always* got wrong in order to keep
his mind tight to the main issue? I tried (in vain) to decide, and at the
same time I tried to explain to him the main issues of Abel-Nottidge's
play. I was worried about this; I feared he might have been an enthusiast
for the Malvinas war; his associations with royalty and those regular
photos in the press of him laughing and joking with M. Thatcher and co-
conspirators were very much in my mind. But he soon put that right:
'God, Jack! the Malvinas—' (not 'the Falklands'; interesting) '—"we die
to gain a tiny patch of ground that hath no profit in it but the name, to
pay five ducats, five, I wouldn't farm it!"—' (oh yes: a quote from
Hamlet, and very near word for word) '—mind you, there *was* a
question, simmering, secret, behind scenes, Antarctic minerals, yeah?
But in that case, why tempt fate by decommissioning the local gunboat?
for that's what set it all off. Or did they decommission in order to
provoke? and yet they'd fixed up nothing with Ron Reagan! and as for
the EEC . . . Bloody bloody fools, Jack, and I *long* to see this play tonight.
If it's as good as they tell me, I'll pay for it, sure. Five ducats? *Five hundred
thou*. Or whatever. Here we are; let's drink.'

We had already reached the liquor cabinet in what I took to be his
private Dublin hidey-hole, an incredibly lush penthouse on the top of
some new offices somewhere south of Baggot Street Bridge: a spacious
irregular room, open-plan, subdivided by a few gauzy drapes like the set
for a TV soap-ad. A four-poster bed in one corner and a huge marble
bath right beside it. (Bath? Poignant memories? No longer germane. . .)
Expensive modern paintings: Irish artists, he told me, the only one of
them who was dead was Jack Yeats, but his canvas was twice as big as
anyone else's. 'I like him best, that's why, I *longed* for this picture for
years. That's a woman in a shawl and two white horses on a hillside, all
that yellow-purple frenzy is heather and gorse, you have to stand well
back to make it out. *You* buy pictures, of course. Tell me the painters. No,
don't. Not just yet. Why don't we do some business? Refill? Of course.'

His proposition was more generous than I could have imagined.
Mega-Cordwain was prepared to back, not just a specific production or
productions, but the company's very existence, for as long as we would
need, until our profits began to break surface. Suppose they never broke
surface? 'How long will it be before you can know for certain?' – he
seemed to turn away as he asked, implying perhaps that he trusted me
for an honest answer without staring me out of countenance; however,
I suspected that his judgement of a tone of voice would be quite as acute
as his eyesight.

I answered, with a hesitant gulp, deliberately hesitant, I did not think he would appreciate my being too cocksure, he preferred to keep that sort of style for himself – 'Two seasons. Three?'

'Okay, call it three. From what you told us in your talk this evening, you want elbow-room to shape the company; Mega-C.'s very happy to give it you. Feel secure, Jack, it's all happening.'

He had thrown, as they say of the gipsy-gang in the ballad, 'the glamourie o'er me'. Which was not at all respectable, I don't approve of millionaires. So why did I succumb to this one? 'Mummydear'? Yes, 'Mummydear'! – always so prejudiced against what she was pleased to describe as the 'business-Jews' of Leeds, she believed them 'the essence of vulgarity' (*she* believed, God save the mark!); even ten years after her death I felt vehemently impelled to contradict her noxious ignorance. Nonetheless, I did not absolutely abandon common sense.

'Strings attached?' I enquired crisply.

'Strings, Jack? Why, of course. I'll want Mega-C.'s logo on every programme, every poster – only the logo, none of your subservient blurbs, I'm not a Robert Maxwell, not quite. And also, I'll want the very devil of a high standard, scriptwise, productionwise, which I know you can provide, but I'm warning you, don't get too contented, don't let it slip. I'll be the judge, not the critics, don't you worry about the critics. I want to see your plays, and I want to enjoy them, revel in them – those are the strings.'

'No qualms about the choice of plays?'

'God, no; that's your business! Make your own mistakes, same as I do; take the consequences, same as I do. I'll tell you something else: this Euro-bullshit, from the perspective here of Ireland, it doesn't quite look to be such bullshit as the English keep insisting it has to be. I felt, from your talk this evening, you've already felt an inkling? If you have, then you're one up on Thatcher. In ten years' time or so, you ought to have your MAFFICK! well dug-in across the continent – a link, d'you see, a link! and, Jack, every day I try to make links. God, isn't she lovely. . .' He had picked up a framed photograph from his seven-foot-wide writing-table: a paparazzo snapshot of a fruity young woman guffawing with abandon in the midst of what appeared to be a thoroughly drunken orgy of very rich people indeed. She had masses of hair full of flowers, falling down about her bare shoulders, and her slippery slipping ball-gown was as lush as Lev's penthouse.

I agreed, she was lovely. He began to explain to me, apropos of apparently nothing, that the original Maria Goretti was a juvenile saint who had submitted to be stabbed to death rather than endure a rape.

This struck me as inappropriate: I told him I must get to the theatre.

He laughed and rang at once for his chauffeur. As the lift took us down, he said, 'You're Yorkshire, like me. D'you know, when I was young—' (Young? What *did* he call 'young'? How old did he think *I* was?) '—I was quite as uptight as yourself. If we're to be good for owt at all, Jack, we all in the end have to let it all hang out, but each one of us has to find his own different road to it. Families are shaped by landscape quite as much as heredity. Aire, Ouse, Don and Dearne are none of 'em big rivers, but begod they'd have us drowned if they could.' His slick accent, Oxford/Mayfair, had suddenly gone all northern. *I'd* been assertively northern ever since I stepped into his limo.

After the show Cordwain told me it was even better than he had hoped, he met the company and warmly congratulated them, he whirled away to intoxicate his Maria-Goretti. I told the company of the nature of his offer. General relief, tempered rejoicing, and no one disapproved. Ideological scrutiny of the principle involved being conspicuous by its absence, straightforward bread-and-butter was the keynote of the response – once they'd asked me my own question, 'Strings attached?', and I'd given them the answer that was given to me.

'Can we trust him?' said Antonia, in her conscientious capacity as trade-union shop-steward ('Equity rep'), guardian of her colleagues' rights.

'Garsdale will check every word of the contract,' I assured her. (And you did, didn't you, Gabriel?) 'I'd say we can trust Cordwain as far as we can see him, no further. And he can only trust himself as far as the market allows him. We *are* in the market, let's face it. Totally dependent upon world sales of shower-gel. Risk! we have to face it, no more featherbedding.'

7

'Oh great!' says you, Gabriel, if you've followed me this far, 'MAFFICK! got its subsidy and Mr Cordwain was a lovely man. But what has this to do with Jacqui Lobscott? Get on with it, for God's sake.' Gabriel, be patient: it is the *obvious truth* that no story can start later than its beginning, for then it's not a story but a mere ejaculation, without context, without significance. The only difficulty for the teller is – what *is* the beginning? and how to discover it? *My* beginning really was the noticeboard in Trinity that advertised *Les Femmes Savantes*. Yet that would make no sense if you did not understand how Cordwain and I were already on converging courses toward our agreement. And *that* would make no sense if you did not understand the Brit-establishment response to *Deepwater Dread* and therefore why the agreement had to be made.

I suppose I could carry it back to Adam and Eve in the garden, a complete chain of cause-and-effect, none of it entirely meaningless – don't fidget: we are now at the coalface!

They'd said they were 'nameless females': not quite.

There were three of them; and they introduced themselves, one after the other, harsh voices rasping out Ancient Greek, French and English: 'Alecto; Tisiphone; and Megaera.' '*Pas Possible, Mon Nom; La Destruction Vindicative; et La Rancune.*' 'Unnameable; Vengeful Destruction; and Grudge.' In short, the Three Furies from mythology, in green tights and black leotards, their faces as heavily painted as Hindu Kathakali dancers, and monstrous great structures, part-wig, part-tiara, on the tops of their heads. Were it not for the contours of their bodies, you would not know them for men or women. They performed to continuous but variable rhythms played upon an array of queer-sounding percussion instruments by two girls at one side of the dais. These musicians had white-and-green faces and were draped in long strips of black ribbon; sometimes they howled or grunted.

Their play was very *French*, in that it had no story but presented a series of meditations upon different aspects of the 'female condition', with philosophical harangues. Alecto spoke chiefly English, Tisiphone, French; and Megaera, Spanish and German; although they all from time to time dropped into shreds and patches of all of the languages. In between the harangues were short dramatic interludes of (I suppose 'archetypal') confrontation between one sex and the other, at times farcical, at times melodramatic, incessantly strident. They shared out the male roles between them in a pitiless vein of stereotyped caricature: one of the musicians handing up an oversized practicable phallus to be clipped into the fork of each woman who was temporarily a man. They seemed on the whole to take a poor view of male anatomy. All of it, spoken orations and smutty interludes, was taken at a great pace, *danced*, one might say, and very excitingly danced.

Technically, there was no doubt they were brilliant (and I felt quite jealous); in terms of content, I thought their show jejune, vexatious, boring.

After forty minutes by my watch it came to an abrupt end: they just broke off in mid-speech and ran out of the hall, while their 'music' went on louder and louder under the echoing vault until the audience understood that only by applause could it be silenced. One of the musicians jumped to her feet, cried, '*C'est tout, fini!*' and she and her colleague fled likewise.

Buzz of enthusiasm, sneers of distaste, cynical Irish mutterings of 'Jasus, what was all that?' What indeed?

And then, the panel.

Antonia, who'd been sitting beside me halfway up the aisle, breathed ecstatically into my ear, 'Golly, Jack, weren't they good?', before mounting the dais to arrange the table and chairs.

She gathered to herself her three or four pundits, all women of some theatrical distinction (according to the programme) from various countries; they fussed about microphones, translators, carafes of water, in the usual way of such affairs; while this was going on, Fid Carver imperceptibly joined them, taking his seat at the right-hand end of the table. Until then he must have been at the back of the hall; I hadn't seen him.

Then there was a pause. They had to wait a couple of minutes for their *Femme Savante*. When she arrived, there was only one vacant chair for her, on the extreme left, and therefore a good distance from Carver. She'd been Alecto, as I could tell from the stockiness of her thighs and the roundness of her rump, and as 'Alecto' she was baldly introduced, no other name, no nationality. She was still in tights and leotard; she had removed her head-dress and much of her elaborate paint – it wasn't by any means all off, there were vertical streaks of blue, green, white and red all blurred together, making it hard to read her expression. And her face was part-hidden behind a most obtrusive microphone.

The debate was much as I had expected. Deadly serious dogma, seriously received by the actresses and the female dons and the female students and the female journalists in the body of the hall; none of it either new or grippingly expressed. To begin with, Antonia asked each panellist to 'respond to the challenge of the theme' – she herself would lead off. So each of them spoke heavily about sexual politics or mainstream theatre or a bit of both (variously mixed) until they'd emptied their buckets, one, two, three, four, and then it was Alecto's turn.

She was the first one to have anything like a fresh idea. I thought it was a mad idea; but it did contain a certain logic; it actually *bothered* me. She said we were living in what purported to be an era of sexual equality and equal job-opportunity, the EEC had declared this as a positive policy, member nations were attempting to legislate for it in practice. All trades and professions were included – except two, the churches and the entertainment industry. About the churches she would say nothing, she had freed herself from theology long ago, let them cling to their old rubbish till it choked them. But the stage – ah! that was different. No clerical ideology was offering impediments here; the objection to equal status was entirely pragmatic, and it was more than high time we got rid of it. A mouldy old convention, she said, that men should play men and women should play women, which wouldn't matter a damn *except for the fact that*—

'Women, it has long been clear (and if it hasn't been, there's surely no doubt of it now, not after the contributions of the previous speakers), do *not* receive acting-roles of 'power and initiative' on the same scale as the men. I can prove this by statistics of the *dramatis personae* of a dozen plays currently running in London and a dozen in Paris, and only today I've been poking my wee nose into all the programmes of this Festival. The same disproportion of gender in each place – d'you want to know why—?'

She suggested historical reasons for it, social reasons, political, all very scholarly, I won't go into them.

Her solution? Let the EEC directive be enforced in the theatre. No cast of any play to have less than fifty per cent females.

She grew heated and smacked her hands upon the table to each beat of her argument – she could have done with her two percussionists, she must have thought of them too late. 'This will not compel the playwrights to write roles to an exact fifty–fifty proportion; if there's more men than women in the script, then women actors play some of the men – whichever way round it falls out, it could as easily be vice versa. Why not? We expect a young actor to play an aged character, an Irish actor to play a Spanish character, a warm affectionate actor to play a cold-hearted dissembling villain – it's no more than the day-to-day skill of the business, we're trained to do it, the public accepts it. So why not the opposite sex? It's often done for special occasions, pantomimes and so forth; Shakespeare wrote for it all the time, he had to, it was the rule, but in his case the cross-dressing was entirely unilateral. But I *don't* mean for special occasions, I mean ordinary day-to-day roles. Dear goodness, I've said enough. If you want, I'll come back to it later.'

I could not understand the strained posture of Fid Carver: he was observing her with such intensity! *And* chewing a piece of his beard; difficult for him, the beard was so short, he could only be attempting the ungainly feat under the stress of severe disturbance. Did he hate what Alecto was saying? Or was it something else about her? Her voice was angry sandpaper and her English was kind of foreign – Spanish-foreign, French? Certainly a hint of Scots in her phraseology – 'wee nose'? 'dear goodness'?

You must think I'm as thick as a plank I didn't tumble to it then and there. But the Blackadder, when I'd last seen her, was no more than twenty-two, she'd now be forty. That can sometimes make a great deal of difference, let alone the fallibility of my memory. I just thought, she reminded me, of – of someone I didn't care to recall – or refused to recall. I just thought, 'I don't want to think. Let me, instead, think solely about what she's arguing. It *is* a point of view; I'd like to dismiss it, dammit, I don't think I can.'

Last person on the panel: F. Carver. God, what an odd display! an impression of a man who has just arrived in Dublin via a breakfast-time flight, full of zeal to make his urgent points, and then suddenly – when faced with a hundred-odd people – is struck down in his prime by rabid stage-fright. Quite uncharacteristic; countless times I had heard him address similar assemblies; he was always articulate, amusing and fluent, muted perhaps, but any diffidence, any hesitancy would seem no more than a *tactic* to highlight his essential coherence. Now, however, he was all in pieces. He fumbled with his few pages of script, dropped them on the table, shuffled them about, and finally let them float out of his ken. He coughed, spluttered, drank some water. It acted upon him like raw spirit. He stood shakily up, thereby placing his mouth eighteen inches too high for his microphone. But that didn't matter, because he began at the top of his decibels—

'Furies!' he shouted. 'Here they were and we confront them. Here they were and we know who they are. *Eumenides*, the Kindly Ones, do we confront them in that guise? Do we agree that that guise is mendaciously accounted for by Aeschylus, when he made them submit to the motherless Pallas Athene, born out of man-flesh only, preaching patriarchy from a woman's shape, a renegade shape, a – a damned lie, to be honest with you, Pallas Athene? Don't tell me you don't understand.'

Nobody did understand him; but we were polite, we waited for more. He lost his flow and stammered.

'Or do we – do we – take them for what they are, what they were, what they will be, Kindly Ones only – only, that's to say, if we absorb them into ourselves, and – and – the Furies, are they not sent here to – to tear us to pieces—?'

He stopped short and stared across at Alecto, his features twitching, his teeth bared.

'Look,' he continued, pausing apprehensively between every phrase, 'Alecto here, what she said, I've nothing to add to it. I hadn't thought of it, ever, and she's right. She's a Fury, she has to be. Has to be.

'I do suppose, on the Left, ever since Karl Marx, one enormous mistake, the exploitation of women by men has *not* been, has *never* been understood – I assure you, it is not a footnote, a postscript, a marginal effect of capitalism. But it's capitalism itself, the very cause of it. There.

'Older than capitalism. Accept that, and understand the – the failure of Leninism – the – the failure of Irish Republicanism – the – the – failure. Understand.'

He was shouting no longer but mumbling, crouched over his mike though not using it, he had it somehow pressed into his chest and it boomed and crackled distractedly, making sheer bloody nonsense of itself. Antonia, alarmed, passed him a note. He looked at it with fuddled comprehension; and sat down. But he didn't finish.

Mumbling on and on: '—on the programme, the poster, it says "mainstream theatre", there is no mainstream theatre, mainstream theatre is a voice from the grave, choked with dust, gurgling with worms, a voice of old bones buried deep deep deep, tossed about in the currents of Lethe, I beg you, beseech you, find the source, find it—'

I slid out of my seat and left the hall as quietly as I could. If he saw me, did he realise it was me? He had his eyes fixed on the table-top, I doubt if he saw anyone. On the steps outside the *aula*, with the door half-shut behind me, I could still hear his ramblings – would he stop of his own accord, or would Antonia have to terminate him? (This being Dublin, I assumed everyone would assume him to be drunk; but *I* knew that when he was drunk his behaviour was quite different.) I had arranged to meet our lighting-man down at the theatre: I'd decided on certain changes to be made before tonight's performance, the last of the Dublin run. If I didn't bestir myself he'd be off to his lunch. And then tomorrow evening we were all booked on the Holyhead car-ferry, my Fiat, a transit van, a freight-truck for the sets and stage-gear, the lot. It all had to be organised . . . Eh dear, poor old Fid, somehow those monkey-trick Frenchwomen had totally fucked him up.

Mind you, the previous year he had had a nervous breakdown. I don't know too much of it, only from Leonore's hints, but I gather it was bad. He emerged more stubborn and combative than he'd ever been. He became impossible at the Napoleon play, refusing to work on it, assuring me he *was* working on it – and, at last, while insisting we talk endlessly about it, he was doing his level best to blacken my character within the Theatre Writers' Union and the Writers' Guild. Some people in *my* union, ACTT, the Cinema Technicians' (which I've belonged to ever since I first directed a TV play), had started to discuss the possibility of directors as well as writers claiming royalties from published scripts. *TV scripts*, of course – upon the premise that TV is basically film and not theatre, a director's medium rather than a writer's, and that no script would in fact be published unless a director had first *made* it, and therefore made it fit to be published. I was honest enough to assert (at a union meeting) that the principle should be extended to the stage, for cockahoop dramatists all over the place were selling the books of their plays, companies were reading them and putting them on, and the director of the first production got nothing whatever out of it. In all likelihood most of the stage directions would be his personal creation, not the writer's at all. Sometimes the printed script did not even name the director of the first production. Unjust, I said; I still believe so.

Word was leaked (and I'd damn well like to know by whom) of my speech; Fid Carver got to hear of it; next thing, he had incited the executive committees of both his unions to burst along in with frenzied objections. Of course our flabby lot took a sharp step backwards, assured the seething writers that we dreamed neither of piracy nor larceny, we dissociated ourselves from 'imprudent Jack Juggler who (in effect) had gone over the top', and there the matter rested. Carver and I no longer on speaking terms.

8

I guessed, when I walked away from Trinity, that I'd seen the last of F. Carver in Dublin. I guessed wrong. For at nine o'clock that night there he was, sitting in the back row at *Deepwater Dread*, chewing his beard, chewing his nails, for all the world like a lunatic expelled from a rundown mental hospital and thrown upon 'community care'.

After the curtain-call he inserted himself backstage. The tiny dressing-rooms (there were only two of them) were filled with well-wishers, and we had thought proper to lay on a lot of drink. I was heavily occupied shaking hands, accepting congratulations, congratulating my actors, thanking the theatre-management, and all the rest of it. I absolutely could not *cut* Carver in such an atmosphere, but I did delay greeting him for quite a time. As I threaded the ruck I came across him inadvertently – I made it look inadvertent – he was in deep conversation with Antonia.

'Well,' says I, intelligently.

Quick as a flash, he says, 'Well . . . Well, Jack, here we are again. I saw the play, you know.'

'Ah,' says I. 'Did he like it?' says I, but to Ms Button.

She gave me an odd look, and growled as per usual. 'He tells me he liked *my* performance. What more have I the right to expect? You married his sister, didn't you? Nuclear families, keep clear of 'em, Button; I'll leave you both to your kinship-bonding.' She drifted away for some woman-bonding with a fat lady from the *Irish Press*.

Carver tried to chew his beard, said nothing for a moment, and then – 'It looks as though your young Christopher is beginning to learn his trade at last. Is he here?' He had always had a bit of a spite toward Abel-Nottidge; I was glad to tell him he'd returned to London three days earlier.

'Were you—' he asked hesitantly, 'were you – this morning, at that affair in the college?'

'Yes. I couldn't stay till the end of it. The lighting-plot, here in the theatre, it had to be—'

'A lot of 'em couldn't stay till the end. I heard the feet. You must have thought I made a mess of it. I'm not sure, in the upshot, that I did. Antonia doesn't think so. Neither did Polly. But Polly being there, I wasn't expecting, didn't know who she was at first, it threw me, altogether broke me up, as the Victorians used to say.' He peered into my face with no shadow of nervous disorder, shrewd and omniscient like a customs-officer on the watch. 'You did realise it was Polly?'

'Yes,' I said. 'Polly.' Steel shutters in my mind were swinging up and open, an astonishing white sunburst came out of the gulf behind them, hurting me, blinding me. I had seen her and I had not seen her. It was not Fid's queer performance that had driven me from the *aula*, but the knowledge, buried inside me, that his performance was as it was because she was as *she* was – of course I had known it then, I didn't need him to be telling me now – and yet I did need it, for how else could my memory, my recognition, be sparked into life? I said, 'Polly. Yes. She has changed a great deal. I didn't think I should try to speak to her. She hates me, you see.' Hates. I'd never said this to him before.

I couldn't tell from his reply whether it was news to him or not. 'I had lunch with her. I'm not sure she does hate you. I only came here tonight because of her – I'm not interested in Abel-Nottidge – I came on purpose to tell you she'll be at the press conference tomorrow. If you want to talk to her, she'll talk to you.'

'Is that her message or yours?'

'Mine, on her behalf. She didn't order me not to bring it. I'll be at the press conference too. But before we go there, why not breakfast with me? I'm staying at the Gresham, yes indeed very posh, paid for by the festival committee; there's a lot you need to know about what she's been up to. I'm off now, Jack, goodnight.'

9

I was at the Gresham Hotel by half-past eight. The press conference would be across the river at half-past ten in another hotel, Buswells; so we had at least an hour and forty minutes to ourselves. Are you surprised I was up and about so early? Dear God. I had hardly slept . . . there had been something out of order with the interior of the guesthouse mattress, something out of order with the interior of my mind, I don't know which was worse. Every night for eighteen years I had thought of Polly Blackadder for at least five minutes, ten, before I fell asleep (whether I had company or not); many nights she stayed with me and wandered through my dreams, now harsh and denunciatory, now close and tender-loving, now blind with bodily desire, crying out like a curlew – and sometimes plain *friendly* as we once were at Pomfretshire before – well, before Owston and his wine-bottle, wherein lay all the blame. Every night for eighteen years: and only yesterday I hadn't recognised her. Any wonder that my cramped bedroom was a wasps'-nest of centrifugal grief? The frozen heart retains the *old image* of a vanished beloved, long-standing and immutable; outside it (and unguessed-at) there are human exigencies, season by season, hard at work to construct the *new one* – such foolishness to believe they could possibly correspond.

No problem at all with green bacon at the Gresham: my mixed grill was a great platter of sizzle-and-tang that would tempt an Ayatollah to break his rules. Alas, I had no appetite. Carver took small mouthfuls of rice-cake (from his own private packet) and a beastly-looking compote of prune. He said he had been unwell; he had found himself some faddish diet. My acrid account of the facilities of the Salve Regina led to desultory talk about living within one's budget. He correctly assumed that MAFFICK!'s budget was very tight; he had read how the Arts Council was being stirred up against us; he asked what I thought I could do about it. I talked at large with careless optimism of European cultural endowments, of the unexplored treasures of UNESCO. I avoided altogether any mention of Mega-C. At last, when I could bear no more of it: 'Damn well you know you didn't fetch me here to talk about all this!'

'Oh, but Jack, I *want* to talk about it. I've got a good reason . . . No, you're right, so let's leave it till later. Polly.'

'Go on.'

'Polly. Extraordinary woman. I'd no idea it was her in that play until some little trick of hers, a knack of timing her words to her movement, brought back to me, *instantly*, a single sharp moment from one of our old

VEXACTION pieces. Did you ever see VEXACTION? No, of course you didn't. No. Well, she and I had lunch and a long afternoon. She said—' He broke off and for a moment it seemed as though he'd completely changed his mind and he wasn't going to tell me anything. Then he started again: 'This is, you understand, absolutely confidential. Nothing of it, whatever, to anyone else, anyone. Swear it.'

I took a burlesque oath on the restaurant menu-card. It was evidently valid, for he went on, not looking at me, crumbling his rice-cake: 'Okay, I'll hold you to that. D'you know why VEXACTION collapsed?'

'Natural wear and tear? These small companies commonly—'

'No they don't, not like this one. MI5, Special Branch, very very dangerous political affiliations, I can't give you the details, I was only – only on the fringe of it. But Fred Owston was bang in the middle; she was living with Fred Owston; he panicked, he double-crossed her, she could have gone to gaol.' ('Jesus!' I interpolated, aghast.) 'They split up from necessity and then, she decided, for ever; she'd rather go to gaol than have anything more to do with him. But she also decided it was damn silly to go to gaol, so she used a few of her underground contacts to get herself out of the country and settle herself down somewhere else. She never really knew whether she was on the run or not. Part of her was convinced that the file on her (whatever it contained) had been closed once and for all, and that no one could be chasing her. Part of her believed herself to be as notorious as Ulrike Meinhoff with her mugshot in police-stations everywhere from Lübeck to – to Liverpool.

'She ended up in Denmark among a treacherous exiled subculture of left-wing 1968 Germans. She got hold of a Swedish passport, adopted a new name, tried to keep going in some sort of avant-garde mime-theatre. She'd no money, you know. All her savings from her few successful years as a conventional actress had either been subsumed into the cost of setting up VEXACTION, or Owston had nicked 'em. He was less a crook than a bloody fool, and she'd truly been in love with him.

'She found his clones everywhere in Denmark, in the circles where she moved. Nobody, but nobody, to trust, she says, and everybody all the time spouting hopeless revolution like kettles left too long on the hob. She'd no money, you know—'

'I know; you've already told me.'

'She had a drug habit. She fell into it in Copenhagen out of her despair for the loss of Owston – for *Owston,* imagine! She was still able to work, but was no longer reliable. She knew she was not reliable; the knowledge nearly killed her; Polly, of all people, unable to plan herself from one day to the next, can you imagine? The mime-theatre wasn't reliable either. It folded. She could still work, in fits and starts, if someone was there as her minder, to ensure she had the right supply at the right intervals and would turn up when needed to be told what to do. For "minder", she says, read "pimp". She'd no money, you know—' ('Carver, for God's sake—') 'She'd found her way into porno-films. And strangely enough, as a porn-personality, she found herself in demand. No: not so strange. Talent is talent; they couldn't hide *hers* by taking all her clothes off. I said "porn-*personality*"; a vivid personality, a real individual, emerging from the welter of faceless flesh, with emotional commitment, critical objectivity, humour.

'However, her first director said she was subverting the tacky essence of his skinflicks. He threw her away, at a price, to another guy, more discriminating. This fellow was a Brazilian, he carried her across to Rio, he made what he called "high-art erotica", and some of the better samples of it were seen by genuine artists. One of them was French; he came to Rio to find her; he wanted to direct her in real movies. She was controlled by a bunch of gangsters who refused to let her go. The Frenchman promised her (if only she would trust him) not only to get her away from them but to get her off the drugs. He seems to have had to recruit his *own* gangsters to effect the escape to France – a regular *Entführung aus dem Serail* – there was shooting and beatings-up and motorcar chases and motorcar crashes and all sorts – bribes to politicians, bribes to the cops – just like life in London – Brixton, Notting Hill, Highbury. . .'

His voice drifted away and I saw him put six or seven spoons of sugar into his herbal tea, quite contrary to his diet. 'Oh, get on with it, man! It's already half-past nine.'

'Yeah. Well, she doesn't remember too much about it – in a stupor half the time, she says. She says he spent thousands on her. He could afford it, he was the son of a successful right-wing publisher, inheriting the company profits in very well-placed investments. He was in love with her. Not her with him even after he'd paid for her cure. But she did trust him; she worked for him; three or four quirky little movies; Roman Catholic philosophical mysticism, highly regarded in certain continental art-house circles, but not capable of export to the UK except for the odd film-club or the National Film Theatre. She was billed as Gudrun Bernadotte – ever hear of her?'

'I don't think so.'

'The name seemed familiar to me when she mentioned it; but no more than the name, I couldn't put a face to it. I'd seen at least one of his pictures (I thought it a polished old load of Redemptorist rubbish, second-rate Robert Bresson), so probably I saw *her* but never knew, I wouldn't have been expecting her, and her dialogue would have been dubbed – she speaks French of course, but not well enough to play a Frenchwoman.

'This brought her up to the end of the '70s. She was living with the director. They had a child. He was in love with her; not her with him; and she gradually came to realise that his reactionary political friends, his pompous artistic friends, were slowly but surely turning her inside out. He gave her a luxurious life. I don't know if they were married or not. But one day she informed him that his principles were misconceived.'

'She would, of course.'

'No she wouldn't, not for nearly ten years she wouldn't. Copenhagen, she says, had purged her of all principle and Rio de Janeiro had made her as much a criminal as the criminals she consorted with.' (Nonsense: P. Blackadder could not possibly be a criminal. She is of the *elect*, always was, always is.) 'But the old Polly,' Carver continued, a kind of clergyman's light in his eyes and beatitudes of "grace abounding" in his voice, 'the old Polly was still there and eventually came up out of the grave – out of "the white rabbit's hole", she says.' ('Oh no,' I interpolated, 'never that, she can't have said *that*.')

'She had just discovered, you see, that her saviour, father of her child, restorer of her career and so on and so forth, who was years older than she was, had collaborated during the occupation with the Nazis, or at least with the Vichy scum, making films for them, so on and so forth. When she challenged him, he admitted it, said he had done the right thing, said did she not know that the hoodlum who ran her porno-work in Rio was a Jew and wouldn't it have been far far better all round if Auschwitz had swallowed him up? To which she retorted as I've told you – though surely with rather more *vigour* – and then she had the nerve to ask him what the devil he'd been doing anyway that he should have ever watched one of those same porno-films – he had to have watched it, how else would he have known what she was like?

'That was it. Total bust-up. He ordered her to go. She went before he could beg her to stay, left the kid, left the house in Paris and the villa in Provence, took what little money he hadn't tied up out of her reach, and lit out for Nicaragua to help the Sandinistas. They'd just won their revolution; there was lots for her to do. She asked to help with the Literacy Project, but her Spanish was too rudimentary. They gave her a job training Nicaraguan students to organise young people's theatre.

She met a pair of Frenchwomen at the same task and got on very well with them. Last year they all three returned to France and set up *Les Femmes Savantes*. And that's just about it.'

'Hardly. What about this kid of hers?'

'The father doesn't know that Polly's come back; doesn't know where she is, doesn't care – so she says. He has the little girl with some nuns somewhere; Polly found out where but can't get at her. Nuns: yeah, it's tragic, like shunting off the wretched creature to bloody old merciless aunts, and an only child moreover, no one at all to give her any comfort. Filth.'

Tragic? I thought not. She'd left the kid, hadn't she? It figured. Because she suddenly came to see that its dad was a fascist, she had never conceived it, it had never been born. I didn't say any of this; Carver would have gone spare. I did say, 'Does she still call herself Gudrun, or is she Blackadder once again?'

'Certainly not Blackadder. Her family in Edinburgh disowned her, d'you know that? when she wrote to them for help from Copenhagen. She told 'em too much of the truth and they couldn't take it. So she swore not to use their name, said she was more ashamed of *it* than they of *her*. For exterior purposes she's known as Alecto, *tout court*, but I called her Polly yesterday and she didn't refuse it.'

'I don't think I want to meet her.'

'Why not?' He looked remarkably grim. (I did want to meet her, intensely; but I trembled with fear; too much of the Freudian aggro, forget about it, hide with it, hide away with my secret hard-on to rub it off into oblivion.)

Carver was doing a most mischievous moral-rearmament job on me and I couldn't discern his motive; there *was* a hidden motive somewhere, if I stonewalled him I'd maybe draw it out of him.

'For some reason,' I said slowly, 'she took against me at Pomfretshire, informed me she was out of my life for ever, and I don't know why today you'd suppose she'll have changed her mind.'

Not to be drawn on any account. 'Okay.' He seemed to dismiss the question. 'If you don't want, you don't want. To talk of the other thing: are you able to continue MAFFICK! beyond this present production?'

'Why?'

'Because I've finished the St Helena play. It is definitely and definitively called *The Emperor's Whore*, I know that's not a title you care for, I don't give a fuck. I want it produced. Yes, yes indeed, pour yourself another coffee. Bit of a shock, isn't it? Finished! a complete script. God's teeth, Jack, who'd have believed it?'

'You offering it to MAFFICK!?' He was altogether a different man –
and in less than thirty seconds. Neither melancholic-moralistic nor
moralistic-conscience-probing, but downright old Fid-style sanguine.
Ah, but would he stay like that?

'How does this sort with your silly-bugger comments yesterday? You
said there was "no mainstream theatre". I assumed you meant you'd
henceforth work with outfits like VEXACTION or *Femmes Savantes* and
leave the rest of us to the waters of Styx, or was it Lethe?'

'Would it hurt your feelings if I told you that MAFFICK! is not
mainstream? With a twit like Abel-Nottidge you've had to try to be
mainstream, and that's what's the matter with your production. By
good luck or shrewd management you've made yourself a company
with sufficient blood-and-guts to take you away in any direction. *Always
provided* you juggle your financial backers so that no single one of them
holds a dictatorial whip over you. Can you do that?'

'I think so,' I lied. 'We're not signed up with any of 'em yet, but . . . I
do have some confidence. Artistic independence, baht strings, should be
t'name o't'bloody game, right?' (Awkward. Edge him off this particular
lay!) 'What d'you mean, "any direction"?'

He looked at me suspiciously and his voice hardened. 'I am suggesting
you find out *my* direction and stop dithering under the signpost. Well?'

Talk about dictatorial whips . . . 'You want a woman to play Napoleon?'
I said it as though I spoke of the ultimate absurdity, but his expression-of-
face was blandly untroubled, his reply quite matter-of-fact.

'Maybe. But I'd say not. Not if you confine the casting to your current
personnel. Button would be the best bet, but isn't she too wolfish? This
is the Emperor in his pasty-faced decline, *jowly*: what about Stropp?'
(Ben Stropp was our General Galtieri, undeniably pasty-faced and as
jowly as a bagful of spuds.) 'But Napoleon's not the lead; let's not make
that mistake again; I've got it right at last, you see – the focus of the play
is upon those who *observe* Napoleon: his mistress, Albine de Montholon,
is a key to the story – I know you have tended to disregard her
importance. But we must cast her with great care. Button could do it,
she'd find a totally different problem than this coarse Maggie Thatcher
Abel-Nottidge has written for her, much more interesting, much more
complex, she has the versatility, I'm sure of it.'

I reminded him that I had yet to see his script. I put it to him tartly that
I might not want MAFFICK! to do it at all.

Again, matter-of-fact, blandly untroubled: 'Of course you'll do it,
Jack, unless you still bear a grudge over your directors'-royalties
nonsense. That gun of yours has been spiked; why not forget it and – and

confront a few of your own Furies? No one's written you better scripts
than I have. Use your practicality. If you throw this away, you're a
simpleton; I know you're not. It'll work or I wouldn't say so.' God, how
he could needle me! but he was probably right. When he spoke with
such confidence about something he had created, his opinion was to be
trusted. He seemed to have more to say, but a certain difficulty about
saying it. I waited, politely, until – 'Apart from Antonia Button, though,
don't you think you are short of strong women? Strong *mature* women;
you've got two very good girls, but—'

'How many mature women will you need for *The Emperor's Whore*?'

'If we're casting across the gender-division, we'll need more than one.
None of my main characters are exactly young, and—'

'Alright alright alright, send me your fucking script, Fid, and I'll
sodding well read it!' In hindsight, I appreciate I should not have
interrupted him. If I'd let him run on I'd have twigged what he was after,
several weeks sooner than I did, thereby saving myself from – saving
myself from having to write all this for you, Gabriel, *that's* what I'd have
saved. Shame, guilt, remorse . . . God knows, though, I was vexed! I had
to interrupt – it was much too much by a mile – he not only assumed the
contract signed and sealed, but already he claimed the right to
reconstruct the company to indulge his newfangled fads. First it was
moral-rearmament, now it was arrogant bullyragging.

I was *not* going to quarrel with him, not again. Think what you like,
the man was a hot property. He'd had his low point, but he was back
now in serious business. The NT or the RSC without doubt would take
his play if we were such fools as to reject it out of hand. Despite my
cocksureness with Cordwain, I had in fact nothing certain lined up, no
new script (that is to say) that I could truly stand fast by. And despite
Fid's contempt for the 'mainstream', if the mainstream made him an
offer, he'd accept it like a rabbit taking lettuce.

Nor did I understand why he needed to despise the mainstream. I said
as much.

'Because the mainstream is the cultural arm of the Counter-Insur-
gency Establishment. SAS expertise and high-art cultural excellence,
Great Britain's chief exports to the world. *As* you'd have heard, if you'd
bothered to hear me out at the college. Okay, you think I'm bonkers.
Perhaps I am. Perhaps even outside the mainstream, we're all of us
employed by the spooks. I know absolutely that sometimes we are. I'm
taking a gamble, though, that we can find occasions when we're not.
Why? Because I'm proud of my play: I want it done. Jack, you must
bloody well do it.'

Employed by the spooks? Shoving this unbelievable suppository right up inside me, *he* got up to visit the gents. A parting shot over his shoulder: 'If you're coming to the press conference, wait for me in the foyer, we'll grab a cab.'

I had definitely stated I did *not* want to go with him. But his tale of Blackadder's life was so intriguing, so baroque in its implications, my curiosity overrode my firm intention. Psychological curiosity, sexual curiosity. I was craving that woman just as I did all those years ago. God damn. I walked through the foyer and out into O'Connell Street to breathe some fresh air while Carver and his prunes completed their routine. God damn, he had thoroughly conned me.

10

On the pavement a short stout peremptory man was harassing the hotel porter and a taxi-driver over the loading of his bags for the airport. He had a plum-in-the-mouth English accent, a fastidiously tailored tweed suit, a tight-knotted dark blue tie with an anchor motif, a curiously old-fashioned starched collar and would you credit? an old-fashioned monocle. His face was red, his head red and shiny and bald, and there were white tufts of sidewhisker in front of his ears. I had a feeling he had fabricated himself a fogeyish *persona* largely plagiarised from some historical source; but for the moment I couldn't place it.

He saw me and broke off his altercation with the underlings; he strode between me and the curb; no nonsense, he was all set for a row. 'I know you,' he barked. 'You're Pogmoor!'

'I don't know you,' I began, 'but—'

'Don't you dare to answer me. I tell you you're Pogmoor. You are responsible for that disgraceful bout of nest-fouling I saw at the little theatre last night, an insult to Queen and Country, a besmirchment of the honoured sacrifice of so many of our bravest young men – by God, you pinko shit, you'd better not attempt to put it on in Plymouth!'

Of course I knew now whom he'd taken for a model – the aristocratic captain of a high-Victorian ironclad, and O'Connell Street of all places (where only a few years ago they'd blown up a statue of Nelson) was metamorphosed into his quarter-deck. I really had nothing to say to him; but if he tried to hit me I was ready to hit him back. I clenched my fist to show him. I was a good head-and-a-half the taller, he saw sense, came no closer. But he didn't stop talking.

'Let me assure you I won't let it lie. I read what they said in the *Telegraph*, I deliberately imposed upon myself the sordid task of coming all the way to Dublin to see your infamy with my own eyes, just to be certain the press hadn't got hold of the wrong end of the stick. And they hadn't. Yourself and this Abel-Nottidge should be hounded out of every decent-thinking – decent—' (He was about to say 'club', I suspect, and then decided it might only make me laugh.) 'Hounded!' he roared. 'I shall certainly write to the Society of Authors. I've been a member for thirty-eight years. God knows if they'll stir a finger. Their committee these days is – is—'

I never heard what their committee was, for the taxi-driver (young and insolent) called out to him – 'Hey, head! d'youse mean to miss your fecking plane or don't youse? Sure the next flight's easy with *me*, head, me fecking meter'll tick up all day.' My assailant took the hint, shut his angry mouth, and turned to compress himself athletically into the cab. It pulled out among the traffic.

Carver had arrived and was standing beside me.

'What the devil,' he enquired, 'does that Prosser do here? Is he still writing tripe about the navy? Or did he hope he might find Leonore? I thought I espied his great pate at the play last night, but I thought, "Surely not, not paying his own way into MAFFICK!, not him." What did he say to you?'

I told him; we made haste to get to Buswells, congratulating each other on our disesteem for Maxwell Prosser. There was between us no comment, dark or light, concerning my unheralded change of mind.

11

These press conferences during the Theatre Festival were daily occurrences. Announcements were made by the organisers about forthcoming items on the bill; newly arrived celebrities met the media; directors, writers, actors, whose work had been seen the day before, met the media and complained about (or expressed gratitude for) their reviews in that morning's newspapers; any possible *controversy* was hyped up and publicly relished. A good time was had by all, and all sorts of people dropped in, whether they had anything specific to do there or not. (Prosser should have come, of course, to rant his rage at *Deepwater Dread*. Maybe he didn't know about the Buswells gatherings; or maybe he'd concluded that Dublin was not the wisest locale for a single-handed assertion of Brit jingoism.)

It was a big reception-room with a bar in the corner, a small podium, tables and chairs. When Fid and I entered, a festival spokesperson was reading out the blurb for *Les Femmes Savantes*, the only new show to be under discussion. She pronounced the crop of reviews to be 'mixed', and proved this by quoting a couple: one of them head-over-heels with praise, the other a sneering misogynist diatribe. She explained that *Les Femmes* were off back to Nantes (where they were based) by an afternoon flight, and if anyone wanted to explore their aims and purposes, now was the chance or never.

All five *Femmes* were present, modest enough in what, by the French standards of the profession, would be regarded as casual working clothes – i.e.: left-bank bohemian-chic. They were as sexy and well groomed as Irish secretaries (which is to say a great deal); outshining even the spectacular spokesperson. They laughingly introduced themselves just as they had done in the play – 'Alecto, Tisiphone, Megaera', etc. The two musicians were 'Fortissima' and 'Pianissima', which seemed to be a new joke made up for the occasion, because they giggled so much they could hardly get it out.

Alecto then took the stand, announced that she spoke the best English so she'd been chosen to represent the group; stated that she'd said all she had to say during the Trinity debate, but she'd be happy to repeat it for those who hadn't been there; and equally she would be happy to answer any questions, particularly about the stage-techniques employed by *Les Femmes*, where they found them, why they liked them, what use such devices might be to the theatre and society in general – the usual sort of thing, and she handled it very capably. The media sucked her blood for a whole hour, and a number of fellow artists, Irish and foreign, joined in the interrogation just to make her feel at home. She handled it very capably. Abel-Nottidge and I had gone through a similar ordeal after the first night of his play. She was, I guess, more charming and at the same time even more abrasive than we were; I had to admire her.

Two things of note which emerged from her remarks: the overall style of the *Nameless Comedy* derived from certain kinds of Central American folk-theatre which she herself, together with Megaera and Pianissima, had observed in Nicaragua; and despite their utter commitment to their present project, neither she nor her colleagues had entirely abandoned all idea of returning, now and then, to regular roles in regular theatre or cinema – 'Our play is appreciably altered from each performance to the next, we improvise more than you'd think, why should you assume that our lives are any less flexible? Forby, we have to eat, to eat we need wage-packets, not always, but now and then.'

Forby? How I'd loved it when she talked pawky, like a minister or an advocate out of – out of Stevenson, or was it Barrie? One of the journalists indeed caught at this very word, and asked her had she had contacts with Northern Ireland, or with Scotland?

'I've lived in Scotland, yes. Picked up the phrases. I've lived in so many places. So have we all, all five of us, yes? Nameless Females, placeless, that's our *gimmick*. If we don't have a gimmick, we'll starve, the very principle of showbiz, why not?'

She laughed and the other four laughed. Some of the crowd, feminists, earnest lefties, seemed puzzled – even pained – by this frivolity. *I* thought that for good or ill she'd come a long long way from Fred Owston.

Oh yes, and there was a query about the all-woman basis of the group, a rather greasy query, nudge-and-wink, posed by a Dublin evening rag: must not such male-excluding *Femmes* be perceived as – unstated but insinuated – lesbian activists? Alecto fended it off, seeming to answer with great frankness, giving nothing away. (P. Blackadder at her most characteristic.) Basically she referred the questioner to what she had had to say in Trinity, and left it at that. It left *me* none the wiser as to her current personal life . . .

What did I think of her when I saw her, no longer half-disguised in theatrical gunge, and myself now made aware of the last eighteen years of her history? Not so much 'what did I think?' as what did I see? She was leaner all round, for a start, *gristly*. I'd even say 'taller', if if wasn't impossible. I remembered her face as a round wide-open flower ('daisy-flower', I'd once rhapsodised to that puerile diary of mine); it was now nearly square, tight with muscles where it joined the neck; neck and chin had a Roman rigour. Her lips seemed coarser, thicker on the left than the right as though some goon had put the boot in and permanently misshaped her – Rio? (In fact, yes: Rio.) Blueish lipstick, narrowly drawn, diminished the lopsidedness. Oh, and her hair! at Pomfretshire a glossy cap, precisely trimmed, all a-shine from the brush like a guardsman's boots. Fid told me how when he last saw her she'd been wearing it long and untended, sometimes gathered up in a loose knot or a tail, but in no sense a *coiffure*. Now she had it cropped, not exactly skinhead-short, but surely much shorter than her student style, and rumpled as though she made a point of running her fingers through it instead of a comb. She'd given it a yellowish tint, not applied all over, but leaving streaks of the natural colour to appear; the natural colour was no longer black but grey. In front of her right ear dangled an odd sort of tassel, or lovelock, or Iroquois scalplock, left uncut, left silver-grey, left to swing at her every movement; at its tip a chunk of silver about the size of a 50p coin.

This unusual arrangement had been the main reason for my failure to recognise her; it had the effect of completely changing her from top to toe. Even now, when I'd been told who she was, I had to shut my eyes and shake my head to make myself believe it. Add to which her manner of dress: it used to be striking but not way-out. Admittedly, ideas of what constitutes 'way-out' have changed since the sixties, but even so . . . Now she displayed bare feet and strong bare calves, out of (I don't know how to call them) long shorts, or drawers, or open-kneed loose breeches, bright red velvet with strips of silver buttons down the side-seams; above these, a sort of poncho in red, gold and black, I suppose Nicaraguan, but (as I say) bohemian-chic, she could have had it made for her in Paris.

When the press conference finished its business, and the crowd in the room dispersed into little knots, seeking friends, seeking drinks, I moved cautiously towards her. She saw me coming, said a quick 'excuse me' to whomever was talking to her, and moved sideways away into a corner. An almost imperceptible nod of her head showed me I was expected to follow. She cut us off from the others by slipping in behind a table, but did not sit down. If she didn't like what I said, she had an easy way out behind her, through a door which led to the foyer.

For the life of me, I had no words.

'Ho-ho,' she said, 'Jack Juggler. The dog returns to its – okay.'

This was not encouraging.

'God you're fat,' she said. Great! but I'd already decided (notwithstanding her florid decoration) that *she* at close range looked ten years older than her age. For her eyes were surrounded by deep shadows and lines which her makeup could not hide; there were lines in her brow, sharp furrows from her nostrils to each corner of the mouth.

'Okay,' she said, low-toned, forceful and distressing, 'there's no mileage in scouring out old pisspots. You were a scabby wee polecat, Jack, for all you were two yards high, yet you called yourself an adult man. Some of the adult men I've met since have made me wonder whether there *is* such a thing. Tell you what, for the past year or two, I've sometimes thought of you without a scunner; aye, with equability. Though when I saw you in Trinity, I bloody nearly collapsed. Why? No obvious reason; I was prepared for it; I'd seen your name in the festival listings; I told myself, "Alecto, you've run from so much, you can surely bloody face this one; he was a scabby wee polecat, that's all, and now he's a man of distinction, puffed-out and puffed-up, famous." Like a doctor who once was a medical student. Like my father, wherever he is. Ho.' (Her 'ho' was not quite a laugh, more of a choke.) 'Tell you what, Jack, I didn't collapse. So when I was talking with Fid, and he asked me did I want to meet you, I was able to prevent myself saying no.' (All this time she was looking slightly to one side, over my shoulder, as though apprehensive of someone else coming up and distracting her. Now she snapped her eyelids in a swift blink; open again, and she stared at me direct.) 'How is it you could bear the thought of meeting *me*?'

I said, 'It was unforgivable. I've been tortured ever since. I made excuses at the time: they were no good. So I'm not going to make any now. Nor shall I ask, "Forgive me," because you can't. I just wondered – is it possible – you could shake hands—?'

'*Shake hands?*' I was afraid, for an instant, she was about to spit right in my mouth. But her own mouth gave a twist. She grunted, 'Ho.'

'Shake hands?' she said again; not (as before) a cold and grinding echo, but a straight question; she seemed surprised she had to ask it. 'Oh, that. There were mistakes made, *I* don't know . . . I'm not malicious. Here.' We did shake hands; just. On her part the gesture was so curt a throwaway, it scarcely existed. No: for whatever it meant – and dammit I can't tell you what it meant – it *did* exist, undeniable, as much a piece of history as the – well, as the *event*, the previous most deadly event. It was there, it was on the record, I could feel it across my palm.

Megaera was beckoning to her: time for *Les Femmes* to get themselves together for their journey. They had a gig, we'd been told, tomorrow at Rennes university. Busy people, in demand. She left me without another word, without even looking at me, but the handshake was on my palm, the load (so I believed) off my back, something foul had been brought to an end.

I watched her through the exit-door, as the troupe paused to gather up their bits and pieces in the foyer. She had woolly socks and wellington boots stashed away there under the coat-rack; she put them on over her bare legs. Why not? in the street it had started to rain. But somehow, I did have to laugh. Images, gimmicks, flexibility, P. Blackadder the all-purpose chameleon.

12

So there you are, you see.

She came back into my life; and almost immediately walked out of it.

I did not expect, from the manner and tone of our meeting, that it would breed any noteworthy consequences for either of us. As for my feelings about it – they were all over the shop, a *whirlpool*, but the hatred was gone, the fear, most of the shame – regret, I suppose, was the strongest surviving emotion, angry and idiotic regret.

It was curious that Fid Carver brought me, at the one breakfast-table, unexpected news of both Polly and *The Emperor's Whore*. This play of his was a Tantalus-game, he had for eight years been holding it almost to my lips and then snatching it away. I had often been reminded of the dramatist in Max Beerbohm's tale who boasts to everyone ad nauseam about his forthcoming tragedy of *Savonarola*, until he's universally known as Savonarola Brown; and then he's killed in an accident, the play is discovered and read; and all he's ever written of it through all of this time is a fragment of one disjointed act. 'Napoleon Carver'? but his case was not quite the same, for whereas Brown had written nothing else, Fid had been working consistently, first at this alternative project and then that, postponing St Helena because of them, postponing St Helena because I was not available, postponing St Helena because he and I could not agree, postponing St Helena because he could not agree with himself.

Two days after my return to London, the script came to me through the post. I almost didn't open it, I had built up such a prejudice against it, a presentiment that it would only prove to be a disastrous miscalculation by Fid of the extent of his own powers. I was wrong. It was the best thing he'd ever done, give or take a few awkward bits of structure and half a dozen speeches that didn't seem to come off.

I phoned him at once to say 'Fid, give-or-take, etc., it *is* your best one yet!'

Of course his reply was, 'Of course it is.' (Arrogant bastard.) 'I know that. I told you in Dublin. When do we cast it? Oh, by the way, Leonore says she's free. You'll employ her, of course.'

This was annoyingly premature. *Deepwater Dread* had a lengthy tour in prospect, and for all I knew now I might, by the end of it, be forced to make some changes to the company. And as for Leonore—

More than one problem here. The designer of *Deepwater Dread* had done a good piece of work for me. He had no contract for further work. But then neither had anyone else, at this stage. He was entitled to hope that I would be able to offer him a regular place with us, once the Mega-C. funds were assured. I wanted very much to retain a consistent design-image for MAFFICK! Several months earlier I had invited Leonore to provide it; she refused because of 'pressure of current work', and I had a notion she was now too grand for us. Her studio in Antioch Gardens had become quite a factory, with a shifting entourage of temporary assistants expanding and decreasing all the year round. She often took assignments at theatres and opera-houses abroad – La Scala, for example, to do a highly-talked-about *Turandot*, an 'accolade' (as the press put it) for a London-based artist. She was very much 'Madame Serlio' these days; would she ever be willing to get down into the muck again with me and her brother? And did I really want her? Fid did, that was clear. It was also apparently clear that his persuasion was succeeding; dammit, he'd gone over my head, it was none of his damned business to rope her in without talking to me first, and yet—

Oh, I *did* want her. Her work, when she chose, could be miraculous, which is more than I'd say of our present man's. But, no, I did not want her if she could not commit herself to a full run of MAFFICK! productions. Had her brother thought of that? Again, it all depended on Mega-C.

So you'll understand my state of flux, my general irritation all round. Which I could not fully explain to Fid, lest he find out about Cordwain and fly into a panic at 'commercial corruption'. He'd have to know sooner or later. I needed everything fixed up before that happened.

Deus ex machina! Mega-C. came through with the goodies. MAFFICK! was playing in Cologne; I phoned Leonore and asked her to fly over (if indeed she was still of the same mind); ditto for F. Carver; I prepared a wad of notes on *The Emperor's Whore* and psychcd myself up for a definitive conference on what now had all the features of an ongoing next-presentation. We met and talked, guzzling cream-cakes, in the glazed forecourt of a café overlooking the Rhine: all went well. I even acceded to Carver's queer ideas about women playing men, but on the basis of what was said in Dublin; Stropp for Napoleon, Button for Albine (nothing too weird at the head of the bill). For those roles which would cross over the genders – I had looked at them very carefully – yes, we did need to bring in two additional 'mature' women. With the two young ones and Antonia we'd have a fifty per cent female cast, which is what he said he wanted; let's hope for God's sake it would work!

So far, so good. *Dread* would travel Europe and Britain for two months and then conclude in London for a short run at the Marylebone Showbox, a useful little theatre with the right sort of clientèle. While we were there, we would enter the first stages of the *Whore*'s rehearsals, carry on until the Christmas break, take up where we left off, and open the show in the early New Year. (In the event that *Dread* proved successful at the Showbox, the management of that venue had an option on the first *Whore* performances; thereafter we would be on tour.) Leonore's designs should be ready for our arrival in London, the music should be ready, no problem except *my* problem of letting our designer know we weren't going to use him any more. I can be brutal, and he was quite old enough to take the rough with the smooth . . . For I had in the end secured Leonore for a series of productions subsequent to the *Whore* – only because you, Gabriel, had the devilish ingenuity to devise in my favour the whole complexity of options, let-out clauses, small print, and all of that.

I did have to be a little *devious*, but I hoped neither she nor Fid would rumble it until too late.

I have found that in theatre everything must always be strapped up tight together, accident-proof, fool-proof, smartarse-bloody-proof, if any sort of company integrity is to be achieved.

13

Before I go any further, let me set out the 'argument of the play'.

∾ Napoleon is banished to the British colony-island of St Helena after his defeat at Waterloo. The desire of the restored Bourbon government in France to have his head is refused by the Brits: there is no point in making him a martyr and disaffecting all those French who will otherwise (grudgingly enough, to be sure) accommodate themselves to Louis XVIII. The reactionary Count d'Artois, brother of Louis, later to rule as King Charles X and to be turned off his throne, has been very frightened by the Emperor's earlier return from Elba; he does not trust the British to prevent the same thing happening all over again. He plots the murder of the dangerous exile.

Napoleon is allowed to take a small staff to St Helena. One of them is a General de Montholon, an undistinguished officer who is blackmailed by Artois. He must spike the Emperor's personal consignment of wine with arsenic, in such doses that its result will be a slow sickness of the liver which will eventually kill him.

Montholon brings with him his wife Albine. In order to establish his utter Napoleonic devotion, he plays the complacent husband and allows her to sleep with the Emperor. Although it seems that she never absolutely *knows* of the murder plot, she contrives (in different ways) to deceive both husband and imperial lover. She returns to France, where Artois's secret agents put pressure on her to keep silence about whatever they think she might be thinking. The Emperor dies.

Montholon returns to France. Effectively repudiated by the nervous Artois, he and Albine live on their wits, an ambiguous, insolvent style of life, blackmailing and being blackmailed. In their grey age she wildly involves him with Louis Napoleon (later Napoleon III) in a disastrous neo-Bonapartist coup. He goes to gaol. ♋

So much for Fid's 'fable': part good history, part conjectural fiction. What does he show by it?

♋ He shows, first and foremost, and against most Marxist opinion, Bonaparte as an authentic revolutionary, even after he has been impelled (for that matter, has impelled *himself*: F. Carver isn't stupid!) toward conquest, toward dictatorship. The mole-like Montholon is also a revolutionary, an idealistic but incompetent republican who has hated the imperial pretensions, and regards Waterloo as a tragic but necessary Nemesis. Immense contradiction: Bonaparte has been driven by his revolutionism into Caesarism; Montholon (by the same driving-force) finds himself in alliance with the unspeakable Bourbons, until at length he is the base instrument of Artois. ♋

(Fid said, 'I think Montholon's a sort of Sam Rammit.' Then he said he hadn't said it. Then he said, if he had said it, it was a slip of the tongue and meant nothing. Odd.)

The overall statement of the play.

♋ A passionate cry that European union *must* be made use of to invigorate international class-struggle and revolutionary solidarity for the eventual emancipation of the human spirit; no good at all if it doesn't, because then all we'll reap will be a cannibalistic new species of bureaucratic Bonapartism, or else a reversion to the worst sort of nationalist extremes. Watch out! ♋

14

Even as I first skimmed through it, I felt that this script was a dodgy number. Despite its historical disguise, it was very close indeed to a variety of sensitive knuckles. Watch out!

All the more so because of Fid's care to make it *internationally* practicable. He regarded with deep scepticism what he called the 'cross-border jumbo-jet culture', i.e. touring productions aimed at prestige festivals overseas, with a minimum of verbal argument and a superfluity of non-specific theatrical sound-and-fury, spectacle and symbolism and music and *musique concrète*, 'the director's dream', he'd say, 'the playwright's death'. I believe he thought *I* was a secret inciter of such stuff. At all events he made sure that the *Whore* would avoid the pitfall.

He interspersed the English text with a succession of Brechtian pronouncements, laconic, decisive and yet complex in thought, to be put into the languages of all the audiences we would encounter on our travels. I had to find a way of presenting these which would be good-humoured and not too dogmatic, and would not hold up the story – difficult enough, but with some *juggling* I managed it.

I was slightly concerned by the blunt phraseology of these inserts. Some of them seemed very rude, in a foreign context, given the general right-wing complexion of the epoch. I did not know how Cordwain would take them – let alone the Ministries of Culture, the British Council, and all the other assorted harpies.

Nevertheless, I made no effort to subdue the tone of the script. MAFFICK! had successfully weathered the Abel-Nottidge tempest; we must build upon that boldness, or we would surely fade away. We began rehearsals in high spirits.

About this time I was being pestered by the wretched Prosser. He sent me a play of his own, challenging me in uncompromising tones to produce it. 'You must allow equal stage-space,' he huffed and puffed at me over the phone, 'for the *majority* point of view, otherwise all your claims to democratic humanism will be exposed as a cynical charade!' I read it – conscientiously, every word of the damned thing – and rejected it by return of post. I cannot deny that the man did display a certain ghoulish talent.

꙳ He had managed to fetch together M. Thatcher and Queen Elizabeth I (as it might have been a pair of magnates' escutcheons carried in the wedding-procession of a mediaeval nobody); the living PM, so far as I understood it, being mystically *possessed* by the vital energy of the dead monarch; between them they enacted episodes in bombastic verse illustrative of their respective contributions to the Greatness of the Realm. The loyal population (particularly the seamen) of both historical periods robustly backed them up. The whole thing was a high-pitched miscegenation bred out of Sheridan's *The Critic* by way of Coward's *Cavalcade*, obviously impossible but curiously fascinating in its own perverted way. ꙳

I tried to be polite; I wrote saying, 'Not for MAFFICK!, but I'm sure that *someone* will want to do it. There are great parts for two forceful actresses. Have you tried the Chichester Festival?'

I think he thought I was winding him up.

He kept sending me extraordinary letters. He sent them to Fid as well. He accused both of us of 'corrupting' Leonore, whom he described as the 'true Muse of his inspiration'. Then he started writing to Leonore herself, in a vein of romantic pornography. She answered him, briefly, with a threat to pass on his correspondence to the cops. That silenced him all right; but all three of us became apprehensive. His final letter (to me) contained veiled threats, a suggestion that 'investigations were in progress' as to MAFFICK!'s 'real agenda', and a sinister question: did we know that *he* knew an influential officer of the Ministry of Defence Police? Fid and I were disagreeably reminded of an unexplained happening in Whitesmith Street several years before. (Did I ever tell you about that? A very queer 'security' carry-on.)

On the subject of 'disagreeable', I was happy to find myself developing a most productive artistic relationship with Antonia. What I had taken, when we worked on *Deepwater Dread*, to be a resentful surliness now turned out to have been sheer nervous tension at being directed by Jack Juggler for the first time. (I am, it appears, notorious for coercing and abusing my cast – a malignant libel.) But her extrovert Abel-Nottidge role had excitingly opened her up; she responded to Albine de Montholon with the utmost empathy, exploring the character's *introversion*, delighting in its contradictions. Without doubt, she was 'giving herself' to me, which was important if she were thoroughly to give herself to the part. She soon abandoned a very bad habit I had noticed during the *Dread* rehearsals, that of appealing privately to the playwright whenever she found a difficulty. She now ignored F. Carver and depended more and more upon myself.

I began, without seriously contemplating it, to wonder if she found me physically attractive. I cannot say that initially I fancied *her*, but the more I attended to her drinking-in my exhortations, the less I was aware of her rodent-teeth and pugilistic body-language. I did not, at first, care to imagine her in the nude; and yet I had to, after all, had to *see* her, as it were, creeping into Napoleon's bed; if I could not successfully do that, how could I create the true sense of their love affair? There must be some melting, some *tenderness*, in her somewhere; something other than perdurable bone and leathery sinew underneath that jumpsuit of hers. Carver undoubtedly thought so, or he would hardly have considered her for his Albine. It was up to me to 'call it home' for him . . .

Thus set going by the needs of the job, my reflections, slow but sure, became voluptuous. The last working-day before Christmas I asked her would she care to dine with me. She shied away like a startled goat, and pleaded a prior engagement. Nervous tension, again, no doubt; for I could see that the idea had not disgusted her. When I smiled and said,

'Maybe after the holiday?', she chuckled and seemed to go along with it. Then she told me she wouldn't exactly be having a holiday; the women at Greenham Common had put the word out for more volunteers; next morning she was off down there with her tent and her sleeping-bag to do her bit against nuclear genocide. I wished her luck, and indeed wrote a Christmas card to the Women's Peace Camp expressive of male solidarity, which she boisterously undertook to deliver.

Well. Eh dear. Nay, it was a damned sight worse than 'eh dear', I can tell you. She never came back.

We regathered on January 2nd, with the intent to start blocking the play in a methodical manner – before Christmas we had worked more or less tentatively, improvisations, dances and games to introduce the actors to characters and mood. Over the interval, I had told them, they were to make themselves word-perfect. Antonia, I was sure, would be word-perfect, she was that sort of professional. Yet what could be more *un*professional than the way she withdrew from the company?

Our rehearsal-room was a social club in a back street between King's Cross and Sadler's Wells. We had all been sitting around there for about an hour, drinking tea in cardboard cups from the sandwich-bar over the road, waiting for the Button to turn up, and wondering what could be wrong. (I refused to start without her, not on this first day of intense application.) No one had had any word of her. Her telephone rang unanswered. Perhaps she was in prison? People *did* get arrested at Greenham, whether they sought it or not. There was a knock on the door and a timid entry by the little old lady who acted as caretaker for the building. She had a letter in her hand, she didn't know the name, but the address was *this* address all right, would one of us by any chance be 'Mr Juggler'?

Yes, one of us was, and he recognised the handwriting, *and* the postmark – Newbury. She'd posted it from Greenham. What the hell? Had she decided to 'give herself' altogether to the peace movement? Not quite.

I handed you a copy of this semi-literate epistle, Gabriel, before I wrote you that earlier statement; it was in fact the beginning of it all, but how was I to know it would lead so inexorably to J. Lobscott and the Vermeer and the ashtray and the Holloway cell? In case you mislaid it in one of your files, here it is again:

> PRIVATE AND CONFIDENTIAL!
> I am sorry to let down the company in this way, and particularly to let down Fid Carver, but I am unable to continue to play Albine or any other part in your hypocritical 'non-sexist'

production. I now know what you did in Pomfretshire University in your last postgraduate year, and I know why they call you what they call you. This knowledge concurs with a number of other things I have heard of you, or have come to see in you. I now understand the inner meaning of your manipulations of me *in re* what you pretended was a 'proper comprehension as between director and performer', inasmuch as you asked me to have dinner with you adding (without my knowledge *then*, but be sure I know it now!) the threat of injury to previous insult. You dripping dick, you bedroom butcher-boy, do you think I'm just meat for your grill? I've written my agent to get release from contract, etc., and I don't care how much money I lose by it. It's simply not good enough and blatant exploitation.

Yrs etc.,
Ant. Button

I read this twice, not looking up from the page, hands shaking, eyes swimming.

My worst fear about *The Emperor's Whore* had suddenly been realised, the secret heart of Albine's mendacity was bursting out alive to denounce me, I was Montholon unveiled. (This was why, this was why I had tried *not* to have to work on this story, Carver could never guess what I was on about, but Potiphar's wife! *she* was aware of it, so was – oh yes indeed, so was Vittoria Corombona, which was why I refused *The White Devil*—

No no no – I'm crossing out that last paragraph, this is supposed to be a legal deposition. Let's have some order here, objectivity.

The extraordinary thing was, I *did* think, after meeting P. Blackadder in Dublin, that all that *whirlpool* was once-and-for-all long gone, behind me, disappeared and swirled away for ever.

What had Blackadder been saying to Button? And where? It can't have been in Dublin, or I'd have heard about it earlier. Could *Les* bloody *Femmes* have actually spent Christmas at Greenham?

I shoved the letter deep into my pocket and announced calmly to the room at large: 'Antonia has some sort of personal problem. She doesn't tell me what, but she's having to opt out. Fid, let's have a talk. Everyone else, break until – until tomorrow at ten. God, it's as well that *Dread*'s done with its run at the Showbox! – we'd be right up into t'creek if we'd come back there after Christmas – think of it, *Belgrano* without Maggie Thatcher.'

There was a big sheet of white lining-paper across one end of the club-room, cutout letters, painted bells and bunches of holly, the relic of a recent beanfeast. As my actors shuffled off to pursue their own devices, it mocked me with its cheery message:

HAPPY XMAS GREETINGS &
NEW YEAR 1984
to all our Phelps Street and St Genesius Estate
PENSIONERS!
Noel Noel!!

Nineteen eighty-four indeed. No, Madame Prime Minister, you said the wrong thing about George Orwell in your attempt to lend humanity to your kleptocratic rule: he had *not* 'got it wrong'! Only it wasn't Big Brother who was watching me today, all eyeballs of ice and baleful ideology, but Big Sister and as *nameless* as they come.

Fid Carver drifted around me, he wouldn't sit down, he nagged querulously with silly little pinprick questions: what was wrong with Antonia? how long would she be *hors de combat*? why would I not show him the letter? it was important that he knew – oh, *of course* it was important! but what in the name of God could I tell him?

'Fid, I said it was a *personal* problem, it smells to me like man-trouble of some sort. But she writes as between actress and director, she wouldn't thank me for showing it to you.' I did show him the superscription – PRIVATE AND CONFIDENTIAL! – and he had to be satisfied, but I could see he resented it. 'Right,' I added, 'nuff said. All we've to do now is to think of a replacement. Antonia's word is final, I can assure you of that. So where do we go?'

15

I did not expect him to reply, 'Polly Blackadder,' but that *is* what he said and I tried to make sense of it without giving too much away. He seemed very certain, as though he'd turned it over in his mind for some time.

Now if, as I feared, Blackadder was the one responsible for defaming me to Ms Button, either she would refuse to join the company, or she had poisoned Button's mind with the incredibly Machiavellian motive of displacing her by stealth. If the former, there was no more need for discussion; but if the latter, then we were up against an adventuress so immoral that – that maybe she and I could come to workable terms! A challenging exigency! Almost exciting. But fundamentally daft. And in any case there were practical difficulties.

'Yeah, but she hasn't got a work-permit. Doesn't she carry a Swedish passport?'

'French, in point of fact. That film-director shit of hers leaned on a couple of bent politicians, ex-Vichyites, to secure her French residence, all the paperwork, police, immigration, etc. Now he *could* foul her up by repudiating her to the authorities; but she doesn't think he will – that's to say, provided she promises not to threaten him over custody of the daughter. He does love her, you understand. And he has some cranky notion about her being under his trust as a task from Almighty God imposed upon him for his sins, he quoted a "meditation" to her – from Thomas Aquinas or one of that lot – about Lazarus and the Magdalene. She guesses he might even help her to stay and work in Britain, it would distance her far enough from his yearning prick and from the child, soothe his guilt-traumas as well.'

'Fid, it sounds fishy. But even if it's as you say – hey, wait a moment, what's all this about 'she guesses'? Dammit, you've been *talking* to her! All that stuff about MAFFICK! needing additional mature women – you were scheming to fetch her in. Weren't you, weren't you? Come clean!'

'Oh, I admit I had hoped, but I couldn't push it. Not at that stage. And if Antonia had stayed with us, I couldn't have pushed it at all. More a long-term speculation. But now it becomes urgent. Do we ask her or don't we?'

He argued at length her unparalleled suitability for the part. I argued against him, but with less and less fervour as the morning wore on. The fact was, I could think of no immediate actress of the right type of talent who could step into the company at such short notice; and I doubted if the agencies would find me one.

'But how soon could we get her here? Isn't she wrapped up with her *Femmes Savantes*?'

'They were to break up for a space at Christmas-time, Megaera has a film-part and Fortissima's doing some work with a small-town theatre in Le Creusot. Polly's free. I know her address, and an agent's in Paris. Why not have your business-manager set the cogs of bureaucracy turning? This afternoon, why not? And make sure that Equity doesn't step in and create difficulties.'

I was wondering about Equity. I could not tell Carver, but it might be much worse than the perennial problem of hiring a foreigner. If Antonia Button was spreading the bad word there about me, MAFFICK! could very well be blacklisted. But in the upshot there was no trouble. I suppose she felt unable to *substantiate* anything against me; and when so many in the theatre were desperate for work, the actors' union would not move upon a question of mere gossip. Nonetheless, where *had* the gossip come from?

Okay, let's get Polly over to us, and then I might find out more. So I agreed, with severe qualms; the telegrams were sent; favourable answers were received; I nervously awaited the outcome.

16

Two days later, Polly turned up at the social club straight from Heathrow; very dashing in fur-lined calf-length boots, black-and-white striped tights of thick wool (on one leg horizontal stripes, vertical on the other), a hairy jerkin of blue and grey plaid, and an embroidered blue skullcap. She carried a great kitbag over her shoulder, all her luggage for the entire visit, it seemed; altogether she looked like business, hard, cold and brusque, shrugging off my cordial welcome with something much in the nature of a sneer, but grabbing the script and diving straight into it, no nonsense, she had a job to do.

And by God, as the days went on, she did it very well. She *moved herself* across the body and soul of Carver's Albine like parallel images coming together in a stereoscope. (It gave me the horrors, but I never let on.)

Clearly she was doing it for Carver: I had the impression she believed she owed him something, though he would not tell me what. I dared not ask *her*. I dared hardly speak to her. None of the 'spiritual fucking' that had gone on so disastrously between myself and Antonia; but direct and to the point; either she understood Albine or she didn't; when she understood, she got it dead right; when she didn't, she asked me curt questions, accepted my answers, submitted herself to my arbitrary instruction without any carping, learned her lines within a week. I have often been teased for my 'metronome techniques': this woman *was* a metronome and upstaged me day in day out.

One evening, after we finished work, I hung back to give some extra notes to Ben Stropp. When I'd finished I decided on a drink with Carver and went to meet him, as I often did, at the Bull and Mouth in Percy Street, a small quiet pub at that hour, which our actors as a rule did not frequent. I wanted to discuss them with him; and was therefore put out to find him heads-together with Polly and Mandy Cakebread.

'Jack!' shouted Mandy, 'the very man. Come over and tell us what you think. It's a question of Polly's name, to put into the programme. I said she should be "Polly Blackadder", same as she always was in Britain, she'll not be forgotten, it's not *so* long since she last worked here, we ought to capitalise on her old reputation.' It was obvious that Mandy was not apprised of certain aspects of Polly's past; and Fid looked as though he wished that the matter had not come up at all. Polly stared at the ceiling with a noncommittal expression, but (I noticed) biting her lower lip with one tooth.

'She calls herself Alecto,' said Carver. 'She's hired under that name as a founder-member of *Les Femmes Savantes*, they'll be credited as a group on our hand-outs, I think she should remain "Alecto". What's wrong with it?'

I glanced at Polly, received no answering glance, offered as my opinion that it was absolutely up to her, so what was *her* opinion?

'"Alecto",' she pronounced slowly, '"Alecto" will sound as though I am a downmarket foreign starlet of astonishing pretension. Unfavourable reviewers will make mock, you are offering them a hostage. "Polly Blackadder" won't do at all. Apart from – from all else – there'll be idiotic talk of a "comeback" and questions asked that I don't want put. "Gudrun Bernadotte"? It's the name on my work-permit; but do any of you wish MAFFICK! to be associated with *that man's* movies? Ho.' She took a deep swallow of her whisky. 'No,' she added, 'none of those. Call me Alice Bluefields. It's nae sort of a name, nae sort of a name at a', but Bluefields is in Nicaragua – it'll no' seem over-exotic – and Alice – aye, Alice. Fid, ye ken weel why Alice. Also Jack, I daresay. Belike it's a species of exorcism. That's it.'

I hoped Carver would not start talking about Alice Trip-and-Go. He had the tact to keep his mouth shut; of course it was all double-Dutch to Mandy, who began to try to remonstrate; but in the face of Polly's firmness, the words died in her mouth. She wrote it, 'Alice Bluefields', and went off to our 'office' (i.e.: her Habitat-bright terrace-house in Battersea) to type up her hand-outs.

Polly said: 'A hundred-to-one no one who comes to see the play'll have the least idea in heaven who I've been. If I'm good, we can make up a story; if I'm bad they won't want to know. Which I'd say was the safest all round. Fid, be a decent wee gentleman and bugger off. I think I'd better have a word with Mr Pogmoor. Don't worry, I'm not about to flit.'

This was ominous and I could see that Fid thought so. He looked dubiously from one of us to the other, finished his drink with an embarrassed gulp, and got up from the table. 'Be careful,' he muttered, perhaps to me, perhaps to her, perhaps as a general warning. 'Remember what I said,' he said, specifically to her. 'We've done very well up to now, we don't want to get – entangled. Antonia was bad enough.'

I started to ask him what the devil he thought he meant, but he was away without hearing me out. So there I was, left with Polly, and no clue whatever to her mood, except that it was dangerously volatile. I had not liked that crack about 'Alice'.

'Sit,' she snapped. 'Don't think of evasion. I've worked with you a fortnight and nothing's been said. But it has to be, hasn't it? Tonight's the night, so gird yourself. Whisky, please.'

I got up again like a bloody lackey. I fetched whisky.

'Antonia's "man-trouble". You see, Jack, Fid has intimated he's had his suspicions. *Juggler-trouble*, was his notion. Well? Ach, he'd never have told me if I hadn't pressed him: I wanted to know, d'you see. A snuff of a mystery at the root of my nostrils, Jack, it had to be cleared. So last night I rang her up.'

'Polly, for fuck's sake—'

'Cut that out! Or else *mean* it, in the dictionary sense. As far as I understand her, you didn't, not with her. But as far as I understand her, you would have, if you could.'

'And what would have been so wrong? As far as *I* understood her, she was keen enough in the first place. Somebody scared her. Put your cards on the table. Was it you?'

'It was not. Believe it, Jack, my secret remains *my* secret and always has. Now she did tell me who she talked to, and there's nothing I can do about it—'

'Eh but there's the devil of a lot *I* can do and dammit I intend. Gimme the name.'

'Oh no. I swore otherwise. If you have to thole your uncertainty, year after year, that's *your* problem, live with it. Or d'you maintain you don't deserve it?' God, she was adamant. Sadistic, into the bargain: there was a flickering gleam of pleasure in her eyes and her lips twitched. She was laughing at me.

At a blundering venture I threw out – 'Carmilla Costello?' At which, d'you know? she blinked and said nothing. And nothing was no denial, was it? But – 'Carmilla's not in England. Or *is* she?' I asked. To ask was to admit weakness, but how could I not?

'Is she, Jack? I haven't met her. To tell truth, I wouldn't want to meet her. But supposing she *were* in England, by my advice you'd leave her be. Okay, she might do you some damage. Be damned sure she'd do far more if she thought you were after her.'

Good advice? Possibly. (As you know, Gabriel, I was to reject it, but not until things got much worse.) At any rate it confirmed me in my very random guess. Carmilla had met Antonia. At Greenham? Only too likely. But what was the point? What the hell was the point? I gnashed my teeth and scowled: 'I thought,' and by God I was angry, 'I thought you had come here to work, to work with *me*, Blackadder, right? On a play, Blackadder, right? In a part that suits your genius. Albine de Montholon, the lady of secrets and slyness. Ah well, I daresay, you do need to get under her skin. I daresay that a good flaying-off of *my* skin'll help you do it. Carry on then, tear my scrotum out.'

At which she laughed full-throated. Alecto's laugh, horrible. Then she suddenly put her right hand over my left, as it lay trembling on the table-top. 'You still fancy me, don't you?'

I do not know what came over me. Because I was shaking with rage and yet all I could say was – 'Fancy? I have *loved* you, loved you fucking-crazy all these years.'

'Go on then, say the rest of it – "you dirty conniving bitch", "you evil wee black-eyed liar", "you *vagina dentata*", ye ken the Latin? It's all true, so why keep whisht? Say it.'

It was all true, and I nearly had said it, but I bit the words back at the last minute. How could she know them so exactly?

'Fair enough,' says she, after waiting five seconds for the answer I did not give. As she said it, she took her hand away from mine. 'So we know where we stand. I wasn't quite certain in Dublin. I do think it quite possible that as a student I was a prick-teaser. Well, I'm not any more.' (Oh, wasn't she? My prick told a different tale.) 'No chance of a repetition, Jack. Or if things should slip, and something should happen, dear God, let me tell you, you'll regret it. Understand me: *I am punishing you*. And yet at the same time, I am doing you a service. *My* part in *this* play will make *your* career.' (No acknowledgement, none, that already I was near as famous as Peter Brook.) 'It may be I've sometimes thought that you and I together could have – should have – but what you did was the death of that hope. What you still do – I mean, Button – is clay on the ridge of its grave. Don't think it isn't hard for me. But these days I am so hard, you could sharpen a knife in my cunt.'

This was the queerest conversation I'd ever had with any woman, not excluding Leonore. I don't count Carmilla, my exchanges with her were in no sense conversations, *car crashes* perhaps, at full throttle . . . But here we both sat, with our voices well under control, and her words conveyed nothing but immeasurable contradiction. Have you ever found the wind blowing strongly out of the north on a day of broken sunshine and clouds – and when you looked upwards, why, the clouds were all scudding from the west?

'In Nicaragua,' says she, 'the Contras put a bullet in me. See.' She pulled up the sleeve of the loose-enveloping white sweater she wore under her jerkin, to reveal a pleated great scar in the thick of her arm from elbow almost to shoulder. 'But that was the risk of my working-arrangement there. I'd to accept it or take flight.'

I shook my head, bewildered; what had Nicaragua to do with—?

'H'mph,' says she, considering, Edinburgh-fashion, 'he seems even now not quite to understand. Let me set it in more precise words. You and I work, and this is our working-arrangement: I, as it were, am tearing your scrotum out, because I need its bloody blood for my heart. And I needed to know I could get it. Now I know. See you tomorrow, Jack, ten o'clock.'

She walked easily out of the pub, Alice Trip-and-Go Bluefields, swinging her silver-tipped love-lock, swinging her insolent haunches (black-and-white as any zebra), as though we'd just made a date for a disco. The few regulars in the bar may have thought we'd done exactly that, grey hairs on our heads and all. Ha! if I'd had a sword I'd have cut her into collops. And yet I wouldn't. As a 'working-arrangement', what she'd said was no worse than many such. I've always maintained, no true theatre without *risk*. Indeed she was well able for Albine; and through Albine, at this strange juncture, let's face it, I was earning my living.

17

Does it occur to you, Gabriel, she was going round the bend, this actress? And I ought to have detected it? (Just as I should have recognised her in Trinity College, right?) Okay, I'm egocentric; when involved in a production, that's what I'm involved in, half-blind, and I admit it. For bizarre as her whole attitude was, it really did not strike me that way; it had this dreadful rationality, and I saw no further than that. 'D'you maintain you don't deserve it?' – those few words of hers went echoing through my brain; I could not deny them; if she had decided to disorientate me, it was no more than I might expect, and would not necessarily imply that *she* was disorientated too.

And then, besides, had she not given me reason to think she was sexually drawn to me, always had been, still was? That small action, small but incongruous, of placing her hand over mine on the table, what was it but a deliberate *rhyme* (no, not quite; shall I say 'half-rhyme'?) to the touching of all our four hands that time years ago in the Pomfretshire postgrad study-room? I remembered; she remembered; nothing unconscious about it at all. Now how can I say that a woman who desires me, however inconveniently for her peace of mind, however ill-assorted with her experience, is for that cause alone to be deemed deranged?

And of course she would not strive, given her experience, given the present circumstances, to fulfil her desire in any conventional way. It would be bound to come out all crooked.

So, I repeat, what she said to me was most certainly weird, but not inexplicable, and above all she *did* emphasise how important was *The Emperor's Whore* both to me and to herself – in short, her approach was essentially professional, and why else had I hired her?

In view of what was to happen, this is the best point in my narrative at which to clear myself of utter insensitivity. So I make my excuses here and now and I leave it at that. Across our whiskies in the Bull and Mouth I really was persuaded she knew what she was about. Maybe, in the Bull and Mouth, I was right and she still did? Hindsight, it's not much help.

18

An apparent digression – or rather, since all this about Carver's play may seem to you (unjustly) a digression in itself – a return to the main theme:

The regular first night of the *Whore* was scheduled at the Marylebone Showbox for the third week of February, following four public previews not open to the press. I think it was January 28th when Jenny deVries threw her agency party; she had one every year for her writers and their friends; why January, I don't know, it was a Siberian night, blizzards of snow and all the cab-drivers making the worst of it. Fid was invited, of course, and brought me as his current director. We were pleased with ourselves: the production was going damned well. Polly had stopped her nonsense where it started and did everything required of her and much more. No suggestion, during rehearsals, of punishment for me; whatever had been said between us, she seemed to have forgotten. I cannot say *I'd* forgotten; I felt, every day, these tides of unassuageable longing . . . Every day, I was King Canute, totally ineffectual against them.

In the middle of the party, when I was already half-seas over (the next day was a Sunday, and I needed to relax), I barged into a man I knew but did not at first recognise. I hadn't seen him for many years; he'd cut his hair and grown a moustache. The playwright Alex McCoy, Irish-Scots, from Glasgow. We had had a falling-out in the old MOUTH-71 days, over *The Woyzeck Variations*, he and Saltmarsh at daggers drawn and both of 'em blamed me. Since then, as I understood, he'd been living abroad, writing novels and poetry. So he'd come back to London, had he? He wasn't one of Jenny's people; but the woman he lived with was; she'd winched him along to the party. All this he told me in a sort of over-friendly drunken bubble. I didn't like him at all after our row, and therefore I didn't pay much attention.

Until he lurched against the mantelpiece and all of a sudden became personal. He normally spoke the Queen's English, but excess of claret-cup made him screech in 'Hieland' gibberish like a Jacobite cateran. Because of Polly, this assertive *Scotchness* rubbed me thoroughly the wrong way. 'So phat then will Mr Pockmoor be toing for his diversions, in his intervals of crêpe-paper, and his metronome whateffer? For certain such a shentlemans, such a braw pretty Saxon shentlemans will neffer lack for lassies' cunny-holes? Or should I say '*Putton*-holes'? De'il grapple ye, ye dirty fucker, Antonia's a friend of my friend!'

In retrospect, I think he was trying to be funny.

I'd had no time to react, either verbally or physically, though dammit I was on the point of tossing him into the fire, when his 'friend' caught the spray of his vitriol and came quickly to edge him away. She was a tall dark neurotic bitch who'd been writing (according to McCoy) little monologues for a women's company somewhere; and she fixed me with a sinister regard. Very much as I remember all those prudes in my last term at Pomfretshire. She didn't speak to me; I've half an idea that she spat; I was a little too drunk to be fully aware of it. But not too drunk to hear *him* continuing to eructate – 'Sshekshual harrasshment by a sshekshual-harrasshmenteer,' he spluttered, 'sneck-draw juggling har-rasshmenteer, hoot! I should kick him betwiksht his hurdies till his arsse-pipe comes oot at his mou'—'

Other people had heard him. I was fortunately near the door; I evicted myself from Jenny's flat without having to say anything to anyone; I half-walked half-ran all the way to Whitesmith Street, never mind the slippery pavements, never mind the wild flurries of snow. If McCoy knew, how many more? God damn, were this to grow, I'd be in serious trouble.

But Fid, on the Monday morning, did not appear to have noticed; and he'd always been quite pally with McCoy. So perhaps the latter's lady had taken her man home in disgrace before he was fully able to amplify Antonia's scandal. The cork was in the bottle for a little while longer – so I hoped. I had to hope.

19

Two or three evenings short of our first preview, I was at home checking through my production-notes, and worrying at a number of things that might go wrong with the lighting-plot and the music, neither of which were finalised. I had been lonely every evening for some time; no good to tell myself I had to concentrate on the work; I needed human contact, sexual contact (for that matter), if only to take my mind off P. Blackadder; yet I knew I couldn't have it. No distractions, Pogmoor, not now! The phone rang.

I answered with a leap of relief – anybody to talk to, anybody! – but knowing all the time it was probably bad news – vexatious news at best – it was bound to be, always, at this stage of a production. Leonore's voice, and not at all a happy voice. (Despite the considerable interval since she had last worked with me, we had so far had no differences; but she *was* becoming rather awkward to deal with, offhand and over-precise, two difficult qualities when running side by side.)

'Jack, you'd better come over. Now, tonight, get a minicab if that car of yours is still in for repairs. Fid's here. You'll have to deal with him. It's the proofs from the printer for the posters and programme-cover. Your fault, not mine.' (She'd designed both of them, of course, and ought to have been capable of handling mistakes.) 'I said, *your* fault. Come. Now.' She rang off.

I was in Kentish Town in half an hour, muttering curses all the way to the annoyance of the driver who wanted to chat about Maggie Thatcher and all the good things she was doing keeping the blacks out of the country. I gathered they were conspiring to take over the entire minicab business from one end of London to the other. I told him, as I paid him (no tip), that he ought to go to Jamaica and start up a cab service there, then he'd really hit 'em where it hurt; but he didn't seem to see it. He was still sitting swearing at me when Leonore let me in. Her manner was hurried and furtive, and thoroughly disturbing.

'My studio upstairs,' she whispered. 'You've been at your tricks, Jack. (What'd you do to set off that cabbie bawling out of the door of his car?) Can nobody, but nobody, trust you for a moment? And be careful with Fid, I beg you; Christ, he's in a terrible state.'

Now, I had seen Carver before when he chose to be displeased with me, as, for instance, over *Poison-Voices*. He would stutter into his beard and then shout in unconvincing crescendos, followed always by absurd diminuendos, and he'd spring about like a tiresome firecracker from one corner of the room to the next. But this time it was quite different. He sat in a revolving chair at Leonore's work-table, his back turned towards me, his head bowed, and not a spark of recognition that I'd so much as come in through the door. I walked round the table to meet him face-to-face; he swung his chair away from me, so all I could see was his back again. On the table was the poster, looking singularly effective. A collage: the cocked-hatted silhouette of Napoleon, on a promontory of the island, staring out to sea where a great blurred classical shape of a wide-eyed woman (based on a mezzotint of the historical Albine) seemed to lift from the waves like the moonrise. The programme-cover, held by Carver against his knee, was a smaller version of the same design. We had, he and I, approved both of them weeks ago, when Leonore showed us her sketches.

What on earth had gone wrong?

I leaned over him from behind and took the programme quietly from the feeble clutch of his fingers. 'What's wrong with it? Well? Fid, I'm bloody talking to you. Will you tell me what is wrong with it?'

'Look at it,' he said. At least, I thought that was what he said, his voice was so muffled and indistinct. I did look. Nothing at all untoward. Until I shifted my thumb and saw what it inadvertently hid. At the top right-hand corner, where the indigo blue of the sky darkened to the deepest black, there was a scribble of angry red ballpoint, an attempt to blot out—

Ah! to blot out (and of course I should have known it!) the white-and-silver logo of Mega-C.

'Oh aye,' I said cheerily and none too truthfully, 'I thought that might be it. But it's nowt to mek a song about. It fits very fairly into Leonore's colour-scheme, and its not half the size of MAFFICK! at the bottom. Nay, it's not half the size of the name of Fid Carver, let alone the play's title. Come on, man, for God's sake, buck yersen up.'

He whirled round in the chair at me, pale as the woman-shape herself, and showing all his teeth like an old sheepdog.

'Keep your stupid Yorkshire for those fools that are still conned by it,' he groaned, 'because I'm no longer one of 'em and you've tried it one time too often. Not a word to me, ever, about Cordwain and their sponsorship. You've got more money from them than from any single source, don't think I can't see it – why, you've gone and hung their monogram right over the top of Boney's hat. For a wonder you didn't put it between the two ears of the woman, as so much more meaningful than the equivocal silly simper of a dead-and-gone French tart – haven't you missed an opportunity there? Oh lord, man, lord above us, I detect you bought and sold. And not one word to me, not one.' (All this in a dreary kind of sob.) 'Bought and sold? It's worse than that. *I'm* the commodity to be reckoned in the bastards' till, I am, I am, I.'

The truth was, I had allowed the whole Cordwain issue, and its possible ramifications upon Carver, to slip from my memory. I should have broken it to him gradually, from the first week of rehearsals onward; or better, Leonore should have. But she did not know that her brother did not know, and in any case she had no ideological objections to these sponsorship deals. They irritated her, to be sure, but she accepted them as a fact of life in our inescapable new Toryworld.

It took us until two in the morning to reconcile the miserable Fid to the liberality of Mega-C. Indeed, he was even then not reconciled within the meaning of the act; he simply took the status quo as (for the time being) immutable; and he sat there like a grey-faced waxwork with his eyes lowered, his hands clasped, his whole body a crumple of chagrin (and of total alienation from Pogmoor, his old friend, eh dear).

I had to do the greater part of the talking. Leonore said very little, except to tell him now and then some absurdity from the Bible about Jesus and the tribute-money, how Caesar might have Caesar's pence quite innocently rendered up to him by those who were lucky enough to hold it in their pockets, how a coin found in the mouth of a dead fish was a fair example of finders-keepers on behalf of that same Caesar – or was it the church establishment? she seemed to think there was little to choose between 'em. For she was not religious, and neither was he: I took it they both used the legends of religion to supplement their private decisions. She hadn't talked like that when she was Mrs Jack Juggler. Or maybe she had, over the phone, through the post, to *him*; her intimacies with *him* had always been out of my ken. In the course of our argument she moved him, as a nurse might move a paralytic, from the revolving chair to a sofa, where she sat down beside him and clasped his clasped hands in hers. A pair of ancient pensioners communing their married love on a park bench in spring: an embarrassing exhibition.

Toward me, she offered no comfort. Her support for my persuasions was very much *faute de mieux*, and conveyed to her brother without reference to what I was urging, without even a glance at my face. 'Married love'? I had long had an idea that that might be just what it was. And then, there'd been certain words I thought I'd heard screamed at me when I walked in all unexpected to an outrageous brand of photo-session. (The latter's result, floor-to-ceiling, was imposing its lewd message even as I strode about there with my improvised eulogies of Cordwain. I had always pretended not to see that orgulous blow-up; whenever I did see it, it hurt like hell.) Well, so I'd been wed to an

incestuous sapphist. Happily I'd packed it in before it buckled me
beyond repair. And who cared? it was years ago; weren't the three of us
sufficiently driven by the art which possessed us not to worry about it
too much? philosophical oblivion, and get on with the next job.

The next job, on this occasion, was to make sure that the playwright
would continue to contribute to the progress of his play. (Did I mention
that MAFFICK! was actually *paying* the soppy sod to sit in on rehearsals
and make adjustments to the script? Unprecedented privilege: and he'd
worn me to a shadow haggling to obtain it, like a Berber in the souks of
Marrakesh.) At last I made him tell me that he'd be at the Showbox for
the dress-parade at ten the next morning. Leonore said, 'I'll bring him.
My stationwagon. I'll put him in with all the costumes. I'll wipe his eyes,
wipe his bottom, bring him in. Won't I, Jacob?' ('Jacob?' Something
biblical again, and again quite out of my ken.) 'Jack, you're a puddle of
weedkiller. Go home.' I let myself out immediately without delaying to
call up a cab. I knew of an all-night bus which would fetch me down to
Chelsea. I had to wait for it in frozen pavement-slush for forty minutes
or more.

Throughout the dress-rehearsals and the technical rehearsals I am
sorry to say that Carver behaved very ill. Moody, negative, often
downright obstructive, he earned his playwright's pittance as sourly as
he could. I assumed, to begin with, that it was the sponsorship business
that rankled. True enough; but only in part. It was slowly borne in on
me that he distasted the play as a whole, now that he saw it at full length
with all its accoutrements in place. I guess he had a problem determin-
ing whether what was wrong could be laid to my charge, or to the
actors', or had *he* himself allowed himself to construct his story out-of-
kilter? Because he could not be sure, he decided he should not speak. All
that was left to him was to sulk, so he sulked and we suffered.

At the first of the previews all was in tolerably good shape – to my
eyes, if not to his. Some performances needed briskening, there were a
few stage-management gremlins, but nothing extraordinary. Let Carver
pout and mutter if he wished, I was pleased and I told him so, sharply. I
saw Cordwain in the audience, and made a point at the end of getting in
his way in the foyer. I had a swift ugly notion that he was on a beeline for
the street, which was well out of order – he knew he was chief
paymaster, he'd a solid responsibility, I needed his comments.

'Jack!' he breathed, double-handshake and all the old warmth, for
ten seconds and no longer. 'Wonderful production. Alice Bluefields,
wonderful woman. Who is she? Pity about the script. Some of it. You'll
be hearing. Got a meeting. Bye-bye.'

If he'd head-butted me I couldn't have been more shocked. At least I was the only person connected with the show to be in earshot of the man when he said it. I didn't have to pass it on. *But what had he meant?*

Was it possible he had seen whatever Carver had seen? Could both of them be right and Pogmoor wrong? No fooling, this must be settled. Tomorrow, first thing. I went straight home, saying nothing to the cast beyond, 'Well done, notes at ten, loads of 'em,' and brooded alone until bedtime. I couldn't sleep. I rang Carver, several times. His phone was engaged, or off the hook. I rang Leonore, to find was he in her flat. Her phone rang and rang but no one answered it. The last time I rang either of them was long after midnight, and still no response. I couldn't sleep. On an impulse, I rang Cordwain, a daft thing to do – you don't call up young plutocrats in their swinging free time, you don't know what disportings you'd interrupt. But it was worth it: he was there, and by the sound of him not at all put out.

'I thought you'd be on the wire, Jack. I didn't talk earlier, too soon after the curtain. But we must talk. Tomorrow. Come round here at five o'clock. It won't take long.' 'Here' was his London pad, a revamped mini-mansion in a Nash terrace beside Regent's Park and conveniently near to the theatre.

Then I did sleep, for maybe two hours. This time *my* phone rang, and it was Carver. 'We've to talk,' he said. 'It's all gone wrong. Before we meet the company. D'you know a little sandwich-bar with an Italian name, bang up against Baker Street tube? Giovanni's? No. Giuseppe's? No. Giacob—, Giacob— . . .'

'Giacomo's,' I snapped. 'I know it. Of course I know it. You and I had a cuppa there last week.'

'Did we?' He was helpless. 'I forget. Forget my head if it was loose. They're open early, they serve hot breakfasts. Eight o'clock. See you.'

(It crossed my mind that Giacomo sounded as though it ought to be the Italian for Jack, and that he seemed to have a hesitancy about hitting it, seemed fixed on Jacob. Stupid prat.)

He was there dead on his hour; so was I. I'll not go into the ins and outs of what he said to me about the *Whore*. Broadly, he felt that despite his viewing Bonaparte's historical role through the situation of Albine, its 'essential complexities had nonetheless become obscured, indeed *merged,* under the enveloping glamour of the factitious Imperial Myth'. The play's revolutionary content was insidiously downgraded. This was far from his intention: through a series of short scenes he had attempted to set off one Napoleon-*persona* against another, none of the *personae* definitive, none of them entirely fallacious. The order of these episodes, he was now positive, had been misconceived from the start. To set about and redistribute them would involve rewriting the links between them – a structure of dialectical demonstration rather than simple story-telling – the mind boggled.

'Good God!' I had to exclaim. 'How long will this take you?'

'Oh, the writing's no problem, it's all in my head, I can do it by tomorrow if I start it at once. I don't need to hear your notes, they'll all be redundant anyway. The question is, Pogmoor, how long will it take to re-rehearse the cast?'

I told him that at least we would need to postpone the first night. Immeasurable difficulties but not insurmountable. I told him I was sick of him. How dared he not tell me his anxieties sooner than this!

'Because I didn't know I had them. And then, when I did know, I was so sick of *you*, over Cordwain and his thirty bloody pieces of silver, let me tell you, that I could barely distinguish a political paradox from a sleazy theatrical trick. Last night I worked it out. Last night it was so hard for me to sleep I tried to concentrate instead. Polly came to see me. Deeply troubled with the shape of the play and her part in the play. She said bluntly, as it stood, it made very little sense to her, not *Carver's* sense, she said; the more she worked in it, the more flawed it appeared. She stayed with me all night. She helped.'

'She stayed? She helped? She slept with you?' My entire world, barren and all as it was, had now become a desert of salt – ashes and salt and brimstone – the Cities of the Dead Sea Plain. It had been obvious, ever since Dublin, that Carver was (one way or another) in love with P. Blackadder. But his sex-life was impenetrable, so hugger-mugger indeed that I never seriously considered his actually accomplishing it, not when 'it' signified an honest-to-goodness attraction to a stimulating woman. Mind you, the stimulation, in the case of *this* woman, was far from the ordinary; 'honest-to-goodness'? an ill-chosen phrase, maybe. Maybe anything. Oh! but I was head-butted, for the second time in ten short hours.

I heard myself asking him: '*She slept with you?*'

'Oh yes,' he said simply. Then he looked up and saw my expression. 'No,' he amended, 'not that way. I mean "slept". That's all that I mean. I told you she was deeply troubled. Unhappy beyond all you could think. So was I. So we talked and came to conclusions. Then she whispered, might she come into my bed? perhaps we could *gentle* one another to sleep—'

'Would you stop it! It's appalling! I don't want to hear.' I was ashamed for him, mortified, that he should expose all his weakness like this.

He took no notice. 'Then Leonore had heard us. She came upstairs, and we all talked. Then she came into bed too. So we slept. It was like Paradise.'

'Why, Carver, you're fifty years old.'

'Bloody nearly fifty-two in point of fact. And I oughtn't to have told you any of it. If you ever utter a word, I'll – I'll *really* do murder, with my own hand, so be warned.' I did not understand the funny emphasis he gave his threat; but a clear threat it was, and no fooling. For a moment he seemed genuinely dangerous. There was foam at the corner of his mouth. I made haste to reassure him of my silence.

We left the café on the understanding that he'd disappear into a back room of the theatre and do his best there with the script and tomorrow we'd hold a meeting of the full company to discuss it all round. I kept quiet about my date with Cordwain. A mistake.

20

In contrast to the quiet of his Dublin penthouse, Cordwain's residence by the park was as bustling as an airport concourse, and its fleeting inhabitants were quite as picturesque as any you might see at Heathrow. There was a swarthy manservant to open the door in traditional butler's gear – a Portuguese? I saw a Filipino maid carrying a tray of drinks from room to room, black stockings, black dress, white apron, cheeky hothouse rose behind her lug; a black secretary-woman, very tall, very svelte, very contemptuous, with a cool Manhattan business-voice; another sort of secretary, a young punk fellow with an ear-ring, string vest, tattoos, rips in his jeans fixed together with safety-pins, and bare tracks shaved longways through his hair; to say nothing of half a dozen self-important suits, some of them sporting ponytails, in and out of the inner sanctum – they displayed their briefcases as crusaders might wear shields.

I suppose this man *was* vulgar, but with the heartiness of jocund power; whereas 'Mummydear's' vulgarity, truly sickening, derived from her *dream* of power craved all her life but never attained. She could not bear informality; Cordwain revelled in it.

He did not keep me hanging fire for very long. The punk boy assuaged my impatience by handing me a coffee-table book of glossy S & M photos – the high-finance equivalent of *Punch* in a dentist's waiting-room. Some of them were a little too similar to Leonore's giantess-picture; not a good time to be reminded of that.

Cordwain's first-floor office (I'd say the largest room in the house) was a surprise. I had expected a flaring art-gallery; but he'd hung no pictures there at all. One wall orange, three walls white, an expanse of plain bright orange carpet, and furniture apparently constructed from Meccano. Sitting *on* his desk, not behind it, he wore a baseball cap to show who was boss.

'About the script,' he said abruptly. 'Problems. What does Carver think?'

I began to explain what Carver thought, but he didn't let me finish. 'No no, Jack, he doesn't see it. He's into it too deep. Only going to make bad worse. Listen.' He left off these staff-officer barks and went into more characteristic free-flow, a long breathless maze of sideways information, none of it overtly germane to the theatre, but all about his business and everyone else's on 'Change, stocks and shares, percentages, junk bonds, mergers, takeovers, diversifications, bankruptcies, stabbing each clause with a household name or several (some of them surely defunct, and only mentioned for that very reason, cautionary examples) – Guinness; Nestlé's; Boots Chemist; Lever Bros.; Kellogg's; ICI; Marks and Spencer; Farrow's Bank; Krueger the Match King; Laker Airlines; Mazawatee; Shell-Mex; Vickers-Armstrong; the Murdoch press; the (fictional) enterprises of Dombey & Son, Mr Merdle and Augustus Melmotte; plus Wood Bros. Barnsley Glass (this last of my native town, a shrewd barb to hook my interest) – until I utterly failed to follow him. Except along one general thread: Mega-C. was about the sole British-based multinational that had any current hope of maintaining and increasing its territory without losing its patriotic complexion.

'—it's vital, Jack, you'll see that, absorbability's a terminal symptom, cancer-cells, 'the worm i'th'bud', *kill it!* Downing Street knows that, even if Threadneedle Street don't, and bugger the wimps in the Treasury. Look at Lloyd's. Look at Docklands. Look at Harrod's.'

Somehow, darkly groping as he rattled on, I conceived the idea that Mega-C. was fighting off, or about to fight off, a heavy attack from somewhere – somewhere in Europe probably, although Tokyo seemed to have a share of it. He was forcefully allusive, and in no way directly informative. Contrary to his assurances in Dublin, he made me feel most insecure. Perhaps *he* was insecure too. Fortune's Wheel about to turn; true 'tragedy' as Chaucer understood it:

> Tragedie is to seyn a certeyn storie,
> As olde bokes maken us memorie,
> Of him that stood in greet prosperitee
> And is y-fallen out of heigh degree . . .

All this blinding me with whizzkid science was no more than

preliminary apologia. Put not your trust in princes: *he was about to renegue on his sponsorship of MAFFICK!*

And yet not quite so. Suddenly he switched his tone again and fed himself into a sparkling millrace of praise for all my inventions in the production of *The Whore*. He was transparently sincere. Then, and only then, did he get to the point.

He told me that Fid Carver had 'written the wrong play'. When he (Cordwain) first heard from me the story's theme and our plans for the women to play men, he had assumed that it was a 'feminist job', a vindication of Albine (so manipulated by power-politics); and to an extent that *was* what he'd seen last night. But only to an extent. By and large the script revealed a very dangerous subtext of proletarian agitation; it sorely hindered the true line of the plot. Now I wasn't to 'get him wrong'; revolution was great! in the right context, and all good writers had a right to it. Carver was a good writer, but Carver hadn't thought of the context. Which was (and he spelled it out carefully, talking very slowly for once) the situation resulting from the London presentation of *Deepwater Dread*. Had I heard of a man called Prosser? Well: this Prosser – 'clearly a frightful prick' – had been moving heaven and earth behind closed doors in Whitehall to get MAFFICK! and Abel-Nottidge prosecuted either under the Official Secrets Act or else for Criminal Libel for Inciting Disaffection in the Armed Services. He (Cordwain) knew for a fact that only the shortness of *Dread*'s run withheld the attempt from success.

'Now,' he said, 'Jack! Is it appropriate for Mega-C.'s logo to be seen on the publicity of a company that's just blacked the Government's eye in such a fashion? It wouldn't matter if your *Whore* was the play that I'd expected it to be; wouldn't matter a damn; we're all for women's rights, even Maggie T. But Maggie T.'s the problem. She has decided – she, personally, the arbitrary hag – decided to – to exert a discreet pressure – you'll know how these things are done – to offer certain inducements – for the general greater good of Mega-C. Movements of public money, concealed, I've given you a hint. This was not the case, I needn't tell you, when you and I confabbed in Dublin. Nor *would* it be the case, I mean the problem concomitant would not be the case, if you could softly lead friend Carver to – to, here and there, revise . . .

'Hell, let's not bullshit! all he has to do is to juggle his scene-structure a little, turn a few things round, it might not take him more than a day or so. I could bloody near do it myself. No sweat. Oh, and you'd be granting a favour to that marvellous Bluefields woman. She needs, shall we say? the elbow-room. And *I* need to be shut of the 'enemy within', notable phrase, d'you get it? Okay?' He smiled, with overwhelming compassion.

I gave him neither black word nor white. Were I to follow his pressing advice, our subsidy was secure. Ignore him, no more money. Yet he hadn't actually *said* so. Neither white word nor black; I smiled knowingly back at him; I said, 'Thanks for the chat, I'll have a think'; I left him sat there and wondering. But he wouldn't wonder long. This play would have to show itself, in some sort of shape. Or else not. In the upshot Mega-Cordwain must pronounce; after waiting, no doubt, for the *spooks* to pronounce first. Prosser and his kind were not to be taken lightly.

21

'Carver, fuck you! you don't understand. They are *leaning* on this man. He is not his own master.'

'Oh yeah. So fuck him. But *I'm* my own master and my rewrites are what I choose. *I* choose: is that clear? Pogmoor, is that clear? All day and all night I have worked at this script till I'm bloodless. I am proud of what I've done. You're not proud of what *you've* done: I can smell it off your breath. Very well, let's meet the company and lay it all before them. All the company, Pogmoor: Mandy Cakebread, the electrician, the lot. This is a crisis.'

We were in the narrow little stage-door passage of the Showbox, Carver, Leonore, myself. I had just broken the news of Cordwain. The actors would be awaiting us onstage; they'd have to hear it too. One hell of a flaming row. Was I going to be able to handle it?

Leonore caught hold of her brother, but he shook her off and marched on into the theatre. She met my eyes in despair. We both followed him. There was no need to call everyone; the full company was there – except for the electrician, and I drew the line at *him*, he had work enough of his own to do without worrying about textual disasters.

Before I could start to speak, Carver was letting all fly. He said of me, charmingly, that the poison for years had been in the wine-casks, I had inserted it, and for years he had sipped it and sipped until the gather of his gut was all but liquefied. Napoleon to St Helena had brought a Judas in his entourage; so had Fid Carver, from Pomfretshire. No rewrites! he stormed, neither his own nor the treacherous Cordwain's – no, he amended that: Cordwain was not treacherous, Cordwain was only doing what a Thatcherite asset-stripper had to do, the market economy, the jungle of stocks and shares, he was true (fair enough) to his own destructive principles.

'This play,' concluded its playwright, 'is under contract to MAFFICK! I shall go to my agent and see can she get it stopped, I shall go to the Theatre Writers' Union and see can they blacklist this Juggler-man director of yours, I don't hold any hopes but I'll *try*! Oh, be sure of it, be fucking sure.'

With a vast idiotic gesture of rhetorical contempt he flung his script into the air. He hadn't properly clipped the pages together after all his rearrangements; they went in every direction, across the stage, into the front rows of the auditorium. He stumbled round on his heel, catching his ankles most awkwardly together, and ran out of the house. As he ran we heard him squall and rattle in his throat, the old sheepdog no longer up to the job . . .

Then he crept back in again. Downcast and stooped. He muttered, 'Lenny, come home. Please.' She met my eyes in despair; shrugged; said to me, 'What can I do? I'll phone you later'; stepped down from the stage; took his arm, and brought him away.

Of course, in threatening the very existence of the company with injunctions and blacklists, in threatening the poor devils' *employment*, he had effectively delivered them straight into my hand. And Cordwain's *diktat*, when looked at with a cool courage, was not nearly so bad as first appeared. I spoke to them earnestly, quietly, demonstrating the cool courage, and inspiriting them to share it. One by one they came to agree with me, came to agree with my suggestion that we should postpone our opening by a week and proceed at once to re-rehearse – a modified script, fit to solve the predicament of Mega-C. The playwright, by his violence, had put himself out of court. The contract to which he appealed would give me, as manager/director, leeway to make all necessary changes – true, it did provide that the author's permission must be obtained, but it also neatly qualified it: 'such permission not to be unreasonably withheld'. Did any of them believe that Fid Carver had been *reasonable*?

They shook their heads all round. So I had them where I wanted them; I began, with the assistant stage-manager's help, to pick Carver's pages up from the floorboards, and to talk, while I did so, about which scenes could be cut, which repositioned, and which of them might need a *soupçon* of new dialogue (which I would be prepared to provide). While I talked, while I shuffled paper, I slowly appreciated the quite alarming fact that one of the heads, Polly's head, had *not* been observably shaken. She was leaning against the side of the proscenium, her arms folded on her breast, her face in dark shadow. A thoroughly unknown quantity; and yet she ought not to have been; as Cordwain had said, her part, by this re-emphasis, was bound to come out stronger – stronger and larger – any actress worth her salt should bloody well be glad of it.

'Aren't you glad of it? Polly!' I had to draw words from her. Her silence was dreadful. She, not Fid Carver, was the play. Without him, we could carry on. Without her, complete collapse. That's to say, for the immediate future.

Well! and I did draw words. Oh God, such a heartache of words. Not too many of them, just these: 'I'm only in this company because Antonia Button isn't. If you rewrite Carver's script I shall walk out as he did. And before I walk out, and after I've walked out, I'll let everyone know why Antonia isn't here. Dear goodness, it's a tale that goes back a long way. Are you ready to have it told?'

This was not said at large: herself and me in the corner, intense and private, her low voice held in behind closed teeth. 'We talked about scrotums, Jack. Now is the hour. Ho.'

I could only reply: 'The script without rewrites is impossible. Polly, I've explained, Cordwain said to me last night that he—'

What was the use? I turned to the rest of them and wound the whole thing up, production, company, all of it. That's to say, for the immediate future. All the legal and financial complications, Mr Garsdale, sir, we were to refer – you'll recollect – to you. You'll recollect there were enough of them. Now that you've read this, you'll have fuller knowledge of their origins. (At the time, I only partially confided in you; sorry about that. It wasn't altogether a cover-up, rather an attempt to ingest the disgusting mess by ignoring its more bristly ingredients – think about it, man, how *could* I tell it all?)

Okay: end of MAFFICK! Utter consternation. When, as a last effort, I broke from their horrified gaze to try once again to bring Polly to see sense, I discovered she was gone.

I had always thought that (at worst) she would always be entirely *professional*. I was wrong: she had committed the ultimate unprofessional offence. She had split from the director and joined herself to the author. She was finished, she was nothing, she was dead.

22

I was asked (very grudgingly) by Ben Stropp, if I'd like to take a drink with the cast, 'drown our sorrows, have a wake, begone dull care?' I said I didn't think so: agents, lawyers, accountants, I didn't dare not go and see them at once. So I went away on my own; and I failed to go and see them, I put it off for twenty-four hours; oh, I'd drink, no doubt of that, but on my own if you please, holed up in Whitesmith Street. Rage, contempt, self-contempt, remorse, whatever else ... How would Stropp and his facile companions have the least inkling? *How?*

I found when I got home that the postman had called; there was a registered parcel awaiting me at the office. To take my mind off ugly matters I set out during the afternoon to collect it. It proved to be a cardboard tube containing a valuable print; I'd had a dealer put in a bid for me at Sotheby's the previous week, and now I damned well wished I hadn't.

It was a propaganda cartoon of the early nineteenth century; the artist was James Gillray. I'd been thinking of it as a first-night souvenir gift for Carver, despite its great cost; I owed him a debt, he had written his play at last, for Jack Juggler, no one else ... Hollow mockery. It was captioned:

CI-DEVANT OCCUPATIONS (1805).
Madame Talian [*sic*] and the Empress Josephine dancing naked
before Barrass [*sic*] in the winter of 1797.
A fact!

There they danced, the two women, behind a gauze curtain, in their dishevelled hair and their skins, flaunting jewels, stockings, shoes and a pair of tambourines. The gross figure of the politician Barras sat at his wine, showing them off to a scraggy little Bonaparte who lifted the corner of the curtain to get a better view. A lengthy piece of prose was inserted into the picture, to claim its historical accuracy: Josephine had been Barras's mistress, he wanted her off his hands, and this was how he succeeded in persuading young Boney to take her – plus a hefty bribe, the command of the Army of Italy. The commentary continued thus:

Madame Talian is a beautiful woman, tall and elegant.
Josephine is smaller and thin, with bad teeth something like
cloves. It is needful to add that Bonaparte accepted the
promotion and the Lady, now Empress of France.

It was a very sexy picture. No better man than Gillray for suggesting dark carnality in a candle-lit cluttered interior, sordid and yet sumptuous; the *chiaroscuro* of lust. Another of my pictures, that copy of a Caron showing the Story of Joseph, had something rather similar (if one allowed for the difference between painting and engraving): the lascivious curtained booth of Potiphar's wife, where poor Joseph fell into such trouble.

Unwillingly (for I knew I was only torturing myself) I sat alone in my flat and I pored and pored over this print. I drew my curtains, switched on a bright desk-lamp, took up a magnifying-glass to concentrate more closely upon the minutiae of the draughtsmanship. I had a bottle of vodka on the table at my elbow; I kept taking slugs of it. I was shattered.

Leonore rang me up.

'Madame Serlio', aloof and haughty, as though she and I were perfect strangers. I wearily narrated the defection of Blackadder (naturally without recounting everything she'd said to me) and the consequent break-up of all our endeavours. 'Are you surprised, Mr Pogmoor?' says she. 'You ratted on your principles. You don't expect to keep in business?'

'Come off it, Leonore – I thought you were on my side—'

'I was, when it was only a question of the logo on the poster. Even then I did not commend you, you've surely not forgotten. I did think my brother exaggerated. Now I realise he did not. He was right, and I see he was right. I ought to have supported him. I blame myself. Today, I *do* support him, immoveably. *And* Polly Blackadder, I applaud your indomitable Polly! Do you know where she is? My brother and I are most anxious to thank her.'

'No, I do not know. No, I don't *want* to know. Is that all? because if it is, I'll—'

'I should tell you, as you sound depressed, that Fidelio is not at all cast down. Resilient and very combative; *and* in good health, the pain in his back quite vanished. Beware of him, Pogmoor. Beware of me. Nothing more to say to you, really. Except – oh, I hadn't known, until you mentioned it this morning, that Maxwell Prosser is somehow involved. For that too I blame myself, although the fault was perhaps chiefly Carmilla's. Oh, and one more "except" – don't ring off till you've heard it – I want a cheque within the week for all the work I completed for you. Otherwise Lewis Hinge will be in touch with your Garsdale.' She put down the receiver.

I turned again to Gillray and the vodka. It was growing dark outside, late afternoon already, hailstones whipped against the windows, a *whirlpool* of squalid winter. 'Carmilla', she'd said? What the hell had Carmilla to do with Prosser? Indecipherable. Yet Carmilla had infected Button, and then Button had allowed herself to expose her infection to Blackadder, thereby *reinfecting* Blackadder with a virus supposedly dormant! – trail of consequence like Ariadne's clue stretching and twining into the labyrinth, into the jaws and stinking groin of the Minotaur – and oh! if just once, at my mercy, I could have Carmilla laid before me prostrate, what *would* I not do to her? Whirlpool.

I pulled myself together, and typed a formal letter to the Marylebone Showbox management (I'd promised it'd be in the post tonight), confirming that the production was off, and expressing my willingness to meet them with solicitors and discuss terms for the breach of contract. It cannot have been well spelt. My boozy fingers slipped all over the keys. I went out to put it in the mailbox in the King's Road; God, was it seven o'clock? I only just made the last collection. Lurched back to the house, vodka, old Jas. Gillray, dirty old mad Scotch drunk he was, but he knew how to draw dirty women . . . His damned engraving had run me up into four figures, good God. I'd sworn I would have it; and now I didn't want it. I found a bottle of Indian ink in what I called my 'arts-and-crafts locker', and a thick-nibbed calligrapher's pen. I jabbed and stippled blots of black all over the caracoling Josephine, obliterating her shape, denying her provocation; ineradicable blots of infamy, the greasy tart.

I must have left the door unlatched. Both doors, hall door downstairs, flat door upstairs. Or did some fool let her in?

I was slumped forward over the table, my marred expensive print fallen to the floor, my vodka-bottle on its side spilling empty, my ink-bottle I don't know where, I was thick in a flounder of bad sleep. A hard hand shook my shoulder, grabbing at it, tugging: it hurt. I bent away to one side and vilely cricked my neck trying to twist around my head to see who was at me. The hard hand gave a shove and unbalanced my chair. *I* was on the floor too, me and Jas. Gillray, both of us pissed out of our skulls.

I lay flat on my back half-stunned, hiccuping, gasping; gouts of vomit shot out of my mouth. Someone was tearing at the front of my clothes, denim jacket, shirt, dragging the buttons open, breaking their threads regardless. My belt was most violently unbuckled, my fly-zip and the join of my underpants dragged asunder. I sprawled, as it were, like an overturned tortoise, being exposed in one great gap from throat to thighs. She was kneeling above me, her knees either side of my knees and pressing against them deadly firm; I could not at first make out who she was, for her head was between me and the lamp. But the glare of the lamp caught the edge of the knife she was holding; I was not too drunk to understand a knife-blade, I tried to scream, but I choked instead. A *gurgle* for instant assistance – who could hear it? Nobody.

I am a biggish fellow, yes? I don't fight much – to tell truth, I don't fight ever – save for one occasion, at Leonore's, that cruel photograph! and *Carmilla* – yet I ought to have been strong enough to free myself now; Carmilla was of small weight, but sinewy hard and as quick in her moves as a biting insect; I rolled and thrashed uselessly beneath her. I managed to throw up my left hand and caught hold of her right hand, the one with the knife – *my* Stanley-knife, from *my* arts-and-crafts locker. This brought her right ear round into the light. Jumping about below the ear was a lock of bright pale hair with a sharp silver ornament. The light hit it and made it a shooting star: *zing*.

(So it wasn't Carmilla. How *could* it have been Carmilla? She wasn't even in England, was she?)

Fury Alecto . . .

Or Alice. Or Polly. (Not Gudrun. Gudrun held no meaning for me; I never saw those lousy films.) 'Now is the hour,' oh Christ, yes. About a full half-day unpunctual, but I guessed she'd been *steeling* herself. Her knife-hand came free of my grip. I was wearing a vest under my shirt. She got the blade in at the top and slit it as far as its lower hem, two inches above my pubic hair. She did more than slit the vest; she cut my bare skin all the way down. She heaved herself backwards a little and fitted the knife into the crotch of my jeans; one slash, and then another; they parted on the inside seams, opening up along both my thighs. And she cut my thighs too (just as she had my torso) through the sodden smelly web of my winter longjohns.

I still could not move; that is to say, not raise my body. I seemed to have no power over the appropriate muscles. But her force now being exerted against the lower part of me, I had a chance at last to lift up my head. It cleared my gullet; I could yell, if my vocal cords allowed me. They barely did; a hoarse, broken, paralytic series of groans. She didn't seem to care. She was sobbing and laughing and spitting; her knife went every which way, flicking and darting and drawing blood; any minute I'd be gelded; she had her handgrip there tight already (razor-sharp fingernails) to mark the place and stretch the flesh for the final chop. Then she let go. She had instantly changed the knife for the ink-bottle from the table-top. I felt its contents pour over me, a miniature River Styx onto my belly and below, it trickled through the hair, mingled with the blood and made a pool under my buttocks as I lay. The bottle's dregs, she tossed into my face.

What had caused her, at that moment, to put the knife aside? Either she played with me barbarously out of sheer stark Alecto-duty, or else she was uncertain how far she wanted to go. To this day I can't work out which. The fact is, she changed her weapon; and Lev Cordwain rushed into the room and pulled her off me and threw her into the corner and picked up the knife and the ink-bottle and eventually picked up Pogmoor.

He had found the front door open, had heard my cries even as he came in, had raced up the stairs to find out what the hell was happening – and now he was here and I was still in one piece. A most indecent bleeding humiliated piece, shamefully stained and dripping, all criss-cross shallow lacerations like a bacon-joint prepared for the oven. There was no other person in the house; every resident was out upon town. I am not sure whether it was better or worse to have Cordwain, of all people, find me in such a state, or one of my neighbours who scarcely knew me.

He said, 'I'll look for iodine. Iodine to begin with, then we'll think about an ambulance. Police?'

I shook my head. Not police. Never police. Besides, Alecto was dead quiet. Sitting against the wall and weeping and gulping and talking to herself, talking to her little daughter who wasn't there, rambling on in French about '*Ah ma petite, ah ma chérie, où est maman? maman viendra vite vite, voici maman, maman écoute son petit chou, sa fleur si précieuse,*' and more of the same without pause.

Cordwain said: 'An ambulance for *her*, yeah? Has she ever done this before? My fault, though; big money talking loudly, you'll know I'd no alternative; my fault, Mega-C.'s fault; can't be helped, it had to be done; I take full responsibility, my cost, I'll get her looked after. What about Carver? Is he going bonkers as well?'

Feebly and bitterly I told him, alas no. Or not in the sense he meant. I staggered around, holding my savaged trousers up, covering my desecrated nudity with a daft scrap of tablecloth, wondering about iodine – he'd forgotten he was going to fetch it – he was crouched beside *her* now, folding her in his arms, putting soft words into her ear in (would you believe?) French – he said almost the same things to her that she herself, unaware of him, was still murmuring to her vision of her child.

It only served me right, you'll say. *I've* said so, many times. The biter bit, the poetic justice. And also you'll say: 'Why, why, after all of that, were you so maggot-brained as to mess yourself *a second time* with Jacqui Lobscott?' Why? This is a statement of fact, not an anthology of solipsistic speculations: I won't even try at this point to say why. Maybe, through the remaining narrative (factual), some reasons will arise which you may think hold water. I *can* say that for a whole year – no, more than a whole year – I lay with no woman, nor even desired to lie. Quite apart from any other consideration, the scars on my body stayed livid through most of that period. They've not quite disappeared even yet. If I have to, I'll get them photographed and enhanced and sworn to by the photographer. But will they do my case more harm than good? You're the lawyer.

To leave no loose ends in passing—

Cordwain's visit to me that evening: he wanted a serious talk about how to salvage MAFFICK! He was genuinely distressed to hear we had collapsed. He'd tried to ring me more than once but my phone was off the hook. (So it was; I'd put it so, as soon as Leonore came to the end of her rubbishing.) It was a mark, a flattering mark, of his tycoonish concern that he'd travelled across London instead of calling me to Regent's Park.

He made me undress completely and – with his own hands – dabbed an agony of iodine all over me. This was long after the ambulance had come for Polly. While its crew were dealing with her, he hid me in the bathroom; no need, he said, to set them talking about grievous bodily harm. He'd held her in his arms right up to their arrival. Then he went with her to the hospital and only returned to Whitesmith Street when fully assured she'd be properly seen to – a private bed, a private consultant from Harley Street, the full flow of a rich man's bounty. He told me what I didn't know, that she'd grooved her own flesh as well as mine with the Stanley-knife, and more deeply: her clothes were all sopping with blood. No arteries, thank God for that. He said it couldn't have been deliberate suicide. Random strokes at all angles, missing me she cut herself, 'she hadn't thought it out, Jack, she was bonkers'.

During the iodine I complained about his leaving me alone. True, I had lain semi-conscious and utterly apathetic, as far as my mind went; my body, you'd have thought, would have been on fire, and (once he began to attend to it) it was. But for the hour or two of his absence I hardly felt a thing. I did not change my ruined clothes, nor even start to wash myself. I must have been temporarily anaesthetised by shock. Plus the effects of the vodka. Nevertheless, I complained. How did he know I wasn't dying?

He replied: 'Because you weren't. She's the one that's been harmed, Jack. You've just been scared. There's more to this than the end of the company, isn't there? What *did* she have against you?'

I snarled a little at that. It was none of his business. But if he thought it was – '*If* you mean to make it your business, finding her doctors and treatment and all of that, you'll have every chance to ask her yourself. She won't tell you the truth, any more than I will. I'm happy to let it go. Can I give you a hint? She has a filthy bad marriage, in France. No access to her child. If you really mean to look after her, *that's* where I'd guess you should start. Just possible you've the resources, the influence, to do something.'

He gave me a very long grave look. He said he'd take me at my word. Then he splashed some dire cleaning-fluid all over my genitals and told me to scrub the ink off. He even read me an Hebraic lecture on the hygenic advantages of circumcision. Well, I had been punished; and now I was punished for having been punished. So say it served me right, say it and say it again.

Would you believe? the bloody man, while clearing up my room for me, found the Gillray print and was *amused*. I'd have expected, bearing in mind his own *objets d'art*, that such vandalism would have appalled him. But all he said was, 'If you paid for it, I daresay you've the right to amend it. I daresay I know why. And I daresay *you* know that you've hugely augmented its value. It's now a unique piece. With a hot little story attached, too. Let me have it, Jack, and I won't tell. Refuse me; I'll spread the word. Name a figure; I've a chequebook in my pocket. God, I love it! "teeth like cloves", eh? But even so, even with all the black ink, her and her quick little friend, hips and tits like damson-plums, a pair of pussies like cupfuls of sherbet.'

As for MAFFICK! We did not discuss MAFFICK! I had now no intention that that company should ever revive itself. If I left sex alone for eighteen months, so also did I refrain from management. In fact, I went abroad, as you know, seeking and finding freelance directing-jobs: the residue of MAFFICK! was all down to you.

In April of '84 Mega-Cordwain was the subject of scare headlines in the financial pages. Takeover bids from every quarter, shares bounding up and plunging down. In May the City editors were able to report 'All Clear': the consortium had sailed safe into harbour, thanks to a government subvention. M. Thatcher performing a U-turn, one of her most brazen, flying in the face of the market. She tried to deny that's what it was, but some of us know different, some of us tap our noses. She did of course pronounce that when there's no alternative, *There Is No Alternative*. Oddly, she failed to point out that her deal, *inter alia*, had defeated an 'enemy within'. She must have held MAFFICK! to be very small beer in comparison with the coalminers. I wouldn't think Prosser agreed. To the devil with her.

Last autumn I heard more about Cordwain and Polly. It seems he'd patched up – at considerable cost – an agreement with her tortuous anti-Semite. Patched up by a Jew: you'd have to laugh. And the Jew was so forceful that the Frenchman in the end (with whatever mops and mows of hatred) conceded permanent custody of *la fleur précieuse de maman*. I

believe there was first some significant communication with the Simon
Wiesenthal people in Vienna: if a threat of a long-delayed war-crimes
prosecution had to be employed, fair play to young Cordwain, wouldn't
you say? (An irony, though: didn't the Frenchman himself use equally
devious means to get Polly out of Brazil? But I didn't hear that this time
she so relaxed her guard as to submit herself to Cordwain's bed. Nor did
she fall for his corporate politics. She continued to abhor them.
Moreover he was proud of her for it.)

I've been told she came out tentatively, cured, fragile, but of sound
mind, from a spell in a private clinic in the home counties.

Now she's back in Nantes, with her daughter, with her *Femmes
Savantes* friends, and undergoing intermittent treatment. Cordwain
pays; I hope he's not rooked by Frog charlatans.

So we arrive at your crucial question: could Polly – whom of course
you met once, but only as Alice Bluefields, only as my leading actress;
what did you think of her, by the way? – could Polly be persuaded to
denounce Carmilla Costello's slanders? I dare not ask her. Plain and
clear: the very idea gives me the runs. But if *you* want to ask her, go
ahead. You might find her in another clinic. You might even find she's
gone off again to Central America. Cordwain will know.

This is hopeless. I've been writing this for days and I've no better
answer?

23

Of course I've no better answer. If I had, I'd have told it you in my first
deposition, wherein I half-pretended I hadn't seen the Blackadder since
1965. I decided I must write it last autumn: I came home then from
Australia to find that my lurid past was known to, and barked out by,
every dog in the street. The end of MAFFICK! had queered my pitch, Fid
Carver and his icepick of a sister had queered my pitch, Button had
queered my pitch, Costello above all had set them all askance at me –
until no one in the profession of any sort of quality would so much as let
me direct a commercial for Smarties. I hoped, I suppose I hoped, if I
could settle the old Pomfretshire distortions, all the rest would be
withering on the vine.

Why, even this shit-heap Lobscott case would be easy enough, if only
Costello hadn't thrust herself into it.

Okay. Now. The Lobscott case. To work on a play of Percy's is one
degree above a Smarties ad, just. Which is why I agreed to return myself
to Knaresborough and see what he'd been up to. It was apparent from

his cheery letter that he hadn't heard the Jack Juggler rumours; he had finished these new scripts; he of course thought of me; come at once, come at once, rewards and glory! come and spend Christmas, we'll celebrate in style! I put my deposition (which I'd already commenced) on one side pending possible optimistic eventualities, and drove headlong northwards to my fate.

Gabriel, d'you know? *I'm sick of this document.* I have to have a break before I can continue, the more so as it's coming to the crunch. CID insist I am not to leave London without contacting them, damn their eyes. They are holding my passport. Is that legal? But if I try to challenge it, they're bound to arrest me, so I won't. Nor will I tell you just what I mean to do, in case *you* get leaned on by the cops. Suffice to say, I need a break, I'm having one. And then I'll get back to my desk.

If any or all of the above strikes you as even slightly approaching the 'obvious truth', you might drop me a brief word of appreciation. I'll find it in my letter box when I'm home again.

All Pogmoor knew, when he brought himself up short in the middle of his deposition, was that above all else he must go! *out of town, away from the law, clear and free from his choking entanglements: a* man on the run, *heedless and senseless. Romantic, perhaps, for some, if they were not (as he was) in a state of paranoia. He must leave his car behind. Car numbers are more easily checked across country than people. So by coach; and then maybe by train.*

He saw no one on the watch outside his house when he departed.

It was mid-May, but the weather was as wet and dark as February. He made irregular legs of journey in a generally north-westerly direction, stopping overnight at various places of antiquarian interest – cathedrals, castles and so forth. He felt thoroughly out-of-tune and not at all in a tourist frame of mind; but he persisted. If he could not soothe himself amongst museums and ancient buildings, what would give him ease? He managed indeed to dismiss the Lobscotts from his thoughts; but the unfinished business of The Emperor's Whore *nagged at him dreadfully – no doubt because of all he had had to write during the last few days. Wild floods of regret swept over him – not for Polly, not for Carver, but (absurdly) for the Gillray print he had disfigured and then lost to another. The scene in that cartoon, however superficially irrelevant, should by some contrivance have had a place in Carver's play; how could author and director (or, for that matter, designer) have missed it?*

Pulp-heads, all three of 'em. Opportunity neglected, thrown away, waste!

Sixth Tale

How Another of Jack's Dreams Gave Shape to Albine de Montholon
(1986)

This whiteness upon him is but the leprosy
Of pure dissimulation.

> (Thomas Middleton, *A Game at Chess*)

My love, my hope, my dearest! O, he's gone,
Ensnar'd, entrapp'd, surpris'd amongst the Black ones!
I never felt extremity like this:
Thick darkness falls upon this hour.

> (Thomas Middleton, *A Game at Chess*)

But what are kings, when regiment is gone,
But perfect shadows in a sunshine day?

> (Christopher Marlowe, *King Edward II*)

At nightfall on the fourth day of his trip Pogmoor was aboard a local train between Sheffield and York. An injudicious choice perhaps: Sheffield was too near Pomfretshire, York too near Knaresborough, this was no region to linger in; no, not in his present mood, no soothing for him in these parts. He distressed, rather than amused, himself with a paperback art-book, Modern Women Painters and the Erotic. *Another injudicious choice. It 'did nowt for him', he disconsolately decided, neither quietened his spirit nor cosseted his lust. Women's singularly crude visions of sexual necessity were not what he sought to know about just now. The train stopped.*

1

Down the length of a scantly lit platform a croaking West Yorkshire voice announced: 'Cudworth! Cudworth for Barnsley! Change here for Barnsley!'

Wondering at himself, Pogmoor got out. He had not visited Barnsley since the funeral of his mother in the early '70s. And surely the Cudworth branch-line had been closed to passenger traffic for years?

Obviously not, but—

He remembered well enough, from his childhood holiday journeys, this melancholy little junction in the midst of a drear countryside; he remembered the coalpits, the slag-heaps, the desultory cottage-rows of the colliers. He remembered the station's windswept open platforms, and their two small brick buildings (hutches, rather), one of them containing what purported to be a waiting-room. There was no Barnsley train in what used to be its usual bay; all the station staff seemed to have disappeared. He must hang about, no doubt for ages. He entered the waiting-room. None of your tacky new British Rail plastics in here: dark woodwork, sooty, stained-and-grained mahogany-brown. A smouldering coal fire. Mouldy timetables in black frames. A set of aged bye-laws; they were (good heavens) endorsed: *by order of the Directors of the North Midland Railway Company, 1853.*

And that couldn't be a *gas lamp* up there in the ceiling? Could it?

He sat, and shivered, and vaguely pondered. A goods train, puffing and clanking, moved slowly along, on the up-line on the far side of the station. Puffing? He peered through the filthy window-panes. White-hot sparks rendered vivid a thick cloud of smoke: no question, a steam locomotive.

He turned back into the room. He saw, without much surprise, that he was not alone. Two elderly people, a wizened bent corrupt-looking man and a haggard-handed woman with a black veil over her face, were sitting very still in the most obscure corner. They had not come in after Pogmoor's entry; they must have been there all the time, so quiet he'd failed to notice them. There was something out-of-place about their black clothes. They seemed, if anything, more old-fashioned than the station. The woman's bulky skirts came to her ankles, the man had a top hat on his knees.

The man blinked forward towards Pogmoor; without rising from the bench he made him a constricted bow. 'You will pardon me, *m'sieur,*' he said shakily, in a French accent, a transparently cod French accent, Peter Sellers playing Inspector Clouseau. 'It is curious, is it not, that for so recent an innovation, these premises of the *chemin de fer* are already in such dirt. It is what we would call, in my country, *un scandale caractéristique de la perfide Albion.* Your men of business no doubt calculate that he who must travel, must and shall, whether cleanly or foul. *Bah! cela me donne de la nausée*. But again, if you please, pardon me; and permit me, if you will. We are to wait, in this *oubliette, le bon dieu* alone knows for how many hours. I am privileged, therefore, to entertain your tedium! I myself, *Monsieur le Comte Charles-Tristan de Montholon, Général de Brigade*, though no longer upon active service, so capably aided by my most charming lady, a personage of inimitable talent, *Madame la Comtesse Albine de Montholon*, who lamentably prede-ceased me in thc year of '48; revolutionary year, *m'sieur*, to turn the whole world on its fulcrum, year of hope *et du désespoir*.' The veiled woman inclined her head and the bony fingers that protruded from her mittens offered a fleeting but graceful flourish.

Pogmoor, embarrassed and baffled by what appeared to be a couple of itinerant bedlamites, inclined his own head in return and made small Gallic throat-noises. '*Enchanté, m'dame, m'sieur,*' were the least inarticu-late of these vocables.

'*Eh bien,*' continued the count (for even were he not a count, we must needs call him something), 'if you should so desire, under my instruction *Madame* will recreate here and now the very substance of that libel so persuasive to your English soul – I mean, the "Choice of Josephine", how our late Empress was introduced to the Man of Destiny in his incandescent youth – as I say, a perfidious libel, but one which twenty years later, upon the Island of Accursed Exile, was so often a solace to us when our so-tragic master was sunk in sorrow, and we his companions played quietly, how you say? *les petits opéras bouffes*, the charades to give warmth to our loneliness. But no, it was more than charade. The poor Josephine, you will say, was by that epoch *une histoire surannée*, an old song! Yet how the Emperor had once indulged himself, so he could and would and did again. To remind him of his greater days, was it not appropriate we should play the game once more? Upon the Island, *voyez-vous*, a new choice, the "Choice of Albine".'

Springing to his feet, twirling his hat, bowing and gesticulating like a showman at a fairground booth, the count strutted almost up to Pogmoor's astonished face – '*M'sieur*, it is permitted? *Alors!* your best attention please' – and then turned smartly in his tracks to beckon to the countess. Obediently, she stood; a tense attitude of expectation. The count made three or four swift passes with his hands. In the gloom of the high-ceilinged room, it was as though he were thus able to expand its walls backwards, to *create* the fairground booth where before there had been nothing but dark wainscot and railway notices. A rustling, transparent drape descended softly of its own accord in front of the countess. Some curious music, a species of farandole played on what sounded like a hurdy-gurdy, augmented from a faint whine into a something near a screech. The countess, very stately, moved to and fro to the tune, barely visible behind the drape, divesting herself of a multiplicity of shawls. The room by degrees became darker and darker.

'Aha!' exclaimed the count. 'We cannot show you everything! *Par exemple*, we have not the personnel. But you, *m'sieur*, you must be Bonaparte; I, your presenter, am that execrable Paul Barras; my dear wife of course is Josephine – ah, but who shall be Madame Tallien? Albine must imagine her. And therefore, because she imagines her, you will imagine her too! *Madame Albine, s'il vous plaît*, imagine for this gentleman Jeanne Marie Ignace Thérèse Tallien, the superb beauty and evil genius of the Great Betrayal of Thermidor!'

And as he spoke, the countess (for a second) held herself rigid. At once, like a breath of wind on a deep lake, another female shape came dimly into view behind her, similarly clothed, likewise moving to and fro, divesting herself with a more than equal dignity.

The music increased its tempo, and was now supplemented by the rattle of tambourines. Slowly the curtained space at the end of the room began to grow light – a flickering warm orange-red flaming light, a glow from a furnace, Pogmoor thought – yet was it anything more than the Cudworth waiting-room fireplace at last beginning to do its job?

What Pogmoor saw, during the next few minutes – it may have been longer than a *few*, for his reckoning of time had mysteriously abated – was pretty much the same spectacle that Gillray drew. There were points of difference—

The two women did not dance naked: they had uncovered only so far as their shabby discoloured undergarments; that is to say, long flounced drawers and loose low-cut bodices of cotton which had once perhaps been white. Mildewed contraptions hung clashing from their waists, cane hoops and leather strapwork – the frames of crinolines, Pogmoor deduced.

Their abundant hair was not dark but brittle grey and filled with scurf, caught up by no jewelled bands but streamers of withered flowers which shed dusty petals at every step.

Upon their bare arms and finally revealed faces (bonnets and veils were their last clothes to be discarded) the skin showed so ghastly and taut as to resemble stocking-masks worn by bank robbers. Yet they smiled as they danced, furtive collusive toothless smiles; their hollow eyes rolled unnervingly in coquettish invitation; and – strangest of all – their features were of identical cast, not so much twin sisters as one skipping crone and her absolute mirror-image. Ah, wait! Pogmoor told himself, that was only to be expected, for was not the second woman but the keen *imagination* of the first?

It was, in short, a grotesque parody of an original grotesquerie: James Gillray out-Gillrayed, the cruel burlesque burlesqued most cruelly to throw its satire first and foremost at Jack Pogmoor himself. It sat on his stomach as queasy as rat's-flesh.

2

The dancing increased in speed, the music in shrillness and clamour, until Pogmoor's eyesight grew disordered; all he could see was a widdershins whirl of pallor-and-shadow, fearfully tinged with fire. At last, in a kind of *dissolve* (easy to be produced, he thought, by the technical resources of a film-studio, but this was no such place), the whole farrago, including the count as its presenter, dispersed into a kaleidoscopic confusion of red light, black darkness, and yellowish-white women-ghosts – the mass of dots of a pointillist painter – three dimensions of them receding ever away from the eye, a perspective so infinite that it sickened his spirit more atrociously than the dance itself. The farandole slackened and stilled its harsh tones. No more tambourines, only the hum of the hurdy-gurdy, now playing a desolate slow march.

At length, a cessation of movement. The array of dots began to change colour.

Pogmoor's depression lifted proportionately. He was intensely curious, that was all; he felt really no more fear, or hardly any.

The dots, little by little, formed a whole new perspective; and coalesced, clarified themselves, as they did so: a wide blue sky, a wide green plain running to a far horizon with a distant church tower and a windmill, a double line of poplar trees bordering a road. Along this road, strolling slowly arm-in-arm in deep conversation, advanced Montholon and his lady. Pogmoor at first was not sure that was who they were; they were too far away. As they came nearer to him, he recognised them beyond doubt, even though they were many years younger – in their late twenties or early thirties, perhaps, and dressed in decent country clothes appropriate to the year. Which year? 1812? Why not?

They were fifty yards from Pogmoor when Albine broke roughly from her companion's arm. She was railing at him, flushed with anger. He stood in the middle of the road, disconcerted, and angry in his turn. She strode on ahead until she was within easy speaking distance of

Pogmoor. The count, running after her, caught her up and held her by the elbow. They showed their teeth in exasperation, one at the other; then both together turned to Pogmoor.

Montholon spoke first – not any longer in his silly comic-actor Franco-English, but in respectable cultivated French. (Pogmoor, whose own French was little better than moderate, was surprised to discover he had no difficulty in understanding. The surprise endured only an instant: this foreign tongue had become entirely natural to him.) 'Sir, I have to tell you, you see a woman who is a liar.'

'Sir,' echoed Albine with a vehement emphasis, 'you see a damnably lying man. He knows it, I know it.'

The count sneered and flicked his fingers skyward – the sort of 'period' gesture Pogmoor would have discouraged from any actor playing the part. 'Oh, why is she impelled to make such a fool of herself in the presence of a third party? If she is a liar and then she says I lie, who will not be convinced I am telling the impregnable truth? Nonetheless it is neither my lie nor hers that brings us so much trouble, but the lie of our entire condition, the lie of revolution, the lie of empire, the lie of war, the lie of France herself. You, sir, will understand.'

'Of course he will understand.' Albine was looking at Pogmoor and talking not to him but about him, an uncomfortable circumstance, considering he was more or less a stranger. 'He is bound to understand. He is a bred-in-the-bone liar himself, and so was his colleague; and yet both of them have presumed to know us inside-out and publicly to declare their knowledge.

'This one was afraid of his presumption and sought to avoid the task, because to know *me* was to know too much about a woman he had cause to fear.

'The other one was not afraid; no, he was on fire; for to know *you*, Charles-Tristan, was to know what you did, what you hid and how you lived without discovery. In his own case, his own *hiding*, he lived in continual terror; for him you were a pattern of imperturbability. He envied you and longed to explore you, while pretending it was *me* he explored.

'Is it astonishing that in the end the pair of them each had their teeth in the other's throat? Their falsehoods were entangled, their fears pulled the knotted skein from opposite directions tighter than a heart that bursts with sorrow, nothing was unravelled, nothing made smooth: hatred alone was the sum of their strivings. He understands.'

Pogmoor did *not* understand.

The other one? Was she talking about Carver? If so, she had an insight that he (Pogmoor) was quite unable to catch hold of; yet what she had said of himself was acute. He had an eager presentiment that if he sat here long enough he would at last learn something neither he nor Fid Carver had had the wit to uncover.

But to hell with it all: it was two damned years too late. *Waste . . .*

He sat, and contained himself.

This short rhetorical episode, a brace of French oddities orating their abstract accusations like characters out of Racine, marked the end of what Pogmoor took to be their awareness of him as Jack Pogmoor. From now on he watched their story unacknowledged by them or by anyone else within it – except when he found himself to be part of the dramatis personae. *Such an occasion was about to come up. He did not expect it; but it did not take him aback; it was all of a piece with the rest of the uncovenanted carry-on.*

As Montholon and Albine continued to dispute, stamping their feet and striding about in the middle of the dusty road, Pogmoor took careful note. He compared them, their appearance, their behaviour, to his actors in *The Emperor's Whore.*

His (or Carver's) Montholon had been conceived as a sly vigilant intriguer, the silent factotum in the background, deferentially pursuing his own deadly agenda. The real man – for Pogmoor was now persuaded that this, in front of him, was indeed real – had nothing of that quality. He was a handsome, careless, vicious fellow, with an overripe countenance framed in luxuriant dark whiskers, the sort of idle charmer to believe (more often than not, to be confirmed in his belief) that any female whom he met would eventually release her pent-up desire into his unscrupulous embraces. He had only to adore – to *seem* to adore – and impudently to whisper this and that – irrepressible, irresistible.

As for Albine: Polly Blackadder had brought to Albine so vital a plausibility that Pogmoor found it very hard to think of the real person unless he also thought of Polly. The earlier Albine-shadow, most earnestly worked up by Antonia, had totally fled his memory. But here, he was confronted by a woman who bore a certain physical resemblance to Polly without any of her attributes of personality – one exception: the twitch of a smile, the uneasy suggestion that she was nursing a private joke at the expense of whomever she was talking to. Even that point of likeness, however, was overlaid by another more immediate reminiscence. When Polly smiled, the expression of her eyes remained clear and sturdily honest, which Pogmoor had always seen as a truly diabolical variety of deceit, whereas this Albine matched *her* smile with most untrustworthy glances and little movements of her fingers to touch her chin, stray among her hair, swiftly pass across the nipples of her breast – *Mrs Lobscott*, to the life. Out of the frying-pan, Jack Pogmoor, and into the fire.

Alpine and Montholon were not on this road by hazard. The place where they had stopped was in fact a crossroads where they were waiting for something, or someone. Probably for a vehicle – one of them was going on a journey – Montholon, it would be, for although the day was so very hot (Albine wore no more than a light summer gown and a straw bonnet), he had a wide Byronic mantle thrown over his shoulder and was vexing himself with a cumbersome despatch-case. A large portmanteau lay in the grass, beside a newly cut stone bollard inscribed 'PARIS 206 km'. Beside the portmanteau a man dressed as a valet was lounging in bored attendance.

His name was Jules; but he was Pogmoor, incorporated without warning. Not necessary to refer to any subsequent intrusions of the dreamer into the dream: sufficient to know that he will be there in almost every episode, in a regular variorum of roles, sometimes male, sometimes female – Albine herself, even, or Charles-Tristan, but never Napoleon. He is to see the latter always through someone else's eyes.

Involuntarily he is to further the plot, playing his part as though coached in it by a natural instinct – like a bird that knows its migration-time and keeps company with the flock without having been told what to do or how to do it.

Because he was Jules, Pogmoor was now aware that his master's lady (who was not yet the Countess de Montholon but Mme de Vassal, adulterous and divorced) was nearly three months pregnant. It hardly showed; but her maid had guessed and had of course told Jules and between them they had told the other servants. In the dilapidated little château where the lovers' runaway idyll achieved its ecstatic climax and then gradually deteriorated, there were not many other servants; Montholon was as usual strapped for cash.

He looked his mistress up and down with the frigidity of a police-agent. 'I do *not* believe this pregnancy. It is a means of blackmail. And if I *do* believe it – I ask you again, and this time I demand a reply! – what assurances have I that I am the father?'

Albine smiled: remarkable equanimity in the face of such an insult (but the argument had gone on all morning and she and he were only repeating themselves, rubbing their sores obsessively, possibly hoping to rub them out). She answered, 'No assurances at all. But if you need to maintain your suspicions, you must clinch them by finding a name. A name, sir, a likelihood, and some evidence of opportunity. You seduced me, eloped, evaded a duel (and none too courageously), lived with me in this desert till your debts overcame you, and now you have to wonder has someone else been following your tracks? To perform the same nonsense that you did, and to look for the same smarting consequence? Why, it is ridiculous: who would be such a fool?'

'I did not evade a duel. I refused, I am a nobleman, I could not fight your husband; never mind the fraudulent '*de*' he's stitched on to his appellation, never mind his gold-braided uniform, your husband is no better than a—'

'—a functionary whose frauds left him open to blackmail, *your* blackmail, oh yes, how dare you talk about mine! Why, he colluded in the romantic elopement, as you very well know. It is a pity that I failed to find it out before last Tuesday.'

'That is not how it was. Vassal offered money to keep the matter quiet and avoid the scandal of divorce, the public exposure of his cuckoldry. I was disgusted by such baseness; I took the money and I took his wife; I told you and you approved; we were, you distinctly said, "spoiling the Egyptians in the style of good old Moses"! Therefore in revenge he went for his divorce, published his own disgrace, alleged my cowardice, in the hope that a lover so shat-upon would make the husband smell sweet by comparison.'

'That is not how it was. For the money you took was nothing. Or if there was more which you haven't acknowledged, you've spent it already, and most certainly not upon *me*. So will you marry me or will you not?'

He changed his tone and looked tenderly into her eyes. He laid his hand upon her arm; she threw it off in annoyance; he laid it again; she let it lie. Her smile told nothing: was she softening toward him, or giving him the rope to hang himself? (None of these cross-purposes would have fallen out at all had she not been absurdly attracted to him. Despite the best efforts of her considerable intelligence, she was not yet entirely disillusioned. When he was tender, she melted. She knew that he knew that; already she had discovered the uses of a counterfeit melting. Their life together had been so far very brief; he had not learned to detect the difference.) 'Albine, how can you ask? You are the flower of my heart. Of course I will marry you.'

Now, was he aware that she had her own money, inherited from the first of her two husbands (the dead one), protected in a fund in the name of her male cousin? If she told this to Montholon, he would surely keep his promise; but then he would be after the money. If he could not get at it, he might abandon her. And in any case, she was doubtful as to the honesty of the cousin; it was alas highly possible she might not be able to get at the money herself. Her first husband had lived, more or less, upon what some would describe as Albine's *immoral earnings* as a semi-public courtesan around the officers' gambling-houses in garrison towns in France and all over 'revolutionised' Europe. The legal status of the fund could suffer from this; be nullified, even. Now that the Emperor was making his peace with the Church, had got rid of his disreputable Josephine and married a Holy Roman, a Hapsburg princess, 'immoralities' were not to be laid open. The cousin could so easily take advantage of such a climate.

It was all very worrying.

If Montholon, on the other hand, remained ignorant of the fund, for what possible reason would he *want* to become her husband? She was socially unacceptable, in the salons where it mattered; she was older than he was and had not worn nearly so well; she had slept, in earlier years, with too many of his rakish friends. (Odd, she never met *him* in those years: accident of circumstance, she supposed. But a pity. They could both of them have been warned by the experience.) Of course, there was always the chance that he really did love her. Stranger things had been known. He was incongruously proud of his noble rank; he probably, like most aristos, desired an heir to the great name. But unlike most aristos, he was also a Jacobin, and a very abrasive Jacobin when he felt like it. None of the old families who had survived the Revolution would dream of providing such an adventurer as Charles-Tristan with a wife of authentic blood.

The more so, as he had not 'survived' the Revolution in any honourable sense. He was no more than ten at the time of the Terror, being brought up within the family of a republican grocer in Poitiers. The old count had put him there as soon as King Louis was hauled out of his carriage at Varennes and restored, a broken captive, to Paris. This fosterage was but part of an elaborate and cynical transaction – the grocer would have the discreet use of money which the count could not transfer from France to his place of exile – at the same time, the count's escape would be facilitated by the grocer's political influence (the countess being already safe and sound beyond the Rhine) – the grocer could betray neither the count nor the count's child for fear lest the count tell the truth about the money. Moreover, count and grocer had certain links of amity: they'd collaborated at one time toward a very successful venture in the West Indian slave-trade – the grocer held an interest in a sugar-plantation of Saint-Domingue – and long before that, when they were both wild young men in a backward Touraine country town, they had actually shared a peasant mistress, a most harmonious relationship that temporarily went far to dissolve the barriers of class and caste, one of her children being acknowledged by the count, the other by the grocer (they complacently drew lots as to which).

Then came the news of the count's sudden death in Austria. The countess, it seemed, was to take another husband. Charles-Tristan, it seemed, was written off from her ledger of love.

Whereas grocer and grocer's wife dearly loved the boy, and indulged him. Without abusing his parentage, they succeeded in rearing him after their own ideologies as a Robespierrean enthusiast, just as they did with their own children. He learned, in a comfortable household, that the old count had been a good man, only compromised by his unfortunate birth for which the bloodshed of the Terror was the regrettable but logical remedy. He believed it without question, for it was taught him by good people and his foster-brothers and sisters showed him an excellent tact (whereas his real family had tended to treat him with chilly reserve, unpleasant to a playful little boy). After the coup of Thermidor and the execution of Robespierre, these doctrines were imparted in secret; it was not long, however, before General Bonaparte, a protégé of the Robespierre faction, seized power, and for a while it appeared to the confused provincials of Poitiers that the old zest for an extreme republic was about to be rehabilitated. These hopes were soon dashed; unfortunately the grocer had already allowed himself too many sanguine words about guillotines and 'enemies of the people'. He was in danger of losing a number of public offices he held in the town; these had brought him personal profit, to be deprived of them in the depressed state of the country's trade might well mean ruin. He needed an insurance with the conservative element – what better device than quietly to proclaim his years of benevolence to the young Count de Montholon?

The young count not surprisingly was flabbergasted by his foster-father's reversal of principle. Was he now to regard himself as a Royalist or a Jacobin? or did practical loyalty to the regime of the First Consul demand a little of both? The grocer, seeing his distress, obtained for him as soon as possible a commission in the army; there the boy need face no greater moral problem than whether to risk his life or preserve it – and obedience to orders would in most cases solve it for him. Once in uniform, he found men – and women – who had some family connection with the de Montholons; his charm and apparent abilities raised him in their esteem. He secured several promotions, first as a headquarters aide-de-camp and then as attaché to various embassies, all of them agreeable posts, none of them exacting. He was never required to take command in the field.

He met Albine in Germany. He had reached the rank of Colonel and as such was appointed to Würzburg, to the court of the allied Grand Duke; they called him Minister Plenipotentiary; in fact he was there as a sort of colonial governor, to enforce the Emperor's demands for conscripts and taxes and the imprisonment of nationalist agitators. He carried out these tasks easily enough, for the little dukedom was thoroughly intimidated. But it *was*, even so, a dukedom. By Montholon's standards it should have been a free republic, full of liberty, equality and fraternity. *That* was what the French army abroad ought to be looking to. And it wasn't. Most of the dissidents whom the duke had to gaol were men like Montholon's own foster-father. Such ironic distortions *could* be explained by the exigencies of continental war, but—

He quietened his conscience with a deal of drinking and gambling and a series of licentious affairs. The last of these was with Albine. M. de Vassal travelled the petty German states to centralise the cash and cannon-fodder which Montholon (and his colleagues elsewhere) busied themselves to raise. He left his wife in Würzburg while he rode his rounds with a large escort, for the highways were no longer safe. Nationalists in armed bands were already beginning to disrupt the imperial system; there were stories of the rape of unsuspecting Frenchwomen.

If Albine thus escaped a brutal violation, her marriage-bed did not remain sacred. When Vassal returned unexpectedly to find the Minister Plenipotentiary merrily whistling '*Marlbrouck s'en va-t-en guerre*' and shaving himself in Vassal's dressing-room with Vassal's own razor while Albine took her morning bath three feet away from him, it was hard to know what to do. A scandal between responsible Frenchmen in an unstable part of Germany would be far worse than scandalous – *politically detrimental!* and the Emperor would be enraged.

There was an ignoble bargain, of some sort: the exact details a matter of sniggering rumour among the Grand Duke's entourage. Montholon applied for a period of sick-leave, claiming an aggravated spleen. When he went home to France to recuperate, Albine travelled with him. (Vassal put it about that she had to take advantage of the Colonel's escort; there might be no other suitable convoy for many weeks; French officials were being advised to get their ladies out of Germany as quickly as possible because the Emperor was recruiting for the Russian campaign and peasant resentment was fierce in the regions.)

Now, after delaying until high summer on the willowy banks of the River Creuse, Montholon was forced to make up his mind. He *must* go to Paris, or his career would collapse. The plea of sickness had lost credibility. The last letter he had from headquarters had been a brusque demand for a doctor's testimonial, or else . . . He did not know any corrupt doctors who might forge something for him, at least not in the countryside; it was more than high time to pronounce himself cured. He explained this, yet again, to Albine, swearing to return as soon as his position was made safe. She was sceptical, as always, but reflected that she *was* well installed in his château; she had made friends with the local prefect's wife; if Montholon renegued on her and decided to evict her, he'd have to come in person to square the prefect. So she softly permitted his protests of a sorrowful yet hopeful *au revoir*.

The Paris diligence, overloaded, groaning along the pavé, was already in sight down the southern branch of the crossroad.

She clasped him in her arms, agreeably aware that her touch did not yet *fatigue* him. Casting a quick glance over her shoulder to make sure the man Jules had the sense not to stare at them, she put Charles-Tristan's hand against her belly. 'Am I indeed the flower of your heart?' she murmured. 'Let me show you how you have been the heart of my flower, you still are, you shall be again; many times, oh my love so many many . . .' With her own hand at the front of his breeches, she tested her assertion, found it well proven, and kissed him until his breath was spent.

The coachman dragged his horses to a clumsy and steaming halt; Jules heaved the portmanteau into the boot and his master into the body of the diligence; he himself scrambled to the roof and sat upon bales of merchandise with the cheaper sort of traveller, peasants, a grubby priest, young soldiers bound for their regiments. They were singing up there and handing round a bottle of wine; the anxious count, down inside, must press for a place sweatily amongst irritated burgesses and their wives. He cursed himself that he had no chaise of his own, not even the wherewithal to hire one. But as he was out of uniform his financial straits were no especial humiliation, no one could say (particularly none of the conscripts on top), 'Something not quite right about that colonel-type, hey?' God, though! at this rate he wouldn't be in Paris before the middle of next week.

Albine waved her handkerchief until the diligence was well on its way. Then she turned herself round to go back to the château. She thought that when she got there, she'd lie on a couch in the garden and make an effort at writing a poem. Alone between the poplars, she put the handkerchief to her eyes. Tears were of no use; but how could she prevent them from running down her cheeks? At any rate, she need not *sob*. A modicum of self-control, if she were able to attain it. She was, after all, well practised.

3

It was Montholon's second visit to the choleric general. His first, on his first day in Paris, had been degrading: his superior officer sat and swore at him, while he, rigid in his regimentals, tried not to flinch and failed miserably. Since then he had hung about in barracks – an environment to which he had of late been little used and which irked him beyond endurance. Not quite under arrest; but damned near it. They treated him like a raw lieutenant, made him orderly-officer five nights out of seven and put him in charge of ill-disciplined new drafts in transit to the Vistula and beyond. His recollections of the sweetness of Albine became clamorous. Oh, if they *were* married, and she could only be living with him, here in his sparse quarters, what a difference it would make!

At last, recalled abruptly to the general's office, he was to know what lay in store for him.

'Montholon? Oh yes, *de* Montholon, apologies, it would never do to demean an ornament of the old regime, would it, Colonel? For fuck's sake.' (The general had been a corporal in the National Guard in '93 and let nobody forget it.) 'Left up to me, you'd be posted forthwith to lead a fatigue-detail into Russia. Too late for the loot and just in time for that winter of theirs. Freeze your bollocks off and good riddance. We'll come to your bollocks in a minute.

'Sacred God but it's not left up to me. I have an order from above that pending the imperial decision you are to be assigned brevet-rank of brigadier and sent to—' (The general peered through spectacles at a closely-written sheet of paper.) '—sent to Metz, where you will take command of what are known as the "ancillary services" of the Moselle-Saar military district. It is *not* a post of honour, nor does this brigadier rubbish advance you beyond a colonel's pay. I should sodding well hope not. You will take it, if you please, as a formal endorsement of the requirements of the post, and nothing more. Your sub-districts have a colonel apiece; you have to outrank them; by as little as possible, God's gut!

'*I* think it's far too good for you. *I* think your record is worthless. But you have friends, it appears, in places which I cannot reach. However, I *can* reach the Emperor. By a very long slow process. I'd not be surprised if he's across the Russian frontier by now. He will not relish being informed of your affairs. But he *will* be informed. I write to him today.'

'Sir.'

'Sir what? Get your fat arse into Metz. And when you're there, man, you'll *do some work*; here's your orders.'

He rudely thrust a document against Montholon's blue-and-gold chest, and opened the next file on the heap that lay before him; the interview was over. Montholon hesitated, struggled to speak, choked.

'Not gone yet? Fuck's sake; what d'you want?'

'Sir, the – the other matter – sir?'

'Eh? Oh . . . Yes, I said we'd come to that. There *are* married quarters in the barracks at Metz. If you want to put a wife in 'em, *I'm* not going to stop you. But you're not to move out of 'em. None of your ormolu apartments in what used to be aristo town-mansions, none of your bijou boxes in the glades of the forest, understood? Sacred God but I pity her. When did the marriage take place?'

'It – ah, it didn't yet – sir, I was hoping that perhaps—'

'It didn't? Then it won't. Or not until the Emperor has given his approval. You are still by the book on attachment to the Diplomatic Corps. Temporarily *de*tached, but the rules for fuck's sake hold good. All marital arrangements to be approved at the highest level, the *very* highest level. You know that as well as I do. Until word comes from Russia you keep your cock in your breeches, is that clear?'

'But sir, she's expecting a child—'

'When?'

'She says, she's known of it two months and more, an approximate guess but that would mean—'

'God's gut, I said it was slow, but not *seven months!* between Vilna or wherever and France. You'll hear the Emperor's word before you hear the brat squall; even if you don't, what's the odds? She's lumbered already with a slimy aristo bastard, a second one from her own twat won't make that much difference. Get out.'

4

Albine did write her poem. Her verses were not stylish, she neither knew nor cared about the correctitude of the Alexandrine measure, but she did know the old country songs and she based her technique upon them. It was not a poem to be sent to Charles-Tristan, who would certainly hate it, if he didn't prefer to laugh at it and pass it round a smirking circle of languid young officers. But it tried to state some matters of truth, which she had not yet confided to her lover.

> Baby in my belly, listen to my word:
> You are not the first there: sweetheart, you're the third.
> – *la la-la* ron-*lon lé*
> Little Number Three,
> Mama sings her song to you –
> Papa, where is *he*?

> Number One was Anne-Marie. Now she's dead and gone.
> Like a summer swallow, fluttered to the sun.
> – *la la-la* ron-*lon lé*
> Her mama was a tart;
> Her papa was a bad man
> With a worm inside his heart.

> Number Two was white and grey, he never lived at all.
> They buried him in winter and I called him Little Paul.
> – *la la-la* ron-*lon lé*
> His papa never knew.
> His papa was in cruel Spain
> Where the red-hot winds did blow.

> At Vimiero papa died where the red-hot bombshells blew.
> But mama had her husband-man fit to make you spew.
> – *la la-la* ron-*lon lé*
> Husbands are no good,
> Neither when they're still alive
> Nor yet when they are dead.

> Baby in my belly, sweetheart Number Three:
> Shall you be a pretty girl, or just a cheating *he*?
> – *la la-la* ron-*lon lé*
> Husband yes or no?
> He promised he would tell me
> Before the winter snow.

> *He promised and I fear he lied.*
> *Don't tell me, child – I tried, I cried.*

She wrote the last two lines several weeks after Charles-Tristan left for Paris; he had sent her not one letter, not even to announce his safe arrival. But the very day she wrote them, a letter came. From Metz. Part of it filled with flowery expressions of love and devotion (which she pouted at impatiently, as necessarily insincere); part of it, however, was businesslike and to the point.

> —enclosed is a warrant, gratuitous, for your journey by diligence (officer's family entitlement, inside seat); you know how to reach Paris; from Paris the daily vehicles leave the Auberge aux Trois Lunes, near the junction of the Rue du Temple and the Rue St-Antoine, at six in the morning. Thus you will spend the night in the city. Enclosed is a note for the landlord of the Trois Lunes, in the name of the Countess de Montholon. I have spoken to this man and left him an IOU upon my next remit of salary. He is impressed by the word 'Countess' – ah! did we have a Revolution or not? – and will make no difficulty, I am sure. At Metz our simple ceremony will be without guests or jollifications. The GOC here believes we are married already; when I introduce you to him, do not fail to convey that *truth*. It is my hope that by this small deception, no one (*who really matters*) will discover our circumstance until it is already too late for it to make any difference. The Emperor, by the latest bulletin, has taken Smolensk; once he meets the dishevelled legions of the Tsar, nothing will stand between him and Moscow. Glory to the arms of France! He will be there without doubt for a long time, re-organising so huge an addition to the immensity of his dominions. And at such a prodigious distance.
>
> Oh, my dearest love, when I contemplate in my dreams the twin-budded *compassion* that swells your white bosom—
> (*etc.*)

There were too many things left unexplained, even the tag to the signature – how *could* he simply write himself 'Brigadier' without any account of the method of its coming to pass? And what was he doing in Metz? A gloomy town, as she remembered it, half made up of crabby Germans. She had no desire at all to share her Montholon with any more Germans. She assumed his 'simple ceremony' would turn out to be a wedding; but nowhere in the letter (and she pored over it time after time) did he actually say so. And as for 'small deception' and 'prodigious distance'! – whatever he might be up to, it was suspiciously two-faced. Oh, the picture of her wretched life, over and over again!

But the travel-pass was in her hand; all that remained was to satisfy the scrutiny of the man at the Trois Lunes. If he knew what that IOU would be worth, she would probably have to sleep in the street. Or, at any rate, to *walk* the street.

Somehow, she contrived to sing as she went to her bed that night:

—*la la-la* ron-*lon lé*
Husband I think yes.
He promised he would tell me:
He's told me now. I guess.

'Countess' . . . For he had at last brought himself to write it down in
pen and ink, which was next best thing (wasn't it?) to the fact.

5

From a damaged despatch, dictated by the Emperor himself from his
Grand Army headquarters in Moscow, to the general in Paris who sent
Montholon to Metz:

> —on the other hand, the action taken in regard to Brigadier
> Count de Montholon gravely displeases us. Why was not the
> commandant of the Metz garrison informed of the situation in
> time? The report upon the woman's history is bad, and . . .
>
> . . . hard enough to find *honest* men to supervise our supplies
> and administrative needs without having continuously to
> inspect their private . . .
>
> . . . possible improprieties. In his present employment, we do
> not suppose this blotched matrimony will do serious harm . . .
>
> . . . to give rise to talk in the Metz garrison would be an
> undesirable . . .
>
> . . . a similar post elsewhere. Find him something *inside
> France*, lest foreign citizens of our Empire have occasion to . . .
>
> . . . and nowhere in the Paris district, mark you. No operas
> and café society for *him* . . .
>
> . . . scandal in a most sensitive department of the army: his
> erstwhile gazetting to the diplomatic branch is herewith
> revoked. We wish him also to know that his marriage is
> disallowed, that is to say *unrecognised*. To cancel the registered
> contract would bring our magistracy into disrepute, so they
> remain man and wife; but neither of them need look for further
> favours.
>
> In reply to your submissions as to the military prison at
> Vincennes . . .

This document arrived blackened with fire and portions of it quite
burned away. The courier had been caught between two houses that
collapsed in a blazing Moscow street: he narrowly escaped with his life.

6

If Albine had felt Touraine to be a desert, what was she going to think of the barren hillsides of the Cévennes? For that was where Montholon was eventually posted.

Before he received his papers, however, he and his bride had to spend an unconscionable time in a barracks on the outskirts of the capital – he had been ordered out of Metz at six hours' notice, and now once again this delay! He made the most of his new brevet-rank; but 'operas and café society' were well beyond his means. He tried to improve the latter by regular attendance at gaming-saloons, where he lost more than he won. Albine did not accompany him on these excursions: she had been there too often in the past, too many people would know her, she was genuinely anxious not to create an embarrassment. Despite every fit-and-start of wounding misadventure, she rejoiced in her marriage, she was determined to keep it sound, she showed constant solicitude for Charles-Tristan's lovely body and his limping career. She knew this to be foolish; she was happy to be a fool. Moreover she was happy, beyond all checks of common sense, to be carrying Charles-Tristan's child.

During one of his disappointing *vingt-et-un* evenings, Montholon for the first time in his life was seriously challenged upon a question of political principle. For the first time in his life he became acquainted with political intrigue.

A man of late middle age, quite unknown to him, wearing civilian clothes (a shabby grey caped overcoat, a frayed old black scarf, a very bad top hat), condoled with him on his losses and offered to buy him a bottle of cognac to 'set him in good heart on his road back to barracks'. A fellow with the look and manners of a disgraced sergeant-major, decidedly out of place in an exclusive establishment; yet Montholon had already noticed that several senior officers there did not disdain to be on courteous terms with him.

So he said yes to the drink, and they sat down at a secluded table. The stranger made conversation about disturbing news from Russia – it was rumoured, he asserted, that the Grand Army was preparing to move west, away from Moscow in the wrong direction, and no one in Paris could say why – Montholon expressed doubts as to the truth of this, but was professedly doubtful about the doubts – then the man suddenly fell silent, scratching his grizzled moustache.

His next remarks were hoarse and nasty, as though impelled through twisted lips by a muscular action of disgust: 'Someone told me, brigadier, that this highfalutin noble title of yours is by way of being a *mask*, dammit; you don't give a shit for it, who does? it wasn't awarded you by the Emperor, it's not sewn into your uniform – but you'll use it when you think it's useful – like a jemmy to a cracksman, yes? like in here, like to bamboozle this turdy crowd of gold lace and snot-noses who'd never admit, no not at all, by no means, that their mothers gave birth to 'em in pigsties . . . Someone told me. Is it true? If it's not, I'll say goodnight and up-your-shite-hole.' He rose to his feet, perhaps drunk; but his eyes were precisely focused.

Montholon was disconcerted. The stranger's words were from the same jealous bag as the sarcasms of that general who'd been so rude at headquarters. But the general had spoken to ensure swift obedience – behaved in fact *like* a rude general, and there were plenty of them in the service. This man on the other hand showed no apparent motive, except to make Montholon feel guilty. Why? Resenting every single circumstance that currently oppressed him, and therefore careless of his tongue (the cognac may have had something to do with it too), Montholon crouched forward over his glass, glared upwards, red-faced, at his interlocutor, and announced in a savage whisper: 'I'd have you know I'm a republican, always have been, always will be. What the devil is it to you what I am?'

The other, still on his feet and gripping the back of his chair, bent his face close toward Montholon's. He grinned, revealing a stench-pit of a mouth only one-third full of uneven yellow teeth. 'Nothing in the world,' he growled. 'Unless you can answer me three questions—

'One, why is our new Empress the niece of Marie-Antoinette? It makes her a sort of Bourbon, don't it? by marriage-kin if not direct blood, and therefore her young son, who's the Emperor's young son, will come to the throne as a sort of Bourbon too – won't he? There'll be no need at all for the foul fat old bugger they call Louis XVIII. You looking forward to that day?

'Two. If it *is* true that the Emperor can't destroy the Russian army, can he fetch his *own* army home again? And what size will it be when it gets here?

'Three (and that's the lot): why d'you think I said "his own army"? Why not "the army of France"?

'Don't answer me now; or rather, don't answer me if you think it might be dangerous. If you haven't an answer, or you *don't* think your answer's dangerous, open your arse and spray it around the world; call on these buggers here to clap me in irons for treason. But remember what *you* said before *I* put the questions: "republican", right?'

He was slowly forcing Montholon, by sheer intensity of his gaze, to meet him eye-to-eye. Montholon sat paralysed, the rabbit in front of the python; eyes met and held; then the stranger looked away. 'Good,' he said quietly, 'good. Not a cheep out of you. And what a public place we're in for a loyal sod to show his loyalty. Why don't you go home to bed? You're stoney-broke, you're pissed. Sleep on it, sonny; and when you wake, *keep* awake. You may need your wits about you sooner than you think.'

He moved quickly away, to be accosted by a major of hussars with a brassy laughing woman on his arm. The major, drunk and hearty, cried, 'Colonel, you'll split a bottle?' and the stranger swore a curse and accepted.

This was queer and far from amusing. Montholon concluded it was indeed time for bed. On his way out of the saloon he buttonholed a waiter. 'The man in the grey coat there, the one with the broken teeth – d'you know who he is?'

'Of course, brigadier, yes: it is Colonel Boutreux, a most heroical officer, so they say, sir. After his wounds he's been unfit for service, so they say. We see quite a lot of him here. It's a shame really, isn't it, sir?'

'Shame? Yes, very possibly, "shame" would be the word. Shame.' Muttering to himself, 'Shame,' Montholon wove his way into the street and fumbled for coins for a cab. There were not enough of them, his pockets were all but empty; he must walk.

He kept this experience from Albine; but she found out about it only the next day. She was buying the morning milk and bread in a street outside the barrack-gate, when she recognised the woman standing next to her at the baker's counter. Fifi, a brassy old friend, a jolly trollop (in fact the hussar's companion of the gaming-house the night before), whom Albine would have much preferred not to have met; or if she did have to meet her, anywhere else but here. Fifi had never had a sou's-worth of tact – a compromising situation, to her, was just a joke. She cornered Albine, discovered she was married and to whom she was married, made several bawdy comments on the rigours of matrimony, expressed alarm as to Albine's pregnancy ('Good God, love, a baby in barracks! and you call yourself a countess? Lord, you can do better than that. If you want the brat *dropped*, Fifi can fix it, you know. No? Suit yourself, dear . . .'); after rattling on for a minute, she paused, and became serious.

'Tell me, dear, this Charlie-T, or whatever his name is, how deep is he into politics?'

'As far as I know, he's not into them at all.'

'Oh, but he is, dear. He was last night anyway. And very funny politics, I can tell you. An old devil with a face like a rhino who can't find his way back to the zoo. If your friend, dear, 's been led to think he's about to re-copulate with the virgin Revolution, just you let him know there's not a virgin left in France – Fifi talks from experience, dear – Fifi knows the brave Boutreux from a hell of a long list of wasted years. Whatever he's at now, there's more than republicans in it. Bourbon monarchists, of the dirtiest sort, they'll *all* be in charge of that rotten little coup.'

'*Coup?*' Albine was so startled she dropped a yard of bread.

Fifi hurriedly caught herself up: 'No, I didn't mean "coup", I meant— Don't you worry your pretty ribbons about what I might have meant, I never said it. I'll have to leave you now, dear: the galloping major wants his breakfast, silly man! but he's at least had the sense to wangle a rented apartment, we don't have to slum it in barracks. Poor you.'

Over Montholon's breakfast, Albine told him the tale. He turned as white as the inside of the loaf. 'You've no business to know this!'

'Neither have you,' she snapped. 'Who's Boutreux?'

'I haven't the least idea.'

'Stay that way.' She was peremptory; he was frightened; he promised her faithfully, no repetition. Moreover, he meant it.

He was put to the test a week afterwards. Colonel Boutreux secured the escape from house-arrest of the inept but fanatical old secret-society revolutionist, General Claude-François de Malet; and Montholon gave no help to either of them, although he knew they expected it.

Simply *because* he knew, his position was not as difficult as otherwise it might have been. The orderly-officer of the barracks was called to the gate at crack of dawn, to find Malet there on horseback between two spectacular outriders (one of them Boutreux): a grim trio of hoar-headed dogfaces in the fullest of full dress, cocked hats, plumes, embroidered baldrics – and, amazingly, tricolour sashes, a garniture not seen on a soldier's uniform since 1804. Malet held a document, a most official-looking document; he read it out. It purported to be a proclamation from the Senate that, due to the 'tragic but criminally irresponsible death near Moscow of the self-crowned "emperor" Napoleon', a provisional government was now formed upon the principles of 1793, the minister of police was under arrest, the prefect of police was under arrest, the infant heir to the throne was formally displaced on account of his mother's reactionary connections, and all garrisons of the Paris district were to mobilise to secure law-and-order in the city.

The orderly-officer called the commandant, the commandant called all the officers, the troops were paraded, the terrible (and yet exhilarating) news was announced to them, and their immediate duties assigned. Most of the men said, 'Thank God. Maybe an end to this fucking war then?' Some of them said, 'Let's have a guillotine.' Only a few said, 'The Emperor *dead*? Sacred Christ, it is the end of France.' (Bear in mind, these were new conscripts; the enthusiasts, the veterans, were eastward with the Grand Army or dwindling to their deaths in Spain.)

Montholon, thanks to his wife's warning, had slipped quietly out of it after the preliminary officers'-orders meeting; his work was in an office at the back of the building; he did not normally attend the parades. Thus he alone of the garrison (save for some cookhouse and sanitary-detail personnel) avoided taking a mass oath to maintain the new government. When Malet's imposture, later in the day, was uncovered by another general more astute than the rest, Montholon was easily in the clear. Indeed, he was congratulated by the Paris GOC.

Old Malet was arrested and shot, Boutreux was shot, a number of others were shot. Montholon toiled through a dismal six months in the Cévennes; but at last he received a most welcome promotion, a reward for his survivalist instinct – his brevet-rank made substantive (the full pay of a brigadier was not to be sneezed at) and his services put once again at the easygoing disposal of the Diplomatic Branch. He knew it had been a near thing.

7

Albine was able to live like a lady. Not perhaps like a countess, the brigadier's pay did not run quite so far, and there was an ominous backlog of debt. But here she was, in Paris, with an elegant apartment overlooking the river, and a husband who had now most happily been given a job at the Imperial Court. It was a run-of-the-mill bureaucratic job which did not afford him any sort of access to the Emperor's presence; nonetheless, he was a soldier-*courtier*; he had to dress very well for it; his wife had to dress well; and (much the best of all) she was accepted without question as his *genuine* wife and the tradesmen all knew it and extended exemplary credit. The strictness of social standards had bent to the necessities of military collapse.

After the splendid Grand Army had fallen to pieces, bone by frozen bone, in the nightmare of the Russian snows, its leader knew that his followers' loyalty was no longer to be taken for granted. The Malet coup had appalled him when he read the reports (beyond Smolensk, in his sledge, in the midst of that first overpowering blizzard): it so nearly succeeded. Any officer, like Montholon, who had shown himself staunch, was excused almost anything. Marriage to an underbred whore became a laughable triviality. Disobedience to orders concerning the marriage meant only that the defaulter had improvised, securing his own base as he best knew how. No matter that his choice of tactic was imprudent: the Emperor himself was now improvising as wildly as when he was young, the Emperor himself was uncommonly aware of the possibility of imprudent mistakes.

But what of the marriage? Their baby, a boy, had been born in icy lodgings in the primitive hillside town of Cassagnas in the coldest January known to the Cévennes for a generation. The midwife was drunk; Albine suffered terribly. One night, back in Paris, she turned upon her husband and told him: 'No more. I thought in Cassagnas I was surely going to die. If you have to keep on fucking, fuck somebody other than me.' Romantic love had not lasted now that hardships were no longer to be shared. It must have fallen off the coach somewhere along the heavy lurching journey from the sources of the Loire to the house-crowded quays of the Seine.

The centre of Paris, for Albine, was agreeable, civilised, amusing, extremely comfortable – and an emotional desert. She met her friends and chattered scandal; her husband yawned, did his work with fidelity but no great energy, wandered the town after dark seeking dubious and expensive pleasures. Little Maximilien was looked after by nurses, several nurses in succession, none of them entirely honest or competent. At times the baby was spoiled, at times repressed, at times neglected; he seemed doomed to grow up incorrigibly tiresome, whining and raging and breaking things, and Albine laid the blame on Charles-Tristan.

Now and then Albine took a lover. Which was perhaps inconsistent with the grounds of her refusal to sleep with her husband; but it may be assumed she took very good care to avoid any act of Eros that could possibly result in another child. Her young men did not always appreciate this; word went around that she 'baulked at her fences', that she was 'soft in the mouth and tight in the tail'; slanders appropriate to those debonair light-cavalry circles where she tended to find consolation.

By 1814 enemy armies were in France. Wellington's Peninsular troops advanced upon Toulouse, Prussians and Austrians threatened Paris along the valleys of Seine and Marne. Every fighting regiment the Emperor could muster was unmercifully deployed in subtle and brilliant counter-attacks; to small purpose. Public morale must be enkindled, and the Spirit of '93; so the Marseillaise was sung in the streets by buskers under imperial orders; revolutionary offices of local government were hastily restored, elderly republicans fetched from obscurity to fill them. But against whom in these days could a revived revolution revolt? Monarchy, nobility, church, were all firmly 'Napoleonic':

Napoleon in despair was laying his own empire under the blade of his own guillotine, and he knew it, he laughed at it, he fought on.

Montholon too laughed at it, from an embittered inflamed conscience, although to be sure he was doing no fighting. 'General Malet was impossible!' – he sometimes (to his peril) cried it aloud: 'But Malet, just conceivably, might have prevented *all this*.'

The bureaucratic job, so gratifying less than a year ago, was no longer worth the paper it consumed. His pay was in arrears. The paymaster, when challenged, threw up his hands: '*You* go and argue with the bank, brigadier; if they won't cash the Emperor's cheques, why don't you assert yourself, just you tell them who you are . . .?'

So Montholon, in Paris, drank and drank and went brothel-crawling. Perhaps because his wife was older than he was, and reviled him as though she were *much* older, he developed an ugly taste in his debauches. The younger the girls the better, and if boy-children as well, so much the better again. One house above all others, *le Pavillon aux Anges Sucrés*: it held a little theatre for choreographed 'exhibitions', every customer secluded in his own ornate box so that none of them could see the others; and an orchestra, of white-faced dead-eyed ten-year-olds in *Commedia dell'Arte* costumes, to play recorders and drums and bells and sing songs that sounded like nursery-rhymes until one actually listened to the words.

Now Montholon had a stepfather, an émigré of the old regime, the Count de Semonville. They had of course never met; Semonville had made his home in England with Montholon's mother, who died while her son was at Würzburg. A formal and contemptuous letter, sent by the stepfather through curious byways of wartime communication, announced her death to Montholon, making no comment on it, passing on no affectionate message: ice-cold factual statement composed in the third person. Montholon did not care. He was in Albine's arms when he read the letter; he said only, 'It would have been grievous news, had it emanated from Poitiers. As it is . . . lie on your side, and we'll do it again, *this* way . . .'

Towards midnight on March 12th, 1814, the very day, by coincidence, that the British navy brought the advance party of Louis XVIII's government out of their English refuge into Bordeaux, Montholon sat in a box at the *Anges Sucrés*, listening to the music and waiting for the show to begin; *les Ballets Roses* was its prurient name; boy and girl dancers, rigorously trained, none of them older than thirteen. He was very tired, depressed, eaten with rage at the depravity he smelt all around him. Nothing, he told himself in impotent frenzy, could have been quite as bad as this before the Revolution, no, not even in the days of Louis XV. If a towering angry priest, a modern Savonarola, had thrust himself suddenly upon the tiny rococo stage to denounce the sinful doings and roar for an instant repentance, Montholon (ingrained atheist) would have fallen to his knees and wept for joy. But such a priest never came, nor would come; Montholon just sat there and caressed his groin, and waited for the sweet little slave-children. His own son had taken his first wavering steps just a fortnight before.

He heard a movement at his back; he swung round in alarm and anger; he had called for no service by the bell-pull beside his chair – who dared thus intrude upon high-priced privacy? The management of this house was falling damnably short of its standards – who? – what? He began to bluster.

Behind him was an inner alcove, with a bed in it: and a man on the bed, unbelievable! reclining there indolently, a long pale white-haired man with a young face, bespectacled and dressed in humble black like a secretary. But his attitude was far from humble: he lay as though he owned the whole building.

The man said, 'Ssh. You'll be heard above the music. Come and sit with me among these cushions. You'll still get your full view of the darlings. You can watch and feed your eyes while we talk. Because we do have to talk and there are altogether too many spies in this city: I thought, do you see? this would be the best place. I told the proprietor to bring you neither Laïsette nor Ganymède until we've finished our conversation and I'm gone. He does what I tell him; and so, I daresay, will you. I am sent, do you see? by the Count de Semonville.'

How the devil did he finger the very names? Why, Montholon himself had not decided which of the brothel-children he would send for. Yet without doubt those two small faces had already crossed his mind.

And Semonville? Where *was* Semonville?

'Not in Paris, brigadier; he was in London when he last spoke to me. But *I* am in Paris and you can trust me as you would trust him. He is now a close associate of His Royal Highness the Count d'Artois.'

This was news, and disturbing news. His Royal Highness, the most *ultra* of all the reactionaries, was said to be the driving force behind the entire Bourbon party; left to himself, their 'Rightful King' Louis would muddle along benevolently and do nobody too much harm. But Artois, the younger brother, wanted France, the whole of France, to sprawl at his feet to be punished, amid cries to the Roman Church for pardon in the name of God, hot tears of a drastic anchorite in a cloister of self-mortification. If the Bourbons were restored (and each day it seemed more likely), Artois would seek and find every irreconcilable Bonapartist, every ancient Jacobin, and screw them tight in the wine-press of his vengeance. The very thought of the man was a hideous gripe to the bowels.

And here was his messenger, seated close upon a bed with Montholon, his arm about Montholon's shoulder, complacently watching seventeen naked and beplumed children who gyrated like full-grown harlots. Seen from the back of the alcove, they had the remote inhuman quality of garishly lit clockwork puppets in a miniature peepshow. 'Your stepfather has heard of what you did – or rather didn't do – in regard to General Malet. He assumes – is he right? – that Robespierre is no longer your idol. But he also knows that neither is Bonaparte. Bonaparte is finished; that is obvious to anyone. Bonaparte will be replaced. The legitimate monarchy requires his replacement made easy. The legitimate monarchy will be a very generous patron to all those who will fulfil such requirement. You may think it difficult to secure your peace with your stepfather. He is prejudiced against you, as is natural.'

He paused and breathed heavily. The flow of the children's dance just then was particularly piquant. He dug his fingers, long strong claws, into Montholon's arm and his other hand crept upon Montholon's thigh. Montholon held his eyes fixedly forward, watching the children, sweating, shivering.

The messenger continued: 'As is natural. Is *this* natural? Of course it is, once you rid yourself of preconceived ideas. These darlings are not old enough to have preconceived their *own* ideas. Under your touch when they come in here, they are *shaped*, are they not? to whatever form of pleasure you may pump from the cesspit of your soul.'

The messenger's mouth was close to Montholon's cheek, stirring his soft whiskers, a wet musky breath, a flickering tongue.

'Charles-Tristan, what you must do is to let me tell your stepfather that you are henceforward His Royal Highness's man, as bound to him in love and duty as *you* expect these darlings to be bound to you here tonight when you name them and send for them. Ganymède, the miniature blackamoor; Laïsette, is she a Swede? your bond-servants for an hour, bought and paid for, lavishly. Your stepfather, returning to France, to his ancestral estates, will forgive you all your trespasses. He may even ensure that you are made a full general. But you have to be *obedient.*'

With a sudden wrench he tore at Montholon's crotch, twisting the turgid genitals like an artisan forcing a padlock.

Montholon gave a cry—

'Ssh!' hissed the messenger, 'Ssh . . . Men will think in the dark your little lusts are unmanageable. And everything these days can be, must be, managed. Would you know the most useful way of managing your present affair, your betrayal of your Bonaparte? you can surely do no better than follow the instructions of the Prince of Benevento, so-called.' (He meant Talleyrand, the discredited minister, widely known to be intriguing with the Bourbons, yet virtually uncatchable in his treasons.) 'He will effect his own contact with you, whenever it suits him; keep awake and *be obedient.*'

Once again the agonising grip, the cruel twist. A skinny yellow-haired girl was lifted up among the dancers, erect, her fragile arms stretched above her head; she sang a shrill little song about fishes, slowly turning her palms in the air like strands of pale waterweed.

'Ah, but that is beautiful! Laïsette herself. So now I am away; I only come to watch, d'you see?' He slid from the bed and, as he did so, bent suddenly down again to Montholon's ear, with – 'When we say *obedience,* we do of course include your lady. You have Laïsette, Albine has her current horse-captain, the horse-captain has a wife. Such trouble such revelations could cause.' With a jerk of his head, he bit Montholon deep in the ear-lobe; the blood flowed down Montholon's collar.

In that instant of pain the strange man must have gone from the alcove. Or had he even been there? was he a living man at all? or—?

One of the servants of the house came to consult the brigadier's wishes. Montholon could only say to her, 'You are old enough to be my mother, I sometimes think you *are* my mother, you are a devil out of hell and a fit mate for the white hair and those eyeglasses. Your bill for what I've seen and I'll pay at the door; I'm leaving, damn you, *now.*'

8

Montholon did prove obedient; along with many other officers and civilian functionaries. He hung close to Talleyrand's hem when the Emperor abandoned Paris and the Prussians and the Austrians (and indeed the Russians) moved in, eliding himself smoothly into the new Bourbon order. The Emperor abdicated, Talleyrand announced himself provisional head of state, Louis XVIII was officially proclaimed. The Emperor was allowed Elba, the smallest of his dominions, to live in and rule: an 'absolute sovereignty', a mockery of regal power. He begged his wife, Marie-Louise the Austrian, to come and rule it with him; to bring their son, young Napoleon, three years of age. They never came; he never saw them again; her father had gathered them in, to Vienna, to political quarantine, Catholic, legitimate, the old world before the flood. The Bonapartes and all they stood for were to be wiped out of history.

While all this was going on, Montholon became aware of a vernacular innovation. The monarchist-ultras were referred to as *radical*; whereas those who still maintained the Jacobin ideal were called *conservatives* and in his heart he knew himself one of them. 'Conservative'? he was not yet thirty-two, and now he was marked – to anyone who could read his mind – as more or less senile.

But then they couldn't read his mind. Not even Albine. His stepfather's uncanny messenger had apparently feared that Albine might defy her husband's change of coat. He was wrong. When Montholon very carefully let her in upon his plans while the court fell to confusion in every corridor and cubby-hole of the palace, she smiled and said nothing: except, 'A man would be a damned fool to refuse his stepfather's patronage. I suppose he's rich, this sneering Semonville? It's time we bought a carriage and pair.'

Her young 'horse-captain', like her husband, became a most fulsome Bourbonist: upon both flanks her life was secure. What better could be looked for when a great nation loses a war?

Semonville may have been rich, but he gave Montholon no money. He took one look at Albine, sniffed, bowed extravagantly, and excused himself 'from burdening any further with my cumbersome presence the charming lady's hours of conversation'. As the Montholons were in *his* apartments when he said it, it could only be understood as 'take yourselves off and don't bloody well come back'. The promotion to full general did however arrive; together with a responsible post in charge of a division of the army's Pay and Accounts Department. For the Diplomatic Branch, as supervised by Talleyrand (who was grabbing all the respectability he could acquire), was to be stuffed with ex-émigrés of unimpeachable Bourbon credentials: foreign governments would need to be reassured.

The Count d'Artois was now officially known as 'Monsieur'; the traditional title of the eldest of the king's brothers. He effectively kept his own court, and anything important to be done in the realm was organised from Monsieur's private cabinet. His secretary (an elderly priest, sidelong and superficially diffident) sent formal word to Montholon to be present at what amounted to a royal levée. Monsieur was gracious, almost affable, a tall mule-faced self-congratulatory pillar of cold steel, white-haired and approaching sixty, wearing a blaze of orders

on the breast of a very narrow frock-coat that came down to the middle
of his calves. His stance was so upright that he looked over everybody's
heads; but he did condescend to meet the eyes of Montholon (probably
because he had been told he would not find them candid, and he wished
to be sure of his man). He said, to the secretary, 'See that the general is
properly instructed as to his informal duties,' and then to Montholon,
with a headmasterly smile, 'His Most Christian Majesty will abundantly
reward every proof of your loyalty, general; I am sure he will find no
lack of occasion so to do. You are heartily welcome to the service of the
New France, a kingdom that has rediscovered its soul.'

Later, in the secretary's office, the 'informal duties' were made clear.
Montholon was to prepare dossiers upon his colleagues and subordinates in Pay and Accounts, with particular reference to their previous
service (Napoleonic, revolutionary, or émigré), to their casually
expressed political opinions, to their assiduity or otherwise in attendance at weekly Mass, to their tendency to drink or gamble, to their
sexual morals. He was driven to protest: 'Sexual morals? You mean I am
expected to uncover bedroom gossip for Monsieur? Surely, reverend
sir—'

'General, you – ah – misunderstand, not gossip, no. Ah, facts. Ah,
consider now, general, there are, oh dear, houses in Paris, deeply
iniquitous houses, flying in the face of God – not only women but, ah,
men and even children – regularly prostituted. It should not be
impossible, by calculated turns of talk, ah, and *other more complex
expedients*, to discover – to elucidate – if any of your fellow officers – do
they know of these dens? frequent them? The police of course are on
the watch; but the police are not yet, ah, fully reformed – bribes, you see,
general, oh dear yes. Your information will serve as a – as a check upon
their reports, useful, most useful.'

Oh, it was transparent: Montholon's vices were no secret from
Monsieur's staff, quite a different matter from the stepfather's messenger and a damnable thing to think of. But was this cleric warning him
off, or was he in fact encouraging him to continue his visits to (say) the
Anges Sucrés, to frequent the loathly place as a spy? Difficult. Montholon
thought it over, and then over again. Maybe best to take things easily –
one or two emollient reports, just to show he was alert – confirming the
soundness of, for example, Colonel A. who was prominent in the
Corpus Christi procession, or Major B. who always kept a lithograph of
His Most Christian Majesty over his desk – and so forth . . .

It may be thought that Montholon, now that he was settled in a
peacetime career in comparatively good odour, would not need his vices

any more. At gambling-saloon and child-brothel he had experienced disquieting encounters; he had indeed determined to avoid both classes of resort for at least a considerable period. Which left him only the dram-shops. And his hangover every morning in Pay and Accounts was eventually bound to be noticed. And yet he could not go home, to endure the cruel sarcasms or the silent secret laughter of Albine. He did not exactly hate her: quite simply – *he had ceased to know her, and yet he feared she still knew him*. It was shocking to live in marriage while keeping constant guard upon his tongue.

He dared not even talk to her about what he felt was his one Good Deed – his successful prevention of the trial of his foster-father, the Poitiers grocer, upon charges of subverting the state. The old fellow had apparently gone mad, and flown the tricolour from his shopfront the very day that King Louis was proclaimed. Montholon only heard of it several months afterwards when one of the grocer's daughters found out where he lived and came crying to him, for God's sake, for the sake of old times, to get her father out of gaol – 'They are saying, if he's convicted, they will send him to the galleys, oh please, oh please, Charles-Tristan, remember your *own family*!' He was stricken with a true instinct, of pity and love, and of 'loyalty' as it ought to be; he went running to Monsieur's office, he besought the sidelong secretary, a personal favour if nothing else, to have the process dropped – 'After all, it was only an emotional outburst, the man is aged, an invalid, no longer in office in Poitiers, and his business (I understand) is very near bankrupt!'

The secretary took snuff, cleared his throat, opened and closed his missal. He murmured something into his hand about 'duties unfulfil-led', about 'establishments of insidious sin', and – in unexpectedly down-to-earth terms – how 'one good turn deserved another'.

Montholon took the hint, went that night to the *Anges Sucrés*, the next night to three card-houses, and sent in reports upon the clientèle of all of them. (He had to improvise about the *Anges*, where there was no public space in which to meet other people; only a cloakroom where he observed coats and hats and made various guesses.) The following week he received a brief note from the secretary: the prosecution of the seditious grocer was not to proceed, an act of special mercy by the minister of police – but General Montholon *must* guarantee the future good conduct of all or any of his suppositional relatives. These dangerous derelictions could not be permitted to recur.

Montholon ought to have been pleased with himself.

But the damage had been done. One footstep once again inside his old haunts and woe! he discovered he could not keep away.

In the first week of March 1815, he was on a winning streak at faro in a saloon behind the arcades of the Palais Royal: he knew he must stop, pocket his gains, get home with them at once. But no! he threw them all upon the table, lost them, and staked again – this time his bankbook for all his savings (such as they were). Had he known about Albine's fund he would certainly have staked that too. And he lost.

He very nearly went and shot himself, as indeed an officer should. But he thought about it all night, while he walked the streets sobering up, penniless; and in the end had a better idea. Next morning, in his office, he committed a forgery, embezzling six thousand francs, cash.

In the course of the afternoon that devout Catholic 'Colonel A.' detected the hapless forgery. He reported it at once to GOC Pay and Accounts. Montholon, under open arrest, went home and told Albine. How could he not? they had posted a sentinel on the landing outside his apartment. She said, 'You bloody fool, you've ruined me, you everlasting liar; and you have ruined your unhappy little son.' She went to visit a friend. She spent the whole night with a lieutenant of cuirassiers whom she just happened to meet there.

Next morning (March 5th) a courier, galloping madly, as blindly as Mazeppa, flung himself into Paris from the south: Napoleon was out of Elba, he had landed near Antibes, all the stakes were miraculously replaced on the table, there was everything to play for, everything in the whole wide world!

9

Of course at such a crisis courts-martial were not to be thought of. Able-bodied generals, left under arrest, were a manifest absurdity. The sentinel was taken away from the staircase, Montholon was ordered provisionally to resume his duties (with 'Colonel A.' as his minder): it looked as though the entire Pay and Accounts office would be mobilised and sent to the front. Except that no one knew where the front was. Every regiment despatched south to intercept the Corsican Usurper had somehow contrived to join him; all France, it appeared, was joining him. King and king's brother, with both of their households, prepared to take flight. Talleyrand sat in Vienna, conferring with the victors of the previous year; unable to do anything but stay there and cagily commit himself to the foundering Bourbons. So Montholon could not consult him.

Whom *could* he consult, but Albine?

Albine lay back and lifted her chin, staring at him from her Grecian chaise-longue, as cool as a great lady in a portrait by Ingres, her breasts half-revealed in a low-cut gown, a provocative ribbon round her throat, one small golden feather curling from her velvet headband. If her get-up was deliberate, to demonstrate total indifference to her husband's plight, she could not have effected it better nor chosen a more insolent pose. He thought: 'This is the end.'

Maximilien (now two-and-a-quarter years old) cried tiresomely in the nursery across the hall; the nurse could be heard remonstrating, smacking him, redoubling his wails. Albine's little black cat, scared away by the tumult, ran into the drawing-room and leaped upon its mistress's knee.

A long silence. And then, as she stroked the cat and murmured to it, subduing its alarm, Albine decided to surprise the beastly man. She was not at all indifferent, she had been thinking very hard, she knew exactly what to do. 'I don't ask what the hell you were after, all those nights upon town, but you've told me about the last of 'em, it was enough to bring my dinner up. I'll talk no more of it: except to say this – as a result of your *ramblings*, you owe the army six thousand francs. Not King Louis's army, not the Emperor's army, but the army of France. It's changing its allegiance, which is what armies do; but it still needs to pay its soldiers. Whoever's in command of it, he's going to want that six thousand. So if you really thought you can change *your* allegiance, put on for a second time your Bonaparte sash, I can tell you – you can't. There's only one thing for you. Run.'

'Where to?' He sat, shoulders hunched, on a low stool; he looked down at his boots, his voice cracking with despair.

'Abroad, probably. Don't ask me where abroad. All Europe seems bent on fighting the Emperor – already from Vienna they've declared him an international outlaw. Anywhere in Europe you'll get mixed up with armies, and I think you'd better not. Try the United States. Every wanted criminal ends up in the United States, even your friend Talleyrand had to live for a time in Philadelphia. Well?'

'Christ, this is fatuous. How can I possibly go to America?'

'Then don't go to America. Go to Touraine. You've a very cosy château, or don't you remember? You can pretend to be ill again. I daresay it'll be some time before they come after you with handcuffs; you can manage to make your peace with 'em before then. You were always good at *managing*. Weren't you?'

'Touraine is impossible too; I cannot afford even to *keep* the château. I'm going to have to sell it, just to live.'

'To live in Paris, do you mean? watching every day for the provost-marshal at your door? Under no circumstances, Charles-Tristan, will I permit you to live in Paris. Touraine, or I'm done with you.'

'Done?' he bleated. 'Done? But I thought you *were* done with me – I thought that this, today, was the last – the last—'

'The last talk we'd ever have? My God, I wish it was. My God, I wish, just once, you'd have stood up like a man and *told us who you were*. If you had refused the Bourbons, I'd have backed you right up to wherever it led, bankruptcy, exile, gaol. And if now you'd refuse Napoleon, I would back you there as well. As a Bonapartist or a Jacobin, one or the other, you'd be honest, you'd be mine. You still have the chance. And I'll give you the chance. But not yet. Don't expect me to back you over six thousand stolen francs, don't expect me to believe you took them to subvert the regime.

'Do what I say: come to Touraine, and wait till you know what you're doing. Because I don't think you *have* known, since – since the day you ran in with Boutreux. If you had not met that man, I could have – could have – I don't know what I could have done with you – but I loved you then. I can't forget it. Come to Touraine.'

He might have noticed the tears in her eyes but he didn't.

Wearily he repeated that Touraine was impossible; did she want him to walk there? why, he had not the money for the coach; the entire six thousand had gone on his gambling debts. At that her whole countenance changed, and she laughed like Maximilien receiving a treat. *She* had the money, she said, and laughed again. Her cousin was holding it; but her cousin was revealed as a damned Bourbon lackey – had been for the past twelve months – he was running away, fast, with all the other Bourbons, and Napoleon's crowd were bound to indict him for treason. (This very afternoon she'd been trawling the town to find out about it.) His legal identity would be null and void within the week. Mind you, she could claim the fund only in the name of her husband, and the name of her husband might not be any good because of the six thousand – and yet was it not true that the question of the six thousand was noted down only in *military* charge-sheets? The civil courts had no cognisance, not until the army thought to serve them the proper documents, and that would take ages – in the present state of emergency, who on earth would have the time to attend to it?

'Are you sure, are you sure?' gasped Montholon, utterly amazed. 'It never crossed my mind! Where did you hear it?'

'From a very very helpful young lawyer. You tell me how you've been spending your evenings, *I'll* tell you what I did to render him helpful.'

'This isn't a matter for jokes.'

'Everything's a matter for jokes. Except we don't seem to have made any, not for two years and more. So maybe there *is* no cause to laugh. But on Wednesday the money is mine, and it'll keep us in Touraine until – until somehow I can say that *you're* mine. You. I loved you, and I loved you, and I loved you . . . Don't touch me.'

He'd had his hand upon her bosom, his mouth toward her lips, he had thought, for an instant, that she – no. He would have to wait, and she meant him to wait. But at least she had the cash. She had saved him.

10

Montholon slept in a closet called the 'guest-room' while Albine had the marital bed next door to the nursery. Sometimes (supposing she were at home and not too tired) she would get up to deal with Maximilien when he cried; usually she left it to the nurse who slept in the nursery itself. The little boy's night-time fretfulness gave a tacit excuse for the separation of beds; there'd been no spoken decision that husband and wife should lie alone. Montholon, sleepless, swam it about in his brain: once they got to the château, one bed for the pair of them, no discussion, no questions, just the arrangement they had had there in the old days. Undressing one another for love. *Voluptuous.*

Meanwhile, he must see (if at last they were to be jolly together) how jokes about nights-upon-town could be evaded or turned sideways, made harmless. It was no great disgrace for Albine to imply that her lawyer was her lover. Many husbands allowed far worse. But one thing led to the next; a huge horror came over him of what she would say if ever she found out about the *Anges.*

All hope of reconcilement would be lost.

He thought (as he often thought) of his own small son in such a den. And of what he would do to the man or men who'd *use* him there. His bright-eyed leaping child whom he so callously neglected – named of course, and compromisingly, after Maximilien Robespierre, a sort of vicarious compensation for the fiasco of the Malet coup – strike it from his brain, strike! The house of the *Anges* was in the past.

Even the gaming-house was in the past. The future was Albine and the gentle green countryside. Albine and her beautiful money.

He sat straight up in bed.

For years she had deceived him; he'd heard nothing about the money. *And now she could only have it if she applied for it under seal of his name.* Married woman's goods and gold, vested in the husband, by—?

He knew well what by: the Napoleonic Code, imperial fiat! deleting the egalitarian principles of the true-revolutionary laws that were drafted in '93 – and *he* was the husband and he had believed – until now – that this trickery of a Code was devised for a husband's advantage . . .

Without *her* he could not live. But without *him* – why, she *had* to pretend that she loved him. Sacred God! she hated him still. All her reconcilement was a *sham*.

And a sham he had no choice but to accept. She had worked him into a corner. 'Management'? Oh yes: how shrewdly, how secretly, she had *managed*. He was now as much her bondman as ever he had been to that unicorn-horn of an Artois. He rolled in the bed, he clenched his fists, bent his knees, jerked them out straight again, he groaned and he wallowed. And he dreamed the most foul dreams. Of Laïsette. Of plump-buttocked little black Ganymède with a bloodstained pair of pliers. (How had Laïsette grown those ten triple-pronged forks where her fingernails ought to have been?) Whirlpools of dreams. Ropes and spiked chains and the old brothel-bawd pulling them tight – his mother? and was she not also the mother of his babe? Horror – and no sense to it. He was *managed*, he was bound.

11

But all these inner rages were without open voice. He brought her under spring sunshine to Touraine; tried to seize the voluptuous chance; tried to live there soft and still, the stillness of the pond by the broken-down old watermill behind the château stable-yard.

It was a mid-afternoon of mid-May and bright flies danced from one shining water lily to the next. At the far end of the pond stood a deep bed of bullrushes; impenetrable brambles, and thorn-bushes full of blossom, crowded down to the brink but curved back for a few yards to leave a patch of warm green grass, the shape of a horse's hoof; dandelions and daisies and late primroses all over it; bluebells in flower; the sombre woods reared up behind, half a mile of them. This corner was protected from the sudden glance of strangers by the rushes or the trees. A rug had been spread on the grass, and Albine lay there bare as Venus, bold as Pope Joan, luxuriating in the sun. She and Montholon had first bathed and then made love; afterwards one of his dark fits of melancholy had crept over him; he had dressed himself and wandered off.

(She was saying nothing these days about not wishing to be made pregnant; she was not saying *why* she said nothing; Montholon was too lecherous to enquire.)

In the distance, in the overgrown garden the other side of the château, Maximilien played with his nurse – Zoé, a good-natured young woman from the village, who had taken the place of the cantankerous Paris servant and was a great deal more suited to her job. Albine could hear their laughter; they were quite out of sight; everyone, every thing, was quite out of sight. Except the flies, and they were a nuisance. She raised herself sharply to flap at them with a bunch of young green fern.

'Oh, madam, my God! I did not see.'

Her movement had brought her upwards, head and shoulders higher than a nearby clump of brambles that extended to meet the bullrushes. It was a man, just come out of the wood (just? he could have been there ten minutes), gazing at her in what he made out to be red-faced embarrassment. She pulled the rug to cover herself; he turned his head aside. He was about half a dozen years younger than Charles-Tristan, tall, swarthy, with a thin black moustache. He wore the blue and red uniform and the wide cocked hat of a captain of gendarmerie. He was not at all handsome, there were pockmarks on his face and the white scar of a sword-cut; even so, he was pleasant to look at, a humorous lad (she guessed) from the way he had spoken. His gesture of apology was something of a burlesque – he did not *need* to feign a blindfold with his hand.

'Would you look at me, sir, please? I am draped, you may do so.'

'Madam, I take it you are the Countess de Montholon? I came to see your husband, by way of the short cut, may I assure you I had no idea that—'

'What do you want him for?' She heard her voice break with anxiety, which would never do. He was only a policeman, she was a lady of title. (She was a lady of title conniving at crime; she must be cautious, very cautious.) 'I cannot, at this moment, tell you exactly where he is. May *I* take your message? I'd be glad to.' That was better; but she should not have stood. The rug was in danger of slipping.

'I'm sure you would – when I tell you I don't want to arrest him. There *are* those that might want. Six thousand francs? But no immediate warrant; and I've come to try to help. Perhaps you'd care to sit down again? If you don't mind, I'll sit with you. I've had a very hot ride.'

He was gentlemanly enough, but far too familiar. It puzzled her and she missed her chance to tell him to keep his distance. Damn him, he was squatting already in the bluebells, a puck, an elf, a leering woodwose.

'Also,' he continued, 'the quieter we keep ourselves, the better. The times are insecure, and politics are still very doubtful.'

Politics?

'Go on. Say what you have to say. I don't like this at all.'

'Oh, don't act afraid; it's mere affectation, you know I'll not do you any harm. The uniform's my guarantee. I take it very seriously. Dishonour from an officer, dishonour to France, dishonour to the Emperor. I believe that! I'm eccentric. Moreover I believe that my foster-brother has ceased to believe it; and I hope, with your aid, to manoeuvre a change of mind.'

'Foster-brother?' What *was* this? She had of course been told something about—

'He has told you something of the grocer's shop in Poitiers? We all feared he'd forgotten about us, until he saved my father's liberty. But he saved it, you see, from within the Bourbon court, which was bloody disgusting, and so I'm here to tell him. *I* lost my place when fat Louis came back last year, and proud to lose it, no mistake. Now, Countess, what's *your* view?'

She suddenly saw her way clear. It was all very strange, but this man and herself were *chiming* together (allowing for their different starting-points); a gambler's wild guess – but was there not something she could do here to further her very purpose in having come to this place at all? Unless—

He had said 'seriously' – but why did he hide a sort of merriment all the time, even as he said it and went on to talk about honour? If he was playing with her, then her guess was not a good one, indeed it was very bad, there could be a vicious development. She noticed he was shifting himself, inch by inch, toward her. She must immediately parry – but what was the stroke she had to guard against? Try a laugh—

So she laughed. ' "Countess"? You'd better know, I'm no more a real countess than you are.'

At which *he* laughed, and his stealthy movements stopped. 'I'm aware of what you are. What you were three years ago, the time you first lived here. I wasn't in the district then, but I've found it out, through the office files. I'm aware. I needed to test you. "Talk to her like – like I'd talk to my sisters," I thought. "Discover just how much of a *Bourbon* she might think she is. As for instance would she call me 'my good man', or 'officer', or 'insolent jack-in-office'?" These little things signify; I take note of them daily; it's part of the business.'

'How'd you like me to call you?'

' "Brother-in-law", obviously. Gaius-Gracchus is my given name. Or else there's always "citizen" – would that suit? If the news I hear is true it's going to have to suit all of us. Thank God. If there is a God. "Supreme Being"? – d'you allow the Supreme Being?'

News. Unaccountably excited, she jumped forward towards him on all fours: 'News, news, what news? Tell me, tell me, before he gets back! Oh, it could be most important.'

He thrust his hand into the despatch-pouch that hung from his cross-belt, pulled out a folded paper, shook it open in front of her face. She saw an official report of some sort, the imperial stamp at the top – it was printed, and headed:

PALAIS DE JUSTICE, *Île de la Cité, Paris*
Confidential until released to the public

'You ought not to be showing me this?'

'Of course not. Highly irregular. Why else did I prowl through the wood like a bandit? But see what it says.'

It was a preliminary warning to all prefects, intendants and commissioners of police that new legislation was about to be promulgated which might (in certain areas) be productive of disorder. A constitutional monarchy with guarantees of all manner of civil liberty, a return to a number of crucial points of the Revolution, a clear diminution of the imperial pretensions, and an unstated but implied renunciation of any further adventures of conquest.

'*This* will produce disorder?'

'It is not exactly Jacobin, but there's more behind it, much more; the Bourbonists will loathe it. Don't deceive yourself, Albine, there are thousands of them still about. I am my father's son, I'm a republican-democrat, unashamed – "Gaius-Gracchus" what else? – the Empire has been a prodigious aberration, but we can't kill it in a week. Malet tried, and look what happened.'

'Look,' she said. 'Yes.' She was thinking, wondering, calculating. So much so that she ignored his use of her first name; she did not even realise that the rug had slipped again and enveloped her no more modestly than a napkin. (He failed to draw attention to it, but he saw it and enjoyed it, and yet he was still serious.)

'Oh! do you believe,' she begged, 'sincerely believe,' she begged, 'that a republican at heart could accept this *in* his heart? Even a republican who's expecting court-martial?'

'If Charles-Tristan does not accept it, we must ask him why not. If he says it's a mere sop to delude the old revolutionists, then we ask him why he thought there was something wrong with Malet. That should stop his mouth. If he says he cannot trust Napoleon, then we ask him what he believes would strengthen Napoleon to keep his word, and if he says – as he must say – "the strength of the men about him", then we have him! He is to go back to Paris and be part of that strength. The powers at Vienna are marching to destroy us. This paper in my hand is the last hope for a people's France. *That's* what they want to destroy! Citizeness, *we need your husband*. My God, he was my boyhood's hero, *I* need him, he must not flinch.'

'Very well, he goes to Paris. If not, Gaius-Gracchus – then that's it! for I'll know beyond question he's a hopping twisting corpse and be damned. Help me, help me to show him his heart.'

Such hard solemnity, all of a sudden, between the two of them. They clasped hands and knelt, face to face, statuesque: a Grecian king (perhaps) in Pentelic marble, binding a treaty with an Amazon, dug up at an Aegean temple-site and bought for a song from the Turks by a wandering dilettante who'd present it to the galleries of the Louvre.

Then a wicked hot-weather insect slid down between the rug and her rump and stung her like the jab of a bayonet. For a few seconds all was wild – she running, yelp upon yelp (rug fallen altogether to the grass), he flailing uselessly with his great hat.

Round the edge of the pond came Montholon, a straw sombrero a-tilt over one eye, his spirits very pleasantly restored; he held an opened bottle of wine and two glasses; he found his wife bent forwards moaning, golden-white among the flowers, while a black-avised catchpoll crouched intimately behind her to smear her with a finger-full of ointment. (Ointment, this incubus was telling her, that he carried always in his pouch when on his rounds in the midst of the year.)

Scarcely a scene to explain itself easily.

Had Gaius-Gracchus not been a gendarme who knew all about the six thousand francs, there might well have been a duel before everything was sorted out. But at last, by way of laughter and storms of anger and fatuous apologies and pompous bouts of sulking and earnest exhortations and tears, it *was* sorted out. Foster-brother and wife together laid every possible pressure, both generous and sneaky, upon Montholon. By suppertime he had grudgingly made up his mind, and covered his grudge with a fine show of political courage: '*Ah, ça ira!*' he declaimed. 'Paris! Tomorrow we set out, and to hell with the consequence.' As an

afterthought – 'Oh, Guy-Gracque,' (using the affectionate old diminu-
tive) 'where are you stationed, Tours? Be assured, dear old fellow, your
career; I shall put in the brotherly hint with the Emperor.'

Gaius-Gracchus grinned; he did not believe a word of it. But he now
knew all about Albine, out of her clothes and in them, and one of these
days perhaps—

He dropped an eyelid toward her; his moustache twitched. She, in
response, opened her own eyes wide and briefly lost her small smile, a
gesture (if you'd call it that) which neither rebuffed nor led him on; it
showed she understood, he had to take it as it came.

12

In fact, nearly a month passed before they set out for the capital.
Montholon had first to write some letters, to various generals of his
acquaintance, to find how the land lay; and none of them replied very
quickly. Not surprising: they had much to occupy their time beyond the
affairs of a pay-officer of dubious repute. Albine too was writing letters.
The business of her fortune was less complete than she had given
Montholon to understand: when she said that 'on Wednesday the
money was hers', she lied. What she had actually meant was that on
Wednesday her clever young lawyer would have arranged to *borrow* for
her on the strength of her expectations from the fund. He managed this
up to a point, sufficient for the visit to Touraine, but to get at the real
money was a much more complicated task.

Also, of course, there was accommodation to be fixed up: they had
had to tell their landlord to let the apartment to someone else when they
left; an absentee rent was far more than Albine could cope with.

At last the various letters were answered, and the answers were
relatively favourable. Pay and Accounts wanted nothing to do with
Montholon; but the imperial household would require personnel while
the Emperor was out on campaign; Montholon had worked there
before; he was 'detached for special duty' as one of the court
chamberlains until the Emperor's return, when his position would be
'looked into' and 'put on a proper footing'. (His full-generalship was not
recognised, as being a Bourbon appointment. He reverted to plain
brigadier.)

Nothing was said about the six thousand, but that did not mean that it
never *would* be said. He had to hope for the best and live for the next
day's salary.

The lawyer found them an apartment, much smaller than their

previous one, and less salubriously situated; but at least it was cheaper. Albine's money was 'coming along nicely', whatever that meant. There seemed to be a quantity of very involved legal business under way; but the cousin had definitely absconded and the lawyer was almost sure he could prove that the man's evasion was indeed that of a manifest traitor. In the meantime, the 'dear countess' must not worry . . .

Montholon took up his new duties on June 12th, the day after the Emperor's departure. They were not onerous; the Tuileries palace was empty, save for a large company of bone-idle lackeys, and decorative officials of Montholon's own caste who sauntered in and out of one another's offices, taking coffee and liqueurs, reading the newspapers, playing cards and going out to the races in the afternoon or the opera at night. Montholon found a pile of unanswered correspondence left behind by his predecessor (now with the general staff at the front); it dealt with all manner of absurd questions of protocol and it had to be *managed*, but there really seemed no hurry.

Montholon was behaving himself. Neither cards nor races nor opera (he could not afford them, in any case), and most certainly no brothels. He was home every evening at a decent hour to the embraces of Albine, which were extremely fervent, almost madly so. The fact was, she was desperate to keep him. Yet she feared she might have to throw him over. His embezzlement had shocked her into two shapeless days of terror. She had rapidly recovered from them and Touraine was full of sweetness; but now she was by no means sure that her scatty little talk with Gaius-Gracchus had made any sort of rational sense. *Political commitment* was a queer thing; scary for a woman of her disposition. True, the new constitutional decrees had been published on the first of June. Montholon had no excuse for failing to support them. France *did* require defending, and it *was* a freshly liberalised France. Nonetheless she was grindingly conscious of a huge strategic gamble: the army confronted the forces of Britain, Belgium, Hanover and Prussia all in the one campaign – Austria and Russia could not be far behind – and there was talk of armed Bourbonists already in rebellion in this or that remote part of the country. What *was* she to do if her husband were to find himself once again craving the patronage of Artois, craving the *mercy* of Artois? And what about the cousin? and the fund?

The bulletins from the front line proved endlessly cheerful. Wellington was outmanoeuvred, Blücher had lost his chance, Brussels would fall within twenty-four hours.

The battle of Waterloo was on June 18th.

Paris did not have precise news of the Emperor's defeat until the 20th.

But at sunset on the 18th something happened to convince Montholon beyond all doubt that there had been a disaster. He never discovered quite *how* this experience could have come about; it seemed, all his life, to contradict the terms of any straight explanation. He was (as we have said) an atheist, ingrained; moreover, until after he took to the sexual misuse of children, he had no superstition.

13

Sometimes he was to wonder if the hysterical satyriasis of his born-again marriage had not had some influence on the balance of his mind. Every morning from June 13th until the 18th he had awoken queasy and drained from a night of erotic turbulence, wide-awake couplings in all sorts of strange postures, half-asleep pokings and lickings and proddings, sleeping dreams of yet more of them but physically impossible and as savage as a running of maenads. He knew it could not go on; the woman was becoming *monstrous*; and yet how could he tell her to stop? He knew he did not want her to stop. Satiated, he still craved for it. And after all, she was his wife. And again after all, until everything at length could be 'put on a proper footing', it was she who held the money.

14

It had been a day of brooding tension at the Tuileries. Everyone knew from yesterday's bulletins that the armies in Flanders were in touch with each other at skirmishing range; a great battle was inevitable, if not today then tomorrow, but Napoleon (it was well understood) preferred to strike quickly, so it should be today; and it appeared that his enemies had divided their strength – would he fight the British first, or the Prussians? How much of a threat were the Hanoverian and Belgian regiments? How was the weather over there? for cavalry were baffled by sodden ground, artillery rendered immobile. In Paris it was raining like the first hours of Noah's flood. Generals and colonels who felt they ought to be in the field (but may have been glad they were not) wandered the corridors, laying nervous bets, sending to the gate to enquire if any couriers had arrived, arguing about possible arrangements for a victory parade. Ill-conditioned little arguments, opinionated gentlemen biting their friends' heads off.

Still no news: after hanging about for three hours beyond his normal knocking-off time, Montholon decided to go home. It may not have been quite consonant with the dignity of his rank to walk in uniform with an umbrella up; but thrift was all-important. Appearances could wait until the Emperor was once more in residence. He must grit his teeth and make his way through the sordid network of slum-streets surrounding Les Halles; it was alas his shortest route, and no one but a fool would struggle the long way round on such an evening. In the violence of the downpour, footpads and foul-mouthed drabs and crazy beggars were unlikely to be out in the open. He saw plenty of them as he hurried past; they were pressed into doorways with sacks over their heads, or swigging liquor from dirty old jugs in the entries of festering courtyards.

A market-cart, loaded with vegetables, came plunging round a dark corner, the big horse flogged ferociously to get to shelter as soon as possible. Montholon jumped aside, his boot slipped, he fell smack! into a brim-full gutter; his umbrella shot out of his hand and his cocked hat swam away from him in a convoy of floating filth. Scrabbling through the muck to recapture it and regain his footing (two incompatible aims), he felt the clutch of small fingers under his armpits. Slowly he was heaved upright and someone put the hat back on his head. The fingers left his body and instead took a hold of both his hands. Cold fingers, gripping tight, urging him to look down.

A boy and a girl, one on either side of him. They were the sort of shattered children you might find at any time about Les Halles, ragged, shivering, sloppy with ordure from top to toe. 'Come,' they said, in high piping voices, 'come with us, you got to come. It's not far, mister, come on; fucking come with us, mister, when you're told.' They pulled at him so strongly that he had no choice but go with them, between them, splashing through the rain-puddles and liquefied horse-dung. Their faces, half-hidden under matted mops of hair, were familiar? surely not? Black hair and a coal-black face: the boy was an African, there were many such in Paris. And the girl – yellow hair, ochre-yellow with all the dirt, but even so – death of God, yes he *did* know the girl! – Laïsette, cursing and swearing while the tears streamed out of her eyes and mingled with the rain on her pinched little face. The boy was weeping too – he was Ganymède of course – the one deliberate point of colour-contrast in the troupe of the *Ballets Roses*; the sooty thumbprint on the pink-and-white tapestry, the crow among the doves, the fly in the bowl of thick cream.

How had they come to be where they were? The *Pavillon aux Anges* was a mile away, across the river, and Montholon knew that the children were never off the premises. The place was in fact their prison; they were fed well, to be sure; were washed and well appointed; but

locks and bolts, barred windows and nameless punishments, were said
to keep them always from the open day – had these two escaped? and if
they had, were they starving? He asked them – out of breath, for they
hastened him along at such speed – all they would answer, repeatedly,
was, 'Fuck you, mister, come,' and 'Shut your hole, fuck it, you've to
come with us, come.' And still they sobbed and sobbed.

The door to which they brought him was a thieves' door, a poisoners'
door, a door of split planks green with mildewed rot in an alleyway a
yard wide between two tottering tall tenement-pilcs; nettles sprouted
rank through the cracks in the stone threshold. It was opened suddenly
from the inside; the children caught him off-balance and pushed him
through into the house, their sharp fists hard against his kidneys.
'Goodnight, mister,' they squealed (could it be a deliberate echo of the
brutal tones of the late Colonel Boutreux?). 'Up-your-shite-hole. IN!'
Then the door shut behind him; the children were left in the street; and
there he was, groping and barking his shins in a dark passage full of old
lumber and a horrible stink of piss.

Whoever had unlocked to him seemed no longer to be at hand.

He saw a light under a door at the bottom of a short flight of steps.

Remembering at last he was a brigadier with a sword at his side, he
pulled himself together, struck an indignant attitude, boldly went
down, flung open the door – he required explanations! he required an
apology! he found himself peering into a room so unusual that he came
to a halt on the bottom step, at an absolute loss for words.

It was large, bare and very grimy, with only a few sticks of worm-
eaten spindly furniture. There was a blazing fire of logs in an old-
fashioned iron basket set within a cavernous chimney-place. The June
evening, so wet out-of-doors, was notwithstanding sultry; the fire was
surely needless, the room was like an oven. There seemed to be no
windows. A pair of oil lamps smoked on a rickety dresser. A shoddy
virgin-and-child plaster statuette in a niche in one wall; on another one,
a torn print of the crucifixion. Opposite the fire, a great wooden tub full
of steaming water. A few scraps of carpet littered the floorboards beside
it. A black suit and a white shirt (together with stockings and
underwear) were draped across the back of a kitchen chair.

Montholon thought immediately of the famous picture of murdered
Marat; but the man in the tub was not Marat. Nor was he dead. A young
face, long white hair, steel spectacles with tinted lenses – the man of the
Anges Sucrés.

He was writing something in a notebook on a shelf laid over his knees
– again, the very shape of Marat. 'It's a bad night,' he said, without

looking up. 'You're soaked; you'll run a fever. Here is a fire to dry your clothes. Strip and get into the hot water with me.'

'I will not.' Montholon was trembling uncontrollably; but he refused to be *overpowered*.

'Suit yourself. Then you wish to be quick? So I will be quick: listen very closely. Bonaparte is finished. Tonight, now, without remedy. He will abdicate again; he will very soon be made a prisoner; but by whom is an open question. We cannot risk his resurrection, not twice in one year, no. If those who take him do not deal with him, some other arrangement must be made. We have to know *what* arrangement, how. Someone must be there to tell us. Monsieur thinks it could be you. Should be you. Shall be. Don't speak. Pay attention. *Be obedient.*'

Montholon felt his scrotum shrivel. He tried to speak. No use. His attempted words were mere clicks and groans.

The man went on: 'When the usurper flees from the battle and comes back to his stolen palace, you will attach yourself to him as closely as a snail to a wall. Wherever he goes, you will go. And you'll wait to receive your instructions. For if you do not, what else can you do but remain in your own filth until Monsieur shall think fit to deal with you? There are penalties for embezzlement, even when the criminal is a nobleman of ancient lineage. There are galleys, there are gaols, there is the guillotine. And no leniency. Bonaparte stole His Majesty's realm; *you* stole His Majesty's gold. Set the smaller thief to punish the greater, and then let him seek for forgiveness. There! that's the wish of Monsieur. Malséant, I am ready! Dry me and dress.'

15

A sour slouching young fellow came through a door behind the bath. He wore a market-porter's blouse, loose trousers and sabots. He was not at all cleanly. His shining dark hair lay slicked across his forehead and twisted over one eye into a pickpocket's quiff. There was a certain glowering beauty about his saturnine face, the beauty of an eagle that has chosen to live like a vulture. He carried towels over one arm and extended the other to assist his master up from the water. He dried him with a sedulous gentleness, patting him around his unashamed (and apparently unmoved) secret parts like a mother with her baby.

The white-haired man purred and stroked Malséant's head.

We have said Montholon felt his scrotum shrivel; and so it had, through fear. But now he felt something else, not exactly a sexual thrill, not exactly physical, but nonetheless akin. He was filled with a tingling anxiety, a presentiment, a longing – he attempted to put a name to it. He found only the one word – *envy*. He was envious of this Malséant, of the service he saw him perform, of his sinister self-possession.

'Leave my clothes for the moment. I will air myself by the fire.' The white-haired man walked across the room in three long naked strides and stood barefoot and preening himself on the hearth. His tall lean body was deadly pale, and hairless save for one white little tuft round the root of his penis. He slid his hands up and down inside his thighs. 'Now,' he said, 'Malséant, get this very dirty chamberlain out of my sight.'

Malséant was small but extremely tough, quick and violent. He flung himself at Montholon with the fury of a wild cat and drove him out of the room. He drove him stumbling up the steps and kicked him on the ankles all along the passage. He dragged open the door and turned to seize hold of him to manhandle him into the alleyway. And then he stopped, raised his hands, clapped them together.

For Montholon, *overpowered*, had fallen to the threshold in a faint.

He came to his senses in a rattling squalid hackney-cab, a few streets from his own dwelling. The cabman brought him to the right house without having to be told, and refused to accept any money. He'd already been paid, he said; he knew better than to try to get two fares for one journey – at any rate when his first customer was *that* customer. 'Sacred God,' he said, 'we don't play no games, not with the likes of *him*. Do you know him well, sir? Take an old man's advice and stay clear.'

16

Had it really happened? Had he dreamed it? Of course he had dreamed it. Of course, on his way home he had stopped off for a drink, had allowed the apprehensions of the day to combine with wine or brandy to make him drunk, had in consequence suffered a drunkard's delirium which laid him in the gutter – whence a comradely citizen and a good-hearted cabman had providentially rescued him. Of course?

But he knew that the battle for Brussels was lost.

Nothing could expel that from his mind.

That night he said little to Albine; he went straight to bed, pleading a severe chill – true enough in all conscience. Moreover it meant she made no carnal demands on him. He was sure he could not bear them if she did. He wondered, would sexual intercourse ever be possible for him again?

He could hardly find the strength, let alone the will, to fetch himself up next day. Albine shook him and slapped him and threw his clothes into his face – 'You must, you must, you must go to the Tuileries!' she railed. 'This morning of all mornings, did they win, did they lose? – Charles-Tristan, what will become of us if we don't know in good time what's been done, who is dead, who is alive? – who, who, today are our masters?' She went off to make the coffee.

He could only afford an inferior brand of valet. (The expensive and ambitious Jules had long since departed his service.) This dithering man was useless at helping him dress, unable to understand that, for Montholon, the stockings went on before the shirt; shirt and cravat before the trousers; before waistcoat and coat, the boots (to be polished while on their owner's legs) – such had always been Jules's way and Montholon was not about to change it for anyone. There was a stupid repetitive row, daily. This morning it was made worse by Montholon's state of mind. He roared, 'Boots! you mudwit, boots!' while the oaf stood and gibbered with a waistcoat. The boots, long hessians with gold tassels, had already been thrown by Albine and lay separated, one at one side of the bed and one the other. Nervously picking them up, the valet held the first of them upside down: 'Beg your pardon, sir: this here, like, it just fell out of it.'

He stooped again, for a folded paper.

'In the boot?'

'Yessir, seemingly. Was you aware of it, sir?'

'Give.'

One glance at the paper and he ordered the valet out of the room.

He sat down on the bed, his head swimming. It was a pen-and-ink note in a very tiny, almost illegible hand, on a page torn out of a notebook. The same notebook in which he had seen the man in the tub writing, or had seemed to see writing, or had *dreamed* of him writing? – the same? How could he be sure? Of course he could not be sure. But the written message was no illusion.

> He who is to tell you what you are to do will make himself known to you by a hook instead of a right hand, and the words, *lost on behalf of my much-wronged nation, France*. To forestall mistakes, you will ask him, *Which France?* Thereto he will reply, *That of my long-suffering father*. Impossible to inform you where or when you will meet him. Remember: 6000. Obedience, no leniency.

If this was no illusion, then it had been stuck into the boot by

Malséant in the very act of hurling him from that abominable house. Then the house did exist, and the white-haired man, and the bath? but what of the – of the destitute children? NO! *their* intervention could not be possible, a figment of his ill conscience, the devil's pictures in his brain. (No, he did not believe in the devil!) His brain whirled accordingly, as he forced himself to ask himself: was he, Montholon, now, in a fit state to be certain that it *was* no illusion? To prove it, beyond all doubt? He would only be able to do so by showing the paper to somebody else. Who? Not Albine, at any rate. She must not know, must not. The valet? He might be more cunning than he seemed, his suspicions might already be aroused. So show it him, and quieten them. Make a melodrama (as if it needed one) – thus: 'Here, you, come in again! I am sick this morning, have you noticed? My eyes are thick and streaming. I can't read a word of this. I believe it is a message from the Emperor's secret service. Of the utmost importance you say nothing about it to anyone. Your life as well as mine depends upon it. Read.'

The valet, awestruck, took the paper. Slowly, for he was all but illiterate, he read out what Montholon had read.

Oh God.

'Very well. You understand, if ever you see a man with a hook for a hand, you will not, *you will not* talk to him. You fetch him to me, or you tell me about him. At once. As soon as I've had my coffee, go and find me a cab for the Tuileries. I am too unwell to set a foot on the street. Look sharp, you bloody incapable.' That ought to do it. The important brigadier, suffused with every secret of state; and therefore the important valet, but the fearful valet too, in salutory danger of secret death.

Oh God! let it truly be the arrant nonsense it appeared to be. A cruel practical joke, or the revenge of a frustrated pervert. 'Suppose I *had* got into the bath with him? Would the end of it have been any different? What's the use, it's too late now. And who am I to talk about perverts?'

Suffused with every secret of state? Suffused with but one secret, which burst out the sweat from every pore of his skin: that he was now a spy in the pay of Monsieur. And not even to be paid in money, only by an unreliable assurance of his own safety. Well, he had lied enough to Albine; Albine had not found out *everything*. No, he'd contrived to manage. It was his nature. (Born and reared an aristo-Jacobin, neither the one life nor the other.) But was it his *talent*? In truth, he could not tell; he was no more than an apprentice. Now he must learn to be a master.

17

Forty-eight hours of despondency, revived hopes, dashed hopes, cross-purposes, hopeless confusion. Montholon was at the Tuileries at dawn on the 21st – indeed he had been there all night as the post-riders straggled in with contradictory news of the defeat – some said Napoleon was dead, others that he was a prisoner in Wellington's hands, one ranting idiot (admittedly with a ghastly head-wound) claimed that he had seen him tied to a tree by Blücher's Prussians and about to face a firing-squad. All agreed that the battle was decisively lost; and the disagreements seemed to show that it had also been disgracefully lost – the army at the end had broken and fled, there were panic-stricken soldiers scattered all over northern France, no regiments left in being; no generals with any forces at their command, nothing but death, waste and terror.

But not long before first light another courier came crying at the gate, this time a man of sense, undaunted. He was General Gourgaud, GOC Field Artillery; he knew exactly what had happened and what was to be done. He called at once for General Bertrand, the grand marshal of the Tuileries and Montholon's chief. Bertrand called at once for the officers of the palace and explained the situation. The Emperor was arriving within an hour, in his carriage, with what remained of his personal staff. He would not come to the Tuileries but to the Elysée, as more easily secured in case of public disorders. The senior members of the Tuileries establishment must immediately move themselves the short distance to the other palace, with all confidential papers and financial strongboxes; the Tuileries guards would go too, as an escort for the documents and cash, and to double the strength of the companies already at the Elysée.

More confusion, speedily resolved by Gourgaud's parade-ground bellows and a rapid set of decisions from Bertrand. Montholon found himself in a closed carriage with four entire filing-cabinets and a civilian chamberlain, the Count Las Cases. An attempt by General Gourgaud to further overload the coach by piling in two great canvas bags, full of jewelry and small change, was vetoed at the last minute by Bertrand, who took one look at Montholon, remembered something he had heard about that particular brigadier, and at once, without comment, found another vehicle.

Las Cases, a finical aristo of literary leanings, told Montholon tearfully as they bumped and banged over the paving-stones that these were the days for any gentleman who kept a journal: Fortune's wheel (Brigadier Montholon would recollect the poets), Phaëton falling from the height of the aerial element, Themistocles, Alcibiades, it was to be hoped neither Pompey nor Caesar – although they *would* murder him if they could. He was going to have to go, Montholon surely knew that. It was the *process* of his going that required to be recorded. Majesty eclipsed in sorrow. Sorrow eclipsed in courage. He himself, Emmanuel Las Cases, would do his humble best.

Montholon was ready to talk of anything but murder. 'D'you know, count,' he said, 'I have not seen the Emperor since before he departed for Elba. I – ah – I thought at that time he was beginning to look – ah – old. How is he these days?' This was the sheerest twaddle: had all his years in the Diplomatic Branch taught him no better? He blushed for his own words, but Las Cases was too upset to be listening critically.

'Keep your own journal, brigadier, commence it today. Start with a description of the Emperor's demeanour in defeat, his philosophy, his magnanimity; yes, his appearance. He's been growing very corpulent, you know, his face is yellow, yellow and green. He's only forty-five, he looks fifty-five; looks older than me, you know; I'm forty-nine, I look forty.'

Their carriage rolled into the great court of the Elysée, immediately after the arrival of the Emperor's. The yard was a vortex of guards and flunkeys carrying torches, horses rearing, exhausted officers and troopers dismounting. A turbaned and scimitared Mameluke, one of the imperial body-servants recruited years ago in Egypt, leapt at once to the Emperor's coach-door. Napoleon stepped painfully out into the torch-light, hunched-up and unaware that his greatcoat was wrongly buttoned and his hat askew. He peered all about him as though bewildered. He *was* corpulent; he was also hollow-eyed, hollow-cheeked, in need of a shave and pitiably uncertain as to what sort of welcome to expect. A nervous little fat man, stuttering for something to say.

At last he said it; snappy and irritable; 'magnanimity' would have to come by degrees. 'Where's Bertrand? He should be here. Why isn't he?' His eye caught the glitter of Montholon's palace uniform: 'You, who are you? Where's your chief?'

Montholon felt himself about to twaddle once again. But if you fear to be a fool, *be* a fool, in all good courage, if that's what your employment would seem to demand. A chamberlain, after all, was not quite serious, neither warrior nor politician: the appropriate pretence came easily enough. He combined a salute with a species of bow, sweeping off his hat and declaring himself: 'De Montholon, sire, brigadier, appointed court chamberlain in your absence. Allow me to escort you, sire. Your private suite? A bath? Bed?'

The Emperor stared at him, incredulous; and grinned. An infectious boyish grin, a backstreets-of-Ajaccio grin, full of mischief and hidden delight at the extreme possibilities of pomposity. It totally transformed him. 'I'm quite sure, brigadier, that you *were* appointed in my absence. What did you run before that? An hotel? And why, sir, full-dress uniform with an undress hat on your head?' (Because the best hat with all its feathers had been drenched in a stinking gutter; neither time nor opportunity since then to buy another. Was an explanation possible? Here and now? No.) 'Never mind, never mind, you're as imperturbable as a Swiss head-waiter – a bath, he says, bed? Why aren't they all as cool as you? All I want is coffee, and a boxful of good snuff. Send for 'em fast and come and talk to me. The rest of the day's all politics. Let's have some silly chatter first. Domestic. Bath-towels. Don't bring Las Cases; he'll write every word of it down. Where the hell *is* Bertrand?'

He took Montholon's arm and walked him into the palace. Montholon explained how Bertrand was still handling the logistical difficulties of the transfer from the Tuileries, and the Emperor grinned again at all the trouble he seemed to be causing: 'No, but they mustn't blame me. Blame Wellington, blame Blücher, blame that idiot Grouchy who took an entire army corps at hare-and-hounds across the landscape instead of being where I'd told him to be. Well, in that case you *must* blame me. God knows, the Man of Destiny is fallible. Who else gave Grouchy his job?'

18

He did not really want to talk about bath-towels. It became obvious after five minutes that he had latched onto Montholon simply because he did not know him, because indeed Montholon was the one conspicuous man in the hubbub of the Elysée yard whom he did not know, and therefore he could tell him things which, spoken to his accustomed confidants, would only be compared with what he had said on some other occasion, and so be seen as symptoms – of what? stubbornness? changeability? consistency? inconsistency? Montholon could not compare. Montholon could only receive them as they came.

Napoleon was trying out, on a 'new' officer, a new pattern of invincible Napoleon, a Napoleon twice defeated within a year-and-a-quarter who was trying to find a reason for the rest of his life. A reason to be found before he could determine what *sort* of a rest of a life – even supposing that such determination would be his. Others were bound to have a say; but he needed to settle his own mind about it first. He gulped black coffee, sniffed snuff (and let it fall from his fingers' ends to sprinkle the carpet without entering his nostrils, an odd habit abhorred by the palace cleaners), reminisced vaguely about an innkeeper who did him a good turn in his first Italian campaign; and then slewed the aim of his discourse at an obtuse angle toward a venomous dissection of the character of Fouché, minister of police.

'Fouché will betray me as he betrayed me before. Fouché will play me a Talleyrand. The soldiers who flocked to me on my way inland from Antibes cannot flock now – they are dead – or *will* not flock – they're broken.'

Montholon muttered some platitudes about 'the people' – how the Emperor's popularity had never been so manifestly strong as upon his 'miraculous resurrection', how enthusiastically the public had greeted his revised constitution – he brought Gaius-Gracchus into the consolatory argument as 'a simple rural gendarme' – but Napoleon rounded on him with a giggle.

'The "people"? Dear good brigadier, which people? The ones who rebelled against the conscriptions in the hour of disaster and danced in the streets when I abdicated? Danced the Carmagnole, revolutionists every one: Boney to them was just another damned Louis to be given the chop, could they get at him. Have you heard how, on my road to Elba, I had to change hats with my servant, like a clown, in order to avoid being lynched? And then to disguise myself as an Austrian? Imagine me, an Austrian. Did I ever in my life look at all like an – oh, you *are* a good man, you're a Jacobin, aren't you? but don't talk to me about the "people".' The strange jocular femininity that had run through these words disappeared to be replaced by a darker, deeper register of gloom: 'I found them poor, I left them poor. They owe me nothing. Last year they understood it, so they hated me. Then the Bourbons came in and the Bourbons were as bad as they always were, so they left off hating me and hated *them* once again. Maybe today they are still in that frame of mind. Maybe.'

He asked, gently, for more coffee. While Montholon was pouring it out, a noise of shouting and cheering could be heard in the streets – a gathering noise, a crowd of demonstrators growing larger every minute to bawl a vigorous rhythm of, 'Napoleon, Napoleon! Citizen Napoleon! we want Napoleon!'

'Oh yes,' he said, cocking an ear, 'maybe. Maybe a man of mine is paying them to roar? I didn't give any orders but some of my staff have initiative – even when it's not required. And if there are enough out there I could march at their head to overthrow the Chamber of Deputies before the Chamber deposes me. As Citizen, you note, not Emperor: Danton *redivivus*. A new guise, a new voice – it might very well save my life! But my life is not worth it, not worth anybody's fury and death. I am not Gaius Marius (you know your Roman history?) to make Paris a bloodbath, because Fouché, let me tell you, Fouché would ensure that that's exactly what would happen.' He was now speaking urgently, breathlessly, gripping Montholon by the arm and thrusting the quick words into his face – 'I would be perceived, if Fouché had his way, as punishing the Parisians by the power of the sword, the whiff of the grapeshot – and why? for no better reason than that they are Parisians, which is to say as fickle as the favours of their own mothers, the trollops of the street, the dancers of the Carmagnole – don't they call it the Cancan these days? – lifting their skirts to hurl their indecencies against anyone – anyone at all – who has not in two minutes been able to make them rich. Poor creatures. Unfortunate deluded little fuckers. We've betrayed 'em, every one of us.

'What did you tell me your name was? De Montholon? Let me remember. I used to know the name of every man in the Old Guard – or rather, I had an officer just behind my shoulder who'd mugged up the names and their order in the ranks and could prompt me with decorous whispers. But he isn't here now and my memory is not quite – I even think it possible I *forgot* to give Grouchy the very exact orders such a man has to have if he's going to do his job at all respectably. But, de Montholon? De Montholon . . . no! I don't forget, no! I told you not to marry, and you did. I remembered my Josephine and told you. *Did* she deceive you? *Was* she the trollop I'd been advised that she used to be?'

'No, sire,' (stiffly) 'no. We are most happy together, very.' It was difficult to keep track. How personal was he going to get? The coffee was too much of a stimulant for this excitable, this tragic, little man who ought – he really ought – to be in bed.

'In that case I'd like to meet her. Present her to me, when we know where we are. Brigadier, she is unique. And does she share the sentiments of this noble rural gendarme of yours? Name of God, *he's* unique too. And therefore, in any bloodbath, he'd surely be the first to die. Dear good brigadier, *I will not lay waste such virtue.*'

This austere abnegation should have been impressive. Allowing for the Emperor's total weariness and the shock of his defeat (which led him astray into little cul-de-sacs of spite), he was certainly uttering thoughts commensurate with the revised constitution – the people were to be spared the barbarities of civil conflict, as indeed they had not been spared the destruction of international war – although *this* international war had truly been a war of self-defence for all of France. If the constitution held, and if the victorious allies would proffer generous peace-terms upon the strength of it, then possibly Gaius-Gracchus would find himself justified – *if*.

But Montholon, as Monsieur's spy, could not allow himself to be impressed. There was too much, far too much, going on behind the scenes. Knowledge of this made him thoroughly suspicious of Napoleon's play-acting. Very clever play-acting, to be sure: to lament his forgetfulness and at the same time to remember Montholon's personal history and at the same time to expose how the famous feats of memory had always been something of a cheat. It was much the same technique as that employed by a notorious Harlequin at the Théâtre des Variétés: in the middle of some sentimental sequence, played for full pathos and beginning to draw tears, the man would appear to be so overwrought by the treachery of his true love that he would knock his own mask off in the violence of grief; weeping, he would call in the prompter to help him fix it – and then, he would proceed with his Wertheresque passion just as though nothing had happened. He may have done it the first time by accident; and then he did it every night, the audience loved it every night. 'Oh, I'm that buggered up,' he'd sob, 'I can't even keep me face straight, look!' But Harlequin, in the end, was *supposed* to be ridiculous. The love he inspired was of a quite different order from that needed by an emperor.

Or was it?

Montholon, in short, had been only partly disarmed by being joked at as 'head-waiter'. Three years ago he might have liked it. Three years ago he might even have fallen for Napoleon's wretched trick of pulling his subordinates affectionately by the ear; at any rate, this morning, he was to be spared that. For the Emperor suddenly buttoned himself up properly, straightened his cocked hat, dusted the snuff from his fingers, said in a touching undertone (almost to himself): 'Today, maybe tomorrow, I shall abdicate of course. Stay with me, dear young man, I'll be grateful for some friends.'

Hands under his coat-tails, head thrust belligerently forward, he stamped out of the room to attend to business, calling harshly and impatiently for first this officer and then that: unpredictable, alarming, the indefatigable military genius once again at the top flight of his improvisation. Hoping against all obvious probability he still had something left with which to improvise.

19

'Stay with me.'

'Attach yourself to him as closely as a snail to a wall.'

Two masters, incompatible, yet both gave the same command.

On June 25th, Napoleon, no longer Emperor – Fouché had effectively seen to *that* – departed – with Fouché's permission and indeed collaboration – for Malmaison near Paris, the country home of his first marriage where repudiated Josephine had lived until her death. Montholon, obedient to both masters, joined the melancholy rendezvous of those few imperial followers whose loyalty had not yet turned.

Napoleon spent four days there, an inconvenient overcrowded scrambled four days, with people sleeping on camp-beds and palliasses all over the house and stables. The entourage were sometimes called in for extemporary councils-of-war. And then for hours they would be ordered to keep clear and amuse themselves, to give the Bonaparte family a chance for some privacy, Corsican rituals of farewell and sworn vengeance, the clan-hiring (for aught Montholon knew about it) of assassins to dispose – of Fouché, perhaps? or Blücher? or King Louis? or Artois? The Emperor's stepdaughter was there, two illegitimate sons, three former mistresses, and finally Madame Mère, his mother, the iron-nerved old lady who had never stood any nonsense from him and who now was so ready to take upon her grim grey head the Roman characteristics of a Volumnia or a Cornelia. She had given her child to his Destiny and his Destiny placed the sword in her heart.

It was (Montholon thought) a very dreadful séance; not improved by the fleeting appearances and reappearances, up and down the staircases and in and out of the garden-doors, of Albine and Zoé the Touraine nurse and Montholon's own damned valet, all constantly in chase of screaming toddling chuckling Maximilien who seemed to believe the whole of Malmaison and its people to have been especially ordered as a full-sized toy fort for him to pull to pieces from cellar to roof. Montholon had had Albine and his household come with him because the Prussians were fighting their way toward Paris; rumour held that they were far more inflamed against the French than the previous year; they'd had severe losses at the battle of Ligny immediately before Waterloo; a devastating sack of the city was not impossible, however many deals Fouché might try to make.

Bertrand was there too, and Mme Bertrand, and three children. Las Cases had with him a teenage son, a conceited little whippet whose advances to the Malmaison servant-maids caused daily complaints. Albine smacked his face for him when he shoved his hand into the

Touraine girl's bodice, and then his father came to Montholon to say 'the boy's manhood had been insulted by the blow' and at any other time and place – *etcetera* – the brigadier should 'think himself fortunate not to be asked for the length of his sword'.

On the 29th, Napoleon announced his intention of leaving, incognito, that evening. A message had come from Fouché that the Prussians were attacking Versailles – indeed, their cannon could be heard from Malmaison – and Blücher had ordered any of his troops who saw the ex-Emperor to shoot him on sight 'like a mad dog'; more precisely, like an *international outlaw*, as defined by the allies at Vienna. The British were thought to be less bloodthirsty; but Wellington's regiments were further away. At all events, Malmaison was no sanctuary, nor the countryside around it.

The ex-Emperor decided he would be less conspicuous if he travelled without escort, an innocent private gentleman, for at least the first stage of his journey. Various meeting-places were arranged, to which such members of the party who were able to catch up with him should make their way in small groups. He was heading south-west for Rochefort on the shore of the Bay of Biscay. Fouché was permitting a naval ship, or ships, to take him and his train on board and bring them to the United States, if that's where they wanted to go. They would have to run the risk of interception by the British blockade-fleet; and upon land there were risks as well, for Fouché had refused a safe-conduct as far as the coast, 'for who knows whose signature can possibly guarantee anybody's life anywhere just now? Use your wits, "General Bonaparte", get out while the roads are still open.'

So it was, on a small scale, a hazardous expedition. Some of the entourage were already defecting. Bertrand kept saying that it really would be better if his wife (who was Irish, 'connected with the most distinguished family Dillon') should make her way to England and enquire if the London government would not accept *him* in due course as a refugee, although naturally he would follow his Emperor wherever commanded – 'Just my wife, you see, not French, she has her relatives – Dublin, perhaps, rather than London? – just my dear wife, you see . . .'

Montholon could not defect. Nor could he tell Albine why. She was suggesting that the road to Rochefort led through Touraine; and she asked him, what hindered them from staying there? A voyage to the United States was too huge a step by far. He told her he had heard that the Touraine-Poitou region was being 'purged' by vindictive Bourbonists (likely enough; it may even have been true). He must make, he asserted, a considerable detour via Vierzon and Limoges. Tours lay to the north of his château, Poitiers to the south; Gaius-Gracchus lived in the former town, the old grocer and the rest of his family in the latter. He yearned to see all of them; they would certainly welcome him as a stalwart of the Emperor's last fling; but he could not bear to be so welcomed when every day his mind seethed with weird visions of a *hook-handed* man. He did not dare, he was ashamed, to enter his own region: impossible to admit it.

Albine believed his tale, for the current atrocity-stories were more lurid every day. She resigned herself to the hectic adventure. She was chiefly concerned with the welfare of Maximilien; it was the first time since the child was born that she really seemed to worry about him. Because she had not been with her husband at the Tuileries or the Elysée, the political catastrophe had smitten her with a violence unmoderated by days or hours of augmenting portents; she had ridden to Malmaison as though stunned; to concentrate upon her baby was an expedient of refuge. Apart from the one protest – 'Touraine?' – she had very little to say to anyone else.

So they loaded themselves into (and on top and in the dickey-seat of) a post-chaise and set off.

20

The hook-handed man had taken several successive shapes in Montholon's imagination. It seemed, at last, most probable that he would turn out to be a tattered and sinister cripple, pretending to be a brave old veteran of the war; or else a dashing young dragoon in full uniform, his mutilation only adding to his farouche bewhiskered charm. Surely the missing hand must derive from some military exploit; the arrangement of passwords would imply nothing else. There was always the danger that by making this detour Montholon might miss the man altogether; and then he would be in trouble; Vierzon and Limoges were scarcely 'snail to a wall' in their closeness to Napoleon's route. But they had been told to travel separately; and what could he do but what he was told?

The slipway to the ferry over the River Cher near Vierzon was blocked by a farm-cart drawn up across the entry. This impromptu barricade had a guard on it, gendarmes with muskets and fixed bayonets. Every vehicle and passenger was being carefully checked before being allowed through. Montholon did not realise the nature of the stoppage until a fair-sized queue of carriages and wagons had trailed in behind, making it impossible for his own chaise to turn and retreat. He was in civilian clothes and a clerk at Malmaison had provided him with false papers –

M. and Mme Dumain, vintner and wife, of Châlons-sur-Marne, travelling to Bordeaux with one child, two servants, and a hired postilion. It was not very convincing. All Montholon knew of the wine trade was the taste of the stuff; if he were asked any questions about his supposed business, he'd be sunk. However, a bold front! and hope for the best.

The officer in command of the gendarmes, twenty leagues away from his regular field of duty, was Gaius-Gracchus.

At least the police here were not taking their orders from Fouché. No question of arrest therefore, but—

Montholon could not think it a joyful reunion.

Albine and Gaius-Gracchus were delighted. Indeed, the latter went so far as to leave his post in charge of a sergeant and take them all three across the road for a good lunch at the Auberge au Grand Bac. He carried Maximilien in his arms and gave him his hat to play with while they ate. He was fiercely sardonic about the future; he would lose his job again, of course. If his father were not interfered with by the Bourbonists (maybe he wouldn't be, they'd already had their thick cut off the steak) he thought that he himself should go abroad to the West Indies: the family still had its trade affairs there: sugar! Everyone, he said, even filthy reactionaries and filthier priests, liked a spot of sugar in their coffee. They wouldn't think to ask, was it *Jacobin* sugar? Of course, a Jacobin ought to ask, was it produced by black slaves? Of course, of course, he said, *but!* sufficient unto the day was the evil thereof. He laughed and recovered his gaiety. He reckoned within a week he'd be on shipboard; just like Charles-Tristan and Albine. Sacred God, though, *theirs* was a journey with honour in it! He would ask to accompany them; but it was essential, beyond everything essential, to secure the communications of the Army of the Loire, an army still fervent for the Emperor: and that was what he did at this ferry. 'Leonidas, if you like, in the pass of Thermopylae.' Oh yes, he might be killed . . . it was all part of the bloody gesture, wasn't it? 'Talking of gestures, Charles-Tristan, this is your chance to let the Emperor know that his loyal men along the Loire will fight any battle he calls for – he's only to give the word! Of course, if he thinks not—

'Well, he's the strategist. But just you make sure that he knows we're damned well ready.'

In a splutter of feigned good humour, Montholon burst out: 'I'll tell him, Guy-Gracque, be assured of it, ah! *ça ira!*'

So Gaius-Gracchus sent them on their way; nor did he forget, as he vaingloriously gave voice to the furious words of the *Ça-ira* street-fighters' song, to write out for them a Bonapartist pass . . . just in case any other patrols should suspect M. Dumain of Bourbon tendencies. He kissed Albine's hand, met her eye with a warm twinkle, allowed his moustache its suggestive twitch. She did not think she would see him again; and she wept a little in the carriage, taking care not to let Montholon observe it.

Montholon's thoughts were a whirlpool.

21

At long last, as it grew dark upon the wet windy evening of July 8th, they drove into the outskirts of Rochefort. Albine had taken in Maximilien from Zoé in the dickey and was holding him in her arms, endeavouring to still his constant whimpers. 'Charles-Tristan, this child is sick, he's been sickening for the last two days, I am truly getting anxious, I tell you he has a fever, this journey is wearing him out. Look, look, there is a pharmacy! Stop the coach! send the man over there, he must ask him is he qualified to prescribe for Maximilien? and if he isn't, where in God's name is the doctor who is? I tell you we report to no Emperor until my baby is safe and sound.'

The valet obeyed, trotting resentfully through the swirls of drizzle into the shop and rapping with his knuckles on the counter. An unfriendly-looking young fellow came out from behind the dispensing-room screen, prematurely bald, cadaverous, with a down-turned morose mouth and sandy sideburns. He was in his shirt-sleeves; his cravat was black and greasy, his waistcoat black and shabby, his apron of green baize. A green canvas eyeshade was pushed up on his brow. 'Yessir, what can I do for you, sir? Make it sharp, can't you? Past me closing-time by ten minutes. I was just about to call the boy to put me shutters up.' He had his left shirt-sleeve rolled tight above the elbow; the other one hung fastened at full length to his wrist; his wrist was the butt of a bright steel hook.

The valet contrived, despite stammers of transparent alarm, to convey his mistress's needs; he kept his eyes, fascinated, upon the hook. The chemist in return peered at him shrewdly and thought for a moment. 'You don't let her bring the child in here. The night air's deleterious, right? I'll just light me bullseye, follow you out to the carriage, take a looksee.'

The valet contrived, back at the coach-door, to speak a quick word from the corner of his mouth to Montholon, who was out of the vehicle and hovering impatiently in the street: 'Hook, sir, the chemist, sir: hook for a hand. Watch him when he comes out.'

'Sacred God, a *chemist*? Go to the devil.'

'Very good, sir, as you say, sir; you did say to forewarn you. Hand, sir, right hand, sir, most highly conspicuous – oh, sir, d'you think we're all *safe*—?'

The chemist came running towards them, with a small lantern clipped ingeniously to a ring-attachment on the curve of his hook. Half-in half-out of the chaise, he turned the light upon Maximilien's flushed face, and gently felt his brow with his left hand.

'Right then, sir and madam, it's clear he has an occasional fever. No doubt, sir and madam, the fatigue of the journey will have made its contribution. Come far, have you? To be sure you have.' He was shining his lantern on the thick coat of mud that disfigured the coach-wheels and panelling. 'Into the shop for a moment, sir; I can put you up a bottle or two. I doubt if it's needed. A night's rest in a warm bed'd do him more good than physic. By rights I should have locked me door by now: but come on.'

Inside the shop, with his one hand he contrived to lay out bottles and a pillbox on the counter. 'Cooling-draught; aperient if required; tablets to *close* the bowels if required; and this here's what we term decongestant if he's symptoms of what you might call a catarrh. Don't let him have 'em all at once, don't exceed the stated dosage, and really he oughtn't to eat. Not for twenty-four hours. Right? Plenty of fluids, though. Oh yes. Don't let the lady carry on about a doctor, *he* couldn't do no better. Just oblige me, sir, if you would, by putting the bottles into this here basket for me. I being handicapped, as you as a gentleman making a journey will surely have noted, with a mechanical device that knows its limitations. Right.'

'Ah,' muttered Montholon, uncertain whether or no this was his cue. It was scarcely conceivable that here could be Monsieur's man. A pharmacy in Rochefort? a sick child, an unexpected stoppage? these were not contingencies that could have been planned for. Nonetheless—

The chemist did seem to be waiting for him to say something: something must be said, willy-nilly. 'Ah. Yes, a handicap. It could have been worse? At least you have learned a – a dexterity? – but how did you lose it?'

'When I was just a prentice, sir, stupid boy, me, straight out of the orphanage, no sense at all, clumsy as a bullock. Aren't they all? Spilt a jar of corrosive all over me wrist; proper treatment was neglected; me burns took the gangrene; surgeon took me hand. Very near took me whole arm. Stupid business; but I survived. Incident to the trade, I suppose you might say, really. I had ought to ask you, sir, being as the times is so queer, and the national police not quite all they might be in the way of current trustfulness, but you do have a permit of travel?'

This last sentence was in a quite different tone: the man suddenly spoke as though he were a policeman himself, and a most unpleasant one. And yet the obvious chance for the password had been missed. Montholon was thrown off-balance. 'Of course,' he snapped, 'why would I not? Pray inform me, how is it *your* business?' – he did his best to sound disdainful. The chemist was not deceived. He smiled like an alligator and very slowly looked all around him, a sly wordless warning of possible eavesdroppers.

'Of course you do, sir,' smoothly, insidiously, dismayingly collusive. 'It was only I took the liberty, to warn you you might be required of it a street or two further up the town. Being that I myself the other day was put to ill-convenience by the temporary loss of my own residence-paper, just a few hundred yards away, you'd never believe it, a few yards from my own shop-door. That's to say, it's not *my* shop: I belong in Paris, only here for a couple of weeks to help out a – a friend of mine, a colleague in the trade. So you'll see that the officer was suspicious. "Lost it?" says he, "lost? How *can* you have lost it?" I tried to make a joke of it, didn't I? Bad mistake. Said I'd lost it in the service of France, my much-wronged nation. Well, in a sense I had. Being it's queer times and violent, the healing arts is a national asset, right? Of course, he ran me in. Hours at the prefecture, hours, interrogated and that. I just warn you, because—'

Time to give the countersign, the ambiguous and dangerous counter-sign. (How the hell had they thought such a rigmarole up?) 'Which France?' snarled Montholon abruptly.

The alligator-smile became a rictus of rage and contempt. 'Oh, I wasn't born an orphan. I had a father, long-suffering; lost him to the lynch-mob, didn't I? La Force prison, the massacres, September '92. *His* France and be damned to it. Who on God's earth *knows* what sort of a France we ought to have?' His hard low-toned voice had risen to a strident bray, proclaiming what? – cynicism? outrage? hatred of *all* society, revolutionary, hierarchical, or simply mixed-up murderous? Then he contained himself, and took a quiet breath. He was properly aware now with whom he was dealing; he had had his instructions. 'Right: so here we are.'

He rummaged with his hook under the counter and brought up a thick waterproof packet, like an angler landing a fish. 'We wasn't expecting you here and now. I've had me ears out, waiting and wondering had you come into town yet: that slow you've been, we thought you'd funked it. *He's* here before you nigh on a week – which is *not* in accordance with the orders you was given. No knowing whether his ship's going to be able to sail or not, for America or the quays of Lethe. There's a British line-o'-battle wagon of what they call the second rate, standing on and off in the roadstead: *Bellerophon*, Captain Maitland. Causes a difficulty, right?' He reached out his hook with a jerk to jam the waterproof packet against Montholon's closed fist until the fist reluctantly opened and Montholon took it. 'That'll do the business. Don't open it now. The dosage is wrote inside. I wrote that part of it meself. Invisible ink, lemon-juice: borrow a smoothing-iron from your good lady, run it warm over the paper, it'll show. You're to wait till he gets to where he's going and then you give it him ever so gradual. Too much and too quick, the paroxysms (what we might term them) will stand out a mile – and point it directly at *you*; for your own sake, no impatience.'

'I don't understand,' said Montholon. But he did.

'Of course you do. And if you don't? We've words to be put in your ear. First, I've been told you might think you'll be far enough off for a mention of *six thousand* not to make that much difference. So we give you two more words. *Sugared angels*. Some sort of a confection? like, in one of them boulevard pâtisseries? Very nice. *I've* not been confided just what they might signify. But *you* know: I can see you know. (I've a privy out at back if your bowels are as loose as they look to be.) Wherever you go with him, there'll be one means or another to pass them two words on, whispering, disseminated, right? Slowly but surely. Which is what we've been told we're to tell you. *He'll* get to hear of 'em. *She* will. Which of 'em would you like least to hear them two words first?'

His manner changed again, to the regular whine of an overtired shopman anxious to get his shutters put up. 'Now, sir, if you'll just take the package, put it into your inside pocket, and hook the basket with the bottles onto me hook, I'm all right and ready to fetch it over to your good lady. Just settle up me little bill first. That'll amount to – ah—' He named a price, small enough, perhaps no more than four times the normal cost of the drugs in Paris; Montholon paid without question. Montholon indeed had nothing to say, neither remonstrance nor acceptance. He himself was on the hook, held there more acutely than any bottle at any price, Parisian or provincial; worse, he could see no end to it. The ingrained atheist, at such a strait, wanted very much to have Somebody to pray to.

22

Six more days, on the Atlantic coast, of uneasy deliberation. The Emperor moved out of Rochefort to a naval-base island in the estuary of the Gironde, and all his hangers-on came with him. He himself commandeered the port-admiral's house, and everyone else had to flounder about, finding what billets they could in a harsh little place devoted to the doldrums of war, where there was scarcely a dwelling that was not primarily some species of workshop or barrack. By mid-July there were scores of them – officers, civilian functionaries, wives, children, servants. Joseph Bonaparte, the Emperor's brother, had arrived (from no one knew where) with his own suite, larger and more heavily decorated than Napoleon's – he still regarded himself, prepos-terously, as King of Naples, King of the Two Sicilies and King of Spain, and kept turning people out of their lodgings in favour of his favourites, none of whom had been anywhere near Waterloo, or even in the train of the army or at its Paris headquarters upon the day of Waterloo.

The weather remained poor, westerly winds bringing mists and rain-squalls in from the Bay of Biscay for most of the time – not heavy enough to deter vessels from putting to sea, but closing down the visibility. How much of the British fleet was lying in wait offshore? How near were they? What were their orders in the event of an attempt to run their blockade? Impossible to tell. At the same time, word kept coming from inland France: regiments en bloc were transferring allegiance to King Louis (not that they wished to, but they felt themselves cut off and unable to mount any adequate resistance); while Wellington and Blücher extended their occupation over greater tracts of country every day.

The Montholons and their two servants were bedded down, very uncomfortably, in a great barn of a sail-loft, which they had to share with five other families and *their* servants. There was only one stove, in what had been the master-sailmaker's quarters; there was quarrelling all day long as to whose dinners should be cooked on it first. Most of the bedding was sail-canvas; there was an ineradicable smell of old tar; the sanitary arrangements were disgusting and caused as much disharmony as the stove.

'Borrow a smoothing-iron from your good lady'? No such implement to be found. And even if there had been, Albine's obsession with poor sick little Maximilien would have prevented her husband from making any approach to her on the subject at any time of the day or night. He would have to use the stove: but when, in God's name? Every time he went toward it, fumbling for his appalling packet, he found a colonel's manservant or a police commissioner's maid-of-all-work or a minister-of-state's dragon of a wife frying herrings there or stewing up yesterday's soup. Whenever it chanced to be vacant, Albine herself and the Touraine girl would be messing with pots of gruel and wretched bowls of arrowroot. Maximilien was not so ill as all that (Montholon thought): but he certainly lacked peace and quiet, for the children in the alcove next his bed-space sprang and yelled and squabbled from dawn to dusk, while their parents (a fat commissary and his blowsy vivandière spouse) sat and smoked their clay pipes and spat upon the floor and took no notice.

In the very early morning of July 14th – at last a brilliant sunrise with neither rain nor wind to mar it – Montholon crept from the pile of abrasive wrappings he called a bed and moved cautiously barefoot down the length of the great room. Albine, flat on her back a few feet away, alongside Maximilien, lay snoring open-mouthed, a bare shoulder and one of her breasts exposed above the covering: a shameless and pathetic sight. He had been sleeping in most of his clothes; he had shaved but irregularly ever since he came onto the island; he looked something like a tramp who had spent the night in a cowshed. All about him the families still slumbered. Improvised pisspots, portmanteaus and scattered footwear lay everywhere between the bed-spaces. A few strips of canvas had been strung up to give privacy to the more fastidious; articles of clothing, swords, women's bonnets, cocked hats, hung from the roof-posts and from nails driven into the wooden planks of the wall.

But in the cramped kitchen-place at the end of the loft, aha! no one.

Not even the vivandière's maid, who had lately developed a habit of sleeping there, practically inside the stove, under orders to be quite certain she was the first to boil coffee and heat up her employers' breakfast rolls. This morning she had defaulted. Montholon thought she might be keeping his own damned valet warm in whatever corner the lazy halfwit had stowed himself; he had noticed a series of sensual preliminaries the previous evening and had wondered should he put a stop to them. Now he was glad he had not.

The stove was out, of course; but it had burned for a good part of the night to supply hot punch and devilled kidneys for the minister-of-state and a gang of his rackety friends (who had kept it up until all hours); its top surface was still warm. Nearly as warm as a moderate iron; it would serve to flatten out a damp handkerchief; it might very well reclaim the dried and vanished tincture of an old squeeze of lemon-juice. First he must light the fire: if anyone came in, he needed good reason for being there. There was kindling-wood and charcoal; and the sailmaker's tinderbox, which remarkably had not been stolen. The flames began to crackle; Montholon filled a kettle from the rain-cask on the outside stairhead. Now he was well established: he was busy upon his duty, to make Albine's tisane. Her herbs were in a pot on a shelf; even more remarkably, they too had not been stolen. (These castaway officers had managed to restrain at least some of their propensity for continuous looting.)

The chemist's packet was pinned inside the waistband of his trousers just above his left groin, where it merged with the generous curve of his lower belly and was partly concealed by the watch-strap and seal-ribbon that hung out of his fob. He undid a couple of buttons, hitched it up and unpinned it, with many glances over his shoulder and under his elbow. No one to see him: good. He took a paring-knife and slit the packet open. Inside were a number of similar, smaller, packets, as cosy and cuddly as unshaped baby rabbits enfolded in the mother rabbit's womb. There was also a tight screw of paper, demi-foolscap (which seemed unduly large for the occasion), and apparently blank. Again with many glances, he spread it out upon the plate of the stove, near enough to the big black kettle to be hidden by its bulk from casual view. He stood with his back to the stove, watching for intruders, waiting for the heat to do its work. While he waited, he stuffed the packet back where it belonged. After a few minutes he groped behind him, burnt his fingers, snatched the paper, and carried it two paces into the sunbeam that streamed obliquely through the window.

A faint brown screed; in parts almost too faint to decipher. Nonetheless essentially clear: it would not be necessary to warm it a second time. He stuck his smarting fingers'-ends into his mouth and began to pick out the crabbed lines of narrow handwriting – he thought he saw a similarity with various letters he had once received from Monsieur's priest-secretary: but he could not be quite sure. (It was certainly not the same writing as on the note slipped into his boot in Paris. *That* particular messenger was now out of the picture; and a damned good thing too.)

Vital preliminary instruction!
Disobedience will be regarded as disobedience in every respect
and appropriate sanctions will follow:
SO COMMIT TO MEMORY AND BURN WITHOUT DELAY

Whether *this man* goes to America or into exile (as of late Elba) or into captivity or anywhere save before a tribunal determined to inflict the sorely deserved death-penalty, these orders will apply. *This man* is to be removed from temporal life (and placed where we must all be placed, at the eternal mercy of Omnipotent God, to Whom all devotion and prayer); but in such a way that his progress thereunto shall seem willed and directed by none but Our Lord God Himself, whose Name and due Worship according to the revealed traditions of our Holy Catholic Church shall be hereby safeguarded by those of us still humbly faithful in His renewed Kingdom upon earth. For twenty-two weary years, blasphemy, atheism, heresy, schism and idolatry have usurped the true Christian Way. Should *this man* continue, such courses must inevitably recur: the dogs of hell to their vomit returning (*etc.*)

You shall – when the time is ripe – ensure a slow admixture as hereunder designated.
Bottles of wine the best mode?
For it is known that *this man* has always reserved, and doubtless still will reserve, his own special vintage for his own special use. Such being his cowardice that it seems he has feared poison ever. Well may he have suffered such fears, for now all his terrors are white unto the harvest of their guilt.
Eripe a gladio animam meam, et de manu canis vitam meam.
(O God, deliver my soul from the sword: my darling from the power of the dog.)
—Psalm XXI

In the Name of the Father, the Son and the Holy Spirit:
in the Name of the Most Blessed Virgin Mary, Mother of God, Queen of Heaven:
to Whose abiding care the land and people of our holy France shall forever be dedicate, as it was in the days of grace of St Denis, St Geneviève, St Louis; and of Joan the Courageous Maid martyred, victorious, unsullied.

Quite the oddest commission for murder that Montholon could imagine: but it surely did not need to be memorised. Wine? Well, he'd not forget that. But how oh how did they expect him to—? Would he have to suborn a *butler*?

At the bottom of the paper, something else: another style, another writer. A coarse back-sloping scrawl, just exactly what you'd look for from a hook-handed man.

ARSENIC, in form of powder. Microscopic dosages absolute maximum for purposes as stated below: must be measured on the thumbnail if (as probable) no druggist's scales available. (*Nota bene*: DO NOT EXCEED, else requirements defeated *in toto*.)

Thence followed a graduated table, divided into sections with such subheadings as – 'Extremely Slow, no apparent Symptoms', 'Prompting Symptoms of Physical Disquiet', 'Causing Nausea and Debility', 'Coup de Grâce, if called for: *NOT to be administered without Unimpeachable Authority*'. Quantities were specified, precisely by grain, approximately by thumbnail, half-thumbnail, *quarter*-thumbnail for God's sake; time-intervals annotated. Montholon was accustomed to administrative documents, and the last pharmaceutical portion of this one was not so very different from certain pettifogging varieties of military order. He conned it, fixed it in his mind, checked it over to ensure that it *was* fixed, and finally thrust the paper into the stove. He turned to find Albine staring at him, barefoot like himself, haggard and unwashed in her dressing-gown, all her hair down about her shoulders.

Every hair on *his* head seemed a gorgon-snake of guilt.

What had she seen?

For he was no longer merely a spy: he was a branded assassin, fixed to his crag like Prometheus, no hope of parole. The vulture was now at his liver; it would tear and ravage irremediably, let him hold himself solitary or pretend loyal duties or pretend social ease – or pretend (as at this moment) the overriding responsibilities of love. For from today forward, there was *nothing* that overrode. The vulture would chew, and the vulture was himself. He lived only for the packet at his groin. (And damn it, the pin had come loose: the damned incumbrance was halfway to his knee.)

And yet it appeared that Albine had seen nothing; she was vexed and vexation made her blind.

'Charles-Tristan, what the devil are you at? Maximilien's awake and crying, Zoé's got the stomach-flux and won't get off the nightsoil-bucket and that man of yours has fucked off to fornicate. If you had to light the stove, why wouldn't you have waited for me? I could have told you to make the gruel. As it is, all you're doing is boiling your own coffee. Selfish pig.'

She seemed ready to weep with annoyance, but something about Montholon's attitude (his shirt all undone, his trousers slipping unbelted round his hips, and such a queer childlike look of naughty despair on his face) stirred her to laughter; and after the laughter, an unexpected tenderness.

Also, she had noticed the herb-jar; she realised he had risen so early for her benefit, not his. But it should have been for Maximilien's: she did not quite abandon her reproaches. 'No,' she pouted, 'I take back "pig". That's all I'm taking back: the child's gruel comes first before everything.

Fetch me the oatmeal, clean water in the pannikin – what have you there? *salt?* Nonsense! you ought to know better than that, come on come on come on – he's awake for it already, and if he doesn't sick it up I think he's turned the corner. He did sleep all night, you know, and nothing worse than wetting the bed. Come, come on, gruel! Ah, you're a sweet creature when you want to be.'

A quick impulse: she gave him a kiss.

'So am I, though you mightn't think it,' she continued as she stirred the gruel, all of a rattle of highly strung chatter, the first chatter she had found in herself since Paris. 'I do know I haven't been, not lately. Can you blame me? Even if you blame me, forgive. It's been hell. What with Maximilien, and Gaius-Gracchus – what's going to happen to *him?* he'll be killed and he's such a nice man, so good for us, his jokes and his not-jokes, so good. And of course I ought to be fretting for the Emperor, I know of course that *you* are, but oh, Charles-Tristan, what will he do? America? are we *all* supposed to go?'

She looked up at him anxiously. A shadow was crossing his face. He had been told, she decided, that *he* was for America and he did not want to go. Why not? Because he must leave her behind? Why, of course! he believed she would refuse to accompany him; for she had, had she not? been stupid and unhelpful about coming to the coast, sulking all the journey (except for the Gaius-Gracchus interlude) and now heaven knew what confusion she was causing him, conflicting with his duty, wrenching his poor old affections. She shoved the pannikin to a cooler part of the stove-top, and fastened both her arms around her husband, for 'husband' was what he was and let her not forget it! lovely as he had always been (even that telltale little pot of a belly was not yet uncomely, and could with proper care be reduced): tight arms, protective, pleading for protection, pleading no longer for a return to Touraine but only that those golden Touraine days (dear God, only a month-and-a-bit ago?) should be carried with them always, to travel with them *now*, to wherever they should be bound, comfortable quarters or not – for she and he were now together, *must* be together, he must truly understand it.

This was not the acrid lechery of that apprehensive week in Paris while Waterloo crept nearer and nearer. This was true love from a full foolish heart and she meant him to feel it. Oh, why would he not meet her eyes?

She put a hand to the back of his curls and bent his head round to hers. He did meet her eyes and all hint of a shadow was gone. 'Charles-Tristan, this is important. I am telling you, I was *wrong*. A voyage to

America is *not* too huge. Maximilien is getting better, *I* am better already, of course we will go where you go. I love you.' She kissed him again, and he kissed her in return, layering it on, lips, tongue, cheeks, eyelids and each of her ears, until she squawked like a milkmaid and begged him to leave off, there were others in the building, they'd be coming in to use the stove—

'Oh,' she said, on an afterthought, a sudden recollection of something she had not quite liked but which she would not now allow to spoil her mood. (They were carrying the pan of gruel and Maximilien's bowl and spoon through into the sail-loft, where their fellow lodgers one by one began to lurch out of their beds.) 'Oh, what was that paper I saw you read with such attention and then burn? The minister-of-state's wife been slipping you love-letters, has she?'

Montholon laughed. An easy laugh, charming, entering into the spirit of her banter. 'Not at all: the vivandière. But it's quite out of the question. She expects me to purchase her brandy as well.' He dropped his voice to a consequential murmur: 'No: to be serious. There are *secret orders*. Passed around by – ah – Bertrand, Gourgaud. Some of the hangers-on are – well, they are not to be trusted. You understand?'

And of course she understood. The Emperor's fate in her husband's devoted hands. At last Charles-Tristan lived at the height of his capacity. How tragic, though, it had to be sheer defeat that brought him there. Proud exiles, to America! and her bosom swelled with pride.

Exactly at that moment, before Maximilien had even opened his mouth for the first spoonful, a naval petty-officer came banging amongst them: 'Ahoy! Ladies, gents, officers, civilians, the lot: port-admiral's compliments and you're all to go directly to the boat-shed abaft of his house: council-of-war with the Emperor, no exceptions, lackeys and skivvies included, just as you are, never mind your little washings and brush-ups. Begging your pardons, show a leg!' The French fleet of late had not had much glory: to hector senior soldiers was some compensation, and none of them could effectively complain. He hammered on a tin plate with a marlin-spike until all pretence of sleep was useless; and then he banged out again, to harry more of the general staff in their billets along the quay.

The boat-shed was the nearest covered space to the Emperor's quarters that could accommodate upwards of two hundred people, for that was by now the size of his entourage – it seemed a large number until one recollected that it could also be described as the size of his entire Empire. There was a wide tiled roof supported by wooden posts, and no walls. When Albine got there, hurrying in the wake of Charles-

Tristan, both of them dressing as they ran (Zoé groaning behind under the weight of Maximilien and the discomfort of her stomach-ache; the valet nowhere to be seen), she found baulks of timber pulled by seamen into an arrangement of makeshift benches, as for a law-court or elected assembly. Montholon had thrust himself up to the front with other generals and officials, adjusting his sword-belt, straightening his hair, giving his cocked hat a surreptitious polish on his sleeve. Bertrand supervised two ratings who carried in a mahogany table from the port-admiral's office and laid out on it paper, pens and inkwell.

The boat-shed filled rapidly, with some attention to seniority, the higher ranks asserting themselves around the table. Wives sat behind the lower ranks; servants and children behind the wives. Soldiers with fixed bayonets were placed round the edge of the shed, facing outwards: no mere formal guard but a vital security precaution – they could not defend the Emperor against the onset of a Bourbon regiment (a possibility every day growing more and more probable); but they could deter assassins, and who knew how many of *those* might not already have been infiltrated onto the island, for ferry-boats kept coming and going, stores were being landed, the very sailors of the frustrated fleet were not beyond suspicion?

Albine, out of the corner of her eye, saw Montholon's valet slithering in at the back – his name was Grâcepardieu, and a name he had good need of, she said to herself, she hated him, always late, never ever aware of what he had to do next – the vivandière's maid at the tail of his coat – oh, to be sure, with her bodice all undone!

No sooner had this flurry of spite passed her mind – worse than spite, inconsistency – she herself had no skirt over her petticoat and had to hide the fact under a great shawl – than dapper little Las Cases popped up at the table. *He* was dressed impeccably, not in uniform but very much *ex officio*, as smart as a notary's copying-clerk with his hair-powder, black suit and fastidious black cravat. He began to announce something; Albine could not hear what it was; he seemed to have a cold; and in any case he was not allowed to finish, for feet stamped outside the shed, a sergeant-major bawled, the rank of guards presented arms with a vehement succession of clashes and claps, and the Emperor was under the roof and holding forth at strenuous speed before anyone had time to take breath.

'—and I seem,' he was saying – it was as though in his urgency he had begun his address before leaving the port-admiral's and was already halfway through it – perhaps he was? – brother Joseph was at his elbow and had no doubt been harangued all the way across the yard – 'I seem to spend my life frustrated by islands, Corsica, Elba, this infernal stone-crop here, and you'll all be as sick of it as I am. Where next? At last, you see, this morning, God's given us a clear horizon – with one of Hanover George's men-o'-war pasted to the very middle of it like a wafer on a debt-collector's summons, and in sight, more to the purpose, of an entire Anglo-Saxon squadron, hull-down in the distance. We don't even need a telescope to see them. Our own ships are ready to sail; the captains inform me that if they catch tonight's tide there is a chance, if we dare take it, of evading our foes and breaking out into open ocean. A chance. And have we not many a time taken our chance? My children, how many chances, more perilous than this? Of course we have; you grin at me; you are alive to the danger and you *live!'*

This was hard-knuckled vigour, humorous as well, Napoleon at his most captivating; and Albine was captivated, warm and fervent from her tousled head to her black stockings with all those holes in them. She had not been so close to him more than once or twice before, and only at Malmaison where he had lowered like a thundercloud, striding the corridors with scarcely a word to a dog; now she saw suddenly the Man of Marengo, the Sunburst of Austerlitz, she would *die* for him, here, this very minute, at his feet in this wide-open shed; in mucky old underwear and never give a damn what he thought of it. She could not deny; his power was directly *sexual*; there was no rationality about her surge of devotion; first her husband, now her monarch; everything today was conspiring towards orgasm.

She glanced around her. She was not alone in her emotion. She saw flushed faces, parted lips, fingernails driven into palms. Men and women, overtly aroused. But she must listen; he was talking not alone to these others but most personally to *her*, shaping *her* life as well as his own—

Deflating his own rhetoric, too. He shrugged, waved his arms, offered his laughter to mock the very glory of his glorious Last Chance. 'Dear comrades,' he smiled, 'foolhardiness is not enough. I've had hot-headed marshals, foolhardy subalterns, grenadiers with their eyes blind with blood; and nothing they ever did would have won us any battles if *I* had not known how to utter just one small word: "Stop!" So let's be quiet, let's be cautious, shall we think about what might happen if King George and his sailormen are *not* evaded? Shall we think how fat Louis and his breech-sucking sycophants, Talleyrand, Fouché, *patati, patata*, are to be told the grotesque story? – oh yes but yes I said "fat Louis", you'll wonder how I have the nerve? but *I* am not fat in my soul; this paunch is a phantom, pouf! and it's gone, little hobgoblin Boney as lean as when he first crossed the Alps! – and then let's just think how fat Louis and his friends will be telling the story themselves – to Blücher, to Wellington, to Castlereagh, to Metternich, to the Tsar – and oh dear, to the people of France.'

He conjured up a picture, a cameo of caricature: of 'the horrible hobgoblin' hauled out of the hold of a captured ship by ruffianly British marines, their red faces, their fartings from all that intolerable roast beef, their 'Shakespearian clownish glee' at finding their ancient enemy hid away to save his life among wine-casks, sacks of biscuit, rat-eaten coils of rope.

'Dear oh dear, it would not do. For whatever we now plan, must be planned toward dignity, toward a soldier's nobility, above all toward the utmost *magnanimity*.' Albine saw Las Cases preen himself. Had he had a hand in the Emperor's phrases? There must certainly have been some rehearsal; she did not care; it was a hot romantic play, all the better that its lines were well studied. 'Another notion has been put to me. My beloved brother had a notion. I thank him from a full heart for it; I reject it. Because he thought he might take my place, pretend to be me, and courageously, deliberately, deposit himself in the way of capture. Ah, Joseph—' He flung his arms around Joseph in an excess of affection; no, a parody of affection, he clearly thought that the brother was a fool: '—dear Joseph, you are taller than I am, alas a great deal thinner, the coat would be too short, the breeches half-empty. Flat-arse!' He smacked Joseph's backside, laughed, and led everyone to laugh. 'No! these expedients are no better than half-baked; send them back to the kitchen and consider instead the solution of the *cordon bleu*.'

He talked rapidly of a scene from ancient history, how Themistocles, who saved Athens from Persian invasion, was in the upshot betrayed by time-serving Athenian politicians, and sought sanctuary at the Persian court, the implacable den of his enemies – but he walked there, head held high, and defied the Persian emperor to degrade him. 'Nor was he degraded. His noble foe responded to the great admiral's nobility, and received him with incomparable honour. Now, will anyone do this for Napoleon? The Prussian won't, the Russian won't, the Austrian – no no no. Against my will I have ravaged their territories, their great landowners will never forgive. Moreover, they have sworn to hand me over to the Bourbons. So what of the most ancient of all our national adversaries? H'm?'

He spoke what did seem to be realistic good sense about his failure to invade Britain, about the feeling of immunity from the atrocities of war which this had bred in the ox-like British soul (if such an entity did indeed exist), about the degree of admiration for him even now continuing (according to his spies) among vast sections of the British public, about Lord Byron's enthusiasm for him and Lord Wellington's notorious respect, about a moment at Waterloo when the chance of battle brought him personally under the mouths of Lord Wellington's cannon and those cannon fell suddenly silent. No, the British were not rancorous: their aristocrats were too absurdly chivalrous, their merchants too wedded to the 'ambiguities of the material *main chance*' – if anyone would accept him as a conquered but proud suppliant and thereafter a loyal friend, it would have to be Perfidious Albion, who had never liked the Bourbons and would be only too glad to turn the perfidy against fat Louis. 'Incorrigible perfidy, dear comrades, and we use it to the height of our cunning!'

It was, he admitted, a gambler's final throw. But the odds were closely calculated. The risk, he firmly believed, was less than all the other risks from all the other possibilities. Therefore he had written a letter to be delivered, under a flag of truce, to the *Bellerophon* offshore. It was, in effect, an appeal from the new Themistocles to George the Persian Emperor in the guise of Regent Prince of Great Britain – Las Cases would read it out – but Las Cases having lost his voice, the Emperor snatched the paper and declaimed it himself—

> I have finished my political career, I come to sit at the hearth of
> the British people, I put myself under the protection of the laws
> which I claim from Your Royal Highness as the most powerful,
> constant, and generous of my enemies.

'I shall, if I am permitted, call myself by a simple name – Colonel Duroc, perhaps, in memory of a brave officer who died at my side, many of you will have known him? – and I shall seek a country house within the neighbourhood of London, surround myself with you my dear friends, dig my garden like Candide, write my memoirs, entertain old soldiers from the army of Lord Wellington, now and again go to the city to hear Shakespeare in the mouths of Kean and of Mrs Siddons – is she still alive? Perhaps I might teach French – with a Corsican accent – to the little English children of the village.'

He paused to allow this sentiment to penetrate all hearts. Gourgaud, himself a Corsican, sobbed uncontrollably; Mme Bertrand (her mind full of her Irish kin) smiled in ecstasy at her husband, who smiled back and mopped his brow with obvious relief; Montholon wiped away a tear and awkwardly appeared to be adjusting the fit of his trousers; Albine made a mental note to tell him on no account must he grope his crotch when sublimities were in progress. She herself was overcome. If the

British really were to respond to such a gallant, such a truly *Gallic* supplication, worthy not only of Themistocles, but also of the great Vercingetorix, and if she and Charles-Tristan were able to accompany their chief, then would not the future be almost as gentle and entrancing as Touraine?

She envisaged herself in a rose-embowered cottage at 'Colonel Duroc's' rural gate – why, the whole district, wherever it was (Sussex-shire? the Hamptons? East-Anglian Kent? her geography was lamenta-bly vague) could well become a small colony of elegant French, and the very best class of French, versatile, sanguine, men and women of Olympian tenacity – such a change for the English from those leeching Bourbon émigrés! – she wondered was it true that a handsome woman in a box at the Theatre of the Drury Garden Lane might receive invitations from two or three milords at one time, and not one of them would presume to offer force against her chastity? 'God, I'm a silly bitch! but I do have to dream about *something*; would Charles-Tristan not make an effort and hunt up Gaius-Gracchus to join us?'

For some undecided reason, she was having her little doubt about Charles-Tristan. In proximity to Napoleon, he seemed suddenly a quite servile small fellow. And yet he was near six foot tall. Was it the pallor of his face? Or a suspicion of a crouch to his posture? But then, they called him a chamberlain. It could be so; he was just doing his work. At the stove, half an hour ago, she had thought he was like – well, like Themistocles, or another such, upon one of those huge canvases by David. Or had she? Not really, no, admit it. But David's heroes were naked, and she had thought of her husband naked – she had not seen him so for what appeared to be ages – how could she, with all these gatherings and dispersings and rushings and post-chaises and escapes and gendarmerie at the road-blocks and crawlings fully dressed into bed in all sorts of sordid stopping-places? And Maximilien falling ill. And would Zoé be included for England? Indeed, would the poor girl want to come? She could hardly be kidnapped. But how would an English nurse, all brawn and raw-boned energy, have the first possible idea of a delicate French baby?

She wondered, would the Emperor's paunch be comical or awe-inspiring, were one to see him without his clothes?

She was, altogether, in an overheated state of mind. Probably not at all well. She listened, distractedly, to Bertrand who was enquiring which of the entourage definitely did *not* want to ask to be taken on board the British fleet. He had a pen in his hand and was writing down names. Montholon did not speak. He knew his duty. So did Albine. So she kept her feverish silence as feeble women around her threw up their hands and begged plaintively that they should not be compelled into exile from 'beloved France so clear and beautiful'. Husbands were remonstrating: some of them agreed with their wives, some prepared to abandon their wives, few of them seemed able to respond with good sense. The Emperor lost patience and walked away, pushing through the sentries to stand in gloom at the edge of the dock: his grand gesture must hold back until the sentimental nonsense (of his own skilled conjuring-up) had worn itself out.

At a low oblique angle the sun poured under the eaves of the boat-shed; direct and glaring, far too hot; and far too much clamour in the boat-shed; enough to turn one dizzy; was there nothing at all at hand, like a jug or even a bucket, whence a person could draw forth a drink? She had missed her morning tisane; she was dizzy beyond endurance. She crumpled into her own lap, a dead faint, and from her lap she spilt down onto the stone flags of the boat-shed floor.

While she lay there she thought she felt none other than Napoleon raise her gently in his arms. But that was a mistake: it was only a sailor, and he dumped her straight back on her bench. The listing and un-listing of volunteers and defectors was to take ages, so it seemed, idiotic talk and cross-talk, stupid wranglings. The Emperor's grand gesture (which should have been as keen as a sabre-blade) was being blunted under the sunlight before it even began to flash.

So she thought.

And then again she thought: unless there was glory and defiance, a surrender must be merely a *yielding*; the Emperor knew this; why could not everyone else see it, and help him? Courage, for God's sake! that's all that was needed. Despite her physical weakness, she herself now knew herself to be utterly determined.

23

Tottering to her feet, she spoke up and would not be hushed, with a hurtling red-faced excitement that stilled the croaking all at once, put the worst of the croakers to shame, and brought a gleam of quick pleasure to Napoleon's darkling face. Indeed, he looked at Albine as though he had never seen her before.

Montholon looked at her as though he was seeing her once too often. What was wrong with him, she asked herself, that he could not bear to hear what should have been his own thoughts expressed in public by his wife? If he would not speak, she had to. Some foolishness about officers' protocol? Or was he simply mean and jealous?

July 14th: twenty-sixth anniversary of the storming of the Bastille; the cuckoo-child inheritor of that historic stress and frenzy sent off a coastguard ketch to HMS *Bellerophon* with his letter of submission. Captain Maitland, when he read it, did not know just how Plutarchian the Prince Regent was likely to prove; but he personally was sure he would make every effort not to besmirch his own place in history by the smallest discourtesy, from himself or his crew, toward this supposed ruin of an Emperor, and then – upon the 15th – toward the large and chattering gang who came jostling aboard at the imperial coat-tails. Over a hundred of them; the ketch had to make three trips.

The *Bellerophon* set sail for Torbay in almost the mood of a pleasure-voyage, as it were the great yacht of some immensely rich potentate, delighting in a sudden access of calm weather, with music and dancing under deck-awnings, servants carrying trays of wine-glasses, ladies with parasols lining the rails of the poop and tossing crumbs of biscuit to the seagulls. Children skylarked with sailors; officers of both nations made grave conversation about respective styles of fighting-technique; Captain Maitland was delighted by Napoleon's keen interest in the naval routine and his flattering comments upon the demeanour of the ship's company. Napoleon pinched midshipmen and tarry jacks by the lobe of the ear, and made jokes in French and Italian; they did not understand him but they laughed at him and he winked. He borrowed the master's sextant to beg a lesson in shooting the sun. He seized hold of a marine's musket and demonstrated the French method of fixing bayonets and presenting arms.

Torbay was an aquatic circus, with the ship at her moorings increasingly beset by every possible small boat from every port along the south-west coast, chartered by families, individuals, clubs, and impromptu yelping groups of shop-girls and office-boys – persons of all conditions prepared to pay *anything* for just one short sight of the Corsican – some hoped he would be in chains – most were prepared to cheer him, and did cheer him, every time he appeared at the rail to smile upon the floating crowds, to kiss his hand to the ladies, to wave his notorious cocked hat. Captain Maitland was worried. He announced to his first lieutenant: 'This holiday humour assumes, and far too rapidly, a political complexion.'

'Oh, it does, sir. Almost farcical. But a prejudiced observer—'

'You mean a government spy?'

'More or less, sir, yes. They are, they say, ubiquitous. To such a fellow, it could appear that our ship's company has connived at – ah—'

'—at a radical demonstration. Exactly. We are ordered to wait here for orders: but I am formally declaring to you my considered opinion that the *Bellerophon* would be more judiciously placed within immediate reach of the forts and dockyard at Plymouth. Wind and tide are advantageous; be so good as to ask the master to lay a course for the Sound.'

But Plymouth was even worse than Torbay. Captain Maitland had a midshipman count the number of sightseeing boats; the young man reached nine hundred and fifty-five before a sudden rainstorm blotted the mass of them out of his vision. He estimated an average of eight people in each boat. In some of the larger boats, entire brass bands. Brass bands that played the Marseillaise, and *Ça ira*, and the Carmagnole.

And in the meantime: no orders. Somewhere there must be grave indecision – Downing Street? – for the Admiralty as a rule was vigorous enough in its replies to captains' reports. Clearly this was not a matter the First Lord could decide on his own.

However heavily the suspense may have dragged at Napoleon's spirits, his followers on the whole did not share it. The almost gleeful hospitality with which Maitland and his men had treated them, their sense of being in some way a treasured gift to the English and one well worth treasuring, their self-important awareness of themselves as the heirs of the (paradoxically Anglophile) Voltairean tradition, all this confirmed their certainty that Bonaparte in his defeat was about to be recognised after all as a spiritual conqueror. Albine said so to her husband as they stooped staring through a gunport at the clustering boats: 'You see, the English love him. Impossible for London to fly in the face of such a warmth of popular feeling.'

'Really, my dear? You suppose that in a very short time our Emperor will be the ally of King George, and King Louis the enemy of them both? Ah, well, it may be so. If it is, you and I could be very very comfortable . . . Don't bank on it.' Montholon's hand was pressed to his groin as though he'd been stabbed with an indigestion-pang, *he* did not look at all comfortable. The heave of the ship, he said, a nauseous calm, he said, even at anchor, absurd . . . Albine was sorry for him, but happy nonetheless to be where she was, and soon she would be even happier – received, a long-lost sister, into the bosom of a friendly nation where all would be forgotten and forgiven.

24

God, what a fool she was. 'What fools,' she cried, 'we all are. Even the Emperor: the biggest fool of all.'

25

Friendliness, bosoms, forgotten and forgiven? oh dear God, never: their entire reception until this day had been the cruellest of practical jokes. July 31st, at moorings in Plymouth Sound and the jocular brutality of the Anglo-Saxon character revealed at its very worst: the bull-baiting, cock-fighting, rat-catching, barefist-bruising English had merely been refreshing themselves sportively for a fortnight, before delivering the Letter of Doom.

It was brought to the *Bellerophon* by an aged bent-backed admiral who read it to Napoleon in privacy, the pair of them alone with Captain Maitland in the latter's cabin. Napoleon's rage could be heard all over the after-quarters of the great ship, from the open deck above to the rat-infested trench of the cable-tier.

'St Helena?' he roared, 'the most lonely of the loneliest of all the islands in the world! I shall go mad there, I shall die, and *that is your master's intention*.' Wolf-like he howled, owl-like he ululated: he was Talma the tragic actor as vanquished Mithridates betrayed by his kith and his kin. And then, like a low-class *comic* actor frantic to grab hold of some laughs, he flung crockery and smashed glasses (which belonged to Captain Maitland). He tore up the fell decree of the ignoble British government and then called for his servant to bring him gum-arabic to stick it together again. He said to the servant: 'You can read to me, from Plutarch. But first I must breathe some fresh air.'

He climbed to the quarterdeck, smiled and bowed to Captain Maitland (who had preceded him there with the admiral), took off his hat yet once more to the gaping public in the bumboats, caught Albine's eye, winked at her and twitched his lip for all the world like Gaius-Gracchus, shrugged his shoulders to everyone at large, and so below-decks again to hear his man read of the suicide of Cato, how the victory of the autocrat Caesar caused that severe republican to fall upon his sword *in glory and defiance*. (The valet said later that he had believed the chapter of Plutarch to be the prelude to his master's own suicide, and he trembled as he pronounced each deadly sentence. No such thing: Napoleon lay back listening, got up from his bunk, demanded a bath, 'You can help to sponge me down, I sweat in this heat till I stink.')

That evening upon the maindeck he addressed all his followers with sombre emotion. There was, he said, a choice to be made. First for him, then for them. Fortune of War! they must not kick against Fate. For Fate, once insulted, might never reverse herself.

26

The Island of Exile, he was appalled to inform them, was very small, much smaller than Elba, and totally devoid of civilised amenities. It was not a proper colony with a native population and indigenous industries and produce; the only reason the English held it was to provide a convenient watering-station for their ships of the East Indian traffic. Impossible that a hundred friends could accompany him thither and find accommodation appropriate to their rank, to their deserts, to the fervent aspirations of their loyal hearts – and even were it possible, the English had forbidden it. 'Elba, humiliating as it was, had been a sovereign kingdom under my unquestioned rule. St Helena is a prison; the only ruler there is a chief gaoler – whatever kind of rank (governor-general of some sort, admiral?) may be allotted him to cover up his true function. Into that gaol I am permitted to bring with me no more than three household officers, military or civilian, and a servant for each of them; their wives and children if they wish, and a servant for each wife; my personal physician and my personal servants, to the number of no more than—' He referred to a sheet of paper in his hand. 'I enjoyed myself at this point with a smart little skirmish of Cairo-bazaar haggling – the abominable Talleyrand could not have done better – the English admiral said eight servants, I demanded sixteen, I forced him to split the difference at twelve.'

If he had hoped for his people to laugh with him, or even applaud, he was mistaken. They were all far too anxious about what was coming next. So he bustled his discourse forward: 'Very well! Do I pick my companions? Do I call for volunteers? Perhaps I should pick and then allow the chosen gentlemen to refuse, if they will. Emperor I may still call myself but I cannot compel. So let you all understand the implications: upon St Helena we will be allowed to draw cheques upon any bank account we may retain in France or elsewhere; I understand the Bourbon Pretender has been persuaded to agree (with some reluctance) to that concession. If the English are to keep us, they at least avoid the infamy of conspiring to rob us as well. Out of my savings, such as they are, I shall be able to pay appropriate salaries to officers and servants. It is important you should know this: I am not asking you to be beggars. Chances, however, for augmenting your incomes will be

limited, it goes without saying; so too will chances for spending them.
Mind you, I don't ask you to commit yourself for my entire lifetime
(which will in any case be short enough); unlike myself you will not be
prisoners. I leave it to your sense of duty to determine the duration of
your stay; there is no doubt that a lonely island will – eh, what? – lack
entertainment. The climate, I am told, is more healthy than you might
imagine. Perhaps.'

He paused; but no one responded. Faces were working, fingers
clasping and unclasping, convulsed with indeterminate passion; clearly
no one wanted to go under such conditions to the huge emptiness of the
South Atlantic, and yet no one wanted not to go – or no one wanted to
be *seen* not wanting to go. Moreover many did not know where *else* they
could go: general-officers who had deserted the colours of King Louis to
rejoin Napoleon after Elba would be almost sure to face the death
penalty if they fell into Bourbon hands. Maybe England would make
allowances, despite this present cruelty – maybe parts of Italy or
the Low Countries – Scandinavia? a renegade Bonapartist marshal was,
after all, being adopted as King of Sweden and was unlikely to keep
friends with the Russians for much longer – oh, America, certainly,
but how to get there? with what papers? they were now absolutely at
the mercy of the British and naturally feared every possible brand of
duplicity.

Napoleon nodded his head: 'Too great a burden upon your loyalty? Of
course, I understand. Let me solve your dilemma by naming some
names. First: General Bertrand! you served with me in Italy in '97, Egypt
in '98; my dear indispensable friend, every triumphant year thereafter,
every year of disaster as well; you came with me to Elba; we know each
other profoundly; we trust each other, I do believe. But general, your
excellent wife has already pleaded with me to excuse you this ordeal –
she pleaded this afternoon in tears, I was deeply moved – you stand
between myself and her. So what do you say?'

It was apparent from Bertrand's taut and devoted profile that he was
indeed nerving himself to volunteer; but Mme Bertrand at once
usurped his opportunity. She did not speak either on his behalf or her
own, she rushed in silence across the deck, she paused to give one loud
cry by the sill of an open gunport and she threw herself out of the
aperture. There was a netting stretched beyond the gunport, not so
much to inhibit suicide as to prevent sailors deserting, sailors fetching
women in, Frenchmen escaping, miscreants climbing aboard to steal
rum or assassinate Boney; she hung in the mesh like a giant white
spider, her summer straw hat fallen half down her back, her tangles of

thick fair hair all spread across her blubbery face by the breeze. Several French gentlemen hauled her inboard again, several ladies bent over her to comfort her. Her three children, screaming in terror, were hustled away by their nurse. Bertrand stood rigid; Napoleon smiled grimly. 'My poor Bertrand,' he said, 'I don't think she meant it. That netting has been rigged ever since we dropped anchor, she cannot have failed to observe it. Shall we call this little theatre-piece positively her last appearance in the role of – of pathetic female victim of military stupidity and political ruthlessness, h'm? I know you will come with me to the Island. I rely on you to persuade your dear Irish Fanny, for your own happiness, to come too, along with your captivating little ones. If she utterly refuses – well, the English will assuredly let her stay in this country, if her relatives are prepared to make sufficient fuss; I have told her that already.'

Albine, to her husband, while all this was going on: 'That very tiresome woman is not so stupid as she seems. To begin with, her relatives here have cast her off for marrying a Frenchman; nor has she been able to be reconciled with them – I know how many fruitless letters she has written since we arrived. She has no choice but to go with the Emperor; and then you know, she would wish to be thought in love with him; she must show him the huge sacrifice she makes for his sake – *his* sake, not her husband's – oh, we'll hear more about it, *all* about it, in the process of time. At least, I suppose we will? There will be *some* news permitted between this St Helena and New York, or wherever we are finally to settle?'

For Montholon of course was not bound to St Helena; the Emperor scarcely knew him and would never single him out; nor had he the qualities for such a wan and self-mortifying duty. Her own fervour of service was perfectly quelled by this spectre of a rock in the ocean – (and yet perhaps – even now – were the Emperor suddenly to turn to her and beg *her* to share his exile, without Montholon, without indeed any reason or excuse except that he 'had seen the truth of her heart in her eyes!' or some such, and could not live without it – ah, then, perhaps? – ah, no! speculations neither honest nor truly romantic, indeed they were no better than the sickening egotism of Fanny Bertrand) – and yet she was ashamed that she and Charles-Tristan were not to be numbered among the last few faithful friends.

Deeply as she despised the plump and facile Fanny, she wished she was her, she wished *she* had a husband from whom the Emperor could not bear to be parted; she wished *she* could struggle with the Emperor for the love, for the duty, of such a husband. She was violently upset and wished *she* had just now thought of throwing herself out of a gunport. This was a day for the strongest emotions; and yet everyone all around her (Fanny excepted, self-indulgent lard-cake!) did their best to choke them back . . . Because they were on an English ship, was it necessary to behave like so many damned English sticks of chalk?

Napoleon was demanding Las Cases be one of the party. 'I must retain,' he cried, 'my chronicler. I need a man to write my life upon the Island, day by day, just as it happens, eh what? like the Robinson Crusoe! with my parrot and my hat of goat's-hair! I need a man to write my memoirs as I dictate them; for what else am I going to be able to do there? I must vindicate my life to the whole world before I am compelled to say farewell to it; the very last task my Destiny imposes, you are the man to ensure that I carry it out! You will come? Why, of course you will . . .'

Las Cases, enormously flattered, was no stick of chalk. 'Yes! oh yes, Majesty!' he intoned, 'how could I *not*?' He fell upon one knee and raised his clasped hands in the air. His young son came up behind him, whispering furiously in his ear. Albine knew Las Cases was a widower; the boy must be remonstrating, alarmed for his own future; was his adolescence about to be stunted upon a mid-ocean crag, or would there be found for him some unappealing boarding-school in a friendless foreign country? Albine thought a boarding-school would do the boy a power of good, the harsher the better, flog his slick buttocks to pieces; but why should she worry? it was none of her business; except that it caused her to snigger – ill-muffled hoots, explosive neurasthenic snorts, that the father's conceited posturing was so easily marred by the unthinking conceit of his son.

The tensions among the company had not so much broken down as flown out centrifugally; the awkward silence had evolved into a babel of everyone talking at once, God only knew about what – the Emperor's choice of Bertrand followed so swiftly by his turn to Las Cases (and the two familial interventions, so demeaningly public) were loosening tongues all round – protests, protestations, assertions of loyalty, denials of denial-of-loyalty, jealous accusations mixed up with sudden outbursts of sobbing from both men and women packed together in the ship's waist between gun-carriages and the thick shaft of the mainmast, the seamen and marines looking down on them in wonderment from the gangways on either side.

One more companion for the Emperor to pick. His eye roved round the deck; Albine guessed he was looking for Gourgaud as the obvious third choice; but Gourgaud, for some reason, was immersed in hot conversation in Italian with – of all people – the ship's surgeon, a wilful Irishman who should not have been present at all at this delicate discussion of internal French affairs, and whose gesticulations (when excited) were almost as fierce as Gourgaud's. Just now he appeared *highly* excited; and neither of them immediately realised that Napoleon was waiting to speak.

A very brief pause: the doctor was caught by the Emperor's eye, fell instantly silent, and strove without speaking to alert the noisy Gourgaud to the imperial intention.

Before Gourgaud's windmill arms had quite come to an embarrassed halt, the pause was filled up with a wrench of clumsy movement from within the very crook of Albine's startled right arm.

Charles-Tristan, Count de Montholon, was volunteering pell-mell to accompany his master into limbo.

27

He strode forward; he raised his voice; he demanded that his earlier failures (involuntary failures, as everyone who knew him knew perfectly well, due in no sense, so he stammered, to negligence, idleness or treachery), his failures to be where he ought to have been, with Napoleon in Elba, with Napoleon at Waterloo, must now be expunged by a lifetime's immolation 'upon the – upon the – ah – altar of revolutionary devotion to which I myself in my youth was devoted by my own adopted father as was Hannibal by Hamilcar in the temple of the Punic gods!' He added, in a more matter-of-fact tone, that as a court chamberlain he would be well able to organise whatever sort of household the Emperor should establish in St Helena; attention to protocol, to dignity of ceremonial (even curtailed ceremonial), to diplomacy of contact with British government officials and possibly with representatives of other governments, neutral or hostile – all this was well within Montholon's experience and he could not think the Emperor would find anyone else as good, 'I mean, look around you, sire, let everyone look around! aboard this ship no one with the breadth of my international acquaintance; I mean to say, *is* there? No . . . Why at Würzburg I was . . .'

As his vehemence died away into an apologetic mumbling of the better parts of his curriculum vitae, Napoleon stared at him with undisguised astonishment; and so – even more so – did Albine.

What the hell was the stupid bugger up to?

At last the Emperor answered him: 'What does your wife think?'

What *did* Albine think? She had castigated the lukewarm loyalty of so many of the others; she had believed that once again and at last she truly loved Montholon, only because he did in the end (and without too much trouble) accept her plea to return to the imperial obedience. If she had founded that plea upon his fear of prosecution, she did not now choose to remember the fact with any degree of sharpness; her husband was proving himself a man of courage and commitment, silly and selfish but what would she have? he was what she had tried to make him, how could she complain? 'Oh God!' she cried out, a desolate wail of internal confusion, 'what do I think? I cannot think! This is the very greatest tragedy in the history of the world. Of course I don't want my husband to destroy himself. But if you, sire, are destroyed, what in God's name is left for the rest of us?' She plunged forward after Charles-Tristan, close up to the Emperor's shoulder in defiance of all etiquette to speak urgently, confidentially, into his ear – 'Sire, the point is, do you want him? I can't imagine why you should want him. But if you say you do, then I have married more than I thought I had: for my own comfort I would wish to leave him, for my self-respect I must stay with him. Sire, it is for you to say.'

Napoleon was looking her up and down, and then, from her to Montholon, a strange speculative regard, as of a man who all his life has eaten nothing but plain bread and butter and has suddenly been offered a pot full of jam. 'Yes,' he said slowly, 'I had not considered the need for a trained diplomatist; nor had I imagined I would be making a *court* for myself upon this island. An impromptu encampment was the extent of my presuppositions; and yet of course, Monsieur de Montholon, you are right, you are quite right, upon further thought; my own self-respect will tolerate nothing less. And you, madame, are quite right to relate *your* self-respect to the fulfilment of mine; I am unconscionably grateful to you both and look forward with keen—' (for a moment Albine had the impression he was about to say 'keen amusement') '—with keen appreciation to your regulating my household, the pair of you indeed, at least when we discover just what kind of a household it will be. Good. I have your voices. What can I do but rejoice? My three gentlemen; I chose two, one chose himself, nobody else wanted to be chosen; repulsive expedient! I am sorry, I am wholeheartedly sorry; permit me, dear friends, to be alone for an hour or two! Please!'

His voice quavered and cracked and shot up into an unusually high register; he pressed his hand against his brow and hastened, almost ran, to climb the companion-ladder into his cabin beneath the poop.

At which Gourgaud came floundering away from Dr O'Meara; his arms whirled again; he was mouthing like a drunkard: 'Alone! if he's left alone he will kill himself this time for certain. I and only I can prevent it. Am I not also a Corsican? Montholon, you bastard, who's a bloody Corsican? Me!' And he too ran up the ladder, to the amazement (and disgust) of all the rest. For they all were emotional; and all of them hated the emotions of all the others; guilt, thought Albine, for the collapse of the Empire; guilt for their own collapse as the Empire's pretended champions; guilt for the secret blame they held against the Emperor for allowing his Empire to collapse.

She turned to her husband: 'You have truly, beyond all error, put yourself and myself into the pigswill; truly the only place for us. Wallow!'

28

Another week at Plymouth moorings, of dismay and recrimination, before Napoleon and his chosen party were transferred from the *Bellerophon* to HMS *Northumberland* for the voyage south. (No glory left to them, and the minimum of defiance.) Gourgaud was now one of the three permitted officers – he was a Corsican; he would not keep quiet, even though he had very nearly missed his chance by garrulity at the wrong time in the wrong direction; he had once by his personal valour saved the Emperor's life on a chaotic battlefield – the Emperor, it was conceded, owed him a debt. Las Cases was now rated as a mere secretary rather than state-chamberlain; a loophole whereby Napoleon could keep him; but it bred a little germ of bad blood. In so very small a court, precedence would be highly important. It was Montholon's business to adjust all such matters, which he managed capably but fussily, causing everyone else to resent him, and Napoleon to make fun of his punctiliousness.

Albine made unmerciful fun of him. Herself and the maid Zoé spent much time together in their narrow sleeping-quarters or above on the open deck, playing with Maximilien, laughing at private jokes, and laughing at the pretensions of both Napoleon's Empire and King George's Royal Navy. A new intimacy between them and a comforting one; the instant willingness, almost glee, with which Zoé had agreed to share this most ominous adventure, turned her imperceptibly from servant into friend. The girl said (early one morning as she and Albine stood at the rail and looked out at the oily leaden swell of the North Atlantic, the humped masses of leaden cloud obscuring the feeble sunrise), 'A dirty day in the countryside's no more than a dirty wet day. But at sea, who can tell what'll it do to you by nightfall? I often thought, back in Touraine, "Oh God, for a way o'life where you'd never know how you'd end up!" Ah well, now we've got it and we might as well make the best.' Albine was reminded of her own teenage years when she followed the conquering army and looked out for whatever should befall, young men, rich men, men of destiny. After a fashion, had she not found what she sought?

Aboard the *Bellerophon* she and Charles-Tristan had had no chance of amorous enjoyment. Napoleon alone excepted, the hundred-odd French passengers had been crammed into sailors' hammocks along the common gundeck; but the *Northumberland* now carried no more than twenty-seven of them; the ship's carpenters divided the space with canvas screens into a series of small cabins with makeshift cots to sleep in; if Montholon had been willing, there was both room and time to make love, discreetly, of course, *soberly*. So why was he not willing? He said he felt too seasick. It was true that the weather became blustery. But Albine grew used to the vessel's motion; and so, it appeared, did most of their companions.

She feared he was disheartened by his own ill-judged decision. Had they been sailing on their own to America, it was probable his sensuality would have recovered its spirits whatever the state of the waves. She put it to him so, during the third week of their passage: he replied, sulkily, 'Maybe. If you paid me more attention. You are ready enough, I observe, to gain flirtatious compliments from the English officers when we dine with them.' Which indeed was undeniable; a fashion of formal dinners was established in the great stern-cabin; selected French and English guests every night at the long table, the Emperor as guest of honour, a routine of social intercourse where much was made by the gentlemen of the attractions of Fanny Bertrand and herself.

On those days when he chose to captivate, Napoleon could and did play his *Bellerophon* game with all the old gaiety; but it seemed he now thought it less important to be charming; there was little to be gained by it, his luck was exhausted. (It never occurred to him that maybe that very charm, exercised too persuasively aboard a British ship, had sealed his fate with the British government?) And also he was tired. He spent long periods with Las Cases, dictating his memoirs, which drained him emotionally and gave him bad headaches.

Dr O'Meara of the *Bellerophon*, for some reason of his own – scientific curiosity? Hibernian anti-British hero-worship? or straightforward tuft-hunting? – had attached himself to the party as the Emperor's physician-in-exile. The Admiralty had given permission, in the hope (it was rumoured) that he would also do some spying for them. Despite his rattling bedside manner, he was not the best doctor in the world; the pills he gave for the headaches had unhappy side-effects, increase of indigestion, constipation, wind.

Fanny Bertrand offered remedies, behind the doctor's back, powders of her own composition in collaboration with the ship's loblolly boy; they did not work. Albine offered massage; she would sit for long periods by Napoleon's chair while he dictated, rubbing his neck and shoulders; it did work, up to a point. He would twist himself round and look deep into her eyes and say, 'Yes.' It seemed to her a potentially significant remark, if only he would enlarge upon it; but he didn't.

Montholon, she discovered, was tucked away reading throughout most of his spare time; and he had not said a word of it to her. He knew that *she* craved for books, any books, heavy or light, for this tedious voyage where all she had with her was a pair of dog-eared mawkish novels of unrequited love in the exotic high-life of Stockholm and London – having read them three times over since leaving Paris she was thoroughly sick of their improbabilities – how could any woman credit so high a pitch of sensibility among English or Swedish lovers? and yet the authors were apparently French. Las Cases had books. Packing-cases full of them; but when she asked to borrow he pretended he had nothing but philosophy and theology and the theory of political history and – what was the fourth? – etymology? bah! He lied of course. He disliked Albine and he wilfully deprived her. That business at Malmaison of his wretched son and Zoé. Grudges and malice from stem to stern of this ship-of-fools: so ill-favoured a prospect for their life upon the island . . .

She challenged her husband, 'Where the devil d'you find these books and why haven't you told me?' All he would say was he picked them up on loan wherever he could, and Albine should do the same – Mme Bertrand had some fiction from a Plymouth bumboat, one of the Royal Navy lieutenants had lent him a volume of Byron, O'Meara carried Gibbon in his portmanteau and the plays of a 'parliament-man', Sheridan. But these were all in English; Montholon read English easily; Albine not at all. And she knew he had access to reading-matter in French, although the titles were unfamiliar to her; he only seemed to deal with one book at a time and she had no idea where he kept it when it was not in his hand. The lackey Grâcepardieu should have been able to inform her: against expectation he travelled with them, sulkily, in default of any better opportunity; but she and he were not on speaking terms after a bitter little row at Torbay about the proper care of

Montholon's spare trousers. She had to beg Zoé to *inveigle* Grâcepardieu; a humiliating expedient for both herself and the girl, but the very air they breathed these days was tainted with petty abasements.

Zoé reported that Grâcepardieu kept a tarpaulin-covered basket-trunk in his berth on the orlop deck; it was tightly strapped and padlocked and only Montholon had a key. Albine went to considerable trouble to purloin her husband's key-ring, one muggy afternoon in the equatorial doldrums, while he slept. She sent Zoé with some small cash to tell Grâcepardieu that Montholon needed a bottle of brandy from the purser's store (where such items were sold to passengers at an extortionate profit); as soon as the man was away down to the bowels of the ship to chaffer with the storeman, she slipped with a lantern into his dark little cabin – exactly like a thief – with Zoé keeping guard lest anyone should come. Grâcepardieu's berth was shared by two other servants, a Mameluke of the Emperor's and Bertrand's old-soldier batman – the Mameluke, a lonely Mussulman, spent most of his hours off-duty telling prayer-beads at the peak of the forecastle, and Bertrand's man (according to Zoé) was just then hanging out his master's washing on the designated portion of the rigging – so she guessed she was safe enough.

Well, the basket-trunk was there, she had seen it before of course, she had not thought there'd be anything in it but odd garments and items of footwear, nevertheless why all the mystery? She opened it and found the odd garments. She found shoes. She found a squashed cocked hat and a queer little package tucked into it which she took to be some sort of drug-supply. (Montholon's recurrent hypochondria; no surprise he'd fitted himself out with apothecary-stuff; but unlabelled? she could only trust he'd kept a note of the proper dosage.) Ah! so here were his books. Quite a bundle of them; all in French. She whipped up two or three under her shawl and hastily refastened the trunk.

Zoé called softly from the alleyway: someone was coming down the ladder. Albine in a panic shoved the trunk back under Grâcepardieu's cot, took a deep breath and emerged from the cabin. It was not, thank God, Grâcepardieu who approached, but the Emperor's confidential man, Franceschi Cipriani, a specious Italo-Corsican who knew too much of everyone's business. It was hard to let him walk past without offering him an explanation, for otherwise who could say what tale he would pass on to whom? Yet to think of an explanation was a damned sight harder; Albine stood helplessly and gaped. Zoé's wits were well in place: she grinned at the Corsican – 'Oh Signor Franceschi, the very man! can you tell us, I'm sure you can, whether the Emperor ever spoke to Monsieur de Montholon about court-dress? If he did, Monsieur de Montholon would for sure have told Grâcepardieu; but we can't find Grâcepardieu and it is important to Madame. Monsieur, do you see, is both seasick and asleep.'

Cipriani shrugged and looked bored. 'Ladies, I am sorry, I have no information. I fancy Grâcepardieu will be as usual at the purser's store. I hope you find him.' He left them and they scurried away: Zoé to her own berth at the other end of the orlop, which she shared with Maximilien (who was also asleep, or so they hoped); and Albine aloft to the leeside gangway to find herself a hammock-chair and read.

29

The first book she opened was Laclos's *Dangerous Liaisons*; which she had read, and been distressed by, several years ago, a cruel immoral tale (of diabolical breaches of the trust of trusting women) with an even crueller moral conclusion: not quite the type of story she rejoiced to find in possession of Charles-Tristan's private thoughts.

The next one was new to her, *Justine, or the Ill-Fortunes of Virtue*, by somebody called the M****** de S***. It was very badly printed; no printer's name, but illustrations of some quality. Extraordinary small-scale engravings, so icily imagined, of doll-like men and women with their nude pudenda (as it were) on fire, their parsnip-pallid bodies all but overbalanced by the heavy powdered wigs of the old regime; they submitted to and committed acts of more intimate wickedness than Albine had ever dreamed of. Deeply troubled, she was forced to wonder had her husband known the book's contents before he bought it? Where had he bought it? She was not sure she wanted to find out.

And a third volume: *The Lives and Crimes of Secret Murderers (as Historically Encircled by the Infected Crown of France)*. A revolutionary polemic published at the time of the Terror, it began with that heinous Queen Marguerite de Bourgogne who slew her nightly lovers in the upper chamber of the Tour de Nesle, continued with a leering account of Gilles de Rais and his slaughter of hundreds of innocent children, and then settled itself down to luxuriate in the seventeenth-century mass-poisonings of Marie-Madeleine de Brinvilliers. The anonymous author purported to show how monarchy, of its very nature, encourages its hangers-on to irresponsible atrocity. In Albine's opinion his argument was largely correct (and dear God, there was not much to be done about it!); it was a pity he had defeated his theme with his ghoulish overemphasis, his incessant and bloodthirsty reminders of 'the social value of the guillotine'.

An even greater pity she had ever allowed her husband to compromise himself with that deadly Artois. She had saved Charles-Tristan from the fanatic Malet; how had she failed to keep him clear of the even more noxious Bourbons? Between both extremities she was sorely afraid that his character might have been ruined. For his choice of books was horrible – and he meant to study them, *all alone*, in the creaking nooks and crannies of this dark oppressive ship?

30

So she told him, with a pale face and a quivering small voice, that she had found out his trunk and found out its contents, so what had he to say to her? No less pale and trembling, he assured her in a torrent of words that the books had not been *chosen*, he had grabbed them unseen as a second-hand job-lot from a ship's-chandler in Rochefort, for the forthcoming voyage to wherever they'd be going, the man had wrapped them up and he'd not even unpacked them until – well, until they were all embarked on board the *Northumberland* – and was she surprised he had not wished her to examine them? There were other things in the trunk, shoes, a hat and so forth – she hadn't disturbed them, had she? He'd left them in the servant's berth just to keep them out of the way – there was nothing, he thought, of hers in the trunk – or had she seen something she needed?

She said she hadn't bothered with anything else. She was only concerned with the books.

He let out a long deep sigh; he took her softly in his arms; he told her, very gently, that he had not been a good husband to her lately, there was too much on his mind; but now, perhaps, this evening, with his seasickness (he believed) thoroughly mended, they might try if one of these deplorable English sea-cots would perhaps hold two people? Two people as quiet as mice, as little creeping shipboard mice, for with Gourgaud behind that partition and Las Cases behind this one, even the sweetest little squeaks would be heard and made matter of gossip . . .

Ah, at last, at long last! his warm whisperings.

She only *pretended* an immediate reluctance; nor did she really mind that (despite his initiative) to arouse him to erection proved a lengthy and toilsome process. Honey fingers, fruit-juice lips, sharp teeth, abrupt pinches and slaps; she succeeded in the end and the noise was not excessive.

31

They reached St Helena in the month of October after seventy-one days at sea: the *Northumberland* and a convoy of nine other vessels, troop-transports and storeships bringing an entire regiment and all its goods and gear and preserved foodstuffs to garrison the island and utterly to deter any possible attempt at rescue, any hope that the escape from Elba might conceivably be repeated. A squadron of men-of-war would be stationed perpetually on and off the horizon; no ship of any flag must ever approach without first being boarded and examined.

Albine stared from the poop at this bleak precipitous lump in the middle of – the middle of 'nothing but grey wave-tops and the howl of a vicious wind. Even worse than anyone told us. Lord Christ,' she cried, 'it is as though the devil upon his passagings has swooped like a bloody albatross and dropped a gobbet of his dung, and we have to set foot there and *live*?'

Yet they did contrive to live. And they had hardly begun to discover the necessary ways and means when Albine discovered she was pregnant.

Oh 'as quiet as creeping mice!' it had been, tight together in a swinging sea-cot over many weary weeks – the most uncomfortable copulations she ever remembered since she first lay, a small scared virgin, with a drunken quartermaster in his ration-wagon on the march of '95 through Flanders into Holland – but quiet mice bred a noisy consequence, an importunate roaring girl-child, born at the start of July and without too much pain – St Helena was not the Cévennes; Dr O'Meara, although nonplussed by Napoleon's neurotic symptoms, had gentle hands and gentle words for a woman's travail; and Zoé was unfailingly competent.

Towards the end of her confinement the Emperor was so kind as to pay her a congratulatory visit. He was now set up in his permanent quarters, the house of Longwood on the plateau of the island, scarcely more convenient than the cabins of the *Northumberland*; the Montholons' two rooms backed immediately onto the imperial apartments; whenever the baby yelled, conversation in the state-parlour was grievously interrupted. Nevertheless he spoke to her as though he had made a special journey across half of Paris to see her. He sat at her bedside with Charles-Tristan standing at his elbow and Gourgaud wreathed in smiles just behind him in the doorway. Outside on the verandah, peeping in with discreet benevolence, Bertrand and Mme Bertrand, Las Cases and his ogling son; a flattering group of notables which somehow recalled to her the Arrival of the Magi in Bethlehem. Insincere? But who cared? God damn it, she deserved it.

Napoleon played with the baby, gingerly taking it from Zoé's arms and jolting it up and down. 'Aha, ha ha,' he chuckled, 'the first addition to our new Empire. And what shall you call her, madame?'

Albine was rather dreading this question. She and Montholon had discussed their daughter's name at some length without reaching any definite conclusion; but now she asserted herself and placed *her* choice firmly before his. ('Honesty before obsequiousness,' she said to him later in the day when he launched into a tetchy complaint.) 'Henriette Laetitia, sire, if it meets with your approval.'

'So so, Laetitia! Beautiful: the noble name of my beloved mother; whom I fear I shall never see again on this earth. You met her but the one time, I think? at Malmaison during the Days of Farewell. I am so touched, madame, by your remembrance: I will write to her, I will tell her, she too will shed a tear for you. Your idea, or your husband's?'

'First, sire, my husband's wish, and then of course mine.'

'Thank you, Montholon, thank you, you are a very good friend. I do not only weep because of my mother; but for my own small son and *his* mother, whom also I shall never see, not because I had to leave them but because they were *snatched* from me – an act of such unparalleled international malice I can hardly to this day believe it actually took place.' These laments for his Empress and their child the King of Rome occurred almost by the clock; usually in the morning between his coffee and his daily walk when he most missed a familial routine. But this time it was mid-afternoon; Albine sitting happily propped up against her pillows, with the baby now squirming toward her breast, was a painful reminder of all the humanity from which he had been cut off. (From the less humane phenomena, his military staff in their gold-braided uniforms, the martinet protocol of pseudo-sovereignty so incongruously persisting in this rat-infested rain-leaking jerry-built colonial grange-house, he was not at all cut off: rather did he cling to them like a sloth upside-down on a tree-branch.) But his melancholy only endured for a minute; his handkerchief went back into his cuff; and his versatile tongue turned to sharpness. 'So why Henriette? A family name? Your mother's, madame, yes?'

'No,' she said, timidly, and yet boldly behind the timidity. 'We have called her Henriette – *I* have called her – because Henriette Le Bas was the lady who loved the revolutionist Saint-Just. My husband told me of her and when he told me I admired her. They never got married and once they had parted, Saint-Just without her became – became—'

'A dried-up murderous husk is what Saint-Just became, madame, and they took off his head very properly, a Political Idiot; even though I myself had been attached to his faction in those days. Why did this Henriette leave him? Can you tell? Montholon, can *you* tell?' The Emperor was annoyed. He had enjoyed himself in a miserable sort of way thinking back six short years to his marriage with the Austrian princess; but to be compelled without warning to relive the Jacobin ardours that surrounded the uncertainties of his youth, that was very different, and this parvenue countess was a damned smirking meddler. 'Montholon, I asked you a question.'

'Sire, I always assumed she could not recognise the lover in the zealot.'

'And that's how you'd prefer to see your daughter? Always ready with her scorn and censure for any *man of vision* who might happen to admire her?'

It was possible that a joke was being made here; Montholon decided it would be tactful to suppose so; he laughed and replied, 'No, sire, not I. I think, though, my wife might like something of the kind. Might you not, my dear? eh, what?'

He screwed up his features toward her, silently begging her to laugh too. She turned an illegible face away from him, away from the Emperor, and looked only at the baby.

Napoleon's glance passed from one to the other of them; and then, very intently, focused upon Albine alone. Aware of his hard scrutiny, she deliberately put aside the front of her bedgown and set her nipple in Henriette's mouth. Established thus, an absorbed mother fulfilling her sacred function, she need not be expected to join in any more talk; to be sure she had had quite enough.

The Emperor rose to his feet; he was perhaps embarrassed; it should have been *his* prerogative to bring an audience to an end; but when a lady was giving suck, special circumstances obtained. He cleared his throat and cast about for a courteous excuse to take his leave. There were two books on the bedside table, he fiddled with them indecisively. La Fontaine's *Fables*. (A school-text from the Bertrand nursery.) 'A very rational writer,' he pronounced. 'Cool but perceptive satire, an admirable plain style of regular prosody: d'you enjoy it?' Without waiting for an answer he picked up the other one, the anonymous *Secret Murderers*. It fell open at a well-thumbed page, the start of a chapter which must have been constantly referred to.

He opened his eyes in astonishment, flicking through the leaves and muttering.

Then, with stiff pomposity: 'The Marquise de Brinvilliers? You find her depravities appropriate to a childbed? Great heaven, madame, she gave arsenic in small doses to her own father, and it took him nearly a whole year to die of them. I really do *not* recommend the case as a suitable ingredient to mingle with your little Laetitia's repast. Breast-milk, d'you know? while accumulating in a woman's bosom is immediately affected by the process of her brain; it is a fact well attested by science.'

He shoved his hands under his coat-tails, turned his back on her reproachfully, and walked out without any more words.

Albine complacently moved Henriette from one breast to the other. She had nothing to say just yet to Charles-Tristan, so she held her peace and watched him from the corner of her eye, a sly twist to her mouth, neither a smile nor a sneer; she knew he would soon remonstrate with her for putting their master into an ill temper, but she had not determined whether to laugh at him or retort with anger. To her surprise, he too said nothing; he had sprung to attention as the Emperor left, but now he was livid and shaking as though struck with an ague; he reached out and snatched the book that had caused all the trouble; he blundered backwards through the door, hitting Zoé accidentally with his elbow – 'Girl, I am not well. Help me to lie down on the couch in the other room.'

Albine thought to herself, 'Maybe . . . Not the first time he's had fever since we came here. But he might have found the strength to apologise to his wife and daughter *before* he fell to pieces. Of course I should have told him I had borrowed his nasty book.'

Outside in the gardens the Emperor strolled with Gourgaud. He gave a whimsical lift to his eyebrows, and remarked with a harsh gusto, not perhaps entirely jocular, 'If I were our friend Montholon, I would worry about my wife's reading. She's an odd woman with an odd history. Does she intend to poison *him*, must we suppose?'

Gourgaud appeared shocked. 'Oh sire, surely not. You cannot think she would leave the incriminating dossier by her bed for him to notice at any hour of the day or night?'

'Well, if she does, she perhaps cannot be blamed. Most women at some stage have in mind to be rid of their husbands. Is it a natural consequence of the oppressive laws of marriage, or must we create such oppressive laws simply because we know too well what they all have in their minds? Mind you, Brinvilliers's infamy was altogether beyond bounds. It began because she had a scandalous lover and feared to be found out. It was her father who found it out, so he was her first victim. Now *that* was a murder that went quite against nature. The father had a right to his rage; her husband, probably not. Now if the father had poisoned *her* . . . well, the Romans would have said he was justified.'

'Poison, sire,' affirmed Gourgaud stoutly, 'is the weapon of the coward. On the other hand, the sword, or the pistol—'

'No no, my dear young Gorgo, Gorgotto, you misunderstand. I am not thinking of the weapon but the complexity of the intention. I am thinking of it in terms of all the legislation I did my best to give my peoples. Murder of course, forbidden, all shapes of assassination; duelling forbidden; public hatreds, riot and faction, brought to heel by every shape of restrictive decree: and yet private hate, within the family, within indeed the bedroom – why, yes, within the very bed! – not one of my laws could touch them. We cannot even *see* them. Sometimes the beginning of homicide looks exactly like the burgeonings of love. You know, I *gave orders* to Montholon he was not to marry this Albine. He was a soldier under discipline; if I'd commanded him in battle he'd have killed whomever I told him to, not in pursuit of his own hatreds but of mine – or if he didn't, my court-martial would certainly have killed *him*. Whereas, in regard to his woman, he disobeyed me and it seems I forgave him.'

Murmuring thus, more to himself than to his companion, he had walked without thinking to the far end of the vegetable patch. Beyond the boundary wall was the cordon of British sentries, their shakoes and bayonets visible above the coping, moving silently right-to-left left-to-right, as they trod their unceasing beat. Beyond the soldiers lay two or three miles of scrubby plain, a dreary prospect; and beyond the plain the jagged hills whose cliffs on their far side fell steeply away into the ocean with never an interval of beach.

'Ah, Gorgo, we must not walk further, not beyond the red sentinels, without a donkey of a British lieutenant to dog our every pace. This new governor is intolerable. Restrictive decrees? He's made more of 'em against me in one month than I made against all Europe in seventeen years. If we do not defy him, we shall die. But not, I think, today . . . Back to the house.'

They turned to retrace their steps. A black-skinned gardener, a government slave, was on his knees beside the path, weeding one of the patches. He touched his ragged hat-brim and smiled at Napoleon. Napoleon smiled at him. The slave said something to Napoleon in a strange island patois of African-English; Napoleon could not understand it; he said to the slave, in French, 'You weed the garden, I walk in the garden, I *work* in the garden as well, I plant cabbages. Both of us torn from our homes, for no reason except to satisfy somebody else's peace of mind and unwarranted bodily ease. Gorgo, give him some money.'

Before re-entering the house, Napoleon stopped Gourgaud with a hand on his shoulder, and a confidential half-whisper into his ear. 'D'you think we did right to bring these wives to the island? You had the good sense to leave yours behind you in France. Whereas Bertrand's has insisted upon him finding his own house a mile away, two miles, it's ridiculous. He might just as well never have come. And the winsome Montholon at times becomes so effusive she curdles my bile, and then again she'll turn and answer me as tartly as a – oh, what the hell? as tartly as a bloody tart.'

As he spoke, he leaned forward, chin raised, eyes narrowed, staring from under the brim of his tropical straw hat as a man in a trance, away from the house towards the bright sharp horizon of the sea between the rocky peaks. 'This pregnancy now, count the months: d'you realise they must have been at it on the very ship that brought us here? In the intervals, it appears, of all those compassionate massagings of my neck! It is almost a personal insult.'

He growled like a gathering thunderstorm, forcing out a savage burst of military joviality – 'Which makes me think, general, once she's done with all the indulgence of her lying-in, someone should give her an hour or two's hard packdrill.'

'He'll never do that to her,' said Gourgaud, suddenly malevolent. (The Emperor's tone had passed him the cue for otherwise unutterable words.) 'He needs her too badly. Haven't you seen, sire, he depends upon her to test out your moods for him? Haven't you seen how he caused her to freeze Mme Bertrand away? He has taken control of nearly all the work you gave Bertrand to do. And only because he knows you are always in her company; ah, sire, you may dislike her, but isn't it true you never leave her alone?'

His remarks were not appreciated; he had obviously misjudged the tone.

'Jealous, Gorgo! jealous, jealous, family hatreds, didn't I tell you? Bah, let me hear no more of 'em! I do not approve of discussing my people, one with another, behind their backs.'

'But sire, you did ask—'

'Be silent, sir! You go too far.' His brow was black with quick anger; but then it cleared and he laughed. 'Of course he will not discipline her. If he did he would be poisoned, he knows it: he has read her bedside book.'

32

Montholon at this stage had done nothing with his chemist's packet beyond removing it from his vulnerable trunk and hiding it under a loose brick in the floor of Zoé's scullery. He kept telling himself, 'Let us first see exactly how we are fixed, upon this island. A proper routine, for him, for me, for Albine (Lord God!), and for everyone else of the entourage. *Then* it may be possible to discover a routine for the – (Lord God!) – for the Deed. Small doses, spaced out, it is a matter of calendar precision: I must wait a little while, wait. No one can know in France just yet that as yet I am doing nothing, so I do have a little time. I must be allowed, ah surely surely? to – ah – to make my own arrangements and upon my own to determine when the time *shall be ripe*. They cannot be so unreasonable as not to appreciate my difficulties.'

These thoughts used to come to him when he awoke (as every night now he did awake) at about two o'clock (dead dark and silent save for the distant calls of the night-guard, sentinels changing post and reporting, 'Number four, all's well!' 'Number five, all's well!' 'Number six – *etc.*') to feel his bladder swollen full and urgent for the chamber-pot (however carefully he had avoided drinks between supper and bed-time); he would clamber from bed to ease it; and then scramble back in again and try every expedient to recapture his sleep. But sleep would be gone from him for at least another hour. And how dreadfully throughout that hour he would contemplate the murder and tell himself over and over, 'Let us first see exactly – *etc., etc.*' And then Henriette would wake up and wail for her feed and Albine would have to clamber out to take her.

During the day he was able, for all practical purposes, to forget his looming burden. Which is why, when the Brinvilliers story was so unexpectedly exposed, he behaved like a murderer in a melodrama. But as most people (even the stage-struck) do not imagine that melodrama's characters in fact occur in real life, no inferences were drawn either by Albine or Zoé; and his 'ague' was accepted without question.

But this in turn had an awkward consequence. Concerned for his health, Albine asked him ought he not to be taking some of the drugs he had carried with him in his baggage? Luckily, when she put the question, he was reaching to return the pot to its place under the bed after one of his small-hours urinations (another reason for her concern); the expression on his face and the sudden stiffening of his bent posture were out of her sight in the moonlit room. There was a pause, and quite a natural one, before he straightened himself and answered her. 'Ah, no,' he breathed, calmly enough, 'I purchased powders against the yellow fever and the cholera; no need for them, you see: O'Meara says neither plague is endemic here. All that's wrong with me is maladjustment to the climate – it's either too wet or too hot and there are no regular four seasons as we're accustomed to in Europe. O'Meara says, "Get used to it!", that's all we have to do. He tells the Emperor the same thing.'

Albine then began to worry about the well-being of the children; which gave him the chance to argue with her and so lift off the horror from his mind until both of them fell asleep – almost at once of course to be awoken by the clamour of Henriette.

Albine could not see why Montholon's pissings and the baby's demands were never able to coincide: her rest was disturbed twice as often as it should have been. In the end, and against her will (because at this juncture she badly needed her husband's nearness and continued affection), she decided he must sleep on the divan in their living-room while Zoé on a truckle-bed kept her company at night. A reversion to the bad old days in Paris. But no lover to make it palatable: how *was* she to organise her life?

Meanwhile the Emperor's life was being drastically *re*-organised by the new governor, Sir Hudson Lowe, an undistinguished lieutenant-general whose only reach of imagination was to picture the court-martial that would break him were Napoleon to escape. This character-istic was no doubt the chief reason for his appointment. The British government had had a hard time convincing its allies and the Bourbons in Paris that Bonaparte a remote and permanent prisoner was a far safer political solution than Bonaparte a slain martyr. Yet even from St Helena escape might be possible if any laxity were allowed in the conditions of captivity.

Prior to Lowe's arrival, the Emperor had been billeted on a pleasant English merchant family, the Balcombes. Here he had lived like a much-valued guest, and had struck up a happy friendship with the Balcombes' fourteen-year-old daughter Betsy. Some people said he was in love with her; certainly she adored him and teased him and flirted with him in a way which, had she been a Corsican girl, might not have been so readily interpreted by her parents as touching and innocent. (Albine and Fanny did not interpret it in such terms: they had watched it, as it were from the side-seats of the pit, with beady reprehension.)

And then came Lowe. These friendly contacts were at once to cease; the Emperor under no circumstances was henceforth to be accorded his imperial title; he was to move into Longwood and stay there with the cordon of troops all around him and no casual visitors save by official permission, obstructed quite as often as granted. Betsy wept inconsolably to see him go. Sir Hudson was just the man to cause a schoolgirl bitter tears; but being the man he was, it never occurred to him that that was what he'd done. Nor would he care if he *had* understood. His rigorous *duty*, or rather his terror of being perceived as insufficiently rigorous in pursuit of a *dutiful* rigour, overrode all possible sympathy. And not quite without reason: for if there was one person on the island more than any other who might have helped Napoleon escape, it would surely have been Betsy: although the English in general would have laughed at so foolish a notion, fit only, they would have said, for an archaic rebel episode in a tale by the author of *Waverley*. Betsy, for all her foolishness, was after all a *good girl*: by no means a romantic Gael.

The Marquis de Montchenu, however, did not laugh. He came to St Helena (at about the same time as Sir Hudson) as the French king's diplomatic commissioner, charged with observing and reporting upon the daily doings of the great prisoner and his harassed keepers. He was ready at all times to issue complaints of liberties taken and dangers ignored. He personally witnessed 'Mademoiselle Betzi and the immoral Corsican' laughing and playing and – he thought – maybe kissing in the garden of her father's house. As an unrepentant reactionary whose dissipated youth had been spent at Versailles, he knew all about games and laughter with nubile 'virgins' of the middle class. He sent to Paris a long account of how an English mistress was in process of being procured for the arch-enemy of France; Paris wrote to London; London wrote to Lowe; and Lowe lost his temper with everyone. All this took months and months; meanwhile poor Betsy was left to weep; and Napoleon to lament the loss of a very charming little friend.

A phrase or two let slip at one of his tense brief meetings with Lowe made shockingly clear to him the sort of thing that had been written; he too wept (in private); in the presence of his entourage, he raged at the nit-witted slander.

Albine smiled and hid her thoughts.

Montholon was ordered to go directly to the Marquis de Montchenu and hold very high words with him; Napoleon himself, of course, refused absolutely to be in the same room as the dirty monkey.

It was not an assignment to which Montholon looked forward. He regularly met Montchenu, for the Emperor's staff were not themselves treated as prisoners; they were allowed to move about the island in comparative freedom; and King Louis's commissioner received and despatched all the permitted correspondence, after reading it and taking notes, between Longwood and France. (Unofficial letters were *smuggled* in various ways, usually under the care of venal ship's-officers: Cipriani's responsibility.) Montholon, as a lapsed aristo with diplomatic experience, could chat quite convincingly about nothing-in-particular with another gentleman of the same caste; Montchenu was always happy to give him news of the Parisian theatres, the ladies' fashions, who at court was making love to whom. Superficially the marquis was a gay dog, with his old-style brocaded clothes and his elegant (if top-heavy) wig; he appeared to find Montholon a kindred spirit. But Montholon was never sure just how much he knew of other, more murky, matters. Was he, for example, in the confidence of Artois?

Such uncertainty injected hazard into every one of their meetings, however noncommittal the agenda. And on this particular occasion it would be prudent to handle things very delicately indeed. Napoleon's 'high words', if literally conveyed, could prove dangerous in all sorts of directions.

Over an hospitable glass of the marquis's wine, Montholon cautiously, humorously, even frivolously, broached the subject: '—it's perfectly preposterous, and I do believe you know it is. When did you or anyone else ever hear of his seducing young girls? Indeed, the reverse: look at Josephine, almost old enough to be his – well, not his mother, but certainly his aunt – and I think every one of his recognised intrigues was with a woman of maturity and experience. The fact is, the Emperor has never—'

'Oh no! my dear count, if you insist upon using that word, I am quite unable to hear you.'

'I do not propose to call him "General Bonaparte", and still less "Buonaparté", as I am well aware you would prefer; for if I did you would crow about it, to the height of heaven and all of Paris, in the next report you send home – and I should be expelled from the light of his countenance, and whom would you be dealing with then? The inflammable Gourgaud? – quite impossible. Let's just say *he*, *him*, *his*, which both of us understand, and thereby we can continue to talk.'

'As you wish. You were saying: the fact is, he has never—?'

'It is a little difficult to express, but shall we say? he has never felt able to demonstrate any great sexual assurance; he has always looked for women who would intuitively feel his desires without his having to stumble through the awkwardness of wooing. In short, he has consistently behaved like an adolescent brought to orgasm – ha! *in statu pupillari* – by a – by a self-confident and fully-grown patroness.'

'Venus and Adonis?'

'Very nearly but not quite. Adonis, I seem to remember, commenced by repelling her raptures. True, Josephine at the beginning had to be *thrown at him* by Barras; for otherwise he would never have nerved himself.'

'Yes, there are stories as to how that "throwing" took place.'

'Yes, we have all heard them. Tambourines and the *tarantella*, Madame Tallien and two pairs of dancing-pumps. He was running mad in those days for lack of a handful of tit! all his bravery at the siege of Toulon and ruthless grapeshot in the Paris streets were no help; he knew neither strategy nor tactic that would serve; all alone without his regiments! – I can tell you, if Barras had offered him a virgin, he would have fled from her in ludicrous panic. Yet we cannot deny that he was to love his first wife passionately, a ferocious idealism, all the more so when she deceived him with her paramours.'

'Ah! these threadbare anecdotes are all very well; but you use them to evade your purpose; just what have you come here to tell me?' Montchenu's languid manner was gone; he became irritable, disagreeable, sharply contentious; to which Montholon responded with a decisive set of the chin and a tightening of the lips.

'—that your tale of the little m'mselle is and was untrue,' he grated, 'and that if you are a gentleman you will correct your erroneous report.'

'His words, or yours?'

'Oh, his; and far milder than he instructed me to repeat. If you and your employers sincerely want him contented in his exile, you'll pay very careful heed. For if he is not contented, he is capable of making very deep trouble for all of you. Indeed, for all of *us*. I have my own peace of mind to think of. My wife (as you know) is not many months out of her childbed; the baby will soon be weaned and will require calm, a gentle space for its nurture. Political confrontation would be – inconvenient.' He tried to look Montchenu firmly in the eye, but his own eye (inconveniently) wavered.

Montchenu sneered. 'If I am a gentleman? What have these sordid exigencies to do with good manners? I must report what I am ordered to report, which I agree ought in principle to be true. Suppose then, it is not true. What *should* be the truth? He is held upon this island without his wife and apparently without the remedy of any other female. He is not an old man and as far as I can tell not debilitated; surely he must by now be in urgent need of – what was it? – a handful of tit? Well?'

Montholon saw the jaws of a trap. Any shift of the conversation towards potential 'debility' was perilous whichever way it went. And even as he saw this, he saw that Montchenu could see that he saw it, and he saw that Montchenu *knew*.

'Well,' he replied, stammering damnably, 'well; it may well be that he *is* – ah – less robust than he was. It may indeed be that he—'

'It may indeed be that he is not yet suffering from a *lingering consumption*. Which ought by now to be gradually manifest, had a certain seedy chamberlain complied with most pressing instructions. But you haven't, have you? NO!' The marquis's petulant voice rose into something like a small scream: '—for do we not find the Corsican on the contrary in excellent health? barring his headaches, his constipation and his general depression at being tossed from the peak of his power! And *at* the same time there are very active plots, both in France *and* America! to assassinate members of the legitimate French government, to haul *him* out back to Europe to *overturn the whole world once again!* Oho no, you are *not* my only source of information. *And* I am fully apprised of what goes on in Longwood House. So why have you failed to obey?'

Montholon, grovelling, could only explain that, although he had carefully taken pains to have access to Napoleon's wine cellar, it was nonetheless a 'very very chancy business – in any case, the consignment of his special vintage has only just arrived and – and as you know, he has this fear of—'

'—of rejection by women. We have covered that already.'

'I was going to say – "poison".' He brought the word out with a ghastly gulp. (It had to be said, and now he'd said it.) 'He is suspicious of every mouthful he takes. Sometimes it is the English who will eliminate him, he says; sometimes – sometimes – the French. At every mealtime he is edgy beyond belief.'

'Then you must contrive to set his mind at rest. A prospering love affair would surely do that? Let him live within the embraces of a tender but demanding woman, he will cease to see enemies everywhere; if he still remains *edgy*, she can soothe him into complacence. She need not know with what end in view; for her own peace of mind she would obviously prefer him to be calm and gently balanced.'

'Her own peace of—? Whose?' Some fool stubbornness inside him compelled him to ask, but of course he knew the answer well enough. And Montchenu knew that he knew; Montchenu smiled, and shrugged, and smiled.

33

How does a husband intimate to his loving but scornful wife that he requires her (for reasons he dares not even hint at) to go to bed with his superior? As Montholon sweated in the afternoon heat, wearily leading his horse up the impossibly steep road that wound its way to Longwood from the little settlement of Jamestown, he tried to analyse the abhorrent task. Reluctantly he concluded that certain essential circumstances must infallibly obtain, if he were not to earn a catastrophic rebuff.

First, the lady must have nourished a hope, whether fully aware of it or not, of some such amorous connection. At any rate, one must be sure that the prospect would not altogether disgust her.

The superior, likewise, should have shown at least an *inclination*.

(Thinking over the events since the start of the ocean voyage, one might have reason to believe these two conditions had approximately been met.)

But then, given the superior's mood and character, the lady ought to make the first move. It had happened before: the Polish countess, Marie Walewska, some ten years ago, was induced by her husband (but not only her husband! an entire cabal of Polish notables had canvassed her patriotism) to give herself to Napoleon in return for national freedom. For so noble a cause, her 'self-sacrifice' – if that is what it was – turned vice into virtue; and all honest folk who knew of it agreed. There was nothing of the sort here. Vice, in the present case, was no better than a step upon the stairway to most miserable *crime*. Unless—

—why, of course, unless a *cause* of equivalent appeal could be confected and put decisively, imperceptibly, into Albine's head! and moreover in such a way as to let her think she had thought of it all by herself.

And at the same time the Emperor must be cautiously led to believe that if he should by chance *want* Albine, Albine already was more than eager to reciprocate. Unfortunate that he and she seemed so often to rub one another up the wrong way; which indeed in itself held sexual possibility; but how to determine that the wrong way became the right way at exactly the appropriate time, the appropriate place – oh God, and in Longwood? that sprawling collection of transplanted Hindustan bungalows, where everyone all day trod upon everyone else's feet . . .

34

The first thing to do was to start the slow work of the arsenic.

Then at least he would be shielded from Artois and his blackmail. Montchenu had mentioned neither the six thousand francs, nor the

Anges Sucrés; but it was perfectly obvious he held the pair of vile secrets (as it were) in his fob-pocket; sealed orders to be brought into play if Montholon continued to procrastinate.

'Bottles of wine the best mode,' the invisible ink had proposed.

No. In a climate of apprehension, any tampering with corks could too easily be detected. It was precisely because there was such fear of poison that the Emperor's private casks were kept so strictly separate from the rest of the Longwood supply. No mere servant was to handle them: Montholon himself had been detailed to transfer their contents into bottles, one cask at a time and only just before the wine was needed. Therefore the powder must go direct into the casks (one cask at a time), inserted through a stealthily bored auger-hole, which then could be stopped with wax and concealed beneath a smear of dust and cobwebs. The tapping of the cask and the bottling should be safeguarded from suspicion by a witness, Marchand the Emperor's head valet, Ali the Mameluke, or another.

It took him several days to find his opportunities, to recover the necessary amount of arsenic from its hiding-place, to measure the dose on a precarious thumbnail, to do the bradawl-business in the cellar without risk of any servant blundering in. At length it was done; the first polluted bottle was fetched to the Emperor's dinner-table; the Emperor (and nobody else) drank it; he showed no ill effects, nor did he comment upon any peculiar taste. Maybe the poison was effective, maybe not; time would tell, one could only wait.

That night Montholon's bladder behaved itself impeccably. He slept until daylight without interruption. How strange that a guilty con-science could so easily be quelled by the Guilty Deed completed . . .

As for the difficult question of persuading the Emperor to lean towards Albine's embraces—

Montholon approached it in a roundabout fashion, enjoying himself even: diplomatic deceit, a Talleyrandish exercise. He was alone with Napoleon very often these days, discussing all the problems of Sir Hudson and his insults and slights. One day he pointed out that Bertrand perhaps ought to be taking rather more interest. The next day he asked the Emperor if it was really true that the Bertrands' separate establishment was the result of Mme Bertrand's insistence. Napoleon replied that that was what Bertrand had told him and he saw no reason to doubt it. 'The lady,' he said, 'is a stiff-necked shrew who cannot tolerate our higgledy-piggledy existence. It is all I can do to get them to come to dine with me two nights in the week. I think she has no notion how sorely she hurts my feelings. At all events, I *hope* she's no notion.'

The day after that, Montholon began obliquely to suggest that it was Bertrand himself who decided his family ought not to live in Longwood and his wife in particular should avoid the imperial household.

'But Montholon, if that is so, I must believe she *desires* to be here. What is the meaning of it, and why has she not told me?' Montholon shook his head and gave no useful answer.

Two days later he suggested, even more obliquely, that Mme Bertrand might perhaps have been aspiring to become the Emperor's mistress; or at least that her husband maybe thought she was aspiring, and out of jealousy placed her under restriction. 'It's perfectly true,' said Napoleon, 'that Bertrand *is* a most silent morose fellow, but really I hardly believe . . .' He fell silent himself and changed the subject.

At the beginning of the following week Montholon told the Emperor a circumstantial tale of an ironmonger in Poitiers at the time of the Terror who had caused his young wife to sleep with the local police chief as a piece of political insurance. He achieved this by pretending momentous and public jealousy and locking her up. Hitherto the police chief had never had a thought of her. But once he heard what the ironmonger had done and why, he came down to the shop in his official capacity and demanded to see the abused citizeness; within a half-hour ('or to be on the safe side, forty-five minutes!') she was his. And as soon as their first transports subsided, as soon as she had time to lie still and talk to him, he willingly swore to her that her husband was safe from all future investigation. And ever afterwards he believed that *he* had seduced *her*. 'Sire, I can vouch for it. The police chief was a close friend of my foster-father.'

That evening at Longwood, General Bertrand came with Fanny Bertrand to dinner. Napoleon treated both of them to a cruel vein of sarcasm throughout the meal. Towards the end of it he announced that he was done with all women for the rest of his life. 'There's not one of 'em I've ever met who has not in some way *colluded!* For every whore a vicious pimp; for every pimp a disreputable ambition. Mme Bertrand, a private word, *if* you don't mind.' He led her briskly – almost violently – into the next room, while every face around the table froze in open-mouthed astonishment. Two minutes, three, and then he returned with her. She seemed scarcely able to stand, her body trembled from top to toe, she ran from the house without a word.

Bertrand rose to hurry after her; Napoleon slammed a flat hand on the table: 'General, you have not asked me my permission to be dismissed. Let me inform you before you go that *I* asked your wife would she join me in my bedroom for—

'No matter! she said no. She refused me. Away with you, you bugger, and make the best of it.'

He was choking with emotion but what sort of emotion? – not at all clear.

He made a huge effort, turned to Albine, swallowed his incoherent passion and hesitantly apologised, 'for so barbarous an outburst, for which you, most dear countess, were in no way responsible'. Montholon was glad to see that Albine had tears in her eyes; they were not, he thought, a token of her sympathy with Fanny.

Best not to say to her too much about the episode; but he had to be sure of his ground. He took her out into the gardens, a romantic starlit stroll, with his arm linked warmly into hers. 'That was,' he began, 'a very odd affair – the Emperor seems to be – seems—'

Albine interrupted, quietly, meditatively: 'D'you not understand? I would have supposed it clear enough, certainly to a café Lothario like you. That fury of his was half-and-half lust. Poor Emperor. Don't you see, she was so blatant in her design that his gorge rose against her? Had she approached him directly – I mean, without manipulation – he would not have rejected her.'

'She rejected *him*.'

'No, not at all. Such a sour proposition, hostile and insulting, she *had* to refuse it. He intended her to do so. Serves her right. He mourns every day for his Josephine. He even mourns for Marie-Louise, who I know they all say was a purely political wife: nevertheless she bore him a son and I have heard she gave him great solace for as long as she lived with him. And now he has nobody.'

'There are slave-women on the island. Surely something could be arranged—'

She fired up when he said that. 'Good God, I'm not talking about concubines! And he loathes the very thought of slavery. So typical, he says, of the English. (Typical of you too, it would seem; and no, you can *not* kiss away your insensitivity!) And you know he is most interested in this English chaplain, Mr Boys, who has attacked the use of slaves ever since he came onto the island. Hudson Lowe hates him for it; nearly as much as he hates the Emperor.'

'Oh, I've met Mr Boys: a most ponderous person.'

'Charles-Tristan, you may mock, but I tell you he's a good man. And, whatever your private thoughts, so is the Emperor.'

'Private thoughts—! Mine? What on earth do you imply?'

'I say he's a good man. As a woman I say so. Come, Charles-Tristan, bed.'

He pressed her bare forearm lovingly. Yes, he did love her, with a love that increased by his very betrayal of her. He detested her as well. For the leaven of his intrigue was beginning to bestir itself – in a way he had not quite expected, or not quite so soon, not quite.

Even so he had to wait several weeks. The Bertrands sulked in their house, the rows with the governor reached many a petty but hard-fought climax, the interminable dictations to Las Cases continued, and the Emperor scarcely shifted from his study. He refused to take his exercise because of Lowe's prohibitions upon where he might wander; and not surprisingly his health began to suffer.

Was it only lack of exercise?

Montholon worried lest the dose of arsenic had been too heavy. He cross-questioned O'Meara; the Irishman was positive there was nothing wrong but inactivity and the climate. Indeed the doctor himself was in trouble with Sir Hudson, who deeply resented his complaints about the prisoner's treatment. 'The man's liver is banjaxed, don't you see, governor? dammit,' O'Meara would insist in a disrespectful tone of voice, 'dammit, sir, inevitable; he needs a regime of good long rides across country – he's been used to it all his life as a commander in the field and begod you won't allow it. Would you just take a look at the swelling of his gut, and the arse he's developing like the haunches of a horse. God knows what London is going to say to *you* if you let him carry on in this deleterious fashion!' But the governor was adamant: security regulations had priority over everything else.

The headaches got worse. O'Meara told Albine that her sessions of massage really ought to be resumed. (Since the birth of Henriette she had let them lapse; and Napoleon had not called for them – annoyed with her perhaps, childish jealousy perhaps, her preoccupation with the baby.) She said she was not sure; she seemed to feel a certain shyness. She obviously worried; and Montholon was content to watch her worry; he thought he now knew where her anxieties were leading her.

Meanwhile he decided, once the first poisoned cask was finished, not to put any arsenic in the next one. The process was supposed to be exceedingly gradual; he must use his discretion whether or no to retard it.

Then one day, at dinner, the Emperor without warning swayed in his chair, clutched his temples and cried out. Ali and Marchand carried him swiftly into his bedroom, the party broke up in consternation, Gourgaud went running for O'Meara, and the Montholons and Las Cases and Bertrand (Fanny was not there) surged brainlessly and helplessly around, asking one another what on earth they should do. The doctor arrived all of a muck-sweat, enclosed himself at once with his patient, and then emerged (after what might have been as much as two hours) mopping his brow.

'Ah, no, there's no danger,' he pronounced. 'He's had an enema, it's worked, he's as weak as a kitten, I've ordered him a hot bath, they've just now got the water to boil. He says – and excuse me, I quote his own words, countess – he says, "Where the devil is that judy with the fingers? I haven't heard, seen or felt her compassion for months!" You'd best go into him now, ma'am, he needs you deuced badly.'

'But if he's having a bath—' Albine all of a sudden was very prim and proper.

'He needs you, ma'am, you'd best go in. And gentlemen, the rest of you, he can hear you all gabbling away here, it vexes him dreadfully. Why don't you slide off like decent men to your own quarters? Quiet, you see, sensitivity; the poor fellow requires quiet. That's it now, *that's* the spirit . . . So.' He sprang about them like a dancing-master, edging them out of the dining-room.

Montholon, on his way, murmured short encouragement to his wife: 'My love, he's a sick man, in his bath or out of it. Don't be like the Bertrand woman. Give him everything he craves. Disaster if he's lost to us like this! Go, go, sweetheart, go, don't lose any time.'

Outside, he ground his teeth, twisted his hands together, stamped his boot-heels on the verandah, and went stooping and scowling alone to his own corner of the gloomy dark house.

35

Napoleon's bath was a capacious vessel; at risk of flooding the floorboards, it could just hold two people. But whatever Montholon in his agonies might have been envisaging, the Emperor did not ask Albine to join him in it. He just leaned forward in the scalding water and begged her to go to work on the back of his neck, as so many times before. He did not trouble to excuse his nudity to her, nor even to conceal it; and she pleasantly pretended to be unaware of anything out-of-the-way. Ali was there, discreet and at hand in an alcove of the room to bring towels when the bath cooled down.

'Thank you, Ali: I'm getting out now.' The Mameluke came forward, helped him to stand, wrapped him – ('I am feeling much better. You may go') – and glided away on slippered feet. 'Now, my dear, if you'll kindly give me an arm to the bed?' Albine brought him across the carpet until he stood beside the bedpost and held onto it, weakly enough. 'Just help to pat me dry, if you would.' She knelt at his feet and dabbed the towel all over him. (He gave no sign of sexual arousal.) When she had finished he sat on the bed and gestured her to sit next to him. He took hold of her hand and caressed it.

'O'Meara says, my liver. Of course it has to be the liver. You remember how Prometheus was chained to a rock, his unending punishment for arrogant presumption, and God's vulture came to chew upon *his* liver? Here's where the liver is.' He placed her hand upon the side of his abdomen and lay back on top of the bedclothes. 'Here. Can you rub it for me? softly, gently, it seems to do it some good. Not so much a pain as an intermittent discomfort, undignified rather than heroically mythical. Prometheus had no friend to console him in his chains, to disarm the implacability of the carrion-devouring bird. But Prometheus had usurped the prerogatives of heaven. I don't think *I* did that.'

He laughed, a warm confiding laugh. 'No,' she whispered, 'I wouldn't say so.' (He gave no sign of sexual arousal, nor did she seek to achieve one.)

'Neither would I. All *I* did was tell the French that their vaunted revolution had collided with itself and could never be saved, never, until the world outside France was induced – or *compelled* – to refrain from interference. I was a man dealing with men, that was all. Everything I saw, I saw more clearly than they could; so they naturally left me to put it into practice; and God help me! I did. Perhaps I shouldn't have?'

He groaned a little; she was pressing too hard with her fingers. He squirmed and put her hand away.

'Should I not have told them to continue as they were, a pack of splashing cattle who befoul their own pond? But then what would have happened to my career? I was young, I was selfish; I think young men always are. Young women as well. Did you in your decisions always consider the Greater Good?'

'Hardly ever,' she said, and laughed with him. 'I'd guess I was the most selfish girl in all the world. I had to make my own way: it was damned difficult.'

'And besides, if I'd refused, would it have saved any lives? The war existed. A monstrous boil: it was bound to be lanced by *somebody*. I could not foresee how many thousands and thousands of lives would be lost by my policy – a man dealing with men, but they too had to deal with *me* – how should *I* be expected to prophesy their brute stupidity? I asked *you* just now to be gentle with my liver, and you were; but then you forgot and you hurt me. I suppose it was not stupidity, just the common-or-garden failure of a beautiful human creature to stay totally consistent.'

He eased himself backwards across the mattress until he leaned against his pillows, propped up there and gazing into her eyes. He took hold of both her hands, clasped them together and pulled them in front of his chest. The movement brought her down, to lie close against him, partly alongside him, partly on top. She strained against it, trying to rise.

'No,' she said.

'No, of course not,' said he, with a wintry little smile. He let her go and she sat up, a foot or two from him on the wide bed, adjusting her disarranged hair, fastening a button which had somehow come undone at the bosom of her low-necked gown. 'A man dealing with men,' he continued. 'Thousands and thousands, first alive and then dead. And now all that is left me is to lie – in my chains – stark-naked and hideously fat, while a woman deals with *me*. "No," she says, "no." Because she knows how very soon I too shall be dead.'

'You mistake me,' she muttered, very low, her face turned away. (But the good humour had not gone from her voice.) 'Dr O'Meara sent me in here to complete his attendance on you; so you see I'm half a doctor for the time being, and you've just had some sort of seizure. I have to think of the Hippocratic oath. When *I* need a physician and O'Meara attends me, I'd never allow him, nor would he allow himself, to—'

'Are you drawn towards that Irishman?'

'No.'

'That's something to be thankful for. He's a careless randy sprig and I happen to know he's found a black woman for his island comfort. He'd do you no good if you fell for him. Stay still. Stay with me. Please.'

He shuffled himself clumsily between the sheets, burying his head into the pillows, his eyes closed as though he wanted to sleep. She remained where she was, crouched on her left elbow. She let her shoes fall to the floor and tucked up her feet onto the bed under her thighs. His hands lay close together beside his cheek; she set one of them above the other with her own right hand, and covered them in its grasp as she might have covered Maximilien's or Henriette's when they were fretful. The posture was awkward; it began to weary her. Cautiously, trying not to disturb him, she relaxed her elbow, crooking it flat under her body, and lay there, very still.

He seemed to be asleep; but she dared not move; he had begged her, 'Stay!' – he trusted her. The night was thick and sultry; even in her light muslin gown (with her shawl left somewhere out-of-reach over the

back of a chair) she felt no chill. She could lie like this until morning if
need be.

She thought about O'Meara and his black woman. Somebody's slave:
the doctor's 'arranged' concubine. She thought about the sail-loft and
the Emperor's oration there – Themistocles! – how she had yearned for
him then, willing herself to die for him – how she had imagined his
naked paunch and the majesty of his virile parts – she'd been as bad as a
young girl in a convent-school with impure dreams of the curate during
Mass – how she had laughed at herself for her foolishness and
ridiculously fainted away. In a queer way it had all come true. She
suddenly *felt* like a concubine; and yet she was no such thing. Nor would
she be. This Hippocratic tenderness was better, oh, so much better . . .

He was stirring in his sleep, thrashing his legs about, groaning and
muttering. Fragments of military discourse dropped from between his
teeth – 'Casualty-lists . . . call for stretcher-bearers . . . must have the full
number . . . No, you bloody fool, I did *not* say the grave-diggers! time
enough for *them* when all of it's finished and done . . . done, you idiot,
done . . . can none of you on my staff ever listen to what you're told . . . ?'

To quieten him she began to croon – for no reason she could think of,
she chose that little nursery-tune to which once she had made a poem
about her babies—

> —*la la-la* ron-*lon lé*
> Little Number Three,
> Mama sings her song to you—
> Papa, where is *he*?

Perhaps the song was effective for him: certainly for her. If it did not
send her to sleep, it at least put her into a species of swoon, where the air
was taken up by many more voices than her own . . .

ॐ She was dancing to this chorus, elegantly in the dark room, between
the Emperor's bed and his bath; there were candles on the dressing-
table; they threw her shadow like a giant bat onto wall and ceiling and
the tall clustered draperies of the bed.

Two shadows. Whose was the other? Fanny Bertrand, intrusive bitch,
imitating her dance and destroying it with vulgar incompetence, every
movement coarsened, enlarged – strutting and trampling and thumping
her fists in the air – and now she was pulling her clothes off! determined
to stop at nothing to ravish the Emperor's attention.

What could Albine do but follow suit?

Odalisques, nautch-girls, slave-women. Concubines.

Disgusting! yet she knew she had no choice. So they swung their wobbling hips, the lewd pair of them, a twin-Charybdis foaming with sweat as they swept their ungirt manes of hair backwards and forwards, side to side . . . How the hell was it going to end?

It ended when the man in the bed suddenly sprang out of it, stretching his arms frantically forward to grab Albine by both of hers, forcing her against his chest, thrusting his open mouth hard into her face, hot breath, wheezing lungs, charnel-house stench of sickness and mortality . . . Fanny Bertrand disappeared, the walls and the ceiling and bed disappeared, the candles were blown out and abruptly there was no more singing.

The room was a cold stone cell, with one small unglazed window high up above her head. Through it she could see, not the sky as she might have expected, but immensely tall mountain-tops covered with snow. He whom she gripped was a black man, short, grey-haired, elderly, so emaciated he was almost a skeleton. He had something the look of the hungry old slave who weeded the Longwood gardens; no, he was not a slave, he wore a gold-braided uniform, a general's uniform, but soiled and threadbare with three-cornered rents in the fabric. There was a heap of straw behind him on the stone-flagged floor. In his skinny but terribly strong arms he threw her onto this straw, rolling on top of her and uttering strange syllables which she could not understand, but she knew them to be words of urgent love.

One of them she did understand: 'Liberty'. He gasped it at her several times as though he thought it was her name; if that wasn't what he thought, the word would appear to have little to do with what he was doing, until she realised that on his ankle was a heavy iron ring from which a clanking chain reached out to a staple in the wall. He may not have been a slave; but he surely was a prisoner.

She was so unbearably sorry for him, so pitiful for his poor starvation state, that for a moment she believed she would willingly let him love her in all the ways he chose. But she recoiled. Not because of his colour – she had had a black bedmate in her youth, a lieutenant of Mameluke horse, a Nubian from far up the Nile, whom she remembered with the utmost fondness – but *this* man, this ecstatic unearthly captive, was a wraith who would *dissolve* her, body and soul.

She contrived to let go of him, croaking her useless apologies, which he seemed to accept with philosophical comprehension. Exhausted by her knowledge of her own failure to understand, she slowly crawled away from him; and then, looking round, she saw that he was dead.

Outside, the wind howled and the mountains were now invisible, hidden from sight in a tumultuous blizzard which blew in at the window-hole, covering her with snow until she shivered and shivered and crept in under the straw, huddling against the corpse . . . desperate to warm him back to life . . . ∾

It was broad morning over Longwood; a wild Atlantic gale had gathered during the night and it rattled all the casements like gunfire. Albine woke to realise she was *in* the Emperor's bed, still fully dressed – although her petticoats and gown were rucked up to her armpits and she was holding him round his torso, bare flesh against bare flesh with all the possessiveness of a veritable lover. His eyes were wide open and gazing from his pillow directly into hers, astonished and delighted. (Ailing liver or not, there was no doubt of his arousal now.)

'Did we?' she enquired, trying not to sound emotional.

'Perhaps,' he smiled. 'Don't you *know*?'

'No: but you seem ready to do it again.'

'Are *you*?'

'I had a dream. This is not a dream. Come.'

Despite his tangible desire, he was not really capable. She did her best for him. He thanked her.

Afterwards, he lay supine, watching the fringe of the bed-canopy flutter and fly in the draught. 'I am grievously distressed,' he said, 'concerning these slaves the English hold here. Had my work been fully completed, there would not be one such left in any dominion of the world. It degrades me more than anything that I have to live here amongst them and helplessly watch their toil. Do you know, that crocodile Lowe has forbidden the clergyman to talk to me?'

'Mr Boys?'

'That's the man. His denunciations of the servitude have cost him most dearly in this colony. The slave-owners demand his deportation back to England (even the genial Mr Balcombe is thoroughly hostile to him); and Lowe will assuredly comply. The brave fellow will be accused of conspiracy with *me*; which would dangerously raise him in the regard of English liberals and so cause a political storm, which in turn would rebound to his harm. And to mine. I don't know how to help him; I can only offer him my moral support.'

'Toussaint!' she ejaculated, and could not imagine why she said it. She could not believe she'd ever heard the word before: had it come to her in her dream? But it acted upon Napoleon as though she'd suddenly run a needle into him.

He cried, '*What?* Good God, how dare you!' The fierce furrows in his brow frightened her, the hard line of his mouth, the unexpected clench of his nails into her arm.

'I don't know what you mean—' She faltered and fell away from his anger. 'I don't know what I said. It was a word – just one word – it went with another word – "Liberty". Please tell me, I beg you, what's wrong with it, why? – why do you turn on me so harshly?'

He reared up in the bed and loomed over her for a paralysing sixty seconds, a gross white shark of a man, all teeth and gasping menace; very slowly he relaxed. He seemed to have difficulty in speaking. She cowered. At last he addressed her with calm and some contempt: 'Toussaint L'Ouverture – it was fifteen years ago, my pretty trull – yes, you'd have been old enough to have read of him in the bulletins – but of course, you forgot, he was very far away; and then, yes, because just now I spoke of slavery – yes – you remembered in your feather head . . . Too well I know such heads, they've been about me all my life.

'He was the leader of the revolted slaves in Saint-Domingue – which I refuse to call Haiti, as the blacks would have it termed . . . atavistic barbarity, yes? Barbarian or not, it cannot be denied he had acted according to the spirit of the Revolution. A Jacobin as smart as Carnot, as devoted as Robespierre. More so than me, though I say it myself. Yet *I* was a revolutionist; and I had every best reason to *retard* his revolution – the time was not ripe! – within four years or five, if all my designs were to prosper, the entirety of Europe would be but a single people – with their many tongues and cultures, yes? – but no frontiers any more, no disputes of national sovereignty, no importunate antique dynasties, no rivalries of insane religion, and – d'you hear it? d'you hear it? – *no war*. The English and the Russians for a while might remain, yes? sullen and undisturbed, but in the end, in the end . . .

'So you will easily see how across the Atlantic black freedom was premature. I was a man dealing with men, I had to deal with the white colonists, essential to the economy of France; there had been prodigious slaughter, an inferno of atrocities, in the war between my troops and the ex-slaves, an impossible diversion. It was necessary to arrest, to *remove*, the brave Toussaint. By means of a trick, a false safe-conduct. He appealed to me in a succession of letters, which of course I disregarded – until I came to this island—'

He heaved himself across her and climbed down from the bedstead; backwards and forwards he paced the floor as mechanically as a sleepwalker, to recite what he wished he'd never read:

'—until I came – until I came here – when the words of one of those letters surged up from the dregs of my brain:

> I dare to say with truth that among all the servants of the state
> none is more honest than I. I was one of your soldiers and the

first servant of the republic in San Domingo. I am today wretched, ruined, dishonoured, a victim of my own services. Let your sensibility be touched at my position, you are too great in feeling and too just not to pronounce on my destiny—

Such a paragraph I myself might have written – Themistocles to the Persian Emperor – Plutarch. "Too great," madame, "too just"? I imprisoned him indefinitely, *and* without trial, in a fortress in the Alps: the first winter he endured there killed him. Starved and frozen. Frozen and all alone. Chained upon his rock; and *I* was the murderous vulture.'

She could not withhold a horrified shudder. 'You are *sorry* for it? Remorse? Despair?'

'Anguish, yes. Remorse: maybe not. It is more that I *understand* what I did. Understand it after all these years. But you know, it is not what I'm punished for. Castlereagh and Hudson Lowe would have *approved* my decision. The British army lost thousands of men in the same country, Saint-Domingue, fighting their own war against the blacks.

'On the question of sorrow: I think I am really sorry that I ever decided to call myself Emperor. Such a title in the upshot did no good to the new order; it reminded the well-educated of how Diocletian, a brute soldier, turned half the known world into a tax-collector's prison-house, only to find in his failing age that his sole consolation was his cabbage-patch . . . Just suppose that instead I had maintained the Republic with the intransigence of Cato, a Republic of All-Europe, submitting myself loyally to the recurrent free suffrage of the multitudinous peoples, then perhaps we could have—'

He broke off, stood still, glanced at her sideways, challenging her to contradict. Well, she couldn't: she was too ignorant of the inner political story. But if he lied, was it not a flattering falsehood, to desire to win her heart through simplicity rather than pomp?

'But I did,' he continued, in a small broody voice, 'I did assume that title: and now I must insist upon it, for it is the chief thing they would take from me; the chief thing and they shall not have it.'

Nervously, fussily, he helped her to titivate, reorganise her crumpled gown, pin her hair up with approximate tidiness. 'You must return now, my pretty, to your saint of a husband and tell him that you love him just as much as you ever did – however much that was? For if you don't, he will hate me; I badly need his cool reason in these infuriating affairs.'

He took her by the hand and kissed it. Although, without a stitch on him, he was so irrefutably flabby and squat and ill, there was in the gesture such gaiety and gallant good humour that she all but forgot every dreadful word he had thought fit to say, every twice-dreadful image of her dream.

36

When she reached her own room, she found Montholon at the breakfast-table, biting his nails and peering gloomily into a cold cup of coffee. He was unshaven. He seemed not to have been to bed all night.

'Well?' he snapped. 'You've come back.'

'Of course I've come back. What did you think I was going to do?'

'Well?'

'Don't be silly. D'you want me to tell you? Tell you what? I know what I'll tell you. He's got practically no hair anywhere on his body. He's got the smallest tool I've ever seen on a full-grown man. And his cod is scarcely big enough to contain a couple of hazelnuts.' Which was perfectly true, but left a great deal unspoken. He was sure now that his plan had been successful, but he did not feel like asking her to add to her account. He had in any case heard it said that *size* in such matters was less important to women than some men liked to think.

'Just so long as you gave ease to his pain . . .'

'I did that, Charles-Tristan, thank God I did that.' She embraced him; he drew away from her at first, and then submitted to her affection; he knew he had no right to deny its validity.

37

From then on she was the Emperor's lady, slipping into his private apartments whenever he asked for her – which in fact for carnal purposes was not very often. Napoleon's sexual energy, already low, observably diminished as the months wore on. His pleasure with her became largely emotional; he might ask her to play chess with him, he might just recline on his bed and let her stroke his pale skin and talk to him at random about anything that came into her head. She told him all sorts of disreputable anecdotes of her early years as a garrison 'follower'. He laughed immoderately if any of the men she mentioned had been known to him; many had.

She was glad to find him most discreet; in front of the others he treated her as he had always treated her, distantly, politely, sometimes with his unnerving sarcasm. She had the good sense to give herself no airs, and she made a particular effort to be cordial to Fanny Bertrand. An unrewarded effort, on the whole; but at least she made it. Of course everybody, little by little, came to understand what was going on. But nobody *said*. From respect for Napoleon? Or self-preservation? open statements meant open quarrels. (The Las Cases boy on one occasion made a smutty remark. It was not properly heard, except by his father who boxed his ears and drove him vehemently out of the room.)

One obvious result of the liaison was the Emperor's attitude towards Montholon. The latter was now relied upon, and trusted, far more overtly than he had ever been. This *was* noted, and talked about. It put Bertrand entirely in the shade; he had little to say to anyone. Gourgaud became furiously jealous.

38

Only a few days after the ear-boxing episode, Las Cases and his son were arrested and summarily deported; it appeared that Sir Hudson's people had caught them smuggling letters. (They had foolishly bypassed Cipriani, using a slave for these transactions; not in principle a mistake, for St Helena slaves identified with Napoleon; when they dared, they were his willing confederates; but this one was already watched by government agents.) Las Cases, as it happened, was glad to be sent away; already he yearned for the libraries of Europe; and the boy's education lay hard on his conscience. A troublesome consequence: his nearly completed draft of the dictated imperial memoirs, kept among his papers, was confiscated by Lowe, who refused to hand it over to the Emperor.

The Emperor raged and threatened; but Montholon was secretly relieved by the whole business. Las Cases had lately been seriously unwell – and so had his son – with symptoms very similar to those affecting their master. Montholon had feared for some time that Napoleon was giving his literary collaborator glasses of the special wine as a stimulus during their work together. Young Las Cases too: he used to help with the copying. If it should, by a horrible chance, be the arsenic that was affecting them, the sooner they were out of St Helena the better . . .

When Albine casually said, 'I miss that little old twerp. He could be a bore, but he was always an *interesting* bore; he was recently so much nicer to me than he used to be,' Montholon lost his temper and astonished her.

'Nice?' he spluttered. '*Nice!* Are you a total fool? He's the most spiteful bloody hypocrite I ever met. And dangerous, moreover, you don't know how bloody dangerous. Have any of us any idea what he was writing in that damned book of his?' She asked him sharply to explain himself; he said he didn't know what she meant, and went off in a huff. Nor was he sure exactly what *he* meant: his own sudden notion was new to him – could there really be a danger in the book? If Las Cases had observed anything odd about Montholon's behaviour, and had written it down, and Hudson Lowe were to read it – oh, this was nonsense! If Las Cases had observed, he'd have spoken to Napoleon direct. Montholon cursed himself: he was like a frightened sentinel, thinking every bush by moonlight to be an enemy sniper. What had happened to his self-control?

39

He had another reason for biting his wife's head off.

Albine had just announced to him her second island pregnancy. Abominably inconvenient in itself, it posed a disheartening question. Was he soon to be the alleged father of the Emperor's child? Should he ask her? *Could* he ask her? Would she even know?

After brooding for a few days, he decided to make a joke of it, to test her reaction. 'If the baby in its cradle sticks one hand into the breast of its little jacket, I must be ready to click my heels, take my hat off, bow. Who knows, it might then pull me by the ear?'

She scratched her neck and curled her lips, meaning anything or nothing. 'Of course you must,' she finally answered. 'Click your heels, yes, whatever it does with its hand. *My* child: it'll demand your respect. I don't know what you worry about. After Henriette was weaned I made love to you whenever you indicated.' And *that* was a two-edged remark: he tried to remember the number of times he had 'indicated' since the night of Napoleon's hot bath. *None?*

She had indicated, fair enough: four occasions, six . . . ? Only once, perhaps, had he complied; and then with perfunctory anger, swearing at her, knocking her about. Was it possible she'd conceived out of *that*? It was true, he recollected, that she failed to complain of his violence, smiling at him, scratching her neck (so maddening a mannerism), and then turning away, passively to wipe a small streak of blood from the corner of her mouth – which did (perhaps) suggest that she—

Christ! she had been, still was, using him, handling him, *moulding* him, for whatever slyboot trick she and that damned renegade confected together. 'Emperor', indeed! – a Corsican bandit who'd subverted the people's trust! – infiltrated, no doubt, into the original Revolution by the villainous agents of Pitt! – why oh why had not he, Montholon, thrown in his lot with Malet when he had the immediate chance? Had he done so, his intervention might well have turned the scale! Well, he hadn't: and now he must suffer this insufferable *droit de seigneur*!

Upon the heel of these whirlpool brain-cramps he amazedly recollected Montchenu. Whose business (for five whole minutes) absolutely he'd forgotten. How *could* he have forgotten? Here he was, bond-slave in the service of the Bourbons; how should they understand it? poor fools, they were *sharing* him with Robespierre's ghost. Why, he had no need for guilt! for traitor's qualms! or murderer's palsy! – by means of his arsenic he vindicated the Revolution, he pursued right and justice, without hope of either fame or reward – by God, he was a marvellous man. Let him at once feel the pride of his actions. He laughed aloud and sauntered out, to hasten his pace down the garden-paths, to stride through the rain bare-headed, laughing and shouting at the British guards along the boundary-wall. They stood phlegmatic in their sodden greatcoats and watched the capering Frenchman with disdain. (They had little else to entertain them; the clouds were down on the hilltops; the plain was grey and empty; desolation and abandonment and a plague of bloody dysentery running through the huts of their camp.)

40

Yet he could not stop himself remembering the night he had assaulted her; for his cruelty had been altogether entangled with an event, mortally dangerous, at the imperial dinner-table no more than an hour or so before. The guests had been the Montholons and Gourgaud. The meal was just beginning; bottles of wine were laid in front of each diner by Marchand, as usual; in front of Napoleon his own half-bottle of Vin de Constance, which (as usual) no one else was to drink.

And as usual there was a silence: Napoleon, according to protocol, must be the first to commence conversation. He was dull, he looked ill, greenish-yellow in the cheeks and the whites of his eyes. He sipped from his glass and pushed his soup-bowl irritably away. 'I do believe,' he offered, at last, 'that this damned ocean reef is the most unwholesome heap of pebbles in the whole of the British Empire. They assured me it would not be. Filthy Hanoverian lies. The ranks of their damned regiment are as full of disease as any expedition to the West Indies. Admittedly not the Yellow Jack, which is what they all died from in Saint-Domingue; but intestinal something-or-other and O'Meara is positive it's entirely climatic. And then again, where are the Balcombes? I'd invited them here tonight; they are soon to return to England and I longed to see dear Betsy once again before they sailed. We've been sending each other presents: I gave 'em a bottle of wine, wrote that if they could secure Lowe's permission we'd drink another one in company in Longwood. Well, it seems they did secure it, rather surprisingly. And then Betsy sends me a note to say they cannot come: her mother has fallen ill, stomach-trouble, vomiting. I only hope the dear child shall not be affected . . . What's this? Roast beef? Oh God, take it away, man. Go and hand it to a British grenadier. I might, at a pinch, try an omelette. No, not even an omelette: green salad, without any oil.'

They took their cue to chatter (as brightly as they could, given his gloomy mood and their own individual jealousies) about their general disaffection with Sir Hudson and his territory. Montholon and Gourgaud found little to say; Albine struggled to make herself agreeable with comic imitations of the governor's rebarbative manner, in what she took to be idiomatic English. But the dullness soon settled even upon her. Conversation faded away.

Gourgaud, greedily in the midst of roast beef, after the style of a sour-tempered dog, chopping his teeth into the food and glancing warily up and down the table at the same time, abruptly swallowed a large portion of fat and spoke while still wiping his mouth. 'Did you say, sire, a bottle? Your own wine, and immediately the lady falls ill? I am, sire, a rude rough Corsican, and you know well my ill manners are a token of my love for you.'

Without further words he reached across the mahogany, laid a hairy brown hand upon the Emperor's carafe and poured himself a brimming glassful. Napoleon, startled, sat up to roar at him, thought better of it, said simply: 'So continue your ill manners. You've filled it to the very top. Now drain it to the bottom. Go on, Gorgotto, one gulp: demonstrate to us your old battle-courage, *now*.'

Gourgaud blenched, but obeyed him, showed the wine-glass quite empty, and that was that. Or seemed to be. Montholon held himself motionless, erect, pale as death in his chair. Albine gave him a quick sideways look, looked at Gourgaud, looked at the Emperor, and began again to talk rapidly about how Lowe had been heard to refer to her children and the Bertrands' as 'the enemy brattery', and so forth and so on, malice and scandal as usual . . . Napoleon had no more to say to anyone: until Gourgaud during dessert rose suddenly from his seat, thrust his napkin against his mouth, and lurched out of the room.

Everyone could hear him being sick on the terrace outside.

Then he came in again, gave no apology, stared at the Emperor from the threshold of the French window. The Emperor said, 'Roast beef. You should have sent it away like I did. *I* saw you guzzling the grease.'

'Maybe, sire. I *am* a glutton, I don't deny it. But sire, if we all drank out of *your* bottles, they would never dare poison the whole pack of us. I do but suggest an intelligent precaution.'

'No, Gorgo *mio*, no. The private wine *is* my precaution. We know where it's kept and who looks after it. There are loyal witnesses every time a cask is tapped. I told you, this island is altogether unwholesome; speak to O'Meara; I have it from his own lips.'

And then later, in the bedroom, Albine asked Charles-Tristan to undress her, 'very slowly and wickedly. In the way of the old days in Würzburg. I am prickling all over with a cold grue (as Zoé says when she's upset), I need your warm hands to abolish it. Tender, Charles-Tristan, I need you to be affectionate and tender.'

He tried to be; but as he unbuttoned and untied and slipped the garments from her body, his own 'grue' overcame him and he mishandled her like a ruffian in an alleyway.

41

One furnace-hot sunshine morning in the seventh month of Albine's pregnancy, Gourgaud (who could these days hardly ever bring himself to speak to Montholon) accosted him in a corner of the courtyard. 'It's over half a year since I threw up my *roast beef*,' he snarled. 'From then on His Majesty's condition significantly improved. Several of the servants saw what happened at dinner that night. In my candid opinion – which I am sure you will despise – a message was transmitted to – well, to certain persons unknown. And the tampering with the bottles came to an end. Count, I have to ask you: your duties in the wine cellar, have you between then and now noticed any change as to who goes in and who comes out? Specifically, in recent weeks. I ask this because Dr O'Meara was called to the Emperor last night. I understand the symptoms have returned.'

'Oh, my God, have they?'

'You didn't know? I thought your charming wife might have told you.'

'What the devil do you mean, sir?'

'Whatever you care to imagine I mean. But I asked you a question.'

'Then I give you an answer. No. I do not believe there is anything queer in respect to the wine. You made yourself sick by gorging, *Gorgotto*. And that's all there was to it.'

'You insult me, you aristo pig.'

O'Meara, crossing the yard with his battered old medicine-bag in his hand, saw the imminent challenge to a duel. Without wasting a moment, he intervened. 'Gentlemen, for the Lord's sake, what on earth has come over you? His Majesty's extremely ill; I have him lying under cupping-glasses this minute; am I to tell him his staff are threatening to kill one another? For shame, for shame, the pair of you! Jasus, but you're worse than the squireens of Galway!'

'Sir!' bellowed Gourgaud. 'We are officers of the Imperial Army! The satisfaction of our honour is no concern of any Irishman.'

Rather than risk an escalation of challenges, the doctor turned in his tracks and went straight off to warn his patient. Which was not perhaps what he *should* have done; indeed his upbringing quite strictly forbade such middle-class timorousness; but as a physician he felt he had a prior responsibility.

Napoleon sent him back with a message to the raging Cyranos; no pistols, no swords, and if they did not like it, they knew what to do. Montholon replied with apologies and instant acquiescence; Gourgaud erupted into the Emperor's sickroom, entirely out of control. He was staggered by his master's response. 'You Corsican lunatic! I have told you before about your damned vendettas. All I want here are men who are useful, and only *for so long* as they're useful! You have had your last chance: the next ship back for Europe, you're on board. No, sir, I will not relent. Get out.'

So Gourgaud left the island, thoroughly eaten up with grudge, bewailing 'unheard-of ingratitude'.

42

That was in the February of 1818. And Gourgaud's departure was followed at once by an even more drastic diminution of the Longwood household.

The enigmatic Cipriani had overall control of the domestic establishment; he used to flit from room to room, avoiding irrelevant contact with anyone save the Emperor; he would take odd and unexplained journeys into Jamestown at all hours of the day and night. (In fact, he was by way of being a double-agent, justifiably trusted by Napoleon to co-ordinate external plots for escape, unjustifiably trusted by Lowe to pass on any news of such plots to Government House.) When Gourgaud rode down to the landing-stage to embark for his voyage, Cipriani went too and held a lengthy conference with him while they waited for the ship's longboat. Later in the same day, he knocked softly at the door of

Montholon's quarters to ask for a private word. He found Albine alone, very great in the belly, attempting to rest, playing with Henriette and wishing Zoé would come to relieve her of the overactive little girl.

Montholon's man was lurking in the back-entry – he heard Albine making excuses to the Corsican – he shuffled in, gracelessly enough, through the fly-screen from the scullery: 'You'll forgive me, madame, but I think I can inform Signor Franceschi of the whereabouts of the count—'

'My message is as much to Monsieur Grâcepardieu as it is to His Excellency. If we can just take a step outside . . . Thank you, madame, I will not disturb you further.' He led the valet out to the verandah and shut the door behind them. Something about his expression struck Albine most unpleasantly. Scared at she knew not quite what, she crept to the door, hushing the puzzled child, kneeling down and putting her ear to the keyhole.

She could not hear very much. Grâcepardieu did not seem to be talking above a whisper; only Cipriani's voice was audible, a few fragmentary phrases, that was all, delivered with peculiar emphasis. 'You're to tell him, without nonsense . . . affair of General Gourgaud . . . wine cellar, oh, yes . . . please don't play ignorant . . . Exactly as I've told you, you tell *him* . . . And *tonight!* it won't wait. Tell him or I'll know what to think.'

Grâcepardieu's footsteps returning. She rose quickly from the door and had reached her divan once again before he entered. 'Well?' she asked, attempting with difficulty to control her hasty breathing.

The valet seemed deeply disturbed. 'Madame, I don't know – it's not right he should take that tone with me – like, accusing me, wasn't he?'

'*Was* he? What of?'

'How should *I* know, madame? Oh, he's sinister, that man is; he'd make anybody feel they'd had the *Black Spot* put onto 'em. I'm forced to tell His Excellency. No delays. He was walking with the Emperor in the shrubbery, but the Emperor came back in on his own, I daresay he'll still be there. Begging your pardon, madame, yes . . .' He crammed his hat on his head and departed.

Just then Zoé arrived from whatever she'd been doing. Without any kind of explanation to her, Albine dumped Henriette into her arms, found a bonnet, found a shawl, and hurried off after Grâcepardieu. It was dusk. Slipping quickly from bush to bush, she tracked him across the deserted garden until he came to the shrubbery, where he gave a low whistle and hovered anxiously about. His whistle was repeated from the gloom of the trees; Montholon emerged, furtively; the two of them held a consultation. Alas, quite out of earshot.

Would it not have been appropriate for Albine to have confronted her husband there and then, demanding to know what the devil went on? She told this to herself; she felt unable to do it. Yet it was utterly outrageous that he and his bloody valet had these secrets between them, excluding her. Grâcepardieu was an insolent hound.

So what was wrong with her that she could not speak?

The truth was, she did not dare hear him put words and therefore *shape* to the inchoate cloud of terror that for some time had possessed her imagination. Or was it no more than a phantom of her pregnancy? She was in any case full of absurd premonitions: this new baby – her fifth (a fact of which Montholon, even after all these years, was unaware) – did it come now too late in her life for safety? She knew many women who had undergone untroubled deliveries at a greater age than hers – she was not quite thirty-eight – but sometimes she felt as old as eight-and-fifty. Sometimes? oh God, *most* of the time! And she knew too that O'Meara was not as confident as he might have been . . . He made far too many reassuring jokes. Scarcely surprising she would fabricate Gothic mysteries at every turn . . .

She began against her will to remember things . . . Strange pieces of behaviour on the part of her husband, going back to their sojourn in Rochefort . . .

She remembered, all of a sudden, that curious piece of paper in the kitchen of the sail-loft.

'Secret orders'? *Whose?*

And for whom, in heaven's name, did Cipriani really work?

She made haste to the house before the two men caught sight of her. She did not go to the Emperor's table that night; she pleaded an expectant mother's privilege; she lay on her bed and tried to calm herself by reading; most unwisely she jangled her overwrought nerves with the beastly images of *Justine*, which she had recently turned up in a discarded frock-coat of Montholon's, buried in a most untidy cupboard; she was unable to find that other loathsome book, the one with the story of the Marquise de Brinvilliers, but why the hell should she want to find it? What was wrong with her? Was she mad? She threw *Justine* aside and rummaged for the *Dangerous Liaisons*. She skipped to and fro among its pages: unscrupulous persons plotting other people's love affairs for the worst possible motives. How exactly, she wondered, and why, had the Emperor been induced to take her into his bed?

These days the children and Zoé slept in the living-room; herself and

Montholon in their own double bed. But tonight when he returned – from dinner, she supposed, though unusually early – she pretended to be in deep slumber, sprawling herself deliberately right across the mattress so that he could not get in without shifting her. He fetched some cushions, some coats and a tablecloth, and lay on the floor fully dressed like a beggarman under a penthouse.

Three times she heard him hunting for the pisspot with *sotto-voce* curses, and groaning as he used it. It was possible he was drunk.

He was not drunk; he was simply terrified and thinking hard. He had spoken to Cipriani, and Cipriani had told him that Grâcepardieu had been poisoning the wine – only a suspicion, to begin with – but then a suspicion confirmed by the valet's looks, when he heard Cipriani's deliberately ambiguous message. 'I said "the affair of General Gourgaud": every tooth in the villain's head was a jumping-jack!' Montholon could not make out whether the Corsican really believed this, or whether it was a subtle trap to uncover the real guilt of Grâcepardieu's employer.

But it did appear that Cipriani knew that Grâcepardieu had bought a bradawl from the general store in Jamestown (such a long time ago! how on earth had it come to light?). It was the only precise piece of evidence mentioned; but it *was* evidence, of a sort. Montholon's clear duty was to search Grâcepardieu's quarters – the scullery! And Cipriani was determined to help him with the search. Grâcepardieu would already be in bed. They could turn him out at once and search now (Cipriani said), but it would have to be done by candlelight. This would be a very small packet or sachet or vial, *minutissimo* (Cipriani said); in the dark it could easily be missed. No (said Cipriani), they must wait until morning; so let Montholon make sure that his servant did not leave the scullery – 'A key in the lock, Excellency! let him wonder, if he wishes; let his conscience enfeeble his heart! Let him even, if he wishes, devour the poison *before* we come in! and *ecco!* incontrovertible proof.' But no (said Cipriani), not to lock him in: suicide would leave too much undiscovered. Meanwhile, not a word to the Emperor!

Altogether the Corsican's mental processes seemed so tortuous as to be virtually unmanageable; he was wrapping himself up in his own devious subtleties, balancing one bizarre possibility against another. Was he as clever as he seemed? Or excitedly making much out of nothing? Or merely bewildered and frightened? Frightened, above all, of precipitate action in the dark?

Careful. Go careful.

Now, if Grâcepardieu was lying there on his pallet, Montholon could not remove the arsenic until morning. But by morning it *must* be removed . . . And how to find an alternative hiding-place?

Cipriani had said, 'I'll be at your door at a quarter to five, Your Excellency, if that creates no inconvenience.'

At four o'clock Montholon pulled himself from his sleepless bed, checked to see lest Albine be awake (she was, but she did not show it), and went through into the scullery. He struggled with the tinder-box.

When the candle was lit – 'Grâcepardieu! Up you get. It's bloody early and bloody dark: I've a job for you to do. Go at once to Monsieur Cipriani and tell him he was quite right, I am ready for him now, never mind about a quarter to five, he'll know what I mean, it's urgent! See that you get him here without waking anyone else. You'll have to bring him round the paddock, *not* through the house, d'you understand?'

'Oh Lord, sir, is it yet more of this dreadful "secret service"?'

'Of course it is. Don't ask questions. Just look sharp.'

As soon as the valet was gone, Montholon prised up the brick, took the poison from the hole underneath, placed one sachet in his pocket, and crept through into the living-room. He pressed the remainder in its packet under Maximilien's cot-pallet, very carefully, very slowly; the child did not wake up. Then back to the scullery, to blow the ashes of the stove, lay more sticks in it, set a kettle on to boil. (Like Albine, he too was recollecting the sail-loft.) He found the coffee-pot and a pair of cups. He laid a tray and did his best to give himself the appearance of a busy efficient officer about to start an important day's work.

When Cipriani arrived with Grâcepardieu, Montholon sent the valet into the courtyard to stand guard – 'We must *not* be interrupted! If anyone comes, keep 'em out with a plausible tale.' And then he showed Cipriani the hole in the floor. 'Yes, it's empty, but I saw the scratches on the other bricks and the broken mortar in the cracks where a knife or a screwdriver's been used to fetch it up. Several times, I'd imagine. The wash-bucket usually stands there; it could have been like this for years and no one would have noticed. And the bradawl you talked about: my man had it underneath his bedroll. What'll we do?' (Cipriani said nothing. He sat on a stool with his chin in his hand, writhing his lean frame, meditating darkly.) 'Ah, the kettle! *My* coffee black, plenty of sugar. And you, Monsieur Cipriani?' (Montholon turned to the stove and then to the tray; he bent closely over it, fussed and clattered cup and spoon and sugarbowl.) 'While we drink it, we can think of an expedient. You see, what worries me: if we get him to confess, who is he going to incriminate? This could be a Bourbon device, in which case His Imperial Majesty will presumably make representations to the governor, who in turn will have to tell London. But suppose Grâcepardieu confesses to *us*, and refuses to confess to the British? What on earth will happen then? And then again – no! I cannot think that London would be ordering a gradual murder; it's quite against their policy, though the Emperor *has* often talked of such a thing. And yet suppose, just suppose, the Emperor should be right? Or suppose Sir Hudson Lowe has been making his *own* plot without London knowing anything about it? He's a most *tortuous* man, driven to distraction by His Majesty's courageous demeanour. What do you think?'

'Excellency, how can I *know* what to think . . . ? Yes, coffee, thank you. Sugar. There are, as you infer, very large considerations here of politics quite as much as – quite as much as *police-work*. And I am not sure, not yet sure, of the police-work. See now, this valet – where did you hire him? I ask, is he a stupid dupe or an extremely cunning operator . . . ?' As he spoke, he absently shovelled several spoonfuls of sugar into his cup. Immediate suspicions were tortuously giving way to the problems of a broader analysis . . .

Montholon began to tell him the history of Grâcepardieu; but the Corsican, after a few minutes, did not seem to be listening. 'Excellency, forgive me, you fetched me out of bed very early, I was not prepared – my morning toilet, my – *Porco Dio!* I need the privy. *Santa Maria, Beatissima Vergine!* – oh, my bowels, how they burn!'

The privy was along the verandah at the end of the yard. Doubled over with pain, he staggered out there; he pushed blindly past Grâcepardieu as he went. Montholon came after him, holding him up by the elbow, guiding him to the door in the dark. 'Grâcepardieu, go for the doctor! I think Monsieur Cipriani is ill. Galloping dysentery, *cholera*! It could spread through the whole of Longwood. Quick!'

He stepped again into the scullery. Albine, peeping in, saw him empty the sugarbowl down the drain-grate in the corner of the floor, saw him rinse the bowl several times with hot water from the kettle, saw him wash his hands over and over, first with hot water, then with cold.

43

Montholon was able to withdraw the packet of arsenic from Maximilien's cot; unobserved, or so he thought. This time he hid it actually inside the wine cellar. A risky trick; but a very dark place; it might work.

O'Meara did diagnose dysentery.

Cipriani lay delirious for four days and then died.

44

If Napoleon still retained any of his high spirits, they were now altogether laid waste. An interval of silence and glowering withdrawal: then at last he sent for Montholon. 'My confidential man for so many years and his loss is irreparable. Lowe had him poisoned of course.'

'The doctor does not think so, sire.'

'The doctor does not understand. He's a good man but a stranger. He is ignorant of the transactions. (I *hope* he is ignorant, for if not, he might too easily have done the poisoning himself. How authentic is the hostility of the Irish to the British? Never mind. No point in these wild suspicions . . .) Tell me again what happened. Franceschi came to you before five in the morning? Already, you say, ill?'

'As soon as he sat down I saw the sweat pouring from him; a dizziness, he said, a gripe in the bowels – burning, he said.'

'So why had he come?'

'I had asked him to come. I could not sleep. Your own illness, sire, was preying on my mind, I *had* to consult him. And besides, it was a secret hour: we could not discuss these matters with the whole household up and about.'

'He should have stayed in his bed and called O'Meara. Ah God! he was conscientious. Loyal. Brave.'

'He ought not to have drunk my coffee. He thought it would do him good. Oh, how was I to know—?'

'You weren't to know. Don't reproach yourself. Had he found anything out? I suppose he didn't have time to tell you.'

'He did, sire. He said he was utterly perplexed. If there was poison in Longwood, he held not one clue as to the source of it.'

'So *that's* not why they killed him. No! he was murdered because Lowe had at length discovered he was *my* double-agent, not *his*. Which means, as I see it, two things. One: all the currently operative plans to get me off the island are useless and voided. Now I am quite sure I shall die here. But then, two: even had they spared his life, I would never again have been able to employ him; he was exposed. So his death changes nothing. Nothing. Nothing . . . How is your wife?'

Everyone was asking Montholon that. For no sooner had Cipriani been carried from the privy to his bed, than her labour-pains began, five weeks prematurely. The birth was shockingly painful; a breech presentation with which O'Meara was barely competent to deal, distracted as he was by the confidential-man's collapse, and also by fear of an epidemic – if the chronic disease from the army camp had definitely reached the community of exiles, was it possible for him alone to control it? (He'd more than once warned the governor, but had been packed off each time with a flea in his ear and finally a threat of deportation.)

Albine's screams had been heard all over the estate. And yet this was the first time the Emperor had mentioned her. A whole week had gone by. The baby was alive and more healthy than might have been expected. But its mother, torn in body and wandering in her mind, lay in Gourgaud's vacated room, refusing to see anyone but Zoé, cursing the names of both Napoleon and Montholon, possibly (said O'Meara) about to die – while the child, a girl as yet unnamed, was fed by the wet-nurse whom Fanny Bertrand had hastily found for her from the slave-cabins of a neighbouring planter.

Montholon kept quiet and endured the situation.

45

After nearly two months Zoé came with a message: his wife would see him, she was lucid, she had a great deal to say but was easily tired, so he was to hold his peace and listen and not argue.

He sat by her bed and took her hand. It was as thin as a spiderweb and no less tremulous. But with her other hand she stroked and scratched her neck. She might have been trying to smile; but not an agreeable smile. It occurred to him she looked like a ship-destroying mermaid.

'You've seen her of course. What do you think of her?'

'She – she's very small. The nurse is stout enough. I'm sure she'll fill out in good time . . . Did you *have* to call her Napoléone? And without one word to me of your choice?'

'You were told not to argue: I can't cope. Whatever her name, the child is yours. She is the daughter of rape, and never forget it. Maybe the name means that, maybe not. Allegory: work it out.'

'*Rape?* How *can* you say—'

'I can because I do. You cut my mouth and broke a tooth. There is a scar on my lip, it won't go, it never *will* go. You know what you did that time. With your bloody great garnet on your ring-finger and everything.'

'It was months ago – you never said a word—'

'I didn't then. I do now. As soon as I am well enough, and Napoléone is weaned and fit, I shall go back to France. With all of them, Maximilien, Henriette, Zoé. You can keep your Grâcepardieu.' Her hint of a smile had broadened. Vindictiveness blazed from her shrunken white face. 'In the meantime, I am Bonaparte's, *his*.' ('Bonaparte's'? Deliberately she was using his pre-imperial surname? Unbelievable . . .)

'I shan't sleep with him, you needn't worry. I shan't sleep with anyone again: I'm all in pieces. Like a ransacked strongbox.'

'You said the same after Maximilien.'

'I said it and I lied. Maximilien was the child of love. Henriette was the child of deceit; so there was no pain about *her* birth – or not much. But this time you can assure yourself it's true. Why did you poison Cipriani? Was the *greatest man in the world* not enough for you?'

She cackled with a threadbare laugh to see the horror and hatred and panic that seized him. She tightened her hand into his and kept him firmly in his chair. 'Remember: I can shout for Zoé. She's just behind the door. With the nurse and Napoléone. She can't hear us if we talk in whispers, so don't raise your voice . . . I said, "the greatest man". If that is how *you* think of him, then I know you for a treacherous viper, bribed or intimidated to do it. Because you did do it, you *are* doing it, Zoé saw you take the packet from under the cot, I saw you wash away the sugar, Grâcepardieu tells the tale of his "secret-service orders" as long time ago as Paris and the week of Waterloo.' She looked at him, very exactly, up and down his slumped body from lifeless eyes and bloodless lips to the fly of his trousers: she might have been a tailor assessing his buttons for all the meaning she put into her gaze.

And yet she did mean something, for she went on – 'You could have another reason, your good reason, your *honest* one. It's just conceivable. You could. Even you. For if *I* had done it – and I might have – I would have been able to find an honest word when they asked me. *Toussaint.* How about *that?*

'After he told me, I believed I was sorry for him – the emotion of the tingling hour, in his bedroom where the whole universe was no wider than a half-closed eyelid – sad little naked Punchinello with his headaches and his hairless fat groin. I melted within myself for the torment that I thought was in *him*.'

Montholon was wondering: should he murder her, and by what device? No, not yet . . . for just now he was far too nonplussed.

Toussaint? Unwise to admit perplexity? But he *must* discover, must, the warp-and-woof of her arbitrary mind. 'Albine, is it possible you could talk a bit of sense? Toussaint? – "All Saints"? – is this a religious melancholy, or what?'

'Shut up. I'm an atheist and you know it. I've been having that dream again, never mind *what* dream, I don't want nonsense. Of course you have heard of him! Why, I'd not be surprised if you'd been that poor Negro man's gaoler. Where *were* you in the year of 1803 . . . ? But we talk about your honest reason. Your best reason, your only acceptable one – I wish to God (whom I deny) that you could affirm it and *I* could accept it! – your best reason would be that *your brother Gaius-Gracchus had asked you to do it.* Nobody else! – I don't want to hear of any other motivator. Montholon, you raped me. *He* raped the world. *He* says he's not sorry. But oh yes, he "understands". That's all he does. Revolution was "premature", just like Napoléone. *Unlike* Napoléone, he deliberately had it aborted. So now he understands he might just as well die. I'm dead already; but maybe not my Charles-Tristan, oh please not Charles-Tristan!' – inarticulate but pathetic appeal: she strained him toward her, he resisted, clutching tight to the arm of his chair.

'Well?' she said, faintly, almost without hope but not quite.

'Well . . .' He was lost. Or could she be trying to tell him—?

'I am waiting for your good reason. Charles-Tristan, I have given it you as I once gave you my love. Catch hold of it, hold of it – please!'

Gaius-Gracchus? He tried to remember. For a moment he could only think of the foster-brother in full uniform grinning like a goat and patting her bare backside, but that couldn't be what she meant. Ah! now he had it! He'd heard from her, of course, the man's words on that occasion: 'The Empire has been a prodigious aberration.' The integrity of Gaius-Gracchus; why, the very thrust of Montholon's own thoughts, and recent thoughts, by God! By God, he was a marvellous man: vindicating the Revolution, pursuing right and justice, so honourably serving the pale ghost of Robespierre . . . If that was what she wanted to believe, what harm then if he assured her that he believed it too?

He summoned up a series of deeply sincere tears, begging her to credit them, begging her to appreciate the necessity of his Deed. 'When we met him at the ferry, he told me what I ought to do and how to do it. He was a policeman, experienced, he knew all about slow-acting powders, he even knew the type of venal apothecary who might be persuaded to purvey them.'

He fondled her hands and kissed her breasts. Was she satisfied? She said she was. Could he believe her? Had he ever believed her? She said she was satisfied, and he had no choice but to be satisfied with what she said . . .

He forgot there was a loose end to his story: she knew of Grâcepardieu in Paris and the letter in the hessian boot. *Before* their last meeting with Gaius-Gracchus . . . Weeks later he would remember, and curse himself . . . Ah.

(Albine had not forgotten. But she pushed the anomaly down into the pit of her self-deception, told herself her mind was not yet quite clear. Better, perhaps, it should stay that way.)

So the danger was over? Up to a point. And now he must make that point, now, this very moment, while they were both still so warm together. He breathed it against her nipple as though the nipple were an ear: ' "The meantime"? As you said? You are *his*? How can you be? When you know, and do not denounce, what is – what is *happening to his wine* . . . How will you even be able to speak to him?'

'You've been able, very able, ever since we were on shipboard.'

'It's not the same thing.'

'Of course it is.'

'No. For I have been working in accordance with a plan. I joined him to deceive him. Whereas you—? Explain yourself.'

She shook her head.

(She wanted to say, that between her and Bonaparte there was in fact so hideous a gulf it was almost as great as that between Montholon and herself. Yet here she lay and allowed Montholon to put his mouth to her intimate flesh. It could be no worse were she to sit with the Emperor in his room and make him merry conversation over the chessboard to divert him, even loving conversation. Each one of the three was as false as the others; and she had bound herself fast, to Montholon by six years of comparative fidelity, to Bonaparte by her submission to his frustrations-in-defeat and his ever more childish desires. She had made of herself a *thing* for the pair of them, for murderer and murdered; and so she must continue until it was possible for her to go. She had thought, several times since the agonising childbed, of drinking that poison herself. But despite her apparently casual neglect, she loved her three children, clung to them, dreamed of them nightly in the calmer interludes of her continual nightmares: impossible to abandon them. She wanted to say this, tried to think of the words for it, but the illogic was inexpressible. All she could do was shake her head, and sing.)

Her own little verses; she had made them up two days before; they were fitted to a very ancient tune, nowadays known as '*Marlbrouck*':

> I'm dancing with a dead man
> I'm dancing with a dead man
> I'm dancing with a dead man
> *And the music never stops.*
>
> We're dancing for a dead man
> (etc.)
> *Oh, throw your fiddles down!*
>
> The children play the fiddles
> (etc.)
> *Every note is out of tune.*

> If the dead men kill the children
> (etc.)
>   *There'll only be me to die.*

Her husband against her breast was staring wildly up at her. Was she running insane or what? Did she imagine this crooning was explanatory of anything? By the look in her eyes you'd think she did. And then she managed to speak: 'Let's make an agreement. For as long as I stay on the island – which I swear will be no longer than it has to be – you put no damned poison into anything or anybody. For my part I'll give to *him* not a hint of my discoveries. Break the deal and I tell what you've been up to. Fair enough?' She thrust him roughly away and her voice became coarse and disgusting. (A style of speech he'd never heard from her, but he hadn't known her, had he?, when the hairs were scarce grown in her secret ravine and yet she must claw for her fortune among companions twice as rough as herself.) 'Get your neb out of my bubbies, you hocussing mot-faker. It should never have been let there in the first place, no, not in Würzburg, not in Touraine, Metz, the Cévennes, Paris – never! I don't want to grass on you, cully, not if your motives are what you say, what you fucking say (do I *believe*?), but I won't be your slag of an accomplice. I asked you, fair enough?'

Montchenu had given him no orders to hasten the poison . . . For a few months, it could doubtless be managed . . . for as long as she stayed . . . Hey, Satan of hell, let her *go*! 'Fair enough.'

46

For many clumsy reasons, chiefly the recurrent ailments of the little Napoléone (a sickly child, as it proved), she did not succeed in arranging her departure until a year and more was past. Throughout that time the Emperor suffered only the chronic liver-trouble, digestive disorder and piles that had afflicted him since the Russian campaign. (Montchenu had now no suspicions. So long as suffering was reported, he assumed the plan went well.)

When she went to the Emperor – no! to Bonaparte – to announce her intention, he turned his back on her, stuck his hands under his coat-tails, and sulked. Then he half-moved his head so that he looked at her over his shoulder. 'I suppose,' he muttered cantankerously, 'you now mean to tell me that your third child is *my* child and you need to be paid for her.'

He had never said anything of this before, except for a painful short intake of breath when he first heard Napoléone's name. And Albine had given him no sort of intimation, one way or the other.

She was ready for him; these days she was ready for anything; she laughed and replied: 'I didn't put your sperm through a sieve to separate it from Montholon's. There's no rule that says you can't be her father, except your own encoded laws and what do *they* say? A married woman's children are her husband's: no exceptions. As for pay, of course I need it. Six thousand francs, properly invested, would do me very nicely. And I'd like that set of chessmen with the imperial crowns on 'em. You give me all that and I'm off your back for ever.'

He had his snuff-box out now, and was spilling the dark powder all over the floor as usual.

'You are a mercenary bitch. I knew it when he first applied to marry you. But you're also a fool. If you'd stayed till I died you'd have got far far more from my will. I'll write you a cheque. The house of Rothschild, of course: you'll be able to draw it anywhere in Europe or America. I ought to make it out to *the Emperor's Whore*. "Countess" is ridiculous, although I daresay the Bourbons will recognise the rank if you turn up in France: it *is* one of theirs, is it not?'

He dropped the mockery and assumed a tense and disturbing *hauteur*: 'Could you never understand? This exile is no disgrace. My career heretofore lacked the needful adversity. Now it is complete. People can review it, complete; and see me at last for what I am, in every condition of life, high, low, and stark-naked *human*. Yet you choose to abandon me in the very midst of my final phase. My final, *greatest*, phase. Let me tell you, Racine would have made no such mistake with one of his heroines.

'Why will you not stay till I die?'

She ignored his poignant question – for how should he know how unanswerable it was? – she ignored the sudden tear in his eye. She took the cheque, curtseyed, and backed out of the room, as one must upon saying goodbye to royalty, even to royalty shorn not only of its power but also its last true lover.

That was July 1819. Thereafter he fell ill again, gradually worse and worse until in May of '21 the poison ate him up and he died; he was fifty-one years old, that was all. The Bourbons (so they thought) were now painlessly relieved of every threat to their dynasty.

And Charles-Tristan, Count de Montholon, sailed 'home'. To a boarding-house in Brussels. To his children and his wife. What *would* she have to say to him?

Pogmoor was looking at another hazy maze of pointilliste dots; they formed a brief outline of an unspectacular funeral-car grinding down the hill from Longwood to the valley of the grave; and then they regrouped, making of themselves a ship, northward bound and little-by-little diminishing as it sailed toward an unclear horizon. One passenger at the taffrail, magnified in a very precise focus: unapproachably alone, he spoke to none of his fellow voyagers as they tediously paced the deck to tell over and over the great days of the greatness of the great man . . . Pogmoor saw his black top-hat tilted down over his eyes, saw his whiskers already grey at the age of thirty-eight, saw his folded arms like a tight-screwed vice – and saw too his thoughts (saw, as in an X-ray, as opposed to merely 'deduced', swarming microbes of another person's mind) – saw his thoughts lying deep in a fathomless emptiness – saw the man's self-knowledge in what he had done, saw the total self-ignorance of who was the man that had done it.

And then a further shift, a final one.

A violent one too, sharp noise and sharp pain of electric light into Pogmoor's eyes, the clatter of a diesel train speeding up over crossover points – he was where he had begun, between Sheffield and York, and a farouche youth in uniform pulled him by the shoulder. (Christ, was he police?*) 'Ticket, I said, ticket. That is, if you don't mind my boring bloody job, sir, interrupting your titillated slumbers?' The scurrilous fellow peered, of course, at the book of women painters which lay open on the seat in all its impudicity.*

This dream had been useless; but it posed a question and failed to deal with it. Carver in his play had also failed. When Montholon found she'd found out, why didn't he kill his wife? *Perhaps no proper answer; nor any answer to the other question either:* what prevented Pogmoor confronting Carmilla (and Polly) with their lies, all those years ago in Pomfretshire? *Pogmoor knew, he damned well knew, he'd never been Inclined to Sexual Violence. Why, it could all have been sorted in five minutes.*

At York he immediately took a late-night express to London. No point in travelling on. Like Montholon, in the end, he must return all on his own to the fumes of his own stench, and inhale.

How Jack Had to Juggle Himself a Long Long Way Away

(as further told by J. Pogmoor,

1986 and 1987)

. . . in the scapes of virtue
Excuses damn her: they be fires in cities
Enrag'd with those winds that less lights extinguish.
Come, siren, sing, and dash against my rocks
Thy ruffian galley, rigg'd with quench for lust.

(George Chapman, *Bussy d'Ambois*)

Her act! a woman!
Where's the body?
There.
. . . *Never follow her;*
For she, alas! was but the instrument.

(Beaumont and Fletcher, *The Maid's Tragedy*)

Pogmoor reached Whitesmith Street in the small hours of Monday morning. Yes, there was a note in his letterbox from Gabriel Garsdale, and not at all a happy one. There were also two policemen, waiting in a car at the curb. They had several unpleasant words for him. Later in the day he sat down again to his typewriter.

1

—okay okay, Gabriel, you really had no need to write in such a tone of voice; I thought I'd done very well with all the pages and pages I sent to your house (and by courier!) on Wednesday night. Okay, I could have used only *two* pages, or even one, to report how Polly Blackadder was mad, overseas, and no use to us. But I owed it to myself to make sure that *you* knew the full story behind that development – I truly thought, Gabriel, you were interested in the truth and in salvaging my reputation.

And okay, I ought not to have gone walkabout. If I'd known that Percy Lobscott was going to *die* while I was away, of course I would never have left.

But I can't see it makes all that much difference. His wife is now up for murder instead of attempted murder; and the case becomes a trifle more malodorous. But they can still get her off by laying all the blame on me, and I still have to give you the facts. As you so churlishly point out, I have not yet done so. But I will and I do; and it's not easy.

I'm only sorry the police have been rude to you. And I suppose I must be grateful you did not blankly disown me when they warned you on Friday I'd 'apparently absconded'. (The sergeant who belongs to the dog-like Lestrade has been staking out my flat, I gathered, and was dangerously gruff about it. He told me of the death before I had a chance to open your envelope, so at least I was prepared for what I read . . . I assured him I'd left a phone message at the local nick for his guv'nor the day I went off; can it not have been properly noted? Somehow he didn't seem to believe.)

There's one troubling aspect to Percy's demise: I was still holding fast to a very small hope he might wake from his coma and exonerate me. But probably a damned false hope. He'd have been equally likely to accept his wife's story 'for the sake of the children', help her to be acquitted, and leave *me* where she currently wants me, struggling to prove I'm no rapist. Or else (sheer *vindicta erotica*), he might have sworn I helped her bash him. Not to be trusted an inch; it's just as well he's out of the picture; if you need me for tactical reasons to show remorse that he's succumbed to his injuries – Gabriel, I'm sorry! I just can't.

But whatever my feelings, whatever the perils arising from the new state of affairs, I've to carry on this deposition from where I left off – back in Knaresborough last Christmas to discuss Percy's play. When I arrived there after dark – December 23rd, wasn't it? – he came to the door to greet me and to show me where to park my Toyota. (What was I doing with a Toyota, being so financially strapped? Expecting it to be repossessed, that's what.) There was something not quite right about the way he made haste to apologise for the absence of his wife. 'She was most anxious,' he grinned, 'to see you again, but sadly, tonight, a small family difficulty – her old aunt, you know, in Ripon. . .' An implication, a sly assumption, that I was so close to the pair of them I must understand at once what he meant. This putative aunt, in fact, had cropped up before, but I still was unable to discern his exact point. I thought—

Aha! but what *did* I think?

At the very start I explained to you I could not possibly undertake to tell what Mrs Lobscott thought.

And now I'm home from my trip across country – which wasn't worth it, I may say – the wrong vibes altogether – and unmitigated rain – and then I started *dreaming*, in railway trains, to no good end – after the trip, I am forced to consider how far I even know what *I myself* have been thinking.

It all comes out of the dream. Never mind the dream as such: it's not evidence, you don't want to know. But it did help me see how in terms of what *can* be called evidence, even so-called 'clinching evidence' that finally sways the jury to convict or acquit, *hypothesis* must inevitably play a cardinal role.

It was a *hypothesis* adopted by a shrewd-nosed Nordic scholar, that brought him to announce that Napoleon had been murdered. The *Emperor's Whore* play accepted a further *hypothesis*, that the preliminary hypothesis was good enough to work from. Carver showed the murder taking place and offered no hint that it might never, in real life, have been perpetrated. His script did not prove anything; it merely took the Deed of Poison 'as read', and went on to ask, *hypothetically*, how? Historians, I understand, continue to deny the *hypothesis* he accepted. They may very well be quite right. There are all sorts of other reasons for arsenic getting into Napoleon's tissues; any one of them, as I see it, would in itself be a worthwhile *hypothesis* – though probably not fit matter for an interesting play . . .

So please understand, however truthful I try to be, I ask you from the start to accept from my pen one bloody big *hypothesis* – that if J. Pogmoor (although professionally able to see every side of a situation, or how else could I have worked with Fid Carver?) deals with his *own* situation, that is to say his own *thoughts* as well as his actions, there is bound to be one side he *cannot* see. Because day by day these thoughts have changed and merged and gone back upon themselves in the light of subsequent events; how can I pick them up at any particular juncture, pinpoint them, say 'there! I thought *that*'? In my dream I saw the thoughts of a man called Montholon; on a precise date, May 9th, 1821; and a deadly perspective it was! But a fictional (*hypothetical*) Frenchman is not me and I insist you shall not treat me as though he were. If you can't meet me on that, I'd better look for a solicitor who can.

I tell you of the things I did. And of the things that were done to me. Take it 'as read'. No mystery. Plain fact. Only five or six different ways of looking at it, that's all; and *I* can only look at it from the seat where I'm immediately sat. All the other ways are *hypotheses*: we discard them.

I think now that I thought Lobscott's manner might be due to his knowledge of what had passed between me and Jacqui the last time I saw him and her.

2

I mean, the weeks of his Hermit's Hole *play: the end of summer, 1975—*

If he *was* aware at that time of any adulterous goings-on, he never gave me an inkling. Nor did Jacqui behave as though *she* thought he might be onto us.

Those fun-and-games of '75 began all so very swiftly, without any hassle. I was not staying at the Lobscotts', but in the hotel on the way up the hill. For my first night there I was invited by Percy to his house to dine with the local worthies of the Mother Shipton Playhouse Trust. I found Every Man Jack in a dinner-jacket and every wife with her tits half-out and flounced and furbelowed down to the ankle. There was even a maid-in-waiting (one Deborah, straight from the dairy of old Gaffer Thickpenny's farm, hired by the hour, I guessed, for this momentous occasion, and fitted out with a black-and-white uniform). I had none of the appropriate gear; I hiccuped with underbred confusion. Mrs Lobscott, now and then, turned a sympathetic eye upon me, while the Doc and his friends gave me news in lordly terms of their praiseworthy work for the Cultural Heritage.

I must mention one crucial committee-member – whom I was to meet once again and no more – Rupert Mauleverer-Briggs, a young-looking forty-five or so, as slim as a whippet, corn-coloured sparse hair, inordinate scholarship worn with easy patrician disdain, a sort of Lord Peter Wimsey type if you want a pop-literature analogy. A genuine professor he was, of Regional History, University of Newcastle (I think); at all events he didn't live locally; he made a great to-do of not drinking more than one pint of claret on account of his long drive home. He seemed to have had a large involvement in the resurrection of the Georgian theatre; and it was obvious that he and Percy did not entirely hit it off. He kept referring to Mrs Lobscott as 'our Jacqueline the inimitable precellence', which I thought snide; but it caused her to simper, so I concluded she enjoyed it. I also concluded (mistakenly) that he was gay; in fact he was just old-fashioned and outrageously superior.

We did not talk much about Doc Lobscott's actual play. That was to be kept for a series of tête-à-têtes over the next few days. Shy of hearing in public my opinion of his writing? Maybe 'in public' should be interpreted as meaning 'in the presence of Mauleverer-Briggs'; all the other guests made it clear that I was to see Percy as the undisputed Nidderdale Genius, at whose feet they happily basked in a trance of congenial awe.

They may have held *me* in awe too, the glamorous Great Director, but not nearly so congenially – I was too much of a surly scruff to be properly *respected*, too urban-industrial, too vitally Yorkshire indeed for all these self-proclaimed *echt*-Yorkshire market-town middle-wigs.

At the end of the evening, when I shook hands in the hall and thanked my hostess, she pressed my palm with an unexpected heat and let her tongue briefly flick from between her lips. *Hypothesis*, Gabriel: I thought she was making a pass at me; and I thought she took the point that *I'd* made a small pass at her. 'You'll be among us for some time,' she murmured. 'Not rehearsing *all* the time, surely?'

'Most of it,' I replied. 'There'll be moments of repose. It all depends how hard-working the actors are. Shall you be taking part in the production?'

'Me? Oh no no, Pogmoor, no.' ('Pogmoor'? No 'Mister'? No 'Jack'? Challenging usage from a lady I'd never met before. But upon what did she challenge me, eh? Aye, well, we'd soon see.) 'I am Percival's inspiration, but by no means a tool of his trade. He'd as soon ask me to prescribe for patients as act in one of his plays. And if he doesn't ask, *I* don't. It'd be as much as my life is worth.' This was an odd way of putting things; and I didn't see it as altogether a joke, there was pain in her eyes as she said it, her thin mouth went all taut and her lips sort of *inward* – but only for as long as it took her to utter the words. Immediately afterwards she was smiling, relaxed, and ready for the next guest to bid goodnight. But I noticed she threw a quick glance behind her, as though wary lest someone overhear. 'Tomorrow,' she added hastily, 'they'll be showing you their treasure-trove – I mean the Playhouse – they call it "exquisite". Be sure you're impressed. I'll be there too. Perhaps not at first. I *do* hope you sleep well in that ramshackle hotel where Percy's put you. There's a rumour they stuff the mattresses with litter from the landlord's ferret-hutch.'

The next day, when I saw the Playhouse, I couldn't imagine why she'd been so derogatory – it *was* exquisite, it *was* a treasure-trove, my heart totally went out to it, I had never before had the chance to work in so delightful a space. It was just like my old toy theatre; I'd have slept with it on my bedroom dressing-table if I'd known about it when I was sixteen. *And* a bloody great drawback: 'No nails, screws, staples or sticky-tape onto any of the backstage fabric except where clearly delineated by thin black lines drawn on the woodwork.' The Committee! preserving Heritage; but it tiresomely limited the décor I might wish to erect. Nor could one smoke in the greenroom, nor even in the dressing-rooms (to say nothing of the auditorium), an impossible tyranny over all of eight weeks for a tobacco-soak like me. However, I was forewarned, and anxious to make no enemies: I showed myself thoroughly impressed, I won golden opinions.

After tea we were to have a casting-session – not exactly auditions – Lobscott already had decided more or less who was to play which parts. But I had to hear them read, dammit. I told him quite sharply I was buying no pigs in pokes. He didn't like it, but agreed to lump it. Too early to have a row with me: he grudgingly allowed me to stake out my territory.

I excused myself for the afternoon, asking (if they didn't mind) for the key of the theatre so that I could mooch about there alone and at my leisure with the script, letting the idea of the building seep into my imagination and combine itself – if it could – with Percy's creaking croaking dramaturgy. That bull very shortly must be gripped, and by horns and balls together: rewrites! and how on earth could I tactfully broach it to him? The personality he'd already shown me was lamentably unforthcoming for so delicate a process. I was beginning to be worried.

I sat in the front stalls, now and then staring at the dim stage, reading and brooding and yearning for a cigarette.

A little white hand, like the flutter of a butterfly, appeared round the corner of the proscenium; it was followed by a long thin white arm. A little voice said, 'Repose? A moment of repose, Pogmoor? They've only left a single light on for you. Are you sure that the treasure-trove is sufficiently bright to your eyes?' Then I saw one bare shoulder and after it, her face, inch by inch above the arm, peeping, like a child from behind a chairback. 'It's quite shadowy here among wings and backcloths – isn't that what you call them in the "business"? But *I've* got a treasure-trove you can perceive through the darkest dark.' She gave me a flash of a white foot, in a sandal tied with vermilion ribbons all up her calf, and then a long bare white thigh, and then she whipped it all away with a tinkling little giggle.

Oh aye, it was winsome, excruciating, enough to turn your guts up – or would have been, in the glare of daylight. She probably believed her approach was appropriately 'theatrical'. *Hypothesis*: I think my chief thought was of the deathly embarrassment she'd feel, were I abruptly to turn her down after so self-belittling a show-off – eh dear! I closed the script, laid it on the seat, sprang heavily up the steps across the footlights, and found her all ready for me between first and second promptside grooves. She was wearing a tangerine sack-dress of some flimsy organdie-stuff with nothing underneath it. A very quick love-making, vertically up against a flat: oh, well I remember that flat! item of their archaeologically correct neo-Georgian stock-scenery, most fussily painted with two attenuated cypress trees and the half of a Roman column. She jerked herself a little too strongly, put her elbow like a screwdriver through the canvas, squealed 'Oh God and I've ripped it! whatever will Percy do to us?' before letting the squeal glissade into the full throat of her ecstasy.

(Knee-trembling at Aldershot, national service, age of nineteen, had been nothing like this . . . And yet it had been *just* like it.)

I don't suppose three minutes passed before she'd slipped from under *my* elbow, her dress-material rustled as it fell back into place, and I could hear her cute red sandals pattering off down through the greenroom lobby and out of the stage-door into the alleyway along behind the marketplace.

(To the devil with Aldershot. Did I recollect Polly, on the set of *Jack Juggler* at Pomfretshire? Yes, I did: hatefully. And choked it back.)

3

She had obviously done this sort of thing many times before, and she knew how to manage it. If Percy hadn't caught her at it then, he wouldn't catch her now. Or if he *had* caught her then, he couldn't have objected – or not much – so he wouldn't object now . . . I was *hypothesising* already; and very irresponsibly, you'll say.

About every other day throughout the ensuing weeks, in between all my struggles with Lobscott and Lobscott's play and Lobscott's conceited gang of actors, we repeated the episode – many variations as to time and to place with queer coded little notes to establish them, but always just as rapid, always just as coy, never any exploration of why we were doing it or what either of us thought it might mean. Straightforward flesh it was, hard, hot, soft and slippery; which suited me down to the ground. I do not pretend I was altogether at ease with the situation; there was a vein of neurosis about the lady and her techniques, and her particular social class was not one that I was used to for the two-backed beast. Too close to 'Mummydear' and the upper-layer pretensions of Barnsley. I'd have preferred to find my 'remedy' between the legs of the bucolic Deborah, whom I ran into on jolly terms quite a lot up and down the town; she affected yellow cowboy boots, motorcycle leathers and noisy gangs of youth on street-corners; for me, I'm sorry to say, she was a practical impossibility, being engaged to a big young tough (name of Greg Bones) who worked in the garage where I stowed my Toyota . . .

In the third week of my stay J. Lobscott took the risk (for the first time) of laying me on her own marital bed. Mid-morning. Her children were at school, and Percy had his medical rounds, with a visit to the Harrogate hospital to keep him away until at least one o'clock. She'd covered the coverlet with black nylon sheets in a fourfold layer, an intelligent precaution against 'traces'; she'd set a bottle of wine handy; she plainly intended something longer than usual, something more indulgently sensual, something even involving conversation – again, for the first time.

We played a short innings and then a protracted one and enjoyed it very much; and then she said to me, abrupt and businesslike: 'Pogmoor, my husband's script. You've been telling him it won't work.'

'Not as it stands, no. There's still a good deal of reshaping to be done. It *will* work, like a dream, once we've sorted it.'

'Who's "we"? You've been to London, you've told him you were talking there with a man called Cutler. You want this Cutler to rewrite Eugene Aram.'

'Carver, Fid Carver. If I can get him, he'll be enormous help. You've heard of him, surely.'

'Percival has. He's very upset. Pogmoor, don't do it. Don't you see, the *Hermit's Hole* is all that he has? I don't count his doctoring: any fool can be a GP.'

'*All* that he has? Don't be daft, he's got *you*. And your little treasure-trove. I'd say he should be grateful.' Oh aye, hadn't I fallen irreversibly into the tweeness of her own kind of talk?

But now she was hard-eyed and scarily serious: 'That's exactly what I mean. Without his precious play, he's *got* me. Nothing but his Jacqueline to torture himself with. For as long as the play is his own, he neglects me, haven't you seen?'

I didn't quite catch the force of her emphasis. I could only say, 'Of course I've seen, and I know, Jacqui, I know. I'm sorry for you, it hurts me, or else why would I have—?'

'*You don't understand anything!*' She rolled herself away, jerking about again to give me a cruel dose of her knuckles in my pancreas. 'Sod *you!*' she cried as she hit me, 'you're no damned good!' After which, in a quieter tone: 'What's this Fid Carver like?'

I told her, in some bewilderment, that Fid was a fine playwright, I'd worked with him often, he could be trusted (if need be) to be decently self-effacing. I didn't think he'd demand to have his name on the playbills, if that was what was bothering the Doc.

'No no,' she snapped, 'that's not what I mean. I asked you, what is he *like*?'

Eh dear, she meant sex. She was hoping already (*hypothesis, hypothesis!*) to switch me for the unsuspecting Fid. I ought to have been glad of it. But d'you know, I'd become addicted. I couldn't bear to let her go. Haltingly, I tried to tell her that Carver as an amorous entity was more than a bit of a puzzle.

'You mean he's queer.'

'It's not a word I use; and I *don't* mean it, in the ordinary sense.'

'That remains to be seen. So what's he like?'

I gave it up. I put my clothes on, and left her there. (I looked round at her as I went. She said nothing: but dug her fingernails into her fiery red face. She was white-limbed and vivid and as sharp a temptation as ever, a Lucas Cranach Venus spreading herself diagonally across those rumpled night-black sheets.) It hurt.

Hurt; and of course she was hurt too. I couldn't make it out. 'Neglects me . . . '? She didn't *want* to have an end put to his neglect? Or she didn't want an end to the compensations she could legitimately find for herself *during* his inevitable neglect? Well, if she preferred to wait for Carver's arrival and see what she could make of him, let it happen: but for the play's sake I had to have him.

In due course he reached Knaresborough.

And in due course they fetched him to dinner, not so formidable an affair as the previous session. But in many respects far more disturbing. Some of the same company; Mauleverer-Briggs (although apparently invited) had a very special lecture-date, they said; he stayed away. Both the Lobscotts behaved abominably. Percy was bloody dour and Jacqui took every chance to taunt him. After dinner (at her impetuous suggestion) we strolled out for a moonlit dekko at the original 'Hermit's Hole', a spooky little Gothic hideaway, where Eugene Aram killed his victim and fruitlessly buried the corpse. On the way I began to chat to Katie Kippax, wife of the Trust's legal man; she was one of my cast, playing the schoolmaster's sister with whom Aram on the run develops a romantic connection.

She told me something about Jacqui – which Jacqui had taken very good care not to mention at any stage of our encounters – 'I shouldn't be saying this, Mr Pogmoor – it's really not, you know, from any love of sordid scandal – but I *did* notice you looking at dear Percy and dear Jacqueline with a – with a *questioning* expression, am I right? And it might be as well if you were put in the picture, in view of your need to keep him happy about the play, and to understand just how his relationship with dear Jacqueline fits in – or doesn't fit in – and – how shall I put it? – how his overall psychology affects him in his theatrical efforts. After all, I'm concerned with this; I'm in the play; and one or two little things have already been quite difficult, and unless you can handle it right – why, it's going to get worse! I'm afraid so. You see, he's never been able to discover whether dear little Jennifer and Tristram are actually *his* children or not.'

This was desperately embarrassing: the Lobscotts were six yards behind us on the path with only Fid Carver in between. Out of the corner of my eye I saw Jacqui break away from her husband and catch up with Fid; if she walked any faster she'd hear every word Katie was saying. So *I* said of course, 'Ssh! We'll be heard . . .' And then of course I had to say, 'If they're not his, whose are they?'

'The current odds are on Rupert – yes, Rupert the suave Mauleverer – spitting image of the late Leslie Howard if you ever remember any of his films. Five times as sexy as Percy: I'm sure the whole affair's kaput for several years, but wasn't it *wicked*? Thereby, Mr Pogmoor, hangs a tale, best not to talk about it any more just now, but one of these days I'll pass it on to you. Look forward.'

In the cave we were all crushed together, doing our best to pay attention to Doc Lobscott's historical prosings, when Carver in his unspeakable individualism decided to fall down in a fit. He could have been drunk; or else Jacqueline had something to do with it; she'd been frotting up against him like a cow at barbed-wire and I knew how he hated such extremes. So we got him back to bed and went our separate ways, shrugging shoulders, shaking heads – 'If that's how these sensitive authors carry on after exposure to normal society – well, perhaps it's just as well we're all solid provincial taxpayers, right?'

But it wasn't quite right. I'd been told half of a story about *one* of the taxpayers; I was incapable of 'repose' until the rest of that mystery was cleared up. J. Lobscott ceased to send me messages, ceased even to look at me when we accidentally met. What was I to do for my out-of-hours diversion? Every troublesome production (and they never are not troublesome) I have to have *something* to keep at bay the looming nervous breakdown. Where possible, relevant to the work, like Antonia Button with the *Whore*, or P. Blackadder in the days of *Jack Juggler*. Or otherwise: anything, anyone. J. Lobscott had served me very well, but she'd left a gap, I had to fill it. If not Katie as a lover, then at least buxom Katie as a source of informative dirt.

I refused to stop rehearsals while Fid and Percy were messing with the text. The basic characters remained the same, and so did most of the musical numbers. Anyway, none of the actors had their lines by heart yet, so it didn't matter if the words were to be changed. Or I *told* them it didn't matter – I wasn't about to have them going cold on me. A few days after the dinner party I spent all afternoon in the theatre with Katie and the composer, running through her songs, la-la-la-ing where it looked as though there might be new lyrics, generally attempting to bring her out of her congenital *Oklahoma!* bounce into more of a Brecht–Weill deadpan recitative, social comment with a stiff back and a colour-serjeant's diaphragm – she could do it if she wanted to; she just didn't see the necessity; I bullied her and at last she lost her temper.

'Right,' I said, all of a sudden as nice as pie. 'We're tired, I can see we are. Believe it or not, there's been progress. Let's go and get a cup of tea before all of our six eyes are scratched out.'

The composer went home to Harrogate. He had students to deal with, as I very well knew. Katie, distressed by the horrid names she'd called me, insisted I went back to her house. Her husband wouldn't be in for another hour; we had time to unwind and smooth things over. Which we did: all very warm and flirtatious, lots of malice about the other actors, lots of malice about the workings of the Trust, but nothing to the purpose on the subject of the Lobscotts. I came out bluntly: 'Why not?'

'Why not what?'

'Jacqui and Rupert: why not tell me? You gave every possible hint on Sunday night and today you're as close as a clam.'

'I was tiddly on Sunday; I'd hoped you'd forgotten; it was dreadful what I said, wicked, wicked. And what's worse, it wasn't true.'

'Yes it was.'

'Wasn't!'

'Was.'

'*Wasn't!*' – and nick-nock-nack-and-you're-another! perfectly infantile, until—

'Oh, Mr Pogmoor, I've a confession: I was jealous of you and her. I thought the pair of you, you see, might have – But you didn't, did you, I was wrong? And if I wasn't, who cares? As far as I can see, you don't any more. So if I told you, it wouldn't hurt. And I was only going to tell you because I wanted it to hurt.' (Knaresborough . . . who'd be without it?) 'Aren't I wicked?'

'Diabolic. I'm astonished at you. Right! so that's cleared up. No one's going to be hurt, so why waste any more time? Out with it, quick sharp, before Tom's back from the office to pounce on us in the very act: quick, Mrs Kippax, give voice!'

She temporised yet again, infuriating hussy, saying that her Tom would be able to tell me far better than she could, but of course he never would, being discreet and confidential as a good solicitor ought to be . . . Obviously he'd told *her*, which said a lot for his discretion, but I didn't criticise, only urged – and at last she let go, in a gorgeous run of narrative which I do not attempt to transmit, it would take me another twelve pages.

I'll summarise it for you. One night, about five years previously when Tristram was four and Jennifer one-and-a-half, and Jacqueline no more than twenty-five, there was a most frightful husband-and-wife row about nothing more serious than the overdose of garlic in a casserole for important guests. It began with a simple sneer by Lobscott at the dinner-table and an intemperate retort from Jacqueline. It simmered through the rest of the evening: altercations in the kitchen, angry disappearances of host or hostess for twenty minutes at a time, and then of both together for as much as an hour until all the guests decided there was nothing to do but go home. Finally it spilt out into the street. The Kippaxes were the last to escape; they were the ones to see and hear the out-of-control climax as they strapped themselves into their Jaguar for the half-mile drive back to their house. (Don't ask why in Knaresborough you need a Jaguar for half a mile: you just *do*, and that's all about it.)

Percy was choking and foaming inside the still-open front door; Jacqui on the steps (where as an afterthought she'd come running to kiss goodnight to Tom and Katie) shouted and screamed and smacked him all over his face and bald head. Open palm and clenched fist: she was a *savage*.

'Are you aware,' he snarled, 'that our children are supposed to be asleep?'

'*Ours?*' – and she clamoured like an ambulance-siren. 'OURS? you blind bastard! Whatever gave you *that* idea?'

Doubtless all the neighbours could hear her; but it was unlikely they'd heard Percy, for he kept his voice determinedly low. So their quarrel might have meant anything, as far as nosey-parkers were concerned (except of course for the Kippaxes, two yards away with the car-windows let down). If she wanted to broadcast, she was baulked: Percy seized her by the wrist and pulled her straight into the house and shut the door with a light click of the latch, very swift but so silent and circumspectly restrained. He reopened to scoop up a shoe she'd left on the steps; he shut the door a second time, even more quietly. End of episode.

For several weeks the Lobscotts were not seen, as a couple together, by anyone. But a curious transaction, very shortly afterwards, involved Tom Kippax as professional adviser. The Mother Shipton Playhouse Trust had originally been founded and chaired by Rupert Mauleverer-Briggs. He, and not Lobscott, had made the chance discovery that there was enough left of the old theatre-structure to justify restoration. He used Lobscott as his local contact, and Lobscott took up the scheme with vigorous enthusiasm. (They were a pair of old pals from some second-rate public school in the north of the county. So much for Rupert's classy deportment! Eton, Oxford and the Guards' Brigade my eye.) And then, for no publicly stated reason, Rupert backed out of all executive functions. He still remained a member of the Committee, but only rarely took part in its business.

The full largesse of high-cultural kudos fell slapbang into the lap of Doc Lobscott, who triumphed like a half-pint Guggenheim until the role of his erstwhile associate was to all intents and purposes forgotten.

To be sure, for a while folk would ask Rupert, 'How come?' He just smiled, wryly, snootily, a true gentleman's self-deprecation: 'Pressure of work, don't y'know, Newcastle, the very devil of a long way off . . .' Katie believed none of it. She would not tell me what Tom believed. On the other hand she gave no hint that his view might have differed from hers. So here's hers – as delivered to me in her drawing-room over toasted pikelets and currant teacake with every possible nudge and wink, colourful adjectives dropped into suggestive gaps, sentences broken off just before they attained their definitive predicate—

In the wake of the garlic-casserole row, Jacqui had admitted to Lobscott (no, boasted, enraged and open) that Rupert had been mounting her for five years on-and-off, and that all the business of the Playhouse – exhilarating, creative, hot in the doctor's heart – had served since its commencement as a cloak for their chronic intrigue.

Now Percy's love for his children was so possessive as to be positively *ob*sessive – not so much an emotion as a frenzy – anyone who ever saw him playing games with them, hearing their schoolwork, punishing their naughtiness, would immediately perceive his mental slant. The idea that another man could lay claim to the paternity was a double-thumbed gouge at his eyeballs, many times more agonising than the common-or-garden pangs of your average middle-aged cuckold.

Moreover, the circumstances fetched up from the doctor's gizzard all that sediment of envious bile bred gradually over the years by Rupert's lucky hunch about the theatre.

It is not clear who was the first to propound the Ignoble Bargain, as Katie Kippax called it; but somehow – and with what foul recriminations we can but guess – the two rivals agreed between them that if Mauleverer-Briggs should turn over the Trust to Lobscott, then Lobscott would close the book upon Jacqueline's adultery: no divorce, no victimisation, no naming of names, no scandal.

The crucial point concerning Rupert: he was a dilettante spendthrift supported by a very rich wife. If *she* were to find out about Jacqui, he was ruined. Indeed, Jacqui's breach of secrecy infuriated him when he heard of it. He told her, in Lobscott's presence, he wanted no more to do with her; and Lobscott, in Rupert's presence, embraced the weeping sinner and forgave her with momentous pomposity. Tom Kippax, perhaps, was acting as referee – I don't know.

Since then, according to Katie, Lobscott treated the children with an even greater concentration of the ego; as though desperate to prove to the unconcerned world that they were *his* kids and nobody else's. He handled Rupert with distant politeness, inviting him at intervals to dinner – from a sense of social duty? to disarm suspicion? no doubt. It occurred to me he might also calculate that Rupert at his table was a gouge into Jacqueline's womb – I don't know. For I heard how his relations with Jacqueline had by now become observably eccentric: silent, sarcastic, quite probably malignant, dark beyond anyone's perception.

'I do know, Mr Pogmoor, though it's wicked to say so, that she *has* been playing the field, as they say. Ever so cunningly, of course. Utterly blatant, but secret as well. Quite impossible, I'd say, to *convict* her. (Really she can be the most insufferable bitch, as you saw! don't deny it, on Sunday night.) I mean, does Percy know or doesn't he? Does he *let* her do it because he promised Rupert "no victimisation, she's forgiven, let her go her own way"? Does the poor dear silly man even think of her any more as his wife? Or is it the complete reverse: does he *brood*, Mr Pogmoor? sharpen his dagger? mix his poisons?'

I said I'd no idea; I wasn't long enough amongst them to construct a theory; but a close study of his *Hermit's Hole* might render a few clues if anyone looked carefully at the dialogue. We found a few fraught lines and quoted them at one another with a good deal of intimate chuckling. 'Has he never shown in public any rancour to her about these doings? – outspoken? explanatory? I don't mean just sulks.' I was anxious to predict how he'd react about Jacqui and me, if he did know, if he *came* to know . . .

'Well. Perhaps once or twice. Tom's noticed, *I've* noticed, when Rupert's name cropped up, there has been an *aroma* in the room. No more than the odd once or twice.'

'What sort of aroma?'

All her flibbertigibbet nonsense fell away from her at that. She met my eyes for the first time as though she knew I was truly listening, and replied to me with troubled candour. 'Hate, Mr Pogmoor. Fear. From each of them toward the other. And words, single words, like a code of some sort. He would say, "Bathroom." She'd say, "Bicycle-shed." Words like that. Meaningless, comical; except it *wasn't*, you see. Aroma? oh, I tell you, it *stank*. Percy's an awful idiot, but a very old friend. He doesn't deserve—'

She dug her upper teeth into a very pink lip and shifted her gaze away, downward, as though her fingers on her lap somehow surprised her. 'Mr Pogmoor, we're frightened for him. Do his play as well as you can. He needs it. And – and—'

She seemed not to be able to frame what she wished to say next, until suddenly she heard Tom's latchkey at the front door; it acted like an electrical charge; she threw a few quick words intensely into my face and then sat there, all smiles, for hubby's entry: '*Keep very clear of all of it, you don't know what you've stepped into, this town is a charnel-house . . .*

'Ah, Tom, my pet! here we are. We've worn ourselves out rehearsing, we're wasting our time with delicious tea, and I'll make another pot for you directly.'

4

So now you want to know, of course, would Katie Kippax be prepared to make a statement on my behalf? Would she, for example, give her oath that Mrs Lobscott used violence against Doc Lobscott years and years ago? Or that Mrs Lobscott deceived Doc Lobscott with Mauleverer-Briggs in the most hurtful way possible from a mother to a devoted father? Or that Katie herself was *frightened* for Doc Lobscott? It could help eliminate J. Pogmoor as Essential Accomplice, if that's what the cops think he is.

It might also be helpful could she take another tack? – her sinister imagery of daggers, poison, charnel-house? – implying that Doc Lobscott's attitudes were so *permanently* saturnine that he was indeed well capable of thrashing his wife in the Vermeer Hotel, whether or no she'd been having it off with J. Pogmoor on the bed.

And then of course, there's Rupert – does Mrs Lobscott still have any variety of dealings with *him*? Could we hear the Ignoble Bargain fully exposed?

All of the above might serve: to suggest that Jack Juggler was only brought in at the frantic last minute as a neat *objet trouvé* for J. Lobscott's defence, that my part in the whole affair has been totally irrelevant, that my evidence is in no way germane, that (in short) what really happened is the truth!

Eh, dear: it won't do.

Katie would never say any of it. Firstly, Tom Kippax wouldn't let her. (Nor would he, I'm quite certain, consider for one moment opening his own most decorous mouth.) And then, secondly: that pathetic Playhouse Trust was still going strong at the end of last year, a much-touted tourist-draw for the prosperity of the town. The murder has now put it deep down i't'soot-oyle, there's no denying that. But not irredeemably. An unbridled nympho wed to its excellent chairman and whacking him on the head, might just possibly be presented as a human-error mischance to be sedulously blotted out by the wiles of an intelligent PR. It could happen to anyone, right? But if the whole of the present constitution of the Trust itself turns out to be dependent upon said nympho's ancient antics – why, then—

Gabriel, work it out for yourself. The order-of-the-day is the massive Knaresborough Cover-Up. I'll write what I wrote before: 'The only form of testimony any one of 'em'll give will be such as puts Jack Juggler into chokey for the rest of his life.' And for very sound cause. *I* was the underbred interloper, *I* mucked it up. All Knaresborough (save for Jacqui) is cleaner than Persil. They don't mind what happens to *her* – she wasn't liked there, not at all. But Percival must be preserved. They didn't like him either; they did however *respect* him; and no way will they blacken his name.

I'm sorry.

5

To return to my story.

Katie's cosy teatime upset me unduly. It's hard to say why, without getting into far too much of my personal psyche than is appropriate for your purpose.

I think I did, earlier on, make oblique reference to Potiphar's wife. She figures in that picture of mine, the *Joseph in Egypt*, after Caron. You've admired it on my wall. Only a short while before I first heard of Percy Lobscott, I had an Experience with Caron. A sort of subconscious fantasy of what might occur if the people in his painting, as it were, came to life, and hovered, as it were, in my head – or, to put it another way, if my head was conveyed in some manner *amongst* them. I know it sounds awkward, fit case-history for the booby-hatch, or at least for a cardboard-box bedspace in the passageway of Tottenham Court Road underground. You might also be inclined to think I'd been on drugs. But I hadn't. Tobacco, yes, vodka: nothing heavier.

Just accept, please, that my Experience drove me right away from London, away from Carver's Napoleon play, even away from the Royal Shakespeare and a highly promising *White Devil*. At the time I associated it with a certain sleeping terror of P. Blackadder. (Now that you know about Polly, you'll have a notion of what I mean.) If you don't quite remember your Bible, let me remind you that Potiphar's wife made a lecherous attack upon Joseph and then said that *he'd* attacked *her*. It's a classic sexist archetype, which is no doubt why it struck at me so strongly.

A play about Eugene Aram seemed to have no connection; I went to Knaresborough perfectly sure that I could work there, a free spirit, unhaunted, *exorcised* indeed by mingling for several weeks with 'ordinary' people, well out of the professional theatre and the clinging little claws of my time in academia. A great mistake to invite Carver. God damn him, he brought all of it back. And of course a great mistake to be seduced by my employer's wife. For as I listened to Katie and her twisted skein of small-town sin, I saw how once again I'd been Joseph in search of his destiny in Potiphar's uncanny house, with a woman playing tricks, and hordes of spies on every hand, whispering, whispering – 'Now she beckons him, now he goes into her, now she flings up the skirts of her dress and he fumbles at what's underneath, now she grabs him and tears the seam of his shirt, who started it? him or her? who'll finish it? her or him? who'll cry and who'll cringe and who'll tell? and who, in the end, will *believe*?'

And yet I had to get this play done: *Hermit's Hole* was now no sinecure, still less was it a means of escape. And Fid was in a mess with it. He told me so. He was opting out. He'd signed no contract; I was paying him privately. But *I* had a proper contract. Financially, I could afford to break it; and goodness knows, I wanted to! But I was quite without shadow of an adequate reason. I'd be marked from then on as capricious and *unreliable*, and not only among amateurs – oh, Knaresborough would take care that the profession got to hear of it.

I needed to protect myself. I worked out a short list of immediate do's and don't's:

(a) Avoid any further meeting with J. Lobscott.

(b) Manipulate P. Lobscott with extreme care. Never let him think that his play is not the greatest thing since the *Oresteia*. And never go to his house unless I absolutely have to. Certainly never go there unannounced.

(c) Find a new coadjutor writer devoid of all Fid Carver's hangups. That wouldn't be too easy; but Chris Abel-Nottidge might just do. He was very short on hangups, probably because he was short on inspiration. But *Hermit's Hole*, at this stage, didn't need inspiration; only good sense and sharp craftsmanship.

I was lucky: it was possible to fulfil all three conditions.

Abel-Nottidge sat down with Percy, as gentle as a bedside nurse, and led him sweetly through all the misjudgements of the script without its author even noticing how greatly the whole thing was metamorphosed under this new pair of hands. Fid's flailing attempts at a rewrite were thrown out of window there and then; I didn't bother to tell Chris what they'd involved.

I got the work into the theatre as rapidly as the pages of each scene came from the typist. Whenever Percy wanted to talk to me, I made him join me there, and nowhere else. I went so far as to get permission to *sleep* in the theatre (and damned difficult it was to get: I had to tell the Committee such a heap of silly lies about the environmental whims of my huge creative Temperament). I made sure that the doors were firmly bolted on the inside as well as locked. I didn't really expect Jacqui to make further use of her purloined key; but I couldn't leave anything to chance.

In any case, as it happened, she too left the town. The very day of Fid Carver's departure. I didn't know it at the time, I was too busy saying goodbye to Fid, phoning London to assure myself that Abel-Nottidge was on his way, explaining to committee members why Carver had gone off without any formal explanation to them (sudden illness! it was true enough; but I think they thought he'd got the DTs), and dealing with the stage-manager and the set-designer and the costume-lady and actors who couldn't see why rehearsals were proceeding so slowly . . . Katie Kippax, the next evening, without my having asked, informed me that Jacqui was in Ripon. 'Her old aunt, most dependent on her, in a confusion about her property. It happens every year or so. Tristram and Jennifer have an aunt of their own, Percy's most sensible sister, she's travelled over from Bridlington to look after them while mummy's away. Convenient, Mr Pogmoor, or don't you think so?'

I said it was none of my business. She laughed, winked, pressed my hand. I only hoped *she* knew no way of materialising in the theatre once I thought myself alone there. Things seemed to be a *whirlpool*. That night, in my camp-bed on the forestage, I dreamed again about Egyptian spies. 'Ha!' they kept whispering, 'Jack Juggler is observed.'

I forgot to mention: at the station, as Fid and I waited for his train, he turned away from me abruptly after a long melancholy silence, and spoke, as it were, to the mouth of the railway tunnel: 'Mrs Lobscott. Did you know, Jack, that her husband beats her up?'

'Beats her up! How do *you* know?'

'I heard her. I saw her. On Tuesday. And yesterday. If it wasn't him, who was it? If it was him, can you tell me why?' It sounded like an accusation, but I wasn't having any of that.

'There was an affair,' I said shortly. 'A man called Rupert. A long tale. I don't know all of it. Don't know *any* of it, really. But that's what it must be about. I suppose he remembers, at intervals, and goes mad at her. I'd not care to be married to him. Nay, I'd not care to be married to *her*. Eh, Fid, you're well out of it. Charnel-house, aye.'

'Did you tell her I was gay?'

'Dear God, what d'you take me for?'

'Somebody told her I was a man with a category. *Your* category, Jack Pogmoor, is shit on the bloody window-pane, smeared with five fingers and a thumb.'

Whereupon the train came in; he climbed aboard and took his seat, and never looked at me, not once, as the diesel-motor groaned and thrummed and throbbed its filthy carriages out of the station.

That night he was nearly killed by a roaring great lorry at full speed down the road near King's Cross. He went off in all his bandages with his sister my wife to Exmoor, where I don't know what the hell they did. I *never* knew what the hell they did. Except the next time I saw him, he was as chirpy as ever, burbling over Napoleon, over TV plays about Ireland – not a mention of Knaresborough, good or bad.

6

Fid's evidence, his knowledge that Doc Lobscott had hit her in Knaresborough? I do believe he'd swear to it; he *is* a man of principle. Even though, since MAFFICK!, we've quarrelled (I guess) terminally.

Eh, no! they'd only suppose he hit her because of me. They wouldn't accept the Rupert theory. But the theory does hold water: Rupert had telegraphed the Committee to say he'd be in town for Percy's first night. What must either of the Lobscotts have thought about *that*?

7

I made an effort and ignored the Lobscotts' domesticities, sour and all as they were. I had enough trouble with the production. I won't go into it, it's not germane. Suffice to say, the story-idea Chris and I finally worked from was Percy's original, the tale of the frame-up, an innocent man hanged at behest of a guilty woman. I didn't like it then, I like it less now: sod it! it's too near the bone. My own class-based version of Eugene Aram went out of window with Fid's psychodrama: both of them over-elaborate for the exigent state of affairs. Doc Lobscott was delighted, of course.

The first night was a 'spectacular triumph' (*Northern Echo*). It had to be. The restored Playhouse alone brought press interviews and radio and TV from all over, and something called a *quality audience*. I mean Lord and Lady this and bloody that, Arts Council dignitaries, county MPs wild for public notice, county councillors ditto, plutocratic sponsors and benefactors, academic historians and architects and Georgian-drama specialists – to say nothing of the metropolitan critics who'd never have dreamed of coming to Knaresborough to see the work of P. Lobscott; the building fetched them in; the name of Pogmoor fetched them in; and thank God, I didn't screw up. I tell you, I directed that play as though Brecht himself had written it and left it personally in my hands. And many of the reviewers even took it for a *good* play, the wool most effectively over their eyes. Abel-Nottidge, modest fellow, kept his name out of the programme. The full prestige was mine and Percy Lobscott's; I'd had a lot to lose, Percy (by my standards) very little: I let him take all that he could.

After the show, a lavish reception on stage; never mind all those fears about damage to the precious fabric. Rupert Mauleverer-Briggs was there with a chortling horse-faced wife and her paunchy old dad – this latter was a supermarket entrepreneur, said to be very close to what was to be the new-style Tory goon-squad, Thatcher, Keith Joseph, Tebbit and such: think about *them* and you're hooked in fair and square to the general buzz of the evening.

Speeches: in barrow-loads. Mauleverer-Briggs made a queer one. He avoided all themes of Heritage and 'non-partisan' Cultural Values which everyone else was running to death; he avoided congratulations to Lobscott, to the actors, to the brilliant director. He was a considerable scholar! yet he preferred to ramble on, like an inferior political hack, about the Need for Opportunity. 'This new theatre,' he offered, with an artificial diffidence, 'is, it seems to me, not at all new, it's old; but nonetheless new because tonight it is newly re-used. There was Opportunity. It was taken; by somebody or other.' (Aha, the sleek lizard, he was covertly jeering at the Doc and all his works; *I* saw what he was up to.) 'All Opportunity is new. The very purpose of theatre, in new buildings, or old, or old buildings *re*newed, is, it seems to me, speaking as a layman, to *give Opportunity*, to playwrights, to performers, to audiences – every night, on the stage, anywhere, something new, always, even if it's old . . . You see, all my life, I have *seized* Opportunity. And, d'you know? I *do* know that of which I speak. If you don't seize when you have it, then you've lost it. That's it.'

This nonsense must have sounded profound to the guests; they were all pretty well pissed, flushed in the face, spilling wine down their white shirtfronts and glossy corsages; they applauded uproariously. Except Percy, who glowered like Lucifer. I followed the direction of his gaze. For I realised that *he* followed the direction of Rupert's gaze as Rupert spoke his last few fatuous words.

'. . . lost it. That's it,' had been sent right through the gaps in the throng of boozy heads, down the forestage and out across the pit.

In one of the tiny boxes at back of the auditorium (lower tier, dead-centre) sat Jacqueline all gimlet eyes, her lips so close-drawn as to be invisible. She was in raincoat and headscarf as though she'd only just slipped in (in from where? *Ripon?*). It was improbable she'd seen any of the play. She stood up and waved a handkerchief. 'Three cheers,' she called out, 'for the dear little Playhouse! Treasure-trove, jewel-casket, exquisite, ineffable, never to be violated. And *viva la Signora Aram! assassina e adultera! viva!*' (I hated that Italian fad of hers: she claimed to have been brought up in Taormina.) 'Sorry, Percy; sorry, dear people, sorry. I – I think I had a drink.'

She swayed out of the box, stumbling over a chair as she went. 'Dear people' all pretended they hadn't noticed a thing. I gave her twenty minutes to get herself clear of the purlieus; I made my own excuses; I left with my bags via the stage-door and walked in the rain across town to the garage for my car. It had closed at eight o'clock, but I'd an arrangement with Deborah's lad, I'd already settled his bill, he'd lent me a key. I drove direct to the nearest motorway and direct up to London, not altogether sober, trusting to good fortune to steer me past the breathalyser boys. I made Whitesmith Street in time for breakfast and set myself sternly to put every Lobscott in the world out of my life for the rest of my life.

Did I think of them again in the course of those ten years? Often, Gabriel: of course I did. But painlessly. Nothing in fact had happened to make me wish it *hadn't* happened. The love affair, if such it was, had stung like a nettle-leaf; the play had been a crag-climb, but I'd got to the summit unscathed; any *whirlpools* had dispersed themselves into winking bubbles of fizz and unremarkable little eddies. The entire *Hermit's Hole* interlude could (in hindsight) be considered as – well, yes, a sort of holiday.

8

So now for my second visit. December of last year—

Fierce cold sunshine all afternoon down the motorway, frost on every branch and grassblade, freezing fog as I came into Yorkshire, and the decorations in Knaresborough's high street a-strobe and a-glow for the late-night Christmas shoppers. All smiles at Percy's door; Jacqueline in mysterious Ripon.

(You might well ask, why did I agree to be Doc Lobscott's house guest, knowing well how and why I'd shunned his roof in '75? Answer: stark-naked curiosity. And after surviving all that trauma of Polly, Carver and Cordwain and then a trip to Australia and elsewhere, I felt myself absurdly *immune*. I felt old, I felt tired, I even felt nostalgic. Moreover, I needed some intimacy with people in England, however unsettling, who'd never heard of Carmilla Costello.)

I felt old? Forty-five, that was all, but already grey. While Lobscott, who must have been in his mid-fifties, had *seriously* aged; it was quite a shock. His hair (what there was of it) had turned from scanty black to snow-white, his features were crushed and wizened like a portrait of Ebenezer Scrooge, he had a hunch to his back and a twist to his neck: he seemed, as he leered at me, a malignant Arctic-saga troll.

He insisted on carrying my luggage upstairs, talking all the way in a curious clenched-teeth series of small ejaculations: 'Family difficulty. I *had* hoped we'd all be here. But Tristram's in America, exchange-student on one of those schemes. Can't get home. Business Studies, he's quite the "whizzkid". Jennifer, ah yes, Ginny, lovely girl, d'you remember her? Only a tumbling little child when you were here before. She grew up very fast, she—

'Here's your room, I hope it's warm enough. Storage-heating, I've had it full on. Bag on the window-seat, unpack when you like.

'Pogmoor! have you heard of these – these unorthodox people, the Travellers of the New Age? Never wash, never settle, fight with the police? Poor Ginny. Jesus wept. *That's* where she is.'

He writhed himself about, and still kept grinning.

'So here we are, Christmas. You and me. Turkey, plum pud. Oh, and of course Eugene. He demanded to go with his mother, but—

'Her aunt isn't well enough. Not in Ripon, no. They have to be quiet there. No place for a spirited lad.'

'Eugene?' I asked.

'Didn't I tell you? Since you came here before, we've had a third. He's nine, nine-and-a-half. I think Deborah's put him to bed. She knows all about him, she handles him very well, she's living-in to help with him. Until Ripon's over and done with, until Mrs Lobscott's aunt—

'Care for a brandy and soda?'

Well, here was a family where there'd been a devastation. Two teenagers fleeing the coop in weirdly different directions, and a young one who couldn't bear his father. I wished already I hadn't come. But there *were* Lobscott's new plays: they might be of use to me. *He* might be of use to me. I must suffer his misfortunes with good humour. We sat in his study, deep leather armchairs, cut-glass decanters, eighteenth-century prints of old Yorkshire. He told me, with greater ease (now that he'd spluttered out his first bad news), how he'd turned over most of his practice to a partner and had spent the last twelve months writing away 'with renewed vigour'. Obsessively, by the sound of it, which was not an auspicious sign.

He fetched scripts from his desk-drawer and laid them very precisely on a walnut occasional-table at my elbow. Nine of them, no less. To judge from the title pages, he'd drawn all his plots from the history of the county. There was one about St Robert of Knaresborough, one about Mother Shipton, a third dealt with Robin Hood. Hudson the railway king. Dick Turpin. Richard Rolle of Hampole (another mediaeval hermit). Mystical oddities, sensational criminality. He talked about his hopes of a London production. I temporised, suggesting that perhaps we should think of the local Playhouse to begin with; London was 'problematic' these days; shortage of funds meant small casts; I observed that his *dramatis personae* lists were extremely long.

He didn't like that. It seemed that the Playhouse was not what it was. A 'new element' in the Committee had decided to 'follow the market'; which meant (he implied) Agatha Christie and Alan Ayckbourn till the cows came home. They'd even had a 'deplorable *sex-show*', whatever that might have been. Next week there'd be the Christmas Panto, with a 'television personality, so-called' at the top of the bill. Percy was no longer chairman, having been ousted in favour of Tom Kippax. 'A first-rate solicitor, but his artistic taste . . . Jesus wept, Pogmoor, *yaach*! That wife of his, you remember? Just loves to exhibit herself. *She* chooses the plays. And chooses the visiting productions. Jesus wept . . .

'Well well, here's Deborah. Dinner. Off we go. Come.'

Deborah had grown into a young matron, of bulk and capability. She was married to her garage-man, and dressed herself as gaudily as an old-fashioned barmaid. She gave me the friendliest smile; but cast her eye askance at Percy, glancing again toward me to see if I shared her poor opinion of his state. She served us an excellent meal and disappeared once it was on the table. Later on, when I'd pleaded tiredness and was making my way up to bed, she emerged on the first-floor landing and accosted me confidentially: 'Eh, Jack, there's been changes, right? That poor little lad o'theirs, Eugene. I don't know what to do for t'best. Hark at him now; another nightmare. You'll see him i't'morning. Tell me what you reckon. Do.'

I could hear the child's cries from somewhere above us; she hurried upstairs to comfort him.

I'd brought one of the scripts to my bedroom for a look-over before I slept. I'd picked it at random, and I found it rather different from any of the others. Far fewer actors, only one set, and not nearly so uncompromisingly academic.

I skipped through it and felt more and more impressed as I did so. In the end I read all of it.

One-word title: *Head*.

❧ A surreal rehash of events from Part 3 of Shakespeare's *Henry VI*. One long act only: it takes place just after the battle of Wakefield, in a 'store-room full of old junk', a panelled recess in one of the city-gates of York. The only characters are:

> Henry VI himself, mentally deranged and a religious fanatic;
> Queen Margaret, the 'She-wolf of France';

their son, the little Prince of Wales;
the Ghost of 'pretty Rutland', little son (deceased) of the Duke of
   York (deceased);
York's severed Head, which speaks from the top of a sideboard.

The Head has been carried from the battlefield, where it was cut off by
'bloody Clifford', one of Margaret's adherents and also (according to
Lobscott) her lover. This officer having previously, on the fringes of the
battle, murdered the boy Rutland. Most of the play consists of a dialogue
between Margaret and the Head, with interruptions from the two
children, one dead, one alive. King Henry wanders in and out,
mutilating himself for pious reasons; he infers an old adultery, the Duke
of York and Margaret, horrid mixture of hatred and lust.

Head owes little to Shakespeare, still less to the facts and ambience of
the fifteenth century. Short phrases, long pauses, almost like Beckett,
would you believe? – unlikely connection for Doc Lobscott. The Wars of
the Roses are seen to be no broad national conflict but an inwardly-
devouring family vendetta, obliquely recapitulated in a very narrow
space – Margaret as interloper, foreigner, demonised catalyst for all the
swirling strands of atrocity – the boundary-walls of life and death so
indistinct as to be meaningless.❧

Not history, not even historical interpretation, but the map of a
playwright's mind. In my opinion, a most undesirable mind, but who
am *I* to feel superior? 'Deplorable sex-show' indeed (though Percy can
never have realised it), more by implication than direct statement –
hints of homosexual incest, of S & M, of pederasty, of necrophilia, of
coprophagy – you name it, Lobscott has it.

(I'll send you a copy, in case it's useful for dribs and drabs of evidence.
Probably not, it's only what the bloody man was *thinking about*, for God's
sake; not what he did, not what his wife did; judge and jury would
doubtless consider it 'an abuse of the patience of the court'.)

I thought I might very well find the means of staging *Head*. I thought I
could do a lot with it, through imaginative direction and unexpected
casting, to bring out the half-hidden depravities. I didn't *like* the play: eh
dear, no. But that wasn't the point, was it? I was a man under a cloud, I
had to get work, get myself at once stuck into it, earn, exist, declare
myself, defy my detractors, right?

After breakfast, Lobscott and I must engage in a *productive chat*. What
else was I there for? My spirits began to rise; and I slept without bad
dreams.

9

Young Eugene came late to breakfast, creeping in guiltily while his father and I were already nearly through our bacon and eggs. Cold porridge sat in front of him and he looked at it with pale distaste. A lumpy boy, glandular and uncoordinated.

Deborah appeared in the doorway behind him. 'Please excuse him, Dr Lobscott. He had a bad night again; didn't you, pet? He misses his mum.'

Lobscott glowered like Lucifer.

He took no notice of Deborah, but stared at the boy and stared at the porridge. 'You aren't eating it? Then you shan't eat it. Take it away. And then take *him* away.'

'Eh, but Doctor Lobscott, it's a freezing cold day, he's got to eat *summat*—'

'No. Not a mouthful. I *will* not have sulkiness at Christmas-time. Out you go, boy: *out!*'

Deborah was scared of him. I hadn't thought she would have been. She sadly led Eugene away from the room. I saw him later in the back garden, shivering, pretending to play.

Not a good start. In the old days, if Jennifer or Tristram had been difficult over their grub, he'd have sat them on his knee and *seduced* the spoonfuls into them until they were ready to vomit – I've seen him do it, a kind of oppressive over-affectionate blackmail. Not necessarily a happier method; but at least not so shamelessly tyrannical. He read his *Yorkshire Post* in silence. When his cup and plate were empty, he rose to his feet, creaking, and ordered me (there's no other word) into the study.

'So, Pogmoor, what have you looked at?'

'In full, just the one, *Head*. It's extraordinary. It's workable. For a small stage; in London; which I can find; I hope. Are you still using the same agent? He passes on jobs to *my* agent; we can easily fix it up.'

He writhed. 'I shouldn't have given you that one. It's the one I don't want done.'

I can't stand that class of coyness.

'It's the one I want to do.' I put it to him bluffly. 'The only one that's do-able. Without rewrites; major rewrites. You'd best accept, Percy, I *do* know best, right? Oh, come on, man, come on: you didn't fetch me down here for nowt.'

His response was so freakish that he felt forced to twist about and mutter it into the butt of his cigar. 'Do you believe in God, Pogmoor? Probably not: none of you do, these days. I'm not so sure that *I* do, not as such, if you take my meaning. But I *have* had a concept of a Transcendental Motivator, by no means invariably benevolent. HE – or

IT, take your choice – informs me that *Head* ought not to be performed. But you're right: it's my best piece. The first thing I composed after the success of *Hermit's Hole*. I'd have sent it to you then; but I was distressed by – by this Message from Outside. I laid the script away; and when at last I wrote further plays – why, I've been timorous, restraining myself, keeping strictly to my sources. I'm not surprised you're disappointed. Pogmoor, I don't know: I am open to persuasion; if you're sure you can out-argue the Message . . .'

So I argued and out-argued for the rest of the morning.

At last he gave in, part-way. We agreed he should be allowed to think about it over Christmas. ('A festival of optimism, Pogmoor. The Birth of the Doomed Baby, marked in his very crib for cruellest execution. The strongest argument, ever, against Capital Punishment. Jesus wept . . .') On Boxing Day I'd hear his decision.

In the evening Deborah explained her Yuletide arrangements. She was off home for the night to four children and an indulgent husband, anxious to relieve her younger sister from the chore of looking after them. Tomorrow she'd be in charge of two Christmas dinners. The first was for us; as soon as she had it served, she'd scurry back to her council house and get busy on the second. I only hoped Percy was paying her a decent screw.

'At what precise hour?' he asked her.

'Twelve?'

'Inconveniently early.'

'Any later, Doctor Lobscott, and *my* crowd'll not be eating while five: we'll have t'kids up wi'belly-ache at all hours, I'll never settle 'em.'

'Oh. Well, in that case . . . We may need to leave church before the end of the service. Nuisance.' (We? Was *I* included? What had to be, had to be. I wanted his play; I must do what he wanted till I'll got it.) 'One moment, Deborah! what is *that*, that I see in your hand?'

His sudden question had all the force of an unprovoked box on the ear. The poor woman shrank away from him. 'Eh, doctor, it's nowt but Eugene's Christmas stocking. I put in a few extras for him, i't'kitchen, I'm just on me way up to leave it on his bed-rail. I promised him I'd—'

It was no good. He did not forbid the stocking (as I briefly feared he would); he merely *censored* it, removing a plastic helicopter, a cowboy on a horse, a flexible hairy monster, a bag of sweets and a 50p piece, all of them Deborah's presents. These he laid out on the desk for her to pick up and carry away. There remained his own offerings, a miniature cloth-backed book (*The Vest-pocket Archaeological Guide to the Monuments of North Yorkshire*, first edition, 1906), a washed carrot in clingfilm and an apple. He began carefully to replace them in the stocking. 'Much better for him. No commercial rubbish.' He felt something stuck in the toe.

He extracted it suspiciously. (Deborah's face was ashen.) An envelope, folded up small. It contained a passport-sized colour photo of Jacqueline, taken when she was very young and radiant. Sellotaped to it was a thin gold chain with a heart-shaped locket. He opened the locket with his thumbnail: inside was a card, beautifully painted with tiny flowers and the one word LOVE. He sat very still and looked at it, frowning, sucking his lower lip. Eventually he sighed, put locket and chain back into the envelope, and the envelope back into the stocking, which he handed to her with what was left of its contents. He took the cowboy from her and set it aside: 'He can have this one. You meant it kindly. Give it him tomorrow, when you serve the dinner. Goodnight.'

I excused myself for a moment, 'to the loo'. I was just in time to catch Deborah as she came downstairs on her way out of the house.

'Eh, Deb, love! that was horrible,' I told her. 'What does he think he's doing?'

'I'd best not talk about it.'

'But last night you said—'

'It wor a mistake, Jack, I'd best not. Best not talk about folk, *any* folk, when they're not here to talk for theirsen. Leave me your address afore you're off back to London: if I'm let, I might send you a card.' She dodged me and escaped through the scullery door. Useless to follow her; ten years ago I'd discovered the strength of her obstinate evasions.

Why the turnabout? Something had happened since yesterday. It couldn't be just Lobscott's spite toward the boy; he must have been like that for ages.

Christmas morning, for Eugene, was not altogether godawful. I'd slipped out on Christmas Eve before the shops closed, to buy him a kit for making puppets; he had presents and cards through the post from various relatives; an illustrated book of the Wild West from his brother in New York, and a psychedelically decorated home-made hookah-thing from his sister (no sender's address, and I wondered what she expected him to smoke in it; fortunately Percy seemed to think it was an *ornament*). He would have stayed in his room to enjoy them, but we were mustered without mercy for church at half-past ten. Not to the Knaresborough church; Lobscott had fallen out with the vicar; he drove us instead to a village about five miles away.

I remembered Christmas Matins from my childhood, a strangely poetic experience. It was about the only time in the year the Smythe-Pogmoors attended divine service; my parents' motives were entirely sentimental and social; the very rarity made it all the more poignant. In particular, the reverberating language. But on this occasion the parson used a 'modern English' form, which I take to have no merit, either literary or doctrinal. If you recycle the old prayers into the flat tongue of the bureaucratic bougeoisie, you only expose their essential imbecility. I heard Cranmer's Christmas Collect—

> Almighty God, who hast given us thy only-begotten Son to take our nature upon him, and as at this time to be born of a pure Virgin; Grant that we being regenerate, and made thy children by adoption and grace *(etc.)*

translated into something that sounded, to my half-asleep ears, approximately thus—

> Please, God, your sphere of influence is exceptionally extensive, and you assigned to us that son of yours to incorporate himself into our environment by means of a sexually-non-active mother, today being the anniversary; so, if you incline to the view that we've done ourselves some good as a result and have been rejuvenated by the technique that *you* in your caring way thought out and *we* went along with . . .

At which point my eyes closed completely – until Eugene nudged me awake, afraid – and with justice – that his father would cut up rough. Reluctantly I had to listen: Victorian carols in a feebly Pre-Raphaelite mode, accompanied by a teenaged girl guitarist (there was an organ, but nowadays apparently no organist); and then the blandest of bland sermons, all about Good News.

Eugene had of course been fidgeting and rubber-necking about, as children always will when they're bored stiff. Suddenly he gave a start and plunged headlong out of the pew, running back through the congregation, calling, 'Mummy! Mummy! Mummy!' as loudly as he could.

I turned round in astonishment, to see him clasping his arms round Jacqueline in a secluded side-aisle chair behind a pillar. Lobscott was already on his feet; he pushed his way past me; he stumbled after his son; he only saved himself from falling by a grab at the edge of the font; he hissed and spat toward wife and child, incomprehensible phrases of venom, his ugly hunched body all a-quiver in the full view of everyone.

The parson had the best view, not from the pulpit (which he scorned) but the chancel steps (democratic, community-friendly). His Good News died on his lips. He asked helplessly, was there a doctor in the church? because he thought that the – ah – that *this* doctor was very possibly taken ill . . . An old churchwarden thought otherwise: he marched up to the Lobscotts and briskly, rudely, forcefully, chivvied them out through the porch. I dithered for a full minute. But what could I do except follow?

At first, in the leafless bleak churchyard, I was unable to see them. But there they were, closed up together, a sombre little group under the lych gate. I approached them uncertainly. Lobscott did not look at me; his eyes were cast upward, as though measuring the height of the spire. But Jacqueline, blotchy-faced, sick-looking, gave me a socially correct smile to say nothing untoward was taking place; and even if it were, it would be impolite to notice it. 'Merry Christmas, Mr Pogmoor. You didn't expect to see me? Well, what a surprise. Percy, I paid off a taxi. I'll have to ride with you in your car.'

'Ah,' he said with a gulp, still keeping his gaze on the spire. 'Happy outcome after all, Pogmoor. My wife will be joining us at dinner. I said twelve. No time to lose. Shall we go?'

Deborah, when we all appeared, showed only the most perfunctory emotion. 'Glad you could come, Mrs Lobscott. Happy Christmas. Right then, an extra place. Soup's i't'tureen. One more basting to t'turkey, I'll thicken up your gravy, and we're fixed.' A proper degree of bustle and delicious smells. Lobscott administered sherry. Jacqueline and Deborah had a quick word in the passage. Lobscott didn't hear it; I wasn't *supposed* to hear it, but I did.

Deborah: 'It was all right then, was it?'

Jacqueline: 'Not quite, Debbie, no. But it could have been worse. Never mind, you did well. Thank you so much for your call. They could have been at any church in the county, or none at all.'

Deborah: 'I said you'd have to catch 'em i'church. He couldn't slam t'door on you there.'

Jacqueline: 'And the locket?'

Deborah: 'Aye.'

Jacqueline: 'Oh, thank you, thank you, Debbie! We've got a guest. Get the dinner.'

The dinner was eaten with conventional merriment, crackers, paper hats, brandy afire on the pudding . . . We all worked hard to keep it up; but gradually descended into long silences and dismal half-spoken hostilities between husband and wife, which looked like going on for the rest of the afternoon. Something subtler, perhaps, than sheer antagonism: I detected a mutual *yearning*. Towards exactly what, I can't say. There was sex in it, surely – passion – remorse – regret – a long-obliterated romantic love? My position was uncomfortable. If I stayed, I was an interference; if I went out, things might explode.

Jacqueline came to my rescue; more accurately, Eugene's rescue.

'Mr Pogmoor, I think Eugene would like to go for a walk. Would you take him? An hour or so: go round by the castle and the river-bank, he enjoys it there, don't you, darling?'

Maybe he did enjoy it. He had nothing to say about it. He just waved his new helicopter round and round his head with appropriate buzzing-noises. (Deborah must have conveyed it to him in private.) While he mooched, unapproachably, I sat down on a waterside bench and wondered how to persuade him to talk. I reflected on his name. Was it possible he had been conceived as a direct consequence of the Eugene Aram triumph? Had Percy, that night, followed his tipsy wife into some *panelled recess* of the theatre, to couple with her in proud exaltation, fertile at last as a playwright, fertile once again as a married man, driven to her by more than success – the baleful barbs of Mauleverer-Briggs must also have had something to do with it?

Yes: but what about his deeply rooted disdain of the boy? what about the aberrant subtext of *Head*, created immediately afterwards? Unanswerable questions, but I couldn't let go of them.

I realised that Eugene had come to sit beside me. Without any prompting, he began on a long story. Mummy, he said, had never reached Ripon at all. She'd been captured on the way by an Alien Pirate who dragged her into a space-ship to transport her to Mars. But when she informed him that all human beings *have* to spend Christmas with children (or else they die), the Pirate became sorry for her. He reversed his machine and released her, dropping her off at eleven o'clock outside the village church.

'Did *she* tell you that?'

'No. Not exactly. I think I made it up. It seemed sensible.'

He trotted away from me again, buzzing the helicopter, ignoring me, until I said it was time to go home.

Tea and supper were crackling with silence; I went to bed early.

Jacqueline stayed overnight. I don't know where she slept. Certainly not with Percy. I heard her footsteps to and from the bathroom: they indicated a quite different part of the house. I had a notion she was sharing Deborah's room, for Deborah was back in residence (her family once more under care of the kid sister).

I came down to Boxing Day breakfast; no Mrs Lobscott at table, no Mrs Lobscott anywhere else; she'd finished her coffee and left. A used cup-and-saucer sat on the cloth. Clean plate, clean silverware: she didn't appear to have eaten.

I've told how the years had mistreated Percy. What about *her*? I wouldn't have taken her for a decade older if I hadn't known. A few more lines in her face, heavier chin, heavier makeup, a slightly tighter set to that already tight mouth, a thicker figure than I remembered. She'd altered the hairstyle, from a juvenile semi-bohemian collar-length mop and a fringe, to something cribbed off the heroines of *Dallas*, all waves, weight and highlights. A severely girt two-piece suit replaced loose, vaguely 'flower-power' day clothes. I suspected *corsets*, a sus-pender-belt, the full accoutrements of a dutiful doctor's wife. She'd never been dutiful: for whose benefit was she trying to pretend?

In the course of the morning Percy gave me his answer. 'Yes, sir!' he announced portentously. '*Head* shall be performed, if you truly believe it will please. It has all been quite a shock; I'd prefer not to discuss the ins-and-outs of a production just yet; I'll have certain requirements as to style, emphasis, casting, which I ought to communicate before we write a contract, but I have to mull them over. Can you stay another few days? and then we can talk again.'

The idea of 'another few days' was deadly disagreeable. Particularly if they were to be followed by hours and hours of playwright's niggling. I'd had too many discussions of that sort with self-centred authors; they're premature, they confuse the issue, they spark off unnecessary quarrels. I invented some urgent appointments in London, starting tomorrow. I'd have to leave Knaresborough before lunch. Of course we'd be in touch, I'd keep him conscientiously up-to-date.

He writhed and he muttered, but finally bade farewell with an optimistic grace.

Neither of us made reference to Jacqueline or Eugene.

10

As I was bringing down my bags into the hall, Deborah came up behind me, begging me in a whisper to 'just sneak into t'kitchen for a minute'. I did as she said, and was surprised to see her rumage in a biscuit-tin. From underneath a quantity of ginger-nuts she fetched out two envelopes. 'I wor asked to give you these,' says she. 'One of 'em's from Eugene: he couldn't see you hissen today 'cos I took him round to our place to laik a bit wi't'nippers and their dad and their Auntie Becky. Bit of a treat, like: to cheer him up. *His* dad wouldn't rightly allow it, not most days o't'year, but after yesterday – well, tha knows, *yesterday* – eh, dear.'

Then her warm expression changed, a funny look came into her face, she held the second envelope cautiously away from me as though she guessed it contained a letter-bomb.

'Am I to let you have it or not?' she wondered. 'If he ever finds out *I* gave it, he'd sack me, short and sweet. But he deserves it and be buggered. Tek it, you daft ha'porth; and don't open it till you're well clear o'Knaresborough.'

I'd have kissed her but, as always, she evaded. I left her laughing at me, a harsh laugh with the edge of a gibe in it. I could never make out what she thought of me. As always, in her company I felt awkwardly transparent.

(Now *Deb* would give a statement. I can't say what sort of statement. I do know it'd be damned honest. Probably the prosecution's already subpoenaed her. Worth finding out what she's said to them?)

I drove out of town for a couple of miles and pulled into a layby. I opened Eugene's letter first, as being the less perilous.

Xmas Day bedtime

Deer Mr Pogmoor,
     My Mummy says I ouhgt to write to say thank you for the briliant puppet-set, I have allready made the Dragon and Saint George. When I make the Princess I can have a whole story. My Mummy says you are a Freind and I ouhgt not to forget it. I'm sorry you have to go so soon. That was a briliant story about the Allien Pirate, thank you for telling it. Daddy is cross and I am going to be borred again, I think. Mummy says I must ware her locket under my Tee shirt but only when shes in the house. If she goes to Ripon, no. So I'm waring it tonihgt. Not tomorrow. Debby will hide it for me, Mummy says.

Love, EUGENE (Lobscott)

'Jesus wept'? So did I, damned nearly. Did that unhappy kid really think the Alien Pirate was *my* story? For a medical man, Doc Lobscott was so damned bloody blind they should strike him off the rolls. Well, they didn't: they left it to Jacqui.

So what had *she* to say to me?

To *Jack Juggler*, for his Christmas Box (like the *dustman*) on Boxing Day:
     I wanted to talk to you. I didn't have the chance. Things, as you saw, have been *difficult*. I know you *don't* really need to be in London tomorrow; I heard what you said to P. this morning, you

both thought I'd already gone off, but I hadn't (I have now): you told him lies, and so you should.

Is Beverley too many miles out of your way? It's near the Humber bridge; you can take *that* route when you go on, and not lose so very much time. I've booked you a room for the night in the Beverley Arms. There'll be a note (I hope) at the desk when you arrive. If not it'll be because there are no trains on Boxing Day, I'll have to hire a car, it'll probably break down, hired cars in these parts are *hopeless*. Like everything bloody else.

We have to talk.

Yrs briefly, *ciao!*
Jacq. L.

I sat in the car for four cigarettes, no less, rolling it all over in my mind. She didn't say she'd booked *us* a room. Maybe 'talk' was indeed all she wanted to do. She could have found a nearer rendezvous, couldn't she? Maybe Beverley was where she went when they all pretended Ripon. Maybe—

Jesus wept. Maybe anything.

I unfolded my road-map. Would I need to go through York, or was there a bypass?

11

I stopped for a pub-lunch in Pocklington and took quite a time over it. I didn't wish to arrive too early. (I didn't wish to arrive at all. This woman was an importunate thornbush: she could lacerate the hide of a bull.) I propped the *Head* script against the cruet and re-read it with care, marking it up with a few production ideas. He'd forgotten to say how old his Queen Margaret should be. I saw her as about forty, the right age for the right sort of strong actress. P. Blackadder kept coming into my mind and scaring me rigid, but she can't have been in Percy's mind. Percy's mind would have been full of—

Forget it. I'd find out soon enough.

Beverley: a red-roofed town not unlike Knaresborough, but bigger, and dead flat. It is now all but absorbed into the compost-heap conurbation of Hull. University lecturers use it to live in, people who might have *heard* about J. Pogmoor. I must be wary, keep a sharp eye.

The Beverley Arms is a Georgian coaching inn; its interior brought up-to-date in accordance with tourist-office requirements. My room had its own bathroom, a double bed, a TV set and apparatus for tea and coffee. No complaints, except that her note was *not* at the desk. I took a stroll before it got dark. Across the street a great pale mediaeval church was rearing itself up against the purple winter clouds; it was pinnacled and buttressed and carved with Gothic filigree. I drifted in. Seated at the back of the nave, I looked toward the ceiling and saw it, to my delight, all painted with gold stars on blue panels, a little faded but nonetheless gleaming. They had some sort of concealed floodlights up there. A possibility for the décor of *Head*? (Ah, but who'd make the décor? 'Madame Serlio', my old colleague, my old wife, had turned her back on me: 'beware' was her word, I'd not forgotten.)

A voice in my ear said, 'All the Kings of England are painted on the *chancel* roof: care to walk forward and see them?' J. Lobscott, of course, playing her usual sudden-appearance trick. Find an ancient building, you'll find *that* one in a dark corner, Jacqui L. making her home with spiders until in trips the unforgivable fly.

'Okay. We'll inspect the kings.'

She took my hand as we walked up the aisle. Not erotically; more a gesture to show she needed my companionship. *Somebody's* companionship. I didn't refuse; but I can tell you I was wary.

The paintings were curiously powerful. They'd been restored in recent years and were clear and coarse and threatening. Each king sat on a throne, with his ragged great beard, his heavy sword, his cumbersome crown. Each king was very ready to cut off your head. They began with myth and legend: I could distinguish, for instance, King Lear, and (I think) Cymbeline. And thence into regular history: the last was Henry VI.

She said, 'That's the man, isn't he, from Percy's nasty play? Did you come here to talk about plays? Curious if you did, because—' She broke off and pointed at the ceiling. 'Who's that? He looks different.'

One of the most mythical kings had been replaced by George VI, to mark the date of the restoration. In comparison with the others, he was phoney and bland, like the words of the Christmas church service. Kings were intended to chop off your head, not to be meek and democratic.

'Talk,' says she. 'Why not here? I got into the hotel just after you'd gone out; the receptionist said you'd been asking about the church. I thought, "The church, yes, good place, secluded."'

She led me back into the nave because a verger was pottering about among the choir-stalls. We sat down near a column topped with a carved corbel, a woman in a Tudor head-tire holding an inscribed label: THYS PYLAR MADE GODE WYFFES. Jacqui bit her lip and frowned, scratched her neck, looked away from me and up at the corbel. She was temporising, I could see. 'I suppose,' says she, 'they meant to tell us, *good wives made this pillar*. If they got the syntax upside-down, maybe the goodness too? What fundraiser would want to publicise the donations of *bad* wives? Some very shady elements paid cheques in for the Knaresborough Playhouse. But nobody says so. *I* paid a cheque. I've money of my own, you know.'

'I'm sure you have, Jacqui. But you didn't bring me here to explain your bank-balance. Well?'

'Well,' says she, scratching her neck, 'I *can* pay your hotel bill, if you're skint. You are skint, aren't you? Or else why should you grub for a play by Percy? You could have Carver, Abel-Nottidge, Shakespeare, Shaw, any of 'em. Or maybe not. Well?'

'Get to the point.'

But she was finding it very hard.

Then the verger came shuffling up the aisle; he didn't want to disturb us, but they'd had break-ins and vandalism; he must close the church and lock the doors before dark.

'Is it too soon for dinner? I'll pay, if you're skint. Jack, we need to sit and take our time. At least, *I* do. I know a restaurant.'

Italian food, and the place was not busy. We were lucky to find it open on Boxing Day; I guess Jacqui had checked it out earlier; she did seem to be working to a plan. She kept repeating, 'We've got to talk.' She attempted, she failed, meandering on and on, breaking away at all sorts of tangents. I couldn't make out what it was she was trying to say, so I couldn't help her with it. I ate spaghetti, drank Chianti (which hadn't travelled at all well), encouraged her with the odd murmur: no good.

Afterwards we sat in the Beverley Arms bar. Still no good; and too many vodkas. It was getting late. I wondered where she was staying, when and how she intended to go there.

'No problem, Jack. I've a room in the hotel. Don't hurry me, please.'

She went over to the barman and bought a bottle of Chianti. I saw him lend her a corkscrew; I heard him call her 'Mrs Aram', which affected me uncomfortably: if she thought it a suitable pseudonym, she was either very cunning or a bigger fool than I took her for. Then she said, 'This bar's filling up. Too many people. They distract me.' She held me by one hand, grasped her wine in the other, and led both of us (straw-wrapped trendy bottle and overweight gowk of a man) out into the lobby and up the stairs.

I don't say I wasn't still wary. When we reached her bedroom door and she asked me to come in for 'no more than the shortest while, only until I've said what I have to say, please!', I told her it could wait for the morning, I turned my back, I walked off. I could hear her inside her room, before she shut the door, giving way to a burst of angry sobs. I didn't care. I was *immune*. Moreover, hadn't she told me once, 'Sod you, you're no damned good'? I wasn't having that again, nor the hard fist that accompanied it.

I put on pyjamas, but I couldn't sleep. My head swam. Vodka; and no end of mental *whirlpools*. I watched idiocies on TV, changing channels in hopeless frustration. When she tapped on my door, ever so timid and gentle, I ought to have ignored it, but I couldn't.

She came in, with her bottle (still unopened), her corkscrew, and a general ratty appearance as of a woman in drink who had half-undressed for bed, thought better of it, and wrapped herself again into her clothes all anyhow.

'If I promise to behave myself? Please?' (Like a sad little girl in disgrace.) 'Jack, you misunderstood.' (She shut the door quietly behind her.) 'Jack, I don't *do it*, not any more. I did it once too often. Several times too often. It *tore* him too hard; I hadn't intended. It tore him till he tore at Tristram, tore at Jennifer. Tossed one of them out to America, the other one to God knows where. And then, there was Eugene—'

She sat on the bed, all in a mess and a slubber, crying. I was wary, I was unforthcoming, but I did think at last we were getting near the truth. Unwise to turn her out now. I stood away from her and waited. She didn't go on, so I prompted her: 'What about Eugene?'

'I want to tell you about Eugene.'

'Aye, do.' Suddenly I felt myself spleenful beyond anything, ardent only to be done with it, done with her, done with this cul-de-sac of a dialogue, done with all of my damn-stupid mistakes. Whirlpools were throwing up every possible fragment of garbage, I was powerless to stop them. 'He's your son. So tell me how you *made* him, you and Percy together, to spite Rupert, wasn't it? To toss Rupert over your shoulders, while *you* two tossed each other in the bowels of the jewel-casket, treasure-trove, chi-chi little twatful of *Heritage*! Your Percival resented it, right? vilely took it out on the kid, and what did *you* do to help the kid? Why, you ran to sodding Ripon—'

'Jack, I am trying to tell you—'

'Don't bother. I know it already and not a turd of it's true. You're one chancred untruth on top of another, till your child can't even say whether what's inside his head belongs to *his* head or *your* head or *mine*. To say nowt o'sodding Percy's.'

'Jack.' Stuck in the one groove, so preoccupied she was, I might have sung the Metrical Psalms for all the note she took of my insults. 'Jack, I am trying to say—' It must have been about then that she pulled herself up from the bed; a step forward, she stood close to me.

'For God's sake, you've *said* it! You'll "behave yourself", that's what you said. No you won't or *you wouldn't be here . .* ' It must have been about then that I became fully conscious of the throb of my hard-on, its insistence (since the moment she knocked on the door) that pyjamas' buttonless flies were only there to be laughed at.

'Wouldn't I? Jack, is that the sole reason you can think of for—? Oh, the hell with it.'

She seemed to give up, to resign herself to something. How can I describe—?

My wife once, in her studio, about to open a bottle of Perrier water, determined in her finicky way to use a particular cut-glass goblet which she kept on the highest shelf. She stood on her draughtsman's-stool to reach it; the stool toppled over; she did not quite fall but landed ludicrously across the drawing-table, askew, kneeling, banging her funny-bone. 'The hell with it,' she grunted, and picked up a plastic cup near to hand on the table-top. It was there to hold pencils. She tipped them out and poured in the water. Drank from plastic instead of crystal: oh, she was tall but not tall enough.

12

It is a fact that J. Lobscott and I thereupon were 'sexually intimate'. Police wording: appropriate? But I wouldn't say *accurate*: our congress was unpleasant, it was angry, it was despairing, it was addictive. Did we 'know' each other? No. (Scriptural phraseology is unfailingly idealistic.) But there were two of us at it, equal shares. Who put out the first hand to whom? Honestly, I can't tell you. I *can* tell you: all that corset-stuff she was wearing, she undid with her *own* hands. Mine were wet and shaky; they annoyed her, I reckon.

When we'd finished we lay entangled, neither naked nor clothed; we opened and drank the Chianti. On top of vodka, on top of the earlier Chianti, imagine. It must have been about then that she groaned and shoved her face into the pillow, mouthing what was surely the first vague formulation of her current defence: 'This was *not* what I intended. Oh Christ, I've fucked up . . .'

I didn't believe her. Nor did she say it again. She just groped for the bottle to swig the final dregs. I fell asleep with her hand in my privates; while I slept she got up and went away; in the morning she'd left the hotel. A note for me at the desk:

> J-J!
> I said to you years ago, you do *not* understand anything. My

fault. My tongue was cut out, my lips sewn together, they must have been, for why else didn't I talk? Oh well, another time.

I did tell you about the Humber bridge? If you don't hang about, you'll be stuffing your London lady-friends by mid-afternoon. The hotel bill's pre-paid; don't ask about it, don't draw attention. Just because you wouldn't listen, it don't mean I won't be thinking of you, as favourably as you deserve.

I did tell you, I have money? Don't despise. Cast your seed into the cunt and reap it a thousand-fold, *one way or another*. And don't ever think of Rupert: he's finished, gone, dead, absolute bugger-up.

　　　　　　　　　　　　　　　　　Once again – *Ciao!*
　　　　　　　　　　　　　　　　　　　　T-T

'T-T'? Ah yes, she meant *treasure-trove*. Charming. 'Another time'? Not if I could help it. 'Money'? Goddammit, Gabriel, what *was* I to think? I've never been anyone's gigolo.

She was, you see – *is* – a most complicated creature. There's no word in that letter remotely suggestive of rape. I still have it. Or the CID will have it: it can't be long before they search my flat. But I must warn you, she disguised her writing, pen in her left hand no doubt; standing on her head, I wouldn't wonder. No reason to believe I didn't forge the thing myself . . . Her first letter, fixing the assignation, is provably hers. It doesn't commit her to anything beyond 'talk'. Unfortunate, right?

13

Back in town, I set to work against the odds to interest people in *Head*. The subsidised theatres were prepared to consider it, purely as a play, but when they understood it was a play by a scarcely known author fastened tightly to the most dodgy director in their files, they put up all manner of unattributable obstruction: I abandoned them as a bad job. Mind you, I wasn't surprised. I could find a venue on my own. Not the Showbox: my name there was blown-upon for ever. But the pub theatre at the Soldier's Glory in Stockwell was still in business, though by no means as avant-garde as it had been; and the arthritic ex-hippy, who ran it for the beer consortium, didn't care if I ravished his sister so long as I could bring him as much box-office ('in real terms, hard bread, know what I mean, man?') as the grotty 'inner-city' music-groups and 'community drama' incompetents he'd had to depend on in recent years. The trouble was, he himself had no money to venture. The same applied to other places. I talked to my agent: my agent shook his head.

I sent a letter to Lobscott, breathing good hope, skirting round the problems, but asking if he knew of any potential backers up north. 'Let's just get it off the ground,' I wrote, 'at Stockwell or elsewhere! If it receives the reviews it should, the regular theatres'll be queuing up to host it. Alternatively we could organise a tour. All we need to do is *prime the pump!*' I expected an outraged refusal; but he replied most pleasantly, saying he'd see what could be arranged. He was thinking of visiting London very soon. Maybe he'd bring me some news.

I began to look for a cast. Risky at this stage with neither date nor place signed up. I was *juggling*, but had to start somewhere. No difficulty about adult males: but the lady and the two child-actors were going to be hard to get. J. Pogmoor, the Pomfretshire pervert! beware, beware, he's on the prowl! All the agents at once gathered in their precious charges like agitated mother-hens. Someone said there was a confidential warning, issued (if you please) by Actors' Equity.

Then Lobscott wrote again. Mid-March, for a week, at the Kensington Vermeer. He'd ring me on arrival to fix our appointment.

The day before he came I had a (recycled) Christmas card from Knaresborough. The original message was scratched out and replaced with:

> To Mr Pogmoor, *private*.
>
> Dear Jack,
>   He's coming to see you and she's coming too. But he dosnt want *her* to see anyone when they get there. She says, she dosnt want to either. She says, she's only to be in London for Shops and Art Galeryes, all by herself while he's on Busness. But *I* rekon its you, Jack. I rekon it is, realy. I dont know I ouht to tell you. But may be she'll ring you *private*, so best your prepared. Jack, you be decent, now. Their reconsiled now, marvellous, I dont rekon itll keep but they realy are 2 lovebirds now. He treets Eugene so much better, like a proper dad. She says, no more nonsense, but is it true?
>   XXX   Yours affectonly,
>   DEB

The three kisses were damned ironical. So was the whole message. I didn't know what to do. I'd have to stop answering the phone for a week and rely all that time on my recording-machine, a perfect nuisance. And even then, if she was determined, she'd probably waylay me. What the devil did she think she was at? Didn't she know I'd gone off her completely? Didn't she feel my repulsion in the Beverley Arms? Or did hatred just feed her her kicks?

Lobscott rang the following evening: he was tired with his long drive, needed to go to bed directly, would I come round for breakfast tomorrow and we'd spend a useful morning together?

He specified nine o'clock. I was punctual. I always am.

If Jacqueline had breakfasted with him, the waitress had cleared all away; but I observed he'd already eaten the greater part of his meal, he was finishing toast-and-marmalade and had ordered a fresh pot of coffee. He didn't explain this. He didn't need to; her furtive dawn departures were becoming as strong a habit as her Jack-in-the-box pop-ups.

His news was both good and disappointing. That is to say, he'd conned pledges for a portion of the requisite funds from old sponsors of the Playhouse. Those self-styled Yorkshire hard-heads wanted their drama-tist to boost Knaresborough down south, and they sniffed for inordinate profits. (He'd drawn their attention to idiotic press reports of the riches of Ayckbourn, Lloyd-Webber, *et al.* TV spin-offs. Film rights. He was no slouch.) But the regional Arts Council was procrastinating, despite his firm acquaintance with 'a man on one of these boards' – its brief did not extend as far as Stockwell, even for a thrusting native son. We did some arithmetic. The promised cash was insufficient.

I hastened to reassure him. Where we'd already found this much, there must be far more to be uncovered. Not to worry. We should talk about production, actors, scenery. Would he like to have a look at the theatre?

I drove him to Stockwell. I could see he was disconcerted. By comparison with the Mother Shipton Playhouse, the place was a tip. The administrator clearly struck him as a fly-by-night gunge-merchant. I had to explain that London was London with its own eccentric standards, take it or leave. He'd already crossed his Rubicon (*videlicet*, the Trent): he moaned a lot, but in the end he took.

We went to see his agent, we saw my agent, we had more than one expensive lunch (*my* expense), we went through all the motions of vigorous showbiz business, and we even talked of rewrites to *Head*. I had now to juggle *him*, you see, all in-together with the backers, the venue, the actors and the available dates; nothing I told him was quite true, but nothing an outright lie. I've fiddled my crafty way into enough successful work to know where to draw the line.

On the whole, though, the doc seemed more than happy. Excited, even. Raring to go.

It must have been the third day of his stay. Again I came to breakfast, again Jacqui wasn't there. Nor had she left any messages on my answering-machine. I felt considerably relieved; but at the same time apprehensive. Was she plotting something, or had Deb's card been no more than a silly little trick to unnerve me? He had agreed to spend the morning going over the last section of his play: entrances and exits didn't work and he wouldn't believe it. But at least he was allowing me to try to persuade him. He had the script on the table ready to hand.

I'd no sooner alluded to it, however, than he put me off, saying he preferred to skim through the *Daily Telegraph* first. He complained that 'this second-rate hotel' was unable to find him his essential *Yorkshire Post*. I could not imagine why he thought I needed to sit there and watch him snort at a London newspaper; no doubt the rewrites made him anxious, he was postponing the hard moment. He was anxious about *something*. With his face deep in the leader-page, he suddenly muttered: 'Do you have a wife, Pogmoor?'

Why did he ask? He knew the answer. I'd told him before. I told him again, I was married but separated. No children.

'A foolish question from an old man, but . . . Did you leave her for another?'

'Not exactly.'

'No children, of course, makes a difference. Pogmoor, do you *have* another?'

'Not exactly.'

'What d'you mean, not exactly? Either you do or you don't.' He peeped at me round the corner of the *Telegraph*, a baleful bloodshot eye; and his question had the ring of a magistrate's on the bench. (He was, I understand, a JP for a few years in Knaresborough.) I don't *think* I turned pale, or flushed pink, or spilt my coffee. I was able to stare back at him, expressing astonishment and some offence. The eye disappeared, he hummed and hawed, he was embarrassed.

'Don't misunderstand me, Pogmoor. I am aware that London manners are not what I am used to. I myself have a need to understand. As a writer, I must not be out of touch. Let me put it another way. If you and your wife do not any longer – aha-rrhm! – do you consider any lady you meet, married or otherwise, to be – aha-rrhm! – *fair game*?'

All I could say was, 'No.' As emphatically as possible.

He folded his newspaper, laid it down, smoothed it flat. He shook his head and sat frowning, eyelids drooping, fingers drumming on the script of *Head*.

'Pogmoor, I am not satisfied, either with your comments on the play, or with the play itself. Or with any of your suggested production arrangements. There's a dishonesty somewhere. I've been smelling it throughout these three days. I'm not even sure it has anything to do with the play. But I *am* sure that for the time being, I do not wish to proceed any further. I have not signed a binding contract. Tomorrow I'll return to Yorkshire. And thereafter I'll let you know.'

This was shocking. I began to remonstrate. But he cut me off, rising to his feet, picking up his play and his newspaper, walking ponderously out of the room. What *had* gone wrong? Whatever it was – and Jacqui, oh my God! kept buzzing in my brain – he was in no mood to change his mind now. I could only go home.

I drivelled about in Whitesmith Street for the rest of the morning, coming to no good conclusion. I ate a corned-beef sandwich: not for pleasure, simply to keep up my ebbing strength. Obsessive vodka. Neurotic cigarettes. At about one o'clock my telephone rang. I was too strung-up to ignore it. Jacqueline's voice, wheedling, mischievous. 'You got Debbie's card, did you? Well, here I am. I've done all the shopping and art I can do with for six months. So now it's time for you. Jack Juggler in his lair. I'll be round in a cab in a quarter of an hour. Don't run away. Because you really will hear something *to your advantage*. Jack, upon my honour. I *do* have some honour. I do.' I didn't speak. She gave a chime of laughter and rang off.

Honour. Oh, indeed. I wasn't going to put it to the test. If J. Lobscott was en route to Whitesmith Street, there was a fair chance that P. Lobscott would be alone in the hotel. I *must* see him again, he must *not* be allowed to sabotage all my plans. I shouldn't try to ring him, I ought not to forewarn, no! but catch him by surprise at the Vermeer, hold him in frantic talk until he agreed to reconsider! Stupid, stupid, stupid: but remember, I was bang in the middle of all this damned juggling, his bombshell had thrown me off-stroke, my judgement was quite out-of-kilter. I set out on foot, hastening along unlikely side-streets where I would not cross paths with her taxi. I know that part of town well. I was at the hotel in fifteen minutes.

I found the foyer crowded with wide-hipped Americans of both sexes, all exhibiting fluorescent name-cards. Some conference or convention; if Percy had left the building, he could have passed through this chummy mob and the receptionist would never have noticed. But I asked her. 'Dr Lobscott?'

'Oh, I don't know, sir. I've not seen him since breakfast. I don't think he went out.' She twisted her head, checked the slot for the room-key. Empty. 'I'll see if he's in his room. What name?'

She picked up the desk-phone, dialled, and waited for quite a long time. At last: 'Room 509? A Mr Pogmoor to see Dr Lobscott.' She listened to the reply, rang off, told me: 'That's alright, sir. If you'd care to go up?' I took the lift. He hadn't left; he hadn't refused me; so far, so good.

The door of 509 was unlatched; when I tapped on it, it swung slowly open under the very small pressure of my knuckles.

14

On the floor, next to the bed, Jacqui Lobscott half-lay, half-knelt, at an uncanny angle: one arm lolled out on the coverlet, the other hung feebly at her side, still holding the telephone-handpiece. The telephone itself had fallen or been pulled from its shelf. She looked ghastly. Her face was bruised, her nose bleeding, blood and tears were smeared together across the front of her white blouse.

There was no sign of Lobscott. (The bathroom door stood open; he wasn't in there either.)

While I hunkered down beside her, horrified, mopping and dabbing, she managed to give me a broken smile. 'You decided to snub me, you fucker? Wouldn't wait for your little Jacqueline in Whitesmith Street? All to the good, to the good, here you are the exact moment you're needed. Fucking Christ, Jack, what a fuck-up.'

'Who did this?'

'You don't know? Questions, questions. Answer them yourself . . .

'*That man*, for some time, he's been wondering, he has, Jack, did Jacqui come to London to have an affair? He'd no thoughts as to who with. Just anyone at all; isn't that what London's like? Jack, he didn't want me to come. But he thought it would be cruel to prevent me. He promised me after Christmas, you see, he wasn't going to be cruel any more. Promised.

'But just now, when I let him know I was on my way to you, he turned round and—'

I'd gone briefly into the bathroom to put her cotton-wool and iodine back into the cabinet; I called out to her casually enough: 'Why *were* you on your way?'

'Don't play your tricks: you'll be told in good time. At all events, I let him know.'

My tricks? She was incorrigible. And reviving herself now, adopting a more comfortable posture, no longer so choked up with crimson snot.

'You can see he didn't take it in the spirit it was meant. To him it was clear proof the affair was with *you*. He told me there was to be no production of his *Head*. He'd already called it off. Then he was cruel . . .'

Again for a moment she wept, snuffled, dragged a hand across eyes and nostrils, continued with her story.

'He's getting old, he doesn't hit as hard as he used to. But Jack, he was cruel; and then he went off to his publisher. That crappy little book of his, the Nidderdale nostalgic one, *you* know. He'll be there all afternoon. He said to me, "You bitch, you won't want to go out, not with the face I've given you. Order a snack from room-service. Pay for it yourself from your own rotten purse," he said. Oh Jack, lift me up. Hold me! but it doesn't really *hurt*.'

I was clumsy, to be sure, but I got her onto the bed without causing her to wince more than twice. She clung to me. We sat together, warmly and very still, like two sad lovers. We *were* lovers, whether we wished it or not. Compassion is a sly aphrodisiac, clad in a deep hood that quite hides the dark countenance of the exploiter. Jacqui's injuries stirred my emotions; and my emotions locked my body once again into the addiction I believed I had thoroughly thrown off. Mind you, if I was a satyr, I was a damned fearful satyr: no way could the consequence be straightforward, let alone of any positive value. There are some things that *no one* should willingly let himself in for. Moreover I was well aware I'd had just such a premonition before, but not in any sexual frame of reference: alas, I was unable to place it. Today, as I think back and write, I find myself empowered to coerce (far too late!) my painful memory—

1970 or so: about the time I shared my first bath with Leonore in Antioch Gardens and was going through the preliminaries of the MOUTH-71 company, the playwright Alex McCoy got me into a corner. He zealously demanded I copperfastened my links with revolutionary Marxist Thought. How could I hope to run a Socialist Theatre if I refused to immerse myself in Theory? I was going to need his work, I needed to keep him sweet, I agreed to come along with him to a dialectical seminar-evening, one of a series he was attending weekly in the house of a Trotskyite actor. Next Friday, he told me, they were to debate the Revolutionary Aesthetic.

And that's when I had the premonition.

But he said he was sure I could make an important statement. When I thought about it, I too felt pretty sure. To the ravens with self-induced augury! I turned up as invited, in ebullient spirits, an envelope of rough notes in my confident top pocket.

An approximate score of people there, most of them in the theatre business, most of them known to me, all very zealous and shiny-eyed. (No Carver, no Fred Owston, although I had recently seen the latter about town: they doubtless adhered to a rival Tendency.) A pair of authentic proles, aggressive young shop-

stewards, represented the Party's Industrial Base and played Flavius and Marullus to the Cassius of the evening, one Bart Carmichael, sixty-five years old, formidable revolutionary fugleman.

That skulking little bastard McCoy introduced me as the 'internationally known director' who would share with the Comrades his experience of political drama. Polite applause, and I launched into it. They gave me a fair hearing, although I did catch en passant a number of sidelong glances, informed head-shakings, momentary frowns.

I soon reached the end of my reminiscences and impromptu notions for the future, signing off with a short hype for MOUTH-71. McCoy made a speechlet of thanks, very pleasantly; he looked about him to see what would happen . . . Several hostile (and predictable) questions: 'Where's the relevance for the Working Class?', etc. I attempted to deal with them but everyone talked at once at acrimonious heckler's length. I couldn't get a word in. I began to lose my temper . . .

Comrade Bart, throughout, sat contemplative like an Irish priest among parishioners, his pudgy hands folded softly on his stomach, his piggy eyes a-glint behind his glasses, a tiny smile on his pursed-together lips. He continued to sit until a moment of quiet ensued, when with all the gathering impetus of a heavyweight steam-roller, he set himself in verbal motion and totally flattened me. I was an Idealist, he growled, a pseudo Jesus Christ, a covert Defender of a ragbag of Bourgeois Values, a Trojan Horse for Multinational Cultural Capitalism. His rhetoric climbed ladders of denunciation and decibels; his cheeks swelled and reddened; his mouth took on the shape of a trumpet-bell. As he roared, his right hand sawed up and down, maddeningly out of time with the rhythm of his words. All my False Ideology, he finally thundered, was fit only to be crushed and the Historic Task of the Comrades of the Party was to crush it!

Collapse of stout Pogmoor ... Well and truly fitted up. Horse, foot and guns, I was utterly ambushed.

Afterwards McCoy made me a kind of apology, saying the same thing had happened to him upon his first evening there; hard Dialectical Struggle; the point was, to learn from it.

Why didn't I?

15

'Now, Jack,' she murmured huskily, 'what happened in the Beverley Arms was a bad miscalculation. We were drunk. We're not drunk now.'

I was though, just a little. Vodkas.

'Let's make a try, shall we, Jack? to regulate our egos, to keep them in proper shape, to resist one another, if we can. Don't you think we can? Of course we can.

'*That man*, that so-called husband, that walking suit of thermal underwear stuffed with his own shit – did you know he wears a truss, and the elastic's as grubby as a flue-brush? – why, Jack, he plays his games with both of us, haven't you yet caught on?

'Jack, we have to talk, dear, about how to *outmanoeuvre* him. About why I was coming to see you today.

'I'd rather talk *in* the bed than *on* it. Wouldn't you? Enjoy each other, Jack, but keep our cool.'

Slowly, painfully, she took off her clothes, one piece after the other, her damaged features iridescent with a strange ragged smile.

'Come on, do what I do, I've more than enough abrasions on me, you don't surely want to lie down in coarse denim pants and that dusty old corduroy jacket?'

She assisted me to strip. I stammered a few words and then decided to shut up. We were neither of us young; she may have put on a few pounds here and there, but her limbs and breasts retained their elegance (she'd still prove a good model for a German Renaissance master); I say nowt about *my* limbs or any other part of me.

So easy and gentle! She'd never been so before, except once. Things went wrong on that occasion. I did not permit myself to recollect it.

Between the well-ironed fragrant two-star-hotel sheets she firmly delineated our physical frontier. My hand must not go *there*. It was okay to lay it *here*. It was not okay to wriggle. Her face was very sore: not to touch.

'Now!' she said. 'Look at us. No complications. No fuck-up of emotion. No stress. We're just friends, isn't that so? Bare and affection-ate. Beautiful.'

She was right. It was beautiful. But how long could it last? Good lord, I was no Desert Father to mortify flesh with the torments of Tantalus.

Twenty minutes, thirty. She sighed and spoke again: 'So, Jack, have you thought what we should do about *that man*?'

'This,' says I, decisively, inserting myself into her, most careful not to hurt her, but convinced she expected it. Gabriel, believe me! her fingers for the past five minutes had been *there* rather than *here*, her eyes were bright and blurred, she breathed rapidly through a half-open mouth. 'What better fashion,' I hissed, 'to punish the grotty old corner-boy? punish him, punish him, punish.'

All she said to that was, 'Ah.' I can't possibly explain *how* she said it. Did one syllable speak volumes? If it did, though, what were their contents? I had really no idea; I didn't give a damn; I just let myself surrender myself until desire was defeated by exhaustion.

A long time went past. Was it half-past three already? I opened my eyes and looked at the ceiling, I reached out for my jacket to find my cigarettes. I passed one to her. We lit up. She smiled amorously, the bruise on her cheek no longer a distressing blemish – a heart-rending *beauty-spot*, rather – for it stirred me to wonder, had we time for another quick coupling? Let me lie back, finish the fag, try again, discover how much juice was still in the fruit . . .

Opposite the bed's foot was a rococo-ish buhl dressing-table (the Vermeer makes a point of its old-fashioned furnishings: 'family-friend-ly'). The mirror attached to it chanced to be so tilted as to give me a clear view of both our heads. In the split-second of time since I last looked directly at her, her expression had appallingly changed. I saw a mask fit for grisly Electra in that intimidating play by Sophocles, cigarette stuck in the middle of it like a dagger in a wound.

She saw that I saw.

'Okay,' and she ground out the three words: 'That's it.' As far away from me in spirit as the moons of Saturn. Nonetheless our two bodies down the length of the bed were still touching side-by-side at elbows, hip-bones, ankles.

Ground out the words, did I say? They came from her like iron filings, all over my naked skin: 'I offered you a test, Pogmoor, and you've failed it. You have no moral strength. I had thought you might love me, but all you do is use me, *juggle* me, you filthy scratch – don't look at me, you haemorrhoid, shift over in the bed, I do *not* want to feel your gluey meat.'

This was quite unlike that time in her Knaresborough bedroom. No raised voice, no angry knuckles, no tears. A drear monotony of low-pitched *judgement* and it turned me, you might say, to a dried-up onion.

'We had promised, Pogmoor, we had promised each other *not*. You could not keep to it for so much as half an hour. I had longed for your kindliness, your closeness, your generosity. I was afraid I couldn't trust you; so I tested you; you failed. Please get out of the bed.'

Tested? She was nothing less than an *agente provocatrice*. How dared she say 'tested'? I stood among my scattered clothes and stooped for my longjohns. *She* wasn't weeping, but *I* was. I put them on back-to-front and got two feet into the one leg, struggling (Laocoön!) with shame, self-disgust, humiliated incapacity to comprehend anything of what had passed since I had staunched her running blood and taken her into my arms.

She was still talking; not directly to me but into the mirror. 'No: I shan't tell you what I'd hoped I could tell you. I'll just say this much: I am sorry, deeply sorry that there won't be any *Head*, at least not from Pogmoor's hands, in Stockwell or whatever other of your haunts. For at last I understand it's a bloody-awful bad play, a bloody-awful author and *a director even worse*. If you *had* put it on, all the critics of quality would have wiped the floor with both of you. God, I am so sorry that I can't watch them do it.'

It crossed my mind to inform her I knew of no such a thing in 1986 as a 'critic of quality', but smart answers would never never do. I had fouled myself up, Polly Blackadder all over again! – indeed, *because* of Polly Blackadder – if it hadn't been for her, would I ever have revisited Knaresborough? Not on your life.

How had it happened? I didn't know, I *don't* know; Gabriel, are you a man or a lawyer? Can *you* chart the labyrinth and point out for me the wrong path I took? Because, dammit, man, I can't.

My underwear was still entangled, I was hopping on one foot, and the phone rang as though it saw me and had to have its superior guffaw. J. Lobscott spoke into it without looking aside from the mirror. 'Yes,' she said, deadpan. 'Yes . . .' And again, 'Yes.' She dropped the handpiece.

'Pogmoor,' she added (without looking aside from the mirror), 'that was Dr Lobscott. Sooner than I expected, much sooner; he's already just about to leave his publisher's. The office is in Queensberry Mews. Two streets away, Pogmoor. Shall you run?'

Two streets? Too close. But not so close as to require a *Commedia dell'Arte* panic. I remained cool. Cool and most damnably resentful. (I daresay I deliberately slowed down my dressing for the pleasure of giving her a fright: if she *was* frightened, she showed no sign of it.) T-shirt on, trousers on, corduroy jacket, search around for my leather jacket, my Raskolnikov-style peaked cap, where the devil were my socks? Too late! I'd delayed long enough. Put the shoes on without them: ah, there they were. I stuffed them in my pocket and—? No, I did not run; I would not degrade myself by allowing him to *harry* me. I strolled.

I refused to turn towards her as I went; but I could not help catching one last glimpse in the mirror: she still stared straight at herself, her half-inch of cigarette replaced between clamped lips, a hand crooked in front of her partially hiding her breasts, a hand near her cheek partially hiding the bruise. She reclined without moving a muscle, rigid, expectant, *triumphant*. By God, she made me shudder.

I've written the rest already. I turned into the service-stair and, turning, heard and saw P. Lobscott on his way from the lift, thumping his stick along the carpet. I didn't think I'd been observed; I was wrong about that, if she tells truth. But how much truth *does* she tell? Anyway, it doesn't matter. The fact is he walked into the room and threw himself at her like a Rottweiler. The police say the injuries they found on her were wider and worse than the ones I had consoled; there *must* have been a second beating, that much is true. And then he fell asleep. And then she came and picked up the ashtray . . .

What is this word 'rape'? If we allow it means anything in a law court, then it has to be objective, definable, matter of ascertainable fact. We can't leave it to subjective opinion. I do not believe that she believes she was raped. That is to say, she didn't believe it *then*: not in the bed, not when he hit her, not when she hit him. By this time, in Holloway, she may well have *come* to believe it. She says I made a promise. So did she. A promise which we both broke, at one and the same gaudy moment. If she claims she did not break it, then that's *her* opinion. Gabriel, her *opinion*. But Ms Wanhope says that 'for a woman' that's all that ought to count. J. Lobscott did not lie down with me for sex; but she got it; *ergo*, rape.

And of course she's never explained what it was she'd been going to tell me. Get her in the witness-box, Gabriel, ask her *that*, dammit! ASK HER!

16

Oh no no no, I forgot, I forgot, you can't ask her anything. I'm not on trial; my lawyer has no standing; the only one to ask her will have to be the prosecutor. To clear my own name, I'm going to have to help prosecute. And I don't really think they'll want to hear what I need to say. According to *their* story I'm a conspiring co-respondent, a Brachiano of the Cromwell Road, urging his White Devil against her husband. (Except that Brachiano, as Webster lays out the evidence, organised the killing himself, Vittoria Corombona was only the accomplice, quite possibly an unwitting accomplice. Not so in this case; I suppose I should be thankful.) And of course the defence likewise will not hear what I need to say. Who *is* prepared to listen? I thought *you* were, Mr Garsdale; but now I'm not so sure.

Gabriel Garsdale, upon reading all this, sighed hopelessly and sat at his desk for a long space of time with his head in his hands. At last he did the only thing that there was for him to do: he had his client in to swear to a drastically edited and abridged text of the three documents (for he included his own version of the one about Pomfretshire and Polly Blackadder which we gave as our First Tale). He forwarded them with a shudder to the office of the Crown Prosecutor.

The trial was in September 1986. Just before it opened, Leonore Serlio heard from her estranged husband – a cold and yet frantic note, saying she must on no account turn up at the Old Bailey to witness the proceedings. Pogmoor could not endure (he wrote) the thought of giving evidence if she were to be in the public gallery, 'hexing me in silence with your damnable Evil Eye'. It made no difference whether she came to show belated sympathy or to nourish her hostility, either way she would infallibly disintegrate him. 'So please, Leonore, I ask you, I beg you, I plead: stay away!'

She took him at his word and did not come.

After that they held no communication until October '87. He was in Australia then, lonely and depressed; and he began to think of her with a certain ancient tenderness. He finally decided he should write; he had known her, after all, for twenty-two years. Before the letter's end his words became quite personal; but the first pages were stiff enough, embarrassed (which was not surprising), artificially dispassion-ate, J. Pogmoor's veracious history of the chilling preliminaries to the ordeal of his much-wronged mistress—

> 4B Emancipation Acre
> off Glebe Point Road
> Sydney
> 31st October, 1987

Dear Leonore,

. . . you will readily understand this was not at all the sort of case Garsdale had had in mind when he directed his career toward the *glamorous concerns* (as they must once have seemed to him) of artists and show-business personalities. It would do his firm no good; but it had to be done.

First and foremost, he told me, we must secure a guarantee that the 'monstrous red herring of incitement-to-murder' was buried and never mentioned again. If the police indeed were set on it, they had at all events failed to substantiate, or else they'd have arrested me weeks ago. Reassuring; until he went on to speak of 'this awkward little niggle of doubt' – i.e.: the visit to Whitesmith Street which Mrs Lobscott never made. Garsdale could not understand why I wished it brought up. Did I not realise how susceptible was such a event ('or should we say, non-event?') to the most sinister interpretation?

He could already foresee the swift pouncing of counsel in court – 'Do you seriously expect the jury to believe that she gave you no inkling of what she meant? *Something to your advantage?* Oh really, Mr Pogmoor! What *could* be to your advantage more acute than a dead husband who'd abused and outraged your lady-love over a space of ten full years? A lady-love, moreover, with *money of her own*, when you, as you have testified, were 'strapped for cash'? I put it to you, sir, that she intended to explain to you her heinous opportunity to achieve Dr Lobscott's death. You had both already planned it; you waited only for the crucial moment. And indeed I put it further: that she *did* come to Whitesmith Street that day, and that there in your secluded residence your conspiracy did take place!'

For it seemed Mrs Lobscott's movements between breakfast and one o'clock could not be established. The Vermeer was over-crowded, the hotel staff had failed to notice her, she could easily have slipped out and covered the short distance to Chelsea (and back again) at any time in the course of the morning. Nor was there any proof that *I'd* had no visitors. 'Entirely alone, Jack, in your flat, and doing what? – *thinking and drinking?* – good heavens . . .'

'You might well say "good heavens". What *am* I to do? Tell you what, why don't we forget all about her phone call, strike it out of my statement, it never happened.'

'You've deposed that it happened and that's evidence. If I conceal evidence, I am liable to the law. In any case, she has told the police about it. But has she *explained* it to them? We don't know. It must remain as an enigma. We skate over it as smoothly as we can. Of itself it proves nothing. I merely warn you, don't insist on it.'

'Gabriel, I am perfectly sure she intended to come to Whitesmith Street to be fucked. The beating she got from Lobscott distorted the whole business and it all went crinkum-crankum. But if I am right, don't you see? then of course she can't make it out *rape!*'

'I said, don't insist on it. I will leave it at that. This "rape" is the least of your worries.'

He fixed up a meeting. Himself and myself; a prosecuting silk, Alaric Houndsditch, QC; and the taciturn presence of the policeman in charge of the case – I call him 'Lestrade' – he just sat in the shadows and made notes. Houndsditch QC cross-examined me, strictly and coldly, on every point in my depositions. I affected a mulish Yorkshireness. You and Fidelio told me long ago that such a mannerism showed I was engrossed in some deception. (It is, of course, my father's vocabulary and accent; the dubious protestations of the Northern Turf.) But these Londoners did *not* know: they took it for a tone of blunt candour.

At the end of the session, Houndsditch QC pressed his palms

together, tilted his head slightly sideways and spoke in an undertone to Garsdale. I heard him say something about applying to the
bench to have me recorded as a hostile witness. I heard him say
something about dropping the enquiry as regards the 'complicity of
Mr Pogmoor'. I heard Inspector Lestrade cough disapprovingly and
say, 'With your permission, sir, we did think we had the makings of
a case—' Houndsditch QC waved him off with a most gracefully
dismissive gesture, an archangel vexed by a flea-sized demon.

On the stairs, Garsdale heaved a great sigh of relief. 'That really
went very well, Jack. Mind you, the detective ought not to have
been there. Houndsditch seems to think of himself as a Hollywood
DA: highly irregular practice. I did not object because I thought it
might work to our benefit. So it did. For it showed there will be no
parallel line of investigation: their decision has been made and it will
stand. No question now of roping you in as Second Murderer.
Indeed, very possibly, no First Murderer (or should we say, Mur-
deress?), for I'll not be surprised if in the end they reduced it to
Manslaughter. You handled Houndsditch most adeptly. Your reaction to the non-existent Whitesmith Street visit was exactly as I
coached you. They're making nothing out of it, as far as I can see.
So all we have to do is to grit our teeth courageously and allow you
to be exposed as the worst kind of sexual predator. I know you
won't like it, Jack. But *you* are not likeable: every flaw in a man's
character exacts its own retribution, we can't expect otherwise.'

The Old Bailey. As a forthcoming witness I could not sit in court
until I had testified. So I missed the prosecution's opening and
everything else on the first day and a half. I gathered that she
pleaded Not Guilty. I gathered that Houndsditch laid all his weight
on the length of time she spent in the bathroom and how this
proved *premeditation*. I gathered that he insisted that her unprompted admission of the killing indicated little beyond her capacity for
duplicity. I also gathered that the medical evidence was unexpectedly challenged. A female police doctor had surveyed Mrs Lobscott's injuries and (under pressure from defence counsel) was
unable to swear that *all* of them had been inflicted at the same time.
I knew they hadn't. *I* knew that her husband had beaten her twice.
But defence counsel implied that some of the marks of violence could
well have been the consequence of rape. There was severe bruising to
the vagina, it seemed. *I* knew it for P. Lobscott's work (second time
round), done just before he thrust her into the bathroom; but the
doctor became confused by cross-examination and maintained it could
have been part of an earlier assault (mine: nastily sandwiched in
between Percy's pair of *blitzkriegs*). I gathered that the police doctor
had begun by being too positive; when forced to concede doubt, she

laid open a vast area of indeterminate guesswork.

They called me late on the second day. I was very thankful not to
see you there. A decency I had scarcely dared to look for. My
gratitude has caused me to write you this letter. At various times I
treated you abominably; I suppose we will not see each other ever
again; so I cannot repeat my trickeries and wilful blindness toward
you. 'Beware,' you told me – well, I didn't! – I owe it to you now to
inform you of the consequence.

Leonore, I *did* see Fidelio. Could you not have kept him away?
And yet, after all, he knew Mrs Lobscott; he had therefore a very
personal interest; he had not come just to take note of how the
brother-in-law would conduct himself. I recognised other faces.
Theatre people, friends and enemies. A contingent from Knaresborough. I saw them as it were in a haze. They saw *me* with the
utmost clarity: they were the audience, I was the play. But it was
not a Jack Juggler production. Its director, whoever he was, was an
irresponsible pantaloon; most of his cast were under-rehearsed and
none of us were fully familiar with the script, a demoralising basis
for effective improvisation. How deeply I now regret all those times
I drove my actors into floods of frustrated tears.

Mrs Lobscott in the dock sat very still, dressed in a black suit with
white silk blouse, a pearl-and-sapphire brooch at the neck. Now
and then the smallest movement: she bit her lips and fingered her
throat. Her hair was most carefully arranged, loosely braided into a
soft pile with streaks of grey allowed to show themselves
unabashed. She *seemed* to wear no makeup. She was (paradoxically)
young, beautiful, and confident, nervous and sagging and ageing,
all at the same time. I do not think she could have made a more
effective impression. She looked across at me, blankly, just once;
and thereafter kept her eyes half-closed.

I gave in evidence everything I had written for Garsdale that bore
immediately upon the case. The rest of it, he'd told me, was
irrelevant; I was not to disgress; nor did I. Houndsditch QC, and his
junior, dealt with me harshly, a hostile witness, 'in love' with the
accused and therefore unreliable. They feared I would concentrate
upon Dr Lobscott's obsessive behaviour and long-drawn-out cruel-
ties – they needed a bit of these – but *not too much*, lest the jury felt
an empathy with murder. Instead I was induced to lay Mrs Lobscott
in the mire by blaming her for a series of aggressive seductions I had
not had the *soundness* to rebuff. I was pushed into offensive detail
about how, on the day in question, she was the first to take her
clothes off before helping me to take off mine. From the corner of
my eye I saw the press benches seething with glee.

Nothing much about her phone call to my flat, except counsel's
suggestion that I had not told the truth: 'Mr Pogmoor, you are

disingenuous; for did she not ring to *invite* you to the hotel? Her husband had been hitting her; she called to you for help, and you came. She was injured, to be sure; she was also commencing to undress. A simple admission: why can you not make it?' I didn't admit; I shrugged and let it go.

I *did* admit running out on her just before Lobscott returned. Even though I was aware of his violence, I cravenly left her alone with him. That admission hurt me more than anything else I'd had to say.

I began to be horrified. Not for myself but for her. My own predicament, until then, had been all I was able to cope with; but there in court, *for the first time since the killing*, I could see her, twenty feet away. She saw me, though she pretended not to; and she heard. I no longer wondered 'What do they all think of me?', but 'What must they be thinking of Jacqui?'

I began to understand how she'd come to accuse me of rape. Would I not have done the same in her place, and believed it an excellent *juggle*?

Cross-examination. Ms Wanhope had briefed a silk, a soft-spoken silver-haired man of sympathetic 'jury-appeal'. His junior was Ms Naomi Lambert, forceful and scornful. She was the one to take me in hand. She dropped hints about Pomfretshire, merely asking me had I known a Ms Blackadder and leaving the question in the air. She referred no less briefly to Antonia Button. She dissected my account of my relations with Mrs Lobscott, from the first afternoon in the Mother Shipton Playhouse. (She managed to make even *that* outrageous come-hither into a case of a strong fat man catching a slight unsuspecting woman alone in a dark building and grievously taking advantage.) She made ordure and drink-soaked trash out of the sum of my behaviour in Beverley. She came at last to the events of the Vermeer.

'You were told by my client, as she had told you on previous occasions, that all she desired to do was to *talk*?'

'Talk. Aye. In bed. She said in bed.'

'*She* said? Or *you* said, Mr Pogmoor? Or did you even *say* anything? I put it to you that you thought no words were necessary, that in fact your hands did all the talking. That you held her in their grip and remorselessly tore off her clothes—'

'Hey, no! Never! None of her clothes were torn. Whoever gave you that idea—'

'That idea was disclosed by the investigating officer. He agreed under cross-examination that various garments showed signs of considerable damage.'

(She must have forced the police to disgorge something they'd have preferred to keep quiet about. But I *hadn't* torn the clothes. It could only have been Lobscott, rampaging in his fury. Forensics should have found that out, fibres under his fingernails, and so forth. Such analysis would not have helped their predetermined case, so they simply didn't bother.)

And so it went on. When she brought up the brutalised vagina, I realised I had had enough. I had kissed that delightful vagina, stroked it and licked it, worshipped it even, for admittedly short moments, but ecstatic and very dear to me. I fell tongue-tied in the witness-box, sullenly permitting her to rove through her squalid fantasy.

'Let us suppose, Mr Pogmoor, that part of your story is true. Let us indeed go so far as to accept that she invited you to bed, as an ill-advised but sincere attempt to develop an *idealised* relationship. People do do such things, I know. Rarely: but they do. At what point during your talk did you initiate sexual intercourse? and did she, or did she not, say "No"?'

Tongue-tied. I waved my hands inconclusively, I *writhed* (just as Lobscott would writhe, the soundless rhetoric of a defeated man). She demanded an answer. The judge demanded an answer. 'Did she or did she not?'

There are moments during rehearsal when I feel completely flummoxed, finding no possible move or gesture for my actors. The play has reached a certain crisis: how to break from it and continue the flow? At such times I can only pray for a vision of a *coup de théâtre*. And there, in the witness-box, I received one. I asked myself, 'What am I doing here?' The reply was instantaneous: 'Jack Juggler, you are making a most noxious disgraceful spectacle. Your only way out of it is strongly to *embrace* your disgrace. Do it now. Do it. Do it.'

I looked up from my trembling hands and over towards the dock. Mrs Lobscott's eyes were at last open, they gazed intensely into *my* eyes, I declare I saw a smile in them. I was about to astonish her; somehow she appeared to be aware of it . . . No, this is too subject-ive. I had not wished to write intimately. Never mind all the psychology, the phoney telepathy, the slippery inner history of Jack Juggler's 'change of heart'.

Facts. I spoke up. I said to Ms Lambert, 'No. She did not say "No". She said "Ah". Which might have meant anything but I knew it meant "No". I was bigger than her, I held her tightly, and I forced her. I am sure it was against her will. I'm very sorry. She's a nice woman.' I was shaking from top to toe, and Mrs Lobscott stared and stared.

Ms Lambert could not believe her ears. Neither could Hounds-ditch QC. Ms Lambert said, 'No more questions,' but Houndsditch QC had plenty. I stubbornly blocked them, until the judge gave him

warning to desist: 'Mr Houndsditch, I suspect your witness has said
what he has to say. Don't flog a dead horse: it only wastes the time
of the court.' (In hindsight, that judge was very taken by Mrs
Lobscott; he breathed an austere compassion every time that he
looked at her, and he looked at her a lot.)

Ms Lambert then stated that in view of my admission she would
call no more witnesses. One of them was to have been Carmilla
Costello, her second deportation postponed to let her tell of my
Sexual Violence. Deborah, too: to explain the distress of Mrs Lobscott
after her short trip to Beverley, how anxiously she had then sought
to patch things up with Lobscott.

Houndsditch QC asked the bench for a private word. Proceedings
were adjourned overnight. Next morning began with an announcement. Murder had become Manslaughter. The judge refused to
dismiss altogether, 'Because,' he said, 'the prisoner (as I understand it) does not deny striking the deceased with the ashtray; she
only pleads a mitigating circumstance. Whatever the circumstance,
counsel will surely concede that no one is allowed to hit another
person with an ashtray (or anything else) to the point of death.
Perhaps your client would prefer to change her plea?'

Mrs Lobscott pleaded Guilty. She took the stand for a desperate
narration: of a ruinous married life, of alienated children, of
wretched loveless love affairs, of men like myself who considered
her a mere *aperture* to be filled at will by their random sperm. It
culminated in a deed of blood, whereby she had destroyed any hope
of serenity as a woman, as a mother, as a creature with an immortal
soul. Her QC brought all this out of her, tenderly, soothingly, and
very convincingly. About sixty-five per cent of it was true. The rest
was crude perjury; but after what *I* had had to say, who could tell
the difference?

Not the judge, at any rate. He awarded her three years in prison,
and immediately suspended the sentence. He said she had suffered
enough; her youngest son needed her. There was great hope for her
yet, he said. By speaking of her 'immortal soul', she had touched
him (I guess) to the very core.

He also said that the papers concerning the man Pogmoor should
be sent to the Crown Prosecutor. But Mrs Lobscott would need to
give evidence about the rape if proceedings were to follow. I
inferred a desire on his part that she be spared the tribulation. The
man Pogmoor, after all, had done the decent thing. Perhaps he too
had suffered enough?

Garsdale fetched me out of the building by a side-passage to avoid
journalists. We did not avoid them; but their mobbing was interrupted by the sight of Mrs Lobscott, also on the way out through the

side-passage. If her entourage (Lambert, Wanhope and the sturdy Deborah) had hoped to use me as a shield for her escape, they miscalculated. I last saw her shrinking back from a rampant hedge-hog of notebooks and microphones and TV sound-booms, as Gars-dale ran me along the street, manhandled me into a taxi, jumped in after me and slammed the door.

'She is not going to bring charges,' he grunted, 'I caught Wanhope for half a minute in the foyer. She says, as her solicitor, she believes she *should* bring charges, but she reluctantly under-stands why not. I wonder if she does? Who's the biggest liar, Jack? You or Lobscott? My God. Quite apart from the unpleasantness, she won't be in England anyway and she's damned if she's going to come back to be pelted with more of the same.'

'Where's she going?'

'Who knows? You didn't expect Wanhope to *tell* me? It's none of our business, nor should we make it our business. So; what will *you* do? Lie low?'

He seemed not to be pleased with me. I was not going to argue with him. The time for self-justification was over.

(It occurred to me that, like Ms Wanhope, he did not quite understand the implications. *But how could I inform him that my extraordinary about-face was in fact the very best bit of juggling I'd ever contrived?* Had I continued to deny forcing her, no one would have believed me, not when her own evidence was so crammed with plausibility and pathos: I'd have been branded Pogmoor the Rapist as scarifyingly as when I admitted it. So therefore, I'd lost nothing. And moreover, *I'd got her off!* All this occurred to me in the taxi even as we drove up Fleet Street. I kept it to myself.)

Lie low? Yes, for a while, but it wasn't enough. How was I to earn? In Australia the previous year it had been put to me that if I needed a job teaching drama students in Sydney, I only had to write. I accordingly wrote and waited in trepidation for the answer. I had no doubt the Lobscott case would be heard of there soon enough; would it prejudice my chances? The letter I eventually received was rather strange.

The principle of the theatre school, a flint-eyed ironist of an ex-Yorkshireman who greatly admired my work, quoted what he claimed to be an Aboriginal fable: how a dangerous crocodile, who had eaten many women of a certain tribe, walked one day into the camp upon two human legs. He opened his belly and behold! all the women slid out, alive and every one of them pregnant. 'See,' he said, 'I have made myself the mother of all these, your beloved women, and I have made myself father and grandmother of all their children. Shall you hunt me with spears? Or shall you afford me the respect I deserve?' They afforded him respect; but they took very good care never to allow him to sit at the camp-fire without a brace of strong warriors standing over him with a strong net of woven reeds to entrap him if he misbehaved. In other words, I would be welcomed for my talent, but watched closely for my character – any trouble, I'd be out on the instant.

He offered me an immediate production, if I could expedite a permit with Australia House. Some of the students (on his Elizabethan-Jacobean course) had discovered a would-be scabrous play by John Marston which no one seemed ever to have put on – *The Insatiate Countess*. What did I think? The idea was to transfer it from Renaissance Italy to convict-age New South Wales, a sort of Anglo-Aussie hybrid, very suitable for a newly arrived Pom. I knew *The Insatiate Countess*: a corrupt text that craved clever adapting; I was stimulated but disturbed. In my present situation, the subject-matter might be described as – well, at best, tempting providence? Was it given me as a species of *test*? – a glowing young mother-to-be set singing at the camp-fire alongside the rehabilitated crocodile, while grimly behind the latter the men with the net take post?

Oh, Leonore! I'd had more than enough of bloody tests. Yet the 'respect I deserved' must depend on my willingness to be tested. You, of all people, understand that, do you not? I accepted the proffered job, on the unspoken understanding that if all fell out well, other and better opportunities would follow. I'd decided, you see, that I did in the upshot have principles, and they were not incompatible with *juggling*.* (I used not to think so, but things are different now, they have to be.) And I decided, very seriously, that if I and these principles ever got to Australia I was not going to 'rat' on them. *Your* word, 'rat', remember? Choice little word, tasty.

The Australian government made some demur, muttering ominously about 'papers in the case' and the 'prosecutor's office', and how they don't grant visas to criminals. I pointed out to them that I wasn't a convicted criminal, there was no prosecution ascertainably pending, and that what a man may say in court, even though upon oath, need not be proof of anything save his own bloodyminded integrity. A risky approach, right? But some great-great-great-grandson of a Transported Perjurer must have found that it tickled his fancy. At all events, I got my permit.

I've been in Sydney all these months: no effective complaints against me so far. Women on the whole fight shy of me; but then I'm fighting shy of the women. I'd say it was about time.

---

* I'm not quite sure what these principles are, though. If I say, Leonore, 'out of dishonesty the sharpest honesty; out of fiction, reality; out of pretence, the living truth,' would you recognise a logic? At all events, a foundation-stone of *theatre*. Theatre is my life. Yours too.

Of course, among any group of students, even in these deflated reactionary days, you'll always find the occasional unregenerate militant. There was a feminist demonstration against me in the theatre school the first week I was there. Not a large one: most of the kids hadn't read about Mrs Lobscott, and the Australian press-reports had in any case been perfunctory. (The long-running 'Murder-rap Mum Claims "Dingo Took My Baby" ' sensation, from Ayers Rock, drove all other unnatural deaths off every front page in the land.) For a few hours, however, my predicament was serious: I could have lost my new job before it started. I *juggled*, and defused the crisis. I had a weapon to hand; only to be employed with a tactful subtlety. I managed. For as it happened—

As it happened, I'd met with an interesting adventure between England and the Antipodes, which I ought to tell you, here and now. Leonore, you're my wife for what it's worth, you've a right to know. Eh, dear.

I was already in the midst of all my travel arrangements when Deborah wrote me a letter. This was shortly after the New Year; they expected me in Sydney at the end of their midsummer vacation, the commencement of the first term of '87. Her message was awkwardly phrased with many crossings-out. It had obviously been difficult to compose—

> *Numb. 6, St Cuthbert's Close,*
> *Knaresboro.*
> PRIVATE

Dear Sir, *Mr Pogmoor*,
  I know I ouht not to have wrote this, But I know you *ouht* to see her. Its not my Secret, it is hers but she ouhgt *not* to have to keep it allways, its not fair and I dont care if she told me not to tell because I am SURE (Mr Pogmoor) you have to be told. You should of heard it from her own voice. And then you will make up your mind as to whats riht for you to do. I was allways your freind but I cant tell you whats riht, you have to find it out yourself. She said *not* ever to give out her adress, but here it is, And don't you ever let on it was Deb that sent it, that wuoldnt be fair at all.

Villa Cazzorotto
Via Camillo
TAORMINA, Sicily (ask for Greek theatre, its a street alongside)

I spellt it riht, I know, becuase she wrote it down for me before she went. She does have a phone, but I dont give you the number, You ouht not to ring her, best to go straiht to the door so she SEES you before she can say Bugger Off.

> *Yours faithful*, but you *did* behave
> dredful to her until the very end.
> And becuase of the end and what
> you did then (you Saved her) so I'm
> writing you now
> > *Deborah Bones* (Mrs)

No kisses from her this time, no 'Yours affectonly, DEB'. And I was
in more than two minds about the contents. Stark-naked curiosity,
as always, won the day. I did not think Deb would have let me
know the address if she hadn't had some idea that 'bugger off'
might *not* be the only response. On the other hand, shouldn't it be
my response? And yet, and yet – her 'secret'? Deb's wording was
ambiguous: she might have meant no more than the secret address.
But I didn't think so. I *did* think about the never-revealed reason for
the Whitesmith Street appointment: could it be that I was at last to
hear it?

And what in the name of God was this *Villa Cazzorotto*? 'The
House of the Ruptured Prick'? Even in Sicily that ought to warrant
raised eyebrows at the post office. And yet, maybe . . . ? who could
say? Suppose she *was* playing tricks with me? Sicily was not
altogether so far out of my way . . .

I found I could fly Alitalia to Catánia, and then (when I'd made
my discoveries) I could transfer via Rome to a Qantas flight for
Sydney. Overnight stops and extra expense; but I'd take a chance.

Taormina is an astonishing Greco-Sicilian hill-town, perched on a
great rock high above the sea. Every street (except the one along
the shoulder of the summit) is a series of hairpin bends; taxis at full
speed are chariots of sudden death. I had a man drive me direct to
the Greek theatre. I did not dare attempt the villa until I'd settled
myself a little. The building is almost completely preserved: they
regularly put on plays there, and operas; I sat in an upper tier of the
auditorium and envied the chosen directors. I declined the services
of the tourist-guide. I didn't need to know the theatre's history: I
could feel it in every nerve. Looking out over orchestra and stage, I
was able to contemplate the wine-dark sea, miles and miles of it to
the indigo horizon.

It is said that Odysseus, somewhere along this stretch of coast,
had his encounter with the Cyclops. I could well believe it. Captain
Nobody, he chose to call himself.

I asked a jovial constable of the Tourist Police, in my best pidgin-
Italian, was there really a house in the Via Camillo with the name
of *Cazzorotto*? He told me (in pidgin-English), oh yes, indeed there
was. A very ancient family name; no one had laughed at it for five
hundred years; though he did suppose they might have cackled in

the dirty old Quattrocento when some bravo or other had suffered humiliation and had no doubt avenged himself most bloodily. Good: so it wasn't a trick after all and it didn't appear to be personal. But suppose when I got there she was out? Shopping? Strolling down below on the beach? Suppose, suppose . . . Nonetheless the address was confirmed, I had come, I must find it.

Not exactly a *villa*, which suggests a large establishment in spacious grounds; it was in fact a 'detached residence' with a pocket-handkerchief of overgrown garden behind high walls, altogether seedy, a local equivalent of some of the less well-tended properties in Huddersfield Road, Barnsley – give or take the Mediterranean climate and the sure taste of traditional Mediterranean building-craft. I doubt if the place was more than a hundred years old: but it pre-dated mass-tourism, and I liked it.

The latch was broken on the front gate. I pushed it open and went in. She had not gone out shopping. I saw her at once under the pergola at the side of the house, lounging in a garden-chair in dark glasses and a wide straw hat. (By the calendar a winter's day, but edging warmly into spring: windless, brilliant sunshine, already a buzz of insects.)

It pains me to describe our meeting. Let me summarise.

First, she showed no *shock*. She must have guessed that Deborah would tell.

Second, she agreed with Deborah, I had 'saved her', for which her thanks. When I hinted I had *lied* to save her, she shrugged as though that was not quite true, but she was no longer disposed to dispute it.

Third, she was happy to fill me in about Whitesmith Street. She spoke of it at once, and no prevarication. She seemed surprised I had not 'caught on'. Of course, she said frankly, she'd had a *plan!* secretly to subsidise her husband's play from her own private income, not to improve its chances but to pollute the very blood in its arteries. She'd intended to enlist me in this incredible scheme.

She filled me in about the real meaning of *Head*.

I had not known she had actually read it. I remembered how she called it his 'nasty play'; I'd taken her remark for sheer prejudice. She hadn't wanted to have anything to do with it, but he hid it away from her with such precautions that she determined to find it and find out why. She did find out. *One aspect of the plot immediately stopped the breath in her bosom:*

∾ —where the playwright shows the Queen of England driving the King mad by sometimes telling him his son is the Duke of York's son, sometimes telling him he is Clifford's son, and then again telling him the boy is his own. The King's love for the Prince veers in and out of hate. At last the King asserts himself and compels her to marital intercourse, wrapping her in a Gothic chastity-belt (as instructed by God) until she can report herself pregnant again. ॐ

(I *had* guessed some such subtext. I'd assumed it referred to the parentage of Mrs Lobscott's first two children. And without doubt Queen Margaret *was* Mrs Lobscott, observed by one who knew her, through a veil of poison gas. At the time I had let it go; I was none too pleased with her myself just then, the way she'd abandoned her youngest kid to disport herself in Ripon. But yes! I'd been insensitive. No wonder she cut up so queer with me. And now I was to find it went further than that, much further.)

She'd had in mind, she said, to *bribe* me with the prospect of a spectacular production. Insidiously I would follow her wishes, not Lobscott's, and the actors of course would follow mine. I was to work upon her husband, whether it ruined the shape of the play or not, work upon his inexperience, blind him to the distortion of the text (her word was 'reinterpretation') until all that was left of his masterpiece would do long-delayed justice to *her*.

'I knew,' she said simply, 'you were already discussing rewrites. Why could they not have been *my* rewrites? You'd persuaded him so cleverly over *Hermit's Hole*, hadn't you? You could play him the same trick again, but make some useful sense of it. You were a juggler, I relied on you.

'I was sure you'd be able to do this, as an act of affection, of duty, of love, once I'd told you *you were Eugene's father*.'

She gave me no time to react but put her finger to my lip, preventing interruption, and went on: 'Now I never told *him*. I made a very bad mistake when I let him know the truth about Tristram and Jennifer. So with Eugene I was silent as a worm. I even let him choose the name; the names for the elder two were my choice, of course. Did he suspect? Oh, I think so, for I laid hands on his script when I heard he'd invited you for Christmas, and all his suspicions and contradictory self-reassurances were crowded into one devouring tale.

'If that was the play that he wished you to direct, don't you see what he was up to? Jack, he was about to set *you* to lash *me* and flog *me* and scourge *me* and lacerate *me* in public on the public stage, in London, God help us! and then he'd sit and smirk as all the reviewers praised him and honoured his ruthless artistry. His sombre bloody vision of the Human Condition. It wasn't for the first time. Remember his 'Mrs Aram'? Well, she was me. And I swore to myself, 'Never again!' I had to do something.'

Oh yes. And she meant it, Leonore. Here was no perjury.

(Leonore, I'm so sorry. You once wanted your womb to enclose my child. I refused you. And when I thought of Mrs Lobscott's womb – why, she'd implied she was on the pill, I never thought of it at all. Flaws of character. Retribution. We can't expect otherwise. Refer to Gabriel Garsdale for instant moral comment.)

'You were right in the middle of it,' she went on, 'centre-stage in the middle of his drama. You couldn't catch on, could you?

'*You* needed the justice too. For my failure to tell you earlier – I had my chance that night in Beverley, like a drunken slut I let it slide – my failure – my failure—'

She was no longer straightforward and frank. She clutched me fiercely by one wrist and held me off at arm's length, collapsing into sobs, until she brought herself up short with a great gasp: 'Ah! I would have told you in your flat, I never got there. I tried again, in the Vermeer. No good. Ah! by my failure, *I* was unjust to you. Jack, it broke my heart.'

(And Deborah knew all about it! I could think of nothing else but that trivial irrelevance as I stood between two pillars of the pretty little portico with its trellis for a creeping vine. How long had Deborah known? Had everyone in Knaresborough been living like secret agents, double identities in all those neat Yorkshire houses, cleanly freestone and crisp red pantiles?)

Fourth (and there *was* a fourth, even after such an overflow of gobsmacking hokum), Eugene was now with her in Sicily. Enormous improvement in him since the death of his dad. Psychologists were confounded: the trauma of itself must have released him, they supposed, he played and laughed like a normal little boy.

'Jacqueline ... Shall I see him?' See him? I'd no idea what to say to him. Everything was going too fast.

She suddenly showed signs of confusion. 'Oh. I don't know. He's gone to the puppet-show. Sicilian puppets are famous, but you'll know that, I'm sure. I'm living here with a friend. She took him. I can't say when they'll be back. How long are you in Taormina?'

Alas, I was booked on a late-afternoon flight from Catánia, I'd have to leave in a couple of hours. Unless—

She still held me. True, at arm's length; but the sexual electricity was sparking. Unbelievably, it had returned. We both spoke at the same moment.

I said, 'Hey, no. Not any more, no.'

She said, 'If that's what you need, there'll be a brothel in the town somewhere. Mafia country, okay? they provide these amenities. And *I* don't need it, *I* don't. No. Jack dear, you can't stay.'

She let go her hand.

The garden-gate screamed open on its rusty old hinges; Eugene came running in. '*Mamma, mamma, mamma, ecco! il cavaliere nero cattivo*!' He was carrying a marvellous puppet, a Saracen knight with bold black face and a huge Islamic crescent-crest. More decorously, behind him, walked Mrs Lobscott's friend.

Carmilla. I should have known.

I turned my back and walked away a few paces. Ought I to leave the place this instant, or wait? I could hear the two women whispering. Then Mrs Lobscott called me. I looked round and saw Costello going into the house. She too was shirking confrontation.

'Jack, come back here, please. You don't have to meet her. But Eugene you should meet, as he came in so closely on cue. Talk to him.'

The boy was bubbling over with all the excitement of his treat, and he remembered how I had been the first to introduce him to puppets. We held a serious conversation about the ancient wars in the Mediterranean between Christians and Moors, the theme of the play he'd been to see. His mother meanwhile retired to her chair and listened without making a point of it.

Then he said, 'Daddy died, you know. It was best for him, I think. He was very unhappy and too old to be happy again. Mummy said I ought to be glad. I *was* glad, as soon as I heard of it, though Debbie cried, I don't know why. He used to shout at Debbie and she didn't like it, you know. Taormina's a nice place, don't you think so? And Carmilla's nice too. She tells about Native Americans. She's one of them herself, she says. A Mohican. The great-great-granddaughter of a famous woman-warrior. Isn't it brilliant? Her real name is Long-Knife-in-the-Belly. I wish I was called that.'

He said something sprightly in a street-Sicilian slang which I didn't understand, laughed at his own joke, and off into the house like a jolly hopping frog – no doubt for another slice of ethnic roots from his new mentor. But certainly, he *had* improved; his very body had improved; all that lumpishness had vanished; he was almost a little charmer. Would Costello now be talking to him about *me*?

There were some elements of Mrs Lobscott's story that did not quite add up, perhaps. By and large, though, I felt I believed it. Nobody's story of compounded sexual error can ever be entirely true. Our passions (and our genitals) reinvent themselves every day of our lives, making yesterday always into an Improbable Fiction.

But I felt I believed it; and I also felt *responsible*. Eugene was my son, Jacqui was his mother, what was I to do for them both?

I mumbled, daft but dutiful, about asking you for a divorce and then getting married to *her*. She laughed.

'Jack, you don't want that. *I* don't want it.'

'Eugene might. Suppose, if all goes well, I brought you both out to Australia?'

'Pointless. What would I do there?'

'What would you do here?'

'Live. It's my birthplace. *La bella Sicilia, gran'isola sfortunata!*'

'We could work summat out.'

'One of these days, I don't know, Jack.'

'Nay, Jacqui, nay, *I* don't know either.'

Fatuous. But the feeling between us was far better than I'd had any right to expect. Then she thought of a matter of importance (I had not dared think of it myself) – 'Wait for two minutes. I'll write you a letter. You can carry it with you, in case – in case something objectionable crops up.'

She entered the house and very soon came out again with a paragraph of typescript. 'I'll ring for a taxi and we can take this down to a notary I know, I'll swear it as an affidavit and he'll stamp it and make it legal.'

It was a short statement, formally phrased, to the effect that I had never committed rape and had only asserted otherwise in order to clear her of murder.

'It's a lie, isn't it, Jack? You did what you did to me and you know it. And you're lucky to have such a good friend as your little Jacqui to tell such a lie for your sake. Carmilla blew a fuse when she saw what I was writing. But it's not going to do me any harm. I was tried, I pleaded Guilty, it can't be repeated. And certainly I'll never live in England again, fuck it and fuck all of 'em. *La bella Sicilia!* here's the cab.'

When the ructions began in Sydney, I used that piece of paper. Not too outrageously; I didn't (for example) face a crowd of placard-carriers and read it out to them like the Riot Act. I quietly *inserted* it into the communal discourse via my friend the principal, who through a discreet process of hook and crook, nudge and wink, allowed it to drift down into the consciousness of the female staff and thence the students. In the end, it was absorbed, and so was I.

Here is a sort of postscript, Leonore. I really don't know how seriously to take it; but equally it ought not to be ignored. I'll leave it to you to decide what to do with it.

We had a visitor last week at the theatre school, a British writer whom you know as well as I do, Alex McCoy from Glasgow. He is trotting about on a round-the-world *finding-himself* tour (as well he might, for in my opinion he's never been other than lost, stolen and strayed since he first stepped out of his push-chair). The British Council dug up for him various lecture-dates in Australia, one of them to speak to our students. When he and I last met, it was during all the rows about *The Emperor's Whore*, and we nearly had a punch-up. You'll understand I was wary of him. But no! he grinned and greeted me with expansive cordiality. Well, I was a familiar face: he'd be homesick, I dare say.

He asked after Fidelio. He said he knew that Fidelio and I had fallen out, but nevertheless he thought it possible I might still be in touch with him.

'I'd have written him myself,' he said, 'but I don't know where he is. He buries himself in Devon, doesn't he? And then there's that house in London where Leonore lives. But I don't carry either address, I left too many notebooks behind when I set out on the trip. And I'd not want my letter to miscarry, because it's a dodgy one. Listen.' He dropped his voice and led me away into a corner of the staff-room, out of earshot of the others.

It seems he had just come from Adelaide, where a play of his was on at the Festival Centre. He had occasion to call to a tourist office to book tickets for an Outback excursion. He paid for them in travellers' cheques, and the woman behind the counter demanded his passport. She was intrigued to take note of his stated occupation – 'Playwright'. She had a northern Irish accent and a ribald confidential manner. She had apparently worked in showbiz herself back in the UK, but was unaccountably noncommittal about when and where. McCoy thought, 'strip-clubs'. If she wanted to gloze over it, he wouldn't ask questions. But they did have a lively chat, one professional to another, the office being none too busy. She had emigrated and was married to an engineer on the Adelaide tramline; she said her name was 'Toe'.

'Toe?' McCoy was puzzled. 'Toe what? Surname or Christian?'

'Never mind,' she answered, 'he'll know.'

'Who?'

'Fid Carver. You do know him?'

He said he knew Fid Carver.

'Thought y'would. They all do. That's the trouble, so it is. He's conspicuous. He wrote all that stuff about Ireland on the telly, time of the hunger-strike, yeh?'

McCoy (I recollect) was vehement against Fidelio's Irish series: he himself belonged to the Protestant tradition – not to put a tooth in it, his folks were ravening Orangemen, and a scorn of the IRA was built into his psyche from birth. However he wouldn't tell this to Toe. He kept his own counsel and listened.

'Come here till I tellya,' says she. 'What youse are to do is to tell your Mr Carver to watch out. There's a man they call the Wee Priest. He's been here, in Adelaide. And Sydney, Melbourne, I dunno. Infiltrating. We had his fucken number, he's out of the Land of Oz and away home or wherever, just in time before they fetched him out feet first. He used to be a Sticky, like a whole rake of us in them days.'

(McCoy said that 'Sticky' meant the Official *Sinn Féin*/IRA, now defunct. Her use of the word meant she herself was not connected with the party that had replaced it; a pejorative, said McCoy. But what, if anything, she *was* connected with, she declined to disclose.)

'Now the word is he's either an MI5 tout or the loyalists have their cock in his crack. It's a fact, though, your Mr Carver is a name on their index from – from way before the flood. I'd best not say why. Just ask him this, though: say, "Fid, d'youse remember a van with a load of theatre-gear that never found its way to Liverpool?" Say, "This Priest now, when *he* remembers it, he regards himself as *robbed*." He's a terrible vengeful man, so he is, and he never forgets a reneguer. Christ, *he* renegues on everyone, why *should* he forget? He keeps his stack of bullets the way I keep me fucken Tampax.

'Of course, *I'm* the one he ought to be hitting if the world had its rights; but me, I'm a wee cockroach, a dooms-better infiltrator than any fucken Priest, *out*-filtrator too. I'm laughing. But tell him, will youse? tell him quick, or by Christ they'll blow his head off.'

Just then the office manager came in behind her, she stopped talking immediately, turned to a newly arrived customer, and when McCoy tried to ask her to speak to him again, she waved him imperiously away. He left Adelaide an hour later with no time to get back to her. He had no idea what any of it meant, or even if it was more than a tasteless Belfast joke.

I don't know either. I pass it on as requested. 'A van with a load of theatre-gear.' If Fidelio, when he hears it, wants to get in touch with me, I'm here, the address above. If not, Leonore, then not. And the same applies to you. We enjoyed ourselves, didn't we? Once . . .

This letter made Leonore hate Pogmoor as she'd never hated him before. Perhaps because it so clearly showed he wanted to make up his quarrel. The enchantment of distance had sweetened her in his eyes? However, his choice of overture – Jacqueline Lobscott and her child, and Carmilla Costello, of all possible subjects for her *to have to read about! – was of such unthinking callousness that she wondered she'd ever longed for the man at any bloody time of her life. Nonetheless, before tearing the letter and tearing it again and forcing it in sodden fragments round the bend of the WC, she carefully cut off the address from the flap of the envelope. She'd always been a thrifty woman. Addresses were meant to be kept. Waste not, want not: for who could say when?*

She had a word with Fid about the message from McCoy (as baffling to her as it had been to Pogmoor). He was sitting at his breakfast when she mentioned it. He looked wanly up from a plate of apricots and Complan, and shook his head very slowly. 'These things aren't important,' he muttered. 'Many better men than I am get such threats every day of the year. You know Hamlet, *love, don't you? "If it be now, 'tis not to come; if it be not now, yet it will come." One of these days I'll tell you all about that wicked Toe. No one ever was able to credit a single word she said. She'd a bum like a dancing bell-flower; I'd have lusted after her fiercely, for a week or two, at one time, if it hadn't been for somebody else. She was a woman, he was a man. Which d'you think won out?'*

'Fid, it doesn't seem to me to be a laughing matter, truly.'

'Sweetheart, it's a Hallowe'en hoax: look at the date. And I laugh more than you do. Forget it.' He spooned up his food and fell to talking about the Guardian Arts Page. *Leonore went quietly away. One of her biblical stories had come into her mind, as a result of that foul Pogmoor's letter. How Samson, having been shorn by his mistress's trick, grew his hair once again in captivity far from home, simply in order to pull down the roof and mangle all the bodies he could. The legend said,* enemy *bodies; but how could he be sure there were none of his old friends in the crowd? Perhaps he recognised some voices – he couldn't see faces, he was blind – perhaps he* knew *they were there and decided to slaughter them regardless? Perhaps he loathed the very thought of anyone who'd attempted to love him?*

Whereby she saw clearly she misread herself. Pogmoor hadn't said 'love', had he? but 'enjoy'. Had she enjoyed *him? Yes: in brute physical terms. Undeniably, for a space, he had lived between her hands, to be fondled and stroked and slapped in any way she thought fit to initiate. She'd cut him out of his own life and pasted him twopence-coloured into hers like a garish little chappie for the toy theatre.*

But as for love? Only Fidelio, no one but Fidelio. She walked back into the kitchen and kissed him all over his hoary face, knocking off his spectacles, disordering his newspaper, to his pernickety good-humoured astonishment.

Concluding Anecdote

How a Man With No Nose
Made Leonore's Last Word
to Jack Juggler
(as told by Madame Serlio, 1987)

I'll make ye curse religion ere I leave ye,
I have lived a long time, son, a mew'd up man,
Sequester'd by the special hand of heaven . . .
            . . . many a burning sun
Has sear'd my body, and boiled up my blood.

       (John Fletcher, *The Island Princess*)

For several days Leonore kept thinking and rethinking the ins and outs of Samson's revenge. The more she considered it, as a parallel to the behaviour of Pogmoor, the less appropriate she found it. In the end she decided she was quite wrong; and moreover unjust to her faraway husband. Not that she liked him any the better. But she wished to treat him accurately, and that was not achieved by the vulgar expedient of flushing his letter down the loo. She looked for (and found) the Australian address she had preserved; and sat herself soberly to write to him.

That book which Fidelio had had from the public library when he was at work on The Emperor's Whore? *A short tale in it, a caprice of history – how did it go? The book was no longer available, the older library-stocks having been* purged *and not replaced – government-enforced cost-cuts, intolerable! But her brother recollected the general outline; she began her letter.*

My dear Jack,

    For you *were* dear, and would wish to be again, I daresay, so I'll do you the courtesy. How sincere a courtesy is unclear even to me as I employ it; you must therefore make your own guess and value it how you will.

    I have discussed this letter with Fidelio. He is unable to bring himself to write to you. But then he was your *collaborator*, I was no more than your wife, I suppose *his* hurt to be deeper than mine: please excuse him. Nonetheless, he does, with difficulty, send you his good wishes. And he agrees that the ensuing story might well strike you as apposite. You possibly remember it? You and he looked at all those St Helena documents together, did you not? As it has nothing to do with Napoleon, except perhaps allusively, you doubtless flicked over the pages to hurry up to the nineteenth century, and forgot all about it?

Fidelio, over my shoulder, says 'allusively' is too weak an adverb. He says 'subliminally/poetically/prophetically' would be better and what a pity he did not realise it when he missed the chance to fit the episode into his *Whore*. He says he is often gripped with such afterthoughts, long after a play is finished and done: they drive him mad, he says. All the more so because *this* play was neither finished *nor* done. He says he does not need to tell you, you damned well know why.

I am not taking dictation from him. Don't be afraid: the rest of the letter is all my own and I'm sending him out of the room. He is very upset.

When the Portuguese at the end of the Middle Ages sailed beyond the Cape of Good Hope to establish trading-stations and then colonies around the Indian Ocean and beyond into the archipelagos, the first ships they used were unbelievably precarious. Think of a caravel, maybe with three masts, but no bigger than that yacht of Maxwell Prosser's. And a hundred and fifty men in it (together with a parcel of women), lousy, half-starved, sleeping in sodden heaps on the bare deckboards arse-into-gut, and ruinously enfeebled by vitamin-deficiency. Think of such a vessel full of time-expired soldiery from Goa, beating north at daybreak in a wild flurry of tempest during the storm-season of 1516.

There is a boy in the maintop, poor little bugger – or rather poor little *buggered*, for the cook's mate (a greedy fellow with his own illicit access to the provisions) has been at him ever since they set sail. This miserable youngster sees nothing but wind and blown water and grey wind again and again, and then he sees *something!* a hideous black tooth of anger and danger hiding itself, revealing itself, through curtains of driven rain, the breakers against its base like streaks of pus in a sick man's gums. He screams a warning. He is not heard, the wind is too loud. He screams a second time; an officer on the poop does at last hear him and throws himself into the rigging, scrambling up to bring his eyes a little higher than the wavetops.

The horrible rock is not on any chart. Perhaps no more than a dozen fully skilled pilots have been here to make charts; it was easy to miss so unpredictable an outcrop. There is no such thing as a telescope, and no means of assessing longitude: all their voyages are by guess and by God, and from half of them no sailor has ever come home. (And yet the king demands trade; his ships have to sail; God sometimes pays attention and the guesses are sometimes good.) All but one of those pilots, indeed, would have concluded that the ocean hereabout was so deep there would be nothing to waste their eyes on. And *that* pilot lost all his records when his overloaded caravel broke her anchor-cable under a sudden squall, and turned turtle in the roadstead of Belém with nobody aboard her but an old watchman and a drunken boatswain.

The military captain commanding the ship has the advantage of the only cabin. It is five feet from deck to ceiling, cramped in under the narrow poop, and the great tiller runs through it from the quarterdeck to an ever-open hole in the stern where it joins with the top of the rudder. Even so, he contrives to be moderately snug. He has a proper bed, with a bedroll for himself and one for his brown-skinned concubine; when he is well enough he eats off silver plate; there is a painted-and-gilded statue of the Virgin and Child secured to a bracket against the bulkhead. Reluctantly he tips himself from his blankets and gropes his way on deck, stumbling and fumbling, trying to button a gold-braided jacket, his only immediate proof out there of his six-hundred-year line of noble ancestors. Without the jacket he might be any other ragged seaborne soldierman; with it he can still achieve obedience from his officers who are in turn obeyed by the men for as long as they have the strength to keep hitting them.

'Call for the pilot!'

The pilot comes, stumbling, fumbling, his boots slipping perilously on the wet planks. If he went barefoot, he would be safer; but he too has a status to preserve.

'You'd think Satan had *shat* it out, as he flew across these desperate waters. Yet it seems several miles in circumference. More than a rock, it is an island. Have you heard of it?'

'My lord, it is not on the chart. But I think, my lord, I do think, I have some memoranda.' The pilot is endeavouring to turn the pages of a thick parchment pocket-book. They are sticking together with dried salt; their watercolour drawings, their crabbed notes in sepia ink are blotted and blurred with years of exposure.

'Ah, yes, my lord, here! Dom João da Nova Castela made a mid-ocean landing fourteen years ago. I think it must have been here: but because of the later loss of his pilot's observations there is nothing I can say but 'I think'. See, my lord, I have written in my book the words *Quaere: positio ignotus? Inutilis.* But if this *is* Dom João's landfall, then we ought to find an anchorage and plentiful water, also vegetables and fruits growing wild. He chanced to have goats on his ship, for milk, I suppose, it doesn't say why. He set two of them, billy and nanny, ashore in the hope they would breed, and so provide fresh meat for future voyagers. Poultry too.'

'A gentleman of forethought, it would appear.'

'I met his pilot once. A most capable mariner, my lord.'

At this hint that the nobility is as nothing without the artisan's *capability*, the captain bridles, but feels too ill to take serious umbrage. His concubine has been vomiting all night and he is unpleasantly conscious of the stink of his shirt. 'We have already lost two-score men to the malady: if we do not replenish—'

'We shall all die, my lord. Allow me then to take order for wearing round toward the anchorage. I do have rudimentary directions. Ask the chaplains, if you would, my lord, to offer prayers for a safe mooring.' Two woebegone friars come stumbling and fumbling along the tossing deck; already, in plaintive voices, they have started to chant the correct orisons.

And the anchorage is found, on the lee side of the island. There is a small beach, the only one they have seen among all these steep-to crags, and a precipitous valley running up into the hills. 'Better and better,' says the captain. 'Green trees. Dangerous savages?'

'My book says *Insula deserta, sine hominibus.* It is, my lord, always possible that cannibal infidels concealed themselves from Dom João. If our soldiers were to go ashore with cross-bows and hand-guns—'

'Do not presume to tell me of military precautions. They are not your mystery, sir. Keep your place. You have *not* told me, does the island have a name.'

St Helena, of course. Named for Dom João's discovery of it upon the feast of that same most sacred lady, herself an indomitable voyager – all the way from frigid Britain to Rome with her son the Emperor and thence in her great age to Judaea and the True Cross of Christ. A sanctified omen, as the friars are at pains to point out.

While the pinnace is being slung up from its stowage in the waist of the ship, there is suddenly a brouhaha from below-decks. Men who are strapping armour to their skin-and-bone ribs drop helmets and breast-plates, seize partisans, clubs or swords, and run to the hatchway. Shouts of protest in the ship's bowels turn to roars of outraged pain.

'What in the Holy Name is going on?'

'It is the prisoner, my lord, the stowaway. He is crying to come aloft.'

'Why? Does he suppose we are about to grant him shore-leave?'

'They say not, my lord. They say something else, but I was not near enough to hear precisely.'

'My lord,' calls out another man, the master-at-arms, climbing up through the hatch with his whip still in his hand. 'My lord, he will not keep quiet. He begs and prays by the Wounds of Christ that your lordship will be so gracious as to grant him a brief word. For myself I would have given it him with an arquebus-butt in his cullions – which to my way of thinking ought not to have been left on him – but I know your lordship's clemency and thought best to ask you direct.'

'Bring him up.'

Soldiers arrive at the break of the poop, dragging between them a famished filthy naked creature, all hair and beard and heavy chains, and rotten with bloody sores. To add to his degradation, two fingers are missing from each hand, three toes from each foot, and his nose and his ears are cut away at the roots – where they have been, there are loathsome black scabs, the clots of tar slapped onto him when it was done. Months ago it was done: the punishment of the governor of Goa. This is the unspeakable Lopes, sometime a gentleman with a shield of notable quarterings: Dom Fernão Lopes who sold his comrades to the heathen.

(For he refused as 'the dole of a miser' the governor's lawful wage and took service under a hostile maharajah. He was captured; they asked him, 'Why?'; he replied, 'For more jewels, fair raiment and sinuous women than I ever saw in all my life. No, their religion did not deter me. It may be false, but it is a work of art. Sly goddesses who impose no chastity. Seductive gods with six strong arms to them, to reach for anything they might desire, good or bad. The maharajah gave *me* six arms, the command of his crack regiments. Had you let me alone for a year, *I'd* have been maharajah.')

'Not so jocund,' jeers the captain from the height of his poop-rail, 'as you used to be, hey? When the King shall judge your treason and the fathers of the Inquisition your apostasy, the summary justice of the governor will seem but a dog-bite.'

Lopes is indeed not jocund, but all his agonies have failed to cow him. He answers with stubborn bravado. 'You well know there is to be no King's judgement. My sentence has been delivered and served. They cast me mutilated out of Goa but at the same time kept me *within* Goa: to live from a begging-bowl, the exemplary leper of the colony's suburbs. Any wonder I evaded them and sought what I hoped would be the refuge of your merciful ship? For had they, in the first place, sent me to

Lisbon for trial, I might have been acquitted. Treason? No full proof. When I joined the maharajah he was fighting his Mahometan overlords; he was not making war against *us*. Later, I daresay he was; later, I may have been implicated. But I have a most plausible defence, and were I put to it properly before the King's chief bench I would use it to the uttermost.

'The Inquisition will not convict me. I never apostatised. I merely lived for a time in a land with no Christian priests and afterwards I told of the customs I observed there. Some of which were monstrous—'

'Oh, shut your mouth! I did not haul you up to make a speech.'

'But you did, sir; the master-at-arms said so. Sir, this is *important*! I beg you, allow me to finish – sir, in the name of blessed Helena herself! – my words, sir, please—'

He is agitated, he contorts himself in his chains, glistening spittle flows down his matted beard. The captain sneers, but concedes.

'Sir, I said "monstrous" – they have a devil, a blue-black woman as lean as a skeleton, with wolf-teeth and red eyes like coals of fire, she demands continual blood-sacrifice, of beasts in her temple and men under cover of night, secretly strangled. And the worst is, they call her too a *goddess*. How could any baptised Christian conceivably worship her? Unless he were damned already, and *I am not damned*.

'Sir, I have made confession since my capture, I am shriven, Jesus our Lord knows my soul. Besides, it is impossible to *convert* into that religion, if that is what you fear I have done. You have to be born to it, a member of one of their castes. To them I am less than a fish or an insect, quite unworthy of hearing their doctrine, if indeed they have any, which I doubt. It may have appeared I did not sufficiently abhor their idols, but that was only on account of my manner of speech. Too jocund, as you said.

'Ah, sir, how I am paid for it.

'Dear Christ, I am only fortunate they did not geld me as was first threatened for my sodomy, alleged, amongst the Hindoos. Fortunate I knew more than they thought, about the same game as played in Goa by certain of our priests and officers with young men from the native dancing-troupes. But that by the way—

'Sir, upon your own account you determined me a second sentence, gratuitously against all principle of justice. To parade me, *as you see me now!* through the Lisbon streets to exhibit my shame; and thereafter to be immured in a monastery. Sir, within the city live my wife and my young son. I cannot *bear* it they should gaze upon me thus. They are guiltless, I am lost to them in any event, why must they suffer the terror of my mutilations, why?'

'So what do you ask of me? To hang you from the yardarm here and now? I have no such authority. I found you alive upon my ship; my duty is to bring you home alive; if, after that, I make of you a disgraceful trophy, what else do you deserve?'

'What else? else? else? "Immured," you have said. Justly enough, I don't dispute it. D'you think that I *want* to go out and about? Sir, in the name of heaven, if you looked as I do, would *you*? Sir, could I not be immured upon this island? Anything, anything, only that my wife and son do not, not not not *not* ever see Fernão Lopes again—

'For *them* I am asking, never for myself. On my knees.'

He falls kneeling and beats his head against the deck.

The captain considers; thinks slowly and painfully of his own wife and children, not seen for six years (thinks of the concubine to whom he is so sadly addicted, a more venial disgrace than Lopes's, but one he will somehow have to hide): he makes up his mind. He says first, 'I have no authority.' But then he comes down from the poop and whispers with repulsion into Lopes's ravaged ear-hole. Then he gives an order to the master-at-arms: let the prisoner, for his health, be permitted a short spell on the beach. The chains to be removed but his wrists tied by a cord lest he treacherously attack any of the men of the landing-party.

The pinnace is in the water. They dump Lopes into it like a sack of mucky dunnage. He crouches upon the bottom-boards, close to the captain's feet as the oarsmen row ashore. He half-smiles and extrudes a pitiful whine from the depths of his beard: 'No clothes? You maroon me stark-naked? No weapons for my protection? Not even a flint-and-steel? Oh sir, this is clemency indeed.'

The captain whispers scornfully back, 'Man, you are no worse off than was Adam in paradise-garden. Perhaps even better. For I think there will be no "sinuous" Eve to tempt you. As for serpents, you will discover.'

When the boat's prow grinds into the sand, the prisoner makes a leap for it. In the twinkling of an eye. Notwithstanding his roped hands. He staggers upright in the waves, tramples through them to the beach and goes straight as a running rat for the shelter of the tree-lined ravine. His sureness of speed is hampered by the loss of his toes, which gives time for some of the soldiers to level their guns and crossbows against him; but the captain forbids it, angrily shouting that the prisoner is the King's prisoner, his life is *not* declared forfeit, they will easily pick him up again before they leave.

Already the men have seen goats, and run hunting them with urchin halloos. Others of the crew heave water-casks to the stream. The captain, left alone for a while, lays his own flint-and-steel on a boulder at the margin of the forest; as an afterthought he sets down a dagger and a pocket gospel-book as well; and returns to his subordinates to chivvy them at their work. Within an hour he saunters over to the boulder once again: flint-and-steel, book and dagger have disappeared. 'Mary save us,' muses the captain, 'I do not know what the King will say. But he is a good Christian monarch: he may not disapprove.'

It takes the ship's company a whole week to replenish and recreate themselves. Through all of that time, no sign of Fernão Lopes. The day they set sail, the captain announces that the renegade is surely perished by his own act, which will damn him eternally: a stronger object-lesson for potential traitors on their way to the Indies than even a parade through the city. 'There are those who might in their depravity *enjoy* such a cruel sight, but the thought of the man's vanishing all alone and totally friendless into this mid-ocean solitude, by God's Passion, it shrinks the soul.'

The friar (to whom he speaks) concurs: self-abandonment is a very dreadful thing, the inevitable consequence of heathen companionship. 'These colonies of ours, my lord, contain immeasurable perils. May our Saviour speed the work of conversion.'

I stop writing to have a think about it. To contemplate it (as I always do these days; do I grow childish as my years advance?) in terms of the toy theatre. To make drawings for the tiny figure of Dom Fernão in his waste place as he exerts himself to survive – d'you imagine the unabated, unabatable, fear-driven storm of his energy? He must have been needle-thin, as atrociously so as an Auschwitz martyr: how often did they bother to feed him, and on what nauseous scraps, in his chains in the bilge of that accursed starvation ship? (And dysentery, scurvy?) He disgusted them. I think they forgot him, for as long as they comfortably could.

So, Jack, I cannot draw him *plump*; but he will have a few of your features. Your cleverness, for example.

I suppose I should ask myself, how did he free his wrists? Until he could do that, he was dead. Draw him frantic, backed up against a sharp rock, scraping and scraping the rope against it? I suppose that *would* be what he did. Or had he first gathered in the captain's gifts? in his teeth perhaps. In which case, the dagger-blade—

You, likewise, freed your wrists. I mean, you managed to reassure

Australia House and afterwards your students and fellow teachers. Tricksters find tricks. And some of them are lucky enough to have others who will find on their behalf.

You could not face *me*, but you could dare to visit Mrs Lobscott. There you and Lopes part company. His wife and his son, he said. With you, it was only the wife. For your Eugene, you even suggested you might fetch him to accompany your banishment. (No shame? But eventually you'll have to tell him, and *how* will you tell him? Or shall you chicken out, keep silence, let his mother *and Carmilla* do all the explaining?)

Is Australia a waste place? Are you naked and bleeding? Your bowels all a-run with mediaeval diarrhoea? Mutilated, toes, fingers, ears and nose? In one sense of course, no, none of it: you're a thriving fat man in a busy busy country. Like Lopes, you do keep your genitals, and unlike him you may have some proper scope to use them. I suppose I ought to draw him jerking off upon a mountain-peak, or in grotesque attempts at bestiality with a nanny-goat. I don't wish you distress, but I wonder will *your* ejaculations from now on be of any greater value? As you are at present, they haven't done much for you.*

I had hoped, Jack, once—

Maybe *you* hoped. But your hope was never me. Polly Blackadder, if I understood her correctly. Does her face still lie burning under your heart? Let it stay there till you die, Jack. Such women are not to be forgotten.

I shall draw you therefore living in your own waste place (alone?), as complacent, as self-indulgently reminiscent, as I always thought Napoleon must have been upon the island – until the arsenic got at him – or if not the arsenic, then the cancer, the hepatitis, the whatever-it-was your Swede professor does *not* believe he died from. (I leave that particular argument to Fidelio.) *I* never cared for Napoleon; altogether too admiring of himself, both in victory and defeat.

You too always admired yourself. Even your letter, which pretended otherwise, told a tale between its lines.

I wonder did Napoleon ever hear of the first exile who languished on

---

* You'll say (I've heard you say it!) that women always say men are totally cock-obsessed, which means women would not say so unless *they* were cock-obsessed, yes?; and that no woman therefore can create, by writing or drawing, a correctly proportionate male personage. It may well be so. If it is, by what right do I harp here on Lopes's phallic solipsism? There were so many other things for him to think about on that island, literally matters of life and death, to say nothing of the profound problem of the organisation of a human society with no one in it save himself. (I've my own ideas on that latter issue, I think he did have a companion: read on, you'll see.) But how dare I, you will say, narrow it down to just *your* silly prick? To which I can but reply that as neither of us have ever been *entirely* alone, my rancid guess, Jack, is quite as good as yours. Also it may serve to teach you a thing or two.

St Helena? If he did hear, was he heartened? For they rediscovered Fernão Lopes and restored him to the human race.

(After him, of course, others: Alexander Selkirk; Robinson Crusoe; Ben Gunn; Adams upon Pitcairn, the *Bounty* mutineer; those astonishing Japanese soldiers in their bunkers on Pacific atolls, who never knew the war was over. History and fiction, mingled together for an abiding archetype: think of it.)

Thirty years later; 1546: another homebound vessel, also Portuguese (not a cockleshell caravel but a great gilded carrack laden with stuffs and spices like a floating fair), drops anchor at St Helena and sends ashore the usual boats. There have long been rumours among mariners of a man on the island, the ashes of his fires have been found, and unaccountable tracks in the forest which no watering-party could possibly have troubled themselves to make. On this occasion there is no doubt of it. The man himself is *there*, sick unto death, delirious, lying helpless on the very strand where he ran from his tormentors.

They carry him tenderly aboard, wondering at his hacked and healed flesh, wondering at his long white beard, his weather-blackened cheeks and forehead, his cobbled-together garments of goatskin, his belts of twisted creeper, the strange spear they found beside him with a deeply worn-away dagger-blade spliced to the end of the shaft and easily removable if it is needed for use as a knife. They discover in his goatskin wallet a near-illegible gospel-book (the paper torn and stained, the cheap printer's ink faded into oblivion): they know now he is a Christian and an educated Christian – how in God's name did he come here? And why in God's name did he choose to stay so long? For after all, the East India carracks make this landfall every year – any one of them could have taken him off.

Perhaps someone, man or woman, remembers the story of the unpardonable renegade from Goa? If so, it is a kindly soul and keeps quiet.

Lopes does not regain his senses until the carrack is well out to sea, and the ship's surgeon has had a chance to prescribe for him. A chaplain comes to talk; to this good man Lopes tells everything. Once he has got over his pathetic struggles with his half-forgotten powers of speech, it all comes pouring out in a flood of heartfelt candour.

A discussion among the officers and priests. They finally conclude that the treason is old history, its perpetrator has already been punished over and over again, they should honour him for his pertinacity and carry him safe to Lisbon. Indeed, at least once, he shall dine in the captain's cabin.

But the meal is not a success. Lopes is now tongue-tied. He begs to be allowed to live on the open deck like the least of the carrack's menials. He cannot endure enclosure; he has his own dreams now, which will not cohere with chattering company; let him only now and then exchange a few gentle words with the friendly priest; and so, he will be content.

Secretly he dreads what he dreaded before: his meeting with his family. No one can tell him whether they are alive or dead. What to do?

Prompted by the priest, he leaves the ship in the Tagus estuary but does not enter the city. Instead he goes aboard another ship, outward bound for Naples. And from Naples to Rome, where he seeks and (with great delay) obtains an audience with the Pope.

His Holiness, when he fully understands the man's scarce-credible story, is amazed and exalted. He praises God and in person hears Dom Fernão's confession, granting him absolution and ordering cathedral bells, a flourish of trumpets in St Peter's Square and a public declaration that here is a very-near saint.

Within a week, Dom Fernão is again aboard ship, first for Portugal, where he does indeed find his wife dead (twenty-eight years ago). His son is gone away, untraceable; if he lives, he's a middle-aged man. Their shame for Lopes's deed has buried both of them completely.

So aboard yet another ship, the very next East Indiaman to sail, as soon as he is assured that the captain will put in at St Helena.

He has left behind him there, it seems, a patch of tilled ground, a vigorous flock of goats, and a poultry-yard second to none. It will not have survived his absence; but he is positive, with a good consignment of tools, seed, and more breeding-stock, that he can rapidly reconstruct his venture. He proposes to build a chapel. The materials, free of charge, are given him by philanthropic Christians: he is to found his own small trading-post and give aid to every ship that comes in.

One thing he insists upon. No one else is to dwell on the island.

His loneliness is now *himself*; it must not be infringed. And then (I don't know when) he dies there, between the departure of one ship and the arrival of another. His corpse is found by a party of sailors: it is stretched out on the chapel floor, as naked as when he was first marooned, the hands clenched together round his wrinkled old cod.

What I wrote about fucking with the goats . . . I have thought it through more thoroughly. He may have done such a thing to begin with, who can say? But throughout thirty years? Could an officially celibate Pope, no matter how compassionate, have so readily absolved (and with so

loud a ding-dong-ding and tata-tantara) such iniquities *contra naturam*?
Only one degree worse than incest. A 'very-near saint'? Pull the other
one.

There must have been something else.

I cannot believe total continence. Lopes had been a soldier with a
soldier's carnal habits, he had no spiritual director to strengthen him, he
discovered his own remedy. To be sure, it was not orthodox.

I shall draw it for my little theatre-toy. (*Your* little theatre-toy once,
but bugger that, Jack Juggler.) Think—

It is a wild disturbing day in the fifth year of his disgrace. There have
been momentous thunderstorms. The night-black cloud flies off upon
the shoulder of the wind, spitting and flashing as it goes: the sun breaks
through to make a rainbow. Lopes, under a tree, intently observing the
shape-changes and vast whirlings of the sky, presses his gospel-book
between his abridged unhandy hands: he'll look through it yet again
and discover a suitable text. The book contains only St Mark, the
shortest of the evangelists, but it is enough and to spare. He opens it at
Chapter Thirteen. Jesus, in horror at the near approach of betrayal and
excruciating death, prophesies a cosmic turbulence.

> But in those days, after that tribulation, the sun shall be
> darkened, and the moon shall not give her light, and the stars of
> heaven shall fall, and the powers that are in heaven shall be
> shaken. And then shall they see the Son of Man coming in the
> clouds with great power and glory . . .

Lopes, I need not say, is a more receptive vessel for that sort of
apocalypse than most of us up and down the world. His mind runs
backward to his boyhood, when they dragged him from his games to
hear a series of melodramatic sermons: their title, *God's Truth to the Ears
of His Prophets*: a preaching-friar ranting of the Vision of Ezekiel. The
friar's words, roughly remembered, combine with the words of St Mark.
It is Lopes's fifth year since he first made his treasons in India. Ezekiel
dates his own revelation to 'the fifth year of King Jehoiachin's captivity',
when he saw the Wheels of God spinning down out of the sky in—

> . . . a great cloud, and a fire infolding itself . . .
> . . . the appearance of the wheels . . . was as it were a wheel in
> the middle of a wheel
> . . . as for the wheels, it was cried unto them in my hearing, O
> wheel . . .
> . . . the likeness of a throne, as the appearance of a sapphire
> stone: and upon the likeness of the throne was the likeness as
> the appearance of a man above upon it . . . as the appearance of

fire round about within it, from the appearance of his loins even upward, and from the appearance of his loins even downward . . .

. . . as the appearance of the bow that is in the cloud in the day of rain.

And that's what Dom Fernão sees.

Except that it is not a man, or a son of man, carried round and round toward him on a throne above the wheels: but the likeness, the appearance, the *cry* of a woman. She descends to embrace him, to relieve the incessant Venus-fury that is driving him out of his wits. Is she sinuous Eve whom the ship's captain so ungenerously joked about? Only afterwards (after the strong hot fuck) does Lopes understand: in fact, the Hindoo devil-goddess, taut and dripping as a caravel's tarred anchor-cable, and the teeth! and the red eyes! and the string of dead men's skulls hanging round her poisonous loins (all fire, upward and downward).

He flees from her, crying to Christ and Christ's Mother. She swoops after him, spinning in her terrible wheels, from hilltop to treetop to the depth of the valley to the beach, until he runs into the breakers of the ocean. He hurls himself there to drown, there is no other way out.

And, no, of course he does not drown.

Perhaps another vision. Fleeting in music to him along the waters, another woman, like a seabird white and gold, wave-green and silver, glorious but gentle, formidable but loving, to fight with the devil-goddess and chase her, league upon tempestuous league, to the dark side of the moon. This is no temptress but a honey-sweet fulfilment of all the dreams of love and selflessness he had as a vital child, as a troubled boy in puberty, and then (somehow) never again. She nourishes his spirit and satisfies his flesh every day and every night – except—

Except sometimes the first succuba returns. Only intermittently, and only for one night at a time. But she does return, and it is long before he realises that the two are but one; if he lives to love the kindly one he must learn to endure the gruesome *other*.

Finally, after years of this (an old age strangely filled thereby with a growth and regrowth of strength), he experiences a night of black extended terror. The woman of the wheels envelops him: she is to stay with him for ever and ever amen. Terror, horror, heart-shrinking, and the sense of an utter *incompetence*. He flees again to the beach; his exhausted brain subsides like a landslip; when it recovers itself and knows itself, he is lying as weak as featherdown in the tween-decks of the great carrack with the surgeon bending over him.

And you, Jack, so far away, where are *your* childish dreams? The untrammelled young enthusiasms of a bright little Barnsley dissident? By whom are you pursued, hey? and in how many shapes? Shall you drown, or be nourished and coddled and even then find yourself suffering God knows what horror-and-terror of unexpected chop-and-change? Shall you in the end be rescued?

Lopes left Rome to go back to St Helena *not* to rehabilitate an improvised farm, rather to die in the embraces of his woman. The woman of the wheels, or the woman from the foam of the ocean? He had ceased to distinguish, he was at peace. The people of the ship that carried him saw his peace, his state of grace; they put it down to the papal absolution. He did not contradict. But he knew that the Pope only knew so much. He (Lopes) had confessed at large to almost impregnable lusts, at last overcome by heaven's direct intervention. He'd said nothing in the Vatican of either seabirds or wheels. No need, he thought, to fear the concealment of sin and hence the invalidation of the sacrament; he'd kept quiet (that was all) about what anyone could have recognised as *illusions*, a species of sickness, a huddle of dreams. While he was in Rome, that's what he truly felt. But only while in Rome. Once again at sea, once again approaching the island, illusions became truth and truth became stronger than any sense of sickness or indeed any lurking sense that such sickness *might* have been sin. He knew this was going to happen. The Pope did not know. And in any case the Pope never set up to be a physician, it was unreasonable to trouble him with such stuff.

So why do I trouble *you*, Jack Juggler? Illusion is illusion, I hear you say: how can it help either of us? Damn your eyes, Jack, it's your trade.

Practical matters. Your message to Fidelio from McCoy was passed on, and received rather oddly. 'Hoax,' he said. No, I don't know if he believes that or not. Because later I asked, 'A van with gear?' He said there had been such a van, it belonged to that VEXACTION group, it was stolen and he and Toe blamed each other for the loss. One of the reasons, he implied, for the company's collapse. Toe's reminder was by way of paying off an old score. The 'Wee Priest' (yes, you're right) being some sort of Irish joke of hers, indecipherable. Fid says her sense of humour is macabre.

Fidelio, at present, is at another of his Irish plays, a dissection of the workings of the Anglo-Irish Agreement. Which agreement, so he says, is 'a sell-out of the six-county nationalists'. I'm sure it *is* a sell-out; I'm also sure that it's not the right time to say so; the press of both countries will have his guts for garters – that is, if anyone anywhere's daft enough to put the play on. . .

He says, if you see McCoy again, tell him to piss off.

'No,' he says, 'don't.' He won't have 'the man Pogmoor' passing his messages to anyone, particularly to someone who knows you both. In his current mood all he can mutter is that you ruined his life. In fact you didn't. But you tried. The same with *my* life, you bastard.

Jack, for God's sake stay where you have sent yourself!

Be Bonaparte, not Lopes. Don't even come back for so short a time as Lopes did. How would Lopes have reacted (d'you suppose?) if he'd found his wife and son all alive-o to greet him in the old Lisbon home? Well, they weren't and I think they were fortunate.

Goodbye.

from Leonore
(your worst mistake, wasn't she?)

She got no answer to this. She never wrote to him again and he never wrote to her. Now and then she heard something of his doings in Australia, where he eventually took up citizenship and sat prosperously in a succession of academic and theatrical appointments. Occasionally he came to Europe for seminars, or in charge of a prestige-winning production. They were not in touch with one another during these visits. If he married, nobody told her.

When Fidelio was killed in 1992, Leonore left it to his agent to inform Pogmoor. Pogmoor sent a letter of formal condolence, devoid of all personal expression. He wrote a supplementary obituary-note for the Guardian, *humorous recollections of Carver 'in his prime'. The implication was that the prime had failed to last beyond 1975 at the latest.*

When Leonore was killed in 1993, Pogmoor wrote again to the Guardian, *not so much an obituary-note as a deranged conversation between dead wife and living husband. The Women's Page editor, to whom it was passed, refused to publish. She said it was a compendium of hidden insults under the guise of a passionate tribute to a very considerable artist, and she thought the 'unsavoury weasel to be in need of professional help'. Pogmoor got wind of her comments; he tried to sue the newspaper, until a lawyer persuaded him otherwise.*

After 1992, Australian theatre people from time to time let it be known to their English contacts that Pogmoor only held his job by the quick of his fingernails. His lectures had begun to digress into lip-licking accounts of what he claimed to be his dreams, causing many complaints: women students said 'sexist smut', women and men together alleged 'obscurity, irrelevancy, egotistical public wanking'.

There was also a desperate brawl, in 1994, in a restaurant in the Glebe district of Sydney, between Pogmoor and an eighteen-year-old youth fresh off the plane – from Sardinia, was it? Sicily? Wine-bottles were smashed and used as weapons, tables and chairs upset, a bowl of pasta in brodo flung all over the proprietor. The police intervened, but laid no charges when the combatants agreed to pay a handsome compensation. So gossips had little to go on – who was the boy? – why the row? – nobody knew.

Pogmoor's later productions became so incoherent as to be more or less meaningless. His crêpe-paper (the word went) was everything to him in the end; his human actors, living and breathing, might just as well not have been there. He was incapable of working with people. *Similar criticisms had always been made, but never with such severe conviction: Jack Juggler (the word went) was* juggling himself off. *Off the point and offside. Off-course. Off his trolley. Off the wall. To put it brutally:* OFF-STAGE.

*

Let our ship sink and all the world that's without
us be taken from us, I hope I have some tricks in
this brain of mine shall not let us perish.
  (Chapman, Jonson and Marston, *Eastward Ho!*)